The Complete
Dracula

Radu Florescu

Raymond T. McNally

Copley Publishing Group
Acton, MA 01720

Printed in the United States of America

ISBN 0-87411-595-7

Florescu, Radu.
    The complete Dracula/Radu Florescu, Raymond T. McNally.
        p.   cm.
    Abridgement and combination of: In search of Dracula /
Raymond T. McNally, 1972, and Dracula / Radu Florescu, 1973.
    Includes bibliographical references.
ISBN 0-87411-595-7
    1. Vlad III, Prince of Wallachia, 1430 or 31–1476 or 7.
2. Dracula, Count (Fictitious character) 3. Vampires. I. McNally,
Dracula. III. Florescu, Radu. Dracula. IV. Title.
DR240 .5. V553F57 1992
949.8 ' 201' 092–dc20
[B]

92-28644
CIP

Cover: *About the wild bloodthirsty berserker, Dracula Voevod.*
Impalement scene and text page fom a 15th-century German pamphlet published by Matthias Hupnuff in Strasbourg, 1500.

Contents

In Search of Dracula

A True History of Dracula and Vampire Legends

Acknowledgments

This book would not have been possible without the collaboration of Professor Constantin Giurescu, the distinguished historian from the University of Bucharest, George Florescu, Romania's most knowledgeable genealogist, and Matei Cazacu, a brilliant young assistant from the Nicolae Iorga Institute in Bucharest.

Special gratitude is owed to the Dracula team we assembled on both shores of the Atlantic, a team whose members are far too numerous to be named individually. Among our Romanian colleagues and friends whose help we particularly appreciate are H.E. Cornel Bogdan, Romania's dynamic Ambassador to the United States; Professor Stefan Stefanescu, director of the Nicolae Iorga Institute in Bucharest; Professor Ion Pop, director of the Folklore Institute, who provided the assistance of his team of experts; and Lidia Simion, who was in charge of foreign scholars at the University of Bucharest and who became our crucial anchor-woman.

For their editorial assistance, thanks go to Donald D. Ackland and to Pat Lambdin Moore.

Finally, we gratefully acknowledge the genius of Bram Stoker, who created the fictional Dracula; the expertise of Bela Lugosi in portraying the vampire count in films; and America's love affair with the imagined Dracula, which partly inspired our efforts to document the real one.

Introducing the Dracula of Fiction and Folklore

"Welcome to my house! Enter freely and of your own will!"
He made no motion of stepping to meet me, but stood like a
statue, as though his gesture of welcome had fixed him into
stone. The instant, however, that I had stepped over the
threshold, he moved impulsively forward, and holding out his
hand grasped mine with a strength which made me wince, an
effect which was not lessened by the fact that it seemed as cold
as ice—more like the hand of a dead than a living man.

So the vampire Dracula first appears in Bram Stoker's
novel. Published in 1897, *Dracula* is as popular now as when it
was written. Millions not only have read it but have seen it at
the cinema. Among the filmed versions are *Nosferatu*, made
with Max Schreck in 1922, *Dracula* with Bela Lugosi in 1931,
and *Horror of Dracula* with Christopher Lee in 1958. By now
there are more than a hundred Dracula films and still others
are in the making.

As for the book before you, it has been written by two
authors. One of us—but let Raymond McNally speak for
himself: "More than 15 years ago, as a fan of Dracula horror
films I began to wonder whether there might be some historical
basis for their vampire hero. I re-read Stoker's *Dracula*, and
noted that not only this novel but almost all of the Dracula
films are set in Transylvania. At first, like many Americans, I
assumed that this was some mythical place—in the same
imaginary region, perhaps, as Ruritania. I found out, however,
that Transylvania is real—a province that belonged to
Hungary for almost a thousand years and that now is part of
modern Romania. In Stoker's novel there were some fairly
detailed descriptions of the towns of Cluj and Bistrita, and the
Borgo Pass in the Carpathian mountains. These, too, proved
real. If all that geographical data is genuine, I reasoned, why
not Dracula himself? Most people, I suspect, have never asked

this question, being generally thrown off by the vampire story line. Obviously, since vampires do not exist, Dracula—so goes popular wisdom—must have been the product of a wild and wonderful imagination.

"Eventually I read an authentic late 15th-century Slavic manuscript, in an archive in Leningrad, which described the deeds of a Wallachian ruler named Dracula. And after researching the little that was available about the historical Dracula in various other languages, I consulted with my Boston colleague, Professor Radu Florescu, who was in Romania at the time. With his encouragement and enthusiasm, I took up the study of the Romanian language and traveled directly to the very homeland of Dracula to see what more I could discover about this mysterious man and legend. There, underlying the local traditions, so I found, was an authentic human being fully as horrifying as the vampire of fiction and film—a 15th-century prince who had been the subject of many horror stories even during his own lifetime; a ruler whose cruelties were committed on such a massive scale that his evil reputation reached beyond the grave to the firesides where generations of grandmothers warned little children: 'Be good or Dracula will get you.'

"Unlike myself, an Austro-Irish American who knew the fictional Dracula through late-night movies, my colleague Radu Florescu is a native Romanian who knew of an historical Dracula through the researches of earlier Romanian scholars. But his ties with this history go deeper than that. As a boy he spent many hours on the banks of the river Arges, which bounded his family's country estate deep in the Wallachian plain. At the time he was ignorant that several miles to the north, and many centuries earlier, a brutal drama involving a large group of boyars had bloodied the banks of this same river. That knowledge came to light when Florescu and myself discovered along the banks of the Arges the authentic site— and cruel beginnings—of Castle Dracula.

"In addition, George Florescu, Radu's uncle and Romania's leading genealogist, has discovered that the Florescus trace back to a boyar family of Dracula's time, and one prominent in 15th-century Wallachian history."

During the late 1960s, together with George Florescu and the Romanian historians Constantin Giurescu and Matei Cazacu, we formed a team to research the actual sites of the real Dracula's exploits and to probe the folklore concerning not only this fearsome real-life prince but also the vampire. Legends are still very much alive among the Romanian peasants in the mountainous regions of Transylvania and Wallachia, and they were the key to some of the startling discoveries that were made.

It was autumn of 1969 when we tracked down Castle Dracula—a castle in ruins and one known to the peasants as the castle of Vlad Tepes, or Vlad "the Impaler"—a ruler notorious for mass impalements of his enemies. Vlad Tepes was in fact called Dracula in the 15th century, but this is not known by the peasants of the castle region today. As for Stoker's mythical vampire, Dracula, he is completely unknown to these peasants.

Using dozens of ancient chronicles and maps of European provenance, documents contemporary with Dracula, and 19th- and 20th-century philological and historical works, and drawing on folklore and peasant traditions, we have pieced together a dual history: an account not only of the real 15th-century Dracula, or Vlad Tepes, who came from Transylvania and ruled in Wallachia, but also of the vampire who existed in the legends of these same regions. In addition, we have studied how Bram Stoker, in the late 19th century, united these two traditions to create the most horrifying and famous vampire in all fiction: Count Dracula.

What was known of this dual history before these researches? In 1896, a Romanian Slavicist, Ioan Bogdan, noted that there existed various 15th-century German pamphlets which described the Wallachian Prince Vlad Tepes as "Dracole," and the Romanian historian Karadja published the texts, but neither made the connection between this reference and Stoker, nor did Bogdan, as a philologist, concern himself with the folklore. A few pertinent discoveries were later made by others. For instance, in 1922, Constantin Giurescu, then a young scholar, discovered the foundation stone of the Church of Tirgsor, which indicated Vlad Tepes as its founder and patron. And in the 1930s, Dinu Rosetti with George Florescu opened the grave of Vlad Tepes at Snagov, but this was only part of a general excavation at the site, not a deliberate exploration of Vlad's grave. It was not until the 1960s that part of the story began to be unraveled by Grigore Nandris. He studied the philological relationship of the names Dracole and Vlad Tepes and noted that for some reason Bram Stoker had associated these names in his vampire story. The German Slavicist Striedter compared Slavic manuscripts and German pamphlets about Dracula; the Soviet Slavicist Lurie analyzed Slavic documents. But it was Nandris's philological studies which prepared the ground for the present study. Harry Ludlam's *The Biography of "Dracula": Bram Stoker* (1962) was also invaluable. Ludlam, without knowing the story of the historical Vlad Tepes or the folklore traditions, described Stoker's meeting in London in the 1890s with Arminius Vambery, a scholar at the University of Budapest. Stoker learned of "Dracula" from this Hungarian friend who evidently knew—but never himself wrote about—parts of the Vlad Tepes or Dracula story and also the peasant beliefs in vampires.

What follows is a complex story, for it involves a 15th-century prince known in his time as both "Vlad Tepes" and "Dracole"; the fictional Dracula created by Bram Stoker in 1897; and the beliefs of the Romanian peasants in Transylvania and Wallachia both today and in the 15th century. This complex story brings up many questions. Was the real Dracula a vampire? Did the peasants of his time consider him a vampire? What connection is there between the real prince and the vampire-count created by Stoker? What do the Romanian peasants believe today about Vlad Tepes and vampires? And have we been dealing simply with "history" or are there mysteries here beyond the reach of historical research?

Europe circa 1500 A.D.

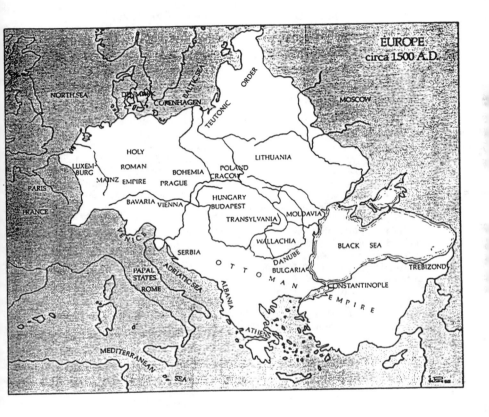

During the 15th century all phases of European life were undergoing transformation. Religious reformers were challenging the authority of the papacy. The invention of movable type, rediscovery of classical education, and development of the arts were raising the level of intellectual life. Feudal localities were becoming associated into states or other units of increased political power. Voyages into unknown seas were expanding man's knowledge of his world. And with the fall of Constantinople to the Ottoman Turks in 1453 came the end of the Eastern Christian Empire, of which the great city had been the center for more than a thousand years. As the Turks pressed outward, dominating the whole of Asia Minor and the Balkan peninsula, throughout Europe fear grew that the entire continent would come under the control of Islam.

Chronologies

Rulers

Princes of Wallachia

Basarab I 1310-52
Nicolae Alexandru 1352-64
Vladislav I 1364-77
Radu I 1377-83
Dan I 1383-86
Mircea (the Old; the Great) 1386-1418
Mihail 1418-20
Dan II 1420-31
Alexandru Aldea 1431-36
Vlad Dracul (the Devil) 1436-42
Basarab II 1442-43
Vlad Dracul 1443-47
Vladislav II 1447-48
Vlad the Impaler (Dracula) October-November 1448
Vladislav II November 1448-56
Vlad the Impaler (Dracula) 1456-62
Radu the Handsome 1462-73
Basarab Laiota (the Old) 1473-74
Radu the Handsome 1475
Basarab Laiota (the Old) 1475-November 1475
Vlad the Impaler (Dracula) November-December 1476

Kings of Hungary

Sigismund of Luxemburg 1387-1437
    (Holy Roman Emperor, 1411-33; King of Bohemia, 1420)
Albert II 1438-39
Interregnum 1444-46
Governor: Ioan de Hunedoara (John Hunyadi) 1446-53
Ladislaus V (the Posthumous) 1440-57 (King of Bohemia, 1453)
Mathias Corvinus 1458-90 (crowned 1464; King of Bohemia, 1469)
Pretender: Frederick III 1440-93 (Holy Roman Emperor; crowned King of Hungary, 1459)

Sultans of the Ottoman Empire

Murad II 1421-51 (for brief period gave power to his son Mohammed II)
Mohammed II 1444-46; 1451-81

Emperor of the Eastern Roman Empire

Constantine XI Palaeologus 1448-53 (last of the emperors of the Eastern Roman Empire; killed by Turks when they captured Constantinople)

Events

1422	Unsuccessful siege of Constantinople by the Turks.
1427	Turkish domination in Serbia.
1431	Birth of Dracula. His father, Vlad II, invested with the Order of the Dragon, an organization dedicated to fighting the Turks.
1440	Unsuccessful siege of Belgrade by the Turks.
1442-43	Victories of John Hunyadi over the Turks in Transylvania and Wallachia.
1443	Dracula and his brother Radu the Handsome are hostages in the Ottoman Empire.
1443-44	The "long campaign" of Hunyadi in the Ottoman Empire.
1444	The Crusade of Varna. Dracula and his brother in danger of death.
1445	The campaign of the Burgundian fleet on the Danube.
1446	Sultan Murad II invades Greece. Mistra becomes a vassal state of the Turks.
1447	Death of Dracula's father, Dracul, and of Dracula's brother Mircea.
1448	Turkish victory over Hunyadi at Kosovo. First reign of Dracula in Wallachia. Turkish domination in the Balkans, excepting Albania.
1453	Fall of Constantinople to the Turks. Death of Constantine XI, last of the emperors of the Eastern Christian Empire.
1456	Unsuccessful siege of Belgrade by the Turks. Death of John Hunyadi. Moldavia pays tribute to the Turks. Dracula begins his second and major reign in Wallachia.
1457	Dracula's cousin Steven (the Great) becomes Prince of Moldavia. Victories of Scanderbeg over the Turks in Albania.
1458	The Turks conquer Athens. Mathias Corvinus becomes King of Hungary.
1460	The Turks conquer Mistra and Thebes.
1461	Fall of Trebizond to the Turks.
1462	Turkish campaign against Wallachia. Dracula taken prisoner by King Mathias.
1463-65	The Turks invade Bosnia and Hertzegovina.
1468	Death of Scanderbeg.
1474	Dracula granted freedom by King Mathias.
1475	The Tartar Khan of Crimea becomes a vassal of the Turks. Hungarian campaign in Bosnia. Dracula given a military command by King Mathias.
1476	Dracula's third reign in Wallachia begins in November; ends in December when he is killed during the course of a battle near Bucharest.

2

Bram Stoker and the Search for Dracula

High up in the Transylvanian mountains we came to a halt. There, atop a black volcanic rock formation, bordering the river Arges and framed by a massive Alpine snow-capped landscape, lay the twisted battlements of Castle Dracula, its remains barely distinguishable from the rock of the mountain itself. This was hardly the grandiose, macabre mausoleum described by Bram Stoker in his famous novel, *Dracula*. Yet, no matter how modest nor how tortured by time, it was an *historic* edifice, one challenging the historian to solve its mystery, to push back an unconquered frontier.

For our party of five, composed of two Americans and three Romanians, this was the end of a long trail. Our search for Castle Dracula had begun in a light vein—over a glass of plum brandy at the University in Bucharest. It continued as an expedition marred by every possible frustration and by mysterious accidents.

This search began, as did so many other Dracula hunts, because of the extraordinary hold the Dracula vampire mystique still exercises upon the popular imagination of western Europe and the United States. Unperturbed by the vampire myth, however, a handful of skeptics have always claimed that there was a *factual basis* for the Dracula story and that the setting indeed lay in Transylvania.

Bram Stoker, at the very beginning of his story, tells of his own painstaking efforts both to consult well-known orientalists such as Arminius Vambery, professor at the University of Budapest and a frequent visitor to England, and to study the available literature concerning the frontier lands between the Christians and Turks. Even Stoker's mention of his difficulties in consulting maps of the area available at the British Museum Library in London are intended to stress the historicity of the plot; he tells us they were not too reliable, but they proved to be far more accurate than he thought.

In Stoker's novel, the town of Bistrita, for instance, is accurately described and located, as are such small villages as Fundu and Veresti (which, by the way, you will not find marked on any modern tourist map). The famed Borgo Pass leading from Transylvania to Moldavia, the northernmost province of Romania, really exists, and is beautifully described to the point of detail in Stoker's novel. The historic context, the century-old struggle between Romanians and Turks that was sparked in the 15th century, is authentic. The ethnic minorities of Transylvania—the Saxons, Romanians, Szekelys, and Hungarians—are known and are distinguished from each other by Stoker.

Dracula was in fact an authentic 15th-century Wallachian prince who was often described in the contemporary German, Byzantine, Slavonic, and Turkish documents and popular horror stories as an awesome, cruel, and possibly demented, ruler. He was known mostly for the amount of blood he indiscriminately spilled, not only the blood of the infidel Turks—which, by the standards of the time, would make him a hero—but that of Germans, Romanians, Hungarians, and other Christians. His ingenious mind devised all kinds of tortures, both physical and mental, and his favorite way of imposing death has caused Romanian historians to label him "the impaler."

In a rogues' gallery Dracula would assuredly compete for first prize with Cesare Borgia, Catherine de Medicis, or Jack the Ripper, owing not only to the quantity of his victims, but to the refinements of his cruelty. To his contemporaries, the story of his misdeeds was widely publicized—in certain instances by some of the intended victims, mostly Germans—from Budapest to Strasbourg. The Dracula story, in fact, was a "best-seller" throughout Europe 400 years before Stoker wrote his account. Many of the German-originated, 15th-century versions of the Dracula story have been found in the dusty archives of dozens of monasteries and libraries.

The names of Dracula and his father Dracul are of such importance to this story that they require a precise explanation. To begin with, both father and son had the given name "Vlad." The names "Dracul" and "Dracula" (Dracule in some manuscripts) are really nicknames. What's more, both of these nicknames had two meanings. "Dracul" meant "devil," as it still does in Romanian today; in addition it meant "dragon." In 1431, the Holy Roman Emperor Sigismund invested Vlad the father with the Order of the Dragon, a semi-monastic, semi-military organization dedicated to fighting the Turkish infidels. "Dracul" in the sense of "dragon" stems from this. It also seems probable that when the simple, superstitious peasants saw Vlad the father bearing the standard with the dragon symbol they interpreted it as a sign that he was now in league with the devil.

As for the son, we now know that he had two nicknames: he was called Vlad Tepes (pronounced tsep-pesh), which signifies Vlad the Impaler, and he was called Dracula, a diminutive meaning "son of the dragon" or "son of the devil." A final point in this discussion of nomenclature: the interchangeability of the words "devil" and "vampire" in many languages may be one reason for the association of Dracula with vampirism.

Other male Draculas, too, were known by epithets expressing deviations of character. Dracul's eldest son was Vlad the Little Impaler; his second son was Mihnea the Bad; and another descendant was Mihnea II, the Apostate. In an age of violence all the Draculas lived violently and with few exceptions died violently.

In his lifetime Dracula had fame and notoriety throughout much of Europe, and rarely has such recognition of a public figure become so lost to posterity. Indeed, when Stoker wrote about Dracula in the late 19th century, few of his readers knew he was writing about an historical character. One obstacle to understanding arose from the fact that the Dracula stories circulated in diverse languages (German, Hungarian, Romanian, Slavic, Greek, Turkish) and in different worlds having little relation with each other. A chief difficulty, however, was the confusion caused by the name itself. Was it Dracula "the son of the devil," Dracula "son of the man invested with the Order of the Dragon," or simply Dracula "the impaler"? Small wonder that the Byzantine scholar reading the chronicles referring to Dracula's deeds of heroism against the Turks, the German reading of the atrocities of the "Devil" against his fellow Saxons, and the Romanian studying the "Impaler's" achievements, failed to attribute these actions to one and the same man. It is only of very recent date that Romanian historians themselves have pieced together some of the fragments of this formidable Dracula story.

If Stoker's Dracula story was essentially correct in points of history, if Dracula existed, why not a Castle Dracula? Since the geographic setting of Transylvania was so minutely described by Stoker, what could be more logical than to begin the hunt in northeastern Transylvania, where the author set his plot on an isolated mountain peak, a few miles east of Bistrita on the road leading to the Borgo Pass.

Over the years, many persons had set out to find Castle Dracula in this general direction. They had traveled the way of Stoker's hero, Jonathan Harker, from Cluj to Bistrita and from Bistrita to the Borgo Pass. They found the countless superstitious peasants; were struck by the majestic beauty of this abandoned Carpathian frontier region separating Transylvania proper from Bukovina to the northeast and Moldavia to the east. But none had found the castle. Half-a-dozen expeditions, undertaken with the same purpose in mind, all ended on the same dismal note— not a trace of *any* castle.

Undeterred by past failures, the authors of the present volume decided to undertake the venture and set forth on the Stoker trail, if for no other reason than to satisfy their curiosity.

From the standpoint of sheer scenery, it is easy to excuse Bram Stoker for setting the story in the wrong part of Transylvania, thus leading the Dracula hunter some 100 miles or more astray. The anchor town of Bistrita, the actual departure point for any Dracula excursion, is a quaint medieval city, more German than Romanian in its characteristics, with a mixed population of Romanians, Hungarians, and those mysterious Szekelys, whom Stoker erroneously took to be possible ancestors of Dracula. The Szekelys themselves claim just as formidable a pedigree of horror, tracing themselves to Attila's Huns. From the crumbling walls of the old city, the most unsophisticated traveler can judge that at one time Bistrita must have been an impressive frontier point; from its oversized marketplace surrounded by the colorful baroque German-styled homes of the well-to-do, he may safely conclude that the town was an important trading center with goods plying northward from Transylvania to Poland and Bohemia and eastward to Moldavia.

Beyond Bistrita, the road finally climbs to the Borgo Pass, along the Dorne depression, passing through several rustic mountain villages where life has not changed much in a thousand years. The peasants still wear their traditional garb— the fur cap, or *caciula,* the embroidered shirt with motifs that vary from village to village, the sheeplined vest, or *cojoc* (lately sold as *après-ski* apparel in the elegant resorts of Europe), the roughly stitched pigskin shoes, or *opinci.* These farm people are not without an artistic side. The women embroider; the men mold clay products with a technique kept secret, although the quality of the local clay certainly contributes to its success. The

Genealogy

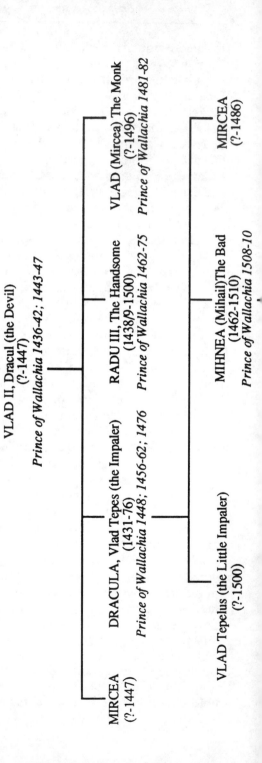

MIRCEA The Great/The Old
(?-1418)
Prince of Wallachia 1386-1418

VLAD II, Dracul (the Devil)
(?-1447)
Prince of Wallachia 1436-42; 1443-47

MIRCEA
(?-1447)

DRACULA, Vlad Tepes (the Impaler)
(1431-76)
Prince of Wallachia 1448; 1456-62; 1476

RADU III, The Handsome
(1438/9-1500)
Prince of Wallachia 1462-75

VLAD (Mircea) The Monk
(?-1496)
Prince of Wallachia 1481-82

VLAD Tepelus (the Little Impaler)
(?-1500)

MIHNEA (Mihail)The Bad
(1462-1510)
Prince of Wallachia 1508-10

MIRCEA
(?-1486)

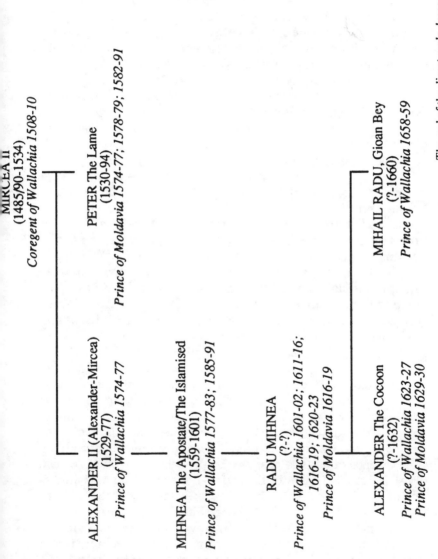

MIRCEA II
(1485/90-1534)
Coregent of Wallachia 1508-10

PETER The Lame
(1530-94)
Prince of Moldavia 1574-77; 1578-79; 1582-91

ALEXANDER II (Alexander-Mircea)
(1529-77)
Prince of Wallachia 1574-77

MIHNEA The Apostate/The Islamised
(1559-1601)
Prince of Wallachia 1577-83; 1585-91

RADU MIHNEA
(?-?)
Prince of Wallachia 1601-02; 1611-16;
1616-19; 1620-23
Prince of Moldavia 1616-19

MIHAIL RADU, Gioan Bey
(?-1660)
Prince of Wallachia 1658-59

ALEXANDER The Cocoon
(?-1632)
Prince of Wallachia 1623-27
Prince of Moldavia 1629-30

The end of the direct male descendants of Dracula.

peasant house, almost entirely of wood, delights one with the imaginative carvings of its *pridvor*, a kind of porch surrounding the house, and the decorative patterns of the main gate, giving the only access to the courtyard. Local folklore is rich: the *Doinas*, the *Strigature* or lyrical poetry, the *Basme* or fairy tales, the ballads, and the *legende* or popular epics, all combine natural and supernatural elements. In the Doinas there are frequent references to the wolves, which, traveling in packs at night in the midst of winter, do their worst to man and beast alike. In the Basme, the bat is often mentioned, and in Romania this creature is an element of bad luck. In the legends of old, the vampire is a supernatural being of demonic origin, fighting Fat-Frumos, the fairy prince who embodies moral power, and is typified as a dragon monster-serpent, the motif used on the ancient standard of the Dacians.

Also interesting for our purposes are the historical ballads which speak of the ancient battleground between Romanians, Tartars, Turks, and Poles. These ballads commemorate countless heroes and villains, though in the Borgo region no Dracula is remembered by the old generation, perhaps the last one preserving by word of mouth a fascinating, distorted history, one quite as remarkable as what the sagas of the Vikings record.

Of late, the more wily peasants, impressed by the number of foreign tourists seeking Dracula's castle, have decided to play along with the search; and they do it well for the price of a few cigarettes and packs of chewing gum. Unwilling to disappoint the Dracula hunter, one imaginative peasant from the village of Prundul-Birgaului made numerous allusions to a "castle" that was *mai la munte,* a favorite expression of Romanian vagueness which means "a little farther up the mountain" (of course, when you reach one peak, as every Alpinist knows, there is always another behind). However, as the historians have often found in regard to folklore, where there is smoke, there is fire. It so happened that the folklore references spurred by gain, implying the existence of a castle near the Borgo Pass, were quite correct. Only it was *not* (Castle Dracula—though Dracula visited it during his lifetime, since he often traveled along the solitary highway winding through the Borgo Pass.

This historic route was initially traveled by Romania's feudal leaders at the close of the 14th century, when they set forth from their haven in the Transylvanian plateau to found the Principality of Moldavia. It goes through majestic country— Stoker's Mittle-Land "green and brown where grass and rock mingle in an endless perspective of jagged rock and pointed crags."

Beyond the lower mountains, surrounding the Dorne depression and rising to 3000 feet, lie the higher peaks, often snow-capped even during the summer; these are the Rodna Mountains of Bukovina, a favorite Alpinist playground which demands the skill and sometimes the equipment of the expert for tricky ascents of upwards of 7500 feet. On the Moldavian side of the border, one reaches the watering spa of Vatra Dornei. Today this town is an important tourist center, not only because of the health-restoring springs, but because it gives approach to a dozen famed monasteries, located in Bukovina and Moldavia proper, and representing extraordinary jewels of 15th-century Romanian artistry. The biblical scenes on the exterior walls of the monasteries, dating back to Dracula's time, are painted in shades of deep blue and purple, and they have survived virtually unscathed through some 500 rigorous winters in this region.

Castle Bistrita, located near the Borgo Pass, may have served as the model for the castle in Stoker's novel. It was John Hunyadi who actually completed Castle Bistrita around 1449, five years before the fall of Constantinople. The Voevod or Warlord of Transylvania, Papal Prince and foremost Balkan crusader, Governor of Severin, hereditary Duke of Timisoara and of Bistrita, and in charge of the Hungarian kingdom, John Hunyadi was, in fact, in control of the political destinies of what was left of the east and central European lands in their last and desperate struggle with the Turks. He died in 1456 while defending Belgrade, the last great Christian bastion on the Danube, the year that Dracula was enthroned as prince. Hunyadi was the father of Mathias Corvinus, the Hungarian king who kept Dracula imprisoned in his citadel on the Danube for some twelve years, from 1462 to 1474. Relations between the Hunyadis and the Draculas, however, were initially friendly, though never intimate for reasons which will be explained later in this book.

During the years 1451 to 1456, Dracula may have lived at Castle Bistrita. We know that he stayed in nearby Suceava with his cousin, the future Prince Steven of Moldavia, from 1449 to 1451.

Not a trace of Bistrita Castle remains today—only legends. It is probable that Stoker heard of these legends connecting Dracula to this region. The Saxon population of Bistrita, who disliked the Romanians and the Hungarians, doubtless heard of Dracula's atrocities against their brethren farther south in the towns of Brasov and Sibiu, where most of the horrors were committed and recorded, and it is quite plausible that some Saxon refugee from southern Transylvania may even have written a description of them in Bistrita itself. However, if there is a Bistrita document about Dracula, it is not known today. In any event, Bistrita Castle was attacked, ransacked, and totally destroyed by the German population of the city at the close of the 15th century, an apparent gesture of defiance against the Hungarian kings, who, as we know, were allies of Dracula. The full story of the precise circumstances which led to the German attack may never be known.

From the few descriptions we have of the former castle, it seems to have been a smaller version of Hunyadi's formidable castle of Hunedoara, located 100 miles to the southwest; a most impressive structure tracing back to 1260 and today completely and beautifully restored. This is the castle of the Hunyadis where Dracula was greeted as an ally and friend in 1452, but as a foe in 1462. It corresponds closely to the "Castle Dracula" in Stoker's novel. With its imposing donjon, smaller towers, massive walls, battlements, and drawbridge, it seems custom-made for the Dracula and vampire setting. In the impressive Hall of Knights, with its lovely marble columns, once hung all the portraits of the "greats" of Dracula's time, including the great John Hunyadi himself and Dracula. A hostile hand, possibly that of a revengeful German, destroyed all these portraits. Fortunately, three paintings of Dracula, plus a number of woodcut portraits, have survived the furies of the past.

In his novel, Bram Stoker describes Dracula as "a tall old man, clean-shaven save for a long white mustache and clad in black from head to foot without a single speck of color around him anywhere." The author depicts Dracula's mustache as heavy, his teeth as sharp and white, and his skin as sallow and pallid. In the portrait of Dracula that survives in the collection at Castle Ambras, the real Dracula is as startling and arresting in appearance as the figure created in words by Stoker, or the character Nosferatu created some years later by Max Schreck in Murnau's 1922 classic horror film.

3

The Historical Dracula: 1430/31-1462

Tyrant from Transylvania

In a broad sense, Bram Stoker was quite correct in setting his Dracula story in romantic Transylvania, even though he located his fictional castle 140 miles away from the site of the authentic one. Dracula was born in Transylvania, in the old German fortified town of Schassburg (in Romanian, Sighisoara). One of the most enchanting Saxon burghs, and certainly the most medieval, Schassburg is located about 65 miles south of Bistrita. The date of Dracula's birth, as close as we can ascertain, is 1430 or 1431. The house in which he was born is identified by a small plaque dedicated to his father Dracul. This marks the threshold of a typical German burgher's house, attached to a row of similar ones of 15th- and 16th-century vintage. Distinguished from each other only by their bright colors, they line a narrow cobbled lane leading up to the site of the old fortress which commands the city.

Dracula spent his youth in this peculiarly Germanic atmosphere, making frequent trips to the Germanies. As an infant, he may have been taken in February 1431 to Nuremberg, site of the Court of the Holy Roman Emperor Sigismund of the Luxemburg line, when his father was invested with the insignia of the Order of the Dragon. On that same occasion, in the presence of a few dissident boyars from his native principality, Dracul was also made prince of the southern Romanian principality of Wallachia as well as duke of the Transylvanian districts of Almas and Fagaras. The formal oath that was taken in Nuremberg affected the future of all the Draculas. The Order of the Dragon, in the eyes of those charitably inclined, baptized the whole family as heirs and successors to the man initially so honored. The Draculas were thus, by their Dragon standard, dedicated to fight the Turks. This formal investiture also bound the Draculas to the hazardous task of seeking the insecure Wallachian throne, ruled at the time by Prince Alexandru Aldea,

Dracul's half brother. This was to mark the beginning of a lengthy feud between rival members of the ruling family, one featuring numerous crimes, of which the 15th century bears many instances, particularly in Eastern Europe.

When the recently invested "Dragon" was finally able to make good his title of prince by expelling Alexandru Aldea from Wallachia in the winter of 1436-37, the seat of Wallachian power continued close to the Transylvanian border, where Dracul essentially drew his support. Historically, Transylvania had always been linked to both the Moldavian and the Wallachian principalities. After the Roman legions evacuated the more recently conquered province of Dacia in 271 A.D. the bulk of the Romanized population withdrew to the mountains, seeking escape from the turmoils of Eastern invasion in the Transylvanian plateau. In this way, the Daco-Romans survived untouched by the Gothic, Avar, Hunnish, Gepidae, Slav, Hungarian, and Bulgarian avalanches, which would surely have destroyed their Latin language and customs had they continually resided in the plain. Only after the torrent of invasions had receded did these Romanians descend into the plain, but cautiously, maintaining tentatively their mountain hideout. By and large, each generation of Romanians from the 13th century onward advanced a little farther into the plain. Eventually they reached the Danube and the Black Sea to the south, the Pruth and the Dniester to the northeast—in other words, to the limits of modern Romania, and also in part to the former limits of ancient Dacia. In the case of Wallachia, nothing is more typical of its tendency to turn to Transylvania for security, and nothing better demonstrates the reticence in abandoning the mountains as a haven of shelter, than the choice of the early capitals of the principality. The first, early 14th-century capital, Campulung, borders the Transylvanian Alps.

Dracula's capital, Targoviste, lies somewhat lower down in the plain, but still provides easy access to the mountains. The choice of this site already marks a period of increased self-confidence in the country's history. Bucharest, Romania's present capital, was fortified by Dracula in 1459, as a defensive bastion against the Turks. It was known as the citadel of the Dambovita river. Lying much closer to the Danube, it reflected the country's power in the continued conquest of the eastern lands, notwithstanding the pressures of the Turks. Dracula's youngest brother and successor, Radu the Handsome, chose to reside more often in Bucharest for precisely opposite reasons; he wished to be closer to his Turkish masters. Rumor had it that Radu, owing to his lengthy sojourn in the Turkish capital, also wanted to be close to Constantinople, as he was not insensible to the pleasures of the sultan's harem. Idle gossip accused him, largely because of his good looks, of being one of Sultan Mohammed's long-haired boys, thus one required to be constantly at his master's disposal. In any case, Radu's reign marked the reversal of the heroic stage in Wallachia's history and the beginning of conditional surrender to the sultan. Conditional, since the relationship of Wallachia to Constantinople continued to be regulated by treaty, with the local princes as vassals to the sultan.

When secure on his throne, Dracul, a wily politician, sensed that the tenuous balance of power was rapidly shifting to the advantage of the ambitious Turkish Sultan Murad II. By now the Turks had destroyed both Serbs and Bulgars and the sultan was contemplating a final blow against the Greeks. Thus, Dracul began the first of his numerous deceptions, treacherously signing an alliance with the Turks against his former patron, the Holy Roman Emperor. In 1438, in admittedly difficult circumstances, Dracul and his two sons Mircea and Dracula accompanied Sultan Murad II on one of his frequent incursions of Transylvania, murdering, looting, and burning on the way, as was the Turkish practice. This was the first of many occasions when the Draculas, who in a sense labeled themselves "Transylvanians," returned to their homeland as enemies rather than as friends. But the Transylvanian cities and towns, though cruelly raided and pillaged, evidently still believed that they could get a better deal from a fellow citizen than from the Turks. This provides the explanation for the eagerness of the mayor and burghers of the town of Sebes to surrender specifically to the Draculas, on condition that their lives be spared and that they not be carried into Turkish slavery. Dracul, sworn to protect the Christians, was at least on this occasion able to save Sebes from complete destruction.

Many such incidents made the Turks suspect the true allegiance of the Romanian prince. Accordingly, Sultan Murad beguiled Dracul into a personal confrontation in the summer of 1444. Insensitive to the snare, Dracul crossed the Danube with his second son, Dracula, and his youngest one, Radu, only to be "bound in iron chains" and brought into the presence of the sultan, who accused him of disloyalty. In order to save his neck and regain his throne, after a brief imprisonment Dracul swore renewed fidelity to Murad, and as proof of his loyalty, he left

Dracula and Radu as hostages. The two boys were sent to Egrigoz in Asia Minor, and placed under house arrest. Dracula remained a Turkish captive until 1448, Radu stayed much longer, and because of his weaker nature submitted more easily to the refined indoctrination techniques of his jailors. To all intents and purposes, perhaps because of his effeminate looks, he became a minion of the sultan and eventually the official Turkish candidate to the Wallachian throne, and in due course he succeeded his brother.

Dracula's reaction to these dangerous years, dangerous because his very life was at stake should his father's policy change, was quite the reverse. In fact, these years of Turkish imprisonment already form a clue to his shifty nature and perverse personality. They taught Dracula, among other things, the Turkish language, which he mastered like a native; acquainted him with the pleasures of the harem (for the terms of confinement were not too strict); and completed his training in Byzantine cynicism, which the Turks had merely inherited from the Greeks.

Dracula from that time onward held human nature in low esteem. Life was cheap—after all, his own was constantly threatened—and morality was nonessential in matters of state. He needed no Machiavelli to instruct him in the amorality of politics.

He also developed during those years, as related by his Turkish captors, a reputation for trickery, cunning, insubordination, and brutality, and inspired fright in his own guards, in contrast to his brother's sheepish subserviency. Two other traits were entrenched in Dracula's psyche because of the plot into which father and sons had been ensnared. One was suspicion; never again would he trust himself to the Turks or for that matter to any man, whether friend or foe. The other was revengefulness; Dracula would not forget, nor forgive, those whether high or low who crossed him; indeed, this became a family trait. The sultan's representative who had arranged the trap which led to Dracul's imprisonment was captured by Dracula in the course of his campaign against the Turks in 1462, and summarily executed after the cruelest tortures—this despite Dracula's promise of safe conduct.

In December 1447, Dracul the father died a victim of his own plotting—murdered by the henchmen of John Hunyadi, who had become angered by the Dragon's flirtations with the Turks. Dracul's pro-Turkish policies are easily accountable, if on no other basis than to save his sons from inevitable reprisals and possible death. The assassination of Dracul took place in the marshes of Balteni, on the site of an ancient monastery that still exists. The father's murder was compounded by the brutal killing of Dracula's elder brother, Mircea, who had fought valiantly on the side of the Hunyadi crusade. There were more legitimate, personal reasons for the Hunyadi-inspired, double assassination, and they deserve a brief explanation here.

At the time of his imprisonment at Adrianople, Dracul had sworn that he would never bear arms against the Turks, a flagrant violation of his previous oath as a member of the Order of the Dragon. Once safely restored to his position as prince, and in spite of the fact that his two sons were hostages of the Turks, Dracul hesitantly resumed his oath to the Holy Roman Emperor, and joined the anti-Turkish struggle. He was, in fact, absolved of his Turkish oath by the Papacy. This implied that he could participate in the Balkan crusades, at that time organized by John Hunyadi against Sultan Murad. Dracul's hesitancy can be readily understood; the risks he took were nothing less than the decapitation of his sons Dracula and Radu. Indeed, it is little short of a miracle that the Turks did not behead these two captives.

The elder brother, Mircea, not Dracul, took the lead more actively in what is described as the long campaign of 1443. From the Wallachian point of view, this campaign proved an outstanding success. It led to the capture of the citadel of Giurgiu, built at great cost to Wallachia by Dracula's grandfather, Prince Mircea. However, the Varna campaign of 1444, though organized on a far more ambitious scale and reaching the Black Sea, was a disaster. The young, inexperienced King of Poland, Vladislav, fell to his death along with the papal legate Cesarini, and Hunyadi himself, it is said, was able to flee and survive only because the Wallachians knew the terrain well enough to lead him to safety. In the inevitable recriminations which followed, both Dracul and his son Mircea held Hunyadi personally responsible for the magnitude of the Christian debacle. "The Sultan goes hunting with a greater retinue," reproached the Wallachian prince, "than the 20,000 Christian crusaders," who had relied upon the support of a shoddy Burgundian and Genoese fleet to prevent the Turkish landing from Asia Minor. A council of war held somewhere in the Dobrogea judged Hunyadi responsible for the Christians' defeat, and, largely upon the entreaties of Mircea, sentenced him to death. But Hunyadi's past services and his widespread reputation as the "white knight" of the Christian forces saved his life, and Dracul ensured him safe passage to his Transylvanian homeland.

From that moment on Hunyadi bore the Draculas, and particularly Mircea, Dracula's brother, a deep hatred. This vindictiveness was to be satisfied by Dracul's and Mircea's assassination. After 1446, Hunyadi once again placed the Wallachian crown in the more reliable hands of a Danesti claimant. (The rival Danesti family traced back to Prince Dan, one of Dracula's great-uncles.)

What is far more difficult to account for is Dracula's attitude upon his escape from Turkish captivity in 1448. We know that the Turks—undoubtedly impressed by Dracula's ferocity and bravery, and obviously opposed to the Danesti princes since they were thoroughly identified with the Hungarian court—tried to place Dracula on the Wallachian throne as early as 1448, an attempt which succeeded for two months. Dracula, then about 20 years old and fearful of his father's Transylvanian assassins, and equally fearful about returning to his former captors, fled to Moldavia, the northernmost Romanian principality, at that time in the hands of Prince Bogdan, whose son, Prince Steven, was Dracula's cousin. During these years of Moldavian exile, Dracula and Steven developed a close and lasting friendship, each promising the other that whoever might succeed to the throne of his principality first would help the other to power swiftly—by force of arms if necessary. The Moldavian princely residence was then at Suceava, an ancient city and today the point of departure for visits to a number of famous monasteries in one or more of which both Dracula and Steven undoubtedly continued their scholarly Byzantine education under the supervision of erudite monks and abbots.

Dracula stayed in Moldavia until 1451, when Steven's father, Bogdan, was brutally assassinated by a rival faction. Perhaps because of a lack of alternatives, Dracula then reappeared in Transylvania, where he threw himself upon the mercies of John Hunyadi, who had instigated his father's and brother's assassination. He was undoubtedly taking a chance, though by that time owing to Turkish pressure the reigning Danesti prince of Wallachia, Vladislav II, had adopted a pro-Turkish policy, thus estranging him from his Hungarian patrons. It was essentially history repeating itself at the expense of the Danesti.

It was in Hunyadi's interests once again to have a pliable tool, a prince in reserve, just in case the Danesti prince might turn to the Turks completely. Thus, mutual sef interest, rather than any degree of confidence, bound Dracula and John Hunyadi together from 1451 until 1456, when Hunyadi died at Belgrade. During this time, John Hunyadi was Dracula's last tutor, political mentor, and, what is more important, military educator. Dracula could have had no finer instruction in anti-Turkish strategy. Like a chivalrous vassal he personally took part in many of Hunyadi's campaigns. He was invested, as his father Dracul had been, with the duchies of Fagaras and Almas. In addition, he rapidly became the official claimant to the Wallachian throne. It was for this reason that he did not accompany his suzerain in the Belgrade campaign of 1456, when the great Christian warrior was finally felled by the plague. Dracula at the time had finally been granted permission to cross the Transylvanian mountains and oust the unfaithful Danesti from the Wallachian throne.

During the years 1451-56 Dracula once again resided in Transylvania. Abandoning the family home at Sighisoara, he took up residence in Sibiu, mainly to be closer to the Wallachian border. In Sibiu, Dracula heard news which had the effect of a bombshell in the Christian world: Constantinople had fallen to the Turks, and the Emperor Constantine Palaeologus, at whose court Dracula may have been a page in the 1430s, had died. Dracula at least could take comfort in the fact that Sibiu was considered the most impregnable city in Transylvania. This may have influenced his decision to stay there. Yet in one of those inconsistent, illogical acts that make a riddle of his personality, barely four years after he had left the city of Sibiu, Dracula mercilessly raided this haven of refuge and its vicinity with a Wallachian contingent of 20,000 men and killed, maimed, impaled, and tortured some 10,000 of his former fellow citizens and neighbors. Pillaging and looting took place on a more ferocious scale than had been the case with the Turks in 1438. As we shall see, the spiteful Germans of Sibiu were to have some retributive satisfaction in Dracula's lifetime.

Hard-pressed by the Turks in 1462, Dracula threw himself upon the mercies of John Hunyadi's son, Mathias, appealing for at least a safe asylum. Mathias, King of Hungary, had previously given some indication of offering military aid, but when Dracula found him at Castle Fagaras (today restored), the king instead of granting sanctuary had Dracula incarcerated on the spot, then sent in chains to Budapest and later to the fortress of Visegrad, 30 miles up the Danube. Here Dracula spent the next 12 years of his life.

What is the explanation of this strange and unexpected reaction on the part of Mathias? Apparently the Germans of Sibiu, hearing of Dracula's predicament, had forged three letters in his name which revealed him as meekly submitting to the Turks, and then had allowed them to be intercepted by servants of the Hungarian king. The original letters were published in the correspondence of Pope Pius II. One can safely presume they were forgeries, since no prince about to demand asylum from a friendly monarch would be so demented that simultaneously he would write to the enemy and promise him military aid against this friend. Such coincidence is incredible even in view of Dracula's notorious perfidy. Surely, the forgery was simply a device of the Saxons of Sibiu for avenging Dracula's depredation of their town two years earlier. Not only was Dracula imprisoned, but his character was defamed by political pamphleteering.

The palace of Mathias was located on a mountain dominating the famous bend of the Danube. Just a few hundred yards below stood the Tower of Solomon, where maximum-security prisoners of the realm were detained. Very early in his long period of incarceration Dracula somehow caught the eye of Mathias' sister. Either because of the intervention of this young lady, whose name has been carefully omitted from the Hunyadi family registers owing to her association with Dracula, or for some unknown cause, the terms of Dracula's imprisonment became progressively more lenient. Moreover, there were all sorts of secret passages under the mountain, one or more of which probably led from donjon and cell to the private quarters of the princess.

Dracula's first wife had died, or, more probably, had committed suicide by throwing herself from the high tower of Dracula's castle shortly before the arrival of the Turks in 1462. He was thus free to marry again. His new marriage to Mathias' sister, plus renunciation of his Orthodox faith, ultimately led to his liberation and his return to the Wallachian throne.

When released from prison in 1474, Dracula was given a house by Mathias in the ancient town of Pest, across the Danube from Buda, but he lived there for only a few months. A local legend circulating at the time spoke of the brutal death of a Hungarian captain who had surreptitiously entered the house and been decapitated by Dracula himself. The event might well have passed unnoticed but for the motive of the killing, so typical of Dracula's egomania in any and all circumstances. He did not kill the man because the house had been subjected to theft, but because his deranged vanity had been insulted. "Is this the way," he asked, "in which one enters the house of a prince, without a formal introduction?" The thief, interesting to say, was allowed to go free.

After leaving Pest, Dracula spent close to two years at Sibiu with his wife. He had seemingly reconciled himself to the German burghers, who could do little against him anyhow because of his marriage connections with the Hungarian crown. In the heart of Sibiu to this day lies the ancient Gothic cathedral with its impressive 200-foot steeple, the construction of which was begun before Dracula's time. Within this church is buried Dracula's only legitimate son, known to history, not surprisingly for a Dracula, as "Mihnea the Bad." Mihnea had fewer opportunities to exploit his evil instincts, simply because he reigned more briefly than his father—from April 1508 to October 1509. He died as did all the Draculas, assassinated by one of his numerous political adversaries, and in the very city where, like his father, he had sought refuge after a turbulent rule. One of Mihnea's male descendants committed the supreme offense, of which Dracula himself had been suspected in 1462; he converted himself to Islam, and thus some of his offspring bore Moslem names.

Another Transylvanian town which is linked with Dracula's name is Brasov (in German, Kronstadt). Brasov seemingly holds the distinction of having witnessed on its surrounding hills more stakes with Dracula victims rotting in the sun or chewed and mangled by the Carpathian vultures than any other place in the same principality. Although statistics are very difficult to establish, particularly for that time, some 30,000 persons were probably killed in Amlas on the morning of St. Bartholomew's Day, August 24, 1460—more than were butchered by Catherine de Medicis on the same saint's-day in Paris more than a century later. Dracula was meticulously accurate when counting Turkish heads, but notoriously vague when the impaled victims were either Saxons or Romanians. Somehow Dracula's St. Bartholomew's massacre has escaped the eye of the historian (though not that of contemporary publicists), while that of Catherine has made her the object of enduring reprobation.

Dracula's crimes, the refinements of his cruelty, deserve a chapter unto themselves. Impalement, hardly a new method of torture, was his favorite method of imposing death. A strong horse was usually harnessed to each leg of the victim, while the stake was carefully introduced so as not to kill instantly. At times Dracula issued special instructions to his torturers not to have the pales too sharp—rather, rounded-off—lest gaping wounds kill his victims on the spot. Such quick death would have interfered with the pleasure he sought in watching their agonies over a period of time, as the stakes were propped in the ground. This torture was often a matter of several hours, sometimes a matter of days. There were various forms of impalement depending upon age, rank, or sex. This is the reason why, in Romanian history, Dracula is known to this day as Vlad Tepes— Vlad the Impaler even though his contemporaries knew him as Dracula.

There were also various geometric patterns in which the impaled were displayed. Usually the victims were arranged in concentric circles, and in the outskirts of cities where they could be viewed by all. There were high spears and low spears, according to rank. There was impalement from above—feet upwards; and impalement from below—head upwards; or through the heart or naval. There were nails in people's heads, maiming of limbs, blinding, strangulation, burning, the cutting of noses and ears, and of sexual organs in the case of women, scalping and skinning, exposure to the elements or to the wild animals, and boiling alive.

Dracula's morbid inventiveness may well have inspired the Marquis de Sade, who was no doubt familiar with his crimes. In regard to the cruel techniques practiced in our so-called enlightened 20th century, Dracula set another shining precedent. He generally demanded confessions prior to punishment, sometimes as a way of escaping partial or even total violence. And often he scaled the severity of the punishment to the instinctively self-preservative wit of his potential victim. There were instances when a man doomed to destruction was able to save his life with some happy or flattering phrase.

The historical ballads tell us that Dracula victims were principally seen in the larger Transylvanian towns such as Sibiu or Brasov, in smaller villages such as Sercaia and Mica, and outside hostile fortresses such as Fagaras. Most of Dracula's Transylvanian atrocities occurred between 1459 and 1461. The decomposed bodies of impaled prisoners frightened the Turks who encountered them at Giurgiu on the Danube. Even the stout-hearted conqueror of Constantinople, Mohammed II, was sickened when he saw the remains of 20,000 prisoners, taken several months before, rotting outside Dracula's Wallachian capital of Targoviste. They included many Turks, perhaps more Germans, some Bulgarians, Hungarians, and Romanians, particularly of the upper class—all those who in some manner had crossed the demented tyrant.

The scene of Dracula's most publicized act of atrocity, which began early in the morning, April 2, 1459, is a small knoll within the city of Brasov. In Dracula's time a small chapel dedicated to St. Jacob dominated the hill until the tyrant prince had it destroyed by fire. (One of the best-known, medieval, local German woodcuts depicts Dracula and his boyars dining and feasting in an open area below this church, while attendants are busily cutting off heads and limbs of the unfortunate.) The story relates that by the end of that April day thousands of Saxon burghers were neatly arranged on stakes around the party. Another incident tells that one of Dracula's more sensitive boyars had the audacity to hold his nose, presumably owing to the stench of the carnage. Dracula, with a twisted sense of humor all his own, immediately ordered one of his officers to impale the man on a stake, but one even higher than those reserved for the rest, so that the boyar might not be perturbed in his agony by the stench of the corpses and blood all around.

In reviewing such horrors, one must remember that there are two sides to Dracula's personality. One is that of the demented psychopath, the torturer and inquisitor who turns to piety to liberate his conscience. The other reveals the disciple of Machiavelli, the premature nationalist, the amazingly modern statesman, who can always justify his actions in accordance with *raison d'état*. The citizens of Brasov and Sibiu after all were "foreigners" who attempted to perpetuate their monopoly of trade in the Romanian principalities. They were intriguers as well. The Saxons, conscious of Dracula's authoritarianism, were busy, as was their wont since earlier times, subverting his regime and granting asylum to would-be contenders from the Danesti clan. It is far too easy to explain Dracula's personality, as some have done, on the basis of insanity alone. There was certainly a method along with his madness.

Although Dracula ruled the principality of Wallachia on three separate occasions and died near the city of Bucharest, which he fortified, both his family homestead—the magnet of authority during his actual rule—and his many massacres take us back to Transylvania. Moreover, the site of Dracula's castle, though technically in Wallachia, skirts the Transylvanian mountains, and the secret passage below the castle leads straight to the snow-capped peaks of the Fagaras mountains. To this extent the tradition borne out in Stoker's story is quite correct. Dracula is inexorably and historically connected with romantic Transylvania.

Prince of Wallachia

But no matter how closely Dracula was bound to Transylvania, his associations with Wallachia are a major part of his story. Dracula's ancestors stemmed from Wallachia, the southernmost of the three Romanian provinces. It was here that he ruled three separate times: briefly in 1448; from 1456 to 1462; and for two months in 1476. It was here, too, that Dracula's capital was located: therein lay the center of his political power, the scene of many of his horrors, and the official headquarters of the Orthodox Church. He also built all of his monasteries in this province, and fought many campaigns against the Turks on its southern frontier along the Danube.

On the northern frontier of Wallachia, facing Transylvania, Dracula erected his infamous castle. On a tributary of the Danube, the Dambovita, he built yet another fortress, which in 1659 became the city of Bucharest, the capital of modern Romania. Close to Bucharest, Dracula was killed, and at the island monastery, Snagov, 20 miles north of the city, he was buried. From Wallachia come our internal sources concerning Dracula, and in essence they tend to confirm the German, Russian, Hungarian, and Byzantine narratives.

At the Military Museum in Bucharest is an assortment of mementos from Dracula's time, and in the park outside is a reconstructed version of the tyrant's notorious castle. The document with the first mention of Bucharest is located at the Academy of the Romanian Socialist Republic. However, the only existing life-size Dracula portrait is located in Castle Ambras near Innsbruck. Ferdinand II, Archduke of the Tyrol, who owned Castle Ambras during the 16th century, had a perverse hobby of documenting the villains and deformed personalities of history. He sent emissaries all over Europe to collect portraits of such persons, and reserved a special room in the castle for displaying them. It made no difference whether the subjects were well-known or comparatively obscure. What did matter was that they be actual human beings, not imagined ones. If such persons could be found alive, the archduke tried to settle them, at least temporarily, at his court, where paintings could be made of them on the spot. A few giants, a notorious dwarf, and the wolfman from the Canary Islands stayed on at the Castle Ambras for some years. Dracula was already dead at the time when this degenerate Hapsburg began his hobby, but the prince's reputation as a mass murderer was already largely established in the Germanic world because of the tales of the Saxons of Transylvania concerning the impalements. We do not know how or where Ferdinand's portrait of Dracula was painted or who the original artist was. It is possible that one of Dracula's descendants took the portrait with him when fleeing Wallachia some time in the 16th century and that following his death it fell into the hands of the Jesuits, who, knowing of Ferdinand's unusual interests, gave it to the archduke.

The fascinating and rather frightening gallery of rogues and monsters at Castle Ambras has hardly been disturbed since the days of its founding. The Dracula portrait hangs between that of the wolfman Gonsalvus from the Canary Islands and those of his two wolf children, who are completely covered with hair. A little to the left of Dracula is the portrait of Gregor Baxi, a Hungarian courtier who in the course of a duel had one eye pierced by a pale. The other eye degenerated into a bloodied and deformed shape. Baxi managed to survive this condition for one year, long enough for the portrait to be completed with the actual pale protruding from both sides of the head—which made medical history. It is strangely appropriate that this impaled victim should be located close to Dracula, whose eyes are depicted slightly turned to the left and seem to gaze in satisfaction at this macabre scene. A visit to Castle Ambras, particularly to the "Frankenstein Gallery" as the modern-day guides insist on calling it, is a startling experience, even for the most stout-hearted.

At Castle Anif, near Salzburg, yet another Dracula portrait once existed. It was discovered at the close of the last century in rather unusual circumstances. A member of the Florescu family, Demeter, a jurist by profession, was traveling through Salzburg in 1885, and by chance was invited to dinner by Count Arco-Stepperg, the owner of Castle Anif. After dinner the count showed his guest the well-known collection of oriental paintings in the large gallery of the castle. To his great surprise, Demeter saw among them a portrait of Dracula, which he immediately recognized, having seen the other portrait at Ambras Castle only a few days before. The owner was not able to explain to him how this painting had come into the hands of his family. In 1968, the authors of this book went back to Anif. They showed the present owner, Count Moye de Son, the notes made by Demeter Florescu concerning his visit in 1885. Unfortunately, the Dracula portrait was no longer in the castle. The Arco-Stepperg family had died out and inheritances had dissipated the collection.

Two other Dracula portraits exist. One, at the Vienna Art Gallery, is a miniature oil painting, probably a copy of the Ambras portrait. The other was discovered accidentally during the summer of 1970 by W. Peters, a German-born scholar of Romanian history. Entitled "St. Andrew's Martyrdom," it shows Dracula—a symbol of evil in the eyes of the 15th-century Austrian painter—as a simple spectator enjoying the scene. Crucifixion, after all, was just a variation of Dracula's favorite torture, impalement.

Several portraits of the prince survive in the primitive woodcuts on some of the German Dracula pamphlets. Whether these are true portraits is an open question since the German artists did their very best to deform Dracula's features. It is a twist of history and fate that the Dracula portraits exist in the Germanic world, and are totally absent in Romania— underlining the fact that in his day Dracula was better known in Western and Central Europe than in his native land. Owing to the popularity of Bram Stoker's novel outside Eastern Europe, this is still somewhat true today.

In Wallachia, Dracula is, of course, commemorated in popular ballads and peasant folktales, particularly in mountain villages surrounding Castle Dracula itself, the region where he is best remembered. Despite the perversions of time and transliteration, or the distortions of the vivid imagination of the peasants themselves, it remains true that popular epic should play an important role in constructing the past. Dracula was not defined as all villain in Romanian folklore, in contrast to the German, Russian, and Turkish traditions which have an obvious *parti pris*. The German-Transylvanians bore him a grudge because he massacred them; the Russians because he abandoned the Orthodox faith; the Turks because he fought them. Romanian folklore—which is, of course, the product of peasant imagery, not that of the boyar chroniclers who labeled him "the Impaler"—has somehow attempted to explain away Dracula's cruel idiosyncrasies. Thus, it records him, in true "Robin Hood style," as cruel to the rich and a powerful friend of the poor. There is a little of the haiduc (the robber baron of the Balkans) in Dracula folklore. This peasant view of Dracula's deeds was probably a whitewash, an exaggeration; nevertheless it persisted. Moreover, Dracula *was* a brave warrior. The peasants were proud of his military accomplishments, no matter what methods he used to attain them. He *was* a national hero, defending Romania successfully against the rising Turkish tide. This one objective, ridding the country of the non-Christian, helped the peasant to excuse the impalement of the boyars, whose intrigues weakened the Wallachian state. It may also have helped them to forgive Dracula's attempts to eliminate those unfortunates, the poor and the crippled, who could not usefully serve the state. In Wallachian villages not far removed from Dracula's castle, there are peasants who claim to be descendants of the ancient warriors who fought for Dracula against the Turks, who defended him at the hour of need and guided him to safety across the mountains of Transylvania.

One thing is certain, the elderly peasants who still cultivate "Dracula tales" are a dying breed, and when the present generation is gone, the folkoric element may well die with them. The authors attempted to stimulate an interest in Dracula tales and ballads, and the first full-scale expedition to collect them was formed in the fall of 1969. As the search continues, it should include exploration of the abundant references to the supernatural, the vampire, and the wolf in Romanian folklore.

In a sense the whole of Wallachia (48,000 square miles) not just the castle region, is Dracula country from the mountains to the Danube, from the plain to the Black Sea. The main sites are Dracula's mountain castle, his capital of Targoviste, the ecclesiastical see at Curtea de Arges, the fortress of Bucharest, and his burial place at Snagov. Also of significance are Tirgsor (near Ploesti), the site of the most famous monastery Dracula built; Comana, erected close to the Danube in gratitude for a victory over the Turks; the tiny grotto of Getateni on the river Dambovita, where Dracula found haven and refuge in his escape from the Turks in 1462; and the proud and isolated abbey of Tismana, where Dracula was a frequent distinguished visitor and patron. Also included are part of Braila, the largest commercial center in the country; the fortress of Giurgiu on the Danube, the scene of Dracula's most successful campaign; Chilia farther up the mouth of the river, a strategic fortress that Dracula held precious enough not to yield even to his cousin Steven of Moldavia; the castle of Floci, a little beyond; and Enisala on the Black Sea, an older fortified bastion built by Dracula's grandfather, the remains of which can still be seen.

Apart from Dracula's famous castle on the Arges, there were minor fortifications erected by him, such as the fortress of Gherghita in the Carpathians. Dracula monasteries are still being discovered. At times one has the impression that the stones in each square foot of mosaic in a Dracula edifice wishes to tell the wayfarer its bloody story. There are no less than three villages scattered throughout the country which bear the name Vlad Tepes. It is safe to assume that they were named in his honor only when his crimes had somewhat faded from memory and his fame as a Christian warrior had helped wipe away his misdeeds.

Although Dracula's reputation had spread far and wide, much beyond Wallachia as we have noticed, the seat of his power was confined to a triangle just south of the Carpathians. At the apex, on the river Arges, a tributary of the Danube, was Castle Dracula, which will be discussed in the next chapter. The base lay between the ancient ecclesiastical seat of Curtea de Arges and Dracula's capital of Targoviste. Located between the two, but closer to the mountains, was Wallachia's first capital, oldest city in the land, Campulung. To the north are the two difficult mountain passes leading from Wallachia to Transylvania—one, by way of Turnu Rosu, reaches Sibiu, Dracula's Transylvanian residence; the other pass, closely guarded by the formidable German fortress of Bran, winds up the mountain to Brasov. This triangle just south of the Transylvanian border was the stage for the central scene of Dracula's six-year rule of Wallachia.

In Dracula's time the capital city of Targoviste was comparatively more significant than it is today, and certainly more imposing, spreading beyond the actual walls of the city. Like Versailles, Targoviste was not only the seat of power, but the nation's center of social and cultural life. Immediately surrounding the ostentatious palace, with its numerous components, its palatial gardens, and its princely church, were the Byzantine-styled houses of the boyars and their more diminutive chapels. On a smaller scale, within the comparative security of the walled courtyard, the upper class attempted to ape the etiquette of the Imperial court at Constantinople. Beyond and interspaced by gardens with stylish floral decorations, still a characteristic of modern Romanian cities to this day, were located the modest houses of the merchants, artisans, and other dependents of the princely and boyar courts. The three spiraled domes of the Orthodox churches and monasteries pierced the sky over the city. Targoviste, like Bucharest later on, was essentially a city of churches, some of which survive to this day, reflecting the intense zeal and piety of an earlier age. The monasteries, with their cloisters, chapels, and decorative courtyards, added to the colorfulness of the city. In fact, one Venetian traveler compared Targoviste to a "vast gaudy flower house." The inner sanctuary, containing most of the aristocratic homes, was surrounded by the defensive ramparts characteristic of the feudal age, though these were built on a far less impressive scale than the walls of the German-inspired fortresses in Transylvania. One almost gains the impression that each boyar household was itself a small fortified bastion, capable of defense not only against the foe without but against the far more crafty enemy within. Suspicion reigned in this Wallachian capital; anarchy was rampant; political assassination was frequent; and rapid succession of princes was the rule rather than the exception—all of which helps to account for some of Dracula's drastic measures against the boyars.

Shortly after ascending the throne in the spring of 1456, so runs one popular ballad, Dracula assembled several hundred of the great boyars of the land in the hall of the Targoviste palace, plus the five bishops, the abbots of the more important monasteries, foreign and native, and the Metropolitan. As Dracula surveyed the wily, tricky, and dishonest expressions of the boyars, he knew that among the guests were his father's and brother's assassins. Then he delivered a most untypical speech for a Wallachian prince (who was more often than not the boyars' tool). "How many reigns," he asked, "have you, my loyal subjects, personally experienced in your lifetime?" There were chuckles and grimaces in the audience, then a tense moment of silence. "Seven, my Lord," was the reply of one man. "I," said another, "have survived thirty reigns." "Since your grandfather, my liege," retorted a third, "there have been no less than twenty princes—I have survived them all." Even the younger men admitted having witnessed seven. In this manner, almost a jocular one, each boyar stood his ground and tested the severity of the new ruler. The princely title and all that it implied had evidently been taken lightly. Dracula, his eyes flashing in a way that was to become characteristic, gave an order. Within minutes, his faithful attendants surrounded the hall. Some 500 boyars who had experienced more than a certain number of reigns (for Dracula knew that his father's assassins would be among them) were immediately impaled in the vicinity of the palace and left exposed until their corpses were chewed up by blackbirds. The lesson of this day did not escape the remaining boyars. Dracula was demanding either their total submission or exile to their respective estates. Woe to him who chose to disobey.

All that one can now see of Dracula's Targoviste are the remains of the princely palace, which was destroyed and rebuilt many times. Dracula's grandfather, the redoubtable Mircea, had placed the first foundation stone at the beginning of the 15th century. Nearby is the reconstructed 16th-century Chindeia watch tower, from the battlement of which the tourist can still survey the whole city if he has the heart to climb a steep and narrow winding staircase. Looking down on the courtyard below, one can clearly discern the remains of the palace's foundation, which indicate a structure of modest size. The cellar was probably used for the princely supply of wine. Here, too, would have been the prison or torture chamber where the unfortunate gypsy-slave or boyar opponent lucky enough to escape impalement was given the traditional bastinado. The notorious throne hall was evidently located on the ground floor. This was where Dracula, his father Dracul, and his grandfather Mircea, were invested princes of the land following a religious ceremony, and where they entertained the boyars, received audiences and petitions, and held official councils of state with the local Divan, which included every member of the upper aristocracy—the bishops, abbots, and the Metropolitan.

In this throne hall occurred a famous scene described in almost all the Dracula narrations: certain envoys of the sultan had come to greet the prince officially, and they refused to take off their turbans. Dracula, who was hyper-sensitive about any slight to his vanity, speedily ordered the turbans of the Turkish envoys to be nailed to their heads. The Turks agonized within a pool of blood at the very foot of the throne.

Many cruel scenes occurred in the throne room of Dracula's palace at Targoviste. Some of them included victims who escaped from the pale by slavish adulation, confessions, and self-incrimination. There was, for instance, the case of two monks from a neighboring Catholic monastery. According to the story, Dracula tactlessly showed them the rows and rows of impaled cadavers in the courtyard. One of the monks, rather than expressing moral reprobation (which Dracula expected and which would certainly have doomed the monk to impalement), meekly commented: "You are appointed by God to punish the evil-doers." Dracula hardly expected enunciation of the doctrine of divine right, and consequently spared this particular monk. His colleague, however, who had the moral strength to disapprove of the ghastly scene, was impaled immediately.

Dracula took particular delight in ensnaring the unwary in a compromising statement. The following incident is typical; it occurred in September 1458, while Dracula was entertaining a Polish nobleman, Benedict de Boithor, who had come as the ambassador of an alleged ally, King Mathias Corvinus of Hungary. The usual trivial conversation was pursued in the dining hall of the palace at Targoviste. At the end of the repast, a golden spear was suddenly brought by some servants and set up directly in front of the envoy, who watched the operation cautiously, having heard of Dracula's reputation. "Tell me," said Dracula, addressing the Pole with some amusement, "why do you think that I have had this spear set up in the room?" "My lord," answered the Pole with verve, "it would seem that some great boyar of the land has offended you and you wish to honor him in some way." "Fairly spoken," said Dracula. "You are the representative of a great king. I have had this lance set up especially in your honor." Maintaining his *savoir faire*, the Pole replied: "My Lord, should I have been responsible for something worthy of death, do as you please, for you are the best judge and in that case you would not be responsible for my death, but I alone." Dracula burst into laughter. The answer had been both witty and flattering. "Had you not answered me in this fashion," said Dracula, "I would truly have impaled you on the spot." He then honored the man and showered him with gifts.

Of Dracula's married life, we know far too little during this period. His first wife, a boyar's daughter, probably died in 1462. From the native Romanian Dracula tales, it would appear that their marriage was not a happy one, for the prince was often seen wandering alone at night on the outskirts of the city, usually in disguise, seeking the company of the beautiful but humble woman who in time became his mistress. This relationship, among many others, indicated both Dracula's distrust of the boyars and his plebeian instincts. Needless to say, this particular idyl did not last; the woman was assassinated— for infidelity, according to peasant tales. Another mistress died in mysterious circumstances, with her sexual organs cut out.

Dracula was always concerned for the survival of the souls of his faithful followers, a reflection of the morbid religiosity inspired by the enormity of his crimes. He was careful to surround himself with priests, abbots, bishops, and confessors, whether Roman Catholic or Orthodox. He often spent long moments of meditation within the saintly confines of individual monasteries, such as Tismana in western Wallachia, where he was known as a generous donor. All the Draculas seemed intent upon belonging to a church, receiving the sacraments, being buried as Christians, and at least being identified with a religion. Even the famous Apostate Mihnea in due course became a devout Moslem. Like the average penitent of pre-Lutheran times, these men felt that good works, particularly the erection of monasteries along with rich endowments, would contribute to the eradication of their sins. Mircea, Dracul, Dracula, Radu, Vlad the Monk, and Mihnea, just to name six of the family, were collectively responsible for no less than 50 monastic foundations or endowments of which Dracula alone was responsible for five. Dracula's half brother, the notorious Vlad, was a monk before he became prince. Even the degenerate Radu, Dracula's brother, who was known as a Turcophile erected a monastery, Tanganul, and was probably buried there. Monastic interest was, of course, a perfect pretext for interfering in, and controlling the affairs of, both Catholic and Orthodox churches in Wallachia.

Dracula had a close relationship with the Franciscan monks in Targoviste and with the Cistercian monastery at Carta, and he frequently received monks from both orders at the palace. But the religious of various orders—including Benedictines and Capucins—sought refuge in German lands after they had incurred Dracula's wrath by refusing to toe the line. One of the monks, Jacob by name, from the monastery of "Gorion," may well have been the original author of the manuscript found at the Monastery of St. Gallen in Switzerland, the oldest document (1462) in the anti-Dracula publicity campaign, which made such a profound impact on the 15th-century Germanic world.

As late as the period of World War I, not a single ecclesiastical foundation was specifically attributed to Dracula. But in 1922, a brilliant young Romanian student, Constantin C. Giurescu, was passing casually through the village of Strejnicu, and stopped to converse with a local priest; by chance his eye noticed an inscription on a half-buried stone which lay in the backyard of the church. The stone had evidently been carved out from the main portico of some medieval church. Suspecting an interesting find and knowing both the Cyrillic script and ancient Church Slavonic, the young historian to his amazement, and that of the priest, deciphered the following inscription: "By the grace of God, I Vlad Voevod, Prince of Wallachia, son of the great Vlad Voevod, have built and completed this church on June 24 in the year 1461." The discovery was, to say the least, revolutionary. Giurescu took the translation of his inscription to Bucharest, where Professor Nicholas Iorga, the internationally known Romanian historian, confirmed the stone's authenticity.

Giurescu, who went on to become a professor at the University of Bucharest, can in many ways be considered the greatest living historian in Romania. In 1968, he came to America for a nationwide lecture tour. He was amazed and elated to find that American students had a strong interest in Dracula, even though much of that interest was due to Stoker's and Hollywood's vampire stories.

The foundation stone accidentally discovered by Giurescu in the courtyard of the village church of Strejnicu belonged to a church located only a few miles away at Tirgsor, where excavations have since revealed two more 15th-century churches. The erection of a Dracula church at Tirgsor had nothing to do with the importance of this town as a trading center. The date coincides clearly enough with the year of the murder of a rival Danesti claimant to the Wallachian throne. Dracula found this man, Vladistav Dan III, at Fagaras Castle in Transylvania, sheltered by his Saxon protectors. Incensed by the intrigue of this rival, Dracula ordered him to dig his own grave and to read his own funeral service, then decapitated him. It should be added that Tirgsor was also near the place where Dracula's father had been murdered in 1447. Thus there were at least two powerful motives that may have led Dracula to erect this particular monastery—a need to expiate his murder of Vladistav Dan and a desire to show filial piety.

Beyond the suburbs of Targoviste lies an extensive network of lakes. These were used by Dracula mostly for fishing stocked trout, and for lakeside picnics and orgies. One outing, probably held in this area on Easter Day of 1459, was climaxed by the notorious mass murder of 500 boyars, a scene immortalized by the 15th-century Romanian painter Teodor Aman. The hilly region is similarly enshrined in popular memories. Here, in 1462, took place the famous impalement of the Turkish soldiers captured the previous winter when Dracula campaigned along the Danube.

Just outside Targoviste, high up in what is essentially an area of vineyards (the famed *podgorie*—hill region), lies an edifice far more handsome with its pure Byzantine profile than any existing church within the city itself. This is the Monastery of the Hill (Manastirea Dealului), known more traditionally as the Monastery of St. Nicholas of the Wines. Although it is reputedly one of the most beautiful ecclesiastical structures in Romania—second only to the Church of Arges, a few miles away—an atmosphere of gloom pervades it. At one time it served as a prison, later as a somewhat harsh military academy. Today it is a retreat for elderly priests and monks. Within the interior, virtually every stone which one steps on marks a tomb. No church in Romania speaks more eloquently about death.

The Monastery of the Hill was initially built and endowed by Dracula's cousin, Prince Radu the Great (1495-1508), one of the few members of the family not linked with bloodshed. Prince Radu (not to be confused with Radu the Handsome, Dracul's brother) gained renown as a patron of learning and a builder of churches; his reward was a majestic tomb at the foot of the mountain altar. Tradition suggests that the body of Dracula's father was brought by some pious monks to a frame church (which preceded the monastery) shortly after his assassination at Balteni. His tomb was unmarked because of the obvious dangers that threatened the monks at a time when a prince of the rival Danesti family was in power. Dracula's elder brother, Mircea, who valiantly fought the Turks during Hunyadi's crusades, is alleged to have been buried close to his father, near the altar. He had been captured by the pro-Hunyadi boyars at Balteni, taken in chains to Targoviste, and executed shortly after his father's murder. When Dracula became prince in 1456 he ordered Mircea's coffin, located in the public burial ground in Targoviste, to be opened. Mircea's head was found twisted and turned to the ground, proving that he had been buried alive and had struggled desperately for breath. Dracula ordered him to be reburied with pomp (in the old wooden church on the monastery site) and proceeded with his revenge against the boyars.

Crusader against the Turks

In the winter of 1461, Dracula hurled a challenge to no less a person than the proud conqueror of Constantinople, Sultan Mohammed II. The subsequent Danubian and Wallachian campaigns which lasted from the winter of 1461 through the summer and fall of 1462 undoubtedly constitute the best-known and most discussed episode in his fascinating career. To say the least, Dracula's resourcefulness, his feats of valor, his tactics and strategy, brought him as much notoriety throughout Europe as his gruesome treatment of his subjects. Whereas his impalements were recorded in what is referred to as *"la petite histoire,"* and, thus, were more easily forgotten, his acts of heroism during the Christian crusades against the Turks, who had reached the climactic point of their penetration of Eastern Europe, were enshrined in the official records of the time.

With the death of the great Hunyadi in 1456, what was left of the Christian forces in this last age of Balkan crusading was in acute need of leadership. The bitter squabbles raging in the Christian camp ever since the disastrous episode at Varna, which had led to Dracula's father's assassination, continued unabated. This absence of Christian unity greatly helped the Turkish cause and had contributed to the capture of Constantinople in 1453, three years before Dracula's second accession to the Wallachian throne.

With the disappearance of the last vestiges of Serbian and Bulgarian independence and the fall of the Greek Empire, Wallachia was placed at the forefront of the anti-Turkish crusade by circumstances of geography alone. Supporting the Wallachian cause, Moldavia lay safely in the hands of Dracula's cousin Steven, who emerged as a hero in the post-Hunyadi Christian world. With the assassination of Prince Steven's father, Bogdan, in 1451, Steven had accompanied Dracula in his Transylvanian exile. There, while both were sojourning in the castle of the Hunyadis at Hunedoara, Dracula had made the formal compact with Steven: that whoever succeeded to the throne first would help the other gain the sister principality. In any event, each committed himself to come to the other's assistance in case of need. Exactly one year after his accession to the throne in 1457, Dracula, true to his promise, sent a Wallachian contingent which helped Steven reconquer the crown of his ancestors. In this way, Dracula helped launch the brilliant career of the greatest soldier, statesman, and man of culture that the Romanian Renaissance produced. For Steven the Great, as he is called, was both a soldier and a lover of the arts. The number of monasteries that still survive in the region of Suceava, Steven's capital, are eloquent testimony to the cultural and architectural brilliance of his age.

The threatened Catholic powers of Central Europe were all interested in the "Reconquista," and circumstances after the fall of Constantinople seemed right for the renewal of a joint Balkan crusade. Following a period of anarchy at Buda after John Hunyadi's death, Dracula formally swore allegiance to the young King of Hungary, Ladislaus Posthumous. Since its geographic location made his realm susceptible to Turkish conquest, Ladislaus was definitely committed to fight the Moslems. Wallachian princes, protégés of the Hungarian court, were virtually pledged to enter the new crusade. The Poles were anxious to avenge the death of their boy-King Vladislav, who had perished at Varna in 1444. The Venetian Republic, as well as the Genoese, was interested as always in any endeavor that might suppress some potential threat to its commercial glory. Besides all this, the conquest of Constantinople was too calamitous a setback for the Christian world to remain unchallenged. Even the protagonists of Western chivalry—particularly the knights in Burgundy—despite how little genuine religious valor and zeal had survived the immoral fourth crusade, could not entirely dismiss their role as defenders of Christendom.

Both the German and the Russian narrators are silent concerning Dracula's Turkish campaigns: the Saxons' aim, after all, was to vilify Dracula, not to praise him; and the Russians were too remote from the Danube at the time to be really interested, and if their hearts were with the Christians, the Grand Duke of Moscow was always suspicious of Dracula's Catholic sympathies. We know the Russian ambassador at Buda was more interested in denouncing Dracula as an apostate than in praising him as a general. We are fortunate, however, in possessing numerous Romanian stories which glorify Dracula and other national heroes, especially as the age in which this folklore was put in literary form preceded the birth of national self-consciousness. In respect to historical events, Romanian folklore can be judged as a more impartial source than the foreign pamphlets which concentrated exclusively on horror tales.

Official Turkish records, including an eyewitness account by a Serbian Janizary, Byzantine chronicles, the report of a veteran in Dracula's army, official dispatches of Venetian and Genoese ambassadors and of papal legates, plus the narratives of travelers are among the major sources of information on Dracula's military affairs. By 1461, Dracula's power at home was sufficiently strong that he could undertake a more active role in the Reconquista. On the Turkish side, the sultan could ill afford to accept indignities unchallenged, but before engaging in warfare, he attempted diplomacy; or, to put it more accurately, to ensnare Dracula by guile rather than brute force. The Turkish governor of Nicopolis, Hamza Pasha, and a crafty Greek interpreter, Toma Catavolinos, were initially sent to the Danubian port of Giurgiu to invite Dracula to discuss disputed territories, nonpayment of tribute, and other matters affecting Wallacho-Turkish relations. Dracula, knowing Turkish perfidy from his lengthy imprisonment in Asia Minor, immediately sensed a trap. These Turks were attempting to lay an ambush identical to that into which his father had fallen 18 years before and which had resulted in Dracula's own captivity as a hostage at Egrigoz. To gain time, the Wallachians pretended to fall in with the Turkish plan, and Dracula informed the Turkish envoys that he would indeed come to the assigned place. When he reached Giurgiu, however, events unfolded in a way quite different from that which the Turkish authors of the plot had intended. Under cover of the forests, which in those days extended virtually to the Danube, Dracula instructed a contingent of cavalry, far larger than the available Turkish force, to surround the appointed meeting place just outside the citadel of Giurgiu. Accompanying the two Turkish envoys, Dracula then forced them to ask that the city open its gates. The garrison was overwhelmed by the Wallachian horsemen. With the two envoys bound to each other, the whole enemy contingent was led in chains to Targoviste. There, in circumstances already alluded to, the Turks were neatly drawn upon pikes in a meadow on the city's outskirts, stripped of their clothes and impaled, some head up, others feet up. Two special pikes, larger than the rest, were designed for the great Catavolinos and Hamza Pasha of Nicopolis. Then they were left for all to see how Dracula dealt with those who attempted to deceive him. After six months, the summer sun and the blackbirds had done their work. This was the spectacle which greeted the Turkish Sultan Mehemet when he finally invested Targoviste in the summer of 1462—a scene so horrible that the sultan is said to have decided personally to quit the campaign.

Dracula knew that this act of atrocity was tantamount to an official declaration of war. In fact, he meant to press his advantage immediately, and in the winter of 1461 he launched his Danubian campaign, the plans for which had been carefully laid. The Wallachians, numbering somewhere between 10,000 and 20,000 men, consisted essentially of a rapid moving cavalry, free peasants, yeomen, and those dutiful boyars who happened not to have incurred Dracula's wrath. The officers were almost entirely new appointees, for Dracula had created a court and military nobility of his own. The terrain, however, was familiar and had already been the scene of skirmishes with the Turks.

The fortress of Giurgiu, built by his grandfather, and a place that Dracula considered to be his own legitimate inheritance, was burned to the ground. From here he made diplomatic preparations for the renewal of a Hunyadi-style crusading campaign against the Turks. He dispatched envoys to all the crowned heads of what remained of independent Eastern and Central Europe; appealed to the Papacy for armed help; and sent King Mathias of Hungary a lengthy dispatch (dated February 11, 1462, and still preserved in the archives of Munich) which reported the capture of Giurgiu. In that letter, Dracula was able to record some remarkable statistics, for there had been an actual counting of Turkish heads, noses, and ears—23,809 in all. Bags of these were sent to Mathias. Though calculated to enlist the Hungarian king in the crusade, the morbid tidings met with failure.

Dracula's famous offensive along the Danube, which was to lead him from Giurgiu to the Black Sea, began as an amphibious operation, since the winter of 1461 was exceptionally mild. Wallachian barges carried the infantry, while the cavalry advancing along the right bank protected their flank.

One purpose of the campaign was liberation: when Dracula invaded Bulgaria proper, countless peasants joined the Christian ranks, greeting the Wallachian leader as their deliverer from the Turkish yoke. Later, when Dracula was compelled to retreat, whole Bulgarian villages sought to obtain the right of asylum on Wallachian soil, fearing the inevitable Turkish reprisal. Dracula's principal aim, however, was to destroy Turkish power along the Danube. Thus his advance became bogged down in a number of siege operations directed against Turkish fortresses from Zimnicea to the Black Sea. Dracula's forces besieged and sacked towns on both banks of the river: Oltenita, Silistria, Calarasi, Rasova, Cerna-Voda, Hirsova, and Ostrov. Local peasant traditions pinpoint one of Dracula's temporary headquarters in a village on the right bank which still bears his name.

It was the Danubian campaign which established Dracula's reputation as a Christian crusader and warrior. Throughout

Central and Western Europe, Te Deums were sung, and bells tolled from Genoa to Rhodes in gratitude for Dracula's endowing the Christian crusade with a new lease on life and taking over the leadership of the Great Hunyadi. Dracula's bold offensive also sent a new hope of liberation to the enslaved people of Bulgaria, Serbia, and Greece. At Constantinople itself there was an atmosphere of consternation, gloom, and fear, and some of the Turkish leaders, fearing *Kaziklu Bey*—the Impaler—apparently contemplated flight across the Bosphorus into Asia Minor.

The winter campaign ended on the Black Sea coast within sight of the powerful Turkish invasion force that had crossed the Bosphorus for a full-scale invasion of Wallachia. With his flank unprotected, Dracula was compelled to abandon the offensive. He burned all the Turkish fortresses he could not actually occupy. Beyond that he could not go; the momentum of the offensive had spent itself.

Mohammed the Conqueror decided to launch his invasion of Wallachia in the spring of 1462; Dracula had hardly given the sultan any alternative. To defy the sultan by spoiling a probable assassination plot was one thing; to ridicule him and instill hopes of liberation among his Christian subjects was quite another—one far more dangerous to his recently established empire. One Greek chronicler, Chalkokondyles, set the total number of the twin Turkish invasion forces as no less than 250,000 men, including a powerful Janizary (infantry) force, the Spahi Calvary, and a massive artillery.

The main contingent, led by the sultan himself, was carried across the Bosphorus by a vast flotilla of barges, assembled for this purpose in the Turkish capital. The other major force had been collected at Nicopolis in Bulgaria, and was to cross the Danube, recapture the fortress of Giurgiu, and then unite with the main force in a combined attack on the Wallachian capital of Targoviste. If these figures are even approximately accurate, this was the largest Turkish invasion force since the one which had captured Constantinople in 1453.

Dracula undoubtedly expected reinforcements at least from Mathias of Hungary, in order to correct the disparity of numbers; he had, according to the Slavic narrative, no more than 30,900 men, even allowing for a levy en masse. In the meantime, he practiced the classical tactic of the outnumbered, namely, the strategic retreat, combined with what is known today as the "scorched earth policy." After preliminary skirmishes along the marshes of the Danube, aimed essentially at delaying the juncture of the two great Turkish armies, Dracula abandoned the line of the Danube and began his withdrawal northward. As the Wallachian troops gave up their own native soil to the Turks, they reduced the country to barrenness, burning crops, poisoning wells, herding the cattle northward, and consuming all that they could not carry with them. The villages were emptied of people, the houses destroyed. The peasants usually accompanied the armies in their retreat. The boyars and their families, hearing of the impending attack, withdrew from their estates to the mountains. Many of them established their headquarters at Cheia high up in the Carpathians, while waiting for the inevitable outcome of the fray. Others took refuge at Snagov, and stored their treasure there. Most of them refused to collaborate with either Dracula or the Turks until the issues were clarified by the fortunes of war. Finally the boyars threw in their lot with Radu, Dracula's brother, but only when there could be little doubt as to Dracula's fate. As the Turks advanced into the country, all they saw was the desolate spectacle of smoke and ashes, vultures hovering in the sky, and howling wolves and coyotes at night.

Dracula's retreat was also accomplished with guerrilla tactics, where the element of surprise played the most vital part. His veterans knew the terrain well, generally maneuvering at dead of night under cover of the vast forests of Vlasie. In these "mad" forests were the lairs of the robber barons, who collaborated with Dracula's forces much as the Cossacks did with the Russian armies in the campaign of 1812. The signals used during the night attacks imitated the sounds of various animals or birds. For speed, which was essential, the best Wallachian horses were used.

The attack known in official sources as the "Night of Terror" particularly deserves inclusion here. In one of the many villages leading to Targoviste, near the forest encampment of the Turks, Dracula held a council of war. The situation of Targoviste was desperate, and Dracula presented a bold plan as a last-resort means of saving his indefensible capital. The council agreed that only the assassination of the sultan might sufficiently demoralize the Turkish army to effect a speedy withdrawal.

The outcome of this plan was admirably recorded by a Serbian Janizary, Constantine of Ostrovita, who experienced the whole impact of Dracula's audacious onslaught. His account describes the complex compound of a Turkish camp at night, with its vigilant Janizary guards occasionally called to order; the smell of lamb roasting over glowing fires; the noise of departing soldiers; the laughter of the women and other camp dependents; the wail of the muezzin; the plaintive chant of Turkish slaves; the noise of the camels; the countless tents, and finally the more elaborate gold-embroidered establishment of the sleeping sultan in the very heart of the camp. Mohammed had just retired after a heavy meal. Suddenly came the hooting of an owl—Dracula's signal to attack, followed by the onrush of cavalry, which penetrated deep into the various layers of guards, frantically galloping through the tents and half-sleeping soldiers, tearing all apart. The Wallachian sword and lance cut a bloody swath with Dracula always in the lead, carried along it seems by demoniac power. *"Kaziklu Bey!"*—"The Impaler"—cried rows of awestruck Turkish soldiers, moaning and dying in the path of the Romanian avalanche. Finally Turkish trumpets called the men to arms. A body of determined Janizaries gradually formed around the sultan's tent. Dracula had calculated that the sheer surprise and impetus of the attack would carry his cavalry to the sultan's bed, and he came close to victory. But as he was within sight of the gold brocade tent, the bodyguard rallied, held the Wallachian offensive, actually began to push it back. Realizing the danger of being surrounded and captured, Dracula reluctantly gave orders for retreat. He had killed several thousand Turks, wounded countless more, created havoc, chaos, and terror within the Turkish camp; but he had lost a few hundred of his bravest warriors and the objective of the attack had failed. Sultan Mohammed had survived, and the road to Targoviste lay open.

The Wallachian capital presented a desolate spectacle to the oncoming Turks. Like the gates of some abandoned Foreign Legion fortress in a later era, those of the city had been left open, and a thick blanket of smoke shut out the dawning light. The city had been stripped of virtually all its holy relics and treasures; the palace was emptied of all that could be taken and the rest had been put to fire. Here, as elsewhere, all wells had been poisoned. As if to confirm the atmosphere of desolation, the only men who greeted the Turks on the outskirts of the city were Hamza Pasha, Bey of Nicopolis, and the Greek Catavolinos, their impaled bodies badly mutilated by the beaks of blackbirds. Adding this awesome spectacle to his experiences of the night before, it is little wonder that Sultan Mohammed lost heart. His despairing comment has often been quoted: "What can we do against a man like this?" After a council of war, the sultan ordered retreat for the bulk of the Turkish army. Then he assigned a smaller contingent, in collaboration with the pro-Turkish boyars and Prince Radu (who had been brought to Targoviste and officially installed as prince), to pursue Dracula in his flight northward to his mountain castle, to capture him alive, and then to cut off his head and expose it at Constantinople as an example for all to see of the fate of those who dared flaunt Turkish power.

There was another, more compelling reason for the Turkish withdrawal. The plague had begun to make its appearances within the sultan's ranks, and the first victims of the dread disease were recorded in Targoviste.

Dracula's appeal for help from his kinsman Steven was answered with treachery. In the month of June, the Moldavian ruler attacked the crucial Wallachian fortress of Chilia from the north; simultaneously powerful Turkish contingents attacked it from the south. This extraordinary double assault was unsuccessful. The Turks abandoned the siege and marched on to their ultimate objective of Targoviste. As for Steven, he was wounded by the accurate Hungarian gunfire from the fortress and withdrew to Moldavia. (He did not renew the attack on Chilia until 1465, and this time captured it, while his cousin Dracula was safely in a Hungarian jail many miles farther up the Danube at Visegrad. Steven had certainly more justification in taking the fortress from Dracula's reigning brother, Radu, who had acquired the reputation of being a pliable tool of the Turks.)

Professor Giurescu explains Steven's betrayal of Dracula in terms of *raison d'etat*. Steven did not think his cousin could hold the fortress against the Turks; he needed it to protect the flank of his own principality; and he was uncertain that the Hungarian members of Dracula's garrison, who were in a majority, could be trusted.

The last episode in the Turko-Wallachian war leads to Dracula's castle on the upper Arges, the prince's final place of refuge from the advancing Turks. Since the Janizary of Ostrovita (upon whom we have mainly relied for a description of the early phases of the campaign) returned to Constantinople with the sultan and the main bulk of the army, and since most of the western veterans abandoned Dracula and hence left no reports, the historian must once again rely for information on popular ballads from the castle region.

The peasants in the villages surrounding Castle Dracula relate numerous tales concerning the end of Dracula's second reign in the fall of 1462. All these stories end at the point where Dracula crossed the border into Transylvania and became prisoner of the Hungarian king. They start anew some 12 years later, when Dracula returned to Wallachia for his third reign. One of the more classic narrations of Dracula's last moments of resistance to the Turks in 1462 runs briefly as follows: After the fall of Targoviste, Dracula and a few faithful followers headed northward; avoiding the more obvious passes leading to Transylvania, they reached his mountain retreat. The Turks who had been sent in pursuit encamped on the Bluff of Poenari, which commanded an admirable view of Dracula's castle on the opposite bank of the Arges, and here they set up their cherrywood cannons. (At Poenari to this day there is a field known as *tunuri*, "the field of cannon.") The bulk of the Turkish Janizaries descended to the river, forded it at much the same place where the Tartars had crossed it a century before, and camped on the other side. A bombardment of Dracula's castle began, but had little success owing to the small calibre of the Turkish guns and the solidity of the castle walls. Orders for the final assault upon the castle were set for the next day.

That night, a Romanian slave in the Janizary corps—who according to local tale was a distant relative of Dracula and who perhaps was inspired by ethnic loyalty—forewarned the Wallachian prince of the great danger that lay ahead. Undetected in the moonless night, the slave climbed the Bluff of Poenari and after taking careful aim, he sped an arrow at one of the distant dimly lit openings in the main tower, which he knew contained Dracula's quarters. At the end of the arrow was a message advising Dracula to escape while there was still time. The Janizary witnessed the accuracy of his aim: the arrow extinguished a candle within the tower opening. When it was relit, the slave could see the shadow of Dracula's wife, and its faint indication that she was reading the message.

The remainder of this story could only have been passed down by Dracula's intimate advisors within the castle. Dracula's wife apprised her husband of the warning. She told her husband she would rather have her body eaten by the fish of the Arges than be led into captivity by the Turks. Dracula, of course, knew from his own experience at Egrigoz what that slavery would entail. Realizing how desperate their situation was and before anyone could intervene, Dracula's wife rushed up the winding staircase, and hurled herself from the donjon; her body rolled down the precipice, into the river Arges. Today this point of the river is known as *Riul Doamei*, "the Princess' river." This tragic folktale contains practically the only mention of Dracula's first wife.

Dracula himself immediately made plans for escape: suicide, no matter how unfavorable the circumstances, was not part of the Dracula philosophy. He ordered the bravest leaders from the neighboring village of Arefu to be brought to the castle, and during the night they discussed the various routes of escape to Transylvania. It was Dracula's hope that Mathias of Hungary, to whom he had sent many appeals since that first letter in February 1462, would greet him as an ally and support his reinstatement on the Wallachian throne. Indeed, it was known that the Hungarian king, along with a powerful army, had established headquarters just across the mountains at Brasov. To reach him was a matter of crossing the Transylvanian Alps at a point where there were no roads or passes. It meant climbing to the summit of the Fagaras mountains, still a challenge to the most experienced Alpinist with the aid of special equipment. The upper slopes of these mountains are rocky, treacherous, often covered with snow or ice throughout the summer. Dracula could not have attempted such an ascent without the help of local experts. The precise way of escape was mapped out by the peasants brought in from Arefu. Popular folklore still identifies various rivers, clearings, forested areas, even rocks, which were along the way of Dracula's escape route. We have tried to use them in reconstituting Dracula's actual passage, but the task has been difficult since many of the place names have changed over the years. As far as we have been able to reconstruct the escape, Dracula and a dozen attendants, his illegitimate son, and five men of Arefu left the castle before dawn by way of a staircase spiraling down into the bowels of the mountain and leading to a cave on the banks of the river. Here, the fleeing party could hear the noises of the Turkish camp located a mile to the north. Some of the fastest mounts were then brought from the village, the horses being equipped with inverted horseshoes so as to leave false signs of an incoming cavalry force.

During the night the castle guns continually fired to detract attention from the escape party. The Turks at Poenari replied in kind. Because of the noise of the gunfire, so the story runs, Dracula's own mount began to shy, and his son, who had been tied to the saddle, fell to the ground and in the confusion was taken for lost. The situation was far too desperate for anyone to begin a search, and Dracula was both too battle-hardened and too cold-hearted to sacrifice himself or his companions for his son.

This tragic little vignette has a happy sequel. The boy, not yet in his teens, was found next morning by a local shepherd from Arefu, who took him to his hut and brought him up as though he were one of his own family. Twelve years later, when Dracula returned as Prince of Wallachia, the peasant, who had found out the true identity of his ward, came to the castle. By that time the boy had developed into a splendid young man. He told his father all that the shepherd had done for him, and in gratitude Dracula richly recompensed the peasant with landed tracts in the surrounding mountains. It is possible that the son himself stayed on in the area and eventually became governor of the castle.

When the fleeing party finally reached the crests of the Fagaras mountains to the south, they were able to view the Turks' final assault, which partially destroyed Castle Dracula. To the north lay the castle and the city of Fagaras, where the armies of King Mathias, it was hoped, were maneuvering to come to Dracula's aid. At a place called *Plaiul Oilor*, "Plain of the Sheep," Dracula's party, now quite safe from the Turks, retired and made plans for the northward descent.

Summoning his brave companions, Dracula asked them how best he could recompense them for having saved his life. They answered in unison that they had simply done their duty for prince and country. The prince, however, insisted: "What do you wish? Money or land? (Part of the royal treasury had been taken along on this difficult climb.) They answered directly: "Give us land, Your Highness." On a slab of stone, known to this day as the Prince's Table, Dracula fulfilled their wishes, writing upon the skin of some hares caught the day before. He endowed the five peasants from Arefu with all the area to the south as far as they could see up to the plain, containing 16 mountains and a rich supply of timber, fish, and sheep—a tract containing perhaps 20,000 acres. He further stipulated in the deed that none of this land could ever be taken away from them by prince, boyar or ecclesiastical leaders; it was for their families to enjoy from one generation to the next.

Ancient tradition in the village of Arefu has it that these rabbitskins are still carefully hidden by the five men's descendants, but despite many efforts and inducements no peasant has been willing to shed light on the exact whereabouts of these alleged documents. Still we have reason to suppose that somewhere hidden in an attic, or buried underground, the Dracula rabbit skins still exist. One Romanian historian attempted to find these scrolls, but the peasants of the area have remained secretive and intractable. Even large sums of money would not persuade them to part with such precious souvenirs of Dracula's heroic age.

Dracula's seal. The inscription is in Old Slavonic and reads: *Vlad Voevod through the grace of God is Prince of Ungro-Wallachia.* "Voevod" signifies a warlord or warrior prince, not a prince who rules by inherited right.

4

Castle Dracula

There are essentially two ways of going from Targoviste, in Wallachia, to the mountains of Transylvania. One of them proceeds north along the Dambovita to Campulung, then to Rucar at the Transylvanian border, and through the mountains, by way of the pass of Bran. This was the route traveled by Dracula during his raids against Brasov, which lay just across the mountains, on the edge of the Transylvanian plateau. The second route is slightly more cumbersome. It takes you west to the river Olt—another tributary of the Danube—north to the episcopal city of Ramnicul Valcea, and then into Transylvania, via the pass of Turnu Rosu (German, Rotherturm).

The first of these two routes is the more scenic. At Campulung, one finds a city of transition between the Germanic and Romanian worlds. It still has traces of what it was in the 13th century—a burgh of the Teutonic order, and in that sense it belongs to the civilization of Central Europe.

Among the medieval customs continued here is the celebration of the Feast of St. Elias, when peasants come from neighboring areas to sell their wares and partake of the traditional entertainment. Dracula often sojourned at Campulung on his way to the north, but only a few local stories are linked to his name. This was largely due to the presence of the Germanic element, who were even more resented in Wallachia owing to the prejudices they brought to local trade.

There are many rustic villages on the route from Campulung to Bran, such as Cetateni din Vale. On a mountain overlooking Cetateni are the remains of a castle and a small church built inside a rock. This castle is not Dracula's, but was built according to popular legend by Wallachia's first prince, Basarab. Inside the grotto three monks still observe a ritual which has been held there at midnight since earliest times, an index to the ageless piety of the region. Peasants in gaily embroidered dress still come from as far as 50 miles away, often walking barefooted up the difficult ascent, to attend the midnight service in this musty, incense-filled, cavern-like place, where faded icons portray their martyrs and saints. One of the monks, who lost part of an arm while working in an aircraft factory, firmly believes that at each midnight mass his injured limb lengthens by an inch—yet another instance of faith-filled superstition. According to local legend Dracula himself climbed this mountain when fleeing from the Turks in 1462, and took sanctuary within the grotto before continuing on to his own castle.

The region between Campulung and Bran is the heart of Romania's historic area. Here a national life was born at the close of the 13th century. There is hardly a mountain, a river, a torrent, or any other landmark, natural or artificial, that in some way or other does not evoke the stormy past—so often recalled in the historical ballads of the peasants. Each village church, disintegrating castle, or fortified manor *(cula)*, challenges the historian to seek the reason for its survival in an area where so much has been destroyed by hordes of invaders.

The peasants along this route are mostly *mosneni* (free peasants). Never having experienced serfdom, most of them are probably descendants of the warriors who fought in Dracula's and the other princes' armies—the bulk of Dracula's military forces having consisted of freeholders since they were more trustworthy than the boyars. Today's peasants proudly remain the owners of their soil, for collectivization has proved generally unworkable in the mountainous districts. Their wood houses are more ambitious than those found elsewhere: the scale larger; the styling somewhat Tyrolean in character; but the courtyards more extensive; and the porches, *pridvors*, more artistically carved. These peasants still tend cattle and sheep, and they take any surplus grapes, prunes, apples, and pears from their orchards to the market of Campulung once they have met their obligation to the state.

In Dragoslavele, the local priest, an amiable man by the name of Rautescu, has written an amazingly well-documented history of the region, in which he traces his own town and many others from Dracula's time.

Rucar is the border town, the ancient customs station, between Wallachia and Transylvania proper. Dracula's frontier guards, whose services he was often compelled by sheer lack of manpower to call upon in order to fight the Turks, had their headquarters in Rucar.

The Hungarian frontier was fairly peaceful in Dracula's time, and relationships with Buda cordial. In a sense, Hungarian-

Romanian relations had to be correct. Struggling with the Turks on the Danube, Dracula was hardly able to challenge the formidable guns and fortifications of Castle Bran, which dominated the valley of the Dambovita.

Castle Bran was allegedly founded by the Teutonic knight Dietrich in the 13th century. Given the number of times it was besieged, burned, or partially razed, it is a miracle that so much of it is extant. In 1225 it came into the hands of the Hungarian kings, and then successively belonged to the Wallachian prince Mircea, King Sigismund, John Hunyadi, and his son King Mathias Corvinus. Dracula was undoubtedly a guest of Hunyadi at Bran.

With its vast halls, dark corridors, multi-level battlements, high water tower, numerous inner courtyards, Gothic chapel, and rustic Germanic furnishings of the period, Bran has an atmosphere which conveys, more than any other castle in Romania, the legacy of the age of Dracula. In the middle of the inner courtyard lies a well, and next to it, hidden by a covering of stone, is a secret passage. Through a winding staircase which sinks 150 feet down into the mountain one emerges into a cell near the bottom of the well. Beyond the cell is a heavy oak door, formerly locked, which opens to another passageway leading to the safety of a mountain knoll and farther on to the citadel of Brasov. The purposes of this intricate passageway were manifold: protection of the castle's water supply; a place of refuge; a place for torture and detention; and finally a secret means of escape. Dracula was apparently impressed by the features of this passageway, for very similar arrangements were later contrived in his own castle on the river Arges. After the death of his protector John Hunyadi, Dracula avoided Bran whenever he passed near it on his way to Transylvania.

After the reunion of Transylvania and Romania in 1918, Bran was given to Romania's Hohenzollern royal family; it was particularly pleasing to the princess who was wife of the heir to the throne, Ferdinand, and who later became the majestic Queen Marie. In fact, this romantic granddaughter of Queen Victoria preferred Bran as a summer retreat to the official royal residence at near-by Sinaia. One wonders if she chose Castle Bran as a royal residence because it accorded so well with Bram Stoker's description of Dracula's castle at the Borgo Pass. The analogies between Stoker's mythical Castle Dracula and the real Castle Bran are simply too close to be coincidental. Moreover, like Stoker, Queen Marie had a great love and understanding of

Romanian folklore, which is so richly invested with the
supernatural.

The second major route to Transylvania follows the valley of
the river Olt, and via the pass at Turnu Rosu crosses the border
into Dracula's favorite city of Sibiu. Turnu Rosu is often
mentioned in documents concerning Dracula. The fortress here
lies on a high bluff on the left side of the pass as one proceeds
north and was built on a much smaller scale than Bran. Only the
ruins of its chief donjons are still visible. The fortress was built
by the Saxon citizens of Sibiu around 1360, on the site of an old
Roman castrum, to guard the southern approaches of the city
and as part of an outward defensive network against Turkish
attack. The name Turnu Rosu, derived from one of its donjons—
the Red Tower, commemorates its heroic role in a specific battle,
when its premises were reddened by the blood of barbarian
assailants. Although the castle was almost entirely destroyed on
this occasion, the Turks were never able to capture the Red
Tower. Nor for that matter was Dracula.

Romanian historical chronicles (which if Stoker did consult
he ignored for his own reasons) do not locate Dracula's castle on
either of the two main routes from Wallachia into Transylvania.
But aside from this, it seems highly unlikely that the wily
Wallachian prince would erect his retreat in the shadow of either
of the two formidable and sometimes unfriendly Germanic
fortresses. In view of Dracula's taste for the inaccessible and his
mistrustful nature, it is equally unlikely that he would build his
eyrie on *any* well-traveled, commercial route. And, from the
standpoint of defense, it would be unreasonable to assume that
he would site his hideaway on a major route that could easily
become a highroad for invasion by Tartars and Turks alike.

For all these reasons, Castle Dracula had to be sought
elsewhere. Fortunately, the oldest Romanian chronicle and
peasant oral tradition speak quite accurately on this point. The
way to Dracula's castle lies somewhere *between* the two known
routes, which follow along the river Olt and the Dambovita, and
it does not include any accessible pass or traveled roads. The
castle itself was located precisely at the source of the river Arges,
which begins as a mere torrent here, collecting the melting
snows of the Transylvanian peaks; then, gaining momentum
little by little, painfully carves its way through the sub-
Carpathian mountains into the Wallachian plain, and eventually
flows into the Danube. To the south, the castle commanded a
formidable view of the Wallachian plain; to the north, it looked

to the snow-capped peaks of the Fagaras mountains. Isolated in this remote spot, Castle Dracula was virtually impregnable.

The road leading to the castle is far less scenic than the one we traveled from Campulung to Bran. The villages are both smaller and poorer; the inhabitants, less hospitable, rather suspicious of foreigners or strangers, much like those in Stoker's story; the houses, less decorative and the costumes not so gaily embroidered as in the usual mountain districts; and the churches, built on a more modest scale.

The road to the castle passes through Curtea de Arges (citadel of the Arges), site of the ancient cathedral, which no longer exists. Here Dracula's ancestors were anointed princes of the land by the head of the Wallachian Orthodox church in full presence of the boyar leaders. The ceremonies following such a religious exercise were normally held in the old princely church of this city, rather than at Targoviste. Generally, however, Dracula avoided the Citadel of the Arges and all it represented, for he got along no better with its church officials than he did with its boyars, who often intrigued against him in Targoviste. Castle Dracula, merely 20 miles to the north of this ecclesiastical capital, acted as a powerful deterrent to potential revolt. In fact, this center of church authority was generally submissive during Dracula's lifetime.

Wallachian chronicles, as well as popular folklore, place Dracula's castle high up on a rock on the left bank of the river Arges, and just beyond the small community of Arefu. By a strange irony, which will be explained, Castle Dracula is also known in the chronicles as the fortress of Poenari, the name of another village located on the opposite bank of the river. In fact, one of the oldest of these chronicles credits Dracula with just two accomplishments: "The 'Impaler' built the castle of Poenari, and the monastery of Snagov, where he lies buried." In this one sentence Dracula, a prince notorious throughout 15th-century Western and Eastern Europe, was summed up by chroniclers in his own land a hundred years after his death. Small wonder that there has been such difficulty in identifying the horrible tyrant and persecutor of the Germans with the castle-and-monastery founder recorded by the Romanians. Bram Stoker's novel, strange as it may seem, probably represents the first attempt at marrying Germany's demoniac to Romania's heroic character. Romanian histories, drawing upon the early chronicles, speak of "a castle known as Poenari, converted by Dracula into an impregnable retreat." Local tradition, however, disputes this idea of a *single* castle; maintaining that Dracula's castle was located on the left bank of the river Arges, and that the Castle of Poenari—a much older fortress, which has now disappeared—was located on the right bank. If this tradition is correct, one can only assume that the early chroniclers confused the two structures and later historians perpetuated the mistake.

It will take the work of the archaeologist to prove this matter one way or the other. For the time being, we are inclined to agree with tradition, and with the elders of Arefu and Poenari, that within the narrow gorges of the Arges, and at a distance of about one mile from each other, these were *two* castles. And we shall now hazard an explanation as to how the identification of one with the other came about.

Of the two villages, Arefu, where Dracula's castle actually is located, and Poenari, which the chroniclers have taken to be the actual site, the latter was by far the more important. In the Middle Ages, Poenari was a princely village; over the years the castle built within its confines gained control of all the neighboring villages, including Arefu. Deeds made by several princes to monasteries and individual boyars, both before and after Dracula's time, all speak of "land endowed to the Castle of Poenari." Moreover, Poenari is the only castle remembered in the documents of the 13th, 14th, and 15th centuries. Local peasant folklore tales clarified the historical problem their own way. The key to the confusion is that *Dracula's castle was literally built out of the bricks and stones of the Castle of Poenari.* Before describing this reconstruction, let us briefly survey our findings about the older Castle of Poenari.

Today, there are no visible remains of it, but peasants from Poenari told us about remains of a low-lying wall at the foot of the hill, which might have formed part of the outward defense of a very ancient fortress. That fact could not, however, be scientifically corroborated. They also stated that when excavations were made not too many years ago in the local church, the workers came across bricks and stone that date back to the time of the Dacians. We were also led to some local mud houses, the chimneys of which contained stones remarkably like the "Dacian" stones found underneath the church. In addition, a small museum organized by the local priest displays an amazing array of stones, coins, weapons, and other artifacts, some of which date to Roman and pre-Roman times. None of this material has been scientifically examined by the Archaeological Institute at Bucharest. Pending such an analysis, however, the hypothesis presented by the local priest, Stanciulescu, seems quite plausible: Castle Poenari was built upon the site of the ancient Dacian fortress of Decidava. After all, the center of Dacian power, Sarmisegetuza, which was destroyed by Trajan's Roman legion in 106 A.D., was only 100 miles to the northwest. In accordance with this theory, Decidava was rebuilt by Romanian princes at the close of the 13th century to resist Hungarian and Teutonic incursions from the north, and given the name of the village which surrounds it—Poenari. It thus figures as a princely foundation with extensive land holdings and occupied a strategic point on the Transylvanian frontier. As a minor fortress, Poenari continued to survive until Dracula's time though it was badly battered by Turkish and Tartar invaders. In 1462, when pursuing the Wallachian prince, the Turks stumbled across the decaying fragments of the fortress and completed its destruction. What is left of Poenari is likely to be found in the foundation of the village church, in peasant chimneys, in the local museum, and in the remaining walls and donjons of Castle Dracula itself.

We must turn now to a further complication in the story of Dracula's mountain retreat. In a strict sense, Dracula was not its founder. When he came to the throne in 1456, the ruins of *two* fortresses faced each other across the river Arges: on the right bank , the ruins of the ancient medieval fortress of Poenari; on the left, the remnants of the Castle of the Arges. One of the two structures deserved to be rebuilt. Dracula chose to rebuild the Castle of the Arges, which had greater strategic advantage, being sited at a higher point along the river. Tradition has it that this particular fortress was founded by one of the early Basarab princes a century before Dracula's time. A few historians claim that the initial fortress was even older than that, and that it belonged to the network of Teutonic fortresses, such as Bran, built to defend the Hungarian frontier at the beginning of the 13th century. If so, since the castle lies across the mountains, directly opposite the Teutonic castle of Fagaras, its usefulness would have been that of a sentinel warning the home base of the presence of hostile forces on the southern slopes of the Carpathians. Here, as elsewhere, local tradition often predates the chronicles and the historians' ordinary sources. The Castle of the Arges (Castle of Agrish, as it was initially known in Hungarian documents) was, in our view, founded by the earliest Romanian princes coming from Transylvania and was definitely not a Teutonic fortress. In a sense it represents one of their first bastions on Wallachian soil. Structurally it bears little resemblance to the much more formidable Germanic fortresses, such as Bran or Hunedoara, located in Transylvania proper. In fact, like Wallachian castles at Cetateni, it is built on a modest scale and bears some of the features of Byzantine fortifications.

There are local tales to the effect that Prince Basarab withdrew to his citadel on the Arges following his encounters with the Turks around 1330. It was considerably fortified by his successors and, like so many other castles in the region, had a stormy history even before Dracula's time. A particular incident in that history requires mention here. On one occasion at the close of the 14th century, the Tartars, who had penetrated the heart of Wallachia—pillaging, burning, and looting on the way—reached the ecclesiastical see of Curtea de Arges farther down the river. The Prince, his bishops, and boyars fled to the Castle of the Arges. In pursuit along the right bank of the river, the Tartars reached the village of Capatineni within sight of the castle, crossed the river, and encamped in a clearing on the left bank (to this day called Plasea—"hilt of a sword"). Next morning they began bombardment with their cherry-wood cannon. When they eventually stormed the fortress, they found not a man within its walls. The prince, his bishops, and boyars had fled through a secret passage, still existing in Dracula's time, leading to the banks of the river. The Tartars in their vengeance left the castle severely damaged. This story has been related because it provides the vital clue to the link between the Castle of the Arges, built by Basarab, and the Castle of Poenari. The Tartars had, in fact, so badly mauled the earlier fortification of Prince Basarab that it was in need of reconstruction. This reconstruction, which could be viewed as virtually new construction, was Dracula's distinctive contribution. On that basis, Dracula might also be named, as local tradition, indeed, has named him, the founder of the Castle of the Arges. Historical chronicles are incorrect only in confusing the names.

To sum up what is surely a complicated matter: Castle Dracula was a reconstruction of the Castle of the Arges, partially with materials from the Castle of Poenari, which itself seems to have been built on the site of the ancient fortress of Decidava.

The story of the construction (call it reconstruction) of Dracula's castle is very succinctly described in one of the ancient Wallachian chronicles:

So when Easter came, while all the citizens were feasting and the young ones were dancing, he surrounded and captured them. All those who were old he impaled, and strung them all around the city; as for the young ones together with their wives and children, he had them taken just as they were, dressed up for Easter, to Poenari, where they were put to work until their clothes were all torn and they were left naked.

A second chronicle states that they worked "until their clothes fell off their backs," a description that has often been quoted. As much as any Romanian document, this one has established Dracula's reputation for cruelty, for these enslaved workers were neither Turkish nor Saxon fiends, rather Dracula's own Wallachian subjects.

As often in this narrative, the chroniclers' story will have to be enlarged, explained, and ultimately accounted for by reference to popular folklore, which is both more colorful than the historian's language and probably closer to the historical truth than documents written a century later. From the village of Arefu come two different tales explaining Dracula's reason for this drastic abuse of his boyar subjects. One of them can be readily dismissed because the offense it relates seems far too trivial, even by Dracula's standards, to justify so severe a punishment. It states that Dracula's brother had been spurned to the point of ridicule by the daughters of a powerful boyar. To clear the family's honor, Dracula took vengeance on the particular faction to which the young ladies' family belonged. The other narrative is far more plausible in view of the circumstances surrounding Dracula's accession to the throne, and his basic hostility toward, and legitimate suspicion of, the boyar class. It runs as follows:

Shortly after assuming power in Wallachia, Dracula investigated the circumstances surrounding the death of his father, Dracul, and particularly those concerning the assassination of his favorite elder brother, Mircea, a gallant hero of war. He found out that Mircea, caught by the boyars with his father at Tirgsor, was dragged to Targoviste and secretly buried alive. He had already been convinced of the boyars' duplicity, in the famous court scene resulting in the impalement of hundreds of boyars outside his palace at Targoviste. The discovery of this later boyar act filled his cup of indignation to the brim, and his servants witnessed a scene of mad rage which must have paralleled those of Ivan the Terrible. However, there was always great cunning in his dementia, and he now planned a revenge worthy of the crime.

Earlier in the course of his journey from Transylvania, Dracula had made a personal survey of the region of the two castles on the upper Arges and was struck by its commanding strategic position, particularly in regard to the Castle of Agrish. The punishment of the boyars and the reconstruction of the castle on the left bank immediately became linked in his mind. "Thus, on Easter Day," states a ballad of Arefu, "our new Prince Dracula assembled both the high and the low of birth for the occasion, with little concern for rank, in this day of peasant democracy, for all to join in the festivities." On the night before, all attended the Easter vigil service, the most important religious celebration of the year. The following morning, there were to be festivities in the princely gardens surrounding the city walls, including a lavish banquet. In addition to the roasted lambs, sweetened cakes, and wines provided by the palace both boyars and humble merchants were to bring provisions of their own.

On Easter morning the boyars came to the meadows, mounted on their fine horses and riding in carriages. The merchants followed in carts or on foot. The Metropolitan and bishops wore their imposing ecclesiastical robes. The boyars imitated the Hungarian nobleman's dress, though a few preferred the more ornate Byzantine style. Turkish dress in those days was as yet unknown. The high headgear with an ostrich feather held by a cluster of costly diamonds, the ermine cape, and the silk embroidered shirt were almost *de rigeur*. The merchants and artisans dressed more simply, some of them wearing peasant dress essentially identical to that still worn today. The men wore the Dacian costume, an embroidered shirt, trousers held by a wide leather belt, a woolen-lined and embroidered vest, and soft pigskin laced sandals. The boyars' wives gathered in small circles, usually in accordance with their rank or court function, and had brought handsome Persian carpets to rest on. Gypsy fiddlers organized both the music and the mirth.

The merchants, craftsmen, and guild representatives were equally conscious of rank and formed small groups of their own. Unperturbed by the feast of the wealthy boyars, the middle estate carefully instructed their apprentices how to settle their less expensive carpets, how to handle their wine, how to serve a table in genteel fashion. On such occasions, they had entertainment of their own at a more modest level. They also came with food and wine.

After the feast, as was customary, the children enjoyed the swings, carousels, and various games provided by a specifically organized fair, their elders rested on the grass, and the younger folk, both boyars and artisans, joined in the *hora,* a traditional Romanian folk dance, while local groups of minstrels and jesters sang or played for the Prince, the boyars, and their ladies. In this fashion, the evening wore on until the sun had set behind the Carpathians.

Observers relate that Dracula was preoccupied throughout the day, rarely conversing with the boyars, nor joining, as was his wont, in the dances. While the partying was at its height, he conversed secretly with the captains of the yeomen guard, issuing instructions, and posting men under trees and bushes surrounding the meadows. As dusk turned into evening, harsh words of command were issued. Within seconds, Dracula's soldiers isolated from the rest of the partying community most of the boyars, their wives and their children, all of whom were easily identifiable by their more gaudy dress. Some 300 of them were enclosed in a prepared paddock, and then manacled to each other.

The operation had been so well organized that few boyars had the time to flee and seize weapons. In any case, because of the heavy quantities of wine consumed, many of them were in a state of torpor. The occasion could not have been better chosen. Dracula was intent upon teaching his boyars a lesson in submission they would not ever forget—if they survived the ordeal.

Persuaded of the unreliability of his own capital of Targoviste, Dracula had determined to build a new castle; it would be closer to Transylvania—on some secure elevation far from any well-traveled highway, or any of the traditional passes, or any powerful Germanic fortresses. The slopes of the Arges satisfied him on all these points. Logistically, he had made up his mind to rebuild the castle of the Arges with the bricks and stone from the Castle of Poenari. Moreover, the outer walls of the new complex were to be doubled in thickness. Castle Dracula was to be made virtually impregnable, able to resist the heaviest cannon fire of either Tartars or Turks. The boyars thus became the instruments of a dual and devilish plot, which combined a punitive operation with the securing of free labor for the construction of a powerful mountain retreat. This situation also neatly solves the problem of identifying Poenari as Castle Dracula. In a sense, it is quite correct to state that Castle Dracula was built "out of the brick and stone of the Castle of Poenari," even though its location lay on the site of the Castle of the Arges on the left bank of the river. This is the obvious way of reconciling both views in an ancient polemic.

The boyar trek from Targoviste no less than 50 miles—was a painful one, particularly for the women and children. Those who survived it were allowed no rest until they reached Poenari. The region here was particularly rich in lime deposits and possessed good clay, and on Dracula's orders ovens and kilns for the manufacture of bricks had already been prepared. The "concentration camp" at Poenari must have presented a strange sight to the local peasants (one bears in mind that the boyars arrived in what was left of their Easter finery). As construction began, some of the boyars formed a work chain relaying the bricks and stones from Poenari to the Arges castle. Others worked up the mountain; yet others made bricks. The story does not tell us how long the reconstruction took, nor the number of those who died in the course of it. People were fed simply to keep them alive; they rested just long enough to restore their energies; they toiled until their tattered clothes literally, as the chronicler would have it, fell off their bodies, then continued to work in the nude. Months later, Dracula had succeeded in both of his aims: the powerful boyar class had been savagely humiliated, and he now had his castle retreat.

The path leading from Arefu to the top of the mountain where Castle Dracula is located is not, by any standards of modern Alpinism, a difficult one. The actual climb takes about one hour. The first element of surprise, as one reaches the small wooden bridge over a sheer precipice which leads to the main gate, is the smallness of the structure, particularly when compared with the vast areas occupied by Castle Bran or Castle Hunedoara. However, the plan of Castle Dracula was limited by the perimeter of the mountain top. The view is superb, almost majestic, both in the southern and east-west directions. One can see dozens of villages scattered among the hills immediately surrounding the valley of the Arges. Behind, barely visible in the sun scorched Wallachian plain, is the city of Curtea de Arges. To the north, lie the snow capped mountains of the Fagaras, dividing Transylvania from Wallachia proper. It is perhaps inevitable that Dracula's eyrie reminds today's visitor of Hitler's high retreat at Berchtesgaden.

The extent of the castle's destruction and decay is already apparent on the way up; one sees a trail of fallen bricks from the top of the mountain down to the river Arges, which is slightly reddened at one spot, not with the blood of Dracula's victims as the local peasants would have it, but with the bricks on the floor of the crystal-clear water.

Castle Dracula is built on the plan of an irregular polygon—the shape of the narrow plateau at the summit of the ridge: approximately 100 feet wide from east to west, and 120 feet long from north to south. One can detect the remains of three of the five original donjons and their connecting walls despite a heavy overgrowth of every variety of Carpathian wild flower, greenery, and fungi. The central tower, probably the oldest, and built by Prince Basarab, was prism-shaped. The other two, probably built by Dracula, are in the classical cylindrical form. The fortress structurally attempts to combine some of the best features of Teutonic fortifications with the more intricate Byzantine style. The thickness of the walls, which were reinforced with brick on the outside, confirms the tradition that Dracula doubled the width of the walls of the earlier fortress. In due course, they were able to withstand the worst cannon fire of the Turks. These walls, protected by conventional battlements, originally were quite high, and from afar give the impression of being part of the mountain itself.

The five original donjons and other elements could have housed not more than 200 soldiers and an equal number of retainers and servants. Within the courtyard, it would have been difficult to drill over 100 men. In the middle of the courtyard the remains of a well are barely discernible. This was the source of the fortress' water supply. An arrangement remarkably similar to one at Castle Bran has also been detected: a secret staircase leading from the well into the bowels of the mountain, and connecting with a tunnel that emerges in a grotto on the bank of the river Arges. This was the escape route that Dracula used successfully in 1462. The grotto on the riverbank is referred to in popular tradition as *pivnit*, which in Romanian means cellar—in this case, perhaps, the cellar of the castle. In the courtyard, a few feet away from the entrance to the secret passage or well, there remains a vault, indicating the presence of a chapel at one time.

Of whatever else there was within the fortress, there is not a trace today. The houses of the attendants, the stables, the animal pens, the various outhouses that were customarily erected in small fortifications of this nature, now have to be imagined. So, too, the drawbridge which preceeded the present slender wooden bridge. We know that the donjons had some openings, probably under the battlements on top, for the peasants' ballads speak of candlelight being visible from a distance at night.

Following Dracula's escape to Transylvania in 1462, the Turks partially dismantled the castle. It was never used by Radu the Handsome, the new Wallachian incumbent, since the place was still haunted by souvenirs of his hated rival and brother. But it was enjoyed as a hunting retreat by Radu the Great, Dracula's cousin, the builder of the Monastery of the Hill. The records at the time speak of a princely governor, a boyar by the name of Gherghina, who was, it seems, a relative of Dracula—perhaps one of Dracula's bastards, or possibly that son who had miraculously escaped the Turks in 1462 and been brought up by a peasant from Arefu. The castle enjoyed renewed prestige under the rule of Dracula's only legitimate son (by his second wife), Prince Mihnea. However, even that half-Hungarian prince could not have felt strong ties to a retreat that was associated with his father's first wife and where a half-brother may have been governor. Shortly after Gherghina's death, the castle was totally abandoned, and during the 16th century the neglect that was ultimately to destroy it set in. By that time, the center of Wallachian power was gradually moving toward the Danube— toward Bucharest. A castle which had existed primarily to survey the boyars in the ancient capitals had virtually lost all meaning. Its location away from all the commercial routes leading into Transylvania deprived it of any strategic value. And even as a hideaway, it had become too remote. For all these reasons, the castle was never used again. Physically, it became entombed in a morass of Alpine overgrowth.

The peasants of the area often talk about it but rarely dare visit it. In the eyes of the superstitious, the spirit of Stoker's "undead hero" still dominates the place. The peasant guarding the castle at night is never seen without a tattered Bible; he reads it constantly while on duty, to ward off, so he indicated, the evil spirits that linger around.

These spirits, in the vivid imagination of the peasantry, take the shape of various animals. Among the actual creatures that are found at this ruin is the Wallachian eagle, which has an enormous wing span, and which was always symbolized in the ancient national crest. The cursed bat, another element of woe in Romanian folklore, dominates the battlements at night. Romania's bat is larger than its North American counterpart though not quite so large as the vampire bat of South America, and is considered dangerous by the peasants. They relate strange tales of people with bat wounds becoming demented and wishing to bite others, and usually dying within a matter of a week. These are the symptoms of hydrophobia. They also concord remarkably well with the Dracula vampire myth and provide a rational explanation of Stoker's horror tales.

The eagles that nest in the castle area are probably attracted by the number of smaller animals. Within the ramparts, rats and mice abound; snake holes are evident, probably nesting the dangerous Carpathian viper; occasionally a stray sheep or mountain goat gets entrapped within the overgrowth of vines; foxes are in large supply; and the Romanian mountain bear is an occasional visitor as well as the mountain lynx. But the most dangerous visitor by far is the wolf. In his novel, Stoker mentions wolves howling while accompanying Dracula's carriage. They will attack men during the winter, driven by sheer despair. Wild dogs often howl here at night—particularly, as legend would have it, during a full moon—sending a spine-tingling shiver through the heart of the most valiant. These are some of the legitimate reasons why spending a night on the site of Dracula's castle has become a sport commanding a high fee. Bets of that nature have been made by the more venturesome, but only one person of our acquaintance has survived the ordeal.

Although the sophisticated, adventuresome students from the University of Bucharest and elsewhere are occasionally willing to try their luck and brave the spirit of Dracula, one can hardly blame the superstitious peasants of the area for shunning it. As Stoker also described it, when a stranger approaches them to ask directions to the castle, they usually turn away and emphatically refrain from giving help. If the tourist persists, they simply shrug their shoulders in quiet disbelief that anyone should be so bold as to tempt the spirit of evil, or they mutter *"nu se poate,"* an approximation of the German *verboten.*

Beyond their superstitions, if such they are, is a strange belief somewhat reminiscent of the medieval German obsession that the great Barbarossa would someday arise again to save the German race. Here, in times of stress, the peasants feel that the spirit of Dracula will be born again, or to put it more accurately, that he never really died; he is just "undead." This feeling is expanded even to the prediction that someday when he does rise again, he will save Romania from its outside enemies as he saved the country from the Turks in the 15th century.

Present-day visitors to the castle prefer to view it from a safe distance, usually from the opposite knoll where the Castle of Poenari once stood. From this perspective, too, most of the sketches, oil paintings, and watercolors of Castle Dracula have been made. Such a distance brings into relief not only the castle itself, but the picturesque mountain scenery surrounding it. Because of the abrupt ridge and the heavily forested area, it is almost impossible to photograph the castle from close by, except when you are actually on top of it. The first painting of the castle was done in 1865 by Hensic Trenk, a Swiss artist, and now belongs to the Romanian Academy.

In spite of the overgrowth, the brick on the outer walls and the three main towers is still quite visible. As late as 1912, a visitor to the castle reported seeing the sunken well already covered with wild vines and fungi, and spoke of other interior details which are now gone. One year later, January 13, 1913, around 9:15 in the morning, the peasants in the area reported a violent earth tremor in the whole Arefu region. To the superstitious, it seemed that the spirit of the "Great Undead" had suddenly awakened from centuries of slumber. At noon, when the tremor was over, the main tower of the castle was no more. Its bricks and stones had toppled down the precipice into the river Arges. This earthquake wrought far more destruction to the castle than either the Turks or ages of neglect had accomplished. In 1940, a severe earthquake affected not only Bucharest, but also the mountainous region. This completed the destruction of the castle.

Because of the tourist interest generated by Bram Stoker's Dracula, the identification of the historical Dracula, and the authors' identification of the castle itself, the Romanian government has appropriated a sum for the castle's restoration. When this is done, Castle Dracula may well become the chief tourist attraction of Romania, vying with the Black Sea towns for foreign visitors. Fortunately our visit to the castle preceded this commercialization. The spirit of Dracula is best preserved the way it is—with sunken stones, Alpine weeds, snake holes, and the trails of brick falling down the banks of the river Arges.

5

Dracula Horror Stories of the Fifteenth Century

More fascinating in a way than official archives, which lead to political and diplomatic history, is what the French refer to as "*la petite histoire*," the more intimate history of a subject, which in the case of Dracula is especially found in the contemporary German pamphlets. In modern parlance, these German pamphlets not only created a "bad press" for Dracula in due course but also became "best-sellers" in the extensive medieval Germanic world from Brasov to Strasbourg. The Saxons' desire for vengeance was realized, at least after Dracula's death, by defaming his character for centuries to come. Although this is a controversial topic, the experiences of, and stories told by, Transylvanian-Saxon refugees may well lie at the basis of all the accounts of Dracula's misdeeds.

It is, of course, impossible to know exactly how the stories in these pamphlets were initially conceived, by what manner the Saxons left Transylvania, and how they eventually came to the West. To date no less than 14 accounts about Dracula have been found, in locations as diverse as the Public Archives of Strasbourg and the Benedictine Monastery of St. Gall (today the Stiff Library), in Switzerland. Most are printed, a few are in manuscript form, and some are illustrated with crude woodcuts. These pamphlets with their woodcuts were the principal medium of the 15th century for transmitting stories and images to the general public. One is tempted to compare this use of the woodcut with television today, not only the screening of late-night monster films but also newscasts.

The Germanic language varies, ranging from Transylvanian-Saxon to High German. Most of the stories concerning Dracula are tales of horror with some sort of a moral for the reader.

NOTE: *The Appendices at the back of the book contain translations of the Germanic St. Gall Manuscript; several tales, including a few variants, from Romanian folklore; and the oldest Russian manuscript about Dracula.*

Though an element of distortion and exaggeration is probable
(after all, it is a part of human nature to exaggerate one's plight)
the amazing coincidence of the stories, and the virtual
impossibility of one model inspiring all of them, leads to some
acceptance of their factual basis. For reasons that will be
demonstrated, the German stories about Dracula can be
considered a reliable historical source, and constitute a much
more intimate account of Dracula's life and times than do the
formal and diplomatic dispatches, which often tend to be written
for posterity's sake. One might well imagine some monk—
serving the chapel of St. Jacob at Brasov, or possibly the
Monastery of Carta located at the foot of the Fagaras
mountains—compelled to seek refuge in the West and relating
there the story of his woes. We know the name of one such
monk, Brother Jacob, from the monastery of Gorion, which has
been variously located in Transylvania, Wallachia, Serbia, or
Bulgaria where there evidently were more numerous Catholic
and Saxon foundations than at one time suspected. It stands to
reason that this monk once having reached safe haven at some
place like St. Gall in Switzerland or Beuron in Bavaria was quick
to relate what he had either personally experienced or heard of.
That others copied what, to say the least, in this age of religious
literature was lively material and that this process was repeated
across generations is quite probable. In time there was an
obvious degree of distortion, and it is safe to assume that a 15th-
century manuscript was more accurate than one recopied a
hundred years later. The details of Dracula's horrors, his
depravity, insanity, as well as his motivation, will be discussed
further. What matters here is the authenticity of the Dracula
tales.

The most persuasive element by far is the remarkable
coincidence of all Germanic manuscripts and pamphlets with
other contemporary sources. For, after all, Dracula was not
merely a subject of great interest in the Germanic world. In the
1480s, a Russian ambassador reported various Dracula anecdotes
to the Grand Duke of Moscow. At Constantinople, the
representatives from Venice wrote lengthy reports to the Doge of
that city republic concerning not only Dracula's valor but also his
misdeeds. The Vatican archives still hold secret reports sent by
the papal legates to Pius II. The Byzantine chroniclers
Chalkokondyles, Sphrantzes, Doukos, and Critoboulos of Imbros
recorded Dracula's formidable military reputation. The Turkish
historians spoke of Dracula as *Kaziklu Bey*. The wily Genoese and

pilgrims and travelers from France, England, and the Italies, fearful but admiring, attributed to him essentially the same traits.

Perhaps most picturesque of all are the local legends of the Romanians themselves, handed down by word of mouth, usually in the form of children's tales. The present authors are the first to have made a comprehensive assemblage of the Romanian folkloric elements concerning Dracula. These have been gathered in villages with Dracula associations, usually from the elder citizens, who best preserve historical ballads—and who are, we believe, a dying breed. A number of local teachers and priests, aware of this threatened extinction, have in recent years been busy collecting such tales, not only concerning Dracula but other heroes and villains of old. The Folklore Institute at Bucharest finally has become concerned lest the fascinating historical tradition be permanently lost, and has organized a number of official expeditions in "Dracula Country." The fact we shall stress at this time is that the Dracula tales collected so far from oral Romanian tradition have an amazing coincidence, even in regard to details, with Slavonic and Germanic stories. In the case of the Romanian sources there evidently could have been no possibility of a common model or pattern. If connections between a fleeing 15th-century Saxon monk Jacob and a 15th-century Russian ambassador Kurytsin are already difficult to maintain, those between a 15th-century Saxon monk and a 20th-century Romanian peasant are impossible to establish. In the last resort the proof of the historicity of the Dracula stories lies in their remarkable coincidence of both character and plot.

The two oldest manuscripts containing Dracula horror stories were written in Low German dialect around 1462, shortly after Dracula's imprisonment at Buda, the Hungarian capital. One, mentioned earlier, is located in the famous 6th-century Celtic Benedictine monastery of St. Gall (St. Gallen) in Switzerland; the other, in the Lambach monastery in Austria. A more elaborate horror story, which fills in many details and brought the account to Dracula's actual imprisonment, was authored by Michel Beheim, a famous 15th-century German troubadour, who narrated Dracula monstrosities in poetic form; it was probably written shortly after Dracula's imprisonment in the winter of 1462 or the spring of 1463. Very similar anecdotes circulated in Central Europe, in the Germanic world, and in Italy. The most authoritative account was undoubtedly one by King Mathias' official court historian, Antonio Bonfinius; the most famous name linked to Dracula memorabilia is that of the *bon vivant* Renaissance pope, Pius II, whose memoirs refer to certain crimes that he may have heard of from his legate at Buda, Nicholas of Modrussa, who had met Dracula and who himself has left us a remarkably accurate literary portrait of the tyrant. Both the legate's and the pope's accounts were written in Latin; the pope's memoirs were initially published in 1584.

The following excerpt from the title page of a German pamphlet indicates the lurid preview of what lay in store for the reader:

The shocking story of a MONSTER and BERSERKER called Dracula who committed such unchristian deeds as killing men by placing them on stakes, hacking them to pieces like cabbage, boiling mothers and children alive and compelling men to acts of cannibalism.

By way of further enticement, the anonymous pamphleteers promised many other shocking revelations, plus mention of the country over which Dracula ruled. For dramatic purposes, the frontispiece of several pamphlets included a woodcut depicting the tyrant Dracula dining happily amid a forest of the impaled. Others simply showed Dracula's face, but with distorted features. One printed in 1494 has a woodcut portraying a bleeding, suffering Christ. Given the fact that the literature disseminated at a time closely coincident with the invention of the printing press was almost exclusively religious matter, one can't help suspecting that the horror plot centering on a lay figure generated enormous interest, even as reading material in monasteries, and provided a welcome diversion from spiritual exercises. It is conceivable, too, that the Dracula "horror stories" were to the 15th century what Stoker's vampire novel was to the 19th century, what horror films are to the age of the cinema.

The deeds attributed to Dracula in the German narratives are so appalling that the activities of Stoker's bloodsucking character seem tame by comparison. The following excerpt is an example of "Dracula's unspeakable tortures unequaled by even the most blood-thirsty tyrants of history such as Herod, Nero and Diocletian."

Once he had a great pot made with two handles and over it a staging device with planks and through it he had holes made, so that a man could fall through them with his head. Then he had a great fire

*made underneath it and had water poured into the pot and had men
boiled in this way.*

Dracula's principal means of inflicting cruel death was, as
we know, impalement. The victim was usually pulled apart by
two horses, after a stake firmly held by attendants had
penetrated the rectum and entrails. Care was customarily taken
to have the stake rounded at the end and oiled lest it cause
instant death.

The German woodcuts graphically demonstrate that there
were other methods of impalement: the stake penetrating the
navel, or as vampires would express it, piercing the heart, which
would of course be instantly fatal. The "berserker" was not
deterred by age, sex, nationality, or religion. The German
pamphlets mention the killing of native Romanians, Hungarians,
Germans, Turks, and Jews; and gypsies, it seems, incurred
Dracula's wrath on frequent occasions. Catholics, the Orthodox,
Moslems and "heretics" perished. Mothers and even sucklings
were executed; sometimes children's heads were impaled on
their mother's cut breasts. There was, it seems, a stake in
constant readiness in the courtyard of the palace at Targoviste.

The German writers relate that aside from impaling his
victims, Dracula decapitated them; cut off noses, ears, sexual
organs, limbs; hacked them to pieces; burned, boiled, roasted,
skinned, nailed, and buried them alive; exposed them to the
elements or wild animals. If he did not personally drink blood or
eat human flesh, he compelled others to practice cannibalism.
His cruel refinements included smearing salt on the soles of a
prisoner's feet and allowing animals to lick them for indefinite
periods. If any relative or friend of an impaled victim dared
remove the body from the stake, he himself was apt to hang from
the bough of a neighboring tree. With the cadavres of his victims
left at various strategic places until beasts or the elements had
reduced them to bones and dust Dracula terrorized the entire
countryside.

How credible are these Dracula horror stories? Were they
based on concrete historical fact, or were they the product of
sadistic-minded 15th-century pamphleteers seeking to awe or
amuse, or to relieve the monks from the daily fare of religious
literature? Or, as some critics of these anecdotes have suggested,
were they in fact contrived, on orders of the Hungarian court, to
destroy Dracula's reputation and justify the harsh treatment
subsequently meted out to him in a Hungarian prison? It would

follow from this hypothesis—a Hungarian plot to defame Dracula—that a common model inspired all the 15th-century Dracula narratives, whether German or not.

The Hungarian court seems to have had strong reasons for discrediting Dracula and having him safely removed from power; aside from other factors, his strong one-man rule threatened Hungarian hegemony in Transylvania and Wallachia. However, even granting that a common anti-Dracula model inspired the accounts by the Hungarian chronicler Bonfinius, by Pope Pius II, and by the German pamphleteers (who by a stretch of the imagination might be conceded as "in intelligence" with the aims of the Hungarian king Mathias), one finds it hard to account for the similarity of the many other Dracula anecdotes published in a variety of languages and circulated over widely scattered geographic and political regions. For instance, there is the Russian Dracula manuscript first written in 1486; it closely coincides with the German stories, yet to assume that it was a translation of them is to credit the 15th century with 20th century standards of transmission efficiency. In addition the Russian story is sufficiently different in terms of ethics and political theory to allow a single source. One major argument against the theory of a "common horror stereotype" is provided by the oral ballads and traditions of the Romanian peasants concerning Dracula. Although more reverential and apologetic toward "the impaler," they contain anecdotes similar to those mentioned elsewhere, but the Romanian peasants could neither understand German or Slavonic, nor read or write even their own language. For that matter, no literary language existed in Romanian lands in Dracula's time. Dracula stories in his lifetime were simply transmitted orally from one person to another, very much as the Viking sagas were. Not until the 20th century were they formally committed to print, and it is safe to assume that a few Romanian Dracula anecdotes still go unrecorded.

One can pursue the argument against a single source for all Dracula anecdotes by pointing out that stories about Dracula appeared in Turkish in the works of official chroniclers; others in Greek penned by Byzantine historians; yet others in the Italian, Hungarian, and Czech accounts written by travelers.

It seems reasonable to suppose that German refugees from Transylvania somewhat embellished the story of their "escape" from Dracula country, as political refugees are apt to do, with the thought that the more sensational their pamphlets were, the better they would sell. The factual basis of their accounts, however, must be taken as generally true. To the determined skeptic, an additional yardstick of credibility might be provided by the serious reports of foreign diplomats stationed in various capitals surrounding Dracula country. Diplomats reporting to their home governments have no material wares to sell; they are usually wary of embellished facts and their reports have to be terse and to the point. Let us quote from the papal legate at Buda, Nicholas of Modrussa, reporting to the Vatican on the subject of Dracula's crimes in 1464. Concerning a specific massacre in which Dracula killed 40,000 men and women of all ages and nationalities, the papal legate wrote:

He killed some by breaking them under the wheels of carts; others stripped of their clothes were skinned alive up to their entrails; others placed upon stakes, or roasted on red hot coals placed under them; others punctured with stakes piercing their head, their breast, their buttocks and the middle of their entrails, with the stake emerging from their mouths; and in order that no form of cruelty be missing he stuck stakes in both the mother's breasts and thrust their babies unto them. Finally he killed others in various ferocious ways, torturing them with many kinds of instruments such as the atrocious cruelties of the most frightful tyrant could devise.

Another papal nuncio, the Bishop of Erlau, who was certainly not prone to fabrications, reported in 1475 that by that date Dracula had personally authorized the killing of 100,000 people. This figure is equivalent to at least one-fifth of the total population of Dracula's principality, which did not exceed 500,000. (Robespierre's notorious reign of terror, 1793-94, was responsible for 35,000-40,000 victims and France had a population of approximately 18,000,000 at the time.)

How did the German Dracula stories reach Western Europe? The German troubadour Michel Beheim reveals in his very poem how he obtained many details of his Dracula story. In the winter of 1462, while residing at the Imperial court of Frederick III at Wiener-Neustadt, Beheim met Brother Jacob, a Capucin monk from the monastery of Gorion (probably located in Serbia) who had obviously fled from Transylvania. Dracula had specific grudges against Catholic monasteries in his lands: many of them were ruled internally by foreigners and all of them were controlled by the Church of Rome, a "schismatic" church in the view of the Orthodox. Dracula's treatment of these enclaves of the papacy was severe. Brother Jacob, and undoubtedly other refugees from Transylvania, knew the area's history well, and were impressive in their mention of not only specific dates but also names of historic personages. The meticulous geo-political descriptions of Transylvania witness further to the basic historicity of these accounts. Many of the ethnic groups in Transylvania at that time are mentioned, as are the religions. The larger Transylvanian towns of Kronstadt (Brasov) and Hermannstadt (Sibiu), administrative units such as the Bursenland (Tara Birsei), the southeastern district surrounding Brasov where many German Saxons live to this day, figure prominently in the German stories. With pinpoint accuracy a German pamphlet published in Nuremberg, 1499, refers to individual sections of Kronstadt:

And he led away all those whom he had captured outside the city called Kranstatt near the chapel of St. Jacob. And at that time Dracula . . . had the entire suburb burned. Also . . . all those whom he had taken captive, men and women, young and old, children, he had impaled on the hill by the chapel and all around the hill, and under them he proceeded to eat at table and get his joy that way.

As noted earlier, a woodcut enables us to identify this area as the Tampa Hill section even though the chapel of St. Jacob no longer exists there. The "Church of St. Bartholomew," which Dracula burned, after "stealing the vestments and chalices," is a 13th-century structure that was built in the heart of the old city and survives to this day.

The mention of smaller townships, even individual villages, monasteries, and fortresses, further strengthens the historicity of the accounts. Although identification is at times difficult since most German names in use during the 15th century have been replaced by Romanian ones and some ancient townships have now disappeared, it has been possible with the help of 16th-century maps to retrace Dracula's path of destruction through Transylvania. In the Hermannstadt (Sibiu) region "he had villages by the name of the monastery of Holzmenge (Holtznetya) completely burned to ashes"; in Beckendorff (Wuetzerland), "those men, women and children large and small whom he had not burned at the time, he took with him in chains and then had them impaled." In these incidents one can identify Holzmenge, where presumably a convent existed at one time, as the Romanian village of Hosmanul a few miles to the northeast of Sibiu (Nocris district); and Beckendorff as being in the vicinity of the village of Benesti. Other Transylvanian villages variously terrorized by Dracula according to the German stories were: Neudorff (the present village of Noul Sasesc, Brasov district), Zeyding (the fortress of Codlea to the southeast of Brasov); Talmets (Talmetch, near Sibiu). Fugrach can easily be identified as the town of Fagaras, a Dracula fief where a castle at one time owned by the Bathorys still stands; Humilach, another Dracula possession in Transylvania, is the present town of Amlas.

Shylta is the Germanic version of Nicopolis, a powerful fortress on the Danube; Konigstein (where Dracula was arrested in 1462) on the Wallachia-Transylvania frontier is Piatra Craiului (literally meaning "the stone of the king"), where a small fortress at one time existed. A few villages mentioned in Michel Beheim's account—for instance, Thunow and Bregel—could not be traced with any accuracy and presumably were completely destroyed. We know from an authoritative Romanian source that at least two other villages, Sercaia and Mica in the Fagaras district, had been so completely decimated by Dracula's raids that they had to be repopulated after his death.

Among the sources that the historian can turn to for verifying the authenticity of the German accounts is the rich primary documentation in the archives of Brasov and Sibiu, two towns which figure prominently in all the German accounts. It includes, among other items, a number of missives by Dracula himself, three of them bearing the awesome signature DRAKULYA (normally he signed himself Vlad).

As the criminal investigator when seeking the truth about a suspect looks for motivation, so the historian testing the veracity of these German stories looks for motives that could reasonably have led Dracula to commit his horrible deeds. Undoubtedly, there was a mad streak in the prince, but we have found all along that this madness was accompanied not by incompetence, rather with keen awareness and enormous cunning. Some of the causes for his acts are suggested below, and very briefly illustrated.

Revenge. The killing of Dracula's father, Dracul, and of his brother Mircea, related in the first episode of the St. Gall manuscript, is an authentic historical fact. The double assassination occurred in December 1447: Romanian sources state that the father was killed in the marshes of Balteni, near Bucharest, and the son was dragged to Targoviste and buried alive by the boyars and merchants in the vicinity of that town. This action may well have prompted Dracula's enslavement of the aristocrats of Targoviste for the construction of Castle Dracula.

The execution in 1456 of Vladislav II (episode 2 in the St. Gall version), who was Dracula's predecessor (1447-56), can also be credited to revenge since Vladislav, along with Hunyadi, was responsible for Dracul's assassination, and also was a member of the rival Danesti faction.

Inter-family feuds. The struggle between the two rival factions of the Wallachian princely family—Draculas versus Danestis—was little less than a struggle for survival, and helps account for many of Dracula's Transylvanian massive raids and individual murders. One German story gives a specific date, 1460, for the assassination of a particular member of the Danesti clan: Dracula allowed him to go through his priestly function and when the service of the dead was completed, he had Dan dig a grave according to Christian custom and had his body slaughtered by the grave.

Political enmity. Because of their defection and subversion in supporting his political enemies, Dracula destroyed two of his own enclaves, Fagaras and Amlas.

Protection of Transylvanian commerce. Most of Dracula's vindictiveness against the German Saxon population of Transylvania, which climaxed between 1459 and 1460, was due to an ill-defined but rising sentiment of nationalism, directed in this instance against the commercial monopoly exercised by the Transylvanian Saxons in all Romanian provinces. This monopoly tended to hamper or retard the development of native trade and industry, which Dracula encouraged in a manner reminiscent of current Romanian policies. A specific incident from the German stories illustrates this intensive jealousy of "national sovereignty." In 1460 Dracula arrested 30 German carriages "on a holiday" from Wurtzland and 400 Saxon trainees (mere boys who had come to Wallachia "in order to learn the language . . . and *other things*"). He had them assembled in a room and burned alive. Dracula undoubtedly saw these persons less as tourists and trainees than as spies sent by the Saxon merchants of Brasov and Sibiu to learn about native methods of production.

Establishment of personal authority. When Dracula first came to rule, in 1456, his native province of Wallachia was beset by internal anarchy, boyar intrigue, rival factions, and Hungarian political pressure. In that same year there occurred at Targoviste the most famous instance of mass boyar impalement; described in Beheim's poem and recounted in other sources. The killings resulted from the somewhat jocular answers of the boyar council to Dracula's question: "How many reigns have you my loyal subjects personally experienced in your lifetime?" Thus Wallachia was immediately and horribly instructed that the princely title, and all that it implied, was not to be taken lightly. Moreover, the property of the victims was distributed to Dracula adherents, who may well have formed a new nobility with a vested interest in the survival of the regime.

Affirmation of national sovereignty. Dracula's motives in his atrocities against the Turks are easily arrived at. Some were surely personal in nature, the result of his imprisonment by the Turks, in Egrigoz, when he was a young boy. But he was impelled by national concerns, too. When his reign as prince of Wallachia began in 1456, Turkish aggression had brought Constantinople and almost all of the Balkans under the sultan's control. In the next year, the Turks began supporting the claim of Radu, Dracula's more pliable younger brother, to the Wallachian throne.

Records state that Dracula refused to make his yearly submission at Constantinople; was slow in paying the tribute; unwilling to supply the yearly levy of 500 children for the Turkish infantry corps; and while the Turkish sultan was busy elsewhere, made frequent incursions on the line of the Danube, raiding villages on the Bulgarian side. It is, therefore, not unreasonable to believe that Dracula's defiance also included the famous scene in the throne room of Targoviste, when Turkish representatives failed to remove their turbans, contrary to Romanian custom at court. When they explained that this was contrary to Moslem law, Dracula's response was "I will hammer in your law." Immediately their headgear was secured to their scalps by "small iron nails." This story, concluding with Dracula's moralizing about the impropriety of imposing Turkish customs upon another nation, clearly indicates his intention of affirming full national sovereignty over limited sovereignty.

The motives that have been assigned to Dracula here by no means exhaust the possibilities. Nor are the illustrations of them limited to the ones we have mentioned.

Another indication of the veracity of the German stories is what they omit. For example: Beheim's poem includes an invaluable, detailed description of Dracula's last days of freedom in the fall of 1462, right after his failure against the Turks, his appeal to the Hungarian king for help and protection, flight to his mountain retreat, and so on. It does not include an account of

Dracula's subsequent imprisonment in Hungary: an understandable omission since German Transylvanian witnesses could hardly have been present in Buda. Beheim's poem also does not mention Dracula's liberation in 1474 nor his third reign in 1476; but it could not, for it was written before these events.

In addition to anecdotes which can clearly be placed in a geographic or chronological historical context are a number which cannot be connected with any specific place or date, but which are nevertheless mentioned in the various German texts and form an integral part of the story. The most famous of these episodes can be identified as follows:

1.   The foreign ambassadors
2.   The nobleman with a keen sense of smell
3.   The two monks
4.   The lazy woman
5.   Dracula's mistress
6.   The Florentine merchants
7.   The golden cup
8.   Dracula's treasure
9.   The burning of the sick and poor

The authenticity of such anecdotes can be substantiated essentially by four considerations: They occur for the most part in all three variants, German, Slavonic, and Romanian and, for reasons explained above, could not have derived from a common literary model. In terms of content, moral and political philosophy, and even specific methods of punishment, they coincide fairly closely with those anecdotes that do have historic validity. They reveal characteristics of Dracula which correspond with traits indicated in the other anecdotes. They describe events and policies which are susceptible to credible explanation. Let us look at two of these anecdotes.

1. There was a famous fountain in a deserted square of Targoviste where travelers habitually would rest and refresh themselves. Dracula had ordered a golden cup to be permanently located at this place for all to use. Never did that cup disappear throughout his reign.

2. A foreign merchant who spent the night at an inn left his treasure-laden cart in the street, being aware of the reputation of Dracula's country for honesty. Next morning, to his amazement, he found that 160 gold ducats were missing. He immediately sought an audience with the prince. Dracula simply replied: "Tonight you will find your gold." To the citizens of Targoviste he gave the ultimatum: "Either you find the thief or I will destroy

your town." Certain of success in advance, Dracula further commanded that 160 substitute ducats plus one extra one be placed in the cart during the night. Duly the thief and the original ducats were found. Having proved the honesty of his capital, Dracula desired to test the ethics of the foreigner. Fortunately, the foreigner was honest and admitted to the additional ducat. While impaling the thief, Dracula told the merchant that such would undoubtedly have been his fate had he proved dishonest.

Both of these stories are in keeping with contemporary references to Dracula's attempt to set a strict code of ethics in his land—a most difficult thing to implement in a society known for its Byzantine cynicism and absence of moral standards, but not an impossible one since Dracula enforced public morality by means of personally directed terror.

Throughout the various sagas of Dracula's crimes, there is a sadistic sexuality: the ritual and manner of impalement, a husband's enforced cannibalism of his wife's breasts, and similar horrors. Here, too, one encounters Dracula imposing morality with morbid measures. The extent of Dracula's indignation against an unfaithful wife almost surpasses belief. Dracula ordered her sexual organs to be cut. She was then skinned alive and exposed in public, her skin hanging separately from a pole or placed upon a table in the middle of the marketplace. The same punishment was applied to maidens who did not keep their virginity, and to unchaste widows. In other instances, Dracula was known to have the nipple of a woman's breast cut off, or a red-hot iron stake shoved through the vagina until the instrument penetrated the entrails and emerged from the mouth.

What explanation might successfully reconcile Dracula's apparent attraction to women with the savagery of his sexual crimes? One obvious conjecture—the very ritual of the penetration of the stake suggests it—is some sort of sexual inadequacy, most likely partial impotence.

There are other, general considerations which must be kept in mind when evaluating Dracula's criminality. One is the proverbial concern of viewing a man's actions according to the standards of his time. Dracula's age is that of the Spider King Louis XI (1423-83); Ludovico Sforza "the Moor" (1452-1508); the Borgia Pope, Alexander VI (1431-1503); Sigismondo Malatesta (1417-68); Cesare Borgia (1476-1507). One could go on and on in enumerating brutal contemporaries. The point is that the

Renaissance, for all its humanism, was marked by extraordinary inhumanity.

Concerning impalement, though never before (or since) in history practiced on so wide a scale, it was not a Dracula invention. It was known in Asiatic antiquity and practiced by the Turks. (The only recorded instance in the West is attributed to John Tiptoft, Earl of Worcester, during the War of the Roses; he had learned it from the Turks.)

Dracula's cruel traits were, in addition, not unique in his family. We know too little about his father, but it seems safe to say that his deeds must have earned him the cognomen "Devil." Moreover, one of Dracula's own sons is remembered as Mihnea the Bad. It should also be borne in mind that Dracula spent more years in prison than he did on the throne; his first imprisonment, by the Turks, began when he was no more than 15, and it involved both physical and moral abuse. But most of his experiences seemed to reinforce one fact: life is insecure—and cheap. His father was assassinated; a brother was buried alive; other relatives were killed or tortured; his first wife killed herself; subjects conspired against him; his cousin, a sworn friend, betrayed him; Hungarians, Germans, and Turks pursued him. *Tout comprendre est tout pardonner?* In reviewing Dracula's life what he suffered and what he caused others to endure—it makes more sense to say that to know all is to reflect on how horror begets horror.

6

The Historical Dracula: 1462-76

King's Prisoner

Dracula's 12 years of imprisonment in Hungary (1462-74) constitute the most obscure phase of his extraordinary career. Romanian oral and written sources are understandably silent about the prince's experiences at that time, since they took place far from the Transylvanian-Wallachian region connected with his name. Turkish chroniclers had no means of being appraised of Dracula's fate, since technically the Turks were in a state of war with Hungary. The German publicists, having triumphed in their anti-Dracula cause, were no longer interested in the subject: Dracula was safely removed from the Wallachian throne, which is all they desired. As for the official Hungarian historians, apart from being generally silent on Wallachian affairs, they maintained discretion in matters of political prisoners.

Despite all this, it is possible to construct some picture of what Dracula's life was like during 1462-74. His presence in Buda when his positive achievements in the Turkish campaign were still fresh in people's mind certainly did not pass unnoticed. Kurytsin, the envoy of the Grand Duke of Moscow, and the Italian diplomats and papal envoys all wrote lengthy dispatches about the imprisoned prince to their home governments.

Dracula spent his first year of imprisonment at a royal fortress in the ancient city of Buda, on the left bank of the Danube. Then, according to the Russian ambassador, he was transferred to Solomon's Tower within the site of the palace of Visegrad, some 20 miles away. This palace was built high on a hill, with a commanding view of the Danube; Solomon's Tower, where political prisoners were held, was located at the foot of the site, on the river's edge. Within this vast complex—today the scene of careful archaeological investigation and partial reconstruction—the flowering culture of the Hungarian Renaissance was focused. Judged by the countless artistic treasures recently discovered in the palace, Mathias appears to have been a true patron of learning and art.

The Hungarian government is interested less in reconstructing the entire palace than in preserving what is left of it. Solomon's Tower, however, has been virtually rebuilt. The cells are tiny; some have barred openings with a view of the Danube. All prisoners were carefully secluded at night, though during the day they were allowed to exercise in the courtyard.

The Russian chronicle of Ambassador Kurytsin relates that Dracula was on good terms with his guards, who kept him regularly supplied with small animals: birds, mice, rats, and other creatures. These he tortured, either by cutting them up into pieces, or by impaling.them on minute sticks and arranging them in rows—as was his wont with human victims—around his cell. It is said that he derived particular satisfaction from plucking chickens bare and then watching them run around in circles, finally slitting their necks. These episodes related by the Russian ambassador form additional proof of Dracula's taste for blood—one so obsessive that apparently he was unable to repress it even in a prison cell. In Stoker's novel, the character Renfield had a similar sadistic pleasure in small animals.

Dracula's ultimate liberation and his marriage into the Hungarian royal family make it logical to assume that Mathias kept in personal contact with his prisoner and in time allowed him to be present at court. Possibly King Mathias—like Archduke Ferdinand II of the Tyrol, who enjoyed entertaining his guests with eccentric personages—could not resist the desire of the curious to meet the legendary demon who had impaled Saxons and the hero who had defeated the Turks. In any event, Dracula did become acquainted with one of the king's sisters, and a romance leading to marriage developed, possibly as early as his first year of imprisonment.

Dracula was at that time, insofar as we can judge from the oil portrait at Castle Ambras, a rather handsome man: the Saxon woodcuts seen on the cover of some of the German pamphlets are crude in technique and doubtless distorted and deformed his true features. A second oil painting, a miniature in Vienna, to which we have already referred, reveals the face of a powerful man. The large dark green eyes have an intense expression; the nose is long and has thin nostrils; the mouth is large, ruddy, thin-lipped. Dracula appears clean-shaven except for a long drooping mustache, and so far as we can judge, his hair was dark and slightly grayed and his complexion deadly, almost sickeningly white. In the painting, he is wearing the Hungarian nobleman's tunic with an ermine cape and a diamond-studded Turkish-style fur-lined headdress.

The literary description left by Nicholas of Modrussa, the papal legate who met Dracula at that time, corresponds fairly well with the painting. "He was not very tall, but very stocky and strong, with a cruel and terrible appearance, a long straight nose, distended nostrils, a thin and reddish face in which the large wide-open green eyes were enframed by bushy black eyebrows, which made them appear threatening. His face and chin were shaven but for a mustache. The swollen temples increased the bulk of his head. A bull's neck supported the head, from which black curly locks were falling to his wide-shouldered person."

Marriage of this man to Mathias' sister inevitably involved not only the political facts of life, but also matters of religion. To Mathias, a descendant of St. Stephen, it would never do for a Roman Catholic princess of Hungary to marry an Orthodox "schismatic." Though union between Orthodoxy and Catholicism had been established by the Council of Florence, it had always been more apparent than real. Now the rivalry between the two churches, notwithstanding the Turkish danger, had once again incurred a fruitless polemic and broken into open hostility.

To Dracula, baptized in the Orthodox faith as his forebears had been, the question of conversion to Catholicism, which was clearly entailed in any marriage contract with the Hungarian crown, posed no particular problem. Like Henry Bourbon in 1593, he may well have calculated that the throne of Wallachia, implicit in his Hungarian marriage, was fully worth a Catholic mass.

Dracula's conversion to Catholicism, however, incurred the wrath of the Orthodox world—and understandably so in a period when religion was closely linked to national identity. The Orthodox world of the 15th century had been threatened not only by Islam, but by a tide of Catholic crusaders. Now Dracula's conversion to Catholicism was an additional threat, implying the convert's reestablishment on the throne of Wallachia, hence loss of that principality to Orthodoxy. The Grand Duke Ivan III of Moscow calculated that Moldavia at least ought to be safely linked by marriage to the Orthodox world. Accordingly, another marriage contract, this time sealed at Jassy in 1463, offered a Ukrainian princess, Evdochia, to Dracula's Moldavian kinsman

Steven. To strengthen the new Orthodox alliance, Steven's daughter Elena married Demeter, the heir to the Russian throne.

Prince Restored

From the moment that Dracula's marriage was secretly celebrated at Visegrad (the precise date is unknown), his return to Wallachia was a foregone conclusion. Even from the Hungarian point of view it was timely. The Danestis, and their German sponsors, had thoroughly discredited themselves by continued petty intrigues in Transylvania. Radu the Handsome, who ruled in Wallachia, was no more than the instrument of the sultan. Steven of Moldavia was considered unreliable, if only because of his Russian entanglement. The mutual suspicions of the still independent powers of eastern Christendom; the rivalry between Poland, Bohemia, Moldavia, and Hungary; the religious problems posed for the Hungarians by Ivan's pan-Orthodox crusade—all these favored Dracula's candidature. Moreover, as a man capable of giving military leadership in the event of renewal of an anti-Turkish crusade, Dracula was a natural choice. Dracula, now safely married into the royal family of Hungary, could be trusted as King Mathias' man. Even Steven of Moldavia, safely identified with Orthodoxy but apparently heedless of any Russian pressure, recalled the old vow that he and Dracula had made years before that whichever of them should be on the throne should help the other gain his legitimate succession. Thus, to the amazement of the Hungarians, Steven sent emissaries from Suceava to Budapest, urging King Mathias to hasten Dracula's return to Wallachia and promising Moldavian military support.

In 1474, after conversion, marriage and 12 years of imprisonment, Dracula was finally liberated and became the official candidate for the Wallachian throne. The Transylvanian duchies of Almas and Fagaras, within the gift of the Hungarian crown, were the first constituencies to be handed back. In preparation for his future role, the Wallachian claimant accompanied Mathias on official journeys to Central and Eastern Europe. It was probably in the course of one of them that the existing portrait of Dracula at Castle Ambras was painted.

Beyond the fact that Dracula accompanied his brother-in-law on a military expedition against the Turks in Croatia, we have few details about his activities from 1474 to 1475. We know he received a house at Pest, that he lived there with his Hungarian wife, and that she bore him a son initially baptized Milhail and later known as "Mihnea the Bad." The Russian ambassador reported one other incident: Dracula's taking justice into his own hands by killing a guard who had entered his house.

After a short stay in Pest, Dracula settled in Sibiu, in Transylvania. From here he began his campaign to regain the throne of Wallachia from the Turks and his rival Basarab Laiota. We are in possession of more internal documentation on this period of Dracula's career than any other. It is possible to follow his route from Sibiu to Bucharest month by month, sometimes week by week, since he wrote numerous letters to the Hungarian king. In a letter dated August 4, 1475, written from Arghiz, Transylvania, Dracula asked the burgomasters of Sibiu to allow construction of a house for him and his family, and interestingly enough he signed himself Wladislaus Drakulya.

Prince Steven Bathory of Transylvania was officially commander-in-chief of the expedition; the Wallachian contingent was supported by Moldavian foot soldiers; the bulk of the army was composed of Hungarians and Transylvanians. As news of Dracula's liberation leaked out, some of the boyars abandoned Basarab Laiota and defected, as was their wont, to the power which seemed on the ascent. On July 25, 1476, Dracula and Bathory held a council of war in Turda. By July 31 they reached the Medias in central Transylvania. In October the citizens of Brasov, where Dracula had committed so many of his crimes, were wooed into subservience by extensive commercial concessions. A splendid reception was offered to the incoming commanders by the harried burgomaster at the city hall. Services were held in all the churches, and prayers were said for the success of the new campaign. The Danesti claimant, who had long sheltered in Brasov, fled the city as Dracula's cohorts entered.

Wallachia itself was reached by way of the pass at Bran during November. Finally the army encamped in the valley of the Prahova river, from where the road led into the Wallachian plain. This time Dracula's aim was less Targoviste, which was besieged and captured by November 8, than the City of Bucharest—the citadel of the Dambovita—fortified by Dracula during his second reign, and now the seat of Prince Radu's power. On November 16 the battle was fought and won in the vicinity of the fortress. Most of Wallachia was once again under Dracula's control.

In mid-November, as a few boyars stood by, the Metropolitan at Curtea de Arges reinvested Dracula as Prince of Wallachia—a prince unacceptable to the Orthodox; feared as a merciless criminal by both Saxons and boyars; intrigued against by supporters of the Danesti claimant; hated by the Turks and Prince Radu, who had vowed to kill him. Thus, when Bathory's Hungarian force and Steven's contingent left the country, Dracula was clearly exposed to great dangers for he had had little time to consolidate his strength. The fact that he was aware of these dangers is suggested by his failure to bring his wife and son with him to Wallachia. It was an irony, and in a sense Steven's expiation for his previous infidelity, that the only contingent which Dracula could now completely trust was a small Moldavian bodyguard two hundred strong.

An Unusual Corpse

According to Romanian tradition, Dracula fought his last battle just outside the city of Bucharest—possibly close to the place of his father's assassination.

The accounts of his death differ in details. One story has it that at this battle the Turks were beginning to break ranks, and Dracula, confident of victory, climbed a hill in order to observe his army cutting the Turks down. However he was temporarily isolated from his men and to maintain his safety disguised himself as a Turk. Unaware of this subterfuge, one of his followers came upon him, and thinking he was a Turkish leader, struck him with a lance. Dracula defended himself with his sword as well as he could, killing five assailants, but he soon fell victim to his own men. Another version states that it was a force of boyars and other personal enemies who confronted him and—despite the efforts of the loyal Moldavians—killed him. Thus death came to "the impaler" when he was 45 years old, and when his third reign had spanned barely two months.

We know that Dracula was decapitated—perhaps in the battle, perhaps by the Turks after their arrival on the scene. His head was sent to the sultan at Constantinople, where it was openly displayed on a stake—proof perfect and gruesome to the world of Islam that *Kaziklu Bey* was dead.

Island Grave

Monks from the Monastery of Snagov secretly gathered up Dracula's headless body and took it to the monastery. Fearing reprisals from Dracula's enemies, they laid it in an unmarked grave.

Snagov is an island in one of the lakes surrounding Bucharest, and is located in the heart of the Vlasie forest. The island is about a mile in length, and a half mile in width. Today, a small brick chapel is all that remains of the ancient monastic complex. This chapel, one of three that originally belonged to the monastery, was rebuilt in 1517. It is here that tradition assigns Dracula's grave. There are other legends associating Dracula with Snagov, and it is difficult for the historian to know how many are founded on fact, how many are fanciful creations of the superstitious peasants nearby, some of whom have envisaged Dracula's ghost rising from the waters of the lake. In this area today, as one sees the motor launches, sailboats, lovely villas—the full paraphernalia of 20th-century relaxation—it is difficult to think back to the bloody era of Dracula; within the walls of the chapel itself with its faded Byzantine murals, it is another matter: as one listens to the stories of the monks, one seems to go back in time.

As in the case of Castle Dracula, one may safely presume that the island monastery with its secure strategic position was originally built on an extensive scale, either by Dracula's grandfather, Prince Mircea of Wallachia, or by one of the boyars at his court. From official documents we do know that Mircea often resided at the monastery and that he endowed it with vast tracts of land from the surrounding villages. Relatively few official documents mention this monastery in Dracula's reign, but in the 16th century a Wallachian prince, in an act of endowment, confirmed those estates bestowed upon the monastery by Dracula. In addition, we know that between 1436 and 1447 Dracula's father endowed Snagov with more land than any other monastery of the realm, and that in 1464 Radu the Handsome endowed it with three additional villages: Vadul Parvului, Calugareni and Stroesti. These along with gifts from other members of the family lead to the conclusion that Snagov is *par excellence* a Dracula ecclesiastical establishment.

In Dracula's time, Snagov undoubtedly was one of the three largest and most important monasteries in Wallachia. Instead of the small church one can see today, the original complex must have reached the full length of the island. It was heavily fortified; the walls extending to the edge of the lake were for additional protection since it is known that in times of peril both princes and boyars stored their treasures here. In addition to the chapels, there were cloisters for the monks, farms and outbuildings for the boyars and their mounts, and according to tradition a prison.

Dracula's son Mihnea the Bad repaired the monastery after extensive damage had been done to it by the Turks, and also had some of his boyar victims interred there. Vlad the Monk, Dracula's half brother, who defrocked himself to become briefly prince, may have attempted to atone for some of the family crimes by becoming abbot of Snagov. Vlad's second wife, Maria, became a nun and lived at Snagov. One of her sons, "Little Vlad," spent all his early years at the monastery before becoming prince in 1510. His son, yet another Vlad, who ruled between 1530 and 1532, may well have drowned in the lake at Snagov and is known logically enough in Romanian history books as Vlad the Drowned.

Though we know very little about the tragedies of Snagov in Dracula's time, or even during the lifetime of the immediate members of his family, a great deal has been written about the violent history of the monastery since that period. A small portion of the tragedy of Snagov is enshrined in its walls and on the cold stone floor of the present small church. One can still read the terse inscriptions in the original Slavonic giving the names of the victims each successive century has contributed to the initial list compiled by the Draculas. Death came to these princes and boyars in different ways and for various reasons, but chiefly they were politically motivated.

In spite of the monks' ongoing prayers the monastery was not spared punishment. It was burned and partially destroyed by the Turks shortly after Prince Radu's inauguration in 1462, and at that time Dracula's treasure is supposed to have been sunk in the lake by the monks, who were in fear for their lives; it is reputed to lie close to the island in one of the deeper spots. In addition to destruction wrought by man, natural disaster added to the tragedy of Snagov. Shortly after Dracula's death, a violent storm erupted with winds of hurricane velocity. Of the two churches then existing, the one built by Dracula's grandfather, the Church of the Annunciation, was torn, steeple and all, from its very foundations and blown into the lake, as was the bell tower. Local tradition has it that only the heavy carved oak door floated on the waters of the lake and that it was blown to the opposite bank, where it was found by some nuns who had established a place of their own. They simply used this providential gift to replace a much less decorative door of their nunnery. The Snagov door has since been deposited at the Bucharest Art Museum. As for the submerged tower, peasants to this day say that whenever the lake is unduly agitated one can hear the muffled sound of the bell.

At the close of the 17th century, the monastery had a fine reputation as a place of learning. It contained one of Romania's first printing presses, the result of the labor of one of the erudite monks of the period, Antim Ivireanu, who printed Romanian and Arabic versions of the Testaments. Because of Antim's excellence as a teacher two famous 17th-century travelers came to the island—Paul of Alep and his father, Patriarch Macarie of Antioch. Writing in Arabic, these men compiled the first scientific "travelogue" of Snagov, which tells of two churches there and of a bridge to the mainland. From their account one might almost believe that Snagov had finally become exempt from tragedy and was launched on a brilliant new cultural phase. This presumed change of fortune, however, was never to occur. Antim, for reasons still obscure, was compelled to leave Snagov and was poisoned and died in exile. His books were dispersed, and the printing press taken to Antioch.

The 18th century period of Greek rule gave Snagov some respite. It was not placed under the custody of the Greek Patriarchates, which at that time were taking over many of the country's ancient ecclesiastical foundations, rather it remained under the jurisdiction of the Romanian Orthodox Church. Even so, the local populace became unsympathetic to Snagov, for many Greek monks served there and all Greeks were regarded with suspicion—particularly because of the vast sums of money that their princes were sending abroad. This may partly account for the peasants burning the wooden bridge linking Snagov to the mainland, making communications to and from the monastery difficult since no permanent replacement of the bridge was ever built. The worst indignity to the monastery, however, was yet to come.

General Kiselev, the Russian-born governor-general of Wallachia in 1830, decreed the conversion of Snagov into a prison for minor offenders. The monks were allowed but a small portion of the monastery for worship. Even in the capacity of a prison, Snagov experienced tragedies. On one occasion as chain-bound criminals were crossing over to the island on a flimsy pontoon bridge, it broke under the weight and sent 59 helpless victims to the bottom of the lake.

Pillage is another, lengthy chapter in the story of Snagov. Since Dracula's time, the monastery had been reputed to store many princely and ill-begotten boyar treasures within its vaults: artistic legacies, valuable religious books printed by the Monk Antim, and a large number of valuable ikons and other religious items. The bait was there, not only for the robber barons, or haiducs, of the Vlasie forest, but also for peasants and priests from the village communities nearby—and the monks were really without means of defense.

At the end of its prison history, which lasted barely 20 years, Snagov, which had always housed a few monks, was virtually abandoned, and by 1867 it formally closed down. The few remaining monks left; no abbot was appointed. Only Sunday services were occasionally said by priests from neighboring villages. During this time vandalism and thievery occurred on a more massive scale, and all joined in—professional thieves, villagers, and government officials. The peasants used the bricks and stones of the remaining outside walls, stole all the wood they could find, and tore doors from their hinges. Roofing material disappeared; stained-glass windows were broken. Inside, the church suffered equally, if not more; pews, pulpits, not to mention holy vases and other religious items, were removed. Tombs were opened, inscriptions torn off, remains of boyars combed for valuables. Abbots and priests from neighboring villages joined in the collection of valuable Bibles and manuscripts, allegedly to save some of them from destruction. In the name of religion, they were sharers in the loot. This pillage could hardly have gone unnoticed by ecclesiastical authorities, and it is inconceivable that the looting of an historic edifice located only a few miles away from the capital was unknown to the government.

In 1890 the administrator of state domains described the ancient monastic complex as reduced to a partially dismantled roofless church. By 1897, the same year Stoker published *Dracula* in London, concerned Romanians—lovers of the antique, historians, and archaeologists—began the difficult task of saving what was left of the neglected Dracula chapel.

The battle to save Snagov as an historical monument, strange as it may sound in this age of national self-consciousness, was as difficult as any single disaster that the monastery has endured— simply through the apathy of the government and of individual ministers. The necessary sums were finally voted and the restoration of the present church began only at the turn of the century—a restoration which, unlike that of many other churches, was done in good taste. The local architects and engineers as well as historians reconstructed the monastery exactly the way it was supposed to have been in the days of Dracula, without the frills of other restored sites. The restoration of Snagov is still being carried out. Like any puzzle long abandoned, there are pieces missing. It is conceivable that the government may someday decide to reconstruct the whole monastery and rebuild the second church as it was in the days of Dracula.

In 1940, during the famous earthquake in Bucharest, when many historic buildings were sent toppling to the ground, the tremor tore the nave of the chapel at Snagov in two. In the eyes of the superstitious peasants, the spirit of Dracula, the great undead, is still there, inviting retribution.

Today, as one surveys the church where Dracula is supposed to be interred, a strange calm surrounds the monastery. Only an abbot, two monks, and a peasant woman attendant pace its grounds. The abbot is a learned man who knows the history of the 15th century and Dracula's connection with the monastery. He has done his homework so well that the Romanian government yearly sends him to Curtea de Arges to train the tourist officials in the complexities of the medieval period. One of his monks, who strangely does not wear the religious garb, spends much time deeply and penitently in prayer inside the church. When questioned as to the absence of religious dress, he confessed that he had committed a "crime" and been assigned by the Patriarch to the island monastery for expiation. Old traditions here, as elsewhere, die slowly.

This story brought to life once again the ancient princes and boyars in similar grief exiled here to wipe away sin. The life of a penitent at Snagov is still rugged since he suffers long periods of total isolation during the winter months, when the ice on the lake is not quite firm enough to traverse on foot. Provisioning, which has to be done by boat, seems to be the main problem. In summer, flocks of tourists are brought twice a day by steamer and innumerable excursionists come by canoe or rowboat to disturb the mystery of Snagov. This daily intrusion in itself is a hardship.

Snagov . . . a place of prayer and prisoners, famous names and infamous acts. Even if one does not believe the popular tradition that Dracula lies buried here, the very atmosphere of this antique site forms an ideal setting for the last phase of the search for Dracula.

7

Vampirism

Old World Folklore

Transylvania has sometimes been described simply as "the land beyond the forest." Even today many Americans, indeed many Europeans, would be hard put to speak precisely about this province. In fact, all of Romania seems to be a place of indeterminable geography, unpronounceable names, and (in the view of film-makers) innumerable violins. As for its people, our knowledge of them is similarly vague. Before going on to look at their vampire folklore, we shall look at them.

They live not in Rumania, but in Romania—a fact stressed by their present government to make clear the land's ties to ancient Rome. Most of them claim to be of Roman descent, but this claim in itself is ambiguous. What does it mean to be a Romanian? There are no specific ethnic characteristics. The people are not all blond with blue eyes, nor all dark-haired with dark eyes; they are not all light-skinned, not all dark-skinned. The chief factor in national identity is that most of the people speak a language which is called Romanian. Even so, one can still hear a kind of Low German dialect in areas like Brasov and Sibiu; one can hear Hungarian in the west near Oradea, or close to the center of Romania at Tirgu Mures. Both Eastern and Western influences affect this culture and give it unique variety and depth.

The people of Romania are still almost 60 per cent rural, and although this basically peasant society is working hard to break into the urban 20th century, its oral traditions are still more powerful than the written word.

Finally, it should be noted that the majority of Romanians are affiliated with, or exposed to the influence of, the Eastern Orthodox Church. This factor, as we shall see, strongly affects the native customs and beliefs concerning vampires.

The notion behind vampirism traces way back in time to man the hunter, who discovered that when blood flowed out of the wounded beast or a fellow human, life, too, drained away.

Blood was the source of vitality! Thus men sometimes smeared themselves with blood and sometimes drank it. The idea of drinking blood to renew vitality became transferred from the living to the dead, and thereupon the vampire entered history. To the vampire, indeed, "The blood is the life"—as Dracula, quoting from Deuteronomy 12: 33, tells us in Stoker's novel.

Vampires have left their mark in all of recorded history. They are cited among the dead in Ancient Egypt. They are defined in 20th-century dictionaries as bloodsucking, walking dead whom some persons still believe in.

Any credence in vampires of course requires conviction that in the afterlife the deceased has a physical body, hence a need for sustenance. According to Eastern Orthodox belief the body of anyone bound by a curse will not be received by the earth—will not decay. The bodies of those who die under ban of excommunication are doomed to remain "incorrupt and entire." Such undead ramble at night and spend only daytime in their tombs until absolution is granted. All this goes a long way toward explaining why vampirism has been so credible in Orthodox countries.

Most Romanians believe that life after death will be much like life now. There is not much faith in any purely spiritual world. So it is reasonable that after death an undead will walk the earth in much the same way as a living person. The walking dead does not always have to be a vampire with a thirst for blood. In fact, the Romanian term *moroi* (undead) is more prevalent than the stark term "vampire" (blood-drinker). But both the undead and the vampire are killed in the same ways. One must drive a stake through their hearts or else one must burn their bodies.

Another Romanian term for vampire is *strigoi*. Strigoi are demon birds of the night. They fly only after sunset, and they eat human flesh and drink blood. In other parts of the Balkans they are sometimes called *vukodlak* or *brukolak*.

Historically, plagues are often blamed on vampires. And sometimes a fir tree is plunged into the body of the vampire in order to keep it in the grave. A sophisticated example of this is the fir-tree ornament which one finds over graves in Romania today.

The belief in vampires is still prevalent in Dracula country. Today at the foot of Castle Dracula, in the small village of Capatineni, lives a gypsy named Tinka. She is the local *lautar* or village singer, and is often called up to sing old stories at weddings, balls, and funerals.

In the autumn of 1969 Tinka told one of our authors two stories about the undead (the moroi). One of them concerned her father. When he had died 30 years ago, he was duly laid out, but the next day the villagers discovered that the old man's face was still ruddy, and his body still soft, not rigid. The people knew that he was an undead. A stake was driven through his heart so as to prevent him from becoming one of the walking dead.

The other story concerned an old woman in the village. After her death many of her close relatives died. So did various animals around her home. Because of these things, the people realized that she was an undead. They dug up her coffin. When the lid was removed, they found that her eyes were wide open and that her body had rolled over in the grave. They also noticed that the corpse had a ruddy complexion. The people of the village burned her body.

Belief in the walking dead and the blood-sucking vampire may never entirely disappear. It was only in the past century— 1823, to be exact—that England outlawed the practice of driving stakes through the hearts of those who had committed suicide. Today, it is in Transylvania that the vampire legends have their strongest hold. As one looks over the following superstitions, it is chilling to imagine their potency and that of similar ones 600 years ago.

In Eastern Europe vampires are said to have two hearts, or two souls, since one heart, or one soul, never dies, the vampire remains undead.

Who can become a vampire? In Transylvania, criminals, bastards, witches, magicians, excommunicated people, those born with teeth or a caul, and unbaptized children can become vampires. The seventh son of a seventh son is doomed to become a vampire.

How can one detect a vampire ? Any person who does not eat garlic or who expresses a distinct aversion to garlic is suspect.

Vampires sometimes strike people dumb. They can steal one's beauty or strength, or milk from nursing mothers.

In Romania, peasants believe that the vampires and other spectres meet on St. Andrew's Eve at a place where the cuckoo does not sing and the dog does not bark.

How does one kill a dragon? St. George killed the dragon with a lance. One must impale the dragon, as one must impale the vampire.

Vampires are frightened by light, so one must build a good fire to ward them off, and torches must be lit and placed outside the houses.

Even if you lock yourself up in your home, you are not safe from the vampire, since he can enter through chimneys and keyholes. Therefore, one must rub the chimney and keyholes with garlic, and the windows and doors as well. The farm animals must also be rubbed with garlic to protect them.

Crosses made from the thorns of wild roses are effective in keeping the vampire away.

Spread thorns or poppy seeds on the paths leading to the village from the churchyard. Since the vampire must stop to pick up every one of them he may be so delayed that he cannot reach the village before sunrise, when he must return to his grave.

Take a large black dog and paint an extra set of eyes on his forehead with white paint—this alienates vampires.

According to Orthodox Christian belief, the soul does not leave the body to enter the next world until 40 days after the body is laid in the grave. Hence, the celebrations in Orthodox cemeteries 40 days after the burial. Bodies were once disinterred between three to seven years after burial and if decomposition was not complete a stake was driven through the heart of the corpse.

If a cat or other "evil" animal jumps or flies over someone's dead body before it is buried, or if the shadow of a man falls upon the corpse, the deceased may become a vampire.

If the dead body is reflected in a mirror, the reflection helps the spirit to leave the body and become a vampire.

One of the most common ways of locating a vampire was to choose a boy or girl, young enough to be a virgin, and seat such person on a horse of a solid color, all white, brown or black, which was also a virgin and had never stumbled. The horse was led through the cemetary and over all the graves. If it refused to pass over a grave, a vampire was thought to lie there.

Usually the tomb of a vampire has one or more holes roughly of the size through which a serpent can pass.

How to kill a vampire? The stake must be driven through the vampire's body and into the earth in order to hold him securely in his grave. The stake should be made from a wild rosebush, or an ash or asp tree. In some areas, red-hot iron rather than wood is used for the stake. The vampire's body should be burned or else reburied at the crossroads.

If a vampire is not found and rendered harmless, it first kills all members of its immediate family, then starts on the other inhabitants of the village and its animals.

The vampire cannot stray from his grave too far since he must return to it at sunrise.

If not detected, the vampire climbs up into the belfry of the church and calls out the names of the villagers—who instantly die. Or, in some areas, the vampire rings the death-knell and all who hear it die on the spot.

If the vampire is allowed to go undetected for seven years, he can travel to another country or to a place where another language is spoken and become a human again. He or she can marry and have children, but they all become vampires when they die.

Did the peasants of the 15th century consider Vlad Tepes, or Dracula, a vampire? Those who renounce the Eastern Orthodox faith can become vampires after death. Since the historical Dracula converted to Roman Catholicism while in Hungarian captivity and apparently died in that faith, it is conceivable that the peasants might once have considered the possibility of his becoming a vampire. But no evidence of any such notion has survived. Dracula or Vlad was referred to as *wütrich* or "bloodthirsty monster" in the 15th-century German horror stories. As we shall discuss further in the next chapter, this word presumably suggested "vampire" to Stoker. However, we find no reason for thinking this old German epithet was so construed in the 15th century; probably it simply meant "slaughterer" for it can also be translated as "berserker."

As for the views of the vampire in Eastern Europe during the 15th century, one can only infer them from the living folk traditions recorded there in the 19th century.

Current beliefs in the vampire were investigated by the authors. In the region around Castle Dracula, for instance, McNally actually questioned the peasants; he found that there is now no connection between Vlad Tepes and the vampire in the folklore. For that matter, the peasants there are not even aware of Stoker's modern Dracula. They do believe passionately, however, in the vampire and the undead.

Most of our culture has an urban bias against the peasants' belief in vampires. This is reflected in our use of the word "urbane" to describe something positive, broad-minded, and rational; and the word "provincial" to designate something negative, narrow-minded, and superstitious. We tend to look down on peasants and their cultures. To us, peasants are primitive and "unscientific." Even Karl Marx conceded that capitalism at least had saved a majority of the population from "the idiocy of rural life."

But the fact is that so-called primitive, peasant people are not incessantly preoccupied with doubt and fear. They spend most of the day in very practical pursuits which are necessary for them to subsist. They use natural explanations to accomplish these daily tasks.

Some evolutionists have assumed that primitive people have no real capacity for natural explanations. The basis for this assumption is that since primitive man lives at a low technological level he must have a thought process which is opposite to that of modern man. To them, primitive, rural man is "prelogical," a kind of child.

But just as primitive man has some beliefs that are vague and uncertain, so does modern man in an urban, technological society. The point is, attitudes toward death and life have been complex for *all* men—hate and love, attraction and repulsion, hope and fear. The belief in vampires is a poetic, imaginative way of looking at death and at life beyond death.

Primitive beliefs are not any stranger than modern scientific beliefs. Nightly on our TV sets, there is some variation of the man in the white coat who stands up amid bunsen burners and test tubes and declares, "Scientific tests have proved that in 9 out of 10 cases. . . " whereupon everyone in the audience genuflects to the new god science. If it is scientific then it must be *true*, and only the scientifically proven fact *can* be true. Is this any more absurd than primitive peasant beliefs?

The vampire possesses powers which are similar to those belonging to certain 20th-century comic-book characters. During the day he is helpless and vulnerable like Clark Kent or Bruce Wayne. At night, just as the mild-mannered Clark Kent becomes Superman and the effete Bruce Wayne becomes Batman, so the vampire acquires great powers and springs into flight.

Dracula, the vampire-count or the count-vampire, is a kind of father figure of great potency. He, of course, like any good father, is powerful at night. In mythology, opposite to God the Father with his flowing white beard is the father figure in the form of a black satan. Significantly, Satan is usually portrayed with huge bat-like wings.

The connection among Dracula, the devil, the bat, and the vampire becomes clear. In Romanian folklore the devil can change himself into an animal or a black bird. When he takes wings, he can fly like a bat. During the day he lives in hell—quiet there, like the bat in its refuge; when day is done, the night is his empire—just as it is with the bat.

The bat is the only mammal who fulfills one of man's oldest aspirations: it can really fly all by itself, defying gravity like Superman.

The bat is not a flying rat. The "wings" of this small animal are actually elongated, webbed hands. The head of the bat is erect like a man' s head. Like man, the bat is one of the most versatile creatures in the world.

New World Bats

Why is the vampire image linked to that of the so-called "vampire bat" in particular? Vampire bats do not exist anywhere in Europe. Yet it is there that belief in the vampire itself, a night-flying creature which sucks the blood of the living, has flourished.

When Cortes came to the New World, he found blood-sucking bats in Mexico. Remembering the mythical vampire, he called them "vampire bats." The name stuck. So a word which signified a mythical creature in the Old World became attached to a species of bats peculiar to the New World.

The vampire bat, the *Desmodus rotundus,* is marvelously agile. It can fly, walk, dodge swiftly, turn somersaults, all with swiftness and efficiency. Generally it attacks cattle rather than men. The victim is not awakened during the attack. The vampire bat walks very softly over the victim and, after licking a spot on the flesh, neatly inserts its two front incisor teeth. As the blood spurts out, the vampire bat licks it into its mouth. That the vampire bat subsists on blood alone is a scientific fact.

The vampire's existence is a frightening tragedy, *sans* goodness or hope, repose or satisfaction. In order to survive, he must drink the blood of the living. And the option of not surviving is closed to him. He should decompose, but he cannot do so. Thus he continues: wanting to live, wanting to die; not truly alive and not really dead. The folklore about him is not based on science, yet it is essentially true. Ten out of 10 vampire legends and customs attest what no one doubts; man fears death, and man fears some things even *more* than death.

A Real Blood Countess

To many people, the events and personages in vampire legends may appear to be pure inventions or distorted details of actual happenings and in either case the work of simple peasants. We have, however, official documentation concerning an authentic seventeenth-century countess, Elizabeth Bathory, which reveals her to have been a living vampiress. In the view of some persons today, and in that of most of her contemporaries, she was the most fearsome living vampiress of all time. Here is her story:

Elizabeth Bathory was born in 1560 in a part of Hungary edging the Carpathian mountains. The Bathorys were one of the oldest and wealthiest families in Transylvania; one of Elizabeth's relatives was a cardinal, several were princes of Transylvania, and her cousin Count Gyorgy Thurzo was prime minister of Hungary. Undoubtedly, the most famous Bathory was King Steven of Poland, 1575-86. But along with religion and affairs of state, the family had other interests—one uncle was a diabolist, an aunt a lesbian, and a brother a satyr.

As a child, Elizabeth was betrothed to Count Ferencz Nadasdy. She was 15 and he was 26 when they were married on May 8, 1575. King Mathias II of Hungary sent them a wedding present. The bearded Count Ferencz added her surname to his, and thus the countess continued to be known as Elizabeth Bathory.

Elizabeth and Ferencz went to live at Castle Csejthe in the Nyitra country located in northwestern Hungary. The count was rarely home, as he was usually off fighting. A great soldier, he eventually became known as "The Black Hero of Hungary."

It appears that Elizabeth's manservant Thorko introduced her to the occult. In a letter to her husband the countess wrote: "Thorko taught me a lovely new one. Catch a black hen and beat it to death with a white cane. Keep the blood and smear a little of it on your enemy. If you get no chance to smear it on his body, obtain one of his garments and smear that instead."

Elizabeth temporarily eloped with a dark stranger, but upon her return home, the count forgave her unfaithfulness.

Back at the Csejthe Castle, Elizabeth chafed under the dominance of her mother-in-law, whom she hated. Aided by her old nurse Ilona Joo, Elizabeth began torturing some of the servant girls at the castle. Her other accomplices included the major-domo Johannes Ujvary, her manservant Thorko, a witch Dorottya Szentes, and a forest witch named Darvula.

During the first 10 years of her marriage to Count Nadasdy, Elizabeth bore no children. But within the next four years she gave birth to three boys and a girl. In 1600, Ferencz died. Elizabeth's epoch of real atrocities was about to begin. First, she sent her hated mother-in-law away, then she turned to running the household for her own pleasure.

Elizabeth was afraid of becoming old and losing her beauty. One day a maid accidentally pulled her hair while combing it. Elizabeth instinctively slapped the girl hard—so hard that she drew blood which spurted onto her own hand. It immediately seemed to Elizabeth as if her skin in this area took on the freshness of that of her young maid. Blood—here was the key to an eternally beautiful skin texture. The countess then summoned Johannes Ujvary and Thorko. They stripped the maid, cut her, and drained her blood into a huge vat. Elizabeth bathed in it to beautify her entire body.

Over the next 10 years Elizabeth's henchmen provided her with new girls for the blood-draining ritual and her literal blood baths. But one of her potential victims escaped and informed the authorities about the gruesome goings-on at Castle Csejthe.

Upon hearing the news, King Mathias of Hungary ordered action. Elizabeth's own cousin Count Gyorgy Thurzo, governor of the province, led a band of soldiers and guards in the raid of Castle Csejthe on the night of December 30, 1610. What a sight they saw within the castle! In the main hall they found one girl dead, drained of blood, and another alive whose body had been pierced with tiny holes; in the dungeon they discovered "a number" of other living girls, some of whose bodies had been pierced. Below the castle, the authorities exhumed the bodies of some 50 girls.

Elizabeth was placed under house arrest in her castle. A trial was held at Bitcse during January and February of 1611. Elizabeth never appeared in the courtroom. She refused to plead either innocent or guilty. A complete transcript of the trial, made at the time it took place, survives in Hungary today and is the major document concerning this horrifying history.

Johannes Ujvary, the countess' major-domo, testified at the trial that as far as he knew, about 37 unmarried girls had been killed, six of whom he had personally lured to the castle with promises of jobs as serving girls. These victims were bound and then slashed with scissors. Sometimes Dorottya and Ilona tortured these girls, otherwise the Countess Elizabeth did it herself. Ilona Joo, Elizabeth's old nurse, testified that about 40 girls had been tortured and killed.

Everyone implicated in the killings, except for Countess Elizabeth, Ilona Joo, and Dorottya Szentes, was beheaded and cremated. The latter two accomplices had their fingers torn out individually and were burned alive. Countess Elizabeth was never formally convicted of any crime.

Instead, stonemasons were brought to Castle Csejthe; they walled up the windows and doors of the bedchamber, with the countess inside, leaving only a small hole through which food could be passed. At first, Mathias II, King of Hungary, had demanded the death penalty for Elizabeth, but because of the entreaties of her cousin the prime minister, he agreed to the indefinitely delayed sentence, which meant solitary confinement for life. In 1614, four years after she had been walled in, one of the guards posted outside her chamber wanted a look at this woman whose beauty was renowned far and wide. He saw her lying face down on the floor. Elizabeth Bathory, the "Blood Countess," was dead.

The extent of the ties between the Bathorys and the Draculas is not known. It is certain, however, that the commander-in-chief of the expedition that helped Dracula regain his throne in 1476 was Prince Steven Bathory. In addition, a Dracula fief, Castle Fagaras, became a Bathory possession during the time of Elizabeth. It is interesting to note that the dragon motif is common to both families. The awesome Bathory crest displays three wolf's teeth encircled by a dragon biting its tail. Finally, in some circles it is believed that the story of the Blood Countess was known to Stoker.

The Bathory crest, showing three wolf teeth beneath a crown. Not shown here is the encircling motif: a dragon biting its tail.

8

Bram Stoker and the Vampire in Fiction and Film

The time has come to talk of terror and horror. Strictly speaking, they are two different things—but, of course, we seldom speak strictly!

Both are responses to the frightful thing, person, deed, or circumstance. But terror is the extreme *rational* fear of some accepted form of reality, whereas horror is extreme *irrational* fear of the *utterly* unnatural or the supernatural. Moreover, there is realistic horror—the unnatural or supernatural fright presented in the guise of the normal.

Terror is also the dread of the use of systematic violence; horror the dread of something unpredictable, something that may have a potential for violence.

When a mad bomber is on the loose in a city, the inhabitants become terrified; they are aware of the capacities of a seriously deranged person; they understand the devastating effects of a bomb. The nature of the danger is clear, and any attendant mystery is susceptible to rational solution. But if a ghost is heard walking at night, the inhabitants of the house are in horror. What *is* a ghost? What might *this* one do: What *can* it do? And finally, there is the realistic horror: perhaps a man in a tuxedo—he looks and acts very natural at the country club—yet we go into shock when we see him flying over a blood-stained corpse on the seventh green. Horrible . . . mysterious. In short, it is some fundamental, forever unexplainable mystery that distinguishes horror from terror.

Bram Stoker's novel *Dracula* is one of the most horrifying books in English literature. It was published in May 1897, was an immediate success, and has never since been out of print. In America, where it has been published since 1899, it is still a best seller.

In selecting a setting for Dracula, Bram Stoker hit upon Transylvania because it was, and is still, a far-away never-never land in the view of most Englishmen and Western Europeans, a "land beyond the forest" where anything can happen, a perfect setting for a vampire. Even in the recent musical *My Fair Lady,* "the prince of Transylvania" is regarded as coming from a wholly imaginary land.

Stoker chose to tell his story through the diaries of the Englishman Jonathan Harker and his fiancee, Mina Seward; the letters of Mina and her friend Lucy; Lucy's journal; and the testimony of Dr. John Seward on a phonograph record—this last, a rather novel touch for the time. The basic story line is simple:

Harker, a real-estate agent, travels to far-off Transylvania in order to arrange for the purchase of Carfax Abbey, an English property, by a certain Count Dracula. As a guest in the count's castle, he finds "doors, doors everywhere, and all bolted and locked," and rooms in which there is not a single mirror. Almost at once he becomes aware that Dracula is a vampire living with a harem of female vampires—and that he himself is a prisoner. He also learns that the count is planning to leave soon for Carfax Abbey, taking with him 50 coffins. Dracula's ultimate intent: the conquest of England.

The count boards a Russian schooner, the *Demeter,* at Varna on the Black Sea. En route to England, he kills the crew. After arriving in England, he attacks Lucy Westerna, who is on vacation with Harker's fiancee Mina.

Dracula gradually drains Lucy of her blood, and infuses his own blood into her body. She "dies" and becomes a vampire. Dr. Abraham Van Helsing, an expert from Amsterdam, tries to save her from vampirism but fails. The undead Lucy attacks children in Hampstead. When Van Helsing drives a stake through her vampire heart, her corpse finds eternal repose.

Dracula also victimizes Renfield, a patient in an insane asylum who has a taste for small animals.

Meanwhile Harker has miraculously escaped to London, and Van Helsing persuades him to help seek Dracula's many coffins. There is a thrilling search for Dracula's corpse, culminating in its destruction just in time to save Mina, whom Dracula has also attacked in his bloodthirsty campaign to spread the vampire cult throughout England.

In actual fact, Dr. Abraham Van Helsing—whose first name is identical with that of Abraham ("Bram") Stoker—is the real hero of *Dracula;* Count Dracula himself is the underdog. Van Helsing has all the cards stacked in his favor. He knows that Dracula is powerless during the day, and at night Van Helsing can ward him off with garlic or the cross. Abraham Van Helsing may be Abraham Stoker's substitute self. He unites the scientific with the occult. He is all-wise and all-powerful. His mind pierces everyday reality to the reality beyond. Van Helsing is also courageous and relentless when confronting the ignorance of other scientists and rationalists and when up against the vampire himself.

Just a few days before Stoker's vampire novel was published, the character Dracula appeared on stage for the first time, in a play entitled *Dracula or the Un-Dead*; it was solidly based on the book and its playing time was something more than four hours. Its performance on May 17, 1897 was the only one which Stoker ever witnessed.

In 1921, almost a quarter of a century later, F. W. Murnau, a young German film director, decided to make the first horror movie about Dracula. (That same year, Henrik Galeen also adopted the Stoker novel for the cinema.) Though Murnau gave full credit on the screen to Stoker's novel, he had failed to get permission to use it. So he changed the setting from Transylvania to the Baltic area, and he also added a final erotic scene. His silent film entitled *Nosferatu* was released by Prana Films in Berlin in 1922. By this time Stoker had died; his widow, Florence Stoker, brought suit against Murnau and won. Murnau's company folded. Although the courts had ordered that the negative and prints of *Nosferatu* be destroyed, this fortunately did not happen. The film opened in London in 1928 and in the United States in 1929. Since then, *Nosferatu* has continued to be shown in the art cinema theatres of the world.

The central locale in *Nosferatu* is the port of Bremen in northern Germany. Here Dracula has an agent named Renfield, who sends Jonathan Harker to Transylvania so that he can discuss with Dracula the rental of a home in Bremen. During Harker's stay with him, Dracula sees a medallion of Harker's beloved Mina, and becomes attracted to her. He attacks Harker, then leaves by ship for Bremen.

During the voyage, he kills the entire crew. Upon his debarkation in Bremen, the fear arises that the plague has arrived in the city. Dracula installs himself in a house across the road from Mina. Harker, who had slowly recovered from the vampire's attack, has also returned home. He warns Mina against the stranger from Transylvania. At the movie's end, Mina realizes that she must spend the night with Dracula—must keep him at her side until daylight—in order to save Jonathan and her fellow humans. She does it. As the morning sunlight falls upon

Dracula, he disintegrates. Jonathan now enters the room and
Mina expires in his arms. This bizarre ending was invented by
Murnau, and it shows a strange, Teutonic attitude toward the
use of sexual attractiveness. It takes real guts to go to bed with a
vampire in order to save mankind.

An Irish actor-manager, Hamilton Deane, who had read
Stoker's *Dracula* around 1899, tried for many years to persuade
some playwright to write a Dracula play. Finally, Deane himself
took over the task in 1923. His play, entitled *Dracula*, was
performed in June 1924 at the Grant Theatre in Derby. It was an
immediate success. On February 14, 1927, it came to London,
where it had one of the longest runs of any play in English
theatrical history.

For the New York stage, Deane revised *Dracula*,
collaborating with the American writer John L. Balderston. It
opened at the Fulton Theatre, in October 1927, with an unknown
Hungarian actor named Bela Lugosi in the vampire role. The
show ran for a year on Broadway, and for two years on tour—
breaking all previous records for any modern play touring the
States.

While the stage versions were becoming such huge successes
in England and the United States, the film director Tod
Browning decided to make his own Dracula movie. Accordingly,
in 1930 Universal Pictures bought the motion picture rights to
the Deane-Balderston version. Browning's film presents Dracula
the vampire as an accepted fact of existence.

Bela Lugosi, the stage Dracula, played the lead in this
famous American film, which was released on St. Valentine's
Day in 1931. The actor had been born Bela Lugosi Blasko in the
town of Lugoj, which is in the Banat region of Romania and once
was part of Hungary. Most film critics agree that he was a
natural for the role. His deep, thick Hungarian accent and slow
manner of speaking, his aquiline nose, high cheek bones, and six-
foot frame all seemed perfect attributes for the part. The eerie
effect of his almond-shaped, crystal-blue eyes was heightened in
the film by focusing light on them through two small holes in a
piece of cardboard. This Dracula film became Universal's biggest
money-maker in 1931.

In the Tod Browning film, Renfield, an agent for a London
firm, comes to Transylvania to get a lease signed by Dracula for
Carfax Abbey. On the way, the peasants warn Renfield about
Dracula's vampirism. He meets Dracula at his castle, and is
attacked by him there.

Dracula travels by boat to London, accompanied by Renfield, who is now his slave. Needing blood, Dracula kills all the sailors on board. In London, Renfield is placed in an insane asylum. At the opera Dracula meets both Lucy and Jonathan Harker's fiancee Mina. Lucy is fascinated by him, and Dracula later makes her into one of his entourage of female vampires. He also begins the process of converting Mina into one. Along the way, he kills other Londoners.

Then Professor Van Helsing, an expert on vampires, arrives on the scene. He declares, "Gentlemen, we are dealing with the undead, Nosferatu, the vampire." He notes that Count Dracula throws no reflection in a mirror. He repels him with a cross. In the course of this film, the character Van Helsing becomes the archetype of the fearless killer of vampires. Van Helsing convinces Mina's father and Jonathan that they must find Dracula in his grave during the day and kill him with a stake in order to save Mina from his dire control. Together they discover Dracula's coffin at Carfax Abbey. Van Helsing drives the stake into Dracula's heart. He is destroyed forever. Mina recovers from her shock. She is saved.

The American horror film became popular because of the almost simultaneous release of two remarkable creatures: Dracula the vampire (1931) and Dr. Frankenstein's monster (1932). It is interesting to speculate on whether there is any correlation between the popularity of these creatures and the period in which they were released—the Great Depression. The optimistic Dr. Frankenstein created a monster which ultimately destroyed him, just as many optimistic investors created a market situation which in 1929 destroyed them. Dracula drained away the life of his victims, an effect comparable to that of the economic disaster.

Lugosi's only rival as the horror king was, of course, Boris Karloff, who played Dr. Frankenstein's monster. In 1938 the film *Dracula* was reissued; there followed a long line of horror films in which Lugosi participated, *The Return of the Vampire, House of Dracula,* and so on; similarly, the Frankenstein film spawned a series. Lugosi toured in the role of Dracula both in America and in England. He was addicted to drugs, and by 1955 was in a state institution. He had taken morphine, he said, during his filming of the 1931 Dracula story for relief from pains in his legs. In August 1956, Bela Lugosi, the vampire king, the living embodiment of Dracula, died at 73 years of age. Although Dracula and other horror roles had netted him more than

$600,000, he had only $3,000 left at the time of his death. In accordance with his request, Lugosi was buried in his black Dracula cloak lined with red satin.

In 1958 the British scriptwriter Jimmy Sangster produced a new Dracula, for Hammer Films, which was based wholly on Stoker's story line. He made Dracula into a realistic monster in technicolor. Some film critics found the film to be "too realistic." Its director was the now famous Terence Fisher. The erotic element predominated: women were attracted to Dracula; they eagerly awaited his kisses and bites—and kiss them and bite them he did in full view. Christopher Lee, a tall thin macabre-faced figure, played Dracula. The new Dracula movie opened in May 1958 in both London and New York. In less than two years it made eight times its original cost. Several take-offs on this theme have been made, the latest being *Dracula Has Risen from the Grave.* (You can't keep a good man down!) And still more take-offs on the Dracula theme in film come out almost every year. The current Hammer films about Dracula are terror, not horror, films, for any real sense of mystery has been lost.

There are four truly great horror films: *Nosferatu* (1922), *Dracula* (1931), *Vampyr* (1932), and *The Horror of Dracula* (1958).

Presently the leading vampire-Dracula productions come from Hammer Films in Great Britain, and the most impressive Dracula actor is Christopher Lee. A filmography of this genre of films, covering 1896-1971 and including commentary, may be found in the final section of this book. In addition, 1972 will see even more startling variations.

About two years ago Harry Allan Towers, a producer at Britain's Tigon Studio, commissioned the Italian director Jesus Franco to film a definitive version of Bram Stoker's novel for issue by Commonwealth United Releasing Corporation. The film was largely shot in Spain; Christopher Lee played Dracula. Commonwealth United Releasing Company folded and American International bought it out, but due to a legal hassle the Dracula film has not been shown in Spain or the United States. However, the film has played in much of Europe with great success; was especially successful in Paris during the spring and summer of 1972. The film is entitled *The Nights of Dracula;* in France, *Les Nuits de Dracula,* and in Italy, *Count Dracula.* It reputedly encompasses the atmospheric horror of Stoker's *Dracula.*

Another current film is *Vampir,* a documentary about the making of *The Nights of Dracula,* directed by Pedro Portobello.

This film shows how the classic horror effects are achieved with such means as the fog and cobweb machines, lighting, and makeup, and how the stake is driven through the heart. *Vampir* was screened in 1971 at the Cannes Film Festival, where it received fine reviews; at the Museum of Modern Art in February 1972 as part of the museum's Cineprobe series; and at the Olympia Theatre in New York on May 5, 1972 at midnight. It has recently been picked up by Roninfilms, a small company which usually distributes Japanese films.

A film entitled *Dracula vs. Frankenstein* is to be released by Independent International. An all-black modern version of Dracula called *Blacula* (American International) is also being made. The noted Shakespearean actor William Marshall will play the title role, and Denise Nicholas of *Room 222* will portray the heroine.

On American television in 1972 a film with one of the highest ratings was ABC's *Night-Stalker* about a reporter who realizes that a vampire is loose in Las Vegas. All the officials make fun of the reporter, thinking that he is simply looking for a sensational story. In the end there really is a vampire, a Transylvanian count who never speaks in the film but has fantastic physical power. The reporter, who destroys the vampire, is hounded out of town by the officials.

In Search of Dracula was produced in 1972 by Aspekt Films, Sweden; director, Calvin Floyd; screenplay by Yvonne Floyd. The authors of the present book served as historical consultants. This film is an entertaining documentary about the real Dracula and Transylvanian folklore, shot on location in present-day Romania. It is the first film to deal with both the fictional vampire Count Dracula and the genuinely historical Vlad the Impaler. Clips from famous Dracula films are interwoven with scenes from Transylvanian folklore about vampires. Christopher Lee is the narrator, and appears as Count Dracula and, in native Romanian costume, as Vlad the Impaler.

This fad for Dracula the vampire all began with Bram Stoker. But how did *he* get the idea? How did he come to be the creator of this modern horror story?

Stoker was born in Dublin on a November day in 1847. He was named Abraham after his father—an employee at the Chief Secretary's Office in Dublin Castle, but he was affectionately called "Bram" throughout his life. His mother was Charlotte Matilda, daughter of a Captain Thornley.

As a child, Bram was so sick and feeble that he was confined to bed for the first eight years of his life. This was a period as critical in the development of Bram Stoker as was life in "the Land of Counterpane" for the young and sickly Robert Louis Stevenson. During Bram's years of confinement, the Reverend William Woods, who had a private school in Dublin, was brought in to instruct him. He continued as his principal teacher until Bram entered college at age 16. But it was Mrs. Stoker who particularly influenced Bram's early childhood and his fantasy life. Her warm love for this son provokes remembrance of Freud's dictum about the success assured to those sons who are especially loved by their mothers. Charlotte Stoker often declared that she loved her boys best and "did not care a tuppence" for her daughters. She told young Bram not only Irish fairy tales but also some true horror stories. An Irish woman from Sligo, she had witnessed the cholera epidemic there in 1832, and later in life Bram recalled her accounts of it. The vampire pestilence in his novel is comparable to the frightful, relentless spread of cholera.

Bram entered Trinity College, Dublin, in 1864. But his interest lay more in the drama than in his studies for a career in the Irish Civil Service. He regularly attended the Theatre Royal, the city's one large, regular theatre. One evening in August 1867 *The Rivals* was performed there, with Henry Irving as the star. Bram was enthralled by the famous actor.

When Henry Irving returned to Dublin in a comedy entitled *Two Roses,* Stoker was in the audience along with another young unknown Irishman, a 15-year-old agent's clerk named George Bernard Shaw. Like Shaw, Bram decided to be a drama critic. His first review appeared in the *Dublin Mail* in November 1871. At this time Stoker's interest in Sir Henry Irving was to be joined with an interest in vampirism.

A Dublin author with the unlikely name of Joseph Sheridan Le Fanu (1814-73) had just written the short novel "Carmilla," one of the greatest vampire stories of all time. Stoker read it and began thinking about writing his own tale of a vampire. In Le Fanu's work, the heroine Laura welcomes a strange girl named Carmilla into her father's castle and they become close companions. Laura senses, however, that she has seen Carmilla in her childhood nightmares. The author creates an aura of Romantic horror about the almost lesbian relationship between the blond Laura and the beautiful dark Carmilla, and so successfully achieves suspense that not until the story's end does one know whether Carmilla is a vampire or simply a victim of one. Finally, in the chapel of Karnstein, the grave of the Countess Mircalla is opened. Carmilla turns out to be the dead countess, whose "features, though a hundred and fifty years had passed since her funeral, were tinted with the warmth of life. Her eyes were open; no cadavrous smell exhaled from the coffin."

Le Fanu followed vampire mythology closely by asserting that her "limbs were perfectly flexible, the flesh elastic; and the leaden coffin floated with blood. . . ." To destroy the undead countess:

> *The body . . . in accordance with the ancient practice, was raised, and a sharp stake driven through the heart of the vampire . . . the head was struck off . . . body and head were next placed on a pile of wood, and reduced to ashes.*

Le Fanu's description of how a person becomes a vampire is also based upon folk belief in Eastern Europe:

> *Assume, at starting, a territory perfectly free from that pest. How does it begin, and how does it multiply itself? I will tell you. A person, more or less wicked, puts an end to himself. A suicide, under certain circumstances, becomes a vampire. That spectre visits living people in their slumbers; they die, and almost invariably, in the grave, develop into vampires.*

Stoker found in "Carmilla" the basic ingredients for the vampire aspects of Dracula. Enchanted, he began delving seriously into vampire mythology.

In the winter of 1876 Henry Irving was in Dublin again, and Stoker described him in the role of Eugene Aram with phrases that give a foretaste of Dracula: "The awful horror . . . of the Blood avenging spite"—"eyes as inflexible as Fate"—"eloquent hands, slowly moving, outspread, fanlike." Stoker tells us, in fact, that he became hysterical at the performance.

Bram began working in a part-time capacity for the great actor. Two years later, in 1878, he left his job in the Irish Civil Service and with his new wife, Florence Anne Lemon Balcombe, went to London. Irving had just taken over the Lyceum Theatre there and needed his friend's help full-time. The Stokers settled down in Cheyne Walk in Chelsea, where their neighbors included Dante Gabriel Rossetti; and James McNeill Whistler.

In all, Bram worked as the actor's private secretary and confidant for 27 years, which are described in his *Personal Reminiscences of Henry Irving*. He called their friendship "as profound, as close, as lasting as can be between two men." But there was more to the relationship than that. Irving held such fascination for Bram that he achieved an extraordinary dominance over him. Indeed, in life Irving was to Stoker, as in fiction Dracula is to Renfield.

Although much of Bram's time was taken up in arranging tours for Irving and his company, he continued to investigate vampirism. He also explored the Gothic novel, a development in English literature which traces back to the 18th century. The Gothic novel was initially a tale of spooks and had a medieval atmosphere highly charged with emotion. In time such stories— particularly those of Ann Radcliffe were given *rational* endings: all of the mysteries turn out to have natural causes; the supernatural elements prove to be only illusions; the horror is explained away.

When Mary Godwin Shelley (1797-1851) wrote *Frankenstein* (1817), there was a new, *realistic* development in the Gothic novel. Mrs. Shelley achieved horror and mystery through the use of science, or, if you will, pseudo-science. The agent of horror in her book was no spook, no supernatural being, nor the illusion of such. It was a real monster manufactured by the technical expertise of a Dr. Frankenstein.

Both the vampire and the Frankenstein monster were created at the same time in English literature and at the same place. The coincidence occurred during the summer of 1816 in Geneva, Switzerland, where Mary Shelley with Percy Bysshe Shelley, her stepsister Claire, Lord Byron, and his personal physician John Polidori had gone on vacation. The group first stayed at the Hotel d'Angleterre, then rented adjacent villas along the shores of Lake Geneva. Mary later wrote that it was a "wet ungenial summer," and the rain "confined us for days." In order to amuse themselves, this gifted group decided to read German tales of horror. Then, one night in June, Byron said, "We will each write a ghost story."

Before the end of the summer, the 18-year-old Mary, inspired by a philosophical discussion and a nightmare, had written entirely on her own the novel *Frankenstein*. When it later appeared in print, some book reviewers thought that her husband was really its author.

Mary Godwin Shelley wrote her Frankenstein story to show in a sympathetic way the failure of a would-be scientific savior of mankind. The public turned it all upside down, and her creation came to inspire an endless run of stories about the "mad scientist" who tries to go *beyond* nature's laws, unlike ordinary, God-fearing mortals. In so doing, he unwittingly creates a monster rather than a superman. Eventually, the unholy creature destroys its own creator.

Not to be outdone by any woman, Byron sketched out at Geneva a plan for a tale about a vampire, but he never finished it. Instead, the 20-year-old Polidori (1795-1821), an Englishman of Italian descent and a former student of medicine at the University of Edinburgh, took over Byron's idea, and using it as a basis he wrote a story called "The Vampyre."

In April 1819, Polidori's tale appeared in the *New Monthly Magazine* under Byron's name, through a misunderstanding on the part of the editor. Goethe swallowed the story whole and declared it to be the best thing that Byron had ever written. Years before, Goethe himself had given substance to the vampire legend in his *Braut Von Korinth*, published in 1797.

In Polidori's "Vampyre" a young libertine, Lord Ruthven, a character modeled loosely on Byron, is killed in Greece and becomes a vampire. He seduces the sister of his friend Aubrey, and suffocates her on the night following their wedding. This story never caught on with the public, and two years after its publication Polidori, unsuccessful at both literature and medicine, took poison and died. However, the vampire myth itself remained popular. Other writers tried their hands at creating a fascinating vampire figure, and Stoker profited from their attempts.

Alexandre Dumas Père composed a drama entitled *Le Vampire*. In 1820 Nodier's *Le Vampire* was translated into English by J. R. Planche. In 1830 Planche's melodrama *The Vampire* was published in Baltimore.

In *Melmoth the Wanderer*, published by the eccentric Irish clergyman Robert Maturin in 1820, the hero is a meld of a wandering Jew and a Byronic vampire. The character interrupts a wedding feast and terrifies everyone. Soon after the event the bride dies, and the bridegroom goes mad. The vengeance of the vampire is complete.

In 1847, Thomas Preskett Prest published *Varney the Vampire or The Feast of Blood*, which was well received and was reprinted in 1853. Before writing it, the author had studied the vampire legends in detail. His story is set in the 1730s during the reign of George II. It concerns the Bannesworth family and its persecution by Sir Francis Varney. Varney sucks the blood of Flora Bannesworth, captures her lover, and insults her family. Oddly, the author presents Varney as a basically good person who is driven to evil by circumstances. He tries often to save himself, but at the end of the story he is in utter despair and commits suicide by jumping into the crater of Mount Vesuvius.

It was soldily in the realistic horror-story tradition of Mary Godwin Shelley, Maturin, and Prest that Bram Stoker wrote his own horror story. Like them, he presented the vampire as an actual phenomenon. His Dracula is, and remains, a vampire—quite different from, say, the horror in a Gothic novel who seems to be a bloody ghost and then turns out to be a wounded human being. Stoker's novel indeed made no attempt to explain away the vampire. Moreover, Stoker made Dracula a contemporary, a vampire who lived in, and walked the streets of, Victorian England. This, too, differed from the early Gothic romances, which employed historic figures and settings.

Stoker had come to London in 1878, and during the next 10 years he published among other works a book entitled *Under the Sunset,* in which there is a King of Death. He also met Sir Richard Burton, the prominent orientalist. Burton had translated into English the *Arabian Nights,* in which there is a vampire tale, and in 1870 some 11 tales about vampires from Hindu sources. It is fascinating to note that in his reminiscences, Stoker wrote how impressed he was not only by Burton's accounts but also by his physical appearance—especially his canine teeth. Additional food for Bram's imagination was supplied by Jack the Ripper, who terrorized London from August to November in 1888. In reporting Jack's murders, the *East London Advertiser* stated:

> *It is so impossible to account, on any ordinary hypothesis, for these revolting acts of blood that the mind turns as it were instinctively to some theory of occult force, and the myths of the Dark Ages arise before the imagination. Ghouls, vampires, blood-suckers . . . take form and seize control of the excited fancy.*

As the idea of writing a vampire story increasingly preoccupied him, Bram searched for a "matrix" that would give it an air of authenticity. Around 1890, he met with a Hungarian scholar, Professor Arminius Vambery, whose travel talks were already known to him. In the 1890s Vambery was famous in

Eastern Europe for his *History of Hungary*, his autobiography, and his writings about his travels through Central Asia. The two men dined together, and during the course of their conversation, Bram was impressed by the professor's stories about Dracula "the impaler." After Vambery returned to Budapest, Bram wrote to him, requesting more details about the notorious 15th-century prince and the land he lived in. Transylvania, it seemed, would be an ideal setting for a vampire story.

Unfortunately, no correspondence between Vambery and Stoker can be found today. Moreover, a search through all of the professor's published writings fails to reveal any comments on Vlad, Dracula, or vampires.

Whatever information did come from Vambery supplemented items about Dracula that Stoker found in some old books in the British Museum Reading Room. There was, for instance, the Romanian legend stating that "In Wallachia, Vlad the 5th, son of Vlad the Devil, cut his way to the throne, sabre in hand, and maintained it by the greatest terrorism and tyranny"; and that "Vlad was created for the part he played; he hated foreigners, he hated the boyars! He hated the people! He massacred, empaled, killed without distinction for his own pleasure and security."

The Vlad in this legend appeared to be "der streng a tyrannisch man Dracula" who reigned simultaneously with Mathias Corvinus, according to a 16th-century work, Munster's *Cosmographia*, which Stoker also found in the museum's library.

Seeking material on Transylvania, Stoker gathered all the guide books and survey maps he could find about Eastern Europe. He also explored the folk tales concerning Dracula.

Another important source in his years of preparation was E. Gerard's *Land Beyond the Forest* (1888), which included a discussion of Romanian superstitions. Gerard recorded that:

> *Even a flawless pedigree will not ensure one against the intrusion of a vampire into their family vault, since every person killed by a Nosferatu (a vampire) becomes likewise a vampire after death, and will continue to suck the blood of other innocent persons 'till the spirit has been exorcised by opening the grave of the suspected person and either driving a stake through the corpse or else firing a pistol shot into the coffin.*

So Stoker had his themes and the setting for his story: the dominating figure of the cruel ruler, the vampire cult, and Transylvania. It was time to begin writing.

When *Dracula* was completed, there were references in it to an "Arminius"—Stoker's way of acknowledging his debt to Professor Arminius Vambery. Of more importance to us, they suggest what information and conclusions the professor had passed on to Stoker. In the novel, the character Dr. Van Helsing—an expert on vampires (with an uneven command of English) says of Count Dracula:

". . . when we and the habitation of this man-that-was, we can confine him to his coffin and destroy him, if we obey what we know. But he is clever. I have asked my friend Arminius, of Buda-Pesth University, to make his record; and, from all the means that are, he tell me of what he has been. He must, indeed, have been that Voivode Dracula who won his name against the Turk, over the great river on the very frontier of Turkey-land. If it be so, then was he no common man; for in that time, and for centuries after, he was spoken of as the cleverest and the most cunning, as well as the bravest of the sons of the 'land beyond the forest.' That mighty brain and that iron resolution went with him to his grave, and are even now arrayed against us. The Draculas were, says Arminius, a great and noble race, though now and again were scions who were held by their coevals to have had dealings with the Evil One. They learned his secrets in the Scholomance, amongst the mountains over Lake Hermanstadt, where the devil claims the tenth scholar as his due. In the records are such words as 'stregoica'—witch, 'ordop,' and 'pokol'—Satan and hell, and in one manuscript this very Dracula is spoken of as 'wampyr.' "

Shortly before Stoker wrote his famous book, the British Museum had purchased one of the German pamphlets printed in 1491 which related horror tales about Dracula. Surely Stoker must have discovered it there, or been directed to it by Vambery, who was familiar with a similar pamphlet in the library of the University of Budapest. Although the pamphlet does not describe Dracula as a "wampyr," it does call him a cruel tyrant and *wütrich*, an old German term for "berserker" or, more literally, "blood-thirsty monster." This presumably was Stoker's cue for transforming Dracula into a vampire. In addition, we learn through Van Helsing's conversation that Vambery was the source for the link between Dracula and "the Evil One," the devil. And, finally, the conversation indicates that Vambery had made the association between the brave, heroic Dracula known through one tradition and the horrifying tyrant known through another.

Dracula begins with the words, "3 May, Bistritz." In the entry that follows, Jonathan Harker records, "I found that Bistritz, the post town named by Count Dracula, is a fairly well-known place . . . a very interesting old place." The town marks, as described in the novel, the beginning of the Borgo Pass, which leads into Moldavia—a true description of a real location. (Indeed, after *Dracula* was published, Stoker was complimented for his *accurate, firsthand* descriptions of a country which he had never actually seen.)

The link between Stoker's Dracula and the region of Bistrita is not wholly imaginary. There was an old Szeckler family in this region. The family was called Ordog, which is a Hungarian translation of the word *Dracul*, or devil. In the novel the people of the Bistrita region speak the words "Ordog, Satan" before Jonathan Harker takes off in the carriage to the Borgo Pass.

The major elements of Bram Stoker's ritual acts against vampires correspond with Eastern European folk beliefs. According to James G. Frazer: "Among the Romanians in Transylvania . . . in very obstinate cases of vampirism it is recommended to cut off the head and replace it in the coffin with the mouth filled with garlic; or to extract the heart and burn it, strewing the ashes over the grave." In *Dracula*, as in Romanian folklore, garlic has the power to protect men against vampires and a vampire can be killed by decapitation and a stake driven through the heart.

In Stoker's novel Dracula appears in the form of mist or phosphorescent specks; the Romanian vampire of folklore also sometimes comes as points of light shimmering in the air. Stoker's vampire can turn into a wolf or a bat, particularly the latter. The Transylvanian Szeklers, self-supposed descendants of an East Asian race older than the Magyars, link the bat with vampirism in their folklore. Following Slavic folklore, Stoker's vampire moves only at night, casts no reflection in a mirror, and is repelled by the sign of the cross.

These and many other details reveal the range and accuracy of Stoker's research. The persistence with which Stoker worked is expressed via Van Helsing's remark "I have studied, over and over again since they came into my hands, all the papers relating to this monster."

Bram Stoker, creator of Count Dracula, re-creator of the devilish-and-heroic Prince Dracula, died in 1912. Sir Henry Irving had predeceased him by some years, leaving Bram at a loss. The death certificate lists the official cause of Stoker's death as "exhaustion."

Seal of the town of Lugoj, Hungary, birthplace of Bela Lugosi.

9

Beyond the Grave

Where is the precise location of Dracula's tomb within the Monastery of Snagov? Does it, in fact, lie there as popular tradition will have it?

In 1931, George Florescu and the archaeologist Dinu Rosetti were officially assigned by Romania's Commission on Historic Monuments to dig around the monastery and elsewhere on the island. Their findings, published in a fascinating monograph, *Diggings Around Snagov*, included various artifacts showing that the island was the site of an ancient pre-Dacian settlement; also a great number of skulls, tending to confirm popular traditions about the crimes committed at Snagov from the 15th century onward; and numerous gold and silver coins of all kinds, indicating the use of Snagov as a secret treasury and mint for boyars and princes alike since Dracula's time.

One of the sites investigated by the Florescu-Rosetti team was a stone beneath the altar, which, according to tradition, marked the place where Dracula lay buried. Popular legend had various explanations as to why this was the location of his grave. First, it was claimed that the monks had the remains of his body placed close to the altar so that his troubled soul could have the advantage of perpetual prayers. Secondly, this particular tombstone, though not of princely proportion and lacking an inscription, was more ambitious than that of several others. The stone was finally removed, but in the large grave below, no headless skeleton was found, instead only ox bones and various Dacian artifacts.

Further exploration—this time just inside the entrance on the northern side of the church—revealed an unopened grave of exactly the size of the altar tomb. When opened, it was found to contain a casket still partially covered by a purple shroud embroidered with gold. Both coffin and covering were mostly rotted away. Within the coffin lay a badly deteriorated skeleton; fragments of a faded red silk garment suitable for a person of at least boyar rank, with a ring sewn onto one sleeve; a golden crown ornamented with cloisonne and having claws clasping a jewel; and a necklace with the barely perceptible motif of a serpent. All of the grave's contents have unfortunately, and mysteriously, disappeared from the History Museum of Bucharest, where they were deposited.

Rosetti told us that he believed that this second grave, if it was not the original site of Dracula's burial, was at least the final resting place. The two graves had the same proportions— the stone of the one below the altar seeming to fit exactly the grave near the north entrance of the chapel. The necklace with the serpent device resembled others found in the Nuremberg area, and undoubtedly was some insigne of the Order of the Dragon, to which Dracula belonged. The red silk fragments were in accord with the Hungarian-style shirt worn by Dracula in the Ambras portrait. The lost ring could have been either a princely ring or a romantic token. During Dracula's time, one of the dying customs of courtly love in Western Europe was the practice of a knight, when going forth to joust in a tournament, to wear on his sleeve his lady's ring. Dracula could well have known this custom from his youthful years in Germany. But whose ring was it? His Hungarian wife's, or some now unknown lover's? Whoever bestowed this tender token of courtly love, it is a strange item to find in the grave of such a prince.

The absence of a headless skeleton and the presence of the animal bones in the grave near the altar are the most mystifying findings of all. They have provoked a debate among the experts that continues today. As in the case of the mysterious disappearance of the body of Alexander I of Russia, dozens of opinions have been voiced, sometimes almost violently. We are inclined to accept the *original* grave as being the one near the altar, the one approved by local folklore, which has succeeded in giving a clue to many enigmas connected with Dracula. At various times village traditions about tombstones have led to the identification of historic personalities. In the old church of Curtea de Arges, for example, it was long observed that the faithful persisted in standing at a certain place to the right of the altar for no other reason than that it was the place where their elders worshipped. They also lit their candles there. An enterprising young archaeologist excavated that particular spot and discovered the unmarked tomb of one of Wallachia's early princes. At Snagov the peasants for many years were similarly accustomed to stand close to the altar. According to legend, they took their places there to express contempt for the tyrant by walking over his grave.

How and when the remains might have been transferred is suggested by a local priest from the neighboring village of Turbati, the Reverend G. Dumitriu. According to him, at the close of the 18th century a Wallachian Metropolitan by the name of Filaret, under the pretext of some repairs on the church, ordered the desecration of Dracula's body. The body and the other items mentioned above were then transferred from the more exalted position near the altar and reinterred in an unmarked place near the entrance of the church where all could trample upon them. The Greeks were not particularly concerned, as were the Romanians, in praying for Dracula's soul. All inscriptions were removed, and a plain slab was substituted for the engraved one. As an additional gesture of contempt, the ox bones were substituted for Dracula's skeleton, thereby compounding a hoax with a sacrilege. "Thus," adds the priest in an article in which he published his theory, at the rear of the chapel of Snagov "lie the earthly remains of Dracula . . . without trace of either an inscription or memento, under some cold stone that gets yearly trampled by the weight of the tourists." All this to wipe away forever the memory of that degenerate prince.

Had the tomb not been desecrated in the particular way related by the Reverend Dumitriu (and his theory does jibe with the dates of certain repairs made in the altar area during the late 1700s), one could still safely conjecture that since the tomb of Dracula looked more ambitious than most it was bound to have been opened and pillaged by the peasants during the period of neglect and abandonment that followed the closing of Snagov as a state prison.

Historical commonsense suggests that Dracula, who in spite of his misdeeds was after all a prince, would be assigned an important burial place in the church—therefore, one close to the altar—and that his tomb should be a little more ornate than that for other mortals. Thus, on all these grounds we are inclined to accept the traditional location of Dracula's grave as the original.

There is really no need, however, to strain after explanations for the possible transfer of graves or, if the second grave is not Dracula's, the disappearance of his body. They almost seem to suggest themselves. Given Dracula's invidious reputation, the general horror in which his name was held in the Orthodox world, and the desecrations committed on the island at various times, it may even be unreasonable to expect that his tomb would have survived intact. Yet, after all the explanations about Dracula's tomb have been considered, somehow the mystery lingers on.

We have attempted to recreate the REAL Dracula as scientifically as the available sources will allow. We have worked diligently and hard. We have consulted every domestic source of the period available. We have ploughed our way through German, Slavonic, Byzantine, and other foreign documentation. We have studied the traditions of the people, closely collaborated with historians in Bucharest and historians at the local level. Now, having fathered the first massive compilation on Dracula—a body of information which ought on all accounts to have resolved many of the riddles that we began with—we must confess that we have not entirely succeeded in bridging the gap between myth and reality, in reconstructing the full personality of Dracula, in clearing up the numerous ambiguities which stand in the way of absolute historical character. So why not, at the end of our story, take refuge in the myth rather than in the historical reality?

Freed from his monastery or castle, traveling in the shape of man during the day, flying like a bat at night, Dracula rises again to terrify and exercise his vampirical powers. Thus liberated with his powers for evil, the vampire crosses the frontier of his own country and attempts, as he did in Stoker's novel, the conquest of England itself. His frontiers have become infinitely extended. It is this Dracula, the man of fiction, not the historical Dracula, who has conquered the imagination of the Western world. Without him, the real Dracula would be greatly reduced in size, tyrannical and bloodthirsty as he was. The ultimate fascination of the Dracula story lies in its myth, not in its reality. Blood is in fact the only valid connection between the two.

The mystery of Dracula endures. It lives in the vampire fictions, which someday may encourage another Harker to make the scenic journey to the town of Bistrita in northern Transylvania in the direction of the Borgo Pass, or impel some zoologist to study the incidence of large bats in the Carpathian mountains. It continues in Dracula's own castle, where none dare trespass at night and where the peasants have unfolded stories of the plaintive voice of Dracula's first wife at a place in the river Arges reddened by a vague subterranean object. The mystery of Dracula persists in the question of whether he exemplifies some spirit of evil that all men encounter—of whether Professor Van Helsing was an expert as much on human experience as on vampires when he said:

"My friends . . . it is a terrible task that we undertake, and there may be consequence to make the brave shudder. For if we fail in this our fight he must surely win; and then where end we?. . . to fail here is not mere life or death. It is that we become as him; that we henceforward become foul things of the night like him—without heart or conscience."

The warnings of the peasants about the perils of seeking the "great undead" may derive from more than a pedestrian sense of caution—may be warnings from the spirit of Dracula himself. For us a signal finally came through as we were on the point of reaching the last few yards separating us from the castle. Fortunately, it was restrained, spelling a broken hip and six months in hospital for one of our members—it could have spelled death. Was it Dracula's way of saying that despite the ruins of his castle, he still rules in some other, unearthly domain?

Appendix I

German Stories

Translation by Raymond T. McNally of Manuscript No. 806 at the Monastery Library of St. Gall, Switzerland.

1. Once the old governor had the old Dracul killed; and Dracula and his brother, having renounced their own faith, promised and swore to protect and uphold the Christian faith. *[Reference is to assassination of Dracula's father.]*

2. During these same years Dracula was put on the throne and became lord of Wallachia; he immediately had Ladislaus Waboda *[Vladislav II]* killed, who had been ruler of that region. *[The killing of Vladislav II occurred in 1456.]*

3. After that Dracula immediately had villages and castles burned in Transylvania near Hermannstadt *[Sibiu]*, and he had fortifications in Transylvania and villages by the name of the monastery Holtznuwdorff, Holtznetya *[Hosmanul]* completely burned to ashes.

4. He had Berkendorf *[Benesti]* in Wuetzerland *[Tara Birsei]* burned; those men, women, and children, large and small, whom he had not burned at the time, he took with him and put them in chains and had them all impaled.

5. Dracula imprisoned merchants and carriage-drivers from Wuetzerland on a holiday and on that same holiday he had many impaled. *[Confirmed by internal Romanian sources.]*

6. Young boys and others from many lands were sent to Wallachia, in order to learn the language and other things. He brought them together and betrayed them. He let them all come together in a room and had them burned. There were four hundred in the room. *[Confirmed by internal Romanian sources.]*

7. He had a big family uprooted from the smallest to the largest, children, friends, brothers, sisters, and he had

them all impaled. *[Execution of Wallachian boyar family by name of Albu is confirmed elsewhere.]*

8. He also had his men bury a man naked up to the navel, then he had them shoot at him. He also had some others roasted and some skinned alive.

9. He also captured the young Darin *[Dan]*. Later on he allowed him to go through his priestly function, and when he had completed it all, then he had him make a grave according to the custom of Christians, and he had his body slaughtered by the grave. *[Dan's execution is a historical fact confirmed elsewhere.]*

10. Ambassadors, numbering fifty-five, were sent to Wallachia to Dracula from the king of Hungary and from the Saxons and in Transylvania. There Dracula had the lords held captive for five weeks and had stakes made for their hostel. And they thought that they would all be impaled. Oh, how greatly troubled they were! He held them so long, so that they might betray him. And he set off with all his army and went to Wuetzerland. Early one morning he came to the villages, castles, and towns. All those whom he overcame, he also destroyed and had all the grain and wheat burned. And he led away all those whom he had captured outside the city called Kranstatt *[Kronstadt; Brasov]* near the chapel called St. Jacob *[Tampa Hill]*. And at that time Dracula rested there and had the entire suburb burned. Also as the day came, early in the morning, all those whom he had taken captive, men and women, young and old children, he had impaled on the hill by the chapel and all around the hill, and under them he proceeded to eat at table and get his joy in this way. *[Undoubtedly these ambassadors were men sent by King Mathias to learn Dracula's precise relationship with the Turks.]*

11. Once he had St. Bartholomew's Church *[in Brasov]* burned, then he also stole and took away the vestments and chalices. Once he sent one of his captains to a great village called Zeyding *[Zeinding; Codlea]* to burn it, but that same captain could not burn it, because the villagers resisted. Then he went to his lord and said: "Lord, I was not able to bring myself to do what you ordered me to do." Then he took him and hoisted him up on a stake. *[Attack on this church and execution of*

the Wallachian captain who was unable to capture fortress of Codlea are historical facts appearing in other sources.]

12. Once he impaled all the merchants and other men with merchandise, the entire merchant class from Wuetzerland near to Thunow and to Pregel, six hundred of them with all their goods and he took the goods for himself.

13. Once he had a great pot made with two handles and over it a staging device with planks and through it he had holes made, so that a man could fall through them with his head. Then he had a great fire made underneath it and had water poured into the pot and had men boiled in this way. He had many men and women, young and old, impaled.

14. Also he came again to Siebenburgen *[means the seven fortresses of Transylvania]* to attack Talmetz *[Talmetch, near Sibiu]*. There he had men hacked up like cabbage and he had those whom he took back to Wallachey *[Wallachia]* as captives, cruelly and in various ways, impaled.

15. Once he had thought up terrifying and frightening and unspeakable tortures, so he had mothers impaled and nursing children, and he had one-year or over two-year-old children impaled. He also had children taken from their mothers' breasts and also the mothers from the children. He also had the breasts of the mother cut off one from the other and pushed the children's heads through and impaled them. And he caused many other sufferings and such great pain and tortures as all the bloodthirsty persecutors of Christendom, such as Herod, Nero and Diocletian and other pagans had never thought up or made such martyrs as did this bloodthirsty berserker.

16. Once he had humans impaled, usually indiscriminately, young and old, women and men. People also tried to defend themselves with hands and feet and they twisted around and twitched like frogs. After that he had them also impaled and spoke often in this language: "Oh, what great gracefulness they exhibit!" And they were pagans, Jews, Christians, heretics, and Wallachians.

17. Once he caught a gypsy who had stolen. Then the other gypsies came to him and begged Dracula to release him to them. Dracula said: "He should hang, and you must hang him." They said: "That is not our custom." Dracula had the gypsy boiled in a pot, and when he was cooked, he forced them to eat him, flesh and bone.

18. Once a nobleman was sent to him, who came to him among the people whom he had impaled. There, Dracula walked under them and gazed upon them, and there were as many as a great forest. And he asked Dracula why he walked around under the stench. Dracula asked: "Do you mind the stink?" The other man said: "Yes." So Dracula immediately had him impaled and hoisted him up high in the air, so that he would not smell the stench.

19. Once a priest had preached that sins could not be forgiven until one made good the injustice done. Then Dracula had that same priest invited to his house and set him at his table. Then the lord had simmel bread put into his food. The priest took the broken bread up with his tablespoon. Then the lord spoke about how he had preached about sins, etc., etc. The priest said: "Lord, it is true." He said: "Why then do you take from me my bread, which I have broken into the food?" And he immediately had him impaled.

20. Once he invited all his landlords and noblemen in his land to his house, and when the meal was over, he turned to the noblest men and asked them how many voevods or lords they remembered who had ruled that same land. One answered him as many as he could think of. So did the other lords, both young and old, and each among them asked how many lords they could recall. One answered fifty; another, thirty; one, twenty; similarly, twelve, so that none was so young as to remember seven. So he had all those same lords impaled, and there were five hundred of them .

21. Once he had a mistress who announced that she was pregnant, so he had her looked at by another woman, who could not comprehend how she could be pregnant. So he took the mistress and cut her up from under to her breast and said: "Let the world see where I have been and where my fruit lay." He also had similar things

cut or pierced and did other inhuman things which are said about him.

22.   In the year 1460, on the morning of St. Bartholomew's Day, Dracula came through the forest with his servants and had all the Wallachians of both sexes tracked down, as people say outside of the village of Humilasch [Amlasch], and he was able to bring so many together that he let them get piled up in a bunch and he cut them up like cabbage with swords, sabers and knives; as for their chaplain and the others whom he did not kill there, he led them back home and had them impaled. And he had the village completely burned up with their goods and it is said that there were more than 30,000 men.

23.   In the year of Our Lord 1462 once Dracula came to the large city of Schylta [Nicopolis], where he had more than 25,000 people of all kinds of ethnic groups killed, Christians, pagans, etc. Among them were the most beautiful women and maidens, who had been taken captive by his courtiers. They begged Dracula to give them to them as honorable wives. Dracula did not want to do this and ordered that all of them together with the courtiers should be cut up like cabbage. And that he did because he had become obliged to pay tribute to the Turkish sultan, who had demanded tribute from him. Immediately Dracula let his people know that he wished to give over the tribute personally to the sultan. The people there were overjoyed, so he let his people come to him in large groups one after the other and he let all his courtiers ride with him. And then he had these people all killed. Also he had the same region called Pallgarey [Wulgerey] completely burned. He also had others nailed by their hair and in all there were 25,000 not counting those whom he had burned.

24.   Once messengers from Hermannstadt saw the dead and impaled in Wallachia like a huge forest, aside from those whom he had roasted, boiled, and skinned.

25.   Once he rounded up an entire region called Fugrasch [Fagaras], women, men and children, and led them to Wallachia where he had them impaled. Similarly, he had the heads cut off his men who had helped him to bury his treasure.

26. Once he had several lords beheaded and took their bodies and had food cooked up with them. After that he had their friends invited to his house and he gave them something to eat from that food and said to them: "Now you are eating the bodies of your friends." After that he impaled them.

27. Once he had seen a worker in a short shirt and said to him: "Have you a wife at home?" He said: "Yes." Dracula said: "Bring her here to me." Then he said to her: "What do you do?" She said: "I wash, cook, spin, etc." He immediately had her impaled, because she had not made her man a long shirt, so that one could not see the seam. Dracula at once gave him another wife and ordered that she should make a long shirt for her man, or he would also have her impaled.

28. Once he had a donkey impaled and on the earth above it a Franciscan monk whom he had met.

29. Once some three hundred gypsies came into his land; he thereupon took the best three out and had them roasted and made the other gypsies eat, and said to them: "Thus each of you must eat the others until there are none left," or he sent them against the Turks, and fought with them. They were very willing to go there, where he wanted them to go. Then he did something: he clothed them all in cowhide, and similarly their horses as well. And as they came upon one another, the Turkish horses shied away and fled because of the cowhide clothing which their horses did not like and the Turks fled to some water and the gypsies after them, with the result that they all drowned.

30. Once he also had the poor people who were in his land invited to his house; after they had eaten there, he had them all burned in a small city. There were two hundred of them.

31. Once he had young children roasted and forced their mothers to eat them. He cut the breasts off women and forced their husbands to eat them; after that he had the men impaled.

32. Once several Wahlen *[Western ambassadors]* were sent to him. When they came to him, they bowed and took off their hats and under them they had brown and red berets or caps, which they did not take off. So he asked them why they had not taken off their caps or berets.

They said: "Lord, it is not our custom. We never take them off before our ruler." He said: "Well, I wish to strengthen you in your custom." And as they thanked his grace, he had them take good strong nails and had them nailed around the caps into the head, so that they could not take them off. In this way he strengthened them in their custom. *[In most versions, including Romanian, the victims are Turkish ambassadors.]*

Appendix II

Russian Stories

Translation by Raymond T. McNally of the oldest Russian manuscript about Dracula: MS 11/1088 in the Kirillov-Belozersky Monastery Collection at the Saltykov-Schredin Public Library, Leningrad. First translation of this document into a Western language.

Among the very few authentic signed documents which have been preserved from the late 15th century is the Russian "Story about Dracula." Copies of it were made from the 15th to the 18th century in Russia. It is one of the first instances of belletristic writing in Russian literature, and the historian Nicholas Karamzin has called it his country's "first historical novel."

This manuscript was written by the monk Efrosin from the Kirillov-Belozersky Monastery in northern Russia in the year 1490. In it the monk states that he copied the story from another manuscript penned in 1486. No one knows who the author of that earlier manuscript was. Most scholarly opinion has focused upon a Russian diplomat who was at the Hungarian court in the 1480s, Fedor Kurytsin; he could have picked up the tale there since Dracula had been a captive of the Hungarian king from 1462 to 1474; moreover the monk states that the earlier author had seen one of the sons of Dracula.

Whoever the original author was, he was more disturbed by the prince's abandonment of Orthodoxy than by his cruelties. While in prison Dracula "forsook the light" of the Orthodox Church and accepted the "darkness" of the Roman Church because he was too attracted to the "sweetness" of this earthly life and not motivated enough by concern for the next one. Thus, the story has a marked religious tone.

The manuscript supports the notion of a "cruel but just" autocrat in its presentation of Dracula. All that this tyrant had done, however cruel it may have appeared by the standards of the average person, was necessary for the good of the state. In order to ward off not only the Turkish invaders but also the continual threat of opposition from the aristocratic boyars in his own land, Dracula had to take harsh measures. Obviously, the manuscript was written to indicate support of the autocratic ruler in Russia at the time, Ivan III, known as Ivan the Great. Here is the text:

1. There lived in the Wallachian lands a Christian prince of the Greek faith who was called Dracula in the Wallachian language, which means devil in our language, for he was as cruelly clever as was his name and so was his life.

   Once some ambassadors from the Turkish sultan came to him. When they entered his palace and bowed to him, as was their custom, they did not take their caps from their heads and Dracula asked them: "Why have you acted so? You ambassadors have come to a great prince and you have shamed me." The ambassadors answered, "Such is the custom which our land has, Lord." And Dracula told them, "Well, I want to strengthen you in your law. Behave bravely." And he ordered that their caps be nailed to their heads with small iron nails. And then he allowed them to go. He said, "Go tell your lord, for he is a cultured man: let him accept this shame from us. For you seem to think that we are not cultured. Let him not impose his customs upon other rulers who will not accept them, but let him keep his customs in his own land." *[This episode confirmed in Romanian and German sources.]*

2. The Turkish sultan was angered and he set out with an army against Dracula. He invaded his land with overwhelming force. Dracula gathered his whole army and attacked the Turks during the night, and he killed a great many of them. But he could not conquer them with his few men against an army so much greater than his, so eventually Dracula drew back.

   He examined those who had fought with him against the Turks. Those wounded in the front he honored and made them heroes and gave them gifts. But those who were wounded in the back he ordered to be impaled from the bottom up and said: "You are not a man but a woman." And when he set against the Turks once again, he spoke to his entire army in this way, "Whoever wants to think of death, let him not come with me but let him remain here." And the Turkish sultan, hearing of this, retreated with great shame. He lost innumerable men, but he never dared again to set out against Dracula. *[The night attack is confirmed by an eye-witness report.]*

3.   The sultan sent an ambassador once to Dracula, in order that he be given the yearly tribute. Dracula greatly honored this ambassador and showed him the whole treasury which he had. And said, "I not only wish to give the sultan the yearly tax, but I also wish to go in his service with my whole army and with my whole treasury. I shall do as he commands and you shall announce this to your emperor, so that when I shall place myself at his disposal, he will give orders in his whole land that no harm should come to me or to my men. And I shall come to my sultan, my liege, quickly after you get back. And I shall bring him the yearly tribute, and I shall personally place myself at his disposal."

When the sultan heard from his ambassador that Dracula wished to come into his service, he honored the ambassador and gave him gifts, and was happy because at that time the Turkish sultan was at war with many of the eastern countries. Immediately the sultan sent to all his fortresses and towns and throughout his land the message that when Dracula comes, no one should do him any harm. On the contrary, they should honor him. Dracula set out with his whole army. With him were his various yeomen. And he was greeted and greatly honored by the emperor. And he traveled throughout the Turkish empire for about five days. But then suddenly instead of helping the sultan, he began to rob and attack the towns and the villages. And he captured many prisoners whose heads he cut off. Some he impaled, others he cut in two, and others he burned. The whole country which he penetrated was laid to waste. He allowed no one to remain alive, not even the babes in the arms of their mothers. But others, that is, those who were Christian, he spared and set them up in his own lands. After taking much booty, he returned to Wallachia. And he set a few prisoners free and said, "Go and tell your sultan what you have seen. As much as I could, I have served him. If my service was pleasing to him, I shall serve him again with as much power as I can." And the sultan could do nothing against him and fled in shame. [*This episode confirmed by historical documents.*]

4.　Dracula so hated evil in his land that if someone stole, lied or committed some injustice, he was not likely to stay alive. Whether he was a nobleman, or a priest or a monk or a common man, and even if he had great wealth, he could not escape death if he were dishonest. And he was so feared that the peasants say that in a certain place, near the source of the river, there was a fountain; at this fountain at the source of this river, there came many travelers from many lands and all these people came to drink at the fountain, because the water was cool and sweet. Dracula had purposely put this fountain in a deserted place, and had set a cup wonderfully wrought in gold and whoever wished to drink the water, had to drink it from this gold cup and had to put it back in its place. And so long as this cup was there no one dared to steal it. [*Romanian folklore stresses Dracula's maintenance of law and order.*]

5.　Once Dracula ordered throughout the land that whoever was old or sick or poor should come to him. And there gathered at the palace a huge multitude of poor and old people, who expected a great act of mercy. And he ordered that all these miserable people be gathered together, in a large palace which was prepared with this idea in mind. And he ordered that they be given food and drink in accordance with their wishes. So they began to eat, and they became happy. Later on Dracula personally came to see them and spoke to them in the following way: "What else do you need?" And they answered him in unison, "Our good lord, God knows how to give, and your highness surely understands the wishes of God." He then said to them, "Do you want me to make you without any further cares, so that you have no other wants in this world?" And they all expected some great gift and they answered, "We wish it so, my lord." Then he ordered that the palace be locked and he set it on fire, and all of them perished within it. Later he told his nobles, "Know that I have done this so that these unfortunate people will have no further burdens, and so that there should be no more poor in my land but only rich people, and in the second place I freed these people so that they no longer suffer in this world either because of poverty, or because of sickness." *[Dracula's killing of the sick and poor is a favorite theme in Romanian folklore. One critic has suggested that the prince's motive was control of the plague.]*

6. Once there came from Hungary two Roman Catholic monks looking for charity. Dracula ordered them to be honored. And he first of all called one of these monks down below into the courtyard, where there were countless people on stakes and spokes of wheels. And he asked the monk, "Have I done well? How do you judge those on the stakes?" And the monk answered, "No, lord, you have done badly. You punish without mercy. It is fitting that a master be merciful, and all these unfortunate people whom you have impaled are martyrs." Dracula then called the second monk and posed the same question. The second monk answered, "You, lord, have been assigned by God as a ruler to punish those who commit crimes and to reward those who do good. Certainly they have committed some crime and have been punished in accordance with their misdeeds." Dracula then recalled the first monk and told him, "Why have you left your monastery and your cell, to walk and travel at the courts of great rulers? You know nothing. Just now you told me that these people are martyrs. I also want to make a martyr out of you so that you will be together with these other martyrs." And he ordered that he be impaled from the bottom up. But to the other monk, he ordered that he be given fifty ducats of gold and told him, "You are an understanding man." And he ordered that a carriage be prepared for him in order that he be driven with honor to the Hungarian border. *[Note different ending in Romanian Story No. 6. Note, too, that the Russian version seems designed to support one-man rule, however cruel.]*

7. Once a merchant, a foreign guest from Hungary, came to Dracula's capital city. Following his command, the merchant left his carriage on the street of the city before the palace and his wares in the carriage and he himself slept in the palace. Someone came and stole 160

golden ducats from the carriage. The merchant went to Dracula and told him about the loss of the gold. And Dracula told him, "Wait, this night your gold will be returned." And he ordered his henchmen to look for the thief throughout the city and said, "If you do not find the thief, I will destroy the city." And he ordered that the gold be placed back in the carriage during the night. But with one additional gold ducat. The merchant got up and found his gold and he counted the pieces once, twice, and found one additional golden ducat. He went immediately to Dracula and told him, "My lord, I have found the gold, but look there is one additional golden ducat which does not belong to me." And then they also brought the thief who had the original gold with him. And Dracula told the merchant, "Go in peace. If you had not told me about the additional golden ducat, I would have been ready to impale you, together with the thief." [*This tale reoccurs in Romanian folklore. Russian version is obviously meant to stress Dracula's sense of justice.*]

8. If a woman made love with a man who was not her husband Dracula ordered that her vagina be cut and he skinned her alive and tied her skin to a pole. And the skin was usually hanging on the pole in the middle of the city right there in the market place. He did the same thing with young girls who had not preserved their virginity and also widows. In some cases he cut the nipples of their breasts. In other cases he took the skins from their vagina and he placed an iron poker, reddened by fire, up their vaginas so far upwards that the iron bar emerged from their mouths. They remained naked, tied to a pole until the flesh and bones detached themselves or served as food for the birds. [*A favorite theme in the German pamphlets is Dracula's austere standards for women.*]

9. Once Dracula was walking down a street and he saw a poor man with a shirt torn and dirty. And he asked that man, "Have you got a wife?" And he answered, "I have, Lord." Then Dracula said, "Take me to your house, so that I can see her." And he went to the house of the man, saw that he had a young and healthy wife, and he told her husband, "Did you work this spring, did you sow flax?" And the husband answered, "Lord, I

have much flax." And he showed much flax to him. Then Dracula said to his wife, "Why are you lazy towards your husband? It is his duty to sow and to reap and to feed you. But it is your duty to make nice clean clothes for your husband. But you do not even wish to clean his shirt, though you are quite healthy. You are guilty, not your husband. If your husband had not sown or reaped, then your husband would be guilty." And Dracula ordered that both her hands be cut off and that her body be impaled. *[See comment for Story 8.]*

10. Once Dracula was feasting amid the corpses of many men who had been impaled around his table. And he liked to eat in their midst. There was a servant who stood right in front of him. But he could not stand the smell of the corpses any longer. So he plugged his nose. And he drew his head to one side. Dracula asked him, "Why are you doing that?" The servant answered, "My lord, I cannot endure this stench." Dracula immediately ordered that he be impaled, saying, "You must live way up there, where the stench does not reach you." *[Dracula's macabre sense of humor is highlighted in German pamphlets.]*

11. On another occasion an ambassador, a great nobleman from Matei the Hungarian king, came to Dracula's court. Dracula ordered him to stay at his royal table in the midst of the corpses. And set up in front of the table was a very high thick golden stake. And Dracula asked, "Tell me, why did I set up this stake?" The ambassador was very afraid and said, "My lord, it would seem that some nobleman has committed a crime and you want to reserve a more honorable death for him." And Dracula said, "You spoke fairly. You are indeed a royal ambassador of a great ruler, I have made this stake for you." The ambassador answered, "My lord, if I have committed some crime worthy of death, do what you wish because you are a fair ruler and you would not be guilty of my death but I myself would be." Dracula broke out laughing and said, "If you had not answered me thus, you would really be on that very stake yourself." And he honored him greatly and gave him gifts and allowed him to go, saying, "You truly can go as an envoy to the capitals of great rulers, because you are well versed in knowing how to talk

with great rulers. But others let them not talk with me, but let them first learn how to speak to a great ruler." *[See comment for Story 10.]*

12. Dracula had the following custom: whenever an ambassador came to him from the sultan or the king and he was not dressed in a distinguished way and did not know how to answer the twisted questions, he impaled them, saying, "I am not guilty of your death but your own master, or you yourself. Don't say anything bad to me. If your master knows that you are slow-witted and that you are not properly versed and has sent you to my court, to me a wise ruler, then your own ruler has killed you. And if somehow you would dare to come as an ignorant boor to my court, then you yourself have committed suicide." For such an ambassador he made a high and golden stake and he impaled him in front of all and to the master of such a foolish ambassador he wrote the following words: "No longer send to a wise prince a man of such a small mind and a man so uncultured." *[See comment for Story 10.]*

13. Dracula ordered his artisans to make some iron bells. Dracula ordered these bells to be filled with gold and put in the river. And Dracula ordered that these artisans be killed, so that no one would know the crime committed by him except for the devil whose name he bore. *[The story of the person who kills the workmen who hid his treasure occurs the world over, thus this episode can be considered as a mythical one.]*

14. On one occasion the Hungarian King Matei set out with an army against Dracula. He fought against Dracula and in the battle they captured Dracula alive, because Dracula was betrayed by his own men. And Dracula was brought to the Hungarian King, who ordered him thrown in jail. And he remained in jail at Vishegrad on the Danube up from Buda for twelve years. And in Wallachia the Hungarian King ordered another prince to rule. *[Dracula's presence in Hungary is confirmed by Hungarian sources, reports by papal representatives in Buda, and the memoirs of Pius II.]*

15. After the death of that prince the Hungarian King sent a messenger to Dracula who was in jail to ask him whether he would like to become prince in Wallachia as he had been before and if so, he should accept the

Latin faith and if he does not wish it, he wishes to die in jail. Dracula, however, loved the sweetness of the earthly world much more than that of the eternal world, and abandoned Orthodoxy and forsook the truth and light and received the darkness. Unfortunately, he could not endure the temporary difficulties of the prison and he must have been prepared for the unending sufferings of hell by abandoning our Orthodox faith and accepting the deceiving Latin faith. The king did not only give him the rule in Wallachia but also gave him his sister as a wife. From her he had two sons, he lived for another ten years and in this heresy he ended his life. *[Sources given in comment above confirm Dracula's restoration in 1476, and his heresy in eyes of the Orthodox Church.]*

16. It was said about him that even when he was in jail, he could not abandon his bad habits. He caught mice and bought birds in the market. And he tortured them in this way: some he simply impaled, others he cut their heads off, and others he plucked their feathers out and let them go. And he also taught himself to sew and in this way he fed himself while in jail. *[This incident is not recorded in any other known sources.]*

17. When the king freed him from jail, and brought him to Buda where he gave him a house located in Pest, which is across from Buda, and at a time when he had not yet seen the king, it so happened that a criminal sought refuge in Dracula's courtyard in order to save himself. And those chasing the criminal came into Dracula's courtyard and began looking for him. Dracula rose up, took his sword and cut off the head of the prefect who was holding the criminal and liberated the criminal. The other guards fled and went to the municipal judge and told him what had happened. The judge and his men went to the Hungarian King to complain against Dracula. The king sent a messenger to ask him: "Why have you done this crime?" Dracula answered in this way: "I did not commit a crime. He committed suicide. Anyone will perish in this way should he thievingly invade the house of a great ruler. If this prefect had come to me and had explained the situation to me, and if the criminal had been found in my own home, I myself would have delivered the

criminal to him or would have pardoned him of death." The king was told about this, and began to laugh and wonder about his candor. *[Not found elsewhere.]*

18. The end of Dracula came in this way: while he was ruling Wallachia, the Turks invaded the country and began to loot. Dracula attacked the Turks and put them to flight. Dracula's army began to kill the Turks without mercy and chase them out of the country. Out of sheer joy Dracula ascended the hill in order to see how his men were killing the Turks. Detached from his army in this way and from his men, he disguised himself as a Turk. Those in his immediate vicinity thought that he was a Turk and hit him with a lance. Dracula, seeing that he was being attacked by his own men, immediately killed five of his would-be assassins; then he was killed by many arrows and thus he died. *[That Dracula died in 1476 is certain, whether he died in the circumstances related here is not known.]*

19. The king took his sister and the two sons of Dracula to Buda in Hungary. One of these sons still lives with the king's son, the other was with the bishop of Oradea and has died in our time. I saw the third son, the eldest, whose name was Mikhail, in Buda. He fled from the Turkish sultan to the King of Hungary. Dracula had him by a certain woman when he was unmarried. Steven of Moldavia, in accord with the wish of the king, helped establish in Wallachia a prince's son called Vlad. This same Vlad was in his youth a monk, later a priest, and subsequently the abbot of a monastery. He then took the final vows and was set up as a prince and married. He married the wife of the prince who ruled a little later after Dracula, and who was killed by Steven Valacu *["the Wallachian," perhaps this reference should have been to Steven the Great]*. He took the latter's wife and now rules Wallachia, the same Vlad who previously was a monk and abbot. This was first written on February 13, 1486; later, on January 28, 1490, I have transcribed *[the text]* a second time, I, the sinner Efrosin. *[The historical references here are fairly accurate, Dracula's son here called "Mikhail" was also known as Mihnea. Specific mention of Vlad "a former monk" as "the present ruler"*

points to Vlad the Monk and supports authenticity of the date of the manuscript.]

Appendix III

Romanian Stories

Translations by Radu Florescu of folktales handed down by word of mouth. First rendering of this material into another language.

One of the central points made in this book is that the general themes in the oral Romanian folktales concur with those in the printed German and the manuscript Russian sources dating to the 15th and 16th centuries. Since the Romanian narratives are longer, often containing a moral, only a few examples are presented here.

1. **The Foreign Merchant.** [In Romanian folklore there are three variants of this story. Variant A is closest to Russian story No. 7. Variant B is very Romanianized and probably developed later; for instance, the Romanian currency *lei* are cited instead of *ducats*. Variant C takes a new form altogether, thus it, too, is probably a more recent development. It should be noted that Variant C shows that in Romania itself the name Dracula was associated with "The Impaler."]

Variant A

When Dracula ruled Wallachia, an important Florentine merchant traveled throughout the land, and he had a great deal of merchandise and money.

As he reached Targoviste, the capital of the country at the time, the merchant immediately went to the princely palace and asked Dracula for servants who might watch over him, his merchandise, and his money.

Dracula ordered him to leave the merchandise and the money in the public square and to come to sleep in the palace.

The merchant, having no alternative, submitted to the princely command. However, during the night, someone passing by his carriage stole 160 golden ducats.

On the next day, early in the morning, the merchant went to his carriage, found his merchandise intact, but 160 golden ducats were missing. He immediately went to Dracula and told him about the missing money. Dracula told him not to worry and promised that both the thief and the gold would be found. He ordered his servants to replace the gold ducats from his own treasury, but to add an extra ducat.

To the citizens of Targoviste he ordered that they immediately seek out the thief and that if the thief were not found, he would destroy his capital.

In the meantime, the merchant went back to his carriage, counted the money once, counted it a second time and yet again a third time, and was amazed to find all his money there with an extra ducat.

He then returned to Dracula and told him: "Lord, I have found all my money, only with an extra ducat."

The thief was brought to the palace at that very moment. Dracula told the merchant: "Go in peace. Had you not admitted to the extra ducat, I would have ordered you to be impaled together with this thief."

This is the way that Dracula conducted himself with his subjects, both believers and heretics. [Mihail Popescu, ed. *Legende istorice ale romanilor din cronicari*, Bucuresti, 1937, pp. 16-18.]

Variant B

In times gone by when Prince Vlad the Impaler was reigning, a merchant, who was traveling throughout our land, yelled at all the crossroads that he had lost a moneybag full of one thousand leis. He promised a hundred leis to whoever would find it and bring it to him. Not long after that, a God-fearing man, as the Romanians were at the time of Prince Vlad the Impaler, came up to the merchant and said to him: "Master merchant, I found this moneybag on my way at the turn in the crossroad at the back of the fish market. I figured that it must be yours, since I heard that you had lost a moneybag." The merchant replied: "Yes, it is really mine, and I thank you for bringing it to me."

As the merchant began to count the money, he was at wits' end to find a way of not giving the promised 100-lei reward. After he had counted the coins to the amazement of the other man, he put them back in the moneybag and said to the man who had brought it: "I have counted the money, my dear, and I noticed that you have taken your promised reward. Instead of a thousand leis, I found only nine hundred. You did well, since it was your right. I thank you once again that you saved me from the tight spot in which I was to fall. God keep you in his grace." The Christian answered: "Master merchant, you erroneously and without cause tell me that you are missing one hundred lei. I did not even untie the moneybag to look inside, and I did not even know how much money it contains. I took it to you as I found it." "I told you," replied the merchant cuttingly and with a double meaning, "I had lost a moneybag with one thousand leis. You brought it to me with nine hundred. That's how it is. Even if I should wish it, I cannot give you more. In the last resort, make out a petition and put me on trial."

The merchant blushed to his ears for shame when he realized that the peasant suspected him. He did not say a word but left bidding farewell, and he went straight to the prince to complain. "Your Highness," he said, "I bring this charge, not because of the promised one hundred leis, but because of the fact that he suspects that I am not an honest man when I know that I was as honest as pure gold, and when it did not even cross my mind to deceive him." The prince recognized the trickery of the merchant, since the prince himself was a clever fellow, and he ordered that the merchant be brought to him. Both the plaintiff and the accused were present. The prince listened to both, and when placing both versions in the balance of justice, the prince realized on which side it weighed. Looking the merchant straight in the eye, he said, "Master merchant, at my court people do not know what a lie is. It is strongly suppressed. You have lost a moneybag containing one thousand leis and you have found it proper to proclaim this at all the crossroads. The moneybag which this Christian brought you contained nine hundred leis. It seems quite obvious that this was not the moneybag which you lost. On the basis of what right did you accept it? Now, give the moneybag back to the man who found it and wait until the moneybag which you lost is found. While you, fellow Christian," added the prince, turning to the accused, "keep the moneybag until the man who lost it shows up." And so it was done, since there was no way of doing otherwise.

[Petre Ispirescu, ed., *Povesti despre Vlad Voda Tepes opera postuma*, Cernauti, Story 4, 1935, pp. 83 and 160.]

Variant C

Once there reigned in Wallachia a Prince Dracula, also known as the Impaler. This prince was very severe, but also just. He would not tolerate thieves, liars and lazy people. He did all in his power to extirpate such men from his land. Had he reigned longer he would probably have succeeded in freeing his land from such parasites and perhaps even prevented that others of that kind be born. But no such luck today!

At that time a merchant from the city of Florence in Italy was returning to his native land with inestimable wares and a large sum of money. He had to pass through Targoviste for there was the seat of the prince at that time. Since he had heard the Turks relate that half had perished at Dracula's hand, he thought that the Romanians were dishonest—as bad as forest thieves. As he reached Targoviste, the merchant went straight to Dracula with a great gift and told him: "Your Highness, fate has compelled me to pass through the land that you rule, with all my fortune which I have accumulated through the sweat of many years of Jewish work in Eastern countries. This land of yours is supposedly Christian. I don't want to have to relate in the West where I am going that a Christian was robbed by Christians, particularly when he was able to escape the sword of the pagan. On my knees I beg Your Highness to loan me a few guards to look after my goods until such time as I leave."

Dracula who was as quick as fire frowned with his eyebrows when he heard that request and said: "Keep your gift, you Christian. I order you to leave all your possessions in any square or any street, in any part of the city which will appear to you most isolated. Leave your fortune there unguarded until morning. If some theft should occur, I shall be responsible."

This was no joking matter. Dracula's command had to be obeyed—otherwise he would have lost his temper. The Florentine, heart frozen with fright, submitted to the order. He did not sleep a wink because of worry and doubt.

In the morning the merchant returned only to find his possessions intact, as he had left them. He looked at them and could hardly believe his eyes. He went to Dracula, told him that all his possessions were found untouched, and praised his land. He had never seen such a thing in any of the other countries that he had visited and he had been traveling since childhood. "What is the worth of the gift you intended to give me?" asked Dracula. The merchant was somewhat hesitant to reveal it. Dracula insisted on finding out the amount of the gift the merchant had intended to pay. Dracula then told him: "Tell whomever you meet what you have seen in my country." [Ispirescu, Story 4, 1935, pp. 83-84.]

2.   **Dracula and the Turkish Ambassadors.** [Compare with Russian story No. 1 and German story No. 32.]

It is said that during the reign of Dracula in Wallachia, Sultan Mohammed II sent some ambassadors.

The latter having entered the reception hall of the Prince paid homage in accordance with their custom of not taking their fezzes off. Dracula then asked: "Why do you behave in this way? You introduce yourselves to me and then do me dishonor." The Turkish representatives answered in unison: "This is the custom with the rulers of our country." Dracula then spoke to them in this way: "I, too, would like to strengthen your customs, so that you may adhere to them even more rigidly."

He then immediately ordered his retainers to bring him some nails in order to secure the fezzes on the heads of the Turkish ambassadors.

Having done this, he allowed the envoys to leave and told them: "Go and tell your master that he may be accustomed to suffer such indignity from his own people. We, however, are not so accustomed. Let him not send either to this country or elsewhere abroad, ambassadors exporting his new customs, for we shall not receive them."
[Popescu, pp. 15-16.]

3.   **The Boyar with a Keen Sense of Smell.** [Compare with Russian story No. 10 and German story No. 18.]

There were times when for whatever crime, whether judged or not judged, a man would lose his life. It is well that those times are now remote, may they never come back. It is well that we can now afford to relate these methods and not be victims anymore.

Some unruly boyars had been ordered impaled by Dracula. After some time Dracula, being reminded of the victims, invited yet other boyars to watch the spectacle with their own

eyes and see how he could punish—seeing is believing. Perhaps
Dracula simply wished to find out whether he could recognize
some of the boyars—for within his retinue were many of the
other faction *[Danesti]*. One of these boyars either because he
had been involved in the intrigues of the impaled victims, or
perhaps because he had been friendly to some of them, and
fearing not to admit that he was overcome by pity, dared to tell
Dracula: "Your Highness, you have descended to this spot from
the palace. Over there the air is pure, whereas here it is
impure. The bad smell might affect your health." "Do you
mean to say it stinks?" asked Dracula, quickly leaning towards
him and looking at him intently. "This is so, Your Highness,
and you would do well to leave a place which might be
detrimental to the health of a prince who has the good of his
subjects at heart."

Perhaps because Dracula had finally penetrated into the
depths of the mind of the boyar, or perhaps in order to shut up
the remarks of other boyars he shouted: "Servants, bring me a
stake three times as long as those that you see yonder. Make it
up for me immediately in order that you impale the boyar, so
that he may no longer be able to smell the stench from below. "

The unfortunate boyar begged on his knees. He wanted to
kiss Dracula's hands on both sides, all in vain. After a short
time he was struggling on a stake much higher than all the
others and he moaned and groaned so vehemently that you
heaved a sigh.

[Ispirescu, Story 6, 1935, pp. 25-27.]

4. **The Lazy Woman.** [Compare with Russian story No. 9
and German story No. 27.]

Dracula was a man with grey matter in his brains and he
insisted on good order in his state. Woe to any soldier whom he
saw improperly attired, he rarely escaped with his life. He
liked to see his citizens cleanly attired and looking smart.
Around him, he could not tolerate anyone who floundered or
was slow in his work. Whenever he noticed a libertine or a rake
he lost his temper.

One day he met a peasant who was wearing too short a
shirt. One could also notice his homespun peasant trousers
which were glued to his legs and one could make out the side of
his thighs when he saw him *[dressed]* in this manner. Dracula
immediately ordered him to be brought to court. "Are you

married?" he inquired. "Yes, I am, Your Highness." "Your wife is assuredly of the kind who remains idle. How is it possible that your shirt does not cover the calf of your leg? She is not worthy of living in my realm. May she perish!" "Beg forgiveness, My Lord, but I am satisfied with her. She never leaves home and she is honest." "You will be more satisfied with another since you are a decent and hard-working man. "

Two of Dracula's men had in the meantime brought the wretched woman to him and she was immediately impaled. Then bringing another woman, he gave her away to be married to the peasant widower. Dracula, however, was careful to show the new wife what had happened to her predecessor and explained to her the reasons why she had incurred the princely wrath.

Consequently, the new wife worked so hard she had no time to eat. She placed the bread on one shoulder, the salt on another and worked in this fashion. She tried hard to give greater satisfaction to her new husband than the first wife and not to incur the curse of Dracula. Did she succeed?

It is just as well that Dracula does not rule our country today, for he would have had to expend many stakes, which might have eliminated from our land the innumerable drones who wither the very grass on which they sit.

[Ispirescu, Story 5, 1935, pp. 21-25.]

5.   **The Burning of the Poor.** [This tale has a particularly moral bent to it. Compare with Russian story No. 5 and German story No. 30.]

The tale relates that there were a great number of people out of work at the time of Prince Vlad the Impaler. In order to live they had to eat, since the unmerciful stomach demanded food. So, in order to eat they wandered aimlessly and begged for food and they subsisted by begging without working. If a man, as I say, were to ask one of these beggars why they didn't work a little too, some would answer: "Don't I wander around all day long? If I cannot find work, am I to blame?" One of that kind, an onlooker could set straight with the proverb: "I am looking for a master but God grant that I don't find one." The others also always found a pretext for not working, such as: "The furrier strains his legs day and night, but does not get anything out of it; the tailor works all his life and his reward is like the shadow of a needle; the shoemaker bends and stoops until he gets old and when he dies he is buried with an empty collection plate." And in this way they found something wrong with all the trades.

When the prince heard of this and saw with his own eyes the large number of beggars who were really fit for work, he began to reflect. The Gospel says that man shall earn his daily bread only through the sweat of his brow. Prince Vlad thought: "These men live off the sweat of others, so they are useless to humanity. It is a form of thievery. In fact, the masked robber in the forest demands your purse, but if you are quicker with your hand and more vigorous than he you can escape from him. However, these others take your belongings gradually by begging—but they still take it. They are worse than robbers. May such men be eradicated from my land!" And after due reflection, he ordered that the announcement be made throughout the land that on a certain day all beggars should assemble, since the prince was going to distribute a batch of clothes and to treat them to a copious meal.

On the appointed day, Targoviste groaned under the weight of the large number of beggars who had come. The prince's servants passed out a batch of clothes to each one, then they led the beggars to some large house where tables had been set. The beggars marveled at the prince's generosity, and they spoke among themselves: "Truly it is a prince's kind of grace— even this charity is at the expense of the people. Couldn't the prince give us something out of his own pocket for a change?" "Hey, the prince has changed: He is no longer the way you knew him." "A wolf can change his fur, but not his bad habits."

Then they started eating. And what do you think they saw before them: a meal such as one would find on the prince's own table, wines and all the best things to eat which weigh you down. The beggars had a feast which became legendary. They ate and drank greedily. Most of them got dead drunk. As they became unable to communicate with one another, as one might say, incoherent, they were suddenly faced with fire on all sides. The prince had ordered his servants to set the house on fire. They rushed to the doors to get out, but the doors were locked. The fire progressed. The blaze rose high like inflamed dragons. Shouts, shrieks and moans arose from the lips of all the poor enclosed there. But why should a fire be moved by the entreaties of men? They fell upon each other. They embraced each other. They sought help, but there was no human ear left to listen to them. They began to twist in the torments of the fire that was destroying them. The fire stifled some, the embers reduced others to ashes, the flames grilled most of them. When the fire finally abated, there was no trace of any living soul.

And do you believe that the breed of poor was wiped out? Far from it—don't believe such nonsense. Look around you and ascertain the truth. Even today times are not better than they were then. Beggars will cease to exist only with the end of the world.

[Ispirescu, Story 8, 1936, pp. 1-6.]

6.   **The Two Monks.** [Compare with Russian story No. 6 and with German story No. 19.]

A crafty Greek monk who like many others was beginning to travel throughout the land happened to meet a poor Romanian priest, an honest God-fearing man. Every time they met, the two clerics argued and between them there arose a fiery dispute. The Greek monk was constantly belittling the priest and criticizing Romanians. The native answered: "If you find Romanians stupid and uncouth, why don't you return to your land among your subtle and wily Greek compatriots? Who has brought you hither and who has called you like a plague on our heads?"

News about the two clerics reached Dracula's ears. He wished to see them and ordered that on a certain day they both be brought to the palace.

They came on the appointed day. He received them in separate rooms. The Greek monk was proud to have been received by the prince, but he did not know that the native cleric had also been invited. The latter was astonished and could not understand how Dracula had found out about him, but he determined that should he find him well disposed he would place a good word for his parishioners. Dracula, however, wished to probe their innermost thoughts, for His Highness was crafty in this respect. When the Greek monk entered the chamber, Dracula asked him: "Reverend priest, you have traveled through my country in the service of the church. You had occasion to speak to good and bad people, with the rich and the poor. Tell me what do the people say about me?"

To such an obvious question the priest thought that he had the obvious retort. With a craftiness of which only a Greek is capable, he answered in a honeyed and false way: "Your Highness, from one end of the land to the other everyone praises your name. Everyone is pleased with your reign. They say that such a just ruler has never reigned in Wallachia. To which compliment I shall add that you need to do one more thing: Be kinder to those of your subjects who come from the Holy Places *[Greeks]* and give them financial aid, so that they may bring consolation for the misfortunes suffered by their monks at these Holy Places. Then your name will be blessed of the angels with undying praise." "You are lying, you unworthy priest, like the villain that you are," shouted Dracula, angered and frowning with his brows. It was obvious that he had been informed about the priest. Even the proverb states that even the sun cannot give heat to everyone. Opening the door he ordered his retainers who were on guard: "Soldiers, this wicked unworthy being must be executed."

The order was immediately obeyed and the monk was impaled. Then going to the Romanian priest who was ignorant of all that had happened, Dracula asked him the same question: "Tell me what do people say about me?" "What should they say, Your Highness? People have not spoken with one voice. Recently, however, they are beginning to castigate you everywhere and say that you no longer lessen their burdens, which were small in the days of your predecessor." "You dare to speak fairly," said Dracula in a gleeful tone of voice. "I will think about that. Be the court confessor from this point onwards and go in peace."

[Ispirescu, Story 7, 1935, pp. 27-32.]

7.   **Dracula's Mistress.** [Compare with German story No. 21 and Russian story No. 8.]

Dracula had a mistress. Her house was located in a dark and isolated suburb of Targoviste. When Dracula went to see her he was oblivious of everything, for this woman unfortunately happened to be to his taste. For her, he had mere physical attraction, nothing else.

The unfortunate woman tried in every way to be pleasing to Dracula. And he reciprocated all the outward manifestations of love which she showed him. One might almost say that Dracula expressed a certain gaiety when he was by her side.

One day when she saw his expression somewhat gloomier, she wished in some way to cheer him up and she dared tell him a lie. "Your Highness, you will be glad to hear my tidings." "What news can you give me?" answered Dracula. "The little mouse," she answered allegorically, "has entered the milk churn." "What does this mean?" questioned Dracula, grinning. "It means, Your Highness, that I am with child." "Don't you dare prattle such tales." The woman knew Dracula's method of punishing lies and wished to justify her statement. "It is, Your Highness, as I have said." "This will not be," said Dracula, frowning with his eyebrows. "But if it were possible I reckon that Your Highness would be glad," dared she continue. "I told you this will *not* be," retorted Dracula, rudely stamping his foot, "and I will show you it will not happen." Unsheathing his sword, he opened her entrails in order to see for himself whether she had spoken the truth or had lied.

As the woman lay dying, Dracula told her: "You see that it cannot be." He left while she agonized in great pain. She was punished because, hoping to cheer up her lover, she had told a lie.

[Ispirescu, Story 3, 1935, pp. 14-16.]

8.   **Vlad the Impaler.** [In their characterization of the tyrant prince, the following accounts concur with the Russian and German sources.]

Variant A

And the old folks said that this village of ours, "Vladaia," including its property, takes its name from a prince of the land called Vlad the Impaler. This prince had here, where the town hall now stands, a big house in which he sentenced the guilty and impaled them. Even today one may find in the soil the remains of those who had been impaled on the hill near the fountain. And perhaps if so many cruel battles had not taken place at Vladaia during the time of Vlad the Impaler as in more recent days, one would find even today the house where the judgments were made, as well as the dreadful impalement stake.

[Told by Dinu Dimitriu, age 60, of Vladaia, Mehedinti district.]

Variant B

Good God, times were bad because of the Turks at the time of Vlad the Impaler! The tax collectors came and took men either as hostages or to enroll them as their soldiers. They even took our herds—one out of every tenth one—and what was better and more plentiful than sheep at that time? The poor sheep: "Come summer, they sweeten you, come winter, they warm you." Milk was so plentiful that at that time our ancestors made *mamaliga* with milk, instead of water, as the milk was cheap. And all that was the reason why Prince Vlad hated the Turks. He pursued them to the last man and when he caught them, he had them impaled.

Prince Vlad also punished the boyars who were often conniving with the Turks or did not behave honestly with people such as we. On one occasion, in order to trip them up more easily, he gave a great feast and also summoned those boyars against whom he bore a grudge. But when they came, he impaled them.

[Told by Ghita a lui Dinu Radului of Almajel, Mehedinti district.]

Variant C

Mother! It is said that Vlad the Impaler was a terribly harsh ruler. He impaled whomever he caught lying or behaving badly towards the elderly or oppressing the poor. He also impaled the Turks who came, from time to time, to rob our country. It is said that this prince had a house in some bigger villages, where he sat in judgment and where he also had stakes and gallows.

The house where justice was administered was in our village, Albutele, near Beleti. Whomever he caught red-handed was sentenced and hanged there. And after he had taken his life, he impaled them.

[Told by Marga Bodea Matusa, age 76, of Muscel district; recorded in "Legende, traditii si amintire istorice adrurate din Oltenia si din Muscel," *Ac. Rom. din viata poporului Roman Culigeri si Studii,* Bucuresti, 1910.]

Bibliography

Ancient Documents and Modern Works about Dracula

The oldest document concerning Dracula is the manuscript in the Monastery of St. Gall, Switzerland. It was written in Low German, probably in 1462. For our translation of it, see Appendix I. Examples of the Dracula pamphlets printed from 1482 onward survive in various libraries in Western Europe. The only one in the United States is owned by the Philip H. and A.S.W. Rosenbach Foundation, Philadelphia. (See Frederich R. Goff, *Incunabula in American Libraries*, New York, 1964, p. 221.) Most of the modern studies relating to the historical Dracula are in the Romanian language.

Beheim, Michel. *Die Gedichte des Michel Beheim*. Band I Einleitung Gedichte Nr I-I47 herausgegeben von Hans Giele und Ingeborg Spriewald. Berlin, 1968. (Deutsche Texte des Mittelalters herausgegeben von der Deutschen Akademie der Wissenschaften zu Berlin, Band LX.) This is the most recent edition of the troubadour Michel Beheim's poem, which is rich in anecdotes about Dracula, was written in Wiener-Neustadt in 1463, and probably was directly inspired by stories told by refugee monks from Transylvania.

Bentley, Juliette. "Vlad Voivode Dracula," *Supernatural*, no. 2. Bournemouth, 1969. Unscholarly, superficial attempt to link the historical Dracula to Stoker's vampire.

Bogdan, Ioan. *Vlad Tepes si naratiunile germane si rusesti asupra lui.* Bucharest, 1896.

Bonfini, Antonio. *Rerum ungaricarum decades . . .*, 4 vols. Leipzig, 1936-41. Latest edition of the chronicle by the official Hungarian historian at the court of King Mathias Corvinus (1458-90). Bonfini, who probably knew Dracula personally from 1462 onward, may or may not have gotten his Dracula anecdotes firsthand. A part of his chronicles, *Decades tres. . .*, was published in Basel, 1543; the first complete edition, in Basel, 1568.

Cazacu, Matei. "La Valachie et la bataille de Kossovo," *Revue des Etudes Sud-Est Europeennes*, vol. 9 (1971), pp. 131-51. Useful for establishing the chronology of Dracula's first reign (1448), which the author arrived at on the basis of novel documentation.

Chalkokondyles, Leonikos. *Atheniensis historiarum, libri decem. Corpus scriptorum historiae Byzantinae.* Bonn, 1843. Earlier translations in French done in Paris, 1577; in Rouen, 1660. Of the Byzantine chroniclers, Chalkokondyles gave by far the most complete account of Dracula's campaign in 1462.

Conduratu, Grigore C. *Michael Beheim's Gedicht uber den Woiwoden Wlad II Drakul mit historischen und kritischen Erlauterungen.* Leipzig-Bucharest, 1903. A scholarly analysis of the work of the troubadour Michel Beheim; places the song in its historic context. By far the best work on this subject.

Czabai, Stephen. "The Real Dracula," *The Hungarian Quarterly*, Autumn 1941, pp. 327-32. Tendentious and without historical value.

Dlugosz, I. *Historica Polonica libri XIII ab antiquissimus temporibus.* Leipzig, 1711-12. This Polish chronicle contains interesting information on Dracul's crusades against the Turks and on Dracula's early career.

Degaudenzi, J.L. "Mythe et realite: le veritable Dracula," *Midi-Minuit*, no. 22, Paris, 1971. A highly fantasized and in part inaccurate interpretation but based on some original research.

Doukas, Michael. *Historia Byzantina recognovit et interprete ...* Bonn, 1834. Although not so informative as Chalkokondyles, the Byzantine chronicler is probably the most impartial commentator on Dracula's 1462 campaign against Mohammed II.

Ebendorfet, Th. *Chronica regum Romanorum.* Mittheilungen des Institut's fur osterreichische Geschichtsforschung; III Ergangzungsband; Innsbruck, 1890-94, pp. 202-4. A new edition of the chronicle was published in 1968. Includes the early German Dracula manuscript written in 1462.

Engel, Johann Christian von. *Geschichte der Moldau und Walachey. Nebst der Historischen und Statistischen Literatur beidjer Lander,* vol. 1 (actually volume IV of *Geschichte des Ungarisches Reiches und Seine Nebenlander*) pp. 75-80. Halle, 1804. Contains reprints of the Dracula pamphlets, plus an analysis of them.

Giese, F., ed. *Asik-Pasa-Zade. Tevarih-i al-i Osman.* Leipzig, 1929. Although not a direct witness of Dracula's night attack on Mohammed II's camp, Asik-Pasa-Zade left an interesting account of it from the Turkish point of view.

Giurescu, Constantin C. *Transylvania in the History of Romania: An Historical Outline.* London, 1969. The best general synthesis in English; written by one of Romania's leading historians.

Halecki, Oscar. *The Crusade at Varna: A Discussion of a Controversial Problem.* New York, 1943. Of interest in accounting for the Dracul-Hunyadi feud, which led to Dracul's murder in 1447.

Heiman, Leo. "Meet the Real Count Dracula," *Fate,* March 1968, pp. 53-60. Account of "Count" Alexander Cepesi, who has operated a small blood bank in Istanbul since 1947 and who claims to be a descendant of Dracula.

Hirn, Joseph. *Erzherzog Ferdinand II von Tirol.* Innsbruck, 1885. 2 vols. Standard biography of Archduke Ferdinand II, in whose gallery at Castle Ambras Dracula's portrait is to be found.

Iorga, Nicolae. *Les aventures "sarasines" des francais de Bourgogne au XIieme siecle. Melanges d 'histoire generale.* Clug, 1927. Commentary on the narration of the Burgundian De Wavrin, who participated in crusades against the Turks. De Wavrin's chronicle first published as: *Anchiennes croniques d'Engleterre par Johan de Wavrin seigneur de Forestel,* Mlle Dupont, ed., Paris, 1858-63, vol. 2, pp. 1-162. This firsthand testimony is invaluable for Dracula's early career.

——————. *Histoire des roumains et de la romanite orientale. Les chevaliers,* vol. 4. Bucharest, 1937. Somewhat disorganized interpretation of Dracula's reign by Romania's leading historian.

Kirtley, B. "Dracula, the Monastic Chronicles and Slavic Folklore," *Mid-West Folklore,* vol. 6 (1956), no. 3. Superficial 3-page speculative treatment of the Slavic Dracula manuscript.

Kittenberg, Hubert. *Schloss Ambras bei Innsbruck.* Innsbruck, 1949. Useful guidebook to Castle Ambras collection.

Karadja, C.I., ed. "Die Altesten Gedruckten Quellen zur Geschichte der Rumanen," *Gutenburg Jahrbuch,* pp. 114-46, Mainz, 1934. Sketchy compilation of the few German Dracula pamphlets known at that time by Karadja, who was a pioneer hunter of Dracula memorabilia. (Most of his collection is now at the Central State Library in Bucharest.)

Kritoboulos of Imbros. *History of Mehmed the Conqueror* (translated by C.T. Riggs). Princeton, 1954. Of marginal interest to Dracula's anti-Turkish campaign of 1462. A very mediocre English translation of the Byzantine chronicler.

Lurie, I. S. *Povesti o Dracule.* Moscow, Leningrad, 1964. The most substantial and scholarly study of the origins of the Dracula narratives, but has not been entirely accepted by Romanian

Slavicists and Germanists. Reproduces hitherto unknown Dracula pamphlet printed in Leipzig in 1493.

Modrussiense, Niccolo (Modrusa), in G. Mercati, ed., *Opere Minori*, vol. 4. Vatican City, 1937. The reports of this papal legate contain precious firsthand information on Dracula's cruelties and a very complete, unique literary portrait. The legate presumably met Dracula after 1462 and during his period of Hungarian imprisonment.

Munster, Sebastian. *Cosmographiae Universales*, Libri VI. Basel, 1572. Contains most of the early German anecdotes about Dracula and his cruelties; had a wide circulation. Munster may also have inspired the work of the archbishop of Prague, Ian of Puchov, first published in Czech in 1554.

Nandris, Grigore. "A Philological Analysis of Dracula and Rumanian Placenames and Masculine Personal names in a/ea," *Slavonic and East European Review*, vol. 37 (1959), pp. 371-77. Very personal interpretation; has not won general acceptance by other Romanian philologists.

―――――――. "The Dracula Theme in the European Literature of the West and of the East," *Literary History and Literary Criticism*. Edited by Leon Edel. New York, 1965. (Also see "The Historical Dracula," essentially the same theme, in *Comparative Literature: Matter and Method*, University of Illinois, Urbana, 1969.) A scholarly but incomplete study of the German and Slavic texts.

Pall, F. "Notes du pelerin William Wey a propos des operations militaires des Turcs en 1462," *Revue Historique du Sud-Est Europeen*, vol. 22 (1945), pp. 246-66. Firsthand account of an English pilgrim returning from the Holy Land and reporting a Dracula victory over the Turks.

Pius II (Enea Silvio Piccolomino). *Memoirs of a Renaissance Pope; the Commentaries of Pius II*. An abridgment of *Commentarii rerum memorabilium* . . ., Rome, 1589, translated by F.A. Gragg, New York, 1959. See also Pius II, *De Bello Turcorum et Hungarorum*, Cologne, 1472. These commentaries include references to Dracula; although obtained secondhand, they are invaluable for an understanding of the complex diplomatic situation which preceded and followed Dracula's campaign against the Turks in 1462.

Rosetti, Dinu. "Les Fouilles de Snagov," *Sapaturile arheologice de la Snagov*. Bucharest, 1935. Brief summary of the main findings of the 1931 archaeological excavations at Snagov, including reputed site of Dracula's tomb.

Sauter, Lilly V. "Ein Schloss in Tirol," *Du Atlantis,* April 1966, pp. 237-69. Scholarly article in popular magazine on the collection at Ambras castle; written by the current curator.

Seton-Watson, R.W. *A History of the Rumanians.* Cambridge, 1934. Still the best general synthesis of Romanian history by an English scholar. Interprets Dracula's reign rather severely.

Striedter, J. "Die Erzahlung vom walachischen vojevoden Drakula in der russischen und deutschen Uberlieferung," *Zeitschrift fur Slawische Philologie,* vol. 29 (Heidelberg, 1961-62), pp. 398-427. A comparative analysis of Russian and German Dracula narratives to be read in conjunction with that by Nandris.

Schwob, Monika Ute. *Kulturelle Beziehungen zwischen Nuremberg und die Deutschen im Sudosten im 14 bis 16 Jahrhundert,* Munich, 1969. A general monograph on German cultural contacts with Southeastern Europe containing a reference to a Nuremberg printed Dracula pamphlet. In appendix, see rare impalement frontispiece dated 1499.

Tappe, Eric. *Documents Concerning Romanian History, 1427-1601; Collected from the British Archives.* The Hague, 1964. Contains the letter of the English pilgrim William of Wey which reports a Dracula victory over the Turks in 1462.

Thuroczy, I. *Der Hungern Chronica inhallend wie sie anfengklich ins land kommen . . . von irem ersten Konig Athila,* Nurnberg, 1534. (See also *Chronica Hungarorum ab origine gentis,* Latin translation by I.G. Schwandter, Vienna, from 1746.) Oldest Hungarian chronicle referring to the early portion of Dracula's career—during the rule of John Hunyadi and Vlad Dracul. Undoubtedly subsequent chroniclers, such as Dlugosz and Bonfini, drew on this work for information about Dracul.

Wey, William [of]. *The Itineraries of Wey.* London, 1857.

Elizabeth Bathory

Baring-Gould, S. *The Book of Werewolves,* London, 1865. Contains chapter on the Blood Countess which may well have been read by Stoker.

Dezso, Rexa. *Bathory Erzsebet, Nadasdy Lerencne.* Budapest, 1908. Based on the work of Turoczi (see below).

Elsberg, R. von. *Elisabeth Bathory (Die Blutgrahn). Ein Sitten—und Charakterbild mit einem Titelbilde.* S. Schottlander, Breslau, 1904. Author apparently did not use original documents, relying instead on the data gathered by Dezso.

Leydi, Roberto. "Dracula era una dona," *L'Europeo*, no. 1 (January 1972), p. 42. Theorizes that Stoker may have been inspired in part by the crimes of Elizabeth Bathory.

Penrose, Valentin. *Erzsebet Bathory, La Comtesse sanglante.* Mercure de France, Paris, 1962. Romanticized presentation with no new historical evidence.

Ronay, Gabriel. *Exploding the Bloody Myths of Dracula and Vampires.* Gollancz, London, announced for 1972. Argues that Stoker's Dracula is based on Elizabeth Bathory.

Turoczi, Laszlo. *Erzebet Bathory.* Budapest, 1744. First published account of the Blood Countess. Contains record of trial.

Major Vampire Stories in English Literature (arranged chronologically)

Polidori, John William. *The Vampire.* London, 1819. First appeared in April, 1819 under Byron's name in the *New Monthly Magazine.* In this tale Lord Ruthwen, a vampire, saps the life blood from his victims.

Prest, Thomas Preskett. *Varney the Vampire or the Feast of Blood.* The first installment of this penny novel appeared in 1847. Entire work, edited by Sir Devendra P. Varma, published by Arno Press, New York, 1970. A very popular Gothic horror story in which a well-educated, gentleman-vampire, Sir Francis Varney, plagues the Bannesworth family.

Le Fanu, Joseph Sheridan. "Carmilla," in *In a Glass Darkly.* London, 1872. In this novelette Le Fanu created the most famous female vampire in English literature; this masterpiece of Gothic horror inspired Stoker to write a vampire story of his own.

Stoker, Bram. *Dracula.* London, 1897. Numerous editions up to the present day. Contains the most famous, most fascinating, vampire in English literature. If one could read only one piece of vampire fiction, this should be it.

—————. *Dracula's Guest and Other Weird Stories.* London, 1914. Stoker originally wrote "Dracula's Guest" for inclusion in his novel *Dracula,* but it was cut out of the initial editions. His widow, Florence Stoker, saw to its publication after Stoker's death.

Matheson, Richard. "Drink My Blood." A short story first published in 1951; republished in Peter Haining, ed., *The Midnight People,* Popular Library, New York, 1968. This incredibly gripping story is about a strange young boy named Jules who becomes fixated on the Dracula image in movies and literature. Jules wants to become a vampire, steals a vampire bat from the zoo, and in the end is met by Dracula himself.

Rudorff, Raymond. *The Dracula Archives*. Arbor House. New York, 1971. A novel recreating Bram Stoker's style and mixing up Elizabeth Bathory and Stoker's Dracula image.

Modern Anthologies Containing Vampire Stories

Carter, Margaret. *Curse of the Undead*. Greenwich, Conn., 1970. Literary tales about vampires.

Haining, Peter, ed. *The Midnight People*. Popular Library, New York, 1968. Short stories related to the vampire theme.

_____. *The Ghouls*. Pocketbooks. New York, 1972. A selection of short stories which illustrates how they inspired specific horror films; includes Bram Stoker's "Dracula's Guest," which inspired the film *Dracula s Daughter*.

Tolstoy, Alexis. *Vampires: Stories of the Supernatural*. 1969. Includes story of a family of vampires from Serbia.

Vadim, Roger; Volta, Ornella; and Riva, Valeria. *The Vampire: An Anthology*. London, 1963. Includes short selections from major vampire stories, by authors such as Merimee, Le Fanu, and Tolstoy.

Studies of the Vampire in Literature, History, and Myth

Epaulard, Alexis. *Vampyrisme, necrophilie, necrosadisme, necrophagie*. Lyon, 1901. The psycho-pathology associated with "living vampires."

Faivre, Tony. *Les vampires*. Paris, 1962. One of the best of the current serious books on vampire beliefs. The author traces the historical records about vampires from ancient times to the present in a semi-scholarly manner. There are some mistakes, such as claim that in Moldavia the word "Dracul" refers to a vampire. The historical data is not well related to the narrative, but the illustrations of the vampire in art are most interesting.

Frazer, James G. *The Fear of the Dead in Primitive Religions;* especially vol. 2, London, 1934. The famous author of *The Golden Bough* delivered these lectures at Trinity College. He dealt with the walking dead in a somewhat out-dated rationalistic manner.

Gerard, Emily de Laszowska. *The Land Beyond the Forest*. London, 1888. The author includes a good deal of Transylvanian folklore, including some on who becomes a vampire and how to kill one.

Her article "Transylvanian Superstitions" was published in *The Nineteenth Century*, vol. 18, London, 1885, pp. 130-50.

Glut, Donald F. *True Vampires of History*. H.C. Publishers, New York, 1971. A presentation of records about vampire cases; no critical analysis.

Hill, Douglas, and Williams, Pat. *The Supernatural*. Aldous Books. London, 1965.

Hock, Stefan. *Die Vampyrsagen und ihre Verwertung in der Deutschen Literatur*. Berlin, 1900. Vampire themes in German literature.

Hurwood, Bernhart J. *Monsters and Nightmares*. Belmont Productions. New York, 1967.

——————. *Monsters Galore*. Fawcett Publications. New York, 1965.

——————. *Terror By Night*. Lancer Books. New York, 1963. Republished as *The Monstrous Undead*, Lancer, 1969. One of the finest studies of the belief in vampires, including probings into the reality behind reality.

Jellinek, A. L. "Zur Vampyrsage," *Zeitschrift des Vereins fur Volkskunde*, vol. 14, 1904, especially pp. 234 ff. A scholarly treatment of the vampire theme in folk literature.

Murgoci, A. "The Vampire in Rumania," *Folklore*, vol. 37, 1926. A brief but excellent study of the vampire theme in Romanian folklore.

Murgoci, A., and Murgoci, H. "The Devil in Rumanian Folklore," *Folklore*, vol. 40, 1929.

Rogo, Scott. "Reviewing the Vampire of Croglin Grange," *Fate*, vol. 21, no. 6 (June, 1968), pp. 44-48.

—————— "In-Depth Analysis of the Vampire Legend," *Fate*, vol. 21, no. 9 (Sept., 1968), pp. 70-77.

Seabrook, William. *Witchcraft: Its Power in the World Today*. Harcourt, Brace. New York, 1940. Paperback: Lancer Books, New York, 1968. Part Two contains a fine analysis of the vampire and the werewolf.

Smith, Warren. *Strange Monsters and Madmen*. Popular Library. New York, 1969.

Sturm, Dieter, and Volker, Klaus. *Von den Vampiren oder Menschensaugern*. Munich, 1968. An excellent, scholarly work, including texts about vampires from literary and official documents dating back to ancient times and up to the present. The book concludes with two fine essays: one on the literary traditions of the vampire, another on the historical traditions.

Summers, Montague. *The Vampire: His Kith and Kin.* Routledge and Kegan Paul. London, 1928. Republished by New Hyde Park, New York, 1960. Summers was one of the pioneers in the field of the occult. This work, though serious, fails to distinguish between significant and insignificant details.

————. *The Vampire in Europe.* Routledge and Kegan Paul. London, 1929. Republished by New Hyde Park, New York, 1966. A general treatment; has same defects as in work cited above.

Varma, Devendra P. *The Gothic Flame.* 1957. Excellent study of the Gothic Romance, with some references to the vampire literary strain.

Villeneuve, Roland. *Loups-garoux et vampires.* Paris–Geneva, 1963.

Volta, Ornella. *Le vampire, la mort, le sang, la peur.* Editions Jean-Jacques Pauvert. Paris, 1962. Translation by Raymond Rudorff: *The Vampire,* Tandem Books, London, 1965. A look at the vampire from an erotic viewpoint; many bizarre illustrations.

Wright, Dudley. *Vampires and Vampirism.* William Rider and Son. London, 1914. A superficial treatment.

Studies of the Vampire in Film

Borst, Ron. "The Vampire in the Cinema" *Photon,* no. 19. Mark Frank, ed. & pub. Brooklyn, N.Y., 1970. This is the best, most comprehensive listing of its kind.

Butler, Ivan. *Horror in the Cinema.* International Film Guide Series. New York, 1971. First published in 1967 as *The Horror Film;* second revised edition, 1970. Contains brief references to vampire films. Filmography at the end is weak.

Clarens, Carlos. An *Illustrated History of the Horror Film.* Longmans, Canada, 1967; New York, 1968. References to vampire films appear throughout the text. The filmography omits several vampire films, but the general text is adequate.

Douglas, Drake. *Horror!* Collier Books, 1969. First published by The Macmillan Company, 1966.

Eisner, Lotte H. *The Haunted Screen: Expressionism in the German Cinema and the Influence of Max Reinhardt.* University of California Press, 1969. First published under the title *L 'Ecran Demoniaque,* in France, 1952; revised and reissued, 1965, by Le Terrain Vague. A classic. Contains a superb analysis of the pre-Nazi German films of the 1920s by one who understood German expressionism and film. Book includes an admirable chapter on Murnau's *Nosferatu.*

Gifford, Denis. *Movie Monsters*. London, 1969. Chapter entitled "The Vampire" quickly traces historical development of the vampire image in film.

Michel, Jean-Claude. "Les vampires a l'ecran," *L 'Ecran Fantastique*, 2 serie, no. 2, Paris, 1971. One of the most comprehensive filmographies on the vampire, plus perceptive comments on the films.

Reed, Donald A. *The Vampire on the Screen*. Inglewood, California, 1964. A small but pioneering work by the President of the Count Dracula Society.

_____. *Midi-Minuit Fantastique*, nos. 4-5, January 1963, Paris. An excellent summary of cast and credits of all the Dracula films until the early 1960s. Many photos from the films.

Filmography

Dracula-Vampire Films, 1896-1971

Most of the early, and by now obscure, silent films about vampires are actually about "vamps"—female flirts who entice or captivate men. The first real vampire movie is F. W. Murnau's classic *Nosferatu* (1922), which was based on Stoker s novel *Dracula* (1897).

Silent Films 1896-1928

1896. *Le Manoir du Diable*. Robert-Houdin film, France; director Georges Melies. American title: *The Haunted Castle*. English title: *The Devil's Castle*. In one scene a huge bat in a medieval castle becomes transformed into Mephistopheles. A cavalier arrives with a crucifix; confronted with it, the devil "throws up his hands and disappears in a cloud of smoke." Despite the film's imagery, the devil-figure does not drink blood, thus is not a real vampire.

1909-22. This period included among others the following films, which are listed here out of historical interest. *Vampire of the Coast*, 1909 USA. *The Vampire's Trail*, 1910 USA. *Vampyrn*, 1912 Swedish short. *Vampe di Gelosia* (The Vamp's Jealousy), 1912 Italian short. *The Vampire*, 1912 Messter short. *Danse Vampiresque*, 1912 Danish short. *The Vampire*, 1913 USA Kalem film; *director*, Robert Vignola. *In the Grip of the Vampire*, 1913 USA. *Vampires of the Night*, 1914 Greene's Feature Photo Plays. *The Vampire's Trail*, 1914 USA; *director*, Robert Vignola. *Vampires of Warsaw*, 1914 USA. *The Vampire's Tower*, 1914 USA, Ambrosia film. *Saved from the Vampire*, 1914 USA. *Les Vampires*, 1915 French serial; *director*, Louis Feuillade. *The Vampire's Clutch*, 1915, Knight film. *Was She a Vampire?*, 1915 Universal film. *Kiss of the Vampire*, 1915 USA. *Mr. Vampire*, 1916 USA. *A Night of Horror*, 1916 German film; *director*, Arthur Robison. A *Vampire Out of Work*, 1916 Vitagraph film. *Ceneri e Vampe*, 1916 Italian film. A *Village Vampire*, 1916 USA. *The Beloved Vampire*, 1917 USA. *The Vampire*, 1920 Metro film. *The Blond Vampire*, 1922 USA.

1922. *Nosferatu oder eine Symphonie des Grauens*. Prana Films, Germany; director, Friedrich Wilhelm Murnau; screenplay by Henrick Galeen. Released on March 5, 1922 in Germany; in the

U.S. as *Nosferatu, the Vampire* in 1929. Count Orlock, played by Max Schreck, is the vampire Nosferatu (Dracula). The script was an adaptation of Stoker's novel. Since Murnau had not secured the proper copyright, he changed the setting from the Balkans to the Baltic area, and he also changed the names of the main characters. This is the first Dracula vampire film. Visually it ranks as one of the greatest horror films of all time. Murnau filmed it in an outdoor, realistic setting. Despite some technical gimmicks which cause modern audiences to laugh, such as the speed-up of the sequences of Dracula's carriage and his loading of coffins, this film is a masterpiece.

1927. *London After Midnight*. Metro-Goldwyn Mayer, USA. Producer and director, Tod Browning; screenplay, by Tod Browning and Waldemar Young, from a novel by Tod Browning entitled *The Hypnotist*. Film released in England as *The Hypnotist*. Lon Chaney appears as Inspector Edmund Burke, alias Mooney (the vampire). In this film Lon Chaney, "the man with a thousand faces," plays a vampire in human form.

1928. *The Vampire*. United Pictures, USA. Released in France, 1928, as *Vampire a du Mode*. A seductive image is portrayed here, not a real vampire.

Talkies 1931-71

1931. *Dracula*. Universal Studios, USA. A Tod Browning Production; producer, Carl Laemmle, Jr.; director. Tod Browning; screenplay, by Garret Fort, from the play by Hamilton Deane and John F. Balderston, based on the novel *Dracula* by Bram Stoker; additional dialogue by Dudley Murphy. Dracula is played by Bela Lugosi, who had the stage role on Broadway. This is the first real vampire talkie. It remains one of the most popular films of all time, though most film critics do not hold it in high regard. The photography is unimaginative; the music contains snatches from Tschaikovsky's "Swan Lake"; but Bela Lugosi's authentic Hungarian accent and presence reach out to make *his* Dracula image a part of contemporary American "folklore."

1931. *Dracula*. Mexican-Universal; co-producer, Carl Laemmle, Jr.; director, George Melford. Mexican version of the Browning-Lugosi film cited above, filmed at the same time.

1932. *Vampyr*. Les Films Carl Dreyer, France; producer, Carl Dreyer; screenplay, by Carl Dreyer and Christian Jul, freely adapted from the story "Carmilla" by Sheridan Le Fanu. Released in America as both *The Vampire* and the *Castle of Doom; in* England as *The Strange Adventures of David Gray*. This film is an example of what a real horror film should be. The dreadful is sensed rather than seen. Blood-drinking is suggested rather than portrayed. The entire film has a distant, grainy quality which is reminiscent of a Seurat painting. This quality actually was an "accident" in filming, and Dreyer turned it into an asset. Unfortunately, the mood it creates remains unique; no successors have ever duplicated, much less equaled, it.

1933. *The Vampire Bat.* Majestic, USA; producer, Phil Goldstone; director, Frank Trayer; screenplay by Edward Lowe. Lionel Atwill plays a mad doctor who tries to cover up his weird experiments by fomenting a vampire scare among the inhabitants of a far-off Balkan village.

1935. *The Mark of the Vampire.* Metro-Goldwyn Mayer, USA; producer, E.J. Mannix; director, Tod Browning; screenplay, by Guy Endore and Bernard Schubert, from the story by Tod. Browning. Bela Lugosi plays Count Mora (Dracula) in the film. His female vampire is played by Carol Borland. This is an elaborate remake of *London After Midnight* (see above). In the film Lionel Barrymore, an occultist, insists that a vampire is behind the murders in a gloomy castle, but in the end the supposed vampires turn out to be local actors. The real killer was a human who had drained the blood of his victim. This film was re-released in 1972.

1935. *Condemned to Live.* Chesterfield-Invincible, USA; producer, Maurey M. Cohen; director, Frank Strayer; screenplay by Karen de Wolfe. In Africa, a woman bitten by a vampire bat gives birth to a baby who becomes a vampire-like werewolf.

1936. *Dracula's Daughter.* Universal, USA; producer, Carl Laemmle, Jr.; director, Lambert Hillyer; screenplay, by Garret Fort, adapted from Bram Stoker's story "Dracula's Guest" and a story by Oliver Jeffries. Gloria Holden played Dracula's daughter, Countess Marya Zaleska. The daughter tries to conquer her inherited blood lust without success.

NOTE: During the 1940s Dracula-vampire films fell on hard times. Such films as *Frankenstein Meets the Wolfman, The House of Dracula, Abbott and Costello Meet Frankenstein,* toy in a frivolous, titillating way with the main elements of fiction and folklore. One cannot escape the feeling that these films were made to satisfy the public's desire for a ridiculous encounter of monsters and comedians. This encounter reached its nadir in 1952 with *Old Mother Riley Meets the Vampire.*

1940. *The Devil Bat.* Producer Releasing Corp., USA; producer, Jack Gallagher; director, Jean Yarbrough; screenplay, by John Thomas Neville, from George Bricker's story "The Flying Serpent." Bela Lugosi played Dr. Paul Carruthers, a mad scientist who raises huge vampire bats to become his agents of revenge.

1941. *Spooks Run Wild*. Banner Production-Monogram, USA; producer, Sam Katzman; director, Phil Rosen; screenplay by Carl Foreman and Charles R. Marian. Bela Lugosi played Nardo, a stage magician suspected of being a vampire-like monster.

1943. *Le Vampire*. France; director, Jean Painleve. Documentary filmed on location in the Gran Chaco, South America. Includes scenes of the actual vampire bat stalking its victim and drinking blood.

1943. *Son of Dracula*. Universal, USA; producer, Ford Beebe; director, Robert Siodmak; screenplay, by Curt Siodmak, suggested by Bram Stoker's novel *Dracula*. Lon Chaney, Jr. played Count Alucard (Dracula spelled backward). The count emigrates from Europe to the United States in search of fresh blood.

1943. *Dead Men Walk*. (Other titles: *The Vampire* and *Creatures of the Devil*.) Producers Releasing Corp., USA; producer, Sigmund Neufield; director, Sam Newfield; screenplay by Frank Myton. George Zucco played the vampire Dr. Lloyd Clayton.

1943. *Return of the Vampire*. Columbia, USA; producer, Sam White; director, Lew Landers; screenplay, by Griffin Jay, based on an idea of Kurt Neumann; additional dialogue by Randall Faye. Bela Lugosi played the role of Armand Tesla (Dracula) who appears in England during World War II. Here, he seeks revenge against those who first tried to kill him.

1943. *Frankenstein Meets the Wolfman*. Universal, USA; director, Roy William Neill; screenplay by Curt Siodmak. Lon Chaney, Jr. played the role of Dracula. The titillating variation on the traditional theme of horror is now a clearly marked tendency, which crests in the 1940s.

1944. *House of Frankenstein*. Universal, USA; producer, Paul Malvern; director, Eric C. Kenton; screenplay, by Edward T. Lowe, based on an original story by Curt Siodmak. John Carradine appeared in his first role as Count Dracula, alias Baron Latoes.

1945. *The House of Dracula*. Universal, USA; producer, Paul Malvern; director, Erle C. Kenton; screenplay by Edward T. Lowe. John Carradine again appeared as Baron Latoes, the alias for Count Dracula in *The House of Frankenstein*.

1945. *Isle of the Dead*. RKO Radio Pictures, USA; producer, Val Lewton; director, Mark Robson; screenplay by Ardel Wray and Joseph Mischel. Boris Karloff played a Greek general who has come back to the island where his wife has been entombed. He accuses a young girl of being a vampire *(vrykolaka)*.

1945. *The Vampire's Ghost*. Republic Pictures, USA; associate producer, Rudy Abel; director, Lesley Selander; screenplay, by Leigh Brackett and John K. Butler, after a story by Leigh Brackett. John Abbott is cast as a vampire in a small African village.

1946. *Devil Bat's Daughter*. Producers Releasing Corp., USA; producer, Franck Wisbar; director, Franck Wisbar; screenplay by Griffin Jay, based on an idea of Leo T. McCarthy, Franck Wisbar, and Ernst Jaeger. A murdering doctor tries to blame his crimes on the daughter of the "Devil Bat" doctor.

194?. *Dr. Terror's House of Horrors*. U.S. Independent. Reissue of parts of four earlier horror films, including sections from Dreyer's *Vampyr*.

1946. *Valley of the Zombies*. Republic, USA; associate producers, Dorrell McGowan and Stuart McGowan; director, Philip Ford; screenplay, by Dorrell McGowan and Stuart McGowan, based on a story by Royal K. Cole and Sherman T. Lowe. Ian Keith portrays a resurrected body dependent upon constant blood transfusions in order to stay alive.

1948. *Abbott and Costello Meet Frankenstein*. Universal, USA; producer, Robert Arthur; director, Charles Barton; screenplay by Robert Lees, Frederic Rinaldo, and John Grant. Released in England as *Abbott and Costello Meet the Ghosts*. Bela Lugosi played Dracula. A light-hearted satire—typical of vampire films, especially since 1943—on Dracula, Frankenstein and the Wolf Man; Dracula ends up as a bat in the claws of the Wolf Man.

1951. *The Thing from Another World*. RKO Radio Pictures, USA; producer, Howard Hawks; director, Christian Nyby (and Orson Welles, according to rumor); screenplay, by Charles Lederer, based on the novel *Who Goes There?* by John W. Campbell, Jr. First film to link the classical vampire with science fiction. A figure from outer space crash-lands on Earth and survives on blood.

1952. *Old Mother Riley Meets the Vampire*. Renown, Great Britain; director, J. Gilling; screenplay by Val Valentine. Released in America as both *Vampire over London* and *My Son the Vampire*. Bela Lugosi played Van Housen the vampire in this British comedy.

1953. *Drakula Istanbulda*. Demirag, Turkey; producer, Turgut Demirag; director, Mehmet Muktar; screenplay, by Unit Deniz, after the novels *Dracula* by Bram Stoker and *The Impaling*

Voivode by Riza Seyfi. First and only film to fuse Stoker's Dracula with Vlad the Impaler, although the references are slight. A balding Alif Kaptan plays Dracula, and the story is set in Istanbul.

NOTE: The popularity of the horror film declined during the late 1940s and early 1950s; but the late 1950s brought renewed interest and once again Dracula and vampire films were being made.

1956. *Planet Nine from Outer Space.* Distribution Corporation of America, USA; producer and director, Edward D. Wood, Jr.; screenplay by Edward D. Wood, Jr. Second title: *Grave-Robbers from Outer Space.* Lugosi played Specter. This was Lugosi's last film.

1957. *The Vampire.* Gramercy Pictures Prod., United Artists, Great Britain and USA; producers, Arthur Gardner and Jules V. Levy; director, Paul Landres; screenplay by Pat Fiedler. American title: *Mark of the Vampire.* John Beal accidentally takes pills which turn him into a vampire at night.

1957. *Blood of Dracula.* Carmel Production, American International Release, USA; producer, Herman Cohen; director, Herbert L. Strock; screenplay by Ralph Thornton. Released in England as *Blood Is My Heritage;* in Canada as *Blood of the Demon.*

1957. *Not of This Earth.* Allied Artists, USA; producer, Roger Corman; director, Roger Corman; screenplay by Charles Griffith and Mark Hanna. Science fiction and vampirism.

1957. *I Vampiri.* Titanus-Athena, Italy; director, Riccardo Freda; screenplay, Piero Regnoli, Rik Sjostrom, and Riccardo Freda. Released in America under the titles *The Vampire of Notre Dame, The Devil's Commandment,* and *Lust of the Vampires.* Not a real vampire film at all.

1958. *The Return of Dracula.* Gramercy United Artists Release, USA; producers, Arthur Gardner and Jules V. Levy; director, Paul Landres; screenplay by Pat Fiedler. Released in England as *The Fantastic Disappearing Man,* and on American TV as *The Curse of Dracula.* Francis Lederer plays Bellac (Dracula), the vampire come to California to spread the cult.

1958. *The Horror of Dracula.* Hammer Films, Great Britain; producer, Anthony Hinds; executive producer, Michael Carreras; director, Terence Fisher; screenplay, by Jimmy Sangster, adapted from the novel *Dracula* by Bram Stoker. Dracula is played by Christopher Lee. This is a fine work which ranks with the earlier horror films such as *Nosferatu* and *Vampyr,* which surpass the merely terrifying. The final scene is superb: Van Helsing (played by Peter Cushing) traps Dracula as he is rushing to get back to his coffin at break of day. Van Helsing in a desperate leap rips the drapes to let in the light, fashions a cross from two huge gold candelabras, and forces Dracula into the sunlight, where the vampire disintegrates into dust.

1958. *Blood of the Vampire.* Tampean Productions, Great Britain; producers, Robert S. Baker and Monty Berman; director, Henry Cass; screenplay by Jimmy Sangster. Sir Donald Wolfit played Dr. Callistratus, a medical doctor with a blood deficiency who carries on research among the helpless victims in his prison hospital.

1959. *Curse of the Undead.* Universal, USA; producer, Joseph Gershenzon; director, Edward Dein; screenplay by Michael Pate and Mildred Dein. First film to mix the vampire legend with the traditional American folklore of the western.

1959. *El Vampiro.* Cinemagrafica ABSA-Mexico; producer, Abel Salazar; director, Fernando Mendez; screenplay by Heinrich Rodriguez and Ramon Obon.

NOTE: Beginning in the late 1950s and continuing on into the early 60s a series of Italian potboilers emerged. It appears that Italian film-makers tried to give new life to the vampire theme by introducing playgirls or musclemen into the films.

1959. *Tempi Duri Per I Vampiri.* Maxima, Italy; presented by Joseph E. Levine; producer, Mario Cecchi Gori; director, Pio Angeletti; screenplay by Mario Cecchi Gori and others. Released in America as *Uncle Was a Vampire.* Christopher Lee as Uncle Rinaldo, the vampire, in an Italian comedy.

1960. *The Brides of Dracula.* Hammer Films, Great Britain; producer, Anthony Hinds; executive producer, Michael Carreras; director, Terence Fisher; screenplay by Jimmy Sangster, Peter Bryan, and Edward Percy. David Peel performs as the vampire-baron, Baron Meinster.

1960. *L 'Ultima Preda del Vampiro.* Nord Film, Italy; producer, Tiziana Longo; director, Piero Regnoli. Released in America as *The Playgirls and the Vampire.* A sexploitation film.

1960. *Et Mourir de plaisir.* EGE Films-France-Italy; producer, Raymond Eger; director, Roger Vadim; screenplay, by Roger Vadim, Claude Brule and Claude Martin, based on a story by Roger Vadim and also Sheridan Le Fanu's "Carmilla." Released in America as *Blood and Roses.* Vampire enters the body of a young girl, and through her carries out his vampire practices.

1961. *Maschera del Demonio.* Jolly-Galatea, Italy; director, Mario Bava; screenplay, by Ennio de Concini and Mario Serandrei, based on the story "Viy" by Gogol. Released in America as *Black Sunday;* in England as *Revenge of the Vampire.* Barbara

Steele played Princess Ada Vajda, the vampire-witch. An excellent film.

1961. *Il Vampiro dell'Opera*. N.I.F. Rome, Italy; director, Renato Polselli. A vampire haunts an old opera house.

1961. *L'Amante del Vampiri*. C.E.F. Consorzio-Italo-Films, Italy; producer, Bruno Bolognesi; director, Renato Polselli; screenplay by Renato Polselli Giuseppi Pellegrini, and Ernesto Castaldi. Released in America as *The Vampire and the Ballerina*. An imitation of the 1960 film *L 'Ultima Preda del Vampiro*. A vampire and his servant prey on showgirls.

1961. *Ercole al Centro della Terra*. Omnia SPA Cinematografica, Italy; producer, Achille Piazzi; director, Mario Bava; screenplay by Alessandro Continenza, M. Bava, Duccio Tessari, and Franco Prosperi. Released in America as *Hercules in the Haunted World*. Christopher Lee played Lyco. A muscleman epic.

1961. *El Vampiro Sanpriento*. Azteca-Mexico; producer, Rafael Perez Grovas; director, Miguel Morayta; screenplay by Miguel Morayta. Released in America as *The Bloody Vampire*. Count Frankenstein is a vampire, and in the end he remains uncaught.

1961. *Ataud del Vampiro*. Cinemagrafica ABSA-Mexico; producer, Abel Salazar; director, Fernando Mendez; screenplay, by Ramon Obon, after a story by Raul Zentino. Released in America as *The Vampire's Coffin*. A mad doctor resuscitates a vampire in this sequel to *El Vampiro Sangriento* of the same year.

1961. *El Mundo de la Vampiro*. Cinemagrafica ABSA-Mexico; producer, Abel Salazar; director, Fernando Mendez; screenplay, by Ramon Obon, based on an idea of Raul Zentino. Released in America as *World of the Vampire*. Vampire on the trail of revenge ends up on a stake.

1962. *Maciste contre il Vampiro*. Ambrosiana Cinematografica, Italy; producer, Paolo Moffa; directors, Giacomo Gentilomo and Sergio Corbucci; screenplay by Sergio Corbucci and Duccio Tessari. Released in America as *Goliath and the Vampire*. Muscleman-vampire versus superhero.

1962. *La Strage dei Vampiri*. Italy; producer, Dino Sant'Ambrogio; director, Robert Mauri; screenplay by Robert Mauri. Released in America as *Curse of the Blood Ghouls*. Italian Gothic.

1962. *La Invasion de los Vampiros*. Mexico; producer, Rafael Perez Grovas; director, Miguel Morayta; screenplay by Miguel Morayta. Released in America as *The Invasion of the*

Vampires. A vampire called Count Frankenhausen acts in this further sequel to *El Vampiro Sangriento* (1961).

1962. *House on Bare Mountain.* Olympic International, USA; producers, David Andrew and Wes Don; director, R.L. Frost; screenplay by Denver Scott. Sexploitation with all three classic horrors—Dracula, the Frankenstein monster, and the Wolf Man. Comparable to *Abbott and Costello Meet Frankenstein* (1948).

1962. *La Maldicion de los Karnsteins.* Hispaner Films, NEC Cinematografica, Spain-Italy; director, Thomas Miller (alias Camillo Mastrocinque); screenplay, by Julian Berry, after "Carmilla" by Le Fanu. Christopher Lee played Count Ludwig Karnstein. Released in England as *Crypt of Horror;* in America as *Terror in the Crypt.* The third film version of Le Fanu's tale, to which it adheres rather closely.

1963. *Tre Volti della Paura.* Emmerpi-Galatea-Lyre, Italy; director, Mario Bava; screenplay by Marcello Fondato, Alberto Bevilacqua, and M. Bava. Released in America as *Black Sabbath.* Three stories in one film, one of which is based on Alexis Tolstoy's "The Wurdalak" about the Urfe family of vampires. Boris Karloff, the narrator, also played Gorca, the head of the vampire household.

1963. *Kiss of the Vampire.* Hammer Films, Great Britain; producer, Anthony Hinds; director, Don Sharp; screenplay by John Elder (alias Anthony Hinds). American TV title: *Kiss of Evil.* A well-made film about a couple honeymooning in Bavaria, where they become involved in the vampire cult.

1964. *The Last Man on Earth.* Co-production: Produzioni La Regine and American International, Italy-USA; producer, Robert L. Lippert; director, Sidney Salkovo; screenplay, by William Leicester, after the novel *I Am Lepend* by Richard Matheson. Vincent Price portrayed Robert Morgan, the last human in a land of vampire-like creatures following atomic holocaust.

1964. *Dr. Terror's House of Horrors.* Amicus, England; producers, Milton Subotsky and Max J. Rosenberg; director, Freddie Francis; screenplay by Milton Subotsky. Death in the guise of Dr. Schreck, played by Peter Cushing, predicts the death of five passengers on a train. One sequence contains a vampire.

1965. *Dracula—Prince of Darkness* or *Blood for Dracula.* Hammer Films, Great Britain; producer, Anthony Nelson Keys; director, Terence Fisher; screenplay, by John Sansom (alias Jimmy Sangster), from an idea of John Elder (alias Anthony Hinds) based on the characters in Bram Stoker's *Dracula.* In this sequel to *Horror of Dracula* (1958), Christopher Lee played Dracula, who is revived by blood flowing into his ashes.

1965. *Terrore nella Spazio.* Castilla, Italy; producer, Fulvio Lucisano; director, Mario Bava; screenplay by Ib Melchior and Louis M. Heywood. Released in America as *Planet of Blood;* for TV as *Planet of Terror.* Beings from another planet try to take over human bodies.

1965. *Devils of Darkness.* Planet Films, Great Britain; producer, Tom Blakeley; director, Lance Comfort; screenplay by Lyn Fairhurst. Count Sinistre, a vampire, tries to ravish modern-day victims from Brittany.

1965. *La Sorella di Satana.* Italian-Yugoslavian; directors, Michael Reeyes and Charles Griffiths. Released in America as *The She-Beast.* A vampiress in modern-day Communist Transylvania.

1966. *Billy the Kid Vs. Dracula.* Circle Productions, Inc.-Embassy, USA; producer, Carroll Case; director, William Beaudine; screenplay by Karl Hittleman. Dracula, played by John Carradine, preys on a western town until he is killed by the outlaw Billy the Kid, played by Chuck Courtney.

1966. *Blood Bath.* American International, USA; producer, Jack Hill; directors, Jack Hill and Stephanie Rothman; screenplay by J. Hill and S. Rothman. American TV title: *Track of the Vampire.*

1967. *Le Bal des Vampires.* Cadre-MGM, France, Great Britain; producer, Gene Gutowski; director, Roman Polanski; screenplay by Gerard Brack and Roman Polanski. Released in America as *The Fearless Vampire Killers or Pardon Me, But Your Teeth Are in My Neck.* A well-filmed satirical approach to vampires. Polanski correctly uses the occult symbols; ironically this was the last film played in by Sharon Tate—Polanski's wife and one of the victims in the Manson murder case.

1967. *A Taste of Blood.* Creative Film Enterprises, Inc., USA; producer, Herschell Gordon Lewis; director, H.G. Lewis; screenplay by Donald Standford, with characters based on those in Stoker's novel *Dracula.* An American, John Stone, unknowingly drinks the blood of his ancestor Count Dracula and becomes a vampire, killing the descendants of those who executed the original Dracula.

1968. *Dracula Has Risen from the Grave.* Hammer Films, Great Britain; producer, Aida Young; director, Freddie Francis; screenplay by John Elder. Christopher Lee's third appearance as Dracula, in a dull film with a garbled story line. Knocked from the battlements, Dracula is impaled on a huge stake with gore galore.

1968. *Le Viol du Vampire.* An ABC "television movie" presented by SNA; producer, Sam Selsky; director, Jean Rollin; screenplay by J. Rollin.

1969. *The Blood of Dracula's Castle.* Paragon International Film, Crown International, USA; producers, Al Adamson and Rex Carlton; director, Al Adamson; screenplay by Rex Carlton. A poor film.

1969. *Malenka la Vampire.* Victory Films SA (Madrid) and Cobra Film (Rome) Spain, Italy; director, Armando de Osorio.

1969. *The Blood Beast Terror.* Great Britain; producer, Arnold Miller; director, Vernon Sewell; screenplay by Peter Bryan.

1970. *Jonathan, Vampire Sterben Nicht.* Beta Films, Germany; director, Hans W. Geissendorfer; screenplay by H.W. Geissendorfer. An erotic film, freely adapted from Bram Stoker's novel.

1970. *Taste the Blood of Dracula.* Hammer-Warner Pathe, Great Britain; producer, Aida Young; director, Peter Sandy; screenplay, by John Elder (alias Anthony Hinds), based on characters in Stoker's novel *Dracula.* Christopher Lee played Dracula.

1970. *Count Dracula.* England-Spain; producer, Harry Alan Towers; director, Jesus Franco. Based on Stoker's novel. Dracula, played by Christopher Lee, sports a mustache as does Stoker's vampire.

1970. *Count Yorga, the Vampire.* Erica Films-American International Pictures, USA; producer, Michael MacReady; director, Bob Kelljan; screenplay by Bob Kelljan. Released in America as *Loves of Count Yorga.* Robert Quarry played the count, a vampire from Eastern Europe, who appears in a California setting in search of fresh blood. A success among the college youth.

1970. *Blood of Frankenstein.* USA; Zandor Vorkov played Count Dracula.

1970. *Lust for a Vampire.* Hammer Films, Great Britain; producers, Harry Fine and Michael Style; director, Jimmy Sangster; screenplay by Tudor Gates. Yutte Stensgaard played a character reminiscent of Le Fanu's Carmilla.

1970. *The Vampire Lovers.* Hammer Films, Great Britain; producers, Harry Fine and Michael Style; director, Roy Ward Baker; screenplay by Tudor Gates. This is the fourth film version of Le Fanu's "Carmilla." Ingrid Pitt as Carmilla played the role of a vampire who lives through three generations and raises havoc among the village inhabitants. Some of the faint lesbian suggestions in Le Fanu's novelette come through in this film.

1970. *Countess Dracula.* Hammer Films, Great Britain; producer, Alexander Paal; director, Peter Sandy; screenplay by Jeremy Paul. Ingrid Pitt had the lead as a female sadist who bathes in the blood of her victims.

1970. *Scars of Dracula.* Hammer Films, Great Britain; producer, Aida Young; director, Roy Ward Baker; screenplay by John Elder. Christopher Lee played Dracula. This film is particularly good in showing the ways in which the vampire stalks his victim and compels the victim to drink his blood.

1970. *Guess What Happened to Count Dracula?* A Merrick International Picture, USA; producer, Leo Rivers; executive producer, Laurence Merrick. The nadir of horror films. Blatant sexploitation. Made three times on the same set: once with actors wearing clothes, under the original title; secondly with actors in the buff in *Does Dracula Suck?*, and thirdly, as a degenerate romp under the title *Does Dracula Really . . . ?* No taste, no talent, bad filming techniques, and poor acting.

1971. *The Return of Count Yorga.* Director: Bob Kelljan. Superior sequel to the first *Count Yorga, the Vampire* film (1970). At the end of the film the count is destroyed, but one of his pursuers has become a vampire, so the cult lives on.

NOTE: See Chapter 8 for 1972 and current films.

In aceasta casă a locuit
între anii 1431–1435
domnitorul Tării Românești
VLAD DRACUL,
fiul lui
Mircea cel Batrin

Home of Vlad Dracul

Ruins of Castle Dracula

Exploring the ruins of Castle Dracula

Vlad Dracul

Dracula

A Biography of Vlad the Impaler
1431–1476

Introduction

After five centuries of nearly total oblivion, the historical Dracula has suddenly been rediscovered. Of recent date there have appeared no fewer than four books purporting to deal with the historical figure, including our own recently published *In Search of Dracula*. This has aptly been described by some as "a minor publishing phenomenon." Under the circumstances the reader may well question the publication of yet another book about the shadowy vampire king, immortalized by Bram Stoker's best-selling novel and by Bela Lugosi's renditions on the screen.

Of the four works claiming to have connections with.the history of the actual fifteenth-century personage, Raymond Rudorff's *The Dracula Archives* is a pure fanciful dramatic reconstruction, on the avowal of the author if not of its American-edition jacket, which claims the revelation of "firsthand documents." Gabriel Ronay's *The Truth about Dracula* should more honestly have been titled, *The Truth about Elizabeth Báthory*, since the meat of the book and the author's chief interests center on the bloodthirsty Hungarian seventeenth-century countess who, if not a vampire, may well deserve the title of the most cruel woman of history. Leonard Wolf's well-written *A Dream of Dracula* is indeed, as the title suggests, no more than a dream, dealing with the author's obsession with Dracula as a sex symbol in contemporary American society. Its connections with the fifteenth-century prince are dismissed in 4 pages (out of 304). Even the present authors' *In Search of Dracula* was by design a miniature encyclopedic and pictorial essay on all the ingredients of the Dracula story originating from Bram Stoker's 1897 novel. It includes a very brief historical sketch of the fifteenth-century Wallachian prince; it examines the ancient and separate vampire tradition of Transylvania; it sets Stoker's novel in its literary Gothic perspectives and provides a brief history of the Dracula films. Although the historical segment was written almost entirely with the help of primary sources, the intent of the publishers was not to burden the book with extensive footnotes and exhaustive bibliographies. The present study finds its raison d'être in answering the charges of some skeptics, who, because of the absence of a critical apparatus in the prior book, hastily concluded the story might have been dreamed up in McNally's and Florescu's fertile imaginations! At a more serious level the present study is aimed at the layman and scholar whose appetite has been whetted but not satiated by the incomplete research that has so far been done. Given the materials available, this represents the closest thing to a full-scale biography on Dracula in any language to date.

Dracula has aptly been described by one of Romania's foremost nineteenth-century historians, A. D. Xenopol, as one of the most fascinating figures in the nation's history. Yet beyond the confines of Romania, the personality of Dracula, whether as a new-style Renaissance condottiere, as a pre-Machiavellian patriot, as a tactician of war and of terror, or even as a sadist, commanded attention despite the overabundance of talent that the quattrocento produced.

Mention of a few dates will help integrate Dracula within the more familiar context of western Europe and stress connections. His native Romanian principality of Transylvania was thoroughly connected to Western political, economic, and social currents, and the concept of an "iron curtain" dividing East and West exists only in the imagination of a few "survey" teachers who find it convenient to end their lessons short of Vienna. Dracula was born about 1431; he ruled three times, briefly in 1448, from 1456 to 1462, and again during the last two months of 1476 shortly before his assassination. The most dramatic event of his time was the fall of Constantinople to the Turks in 1453—the capital of the East Roman world which had miraculously survived one thousand years after the fall of the Roman Empire in the West. This event so impressed the imagination of a few chroniclers of western Europe that generations of students were somewhat unscientifically brought up to recite by rote that the fall of Constantinople marked the end of the Middle Ages and the beginning of modern times. More significant for Dracula's country was the end of Serbian resistance six years later, which decidedly advanced the Turkish frontier to the common line of the Danube.

The probable year of Dracula's birth was marked by two memorable events in France. One was the burning of Joan of Arc as a witch in the public square of Rouen by an ecclesiastical court under English control. The other was the crowning of a ten-year-old boy, Henry VI, as the first English king in Paris.

Among the veterans who had been fighting in the armies of the Maid of Orleans against the English was a marshal of France, Gilles de Laval, Baron de Retz (or de Rais), the prototype of the ill-famed Bluebeard who was hung and burned alive near Nantes for his diabolical cruelties and massacre of children in his castle of Tiffauges in Brittany. The story of Bluebeard is to be found in the folklore of different lands in some variety, and there are distinctive analogies with the Dracula saga and not only in terms of cruelty.

In spite of the burning of a national hero and a heroine in the war against the English, two months after the fall of Constantinople, the last battle of the Hundred Years' War had been fought at Castillon in Guienne and won by France. The patriotic élan of the Orleans maid had helped bury feudal dissent and particularism and, with the exception of Burgundy, had helped secure the "natural frontiers." The only place where the English standard was still flying when Dracula began his principal reign in 1456 was at Calais. Fourteen fifty-six was the year when the harsh verdict against Joan was revised and she was pronounced innocent; it was also the year when Francois de Montcorbier (Villon), the greatest of the French lyric poets, wrote "Le Petit Testament," a fairly representative rendition of the period during which he lived. While Dracula was killing noblemen to eradicate feudal anarchy, Charles VII rather timidly, and Louis XI, "the Spider King," more forcibly in 1461, laid the foundations of a truly centralized, despotic state. The cruelty of the methods used to achieve this end were different only in degree.

In England a war was being fought to a conclusion—the last of the feudal wars—throughout the Dracula era, which helps account for England's absence from the Continent both in the west and in the east. The struggle between the two roses, the house of Lancaster partisans of the "red rose" and the house of York who fought for the "white rose," was fought from 1455 until 1485, well after Dracula's death, when a certain Henry Tudor, who had the blood of both families in his veins, was the victor at the battle of Bosworth field and thus launched the Island Kingdom on its glorious maritime and insular approach to politics and diplomacy. A few English pilgrims still continued in their medieval ways. One of them was William of Wey, who reported on Dracula's fame and fearful reputation on his way back from the Holy Land. Another Englishman, John Tiptoft, earl of Worcester, a former ambassador to Pope Pius II, even tried using Dracula's methods, placing people on stakes to put down an uprising in Lincolnshire in 1470, a shocking form of punishment unknown in the West and "contrarye to the lawe of the land . . . for the which the people . . . were gretely displesyd." Tiptoft was executed for his crimes that very year and labeled the "incarnation of a devil." The future Yorkist king Richard III, who was born in 1452, might equally have been given that title by the Tudor chroniclers of the following reign. Like Dracula, he was depicted as a monster, and like Dracula, he may have been excessively maligned.

Although England had lost the war in France, it was united within the limits of the island up to the Scottish border. Spain had not yet been solidly hewn into a nation and was still suffering the impact of the Reconquista from the Moors, not really completed until after Dracula's death—Granada fell only in 1492. The Spaniard of the period was still essentially medieval in his approach to life and politics, fanatically Catholic, a crusader by instinct, and despite the feudal resistance of the Cortes, willing to sacrifice his liberty for despotism. The two main components of the future Spanish state, however, looked in different directions, if for no other reason than the circumstances of geography. Castile under its king, Henry IV (1454-1474), looked westward to the Atlantic: the circumnavigation of Africa, the exploitation of the Far East, and the accidental discovery of a new continent. Christopher Columbus was born about the time that Dracula had become prince for the first time. With the new sophistication in map making and the technological improvements in navigation, he was able to sail as far as Iceland—the first lap on the more revolutionary journey that was to follow—at the time of Dracula's death. His intriguing and revolutionary plan to sail westward to reach the Far East was assuredly shaping up in his mind when Isabella, his future protectoress, ascended the throne of Castile on the death of her brother in 1474.

Aragon, the other chief principality, faced eastward and seemed intent on embarking on a premature form of *Orientpolitik:* the Balearic Islands first, Sardinia, and finally Sicily and Naples. The Aragonese viewed Turkish progress in the east Mediterranean with far greater misgivings than the Castilians, and Aragon must be considered as a potential crusading power in the East as well as in the Iberian peninsula.

Roughly at the time when Dracula was marrying a relative of the Hungarian king while technically under house detention in Hungary, a far more "historic" union created the Spanish kingdom. Upon their accession to the throne two years before Dracula died (1474), the two Catholic sovereigns, Ferdinand of Aragon and Isabella of Castile, controlled virtually all of Spain and created the framework for its future "golden age."

Fifteenth-century Italy, the headquarters of the Renaissance, can accurately be described as a "geographic expression." Niccolò Machiavelli was born (1469), and the amoral political principles of his *Prince* were being applied well ahead of publication, though there is no evidence of Italian patriotism among the warring republics and city-states. In the north the most prestigious family was the Medicis, who had made their money in banking—assuredly a symptom of the "modernism" of the age. Cosimo de' Medici became the self-styled sponsor of the classical Renaissance and ere long patronized at his Platonic Academy a few of the gentlemen scholars who chose to flee the beleaguered city of Constantinople. His grandson, Lorenzo the Magnificent, destroyed the last vestiges of constitutional independence, as his most bitter critic, Girolamo Savonarola—like Dracula, a premature Puritan—was entering the Dominican order the year before Dracula died.

In the rival principality of Milan another typical condottiere, Francesco Sforza, took over the city by a coup d'état after the death of his father-in-law, Filippo Maria Visconti (1450). His son, Galeazzo Maria, a villain of history not merely cruel but debauched, was assassinated on the steps of the Cathedral of Milan almost the very day—December 26, 1476—that Dracula was killed outside Bucharest.

The papacy, which controlled the central neck of the peninsula and Rome as a temporal power, was just recovering from some of the most dangerous crises in the history of the Roman Catholic church. Pope Eugenius IV had at least on paper put an end to the split between Eastern Orthodoxy and Catholicism, largely because of Turkish pressure at the council of Ferrara and Florence in 1438. His successor, Tommaso Parentucelli, who became Nicholas V, succeeded in healing the far more serious schism within the Western church by compelling the resignation of the rival pope in 1449 and introducing the dangerous precedent of constitutional government which has been threatening papal authority ever since. This splendid figure made Rome the headquarters of the Italian Renaissance; he collected Greek and Latin manuscripts, founded the Vatican library, patronized dangerous critics such as the humanist Lorenzo Valla, and began the reconstruction of St. Peter's in the style of a Roman basilica.

It was the pontificate of Enea Silvio de Piccolomini (Pius II, 1458-1464) that most closely coincides with Dracula's reign. He began his career as a libertine and a *literati* not devoid of talent and changed his ways only when he became a priest in 1446. If a modernist, Lord Acton calls him the founder of freedom of speech in Europe, Pius II was nevertheless enough of a medievalist to understand the threat of the conciliary movement to his authority and the dangers inherent in the Ottoman conquest for Christianity. From 1459 onward the pope repeatedly appealed to the Christian powers, which included Dracula, to join in a common crusade and raised the moneys to subsidize such a concerted movement. Pius II was sufficiently impressed with the extraordinary feat of the Wallachian prince in his campaign against the Turks to mention him in his memoirs. One of his successors, Sixtus IV, was so impressed with the heroic crusading exploits of Dracula's cousin, Stephen the Great, to give him the title Athleta Christi in 1474, two years before the brutal slaying of Dracula was reported in Rome.

In the southern end of the Italian peninsula and over Sicily, Aragonese power prevailed in the person of one of the most cruel despots of the Renaissance, the notorious Ferrante, whose crimes have been compared to those of Dracula. One gruesome hobby was that of mummifying his political victims and showing them to guests in the royal museum.

Even more complex than Italian politics was 'particularism' in Germany; including the bishoprics and free cities, there were well over three hundred Germanys in Dracula's time, and not all of them were of the same ethnic and linguistic background—Bohemia, for example was a Slavic state. The only common denominators within this amorphous medieval Holy Roman Empire, which according to the wits was neither very holy and entirely un-Roman, were the person of the emperor and the waning influence of the Catholic church. Unlike other Western states where the principle of primogeniture had been well established, emperors were elected—as in Dracula's Wallachia—by a special committee composed of three ecclesiastical and four lay states. The tendency was always to select "weak" candidates not likely to interfere with the power of the feudal states. Powerless within the Germanys, two dangers turned the eyes of successive emperors eastward and established contacts with Dracula and his father, Dracul, both of whom spent a good deal of time in the Germanic world. At the beginning of the fifteenth century the more imminent danger was the Czech Hussites who, even after the burning of Jan Hus at Constance (1415), constituted a religious, national, and social threat. Hussite armies were able to penetrate German soil in 1428. It was largely in order to combat this peril that Dracula's father was summoned by the Holy Roman Emperor Sigismund of the House of Luxembourg at Nürnberg in 1431. The other peril was the Turks.

From 1437 onward, the electors of the Germanys almost invariably selected the rulers of the tiny Austrian state for the imperial dignity. This compelled a shift in the focus of imperial policy, since Vienna, the new imperial capital, lay dangerously exposed to Turkish attack. Frederick III of the house of Hapsburg, the last emperor to be crowned at Rome (1452), had had intimate knowledge both of Dracula's crimes and of his heroic anti-Ottoman crusade from the pen of his Meistersinger, Michel Beheim, who composed his famous poem while both were residing at Wiener Neustadt in the winter of 1463, as the Turks were beginning their invasion of Bosnia and Herzegovina, two provinces very "sensitive" to Austrian security. The year after Dracula died, however, the son of Frederick III, Maximilian, married Mary of Burgundy, the first of a number of historic marriages that were to give the Hapsburgs the illusion that the domination of the universe could be achieved by marriage rather than by war

Three footnotes will round off the historical connections between the Renaissance and Dracula. Historians still speculate today as to who was the actual inventor of the new mobile metal type that made printing on a large scale possible. By 1465 this new type of printing had reached Italy, and within five years (1470), France. Caxton's press in England opened in 1477, the year after Dracula died. In 1480 the first Dracula newssheet was circulating in the Germanic world in the vernacular. Within two decades thirteen editions of the first version of the Dracula horror story were printed at Leipzig, Augsburg, Stuttgart, Strasbourg, and Nürnberg, perhaps the first best sellers in history. Whereas German pamphlets were possibly intended to blacken Dracula's reputation, or perhaps, simply to frighten or to amuse the reading public, in Russia the Dracula narrative was turned into an instrument justifying the despotism of Ivan III. The invention of gunpowder was also closely connected with the Renaissance period; it made killing easy and compelled tyrants like Dracula to add thickness to the walls of their fortifications. Finally the new Renaissance back-to-life style of portraiture has left us the first realistic color and oil reproduction of a Romanian prince.

The name "Dracula," "Dracole," or one of its numerous variants was fairly well established as a sobriquet in the chancelleries of kings, popes, princes, and even ordinary clerics and laymen. In fifteenth-century Europe Pope Pius II referred to the Romanian prince in his memoirs; the Hungarian chronicler Antonio Bonfinius mentioned "Dracula" atrocities in the official chronicle of the reign of the Hungarian king Matthias Corvinus; Kritoboulos of Imbros, the Greek defector who may have witnessed the fall of Constantinople, mentioned Dracula by name in his history of Mohammed the Conqueror. Turkish accounts, though one-sided, occasionally commend the courage of "Dîrakula-oglu." Other papal, Venetian, Genoese, and Milanese diplomats fill in the more subtle details about "Dracula," not always related in the German pamphlets, intended for the vulgar. Like many other rulers of the period—Louis XI, Richard III, Ferrante of Naples—Dracula, to say the least, enjoyed a "bad press," and most of the writings were written by political opponents. There can be no question, however, concerning the epithet under which he was known in his day.

One object of current historical and linguistic speculation is the origin of the sobriquet "Dracula." In essence the name derives from the epithet—"Dracul" (pronounced Dra—COOL in Romanian)— used by contemporaries to describe Dracula's father, Vlad II, of the Basarab princely family. There are two main interpretations of the reasons for that epithet. One links the "Dracul" with the devil: *drac* means devil in the Romanian language, and the suffix ul is the definitive article that is added at the end of words. Inevitably the question comes to mind why peasants or boyars should have associated "devil" with a prince generally known as a builder of churches and monasteries. One possible answer is that it was coined by enemies of that prince. Another is that the propagandists of his chancellery gave the reputation of "devil" currency to frighten and cower the people into obedience. A final explanation, which seems most far-fetched and can be corroborated only by further research, is that Dracul was indeed a wicked prince in league with the devil.

Most historians, and some philologists, however, have rallied around "the Dragon" theory of that epithet. According to this view, in 1431 Vlad II was invested by Emperor Sigismund of Luxembourg with the Order of the Dragon in a formal ceremony that took place at Nürnberg. The order, founded in 1418, entailed many obligations, which included wearing a dark costume as a sign of penance every Friday and wearing the insignia of the dragon at all times. The insignia consisted of a prostrate dragon, wings expanded, hanging on a cross, with its tail curled around the head and its back cleft in two. The green cross worn by the knights had an emblem that bore the motto of the society: "O quam misericors est Deus, justus et pius." The symbolism was designed to recall that Christ conquered the prince of hell by his death and resurrection. The wearing of this insignia could certainly not have passed unobserved by the people when Dracul came to the throne in 1436. Previous to his accession he had been minting coins from his Transylvanian retreat in Sighisoara bearing the dragon symbol on one side. The Romanian people therefore nicknamed Vlad II "Dracul" because he was a Draconist—the dragon being a symbol of Satan.

On all accounts Dracula, the son, whose given name was Vlad (Vlad III), simply inherited the name of his father and he was not so labeled because of his notorious cruelties. Professor Constantin C. Giurescu, the dean of Romanian historians, explains that "Dracula" belongs to the category of Romanian suffixes ending in -*ulea*, such as "mamulea," "tatulea," and "Radulea." "Dracula," or more accurately "Draculea," thus means son of the devil, just as "tatulea" means son of Tatul and "Radulea" means son of Radul—it is a diminutive, having nothing to do with feminine endings within fifteenth-century Romanian chancelleries, as some scholars have suggested. Dracula was the son of the devil either because his father was wicked, was looked upon as being wicked, was made to look wicked, or more probably because the order that he inherited from his father had a wicked symbol.

Romanian chroniclers writing 150 years after the events described used the epithet "Dracul" to describe the father and, illogically enough, did not use "Dracula" when referring to the son. Instead, they preferred the epithet "the Impaler," or

"Tepes" (*tse-pesh*—teapa means stake in Romanian)—in token recognition of Dracula's favorite method of imposing slow death. The nickname had already been used in Dracula's lifetime by Byzantine authors as well as by the Turks. When it came to choosing a cognomen, however, it seems that Dracula himself preferred the epithet "Draculea"; at least this is the way he signed at least three documents in later life at Sibiu. Since this was the name best known in his time, the present authors have chosen to respect the Western transliteration of Dracula's choice, contrary to the usage of Romanian historians who speak of Vlad "Tepes."

In spite of his fame in the eyes of contemporaries, Dracula has been paid scant attention by historians, whether they be Romanian or foreign. To this day both "Dracul," and "Dracula," remain vague, almost mythical characters. One answer for this negligence lies in the fact that Romania's first scientific historians were slow in writing definitive biographies about the nation's early personalities. Internal documentation was too scanty for genuine biographical data. Besides, the gathering of external sources did not begin in earnest until recent years, despite the prodigious, if somewhat unsystematized, pioneering efforts of Nicolae Iorga, Romania's greatest historian. The erstwhile chroniclers and even nineteenth-century Romantic historians were hardly scholars in our modern sense, and were often responsible for errors of chronology and even of names (Dracul and Dracula are often confused), errors that have been passed on uncritically to their successors.

By far the more serious difficulty is the total incompatibility of views concerning Dracula's basic character and reputation. What might be described as the negative tradition was re-created by the German historian Johann Christian von Engel, in his *History of Moldavia and Wallachia* (Halle, 1804), which follows along the line of the fifteenth-century German pamphleteers. The reactions of most Romanian historians from the nineteenth century onward were more positive. A few renowned Romanian scholars, however, such as Mihail Kogalniceanu (*History of Wallachia, of Moldavia and of the Transdanubian Wallachians*) vol. I [Berlin, 1837], Ion Bogdan, the author of the best known monograph on Dracula, *Vlad the Impaler and the German and Russian Narrations Concerning Him* (Bucharest, 1896), and even the Romanophile R. W. Seton–Watson (*A History of the Roumanians* [Cambridge, 1934]), consider Dracula as a degenerate, a monster of inhumanity, and an artist in crime who killed for the pleasure of killing and was comparable to the most disreputable personalities of history. On the other hand, the Romanian Transylvanian school of historians, including George Sincai, A. T. Laurian, and A. Florian; Romantics, such as Nicolae Balcescu; Romania's first scientific historian, A. D. Xenopol; the great Iorga and his most distinguished pupil, Constantin C. Giurescu, take issue with this interpretation. Although recognizing the fact of Dracula's mass impalements, they see them justified in the light of the need for destroying the anarchical power of the boyars, and the politics of *raison d'état*. Furthermore they point out that Dracula's actions were not substantially different from those of other condottieri. In the traditions of the Romanian people Dracula is considered a hero. The great poet of the nineteenth century, Mihail Eminescu, views him as the savior of the race and calls him back to life in one of his well-known verses, "The Third Letter," to redress the iniquities of his age with impaling techniques.

Much of the Dracula debate centers upon the further controversy over whether one may recognize the German and other fifteenth century newsletters as authentic historical sources, or whether such pamphlets were pure "fabrications" and Hungarian, German, or Russian plots meant either to defame Dracula's reputation or to serve political purposes of their own. It is said, for instance, that King Matthias Corvinus needed a pretext to arrest Dracula in 1462 and also to account for his own failure in joining Dracula's crusade after he had collected the funds placed at his disposal by the papacy. In the case of the Russian newssheet it is alleged that the Dracula pamphlet had the twofold objective of discouraging heresy and backsliding within the Orthodox church (Dracula was indicted for espousing the Roman Catholic faith) and to provide the stern example of mass impalement as a way of terrorizing the unruly nobility into obedience.

As against interpretations such as the above, there are at least three valid reasons, which can be briefly summarized here, for not discarding the "anecdotal narratives" too lightly.

1. One should observe the extraordinary coincidence of all Dracula narratives—whether written in German, Slavic, Latin, Turkish, or Greek—in basic theme and plot, if not in actual detail. Given their close coincidence in terms of publication, and taking language

and geographical barriers into account, this would tend to undermine the theory of a "common model" that would imply means of communications and translation that the fifteenth century did not possess. More pertinently still, there is an equal measure of coincidence between all foreign narratives and the oral traditions preserved by the Romanian peasants to this day. These traditions, like the Icelandic sagas, were handed down by word of mouth from one generation to another since the fifteenth century, at a time when Romanian did not exist as a literary language and when peasants could neither write nor read, let alone translate foreign accounts. Although exaggerated by time and distorted by transcription, these traditions could have been rooted in historical fact and probably lay at the basis of all Dracula narratives. Legends, after all, can serve historical science and archaeology. Let us recall that Heinrich Schliemann discovered Troy after the descriptions of Homer's *Iliad* provided the initial scent.

2.   The Dracula narratives are relevant by nature of the material that they contain as well as by their omissions. The accuracy of place names, down to the detail of an individual village or parish, implies authors with a good knowledge of Transylvania, as in the case of the German narrative, undoubtedly written by a refugee. On the other hand, the German narrative is silent on Dracula's fate in Hungary, since the author was no longer witness. Precisely the opposite is true of the Russian story, the author of which reveals details about Dracula's imprisonment in the Hungarian capital, where he undoubtedly resided, but knows next to nothing of Transylvanian atrocities, since he was not a witness. Similarly the Romanian oral tradition is strongest in relating the details of Dracula's reconstruction of his famous fortress, details that the peasants knew firsthand. They are silent, however, on Transylvanian impalements or the period of Hungarian captivity, which they could only know from hearsay.

3.   Finally authentic historical sources, both external and internal, tend to confirm the veracity of individual

episodes. The eradication of the nobleman Albu, mentioned in the German narrative, for example, can be confirmed and even dated by reference to the sudden disappearance of that aristocrat from the upper council. In addition, many of the dates mentioned in the narratives coincide with historical dates otherwise verified down to the day and the month of the year.

Apart from basic differences of interpretation concerning Dracula's character and role in history, controversy has centered on specific problems dealing with separate segments of his career, and on the origin of the Dracula narrative to which allusion has already been made. Debate on such questions of detail has been no less acrimonious. We have already made allusions to the polemic that has centered on the origin of the nickname "Dracula," begun by Professor Grigore Nandris over a decade ago in the *Slavonic and East European Review*. Discussion on the origin and value of the German stories was begun by G. C. Conduratu's brilliant thesis at Leipzig in 1903 (he took the German narrative very seriously), continued by Ion C. Karadja in 1931 (a pioneer in the collection of German Dracula prints) and more recently by G. Striedter (1961-1962), U. M. Schwob (1969), and S. Papacostea (1966), a recent partisan of the "Hungarian Plot" theory.

Far more acute and vindictive has been the debate centering on the authorship of the Russian story, and most of it has interested Slavicist and linguistic specialists rather than historians. The most widely held view is that of Professor I. S. L'urie (1964) and other Romanian Slavicists to the effect that the original author of the Slavic story was Feodor Kurytsin or a member of his suite, representatives of the Grand Duke, Ivan III, at Buda. Others, Pandele Olteanu (1960) and P. P. Panaitescu (1952), by a careful analysis of the language place names and other historical details, believe the author to have been a native Romanian from North Transylvania writing in Slavonic; yet others, such as V. A. Boldur (1971), believe that the narrative was composed by official command of Ivan III; finally, a few believe it was a South Slavic text.

Dracula's notorious campaign against the Turks has preoccupied the Romanian historian Barbu T. Cîmpina (1962). His interpretation, however, has not been accepted either in point of battle sequence or in terms of chronology by E. Tappe of the London School of Slavonic & East European Studies who is to publish his findings in 1974. There is a great deal of difference of opinion concerning the dates of Dracula's early imprisonment between Ilie Minea (monograph on Dracul 1929) and Matei Cazacu (1968), who challenges the much lengthier dates originally established by Minea. Few experts are in agreement on the details of Dracula's lengthy period of Hungarian imprisonment, the circumstances of his remarriage and his conversion to Catholicism, the length of detention, or even the place of incarceration. Most historians, like Bogdan for instance (1896), tend to accept Vísegràd as the place of imprisonment. Panaitescu, however (1952), translates Vísegràd as Vacz, a fortress outside Buda. Even more obscure is the origin of Dracula's principal portrait at Ambras. There is agreement it is a copy of an earlier work still being sought, but total difference of opinion on how it got to Innsbruck. Most mysterious is the problem of Dracula's empty tomb. The theory we have adopted, emitted by Dinu Rosetti following his excavations at Snagov in 1931, is one of a dozen and until more research is done represents sheer speculation.

Polemic notwithstanding, research on specific segments of the Dracula story is far from complete. Despite Anton Balota's excellent start (1962), there is still need for a good comparative study encompassing all the Dracula narratives, not only the Russian and German. The task begun by C. C. Giurescu (1922) and continued by Panait Panait and I. Cantacuzino (1970) of excavating Dracula churches, castles, and other mementos needs to be continued, and a good history of Dracula's castle still awaits a historian. The hunt for Dracula prints and manuscripts, which now command a high price, has barely begun, if our hunch that they were printed in best seller quantities is to be substantiated. The discovery of a new Dracula portrait by W. Peters at the Belvedere in Vienna in the summer of 1970 inevitably attests to the suspicion that still other paintings lurk in the shadows of basements and attics. The rare Leipzig print, discovered by L'urie, presenting Dracula's features and costume in totally different forms, suggests an earlier such prototype on canvas. In the field of Romanian folklore, in spite of the efforts of Petre Ispirescu (1937) and C. Radulescu-Codin (1922) and more recently of Mrs. G. Ene (1972), the specialists have merely scratched the surface, and this is even more true in the numerous gaps existing in Hungarian, Székely, South Slavic, Czech, and Slovak folklore.

With reference to gaps, there is still a documentary vacuum that is beginning to be filled with recent availability of the Ankara and Istanbul archives and the translation of relevant Turkish material into the Romanian language by Mihail Guboglu and Mustafa Mehmet. Still to be researched minutely are the Hungarian archives, those of Venice and Genoa, and above all, the Vatican archives, which alone might hold the golden key to many an enigma.

As should be obvious from the foregoing, research on the present book was a collective international and interdisciplinary undertaking. Two faculty Fulbrights, 1967 and 1968, three grants from the American Philosophical Society of Philadelphia (1969, 1970, 1971), one summer grant from the University of Bucharest, and one sabbatical gave the authors respite from their academic chores at Boston College.

Most of the actual study took place in Bucharest at the Library of the Academy of the Romanian Socialist Republic, which has photostats of Dracula's letters and edicts, the originals of which are at Sibiu and Brasov. Most of the documentation both external and internal is now published. Field trips were undertaken when necessary to most of the locations connected with Dracula's name, to plunge, even if a little, into the atmosphere of his times: the birthplace, Sighisoara, the capital city, Tîrgoviste, the castle, the presumed burial place, the monastery island of Snagov. Dracula was pursued to his Moldavian exile at Suceava, to his chief Transylvanian place of refuge at Sibiu. An attempt was made to reconstitute the destructive path of Dracula's anti-Saxon raids from village to village, and to travel the full course of the Danube from Giurgiu to Braila following the details of his famous campaign. Even potential Dracula excavation sites, including those of the fortress of Bucharest founded by Dracula in 1459, were carefully examined. Dracula's portraits at Ambras (near Innsbruck) and Vienna were studied with care, as were Dracula manuscripts and prints scattered in half a dozen German, French, and Russian cities. A visit to Vísegràd, the alleged place of Dracula's imprisonment, proved unrewarding; his name was not on the roster of political prisoners in King Matthias's time. Equally unfruitful was the search for Dracula's original portrait.

The list of credits is far too extensive to be mentioned at length in this introduction. Our debt to Professor Constantin C. Giurescu, professor at the University of Bucharest, George

Florescu, Romania's leading genealogist, Matei Cazacu, researcher at the Iorga Institute of Bucharest, Mihai Pop, director of the Folklore Institute, and Stefan Stefanescu, director of the Nicolae Iorga Institute, H. E. Corneliu Bogdan, Romania's ambassador in Washington, and Lidia Simion, at the time in charge of the external relations of the University of Bucharest, has already been acknowledged in our previous book.

In addition, among the historians we would like to single out for special gratitude, are Mihai Berza, director of the East European Institute of Bucharest and a leading expert in fifteenth century Romanian history, and Dinu Giurescu, the third generation in a distinguished line of historians who is currently writing a biography of Dracula's grandfather, Prince Mircea the Old. The authors were particularly struck by the acumen and true historical insight shown by local historians, village priests, and schoolmasters, such as the Reverend Ion Stanciulescu, the priest at the village of Arefu near Castle Dracula, and the Reverend G. Dumitriu, serving in one of the villages on Lake Snagov. Of the scholars in old Romanian literature, we feel indebted to Professor Dan Simonescu, of the University of Bucharest, who made available to us certain scarce materials coming from his personal library.

Among the Slavicists we consulted was Pandele Olteanu, whose theories concerning the Russian manuscripts we have alluded to. It is unfortunate that we were never able to undertake a field trip with Professor Olteanu to the castle region where he firmly believes that Dracula donations to peasant leaders are still to be found in individual households.

We used the services of many archaeologists but none so often as Professor Dinu Rosetti, the veteran of the 1931 excavation, who took us to his remote digging site at Cetateni, where he believed he had found yet another Dracula church.

Finally, a word of thanks is due to two folklorists: C. Eretescu, who accompanied Professor McNally in his recording of peasant tales in the castle region in the summer of 1969, and G. Ene, who has written a dissertation on the Dracula castle epic; to one specialist in the history of art, W. Peters, from Vienna, who has submitted a learned paper to us on his invaluable new portrait find; to the librarian of the Romanian Academy and noted literary critic, Serban Cioculescu, not only for making our research easy but for his invaluable insight into any period of Romanian history; to the director of the City

History Museum, Florian Georgescu, who allowed the Dracula mementos in his fine collection to be photographed; and finally, though by no means least, to the Reverend Cazacu, the secretary of the patriarch, who arranged our trips to various Dracula monasteries.

Despite extensive research, the authors do not feel they have written a definitive biography on Dracula, because too many pieces of the puzzle are still missing. Nor do they claim, as some critics have alleged in connection with the first book, to have been the first to have unraveled some aspects of the Dracula enigma. This book does represent the first comprehensive, annotated synthesis—the word "portrait," "sketch," or "medallion" describes it accurately—in which two historians have carefully analyzed all available historical, folkloric, narrative, and archaeological resources to the best of their abilities. As such the present work has both the merits and the defects of a pioneering venture and stands as a clear invitation for others to clarify the many problems left unresolved.

Beyond this the authors hope that this book will serve in casting a little light on the shadowed fifteenth-century struggle of a brave people for survival and independence, a struggle unfortunately rarely covered in our surveys of Western civilization, that has its small place in accounting for the very survival of our cultural legacy. Cruel or not, the personality of Dracula as well as the myth associated with his name, transcends national boundaries, and assumes European importance.

Finally, the value of the international aspects of this collective research, particularly the Romanian-American collaboration, ought to be stressed among historians as undoubtedly a first that deserves to be followed by others. In this tension-ridden world the authors feel it timely that historical investigation continues to cut across traditional national boundaries.

1

Fifteenth-Century Wallachia and the Ottoman Conquest in East Central Europe

Two separate negative traits in the history of fifteenth-century southeastern Europe had serious repercussions for several small, formerly independent states within that general area. On the one hand, there occurred a process of internal strife and disintegration caused by adverse warring feudal noble factions; on the other hand, the constantly ascending military power of the Ottoman Turks exploited such internal weaknesses to further imperial ambitions. This twin process resulted in the eventual collapse of proud medieval Balkan states, such as Bulgaria, Serbia, Albania, and eventually the Byzantine Empire, and caused their loss of independence for centuries to come. In the case of the central European states, Hungary, Austria, and Bohemia, the consequences were less drastic. One might nevertheless notice a definite weakening of military and economic power because of the anti-Ottoman crusade; in the case of Hungary there occurred a partial loss of territory. It was not until the battle of Mohács in 1526, however, that Suleiman the Magnificent was able to destroy Hungarian independence and not until 1529 (September 27-October 14) that he was able to lay siege to Vienna for the first time.

Although wedged between Hungarian power and the growing Turkish menace, the Romanian principality known as Wallachia in Slavonic documents, but called Muntenia ("the land of the mountains") or Tara Romaneasca ("the Romanian land") by the natives, had survived almost by a miracle as an independent state to the fifteenth century. In fact, the very survival of a distinctive Romanian ethnic group in the horseshoe of the Carpathian Mountains has quite justly been described by some historians as both an enigma and a historical miracle.[1] Having been conquered by Rome following two successive campaigns (A.D. 101 and 105-106) personally led by Emperor

Trajan, the proud Dacian warriors of King Decebal laid down their arms while their king took poison to avoid Roman captivity. A Roman occupation followed with massive migrations stemming from all provinces of the Pax Romana. This land of opportunity beyond the Danube was labeled "Dacia Felix," because of the rich agricultural soil of the Danube plain and the extensive mineral deposits (gold and silver) mined since ancient times in the Carpathian Mountains. Roman Dacia, although not exactly coincident with the frontiers of modern Romania, roughly included the Danube plain and extended beyond the Carpathian Mountains into the plateau of Transylvania. In modern terms one can visualize the backbone of the territory inhabited by the Romanians as forming a huge inverted S extending from the borders of modern Czechoslovakia down to the Danube, the S being formed by the mountains themselves. Roman power did not, however, extend either to the Black Sea or to the Dniester River. By A.D. 271, under heavy pressure from barbarian invaders, the legionaries and the Roman administration withdrew south of the Danube to the province of Moesia, the present territory of Bulgaria. Most Romanian historians argue that the bulk of the population, which had within this brief period of time been Latinized, at least in terms of language, stayed behind seeking shelter in the plateau of Transylvania beyond the Carpathian Mountains. Described by the early Hungarian chroniclers as the "land beyond the forest," Trans-silva, it has in the eyes of the Romanians always been considered as the "cradle of the race." The Daco-Romans lived and toiled on that plateau for a thousand years, tending their sheep and practicing agriculture to survive throughout the so-called dark ages of migratory invaders. Cautiously at first, then in small separate segments the Romanian populations began descending into the foothills, later resettling the Danube plain. In the case of Wallachia, the oldest Romanian principality, this migration occurred at the close of the thirteenth century. Around 1352 another migration took place from the Carpathian Mountains of Maramures, where ancient Romanian villages survive to this day, into Moldavia, Romania's second principality, located to the northeast between the Dniester River and the mountains.

Those Romanians who stayed in Transylvania, where they formed the bulk of the population, faced Hungarian domination from the establishment of the Arpadian kingdom (barring the small interlude of Turkish rule from 1525 to 1699) up to 1918.

When the principality of Wallachia was first established as a state, about 1290, its political organization was somewhat crude, though more advanced than political life in Transylvania proper where no state apparatus existed—a number of villages simply belonged to the authority of a local *cneaz* (a Slavonic term meaning chieftain).[2] From the end of the thirteenth century onward in Wallachia there were rulers who extended their authority over a wider area, although even their names are imprecise, and in biographical terms they are mere shadows. Basarab the Great (1310-1352), the second ruler of the land, can probably be described as the founder of the Wallachian state and of the dynasty; he was thus Dracula's first ancestor. Not much more can be said about him for lack of documentation.

More solid biographical detail exists for one of his successors, Prince Mircea the Old, grandfather of Dracula and Wallachia's seventh prince, who ruled from 1386 to 1418 and may be looked upon as a kind of Charlemagne of Romania.[3] From a military point of view, Mircea was successful in extending the frontier of his land to its maximum. These included two districts of Transylvania, the duchies of Amlas and Fagaras beyond the Carpathian Mountains to the north and west, and the banat of Severin to the southwest. On the northern frontier of Transylvania, Mircea constructed a number of small fortifications in the foothills of the Carpathians to protect his land against Hungarian power. To the south he extended his frontier to the Danube, building the powerful fortress of Giurgiu, a strategic defensive point against the Turks who were established in Bulgaria.[4] Dobrogea, the region bordering the Black Sea, which also included the Danube delta and was never conquered by Rome (it derives its name from a fourteenth-century local despot called Dobrotic), fell to Mircea in 1389, and he built several fortresses on the Black Sea to keep it safe. The Milcov River marked the frontier of Mircea's land to the northeast, separating Wallachia from Moldavia. The powerful fortress of Chilia on the Danube delta was in Mircea's possession.

During Mircea's reign the chief danger was the presence of the Turks. By sending a Wallachian detachment to help the Christian crusaders at the battle of Kosovo in 1389 (which signified the end of Serbian independence), Mircea was hopelessly compromised and singled out for punishment. With the final submission of Bulgaria and its transformation into a Turkish province in 1393, the Turkish menace faced Prince

Mircea across the Danube. For this reason the Wallachian prince participated in a famous crusade involving King Sigismund of Hungary, French and English knights, Germans from Nürnberg, a Byzantine contingent, and the Venetian fleet under the supreme command of the duke of Burgundy. On September 25, 1396, in front of the fortress of Nicopolis, ignoring Mircea's advice to lead the attack with his well-seasoned infantry, the Christians suffered an overwhelming disaster. After two decades of continued anti-Turkish resistance, Mircea accepted the inevitable: he recognized Turkish suzerainty and agreed to pay a tribute to the sultan. However, unlike the total submission of other Balkan states, the autonomy of his land was maintained intact. The contrast was not merely a matter of semantics; neighboring Balkan states such as Bulgaria were reduced to the status of *pashalik;* they saw their nobility destroyed by the confiscation of their land, "fiefs" were distributed to a Turkish feudal class, the *spahis,* and a regime of harsh financial and political exploitation was established under a native Turkish pasha. By way of contrast, in Wallachia, a native administration and an independent native church continued, the nobility lost none of its lands, and no Turk was allowed to settle on Romanian soil.[5]

With Mircea's death in 1418 there was a confusing period of rapid succession of princes, not all of them legitimate descendants of Mircea. The first was Vlad I (1394-1397), who briefly interrupted Mircea's reign and whose descendants are unknown to us. There followed: Mihail I, Mircea's oldest, legitimate son (1418-1420); Dan II (1420-1431), a nephew; Radu II, "the Bald," another of Mircea's sons who ruled for successive brief periods in 1421, 1423, 1424, and 1426-1427; Alexandru I (1431-1436), an illegitimate son, also known as Aldea; and finally Vlad Dracul in 1436, equally illegitimate, who was Dracula's father.[6]

During that time the chief danger to the state was not only internal disruption caused by the rapid change of princes but the erosion of power from without, from both the southeast and the northwest. For in addition to the Turkish menace, Wallachia became the object of Hungarian ambitions. By virtue of the election of King Sigismund of Luxembourg as Holy Roman Emperor in 1411, Hungary had been *de facto* united to the Holy Roman Empire, which gave the Arpadian kingdom increasing prestige. This was enhanced by the preeminent crusading role of János Hunyady, the powerful governor of Transylvania and regent of Hungary (1446-1456) and the lengthy and brilliant rule of his son Matthias, who ruled between 1458 and 1490 during the climax of the Hungarian cultural renaissance.[7] King Matthias attempted to continue the annexationist policy unsuccessfully begun two centuries earlier by the Arpadian dynasty in reducing Wallachia to the status of a vassal. The subjection of Wallachia to Hungarian rule and its use as a buffer state was strategically all the more important because of the continuing advance of the Turks along the Danube. Belgrade was the last major fortified city on the Danube before reaching Buda, the Hungarian capital.

Thus during the first half of the fifteenth century, Wallachia became a theater of conflict between Turks and Hungarians, each of the two powers attempting to impose a prince faithful to their respective cause. Notwithstanding this simultaneous twin assault from both east and west on its sovereignty, the Principality continued to maintain its autonomous national statehood and a semblance of national life, relying chiefly on diplomacy to survive, but when all else failed, occasionally resorting to war.

Wallachia was, by the standard of the mosaic of small east European independent states, a very large country if one added the two Transylvanian duchies of Fagaras and Amlas—altogether 48,000 square miles (roughly the state of New York), with a total population of half a million inhabitants, most of them Romanian, scattered in 3,220 villages and townships.[8] The vast majority lived in the country, particularly in the hilly Carpathian districts, the genuine historic region of the country. The Danubian plain, in those days still covered in part by extensive forests, was sparsely populated because of the danger of Turkish incursions. Many of the villages of Wallachia exist to the present day and still preserve their ancient historic names: Balteni, Tutana, Babele, Vacaresti, Ocnele Mari, Bistrita, etc. Some of the original Wallachian administrative districts take their names from the chief rivers flowing to the Danube: the Arges, Olt, Prahova, Ialomita, Dîmbovita, and Jiu.[9] The city of Tîrgoviste was the capital of Wallachia since 1385.[10] Earlier capitals located closer to the mountains, for reasons of security, were Cîmpulung, the oldest city and seat of the government (fourteenth century) and Curtea-de-Arges, the second state capital and ecclesiastical see (1330).[11] Braila, located on the Danube, was the largest commercial port.[12] Other important fifteenth-century commercial centers were Pitesti, Tîrgul-de-

Floci, Rîmnicul, Tîrgul-Jiu and Tîrgsor Vechi, a rather important inland trading center which has long since disappeared. Bucharest, much closer to the Danube, although in existence as an urban center, was too exposed to Turkish attack to acquire much significance. Few of these towns were fortified in the Western sense, the existing cities being at most surrounded by Western-style wooden palisades. Some of these so-called cities were, in point of fact, no more than extended villages. A handful of fortresses occupying remote strategic positions on the mountains, the Danube, or the sea, at the frontiers of the country, had been built by Dracula's predecessors but on a very small scale.[13] Unlike the powerful Teutonic fortresses to the north, their style was of Serbian or Byzantine origin. One, more powerful than most, was the fortress of Chilia on the northern branch of the Danubian delta, which occupied a particular strategic position on the Moldavian frontier.[14] Another important fortress, which had fallen to the Turks in 1416, was Giurgiu, built at great cost (with the revenues of the salt-mines) by Prince Mircea about 1390-95 to protect his southern flank against the Turks. There were smaller fortifications on the scale of the famous castle on the Arges, which tradition claims to have been built by Dracula.[15] These must be looked upon as places of refuge rather than as defensive bastions.

The two main classes of society were the boyars, a Slavic word referring to the landowning class, and the peasants. One could barely distinguish the beginnings of a middle estate. Whether these "boyars" were originally free landowners, wealthy village leaders, or the legitimate descendants of an old military caste, or whether they constituted a genuine native aristocracy in the west European sense of the term, is a problem best left to specialists.[16] However, the boyar's claim to represent a native aristocracy is at least partially substantiated by the fact that, from the very birth of the principality, or even before its foundation at the end of the thirteenth century, the term "boyar" was generally associated with tenure, not necessarily ownership of land. In that sense, boyars possessed vast domains comprising dozens of villages and constantly extended these by purchase, marriage, or princely donations. On these estates, like the feudal aristocracy in the West, the boyar was truly sovereign.

In addition to land, the upper echelons of the boyar hierarchy were also granted certain "titles" of Byzantine origin, roughly corresponding to our Cabinet offices. These titles were usually conferred in recognition of merit, military or otherwise, in the service of the prince. The first boyar of the land was the *ban*, or governor, of the province of Oltenia. The *vornic* was the chief judicial officer; the *vistier* in charge of finance; the *logofat* the head of the chancellery; the *spatar* commander of the prince's cavalry because he kept the prince's sword; the *paharnic*, the cupbearer, was responsible for the prince's wine; the *postelnic* provided for the prince's private quarters.[17] Each of these officers commanded the services of one or two aides, usually boyars of lesser importance. There were in addition countless court sinecures and lesser appointments. The important functions commanded substantial revenues. In the provinces the boyars were appointed governors of districts (the native term is *percalab*) and governors of castles. The title of greater boyar also entitled the holder of that rank to a seat in the state council (later to be known as *divan*) which was, in fact, together with the prince, the sovereign body of the land.[18] In this duality of government it was, at times, difficult to say precisely where true power lay.

On the surface the prince—*domnul is* the Romanian term for that title from the Latin *dominus* (the Slavic *voevod* was less frequently used)—possessed all the chief attributes of power. He was the formal sovereign or the chief executive and the head of the central and local administration; he raised and spent taxes, collected customs and revenues of the mines (both princely monopolies), dispensed justice by virtue of certain unwritten laws established for each social category, minted coins, and was commander in chief of the army and of the police. In spite of these formidable attributes, sovereign power was far from being as absolute as earlier historians have implied. Unlike royal authority in the West, primogeniture, one of the more important weapons in the development of centralized power, had not developed in Wallachia. In practice any relative of the prince, whether legitimate or not, could be selected by the boyar council. This situation often led to factional strife: various boyar factions supporting different princely candidates, a situation that, on occasion, could provoke anarchy, which was endemic with Wallachia's neighbors. The boyar council also had to be consulted to confirm important edicts and even to witness ordinary judicial transactions, such as land donations. These were written in ancient Slavonic, which was the official language of the time, rather than Romanian, the spoken language and also the language of command in the army. On these documents emanating from the prince's chancellery, one can find the signatures—usually the Christian name and the court title—of some of these boyars. In rare instances, we find the family name, which is usually derived from the family property.[19] The case of Vintila Florescu was one of the first in 1486. Very few of these original families of the land have survived. The aristocracy was constantly renewed by individual princes anxious to win the allegiance of a clientele of their own.

One instrument of princely power was the Romanian Orthodox church, vaguely linked to the patriarchy of Constantinople since the conversion of the country by missionaries of the Eastern church during the ninth century. In point of fact, since the foundation of the Wallachian principality, the Romanian church was to all intents and purposes autonomous under the rule of its native metropolitan of "Ungro-Wallachia Exarch of the Plains" (such was his formal title). He was no more than the first and only bishop of the land with his see at Curtea-de-Arges (during the fourteenth century there was another bishopric at Severin for brief intermittent periods of time). Theoretically his authority extended to those of the Orthodox faith in Transylvania. An ecclesiastical organization in the strict sense had to await the beginnings of the sixteenth century.

However, there existed a number of wealthy and powerful monastic foundations, such as Tismana, Govora, Cotmeana, Vodita, Cozia, Glavacioc, Dealul, Strudalea, Bolintinul, Visina, and Snagov—owning vast tracts of land and countless villages.[20] These monasteries also enjoyed immunities and privileges and were exempt from taxation. Princes occasionally resided and hid their treasures there. They often summoned the abbots to court. In times of war the individual monastery was compelled to help with financial contributions commensurate with its respective importance. In addition, there were a few Catholic abbeys belonging to the Dominican, Franciscan, Cistercian, and Benedictine orders; their precise history is still to be written. Undoubtedly some were offshoots of more powerful Transylvanian foundations across the mountains. The abbey of Cîrta in the Fagaras district of Transylvania, although theoretically subject to the princes of Wallachia, was a powerful fourteenth-century French Cistercian monastery.[21] Franciscan monasteries existed both at Cîmpulung and at Tîrgoviste, two of Wallachia's capitals. One abbey at Cîmpulung contains the tombstone of the Western knight, Lavrencius de Lôngo-Campo buried before 1300, and can still be seen today.[22] A Catholic bishop of Arges had also been briefly established in 1370. The Catholic church, however, had no influence in the boyar council. Catholicism was always considered "foreign" and was suspect less for religious than for political reasons, since the papacy was closely associated with Hungarian power.

It makes little sense to speak of a middle estate in pre-Dracula Wallachia. The development of certain towns, however, inevitably entailed commerce, and much of that commerce was in the hands of Transylvanian merchants, particularly the German merchants from the Saxon communities of Brasov and Sibiu, who enjoyed a virtual monopoly of trade in certain Wallachian cities.[23] In exchange for this monopoly the German merchants had to pay customs, which provided a lucrative revenue for the princely treasury. There were two traditional commercial roads from Transylvania into Wallachia, which followed two river passes across the mountains: one along the Olt River from Sibiu to Turnu Rosu, the frontier point; the other from Brasov to Rucar along the Dîmbovita River. Along these two passes, Transylvanian-manufactured goods found their way to such marketing towns as Tîrgsor and Pitesti. The obligation to buy and sell goods only in specific towns led to a considerable affluence of people during the trade-fair days of the year. From the prince's point of view it was important to be able to control foreign trade, since from the beginning of the fifteenth century there began to develop a native artisan and mercantile class looking to the prince for the protection of its interests against Transylvanian and other competition and demanding tariff protection.

In terms of origin, all Romanian peasants were originally free. In actual practice a good many of them became serfs on boyar and ecclesiastical estates. This loss of freedom can be studied by tracing the history of the free peasant village communities, which owned their property in common. Their gradual disappearance coincides with the emergence of a Romanian serf—the rumîni (the term should not be confused with the word "Romanian"). The problem of exactly how, and when, the peasant lost his freedom—the vexed question of the beginnings of serfdom in Wallachia and the birth of the concept of private property within the Romanian village—is a question that has been subjected to as much rationalization and parti pris as the polemic concerning the origins of the boyars.[24] During the fourteenth and fifteenth centuries there is little doubt, however, of the gradual "rumanization" of the peasants under boyar pressure. These serfs paid tithes *(dijma)*, one tenth of every variety of farm produce, to both princes and boyars. They paid the *bir*, a personal income tax, meant for the princely treasury, which increased yearly because of the larger tribute that had to be paid to Constantinople. The peasant had to contribute free work, building roads and bridges and constructing castles needed for defense. He had to work on the boyar's estate and to transport his master's goods. The serf, in fact, fulfilled a role very similar to that of his counterpart in the West—he was the state's and the boyar's "mule."

In cases of national emergency villages had to provide a number of foot soldiers, thus greatly increasing the military capacity of defending the country. During these emergencies, the peasants were recruited by the prince's officials in the districts, thus on a territorial-administrative rather than a feudal basis, which gave the prince enormous power over the nobility. This power was enhanced by the survival of a category of free landowning peasants, called *mosneni* in Wallachia, who were also directly responsible to the prince in case of war. In times of national emergency only a few retainers and servants fought under the banner of an individual boyar; thus the boyars represented but a small proportion of the national army. The Wallachian army therefore had a powerful popular and peasant character which contrasted with the feudal structure of the armies of neighboring states.[25] By comparison with these states, and even comparing figures with some of the powerful Western kingdoms such as France and England, the Wallachian army often reached as many as thirty to forty thousand men, for a total population of half a million, a much higher proportion of soldiers than states with populations in the millions. Barring the possibility of a major foreign war, however, the prince could rely only on a very small contingent of police, frontier, and custom forces for purposes of repression. There was, in addition, the prince's personal guard, the *curteni*, who functioned directly on the princely domains and fortresses. Unlike Western sovereigns, the prince had little land that he could call his own. The absence of military power made the struggle against the nobility difficult in times of peace. A prince could certainly punish "disloyal" boyars or ecclesiasts by confiscating their fortune or land, but only in certain well-specified cases: treason was one of them, the absence of an heir another, nonpayment of taxes yet a third.

Where confiscation was justified by law, the prince could and often would create a new boyar from among his adherents.

In conclusion one might say that a cursory glance at the Wallachian principality during the fifteenth century presents the historian with some rather unique characteristics that clearly distinguish this state from its neighbors. Although sharing many of the internal weaknesses of Serbia, Bulgaria, and even the Byzantine Empire, Wallachia was endowed with far more formidable military strength in defense of its independence. Unlike the weak feudal armies the Turks had encountered previously, Wallachia had an army of peasants determined to defend their native soil. The political weight of the boyar class could also be viewed as a factor of strength rather than a source of weakness in time of need. Although it was true that the prince could not maintain himself in power for long without boyar support, the deposition or execution of any prince did not necessarily spell national disaster or the end of legitimate rule. The boyar council simply took over and proceeded to elect a new ruler from within the family of the defunct prince, not necessarily a direct heir. Despite factionalism, a certain national sagacity ruled during the hour of danger, even among the boyars, which stood the principality in good stead. Peasants, boyars, and princes thus made their individual contributions to national survival. As in the case of Byzantium, diplomacy was always preferred to warfare, but the sword was resorted to when absolutely essential for survival.

---

[1] Title of book by George I. Bratianu, *Une enigme et un miracle historique: le peuple roumain* (Bucharest, 1937).

[2] The most recent monograph concerning the foundations of the principality of Wallachia is Stefan Stefanescu, *Tara Româneasca de la Basarab I "întemeitorul" pîna la Mihai Viteazul* (Bucharest, 1970).

[3] The definitive biography of Prince Mircea the Old will be a work by Dinu Giurescu, to be published in 1974.

[4] Prince Mircea the Old, Dracula's grandfather, built the original castle on the site of an older Genoese foundation about 1390. The fortress was captured by the Turks in 1416, though briefly restored to Vlad Dracul. It remained in Turkish hands until 1595 except for Dracula's brief sojourn in 1462. Michael the Brave, a descendant of Dracula's half brother, Vlad the Monk, burned and occupied Giurgiu in 1595. The Turks then rebuilt the fortress and had a garrison within it until the Treaty of Adrianople in 1829. The fort was used by the Turks as late at 1854. In spite of its thick walls (twenty-four feet wide in Dracula's time), nothing remains of the fortress today.

[5] It had been customary for Romanian historians to accept the capitulation treaties with Turkey as authentic, though there is still disagreement with regard

to dates. J. C. Filitti ascribes the Wallachian Capitulations to the year 1391 and 1460 and the Moldavian to a later period, 1512 and 1529. J. C. Filitti, *Les principautés roumaines sous l'occupation russe: le règlement organique* (Paris, 1934), pp. 3ff. Even if no capitulations existed on paper, the relationship between Wallachia and Turkey was clearly the result of some sort of an agreement based on contract.

[6] The only existing monograph on Dracul is I. Minea, *Vlad Dracul si vremea sa* (Iasi, 1929).

[7] Two different viewpoints on Hunyady: a Hungarian, L. Elékés, *Hunyady* (Budapest, 1952), and Camil Muresan. *Iancu de Hunedoara si vremea sa* (Bucharest, 1957, 1968). For his Wallachian policy also see Francisc Pall, "Interventia lui Iancu de Hunedoara în Tara Româneasca si Moldova în anii 1447-1448," *Studii* 16, no. 5 (1963): 1049-1072; I. Lespezeanu and L. Marcu, *Ioan Corvin de Hunedoara* (Bucharest, 1957). For his son Matthias see Elékés, *Mátyas es kora* (Budapest, 1956); Antonio Bonfinius, *Mátyas Kiraly* (Budapest, 1959).

[8] Ion Donat, "Asezarile omenesti din Tara Româneasca în secolul XIV-XVI," *Studii* 9, no. 6 (1956): 75-93.

[9] For a history of the districts see *Enciclopedia României*, vol. 2 (Bucharest, 1938).

[10] Tîrgoviste served as Wallachia's capital from 1330 until 1660, when the capital was moved to Bucharest. The ruins of the princely palace, which is first mentioned in a document in 1420, still exist, though the palace was greatly extended by Dracula's successors, Petru Cercel, Matei Basarab, and Constantin Brâncoveanu. The Turkish chroniclers claim the original fortress was of wood. About 1430, Tîrgoviste also became the residence of the Wallachian metropolitan, though we do not know which specific church was used as the cathedral. For a recent condensed history of the palace see N. Constantinescu and Cristian Moisescu, *Curtea domneasca din Tîrgoviste* (Bucharest, 1965).

[11] The actual church of Curtea-de-Arges was completed on December 10, 1526, during the reign of Prince Radu of Afumati (1522-1523, 1524-1529). In the course of time the church was extensively damaged by fire and neglect. Extensive repairs were begun in 1885 under the direction of a French architect, André Lecomte de Nouy, who did not understand the spirit of Romanian sixteenth-century architecture. See C. Nicolescu, "Le Monastère d'Arges," *Revue roumaine d'histoire*, no. 6 (1967): 961-971.

[12] The most recent monograph on Braila is Constantin C. Giurescu, *Istoricul orasului Braila din cele mai vechi timpuri pâna astazi* (Bucharest, 1968).

[13] There are few specialists in Romania on the early medieval castles. N. A. Constantinescu, "Cetatea Ciurgiu," *Mem. Ac. Rom.*, vol. 38 (Bucharest, 1916); Alexandru Husar, *Dincolo de ruine, cetati medievale* (Bucharest, 1959), pp. 36-47 (deals with Dracula's castle); Nicolae Iorga, *Studii istorice asupra Chiliei si cetatii Albe* (Bucharest, 1899), and "Cîteva cetati din Banatul de Severin, identificarea lor," *Studii* 15 (1962): 169, 173; G. Musceleanu, *Monumentele strabunilor din România* (Bucharest, 1873). Specifically on Dracula's castle see N. Apostolescu, *Cetatile lui Negru Voda si a lui Tepes* (Bucharest, 1910); Alexandru Lapedatu, "Doua vechi cetati românesti Poenari si Dâmbovita," *Bul. Com. Mon. Ist.* 3 (1910): 177-189; Rev. Ion St. Stanciulescu, "Cetatea lui Tepes, cetatea Poenari," manuscript.

[14] Old Chilia, located on the northern outlet of the Danube bearing the same name, is a very ancient establishment. Archaeologists working in the area found the site of an ancient Greek colony. The famous Milesian colony at Histria, where extensive excavations have been made recently by Professor Condurachi, is located just a few miles to the south. The town was fortified by Alexander the Great in the course of his campaign against the Getae. It was known in those days by the Greek merchants as Lykostomion ("mouth of the wolf"). Upon the ruins of the old Greek port, the Genoese built the city of Licostomo, and after 1405, the castle became a fortified Wallachian burgh and occupied a crucial

strategic importance. In 1476 Prince Steven the Great built a new fortress, New Chilia, which was captured by the Turks in 1484. Chilia is now located within the territory of the Soviet Union. Two good studies on Chilia are Iorga, *Studii istorice asupra Chiliei si Cetatii Albe*, chap. 2, and Constantin C. Giurescu, *Tîrguri sau orase si cetati Moldovene din secolul al X^{lea} pâna la mijlocul secolului al XVI^{lea}* (Bucharest, 1967), pp. 205-213.

[15] Both Baleanu and Cantacuzino chronicles refer to "Cetatea Poenari." N. Simache and Tr. Cristescu, *Letopisetul Cantacuzinesc*, vol. 2, and *Variante ale Letopisetului Cantacuzinesc*, vol. 3 (Buzau, 1942), p. 20. For the Baleanu Chronicle see Constantin Grescescu, ed., *Istoriile domnilor Tarii Românesti* (Bucharest, 1963), p. 15.

[16] Radu R. Florescu, *The Struggle against Russia in the Romanian Principalities* (Munich, 1962), p. 46.

[17] R. W. Seton-Watson, *A History of the Roumanians* (Cambridge, 1934, 1963), p. 30. In the course of time, these offices, in approximate order of importance, were those of *ban*, or governor, of Lower Wallachia (an old military title which became purely honorary); *vornic*, originally a subordinate of the *ban*, eventually in charge of the department of the interior; *vistier*, at one time entrusted with the prince's treasury, eventually minister of finance; *postelnic*, or chamberlain in charge of household guests, eventually minister of foreign affairs; *spatar*, in charge of horses, eventually commander in chief; *logofat*, in charge of the chancellery of the prince, eventually minister of justice. All these entitled the holder to first-class boyar rank. Boyars of the second class were associated with the humbler functions of *aga*, or chief of the capital's police; *paharnic*, or cupbearer; *stolnic*, or chief steward; *clucer*, in charge of army provisions; *caminar*, collector of customs; *comis*, master of the horse (the French *écuyer*). The military rank of general also gave a boyar right to second-class status, though that of *polcovnik* (colonel), *satrar* (in charge of the prince's tent), *pitar* (superintendent of the carriages), and *medelnicer* (one who receives petitions) belonged to the third class. It would be idle to seek Western counterparts to these titles, as has sometimes been done (e.g., *vornic* equal to count, *ban* to duke), since they were not hereditary. Descendants of boyars of the first class could claim the courtesy title of *mazil*, those of the second rank that of *neamuri*. The functionaries themselves correspond much more closely to Western feudal household dependents such as seneschal, constable, and chamberlain. Also see Stefan Stefanescu, "L'institution de la dignité de ban en Valachie," *Revue roumaine d'histoire* 4, no. 3 (May-June 1965): 413-425.

[18] For a history of the divan during the fifteenth century see George D. Florescu, *Divane domnesti din Muntenia în secolul al XV^{lea} dregatori si boeri*, vol. 1 (Bucharest, 1943).

[19] Vintila Florescu (1430-1490) was in turn: cupbearer, 1468; chancellor, 1478, 1480-1489; justicier, 1489; intendant, 1490; he was also a generous donor to Tismana monastery. For his genealogy see George D. Florescu, *Divane domnesti* (Genealogical Table I); Octavian Lecca, *Familiile boeresti române; istoric si genealogic dupa izvoare autentice* (Bucharest, 1899) p. 230; *Dictionar istoric* (Bucharest, 1937), p. 221. For a more recent genealogy of the Florescus: Octavian Lecca, *Genealogia a o suta de case din Tara Româneasca* (Bucharest, 1911), p. 37. The first mention of the Florescu family can be traced to a document dated June 5, 1483—a rather unique instance in that early period of the surname being mentioned. Bogdan Petriceicu Hasdeu, *Archiva historica a României*, vol. 1, pt 1 (Bucharest, 1865). Vintila Florescu's sister may have been the boyar wife of Radu the Handsome, according to a Florescu genealogy by G. D. Florescu.

[20] The best history of the Romanian church is undoubtedly Nicolae Iorga, *Istoria bisericii românesti*, 3 vols. (Bucharest, 1932). For a more recent history of the Wallachian church see *Istoria bisericii Romîne*, 2 vols. (Bucharest, 1957), a manual for theological seminaries.

21 Nicolae Iorga, *Istoria Romanilor: Cavalerii*, vol. 4 (Bucharest, 1937), p. 63. The Cistercian abbey of Cîrta (Kerz) in the Fagaras was founded in 1173 and later destroyed by the Tartars (1241).

22 Cimpulung (Dolgopol in ancient Slavonic) is one of the oldest cities in Wallachia. The city already existed at the beginning of the thirteenth century and was the state capital during the fourteenth century. The Order of the Teutonic Knights eventually constructed a larger stone castle which dominated the town. The latter was destroyed in 1225. The city initially contained a large Saxon population and had strong commercial ties with Brasov. See Rev. Ioan Rautescu, *Câmpulung-Muscel monografie istorica* (Campulung-Muscel, 1943), p. 3.

23 For economic history in general see Fritz Jickeli, "Der Handel der Siebenbürger Sachsen in seiner geschichtlichen Entwicklung," *Archiv des Vereins für Siebenbürgische Landeskunde*, n.f. 39, no. 1 (1915), p. 33–184. Herman Heinz, *Bückerkunde zur Volks-und Heimatforschung der Siebenbürgen Sachsen*, Buchreihe der Südostdeutschen Historischen Kommission, vol. 5 (Munich, 1960). Radu Manolescu, *Comertul Tarii Românesti si Moldovei cu Brasovul (secolele XIV-XVI)* (Bucharest, 1965). p. 53, 94. Though outdated, still of some use is G. Conduratu, *Incercari istorice; relatiile Tarii Romanesti si Moldovei cu Ungaria pâna la anul 1526* (Bucharest, 1898). Specifically on Bistrita, see N. Dan and S. Goldenberg, "Bistrita în secolul al XVI-lea si relatiile ei comerciale cu Moldova," St. Univ. Babes-Bolayai (now Cluj), *Historia* 9, no. 2 (1964): 23–83; Stefan Danila, *Bistrita; mic îndreptar istoric*, Cluj, 1967.

24 Those wishing to satisfy the peasant's claim to original possession of the land (hence in favor of expropriating the boyars) contend that the latter are merely descendants of village chieftains *(judec* or *cneaz)*. See Radu Rosetti, *La terre et les maîtres fonciers en Roumanie* (Bucharest, 1907). Opponents of this theory argue that the boyars constitute a hereditary nobility similar to that of the Poles and Hungarian Magyars. See Gh. Panu, *Un essai de mystification historique* (Bucharest, 1910), and *Recherches sur l'état des paysans dans les siècles passés* (Bucharest, 1910). Iorga, with his stress on peasant institutions, leans to the former view, and A. D. Xenopol, Romania's first scientific historian, to the latter; most historians are somewhere between the two. Some historians state that serfdom existed since the formation of the principalities and that the surviving free peasants were simply descendants of impoverished boyars. Gr. Tocilescu thinks they can be traced back to Roman veterans; T. Bolgiu, that they are unrewarded militiamen; R. Rosetti, that they are escaped serfs. The name for serf *(rumani* or *vecini)* appears in the earliest Slavonic documents. M. Emerit, *Les paysans roumains depuis le traité d'Andrianople jusqu'à la libération des terres, 1829-1864* (Paris, 1937), pp. 34–36.

25 N. Stoicescu, "Contribution à l'histoire de l'armée roumaine au Moyen Age (XVe siècle-première moitié du XVIIe siècle)," *Revue roumaine d'histoire* 6, no. 5 (September-October 1967): 731-763.

2

Vlad II, Dracul, and Dracula's Youth
(1437-1456)

Dracula was the son of Vlad II, Dracul, one of Prince Mircea's illegitimate sons, who ruled Wallachia from December 1436 to the autumn of 1442 and from the spring of 1443 to December 1447. Although historians know relatively little about Dracul—there exists only one monograph specifically centering upon his epoch—Dracula's character and deeds can hardly be understood without some knowledge of the adventurous life of the father whose career bears many similarities to that of Dracula himself.[1]

Vlad Dracul was born before 1395. One historian states that his mother may have been Princess Mara, the daughter of the powerful Hungarian noble family called Tomaj, which owned important estates in the Lake Balaton area of Hungary and in northeastern Transylvania. As a young man Dracul may have been sent as a hostage by Prince Mircea to Sigismund I of Luxembourg—king of Hungary (1387), Holy Roman Emperor (1411), king of Bohemia (1436)—as a token for Mircea's good faith in maintaining the treaty of alliance signed with Sigismund in 1395. It is thus likely that Dracul spent much of his youth at Buda and elsewhere in Germany at the court of the future Holy Roman Emperor. The latter, in fact, described Dracul as "in curia nostra educato."[2] The atmosphere of the Hungarian capital was evidently not to the liking of Mircea's son. In 1423 he tried to leave for Poland but was caught and returned to the king by the court of Ujvar. One reason for Dracul's attempted escape may have been a desire to secure the throne of his father, which, after the death of Mircea's eldest son, Mihail I, became in 1420 the object of bitter dispute between his legitimate and illegitimate brothers, Radu II, "the Bald," and Alexander I, nicknamed Aldea. An additional rival was Dan II, a cousin, whose successors maintained a lengthy feud with the descendents of Dracul, which was so bitter in intensity that some historians were tempted to label it the Draculesti-Danesti feud, even though both protagonists were actually members of the same Basarab family.[3] On this occasion the Hungarian court decided to support the cause of Dan II. Nevertheless, since given Turkish pressures one could never be certain of the loyalties of individual princes. It was expedient to keep a candidate "in reserve," in this instance Dracul himself, who was therefore kept under strict surveillance by Sigismund.

Not until 1430 do we find Dracul in Transylvania—when he wrote the first missive to the municipality of Brasov to the effect that he had been officially given the task of "watching the Transylvanian-Wallachian border," a position that can be described as commander of the frontier guard. His headquarters were in Sighisoara, where his house can still be seen today on a narrow lane in the old section of town. A small bronze plaque with Dracul's name and the dates of his residence (1430-1436), attached to the yellow stucco facade, is the only feature that distinguishes that particular house from the adjacent homes that likely belonged to the wealthy German merchants within the old fortified section of town. Dracul obtained a stipend from the Hungarian king and was granted the right of minting coins bearing the order of the dragon on one side, which had legal tender all over Transylvania. Some of these Dracul coins have survived.[4]

During January or February 1431, two important events took place in Nurnberg that were to give definite shape to Dracul's political ambitions. We are referring to Dracul's selection by the Hungarian king as the Wallachian princely candidate and to his investiture into the Order of the Dragon, which has been discussed in the introduction.[5]

Dracul's formal election as prince of Wallachia was the result of Dan II's increasingly ambivalent attitude toward Hungary, which Dracul as a wily politician had anticipated all along. A handful of dissatisfied anti-Danesti boyars had traveled to Nürnberg for the inauguration to give it a semblance of legitimacy. The second ceremony, Dracul's investiture as a "Draconist," deserves more extensive comment. The Order of the Dragon (Societas Draconis) had been established twelve years earlier on December 12, 1418, by King Sigismund, his second wife, Barbara von Eili, and some nobles of Hungary. Like so many of the secular orders of the late Middle Ages, it had various aims: (1) to fight against the infidel, (2) to defend the person and family of the founder, the sovereign of the order (in this case, Sigismund himself), and (3) to perpetuate the memory of the condemnation of the "heretic" Jan Hus at Constance (July 6, 1416). Because of his nominal selection as Prince of Wallachia and in view of the crucial strategic position of his principality after the fall of Serbia, it was logical to presume that of the twin foes of the order of the Dragon, Dracul's attention would be turned against the Turks. Loyalty to Sigismund was in any event taken for granted.

When Dracul returned to Sighisoara shortly after his double investiture, he learned that another half brother, Alexander Aldea, had just secured the Wallachian throne (February 1431) . He understood then that the support of Sigismund alone was insufficient to transform the empty title of prince, which he enjoyed, into a political reality. For that reason he tried to obtain the support of the sister Romanian principality of Moldavia, where two sons of Prince Alexander the Good, of the Musat family, ruled in rapid succession and conjointly—Ilias and Stefan. It was undoubtedly with the thought of future allies in mind that Dracul took as his second wife the sister of the two princes who is known to history only by her religious name, Eupraxia[6] This provides one explanation for the amity existing between both Moldavian and Wallachian ruling families from this point onwards. Both Ilias, Stefan and yet a third brother, the future prince Bogdan II, were after all Dracul's brothers-in-law. Whether with Moldavian or Hungarian support or singlehanded, Dracul occupied the Wallachian throne in December 1436, ousting his half brother Aldea.

Shortly after that time, Dracul was known to have had two sons, Mircea and Vlad, the future Dracula. The first document mentioning their existence is dated January 20, 1437.[7] At least three other sons were born subsequently: Radu, the future prince, known as the Handsome, who ruled from 1462-1475, Vlad the Monk, illegitimate, who ruled in 1481 and again from 1482 to 1495; and another son Mircea, also illegitimate, of whom we know next to nothing beyond the fact that he existed and is referred to in the Russian narrative. It is almost impossible to state with any kind of precision who the mothers of these boys were and when exactly the children were born. As far as the identity of the mother(s) is concerned, the historian Nicolae Iorga divides Dracul's sons into three separate groups. The elder two, Mircea and Dracula, were the fruit of a first marriage probably to an unknown Transylvanian. The next was Radu, born of the Moldavian Musat princess, and finally Vlad the Monk and Mircea were the sons of Caltuna, a native Wallachian woman, or of other mistresses.[8] Only the first Mircea, Dracula, and Radu were officially recognized by the father and are mentioned in official documents. The very fact that Dracul baptized two of his children by the same name (Mircea) implies that they must have been of different mothers.

With respect to the dates of birth of Dracul's children, the documents are a little more helpful even though not totally precise. In 1442 Walerand de Wavrin, a Burgundian crusader who had campaigned in Wallachia, stated that he had met one of Dracul's sons, Mircea, who was thirteen or fourteen years of age at the time. This would place Mircea's birth about 1428 or 1429. The last possible date for Dracula's birth is 1437, when we have four separate references to his existence. Dracula was thus born sometime between 1429 and 1437; we are inclined to push the date of his birth closer to 1429 than 1437 for one simple reason: since he first reigned in 1448, he must have at least been in advanced adolescence to command the necessary authority in difficult circumstances. If he was born in 1431, it would make him seventeen at the time when he first assumed power, a minimal respectable age. The first mention of a third son, Radu, occurs in a document dated August 2, 1439. Radu was probably five or six years younger than Dracula, thus born about 1435.[9] Since Dracul lived at Sighisoara from 1430 to 1436, there can be little doubt that both Dracula and Radu were born in the famous house that can be taken as Dracul's family homestead.

During the winter of 1436-1437 Dracul finally realized his dream, sanctioned by the Emperor since 1431: he became *de facto* prince of Wallachia and took up residence at Tîrgoviste. He took his new Moldavian wife and his three sons, Mircea, Dracula, and Radu, with him. For Dracula, life at his father's

court marked an altogether new kind of existence, very
dissimilar from provincial life in Sighisoara, which was to
last until his imprisonment by the Turks in 1442. These six years
also represent a significant phase for Dracula's future career
from a formative and educational point of view, which is most
relevant to his psychological makeup. Both formal education
and the accidents of politics were responsible in molding
Dracula's complex personality.

Dracula's early education, up to the age of seven at least,
took place in Transylvania within the entourage of his mother,
his stepmother, and that of other women from that province. It
is unlikely that the father had the means to send his sons to
Constantinople, as was the practice with some of the wealthier
boyar and princely families. At Tîrgoviste began Dracula's
apprenticeship for knighthood; he went through the various
echelons in the career of a young knight that were patterned
upon Western precedent. He was taught swimming, fencing,
jousting, archery, court etiquette, and above all horsemanship,
in which the young prince excelled.

We know very little about his intellectual training. The
first tutor engaged by his father was an elderly, highly
educated boyar who had fought on the Christian side at the
battle of Nicopolis under Enguerrand de Courcy, governor of
Picardy and marshal of France.[10] This boyar taught Dracula
Italian and possibly a smattering of French, in addition to the
humanities, the classics, and history. It is probable that
Dracula had learned some Hungarian in Transylvania, and
German as well. He needed his native Romanian, because it
was the language of command in the army. The official scribes
undoubtedly taught him the Cyrillic scrip and Slavonic, in use
at the prince's chancellery, and Latin, the language for
diplomatic correspondence. A new science that was soon to be
regularly taught to sons of princes was political theory and, in
particular, the theory of divine right and the polities of *raison
d'etat*. Both of these are reflected in the *Teachings of Neagoe
Basarab*, political words of wisdom compiled after Dracula's
time between 1512 and 1521, but accurately reflecting the
theory of government prevalent in fifteenth-century
Wallachia.[11] In essence those principles are not very different
from the principles of Machiavelli's *Prince*, written in 1513.

Some precepts in Machiavelli's text such as "It is much better for you to be feared than to be loved" fairly accurately reflected Dracula's future political philosophy.

In addition to formal training, Dracula's personality inevitably bore the stamp of the uncertain and shifting fortune of his father's political career. When finally secure on his throne in 1436, Dracul, a wily politician, sensed that the tenuous balance of power was rapidly moving to the advantage of the ambitious Turkish sultan, Murad II. Having destroyed the independence of both Serbia and Bulgaria, Murad II was contemplating the final blow against what was left of Byzantine independence. Thus, shortly after the death of his patron Sigismund, Dracul signed an alliance with the Turks in 1437. Sultan Murad received Dracul and three hundred of his boyars in the city of Brusa with great honor as the Wallachian prince made his official submission and paid the tribute, a yearly custom since Prince Mircea's time.[12] In 1438, the year of the great Transylvanian peasant revolt, Dracul accompanied Murad II on one of his frequent incursions into Transylvania, during which murdering, looting, and burning took place on a large scale. The Transylvanian mayors of the attacked cities and towns still believed that they could get a better deal from a conational than from the Turks. This explains the eagerness of the mayor of the town of Sebes to surrender specifically to Dracul, on condition that the lives of the townsmen be spared and that they not be carried into Turkish slavery. Dracul, according to his Dragon oath, was obligated to protect Christians against pagans, and on this occasion at least, he was able to save the town of Sebes from complete destruction.[13]

Dracul's pro-Turkish policies suddenly changed about 1442 in circumstances that are far from clear. Indeed, the precise succession of events in that year constitutes the most confused segment of that prince's career and are susceptible to varying interpretations.[14] Some of the confusion has arisen because contemporary observers have lumped together and failed to distinguish between the separate Turkish campaigns of 1438 and those of March and September 1442. A careful study of the documents that cover that year suggests the following sequel: During the month of November 1441 the newly appointed governors of Transylvania, Janos Hunyady and Nicholas Ujiak, came to Tîrgoviste with a mission from King Ladislas Posthumus, the newly elected king of Hungary (1440-1457), demanding the renewal of the crusades against the Turks which the Wallachians had forsaken since 1438. Persistent Turkish military pressure at Belgrade during 1440-1441 and the civil strife in Hungary made it imperative to secure Wallachian loyalties. The Hungarian further relied on the fact that as a member of the Order of the Dragon, it would be difficult for Dracul not to renew his pledges of allegiance to the Christian cause. As a realist, however, Dracul was only too well aware of the overwhelmingly strong military position of the Ottomans: by 1442 they controlled the whole line of the Danube, and their garrisons occupied important fortresses such as Giurgiu and Turnu, which were located on the Wallachian side of that river. Added to these logistical factors, an argument that had some bearing on Dracul's decision was the continued treacherous game played by the Hungarians who, although invoking the Wallachian prince's support, continued to give secret assurances to the rival candidate, Basarab, the son of Dan II, who had made his headquarters in Transylvania. This last factor may have been decisive in Dracul's final decision, at least in attempting to preserve his neutrality between Turks and Hungarians.

When the Turks under their commander, Mezid-Bey, finally entered Wallachia in March 1442, Dracul refused to take sides, allowing the Turkish troops free access into Transylvania. The result of this particular campaign is well known. The Turks suffered a disastrous defeat near Sibiu, and Mezid-Bey was killed (March 22, 1442). Angered by Dracul's neutrality, Hunyady pursued the Turkish army into Wallachia, chased Dracul out of his capital, and placed Basarab II, the new Hungarian protégé, on the throne (December 1442-Spring 1443). In these circumstances it was natural for Dracul to seek refuge on Turkish soil at the close of 1442 together with his family. He likely was placed under house detention at Gallipoli but not bound and in chains, as some authorities have stated.[15] In the spring of 1443 Dracul was reestablished on the Wallachian throne with Turkish help. Thus, technically, as previously stated, we may divide Dracul's rule into two, with the interruption of barely one year—1442—when he was a "guest" of the sultan. On the first occasion in 1436 Dracul had secured the throne with Hungarian help; on the second, in 1443, he was established prince with the help of the Turks—a fact that once again characterizes his ambivalent policies.[16]

Before lending their support, however, the Turks this time imposed certain conditions for Dracul's restoration which, in effect, amounted to a new treaty: he promised henceforth not to participate in any military action against his Turkish suzerain; he was to pay the usual tribute, to which was also added the obligation of sending yearly contingents of Wallachian children destined for the Turkish janissary corps. Given Dracul's previous unreliable record, one can readily sympathize with the Turkish concern for obtaining certain tangible guarantees obligating Dracul to keep promises that he had made and broken before. It was in these circumstances that the father made the difficult decision in the summer of 1444, to send his two younger sons, Dracula, barely aged twelve or thirteen at the time, and Radu, no more than nine years old, as a pledge for his future good conduct. Dracul took care to keep Mircea, the eldest and favored son, by his side.

Contemporary Turkish chronicles tell us that Dracula and his brother Radu were held captive at the fortress of Egrigöz ("crooked eyes" in Turkish) in the Kütahya district of the principality of Karaman in western Anatolia. The town, located almost three thousand feet above sea level, occupied a beautiful site on the southeastern slope of Mount Kociadag. The whole region was surrounded by small mountains and vast forests of oak, pine, and beech-trees, not dissimilar to the sub-Carpathian region of Wallachia in which the two princes had been brought up.[17] Dracula was to be imprisoned there until 1448, a period just short of four years. Undoubtedly this four-year period of captivity, during an impressionable age when character is molded, constituted at least as significant a segment in Dracula's psychological makeup as his formal education and training. This period is also obviously relevant in accounting for Dracula's cold and perhaps sadistic personality. Initially the circumstances of detention were lenient enough. Dracula and his brother were able to learn the Turkish language, got some training in Turkish methods of warfare, and completed their Byzantine education. Eventually, however, the dark cloud of renewed warfare between the Turks and Christian crusaders imposed difficult days upon the two young hostages. Circumstances, in fact, became extremely precarious.

In the autumn of 1444 the king of Hungary broke the armistice of Seghedin and started a new crusade against the Turks on the entreaties of the papal legate's Cardinal Giuliano Cesarini. When the crusades, led by János Hunyady and the young king of Poland, Ladislas III, finally set out on the ill-fated 1444 Varna campaign, Dracul was once again faced with Hobson's choice. This time as a Draconist he could hardly afford to remain neutral: the papacy tried to quiet his conscience by absolving him of his Turkish oath. Nevertheless, Dracul still attempted to steer a safe middle course, by refusing to participate personally in the campaign, and only sent a small contingent of four thousand soldiers under his son Mircea to collaborate with the Hungarian and Polish armies in their operations along the Danube. The Wallachians, however, were unable to save their allies from their tragic fate at Varna when Ladislas, king of Poland, and Cardinal Cesarini were killed. Michel Beheim, the fifteenth-century German troubadour in his song about the Varna crusade states that the Romanian contingent had fought well. He reminds his readers, nonetheless, of the possible fate of Dracul's two sons at Egrigoz.

> Welt er nit lassen von dem stritt
> e immer botschafft keme(n)
> So wolt er toten lassen
> Sein zwen bruder, die er denn hot
> gevangen an der waren tet,
> Wolt er sich streicz nit massen.[18]

The accuracy of this quotation is supported by a pitiful letter written by Dracul to the city elders of Brasov shortly before the Varna crusade. The father was fully aware of the danger to which he was exposing his two sons in Turkish captivity. "Please understand," he wrote, "that I have allowed my little children to be butchered for the sake of the Christian peace, in order that both I and my country may continue as vassal to the emperor."[19]

The two children were neither butchered nor blinded, as the father believed. Nor were they executed in the following year, 1445, when the Burgundian galleys under Walerand de Wavrin, sailed up the Danube attacking the Turkish fortresses of Turtucaia and capturing Giurgiu with the collaboration of Mircea and possibly even Dracul himself.[20] The purpose of that expedition was to avenge the Varna tragedy and find the bodies of the Polish king and the cardinal.

Although the two boys were not killed, their lives were certainly in danger, and the terms of their imprisonment were made harsher. A Turkish document states that Radu the handsomer of the two, had to defend his honor against no less a person than Sultan Murad II himself, dagger in hand.[21] We know that being weak-natured, he eventually succumbed to the pleasures of the harem and may have become a minion of both Sultans Murad II and Mohammed II. He eventually became Mohammed II's protégé and candidate to the Wallachian throne and did not leave Turkey until his accession to the throne in 1462 following Dracula's defeat. Submission was likely the price paid by Radu for his liberation, which probably took place in 1447.

Dracula proved a more difficult prisoner, and whatever duress he had to suffer hardened his character diamondlike. Being in perpetual awareness of the danger of assassination and, consequently, the dispensability of life, Dracula became a cynic. He also obtained some insight into the tortuous workings of the impressionable Turkish mind, and learned their use of terror. He was to use this knowledge to advantage in his subsequent career. In essence the two boys had been spared because Sultan Murad II preferred to use them as pawns who might yet compell Dracul's defection, even after the campaign of 1445. In the long run this presumption turned out to be correct.

In 1446 Dracul was officially informed of the fact that his sons had been spared, and the Turks offered to renew peace negotiations, which Dracul accepted: a new treaty was signed in the summer of 1447. In addition to the stipulations he previously assented to was an obligation to expel four thousand Bulgarians who had taken refuge on Wallachian soil during the 1445 campaign. The motive for Dracul's final tergiversation goes beyond a belated desire to save his two sons from death. It must be sought mainly in his dispute with the great crusading knight, Hunyady, who had barely escaped with his life from the battlefield of Varna.

Relations between Hunyady and Dracul had never been close. Initial mistrust was compounded by Dracul's ambivalent Turkish policies. In addition the Moldavian marriage previously referred to was not at all to the taste of the governor of Transylvania. Any consolidation of relations between the two Romanian principalities presented obstacles to Hungarian hegemony in Wallachia. However, the basic reason for Hunyady's decision to eliminate Dracul from the throne arose from the circumstances that followed the Christian debacle at Varna. In a council of war held somewhere in Dobrogea, both Dracul and Mircea held Hunyady personally responsible for the magnitude of the Christian disaster. "The Sultan goes hunting with a greater retinue," reproached the Wallachian prince, "than the 20,000 Christian crusaders," who merely relied upon the support of a shoddy Burgundian and Genoese fleet to prevent a Turkish landing in the Balkans. Young Mircea, in fact, argued for the trial and execution of Hunyady, who was *de facto* at the mercy of the Wallachians, the Polish and Hungarian contingents having virtually disintegrated. The Transylvanian governor's past services in behalf of the Christian cause and his international reputation undoubtedly saved his life. Dracul eventually insured his safe passage to his Transylvanian homeland.[22] If nothing else, the humiliation Hunyady endured personally, constituted a sufficient motive for the latter's decision to lead a punitive expedition against Dracul in November 1447.

In the last days of November a battle was fought somewhere south of Tîrgoviste. Dracul and his son Mircea were overwhelmingly defeated. Mircea was captured by enemy boyars, and the citizens of Tîrgoviste tortured and killed him by burying him alive.[23] His father, who succeeded in fleeing from the field of battle, was pursued and assassinated in the marshes of Balteni, not far from Bucharest.[24] Dracul may have been buried either at the monastery of Snagov, a foundation to which he had made numerous donations, or in an early wood chapel at the site of the Monastery of the Hill, no longer in existence. Dracul's tomb has never been found.

At the beginning of 1448 Hunyady was master of the political destinies of Wallachia. In December 1447 he proclaimed himself "prince of Wallachia," a fact that induced some Romanian historians to believe that he actually occupied the throne for a short period.[25] However, detailed study of the documents reveals that Hunyady never had the intention of becoming prince. On the contrary, he merely wished to establish one of his proteges on the throne, Vladislav II, yet another son of Dan II, a brother of Basarab II who had briefly reigned (1442-1443). The Danesti seemed more pliable instruments of Hungarian power. During the second half of December 1447 Hunyady was able to return to Transylvania having resolved his vendetta against Dracul.

The execution of Dracul had repercussions that once again affected the lives of Dracul's two sons, still hostages in Turkish hands, this time to their advantage. The sultan summoned them to Adrianople and told them that they were to be freed. In spite of his youthful age, Dracula was given an officer's rank within the Turkish army. He was also made to understand that he was considered by his Turkish masters as a potential candidate to his father's throne—his stern, unyielding character had evidently impressed them. The actual assumption to the Wallachian throne was to depend upon the first favorable political circumstances.

The expected opportunity occurred the following year, 1448, at the time when Hunyady was organizing a new offensive expedition against the Turks. Crossing the Danube during the month of September, the Transylvanian governor penetrated deep into Serbian territory, where he planned to effect a juncture with the army of the undefeated Albanian leader Scanderbeg (George Castriota). During the first half of October the Christian army reached the plateau known as Kosovo Polje ("the field of blackbirds") where the Serbs had suffered their historic defeat at the hands of Sultan Baiazid in 1389. As Hunyady was preparing to resume his advance, the Turkish army surprised the Christians—Turkish spies and scouts functioned much more efficiently than those of Hunyady. On October 17,18, and 19, a second battle of Kosovo took place, which resulted in a serious defeat for the Hungarian army and for the seven to eight thousand Wallachians personally led by Vladislav II, who had joined them. As at Varna, Hunyady was able to flee with great difficulty. On his way northward he was captured by the Serbian despot George Brancovic, who wished to avenge himself because his principality had suffered from looting during the passage of the Christian crusaders southward. Hunyady was imprisoned in the fortress of Semendria, from which he escaped in December 1448.[26]

During that time, Dracula did not remain idle. Heading a composite force of Turkish cavalry and a contingent of troops loaned to him by the neighboring pashas of Nicopolis and Varna, he invaded Wallachia in the absence of Vladislav II and simply occupied the throne at Tîrgoviste without a battle during the second half of October 1448.[27] Such a bold coup inevitably entailed severe repercussions from the Hungarian authorities. The vice-governor of Transylvania, Nicolae of Ocna, immediately asked Dracula to come to justify his usurpation of authority. He was also asked to give information on the whereabouts of Hunyady, who in the eyes of the uniformed Hungarian authorities had simply "disappeared" after the battle of Kosovo. In a letter still extant in the Brasov archives, which has hitherto been attributed by historians to Vladislav II, the wily princely incumbent responded to the effect that he could not attend the meeting with the Transylvanian vice-governor, since this would arouse the suspicions of the Turks, who would immediately kill him. He also answered that he was ignorant of Hunyady's whereabouts but thought he might have perished in battle. Referring to the battle of Kosovo, Dracula informed the Transylvanian vice-governor that he had some news from a Turkish functionary at Nicopolis whom Dracula ostensibly called his brother. If perchance Hunyady had survived and were he able to return to Transylvania, he (Dracula) would seek peaceful relations with the Transylvanian governor.

In this fascinating letter—the earlier written by the youthful prince—Dracula unfolded the state of his mind at the time: His father had been killed by Hunyady and Vladislav II; he had come to the throne with Turkish help; therefore, a rapprochement with Hungary was scarcely possible—the Turks would simply have deposed him from the Wallachian throne.[28]

Historians know next to nothing of Dracula's policy during this first reign, which had heretofore been totally ignored even by Romanian specialists. The punishment of the boyars who had betrayed his father, Dracul, was undoubtedly one of Dracula's first acts of legitimate revenge. These boyars were probably not too numerous within Wallachia itself, for many had accompanied Vladislav II during the Serbian campaign. Although Hunyady's situation was not known to him at the time, Dracula was concerned about his immediate political future, which did not look too promising. The Turkish victory over the Hungarians, however, had been dearly purchased, and Sultan Murad II had neglected to pursue the retreating and disintegrating Hungarian foe. During three days and three nights he remained on the field of battle to bury the Turkish dead. After that, in accordance with Turkish custom, the sultan ordered tables to be set and held a feast among the corpses of the vanquished, thus losing additional valuable time in pursuing his enemies.

Vladislav II, on the other hand, had succeeded in saving his life at the battle of Kosovo. With the remnants of his small contingent he started northward. Upon being informed of Dracula's usurpation, he decided to ignore Hunyady's plight and made no attempt to free the Transylvanian governor from Serbian captivity. Instead, after winning over the remnants of the Hungarian army, he crossed the Danube into Wallachia. Vladislav II found Dracula's army, defeated it, and compelled Dracula to flee south of the Danube during November 1448. However, the fortress of Giurgiu, which had in the interval been reconquered by the Turks, could not be recaptured. Turkish possession of Giurgiu is confirmed by the chronicles that refer to the repairs on the fortress effected by Karaja Bey, the governor of Rumelia during that time.[29]

All these events took place during the month of November 1448. For on December 7, 1448, it was known in the beleaguered Byzantine capital of Constantinople that Dracula had been defeated in a battle with the White Knight (le Chevalier Blanc). This was evidently a mistaken reference to Hunyady who, because of his Romanian origin, was known by the epithet "the Vlach" (le Blanc).[30] There were also rumors, equally devoid of foundation, circulating in Constantinople to the effect that Dracula had been decapitated following his defeat at the hands of Vladislav II. Such rumors notwithstanding, one fact was clear enough: Dracula had been overthrown and was compelled to seek refuge at Adrianople with his Turkish protectors. His first period of rule had lasted short of two months. Vladislav II was thus able to style himself once again prince of Wallachia. Hunyady, however, would not forgive him for his lack of support during the period of his Serbian captivity.

What happened to Dracula after that date? After some time spent at the court of Murad II, the "son of the dragon" fled to Moldavia where his father's brother-in-law and friend, Bogdan II, the father of Stephen the Great, Moldavia's most famous ruler, was prince. The precise family relationship between Dracula and Stephen the Great is the following: Since Dracul had taken as his second wife a sister of Bogdan II, the reigning Moldavian prince was Dracula's step-uncle and Stephen was his cousin. The Moldavian-Wallachian connection had been cemented even closer by political fate, which had compelled Bogdan some years before to seek refuge at Dracul's court in Tîrgoviste. In addition, Stephen the Great's mother, Princess Oltea, was of Wallachian origin, almost certainly related to the Draculas. These family ties themselves sufficiently account for the good reception Dracula received at the Moldavian court of Suceava, the capital city. Dracula lived at Suceava or in its vicinity from December 1448 until October 1451 in the company of Stephen, who was a few years younger. The two cousins were likely educated together by learned monks from neighboring monasteries and by chancellery scribes. Thus, Dracula was able to complete his interrupted formal education at a time when Moldavia was beginning to experience the initial impact of Renaissance culture coming from Italy by way of Poland and Hungary.[31] The sons of princes also became close friends and may have taken a formal oath obligating each one to assist the other in securing their respective thrones and maintaining each other in power.[32] In June 1450 the princes fought side by side under the banner of Prince Bogdan, defeating an invading Polish army at Crasna and thus gained valuable military experience.[33] These bonds of friendship formed during Dracula's period of

Moldavian exile lasted throughout his lifetime, the only shadow being Stephen's tergiversation in the summer of 1462.

Dracula's stay in Moldavia was suddenly terminated by the brutal assassination of Prince Bogdan II, by Peter Aron, the leader of a rival faction, in October 1451 at Reuseni, not far from Suceava.[34] In those circumstances, perhaps because of lack of alternatives, both Dracula and his cousin Stephen escaped to Transylvania and threw themselves on the mercy of none other than Hunyady, the man at least morally responsible for the assassination of Dracula's father and brother. An official of the governor first mentioned Dracula's presence on Transylvanian soil in February 1452.[35] From Hunyady's correspondence with the municipality of Brasov it is clear that Dracula was certainly *non persona grata* and was taking quite a chance. We possess a letter written by Hunyady on February 6, 1452, to the city elders of Brasov, in which he advises the citizens of that town as follows: "It is better that you capture him and chase him out of the country."[36] On March 30, 1452, Hunyady was able to report that Dracula had indeed returned to Moldavia, where he spent three additional years, since Peter Aron, the assassin of Bogdan II, had temporarily been chased out. It was in Moldavia that Dracula heard of the thunderbolt that sent a shiver through the spine of western Christendom—the fall of Constantinople to the Turks and the death of the last Byzantine Emperor, Constantine XI, of the Paleologus dynasty, on May 29, 1453. Only in 1455, upon Peter Aron's more permanently securing the Moldavian throne (he remained prince until the accession of Stephen in 1457), did Dracula once again seek refuge in Transylvania, asking Hunyady's permission to settle there. The governor of Transylvania was, at this time, at the height of his power. He had just added the title 'Count of Bistrita' (the anchor town mentioned in Bram Stoker's novel) to his numerous other dignities such as Ban of Severin, hereditary count of Timisoara, and governor general of Hungary.

At the time of this second request for asylum, circumstances played to the advantage of Dracula, since the relationship of Hunyady and his protege, Vladislav II, had suddenly cooled. The basic reason for this estrangement must be sought in Hunyady's unilateral seizure of the duchies of Amlas and

Fagaras—traditional fiefs of the Wallachian prince. Technically Amlas was given to the citizens of Sibiu, while the fortress of Fagaras was taken over by Hunyady himself.[37] This led to open hostilities with Vladislav II, seeking to regain control over individual townships within these two fiefs. The feud between Hunyady and Vladislav II occurred at a most inappropriate time. With the fall of Constantinople, Sultan Mohammed was determined to destroy what was left of independent eastern Europe. Since Wallachia was technically under Turkish suzerainty, the remaining Serbian cities still in Christian hands and independent Moldavia, perhaps even Hungary, were the next Turkish objectives in 1454-1455. One of the crucial strongpoints under Hunyady's control was the fortress of Belgrade. Lying at the confluence of the Danube and the Sava River, it protected the southern flank of the kingdom of Hungary. Hunyady's main preoccupation thus centered on the defense of this fortified city. Insofar as Wallachia was concerned, since Vladislav II had proven disloyal, Hunyady merely decided to entrust Dracula with the task of defending the Transylvanian border against any enemy, be they Turks or Wallachians, a situation almost identical to that enjoyed by Dracula's father some twenty years before. By way of precedent this arrangement traditionally meant implicit recognition of candidacy to the Wallachian throne itself, although it is likely that Hunyady still felt a certain reticence toward Dracula. In March 1456 he did introduce Dracula to the Hungarian king, Ladislas Posthumus, as the only candidate who could be trusted as prince of Wallachia. Given the dispute with Vladislav II, the serious military threat existing in Serbia, and the lack of other able candidates, Hunyady had little alternative than to gamble on Dracula's so-called loyalties to Hungary.[38]

Contrary to certain opinions expressed by Romanian historians, Dracula was definitely not yet prince of the land when Hunyady was felled by the plague just outside Belgrade at Zemun on August 11, 1456. It was only after the governor's death that Dracula set out with a small contingent of Wallachians (there were no Hungarians in his army) to try his chances on the field of battle and secure the Wallachian throne for the second time. After he crossed the Transylvanian mountains, a battle was fought somewhere on the Wallachian plain (we do not know precisely where), and Vladislav II was put to flight and later killed at Tîrgsor on August 20, as the Romanian chroniclers state, probably by pro-Dracula boyars and possibly by Dracula himself.[39] Dracula had sufficiently just motives for this act of revenge, since Vladislav II had been partially responsible for the death of both Dracul and Mircea, Dracula's father and brother, and had incited others to assassinate him while he sojourned in Transylvania. Vladislav II was buried in the Monastery of the Hill, where his tomb can still be seen together with the brief Slavonic inscription giving the precise date of his death.[40]

On September 6, 1456, Dracula took his formal oath to the Hungarian king and a few days later paid his formal act of vassalage in front of a Turkish delegation that had been sent to Tîrgoviste. The official investiture as prince likely took place in a ceremony on a field outside the capital during the early summer of 1456. Thus began Dracula's second and most important reign, which lasted until the fall of 1462.

---

[1] There exists only one monograph on Dracul's significant career: *Ilie Minea, Vlad Dracul si Vremea sa* (Iasi, 1929).

[2] Ibid, (1929), pp. 31, n. 1.

[3] The Danesti versus Dracula struggles were as brutal as the Serbian Obrenovic versus Karageorgevic feud and took more victims. For a history of that struggle see A. D. Xenopol, "Lupta între Draculesti si Danesti," An*alele Academiei Române Mem. Sect Ist.*, 2d ser., 30 (Bucharest, 1907). Xenopol dramatized this struggle, though it should be pointed out that both families descended from Prince Mircea the Old and were therefore related.

[4] "Moneta lui Vlad I Dracul, REVISTA DIN IASI 1, no. 4 (April 1908); 210-212.

[5] Discussion of the cognomen Dracul and Dracula has been dealt with in the Introduction. For the latest research on the Dracula name see Grigore Nandris, "A Philological Analysis of *Dracula* and Rumanian Place Names and Masculine Personal Names in a/ea," *Slavonic and East European Review* 37 (June 1959): 371-377. For the Order of the Dragon see *L'art européen vers 1400* (Vienna, 1962), pp. 373-374. One of the insignias can be found in Berlin, Ehemals Staatliches Museum, Kunstgewerbemuseum, inv. no. 0344, "Insignia of the Hungarian Chivalry of the Dragon." For the dragon insignia also see Society of the Dragon in Munich, Bayeriches National museum, inv. no. T3792. In that particular version the dragon is represented in the form of a ring supporting the cross with his wings folded on his back—a symbol of the victory of the cross over evil. This corresponds closely to the plastic interpretation of the insignia.

[6] For a controversy regarding Dracul's marriage. See Minea, Vlad Dracul. p. 74, n. 1.

[7] Two of Draculs sons, Mircea and Dracula, are mentioned for the first time in a document dated January 20, 1437, and again on August 2, August 10, and August 23, 1437. On August 2, 1439, a third son is mentioned, named Radu (Prince Radu the Handsome). P. P. Panaitescu and Damaschin Mioc, eds., *Documenta Romaniae Historica B. Tara Româneasca*, vol. 1, 1247-1500 (Bucharest, 1966), pp. 142-144 (doc. 80).

[8] "Le dit Seigneur de la Valaquie n'avait pour lors que un seul fils âge de XIII à XV ans." Nicolae Iorga, "Cronica lui Wavrin si Romanii," *Buletinul comisiei istorice a Romaniei*, vol. 4 (Bucharest, 1927), p. 63.

[9] Panaitescu and Mioc, *Documenta Romaniae*, vol. I, pp. 154-156 (doc. 89).

[10] This tutor had learned French from the Genoese who had bought him from the Turks after the battle of Nicopolis (1396). He must have been quite old, perhaps eighty, when in the service of Dracul. Minea, *Vlad Dracul*, p. 263, n. 1.

[11] These teachings, attributed to Prince Neagoe Basarab, were destined for his son Teodosie. The original text is in Slavonic. They had in part a religious, in part a historic character, and also contained practical words of advice on such questions as the organization of the army, the reception of foreign ambassadors, and the waging of war. *Istoria României*, vol. II (Bucharest, 1962), p. 1026. The most recent work is Dan Zamfirescu, "Invataturile lui Neagoe," *Studii si articole de literatura rômane veche* (Bucharest, 1967), p. 69. Also see P. P. Panaitescu, "Invataturile lui Neagoe Basarab. Problema autenticitatii," *Balcani*, V-1 (1942): 137-206. *The latest text is Florica Moisil and Dan Zamfirescu, Invataturile lui Neagoe Basarab catre fiul sau Theodosie* (Bucharest, 1970).

[12] Minea, Vlad Dracul, p. 157.

[13] Valuable information on the early Turkish expeditions to Transylvania are contained in F. Pall, "Stiri noi despre expeditiile turcesti din Transilvania în 1438," *Anuarul Institutului de istorie din Cluj*, vol. 1-2 (1958-1959): 9-28. Also see Minea, *Vlad Dracul*, pp. 160ff. The Turkish chroniclers Orudy-bin-Adil in the chronicle *Tevarih al-i Osman* and Mehmet Nesri in *Djihannuma Tarih-i al-i Osman* both speak of Dracul's 1438 campaign. See Mihail Guboglu and Mustafa Mehmet, *Cronici turcesti privind Tarile Române: extrase*, vol. 1 (Bucharest, 1966), pp. 53, 89. The mayor and two hundred leading Saxon burghers were forced by Dracula to surrender. They were later taken to Wallachia, but Dracul saw to it that they were safely returned to Transylvania. The lower classes were at first taken to Turkey, but eventually allowed to return. Only one tower of the city resisted and was burned. Nicolae Iorga, *Acte si fragmente cu privire la istoria Românilor*, vol. 3 (Bucharest, 1897), p. 8. Michael Doukas in Vasile Grecu, ed., *Historia Turco Bizantina* (Bucharest, 1958), also comments on the capture of Sebes.

[14] We have essentially adopted the chronology of Matei Cazacu (not Minea's) concerning the controversial chronology of the years 1442-1448. M. Cazacu, "Vlad Tepes Monografie istorica" (Bucharest, 1969), pp. 38-40. Also, see Cazacu, "O domnie necunoscuta a lui Vlad Tepes", *Viata Studenteasca*, December 11, 1967, pp. 1-3. Also, "La Valachie et la bataille de Kossovo," *Revue des Etudes Sud-Est Européennes*, 9 (1971): 131-152.

[15] Minea, *Vlad Dracul*, p. 79.

[16] Ibid., p. 192.

[17] The Turkish chronicles indicate the place of detention as being Egrigöz. Guboglu and Mehmet, *Cronici turcesti*, vol. I, pp. 88, 121, 311. The city of Egrigöz is known as Emet today.

[18] G. C. Conduratu, *Michael Beheim's Gedicht über den Woivoden Wlad II Dracul* (Bucharest, 1908), p. 29.

[19] Ion Bogdan, *Documente privitoare la relatiile Tarii românesti cu Brasovul si Tara Ungureasca în secolul XV si XVI*, vol. 1 (Bucharest, 1905), pp. 76-79 (no. 54).

[20] For the 1445 crusade see Walerand, Seigneur de Wavrin, *Anciennes chroniques d'Engleterre*, edited by Hardy (London, 1891).

[21] Nicolae Iorga, *Historie des roumains et de la romanité orientale*, vol. 3 (Bucharest, 1937), p. 74.

[22] Minea, *Vlad Dracul*, p. 253.

[23] On the role of Mircea and the circumstances of his death see Matei Cazacu, "Un viteaz frate a lui Vlad Tepes," *Viata studenteasca* (October 23, 1968), p. 8. Dracula's revenge on the boyars was directly inspired by the brutal slaying of Mircea by the citizens of Tîrgoviste.

[24] Apart from narrative chronicles (Wavrin's chronicle and Turkish chronicles), the only internal document referring to the assassination of Dracul is in the National Archives of Bucharest (Snagov Monastery, doc. 4, no. 1) , dated April 3, 1534, signed by Vlad the Drowned stating that he saw the book "of the old Vlad whose death caught him in the village of Balteni." *Documente privind istoria României*, B. Tara Româneasca, veacul XVI lea (Bucharest, 1956) pp. 156-157 (doc. 155). Also see Guboglu and Mehmet *Cronici turcesti*, vol. 1, p. 57. The only scholarly study on Balteni is Popescu-Bajenaru, *Un schit istoric, în codrul Vlasiei-Schitul Balteni si vecinitatile* (Bucharest, 1912). For legends on Dracul's death see Armand G. Constantinescu, Magul de la Snagov (Bucharest, n.d.), p. 119.

[25] Prof. C. C. Giurescu lists Hunyady as prince of Wallachia from December 16, 1447, to August 11, 1456. Constantin Giurescu and Dinu Giurescu, *Istoria Românilor* (Bucharest, 1971), p. 700. Also, see F. Pall, "Interventia lui Iancu de Hunedoara în Tara Româneasca si Moldova în anii 1447-1448," *Studii* 16, no. 5 (1963): 1049-1072.

[26] Cazacu, "O domnie necunoscuta a lui Vlad Tepes."

[27] Cazacu holds the view that the old historical tradition in accordance with which Dracula was placed upon the throne with Turkish help was based upon a confusion between Dracula's first reign in 1448 and the principal reign in 1456. Cazacu "Vlad Tepes" p. 49, n. 42.

[28] This letter is dated December 7, 1448, see in Cazacu, "La Valachie et la bataille de Kossovo," p. 135.

[29] Guboglu and Mehmet, *Cronici turcesti*, vol. 1, p. 58.

[30] See note 28 above.

[31] A good recent study on 15th century Moldavian education is: C. Cehodaru, "Invatamintul in Moldava, în secolul XV-XVIII Scoala Dominasca din Iasi," *Contributii la istoria desvolvarii Universitalii din Iasi* (Iasi, 1960), p. 9-32.

[32] Whether a formal contract existed or not is a moot point. Relations between the two cousins were certainly close, and when Dracula became prince, he sent a contingent of Wallachian soldiers to help Stephen secure the Moldavian throne (1457).

[33] Giurescu and Giurescu, *Istoria Românilor*, p. 299.

[34] For details of the assassination see Constantin Giurescu, ed., *Letopisetul Tarii Moldovei* (Bucharest, 1916), p. 41. Also see Nicolae Iorga, *Istoria lui Stefan cel Mare* (Bucharest, 1904), p. 54; V. Pîrvan, *Alexandru Voda si Bogdan*

Voda (Bucharest, 1904), pp. 57-61; N. Grigoras, *Din istoria diplomatiei Moldovenesti 1432-1457* (Iasi, 1948), pp. 171-172.

[35] Eudoxiu de Hurmuzacki, *Colectiune de documente privitoare la istoria românilor 1199-1849*, XV-I, no. 64 (Bucharest, 1876-1912), p. 37.

[36] On February 6, 1462, John Hunyady wrote to the municipality of Brasov about the peace he had signed with the Turks (which included the Wallachian Prince Vladislav II). In that letter he added the following passage, revealing that Dracula was not yet his candidate: "For as I have ascertained, the illustrious Prince Vlad, the legitimate son of Prince Dracul, who is now living amongst us seeks without our knowledge or will, to oppose himself against Vladislav II. Thus, we order you . . . not to give this Vlad hospitality . . . it is better that you capture him and chase him out of the country." Ibid.

[37] There exists a nondated letter addressed by Vladislav II to the leading citizens of Brasov in which he complains of the injustice committed by Hunyady in taking away the duchies of Amlas, and Fagaras from him. The letter is included in Bogdan, *Documente*, pp. 85-87.

[38] For further details on Hunyady's tergiversations with regards to his Wallachian protégés, see "The Chronicle of Thurocz," in I. G. Schwandtner, *Scriptores rerum Hungaricum*, vol. 1 (Tyrnavia, 1765), p. 268.

[39] For death of Vladislav II see Nicolae Iorga, *Inscriptii din bisericile României* vol. 1 (Bucharest, 1905), p. 100. The last document of Vladislav II is dated April 15, 1456.

[40] The Monastery of the Hill was actually a foundation of Prince Radu the Great (1500-1501), though most of the embellishments were completed by Neagoe Basarab. Prior to 1430, there existed a wooden church (known to us through a donation of Alexander Voiev) where the original family plot of the Draculas was located. Like all Dracula graves, it has long since disappeared. On the Monastery of the Hill see Constantin Balan, *Le monastère de Déalu* (translated from the Romanian) Bucharest, 1965.

3

Dracula's Principal Reign (1456-1462): Domestic and Transylvanian Policy

Documentary material on Dracula's domestic policies during his principal reign, 1456-1462, is scanty.[1] We possess only half a dozen missives or edicts signed by Dracula, granting immunities and other privileges to various beneficaries. A few oblique references to his reign are additionally contained in the internal documentation of some of Dracula's successors, and occasional information stems from diplomatic sources. The richest information by far is contained in the Transylvanian archives of Brasov and Sibiu. Dracula maintained a steady flow of correspondence with numerous officials of that province and with offlcialdom in both Transylvanian towns. This "Transylvanian correspondence," which technically should be labeled *external* (Transylvania belonged to the Hungarian kingdom), often bears on domestic events. Given the paucity of internal documentation, we have had to rely cum *grano salis* upon native oral tradition and folklore, as well as on external "anecdotal" history, to reconstruct the Impaler's internal policies. Finally, as in many instances where traditional historical material is lacking, archaeological investigation of Dracula's period, which has been greatly accelerated in recent years, comes to the historians' aid.

One invaluable help to biographical study is portraiture. Among fifteenth-century Romanian rulers, Dracula is the only one of whom we possess an oil portrait. It is located in one of the galleries in Castle Ambras in the Tyrol, evidently a copy of a lost original.[2] It may have been painted by a German artist during Dracula's imprisonment at Buda, which began in 1462. From the details of the portrait, Dracula could have been in his late thirties or early forties.

The history of this painting is of some interest. Ferdinand II, archduke of the Tyrol, who owned Castle Ambras during the sixteenth century, had a perverse hobby of collecting the portraits of moral and physical degenerates, in addition to celebrities. Odd human species living at the time were sought out by emissaries of the archduke and brought to the palace for sittings to complete their portraits; a few of the deformed became permanent members of the princely household at Ambras. This gave the court artist ample opportunity to paint numerous portraits of each. The paintings of villains who had died shortly before were purchased by art dealers in the pay of Ferdinand. To him, it was only important that the subjects be authentic personalities. In this way, here was assembled in that famous gallery one of the weirdest collections of paintings imaginable, a sort of Madame Tussaud museum on canvas.

There are portraits of giants, dwarfs, wild men, malformed people, mutilated faces, and other unsavory subjects. On canvas there is a savage baron of Münken, with his family, living in a cave; Gregor Baxi, a Hungarian nobleman who made medical history by surviving for one year with the end portion of a lance piercing his head through his right eye, distorting the remaining eye and other portions of his face; the "Wolfman" Gonzaga, from the Canary Islands, who caught a mysterious disease which covered him with hair from top to toe; and his two pathetic, hairy wolf children, one blond, the other dark-haired, and his normal, lovely, melancholic wife. In this company also hangs Dracula's portrait. We do not know the identity of the original fifteenth-century artist who painted Dracula. One fascinating theory of how the original portrait came to Innsbruck deserves to be briefly mentioned. Dracula's great-grandson, a physical degenerate by the name of Peter the Lame, who ruled Moldavia on three separate occasions during the second half of the sixteenth century, was compelled to abandon his throne and sought refuge in the Tyrolese Franciscan Monastery of Bolzano in the Tyrol, not far from Innsbruck.[3] The exile was able to take with him Dracula's portrait, as part of his inheritance. When Peter the Lame died at Zimmerlehen Castle in 1594, his son Stephen inherited the portrait. But Stephen was placed by Emperor Rudolph II in the hands of the powerful Jesuits at the height of their Counterreformation activities and entrusted to a Jesuit seminary in Innsbruck, where he died of consumption eight years after his father's death. Dracula's painting was one of the assets sequestered by the order. Given the archduke's taste for collecting evil characters, which was known to the Jesuits, Dracula's painting was either sold or donated by the society to Ferdinand's gallery at Ambras.

There exists another Dracula portrait in miniature, presently located in the Kunstgalerie in Vienna. In addition to the large portraits of his collection, Ferdinand kept in drawers over a thousand small paintings of famous personalities and villains originally at the Ambras Castle. The Dracula miniature is probably a copy of the larger portrait and was painted by an artist of the Nürnberg School.

In the summer of 1970, yet a third Dracula painting was found by a German-born Romanian researcher, W. Peters, who was accidentally visiting an exhibition of medieval paintings at the Belvedere Palace in Vienna.[4] The painting, entitled "Saint Andrew's Martyrdom," centers upon the crucifixion of Saint Andrew, with a Roman proconsul watching the crucifixion on one side, Dracula on the other. In the eyes of the anonymous Austrian painter, who probably completed the work around 1470, the Wallachian prince was a symbol of the spirit of evil. Crucifixion, after all, was another version of Dracula's favorite torture, impalement.

In addition to these three oil paintings we possess several primitive fifteenth-century German engravings of Dracula, the earliest such woodcuts of any Romanian prince, on the title page or cover of the German pamphlets.[5] Some of these depict Dracula alone. Although in one of these prints (Bamberg, 1491) Dracula is at least recognizable, the woodcuts show a subject in many respects different from the Ambras painting and are highly stylized. One frontispiece is colored (Nürnberg, 1488) and another more recently discovered by Professor I. L. L'urie (Leipzig) shows Dracula in war rather than court apparel. In some of the later woodcuts the artist deliberately attempted to deform Dracula's features. The most terrifying by far are two reproductions printed in Nürnberg (1449) and Strasbourg (1500) that portray Dracula dining and wining among the grotesquely impaled victims (some pierced through the navel or the heart) while an executioner, ax in hand, cuts off their limbs. Romanian tradition mentions a Dracula mural at one time located on an inner wall of the old princely church at Curtea-de-Arges. In accounting for its disappearance that same tradition states that a first bishop of the land, Filaret II, ordered Dracula's portrait to be painted over by that of a saintly figure to make manifest his disapproval of that prince's cruelty.[6]

A careful analysis of the existing copy of Dracula's Ambras portrait reflects the character of a cruel, tortured, and diseased man. One is immediately struck by the large, deep-set, dark green, and bloodshot eyes. They appear doubly framed by deep shadows below and long eyelashes and heavy arched brows above. The artist has captured a gaze that is distant and without real focus, albeit the expression is disdainful and imperious. Dracula's face is emaciated, with high cheekbones; his complexion is sallow and sickly, suggesting jaundice or liver complaints. Dracula's nose is strong and a little bent. The tightly sealed lower lip, which alone is visible, is red and disproportionately thick, indicating sensuality. The historians Ion Bogdan thought that the peculiar formation of the lower lip revealed an uncontrollable nervous twitch which may well have affected Dracula's whole face, in the manner of Peter the Great.[7] The face is otherwise finely chiseled and his features regular. By the standards of the day Dracula might be considered a handsome man, his jutting chin bespeaking strength of character. The moustache entirely covering his upper lip (he was otherwise clean shaven) is peculiarly elongated, straight, and meticulously curled at the ends, unlike the drooping moustache popular among most princes of the period. Between the painting and the literary description left to us there is disagreement concerning Dracula's complexion and the color of his hair. Given the graying auburn reflection on his moustache, one might guess that he was of light complexion. His locks are, at any rate, long, curled, and falling way below his shoulders. From a pronounced bulge below his chest, one might surmise that Dracula was far from gaunt and probably not very tall.

Dracula's costume is that of the Hungarian nobleman of the period. It is in no way Oriental or Turkish, emphasizing his predilections for the West. Covering the mantle and topped by gold brocade, is a wide sable collar, an expensive fur rarely seen on the shoulders of Romanian princes. According to the Vienna miniature, the mantle was closed with three large golden buttons interlaced with red filament. His headgear was made of red silk with nine rows of pearls at the lower extremity, very different from the tall ugly headdress worn by Turks and Greeks. The large star that held the pearls together is a yellow topaz stone, in the middle of which was a ruby between eight pearls. The topaz was used as a clasp holding a cluster of feathers, presumably ostrich.

Proof that the portrait was apparently taken from life is furnished by the only known detailed literary description of Dracula, which came from the pen of the papal legate to Buda, Nicolas Modrussa, who knew the prince during his Hungarian captivity and whose account, except in some details, coincides closely enough with our analysis of the painting:

> *He was not very tall, but very stocky and strong, with a cold and terrible appearance, a strong and aquiline nose, swollen nostrils, a thin and reddish face in which the very long eye lashes framed large wide-open green eyes; the bushy black eye brows made them appear threatening. His face and chin were shaven, but for a moustache. The swollen temples increased the bulk of his head. A bull's neck connected his head [to his body] from which black curly locks hung on his wide shouldered person.*[8]

The overall impression is that of a sensitive man with a keen and lively intelligence. It also reveals an overpowering, haughty, authoritarian personality with cruel instincts. Such speculations are reinforced by what we have already stated about Dracula's education and his belief in the divine right of kings, taught to him by his tutor. In addition we should never lose sight of the hardships he experienced during his youth, particularly as a prisoner of the Turks and as an exile in Moldavia and Transylvania.

Dracula's territories extended the full length and breadth of Wallachia and into the two Transylvanian duchies of Amlas and Fagaras, which reverted under his control after the death of Vladislav II. Because of his close ties with Transylvania, the affairs of that province continued to be magnets of attraction, and he was often compelled to cross the Fagaras mountains either by way of the pass at the fortress of Turnu Rosu on the road to Sibiu, or by way of the Dîmbovita at Rucar—where his frontier guards were stationed—in the direction of Brasov. In Wallachia proper, Dracula spent little time in the more ancient capitals of Cîmpulung and in the fourteenth-century ecclesiastical see of Curtea-de-Arges (we have no letter or edict from either place). He generally resided at the court of Tîrgoviste. In addition, he spent some time at Tîrgsor, the great inland commercial center and, toward the end of his reign, at Bucharest (the citadel of the Dîmbovita River, closer to the Danube and closer to the Turks). From letters we also have evidence of Dracula's residing at the monastery of Tismana and the fortress of Giurgiu.[9]

In Dracula's time the capital city and ecclesiastical see of Tîrgoviste was a sprawling town, with its outskirts spreading beyond the limits of the city walls. Like Louis XIV's Versailles,

Tîrgoviste was not only the seat of power but the center of the nation's social and cultural life. Immediately surrounding the modest palace of the prince were the Byzantine-style houses of the boyars and their more diminutive chapels, of which not a trace remains. Within the comparative security of walled palaces, the upper class, which included the prince, attempted to imitate the Constantinople-inspired etiquette of the royal court. Beyond the boyar houses and interspaced by gardens with stylish floral decorations—one contemporary described the city as one immense floral house—were located the more modest houses of the merchants and artisans and other dependents of the princely and boyar courts. As one crossed the city walls, there extended as far as the eye could see, a network of interconnecting lakes called *elesteile*, richly stocked with trout and other fish which provided for the entertainment and sporting activities of the rich. On the horizon one could vaguely discern the beginning of the hills of the sub-Carpathian region, known in Romania as the *podgorie*, essentially the country's wine-producing region. It is conceivable that on these hills to the north of the city there already existed in Dracula's time a small wooden monastery called Saint Nicolas of the Wines, long since gone—on the site of which the famous Monastery of the Hill was built, where many members of Dracula's family are buried. The city was also dominated by various churches; first the cathedral, of which we have lost all traces, where princes were invested by the first bishop of the land. We do not know how many Orthodox churches and monasteries existed in Dracula's time. The only ruins that have survived to our period are those of a fourteenth-century Franciscan church built on a knoll on the outskirts of the city. Judging from contemporary prints, the city itself was surrounded by a wall and moat, though it was never heavily fortified. The Turkish chronicler, the monk Ahmed, also known as Asîk, Pasa-Zade, in fact, speaks only of a wooden fortress.[10]

One of the chief surviving mementoes of Dracula's Tîrgoviste are the ruins of the princely palace, destroyed several times by the Turks and rebuilt twice: once by Peter "Earrings," 1583-1585, and again after the massive Turkish destruction in 1660, on a far more lavish scale, by Prince Constantine Brîncoveanu (1688-1714). In spite of these reconstructions, little remains of Dracula's palace except for the Chîndia tower, which was poorly restored during the nineteenth century, the ruins of the cellar, where individual rooms can still be noticed, and the remains of the foundation, indicating the general plan of the palace complex.[11] Dracula's palace can still be distinguished from the more massive remains of subsequent additions. The old palace was undoubtedly built by Prince Mircea at the close of the fourteenth century, although we do not know the original plans and can only speculate on its styling, which was probably Byzantine. The materials were brick and river stone. Some historians believe the palace had only one floor in addition to the basement. The north wing was bordered by the Chîndia watchtower, which may have been built by Dracula himself. The princely chapel was also located close-by and may have been connected by an underground passage to the main palace. To the west there lay the prince's gardens, undoubtedly extending beyond the walls. The whole palace complex was surrounded by tall and thick battlements, which may also have been the city walls in the fifteenth century. Under the bell tower to the southeast was the chief entrance to the courtyard. Of the main building itself, judging by the foundations, one can notice that it had a rectangular shape and that it was of modest proportions. Even the main room, presumably the notorious throne or banqueting room, was no longer than about forty feet. It was in this throne room that Dracula held boyar councils, received diplomats, and entertained foreign visitors. It was also in this hall that some of Dracula's famous massacres took place. The only serious problem raised by the exiguity of its size concerned the number of victims who may have perished in the actual room—it could hardly have encompassed more than a few hundred. We know next to nothing of the prince's private or working quarters beyond the fact that they were probably located on the first floor. His wife and children lived at Tîrgoviste, as well as the governor of the palace. Only the name of one such governor, Cîrstian, has been preserved in a document (1476).[12] The deep and roomy cellars built of stone— the walls were over twelve inches thick—have been preserved best. They may have contained the princely kitchens, the baths, the wine supply, and also served as torture chambers for prisoners in Dracula's time. The palace guard, minor officials, servants *(sluji)*, and courtiers *(curteni)* undoubtedly lived in other buildings. All in all, the importance of Tîrgoviste as a political and diplomatic center cannot be overemphasized: judicial and chancellery enactments, decisions affecting peace and war, massacres and impalements, and most of the surviving Dracula correspondence emanate from this palace.

In a legitimate sense one can credit Dracula as being the first prince of the land who used Bucharest as a princely residence and fortified the city, building its outer walls. These have been recently excavated and are located in the old market square of the city.[13] Situated sixty miles from the Danube, Bucharest occupied a strategic position on the Wallachian plain and was a natural stopping place on the road from Tîrgoviste to the Danube. The choice of this city as a princely residence also indicates the greater self-assurance of Wallachia's military might, gradually extending its way beyond the initial mountain hideout. Following extensive archaeological investigations, particularly in recent years, traces of urban life on the site of the present city of Bucharest have been found, dating perhaps since Neolithic times. We have many remains of the Dacian and Roman periods. With the birth of the Wallachian principality there is an initial mention of the "citadel of the Dîmbovita" (the river on which Bucharest is located) as early as 1386, though historians are not quite certain whether this so-called fortress actually coincides with Bucharest.[14] The name "Bucharest," which some historians have derived from a shepherd, fisherman, or boyar called Bucur, ostensibly the founder of the town, can also be traced to an ancient Dacian word, *bucurie*, meaning pleasure or satisfaction in Romanian. Such place names have been found in various parts of the country. Previous to Dracula's period we can only envisage Bucharest as a village or a series of connected villages, possibly protected by wooden palisades.

The initial Dracula document, commemorating this site refers to the location of "Iuxta Fluvium Acque Dîmbovita" and is dated June 13, 1458.[15] The first precise mention of the fortress *(castrum)* Bucharest is dated September 20, 1459.[16] The original document presently located at the Academy of the Romanian Socialist Republic exempts some minor boyars from certain feudal obligations. The fact that the first document (1458) simply states "near the river" and that the second document (September 20, 1459) specifies that there was a fortress, leads one to conclude that between these two dates Dracula fortified the city. A third document (granting boyar privileges) referring to the fortress of Bucharest in Dracula's time, is dated February 10, 1461.[17]

Even though Tîrgoviste continued to remain Dracula's official capital, the prince showed increasing preference for Bucharest, and during his brief third reign after the conquest of Tîrgoviste, he did not consider his campaign over until he had captured Bucharest in the late fall of 1476. We presume, in fact, that during his third reign Bucharest was *de facto* the official capital of the land. At that time Matthias Corvinus described the city to Pope Sixtus IV as the most powerful fortress of the land. It is near Bucharest itself that Dracula was killed and buried. The reason for this preference for Bucharest over Tîrgoviste is easily apparent: as a new town it was immune from the spirit of intrigue and anarchy rampant in the old capital, which Dracula had never really trusted; commercially it was a sound location between Tîrgsor and the Danube; strategically lying closer to the Turkish border, the fortress of Bucharest represented a first line of defense which could prevent deep Turkish penetration of the country.

Radu the Handsome, Dracula's brother, showed preference to Bucharest and formalized the *fait accompli* of changing his residence for different reasons—in order to be closer to his Turkish masters. Of twenty-five documents emitted by Radu the Handsome from 1462 to 1475, no fewer then eighteen were emitted from Bucharest. From that time until 1660, when the palace of Tîrgoviste was destroyed by the Turks, Bucharest remained a kind of winter capital. It then became the capital of Wallachia and subsequently the capital of modern Romania.

Dracula had an obsession for building walls. He probably built the walls of the citadel of Bucharest; he may have fortified the monastery of Snagov. He also built castles and small mountain fortresses, some of which have been permanently lost to the historian. One of the fortresses attributed to Dracula was the fortress of Gherghita in the Prahova mountain region, also known as the "new fortress" (some historians think that the "new fortress" was Bucharest), which acquired a certain importance during the reign of Dracula's brother, Radu. By far the most notorious of these fortifications was Castle Dracula, which has been immortalized in fiction by Bram Stoker (even though Stoker's location in northern Transylvania is incorrect).[18] Castle Dracula is also of particular interest to us because in its immediate vicinity (Capatîneni, Arefu, Corbeni, Poenari) there has grown a fascinating body of oral folkloric tradition concerning Dracula, which can with some justification be labeled "Dracula's Castle Epic." The castle itself is located to the north of the city of Curtea-de-Arges at the source of the river bearing that name, on the peak of a remote mountain rock in the foothills of the Fagaras range. Purposely perhaps, the castle, though lying close to the Transylvanian border, is not located on any of the well-traveled medieval routes or passes from Wallachia to Transylvania. It occupies an eerie position and has a commanding view. The castle can be described as remote and inaccessible. In the course of history, Dracula's castle was known by many names: Castro Agrish, Nerxs, Castro Lothovar, and in Romanian documents Castle Poenari, although technically it lies within the boundaries of the village community of Capatîneni.

More likely than not, the initial castle was built by one of the early Basarab princes in the fourteenth century. This is a far more likely possibility than the theory that ascribes its foundation to the Teutonic knight Count Colard in 1233.[19] According to that theory, it was a kind of observation outpost for the larger Transylvanian castle of Bran on the other side of the mountains. Because of its frontier position near the Hungarian border, the castle was certainly of strategic value to the early Wallachian princes. In the course of conflict with the Hungarians in the early fourteenth century, Castle Dracula undoubtedly changed hands many times. It was in the possession of Prince Basarab I (1310-1352), during his struggle to gain independence from Hungarian rule. One of the early Hungarian chronicles mentioning Castle Agrish recalls an attempted attack by the Hungarian king Charles Robert moving his forces northward from Curtea-de-Arges, which had been abandoned by the Wallachians. The Hungarian king and his army were apparently caught in a neatly laid ambush in the narrow gorges of the Arges just below the castle. By the accuracy of the Wallachian archers aiming from the castle and by boulders hurled down the mountain, the Hungarian army was destroyed within a matter of four days—November 9-13, 1330.[20] The castle was later definitely taken over by the Wallachian rulers and refortified.

One factor is more or less certain: When Dracula came to the throne in 1456, only ruins were left of the castle of the Arges. It had suffered irreparable damage at the hands of both Turkish and Tartar invaders. For Dracula, preoccupied as he was to find a shelter from his enemies from both within and without, as well as a desire to find a safe haven for his treasures, the castle on the Arges seemed an ideal spot. The decision to rebuild it was probably made in 1459, two years after his accession to the throne. The boyars were used as "slave labor," and they refortified the walls of the castle, according to local tradition, by dismantling the bricks and stones of another, older abandoned fortress sitting across the Arges River, the fortress of Poenari.[21] The persistent confusion of names can be accounted for by the fact that the castle of the Arges was built with the bricks and stones of Castle Poenari. Logically, however, from the time of the rebuilding, it ought to be referred to as Dracula's castle or Castle Dracula.

Castle Dracula is built on the plan of an irregular polygon, limited by the shape of the narrow plateau at the summit of the ridge, approximately 100 feet wide and 120 feet long. It is built in the style of a small Romanian mountain fortress of Byzantine and Serbian rather than Teutonic design. From what little remains, one can still detect the remains of two of its original five towers, connected by the remains of walls, resting under a heavy overgrowth of every variety of Carpathian wild flower, greenery, and fungi. The central or main tower, probably the oldest (perhaps built by Prince Radu I (1377-1383), is in the form of a prism. The other two, likely built by Dracula, are in the classical cylindrical form. The thickness of the walls, reinforced with brick on the outside, confirms the popular tradition that Dracula doubled the width of the walls of the earlier fortress. They were, in due course, able to withstand Turkish cannon fire. These walls, protected by conventional battlements, were originally quite high, and from afar give the impression of forming part of the mountain itself.

As one enters the castle threshold, one can clearly see that within the fortress there was little room for extensive maneuvering. Each tower could have housed only about twenty to thirty soldiers and an equal number of retainers and servants. Within the main courtyard it would have been difficult to drill over one hundred men. In the center of that courtyard were the remains of a well, no longer discernible, which was the source of the water supply. According to folklore, there was also a secret passage leading from the well into the bowels of the mountain, emerging in a cave on the banks of the Arges River.[22] This was probably Dracula's escape route, which may have been used in the autumn of 1462. The tunnel, say the peasants, was built solidly and reinforced with stones joined by grooves and by boards so as to prevent any mountain cave-ins. The grotto along the riverbanks of the Arges is referred to, by the villagers, as *pivnit*, which in Romanian means cellar, presumably, by a stretch of the imagination, the cellar of the castle deep inside the mountain. A few feet away from the entrance of the secret passage or well are the remains of a vault. This vault may well constitute the only vestige of a chapel on the site.

Of whatever else there was within the fortress, there is not a trace today, although the houses of the attendants, the princely stables, the pens for a variety of domestic animals providing the castle's needs, the various outhouses that were customarily erected in small fortifications of this nature, and the cell where Dracula's treasure was stored, are readily imagined. So is the drawbridge which evidently existed before the present slender wooden bridge. The towers had some openings, for the peasants' ballads speak of candlelight visible from a distance at night in the various towers.

Dracula's castle, although continuing to serve as a strategic defensive rampart for roughly a century following the prince's death, ceased after that time to command the attention of local folklore. The last surviving story concerning the castle, as related by the villagers of Arefu, refers to Dracula's campaign against the Turks in the summer of 1462, when the castle was partially dismantled.

At the end of the fifteenth century, Castle Dracula was used as a prison for political offenders. There is a document from the reign of Prince Radu the Great (1495-1508) which relates that his father, Vlad the Monk (1481, 1482-1495), captured a certain boyar by the name of Milea, who "was thrown into the dungeon of Dracula's former castle." The governor of the castle at the time was a boyar called Gherghina, who was a brother-in-law of Vlad the Monk and one of the few boyars who had remained loyal to Dracula.[23] In 1522 there took place the battle of Poenari, the local peasants apparently having revolted against their governor. Shortly thereafter the castle was taken over by the Hungarian kings, who exchanged it for two other fortresses in Transylvania. This occurred during the rule of Prince Radu the Great's son, yet another Radu, nicknamed "Afumati" (1522-1523).[24] The castle, however, was eventually abandoned during the sixteenth century. By that time the center of Wallachian power was gradually moving toward the Danube, that is, toward Bucharest. A castle that had existed primarily as a place of refuge from the boyars of Tîrgoviste had virtually lost all its importance. The fact that it lay in the hinterland away from all the commercial routes leading into Transylvania deprived it of any value even as a custom outpost. Even as a hideout it had become far too remote. Externally, Castle Dracula became entombed in a morass of Alpine overgrowth, but it continued to be enshrined permanently in popular memory linked to Dracula's name.

Only two sketches of the castle have been made from the knoll of Poenari facing it across the Arges River. The oldest painting is owed to a Swiss artist, Henri Trenk, who sketched the castle initially in 1860 (the picture is now located at the Fine Arts Museum in Bucharest). Another aquarelle can be attributed to I. Butculescu, an amateur historian who completed his picture in 1885.[25] At the time two of the castle's towers were still clearly discernible. The castle was finally virtually destroyed by an earthquake in 1916.

It is only within the last few years, perhaps because of interest generated by the Dracula story, that the Commission on Historic Monuments has belatedly decided to shore up the existing towers and battlements. The general thought seems to be less to reconstruct the castle than to avoid further deterioration. The walls, however, have been built up to what was probably their original size, two of the towers are quite visible, and the thickness of the brick walls can be noticed. Most of the work was completed in 1972.[26] With the addition of floodlights and the construction of steps, Castle Dracula will undoubtedly become a major tourist attraction. For Dracula, however, this edifice represented his mountain retreat, his eagle's nest in the Transylvanian Alps, essentially a place of refuge, where the awesome beauty of nature provided a substitute for the perfidy of men.

One of the central issues posed by Dracula's advent to power was his relationship to the boyar class. Since the birth of the principality, power had always been equally shared between princes and boyars. It should not be forgotten that given the brevity of individual reigns, the absence of primogeniture (no less than twelve inaugurations had taken place since 1418, which made for an average of just over two years per prince), and the fact that a boyar establishment had predated the very formation of the principality, effective political sovereignty tilted heavily in favor of the boyars, who were encroaching upon the power of the prince. Collective leadership, however, and all that it entails, was scarcely compatible with either Dracula's overpowering personality, his exalted concept of the role of sovereignty, or his premature idealization of the nation-state. Dracula in this respect may well be viewed in the light of the first modern Renaissance prince of the land, determined to crush the power of the nobility, centralize the administration of the state, and create a military force loyal only to himself, a process well-nigh completed in most of the Western states. There were, in addition, considerations of external policies in Dracula's persecution of the boyars. Their cynical realism on the whole tended toward a policy of appeasement toward the Turks, particularly after the fall of Constantinople, in 1453. In addition, from an eye-for-eye, tooth-for-tooth point of view, Dracula wished to settle a personal grievance against the boyar class, to avenge the brutal slaying of his father and the burial alive of his brother Mircea. Finally boyar partisans of Vladislav II and other princely candidates had to be eliminated from the body politic. The stage was thus set for a massive exemplary purge and for the destruction of hostile noble families.

We do not know for certain when the famous scene of the mass extermination of boyars occurred. It would be logical to presume that it took place at the very beginning of the reign, shortly after Dracula's inauguration. The few indirect references to the massacre, however, point to the spring of 1459, probably during the month of April, coinciding with the Easter festivities. In effect, the drama entailing the extermination of the boyars has two acts. Act I has been related by the Meistersinger Michel Beheim in a poem from which we have already quoted. Textually translating his lines from the German (verses 459-476), the troubador refers to the impalement of the boyars in the following words:

> He [Dracula] asked the assembled noblemen
> How many princes have you known?
> The latter answered
> Each as much as he knew best
> One believed that there had been thirty
> Another twenty
> Even the youngest thought there had been seven
> After having answered this question
> As I have just sung it
> Dracula said: tell me
> How do you explain the fact
> That you have had so many princes
> In your land?
> The guilt is entirely due to your shameful intrigues.[27]

Five hundred boyars were then seized by Dracula's attendants as they were finishing their meal in the banqueting hall of Tîrgoviste. This episode is also recalled by the Greek chronicler Chalkokondyles and by an anonymous Turkish historian.[28] As previously mentioned, the small size of the banquet hall at Tîrgoviste poses serious problems concerning the manner in which the boyars were seized (there was hardly room for five hundred boyars in addition to Dracula's palace guard). One might imagine that on their way out of the palace the boyars were apprehended in the courtyard. In any case they were impaled outside the palace, and beyond the city walls, and their disintegrating impaled carcasses no doubt contributed to Sultan Mohammed II's expression of admiration and awe when he reached Tîrgoviste in the summer of 1462.

Only the old boyars and their wives were killed in this manner. Insofar as the young and able-bodied were concerned, their punishment had a utilitarian purpose as well. One variant of the Cantacuzino Chronicle states:

He [Dracula] had found out that the boyars of Tîrgoviste had buried one of his brothers alive. In order to know the truth he searched for his brother in the grave and found him lying face downward. So when the day of Easter came, while all the citizens were feasting and the young ones were dancing, he surrounded them . . . led them together with their wives and children just as they were dressed up for Easter, to Poenari, where they were put to work until their clothes were torn and they were left naked.

Another version states that "they worked and toiled until their clothes fell off their backs." [29]

Local tradition has greatly embellished upon this episode, which is firmly anchored in popular folklore in the villages surrounding Castle Dracula. The boyar trek from Tîrgoviste to Poenari was a long and painful one. It undoubtedly claimed many victims long before they caught sight of the remains of the castle to be reconstructed. Within the villages surrounding the castle site, Dracula had given orders for brick ovens to be built, as well as lime kilns. The "concentration camp" at Poenari must have presented a strange sight to the peasants, since the boyars were still dressed in what was left of their fine Easter apparel. Under the threat of the whip, they formed a huge human chain extending from Poenari to the castle of the Arges, passing materials from hand to hand. While some worked up on the mountainside, others were busy making bricks, one vast army of slaves toiling, sweating, building the present castle. The story does not tell us how long the construction of the castle took, nor do we know the number of victims who fell down the precipice, under the burden of stones, or those who died from sheer fatigue. But the work went on under Dracula's vigilant eye until the castle was completed, possibly taking several months. In the eyes of the Wallachian peasants, as well as in the lines of the anecdotal histories, both these macabre episodes help establish Dracula's reputation for cruelty and were responsible for creating the nickname "the Impaler," which henceforth clung to his name.[30]

Another act of antiboyar persecution, related by Beheim, Chalkokondyeles, and in a Romanian document dated April 1, 1551, refers to the extermination of a single boyar family, that of a man called Albu the Great, possibly a partisan of Alexander Aldea, who at the head of a private army had revolted against Dracula. He was, in consequence, killed (probably impaled) together with his whole family.[31] Like the Italian condottieri, Dracula considered the family of an insubordinate boyar as "chips off the old block," equally dangerous as potential conspirators who might inherit the estate and wealth of their parents and thus would continue to intrigue against the throne. They had to be eradicated as well.

Further comment on Dracula's progressive elimination of the old boyar families is provided by a study of the names of the boyar council. Many of these boyars simply disappeared shortly after 1459. Those that survived, either by taking refuge in Transylvania or by fleeing to Turkey, reappear only after Dracula's demise in 1462, during the reign of Radu the Handsome.

To replace these boyars, Dracula created, "Napoleon style," a nobility of his own. Unlike the custom previously practiced when a nobleman's confiscated land was given to another member of the same family, Dracula offered the confiscated land and fortune to *new* men, some of them of plebeian origin, who owed their power entirely to the new prince and had a vested stake in the survival of the regime. A study of the names of the boyar council from 1456 to 1462 shows that almost 90 percent of the members were new.[32] The same principle applied to court functionaries, diplomatic envoys, governors of palaces and castles, all Dracula incumbents. A particularly useful addition to the new regime were the *viteji* mentioned in the Slavic story, a military nobility recruited from the free peasant landowning class *(mosneni)* who were honored on the field of battle for their bravery. They undoubtedly constituted the officerial corps in the large popular army that could be raised in times of danger. In addition to a wartime army, Dracula also needed an independent military force that he could use in times of peace for repression and policing purposes. For this task he could use his personal guard *(sluji)*, a fairly large frontier force stationed at Rucar, and those forces available in his castles under their individual governor, or *percalab*. By all these actions, aimed at emasculating the power of the boyars, Dracula's "modernism" had violated the spirit of the ancient prescriptive constitution of the land. Even in judicial matters, although we can find edicts that still bear boyar signatures, we may safely envisage Dracula adjudicating individual cases entirely on his own, in accordance with the Roman theory that the sovereign is the supreme fountain of justice. It is interesting to note in passing that for one so jealous of his own prerogatives, no Dracula coins have been found. Nevertheless, government without the boyars was a most precarious policy, which in the long run was ultimately responsible for Dracula's downfall.

In addition to creating a faithful and servile boyar clientele, it was the traditional policy of Wallachian princes, brought up in the Romanian Orthodox faith, to dominate the church at home and to use it as an instrument of despotism at home and national policy abroad. Since he was both Caesar and Pope, Dracula cowed the church into obedience by terror. Two incidents are sufficient to prove the point. Folkloric tradition maintains that one of the abbots of Snagov, according to tradition, Chesarie, Dracula's supposed confessor (1456-1462), dared make known his moral reprobation on the occasion of one massacre. Dracula had him impaled on the spot, and for some time the monks of Snagov fled from the monastery in fear of their lives.[33] There are sufficient anecdotes on this general theme, in both foreign and native narrative sources, to make us presume they were in essence, if not in detail, basically correct. In different words the story of the two Catholic monks who happened to be visiting the palace of Tîrgoviste centered upon the same theme. The monks opposed the idea that Dracula's control be extended over the Catholic church as well. On this particular occasion, Dracula showed the two monks the usual horror scenes in the courtyard below, strewn with impaled cadavers, evidently expecting some reaction. Instead of reproof, one monk meekly replied, "You are appointed by God to punish the evildoers." Dracula hardly expected this enunciation of the doctrine of divine right and consequently spared and rewarded the monk. His colleague, however, who had the moral strength and courage to disapprove of the crimes, was impaled on the spot.[34]

As a nationalist, Dracula eyed the immunities enjoyed by foreign monasteries located on Romanian soil with particular jealousy. Their power and influence offended his medieval patriotism. All Catholic monasteries on Wallachian soil were in his eyes suspect, because Catholicism (in Transylvania at least) had been used by the Hungarian kings as an instrument of Hungarian policy. The Franciscan, Benedictine, Cistercian, and Dominican orders on both sides of the Carpathians were considered papal or foreign enclaves which escaped national jurisdiction. National predilections also provide the explanation for Dracula's replacing the French abbot of the powerful Cistercian monastery of Cîrta in the Fagaras district, who had been appointed by his father, with a native incumbent from Tîrgoviste.[35]

Of Dracula's innermost religious convictions and practices, little is known. We presume that his religion was not deep, that it did not arise from any profound theological convictions, and that it had little bearing on his personal behavior. However, in spite of a certain cynicism toward the church militant, characteristic of the period at least according to anecdotal history, Dracula was often seen in the company of Greek Orthodox and Catholic priests and monks.[36] He was known to be particularly fond of the monastery of Tismana and of Snagov, both of which he often visited. Dracula also liked ritual, a characteristic trait of Orthodox believers. Even when he imposed the death sentence, he insisted upon proper ceremony for his victims and a Christian burial. As a member of the Orthodox faith, Dracula was also sufficiently pre-Lutheran to believe that good works, more than faith, particularly the building of a monastery, could atone for evil. In his tortured mind cruelty and religiosity were deeply intertwined, and Dracula would occasionally justify a crime using theological arguments. In this respect there are indications of a deeper morbid religiosity in the Dracula family. Dracula's half brother, Vlad, became a monk.[37] Other members of the family were deeply immersed or involved in pious deeds and religious exercises and vocations. Radu the Great, for example, Vlad the Monk's son, laid down the first ecclesiastical organization in Wallachia.[38] Dracula himself, his Renaissance condottiere instincts notwithstanding, was enough of a medievalist to take his Dragon oath seriously, as a Christian crusader against the Infidel, a cause that western Europe had long since forsaken.

Patronage—the endowment of land and the granting of immunities and other privileges to monasteries and the building of new religious edifices—was the church's official reward for passive and submissive attitudes. The old Romanian chronicles, as well as oral tradition, credit Dracula with the foundation of several monasteries, the most famous of which was the monastery of Snagov, where Dracula allegedly lies buried. The older Romanian historians have accepted the fact that Snagov was a Dracula foundation. Recent archaeological and historical work, however, has proven beyond a shadow of a doubt that the original monastery, located on the island lake twelve miles west of Bucharest in the Vlasie forest, was originally built either by one of the early Basarabs, by Prince Mircea, or by a boyar called Vlad Vintila.[39] Dracula himself often resided at Snagov, may have hidden his treasury there in 1462, and according to peasant stories, had a torture chamber set up there. With his passion for fortifications it is likely that he transformed the ecclesiastical complex into an island fortress. There also exists an obscure sixteenth-century reference to the effect that Dracula endowed this monastery with land.[40]

Although Snagov was not initially a Dracula foundation, other churches and monasteries built by this prince can be found scattered throughout Wallachia, most of them in ruins. Some of these, such as the church at Constantinesti and the monastery of Comana, located close to the Danube, can be accounted as Dracula churches only in terms of popular tradition. In the ease of Comana the record of a Dracula donation in 1461 does exist.[41] The archaeological find made of the remains of a church on the banks of the river Dîmbovita at Cetateni, not far from a well-known fifteenth century fortress bearing the same name, can only hypothetically be linked to Dracula's period and needs further examination.[42]

There is at least one church which there cannot be the slightest doubt that Dracula was in fact the founder, since the Cyrillic inscription indicating the year of construction has been found by Constantin C. Giurescu, at that time a young student at the University of Bucharest. He published his discovery in 1924. This is the church of Saint Nicolas of Tîrgsor, founded in 1461. The inscription reads: "By the grace of God, I Vlad Voevod, Ruler of Ungro-Valachia, the son of the great prince Vlad, have built

and completed the church 24 June 1461."[43] The work of
excavation carried on at Tîrgsor has also revealed two additional
fifteenth century churches, one of which can be attributed to
Vladislav II. The reason for the erection of this particular Dracula
church, however, has nothing to do with the commercial
importance of the town or to the fact that Dracula had a princely
residence in Tîrgsor. This church was completed one year after
the murder of yet another Dan (a Transylvanian candidate to the
throne) and five years after the assassination of Vladislav II. It
would in either case have represented an act of atonement,
particularly for that prince's slaying, which took place in Tîrgsor,
in 1456, shortly before Dracula came to the throne.

Undoubtedly other Dracula foundations will, in due course,
be found. But even if no further finds are made, the present
record within so short a period of time sufficiently attests to the
importance that Dracula gave religion both in terms of personal
beliefs and in terms of ecclesiastical policy.   .

Given his opposition to the greater boyars, it would be easy
to view Dracula as a protagonist of the "general will" of the have-
nots composed essentially of peasants, who represented the
great majority of Romanians in Dracula's time. Because his social
predilections in raising humble men to high rank *(sluji, curteni,
viteji)*, some historians have been tempted to consider Dracula as
a kind of Robin Hood, who took away from the rich and gave to
the poor. Several factors seem to point to such an interpretation.
In contrast to the disloyalty of the boyars, the peasants as a
whole remained faithful to him and rallied to his cause. Dracula
granted immunities from feudal dues to several peasant
villages—for example, Troianesti in the Olt district.[44] Seven
different documents signed by Dracula granting similar
privileges seem to reflect a social policy of egalitarianism.
Dracula also sheltered the peasants from the commercial
exploitation of the Transylvanian German merchants and
defended them from Turkish subjection by refusing to pay the
tribute in money and kind (agricultural gifts to Constantinople)
and in men (contributions of youths to the janissary corps).
Romanian oral traditions emphasize the same point in a different
way; individual narratives state that in Dracula's time the rich
could *not* get themselves out of punishment as they had done
under previous rulers. Dracula's time meant the end of the rule
of the *"bakshish,"* or tipping, so prevalent in eastern Europe to
this day. The peasants, naturally, rallied to Dracul's cause most
loyally during the Turkish campaign of 1462.

Having stated this, we should not press the point of social crusading too far: it would be a gross exaggeration to view Dracula—a despot and a believer in divine right—as a revolutionary who preached egalitarianism among the masses. Even the documentation that exists (seven or eight documents granting privileges to villages), over a period of six years' rule, says little about the state of affairs in the vast majority of villages. Apart from the few edicts referred to, there is no traditional historical documentation concerning Dracula's relationship with the peasant class. This is the reason why, at least in this area, we are exclusively dependent upon local folklore. The validity for using folkloric sources guardedly has already been discussed in the Introduction.[45] In the fascinating tradition of the people that has been handed down from one generation to another by word of mouth, Dracula's characteristic trait, his cruelty, is always mitigated and justified by a strong sense of justice and fair play. In the manner of a Saint Louis of France, the people's verdict was that he was stern and unbending in order that justice might prevail in his land. As such they have chosen to remember him and the Romanian people have been most discriminating concerning the princes whose memory they cared to evoke.

If we are to believe Romanian narratives, in Dracula's Wallachia, crime, thievery, immorality, mendicancy, laziness, disease, hypocrisy, and unemployment were virtually unknown. Innumerable anecdotes can be used to illustrate this point, many of them also figuring in the Russian and German narratives.[46] Romanian stories, however, have a strong moral flavor. One variant of the Romanian story about the Florentine merchant deserves to be quoted *in extenso.*

When Dracula ruled Wallachia, an important Florentine merchant traveled throughout the land, and he had a great deal of merchandise and money. As he visited Tîrgoviste, the capital of the country, the merchant immediately went to the princely palace and asked Dracula for servants who might watch over him, his merchandise, and his money. Dracula ordered him to leave the merchandise and the money in a public square and to come to sleep in the palace. The merchant, having no alternative, submitted to the princely plan. However, during the night, someone passing by his carriage, stole 160 golden ducats.

On the next day, early in the morning, the merchant went to his carriage, found his merchandise intact, but 160 golden ducats were missing. Dracula told him not to worry and promised him that both the thief and the money would be found. He ordered his servants to replace the gold ducats from his own treasury, but to add an extra ducat. He then ordered the citizens of Tîrgoviste to seek out the thief immediately and if the thief were not found, he would destroy his capital.

In the meantime the merchant went back to his carriage, counted the money once, counted it a second time, and yet again a a third time and was amazed to find all his money there with yet an extra ducat. He then returned to Dracula and told him: "Lord, I have found all my money, only with an extra ducat." The thief was brought to the palace at that very moment. Dracula told the merchant: "Go in peace. Had you not admitted to the extra ducat, I would have ordered you impaled together with this thief."

This is the way that Dracula conducted himself with his subjects, both believers and heretics.[47]

Another story mentions a golden cup purposely left by Dracula in a deserted square of his capital at a fountain where travelers would habitually rest and refresh themselves. Never did that cup disappear throughout Dracula's reign, so great was the terror of impalement.[48]

Perhaps the most dramatic incident mentioned by all narratives, German, Romanian, and Slavic, was ridding the country of the beggars, the sick, and the poor. Having asked the old, the ill, the lame, the poor, and the vagabonds to a large palace dining hall in Tîrgoviste, Dracula ordered that a feast be prepared for them. They ate and drank and made merry late into the night. At the height of the festivities, Dracula made a personal appearance and asked the multitude, tongue in cheek: "What else do you desire? . . . Do you want to be without cares, lacking nothing in this world?" They answered in unison in the affirmative. He then ordered the palace boarded up and set it on fire. No one escaped. The main justification for this particular crime was the following: "I did this," reported Dracula to the awe-stricken boyars, "in order that they represent no further burden to other men so that no one will be poor in my realm."[49] This action can be described as a form of mercy killing, getting rid of the handicapped, the undesirable, and the sick, who were a burden to the state. One specialist in the history of Romanian medicine hinted that Dracula may have been attempting to rid the country of the plague, a constant scourge on the lower Danube.[50] Allusions to the "vagabonds" make it plausible that Dracula may have tried to liquidate the gypsies.

Another kind of misdemeanor against which Dracula vented his full anger in a particularly vicious way was laziness and immorality. The extremity of Dracula's punishment in these matters almost surpasses belief, and the punishment certainly did not always befit the crime. The Romanian interpretation of Dracula's treatment of the lazy wife runs as follows:

One day he [Dracula] met a peasant who was wearing too short a shirt. One could also notice home-spun peasant trousers which were glued to his legs and one could make out the side of his thighs. When he saw him in this manner, Dracula immediately ordered him to be brought to his court "Are you married?" he inquired. "Yes, I am, your Highness." "Your wife is assuredly of the kind who remains idle. How is it possible, that your shirt does not cover the calf of your leg? She is not worthy of living in my realm. May she perish!" "Beg forgiveness, my Lord, but I am satisfied with her. She never leaves home and she is honest." "You will be more satisfied with another, since you are a decent and hardworking man."

Two of Dracula's men had, in the meantime, brought the wretched woman to him, and she was immediately impaled. Then bringing another woman, he gave her away to the peasant widower. Dracula, however, was careful to show the new wife what happened to her predecessor and explained to her the reasons why she had incurred the princely wrath. Consequently the new wife worked so hard she had no time to eat.[51]

Another story stemming from the Russian narrative refers to Dracula's unusual puritanism: if any wife had an affair outside of marriage, Dracula ordered her sexual organs cut. She was then skinned alive and exposed in her skinless flesh in a public square, her skin hanging separately from a pole or placed on a table in the middle of the marketplace. The same punishment was applied to maidens who did not keep their virginity, and also to unchaste widows. In other instances, for similar offenses, Dracula was known to have the nipple of a woman's breast cut off. He would also have a red-hot iron stake shoved into the woman's vagina, making the instrument penetrate her entrails and emerge from her mouth. He then had the woman tied to a pole naked and left her exposed there until the flesh fell from the body, and the bones detached themselves from their sockets.[52]

From incidents such as these, perpetrated against ordinary men and women, not boyars or Turks, one might conclude that like Calvin's, Dracula's mind was narrowly inquisitorial, censorious, and puritanical. He constantly probed into the lives of ordinary subjects, always wishing to be informed of the most pedestrian occurrences. According to a Turkish chronicle, if a single man or woman dared affront him, he would have a whole village destroyed in retaliation. In essence, Dracula attempted to legislate virtue and morality through the use of terror. (Impalement here, as in other instances, was evidently the deterrent.) One might truly say that virtue reigned in Dracula's Wallachia.

What was the reaction of the people to this fifteenth-century brand of Romanian puritanism? Although the peasants on the whole attempted to rationalize Dracula's impalements, one may well wonder whether the self-imposed mission of legislating virtue by terror and even cheating human nature out of some minor frailties, such as laziness and immorality, met with sympathy and understanding from the masses. In matters of ethics, the Romanian people have never been particularly censorious and have always admitted the existence of good as well as the existence of evil. One might almost say that the mentality of the average peasant can more closely be identified with that of Dracula's victims than that of the persecutor himself. There is nothing puritanical or fanatical in Romanian moral philosophy or in the ethos of the national character, which is more Byzantine than Genevan. Like a Robespierre, Dracula's stern, unbending, intractable, and cruel justice, calculated to terrorize, was considered by the people as that of a fanatic. It certainly was not calculated to win the hearts of the peasants. With regards to Dracula's relationship with the people, we may conclude that he was indeed admired from a distance, particularly as a national hero, and with the passing of centuries this progressive idealization tended to increase in Romanian folklore.

Historians have been in the habit of labeling Dracula's Transylvanian policies as involving foreign rather than domestic events. They are, of course, correct, since with the exception of the two duchies of Fagaras and Amlas, Transylvania was a part of the Hungarian kingdom. Such a view, however, is excessively technical. It should never be forgotten that the bulk of the Transylvanian population, even at that period, was Romanian. Dracula was born in Transylvania, he was educated there early in his life, and his first wife hailed from that province. It was from Transylvania that he came to conquer his throne, and it was in that province that he hoped to find the moral as well as the material support against his enemies both at home and abroad. It should also be added that the commercial relations between Transylvania and Wallachia had always been close; most of Dracula's correspondence is to be found in the archives of Sibiu and Brasov, and certainly when things did not work out in Wallachia, Dracula sought asylum in such Transylvanian cities as Sighisoara, Brasov, Sibiu, and Medias. For all these reasons a rigid distinction between internal and external policy, labeling Transylvania as involving external policy, ostensibly breaks down.[53]

Commercial relations between Transylvania and Wallachia had always been close since the very birth of the principality, Wallachia was founded by some Transylvanian leaders descending from the Transylvanian plateau into the Wallachian plain. With the establishment of Brasov and Sibiu as trading and manufacturing communities, it was but natural for the German artisans and merchants of these towns to attempt selling their wares to Wallachia, which became one of their principal markets.[54] These Transylvanian "goods" were either exported into Wallachia to certain specific towns such as Tîrgsor or warehoused in these same towns in transit, to be later transferred farther east and south of the Danube. If they were sold in Wallachia, they became subject to import duties; if they were shipped outside of Wallachia, they required export taxes. The point of restricting commerce to certain towns was that the princes of the land could thereby exercise some control on the influx or foreign goods, and could protect the natives from exploitation from foreign merchants; moreover, the collection of export and import duties benefited the Wallachian treasury and helped to pay for mercenary soldiers. Levying tariffs also tended to benefit the prosperity of the selected towns.

Although in a vague sense, Dracula can be labeled a Transylvanian, he showed little sympathy for the interests of the German manufacturers and traders of Brasov and Sibiu. The inherent patriotism already noted in connection with his ecclesiastical policies made it very difficult for him to accept this permanent foreign intrusion, which profited the Transylvania merchants rather than the natives. Dracula was only too well aware of the fact that apart from exploiting the peasants, the monopoly the German traders enjoyed frustrated the establishment of native guilds and industries. He became the partisan, if not of following a policy of strict autarchy, at least of rigid controls at the borders and increased protectionism.

Despite the opposition of views between Dracula and the Saxon traders, initial commercial relations began well enough. On September 6, 1456, Dracula signed a commercial treaty with the Brasovians and the district of Bursenland (Tara Bîrsei), which contained the following provisions: (1) Dracula would help defend the Transylvanian Saxons against the Turks. In case of need, however, a stipulation gave him the right of asylum in Transylvania. (2) The merchants of Brasov and of the Bursenland were given the right to sell their goods and buy their raw materials unimpeded throughout Wallachia without localizing such transactions in specific towns as had been the practice. They could sell their wares directly to the customers and buy their raw materials from the producer—the only obligation being to pay the usual Wallachian custom duties, upon entry. (3) Both sides undertook not to give protection to their political enemies, and not to confiscate the goods of their respective merchants no matter what the provocation. In the same document Dracula swore renewed fidelity to the new young king of Hungary, Ladislas Posthumus.[55] In essence, the economic treaty somewhat liberalized and confirmed existing privileges. A similar treaty was signed with the city Sibiu. These initial good relations, however, were not destined to endure. Before long Dracula was responsible for some of his worst atrocities in Transylvania, lavishly described and possibly exaggerated by German refugees.

The Saxon-German merchants were, in fact, responsible for besmirching Dracula's reputation throughout Europe and in the eyes of posterity. Whether the original Transylvanian refugee who authored the first Dracula manuscripts in 1462 was Brother Jacob, Brother Bernhard, or Brother Hans from the monastery of Gorion, or someone else, there can be little doubt, judging by the familiarity of the Saint Gall manuscript with Transylvanian place names, that the first refugees came from that province. The troubadour Michel Beheim relates in his poetic account that he obtained some of his information from these monks in the winter of 1463 while he was residing at Wiener-Neustadt.[56]

There were many reasons for Dracula's feud with the Transylvanian Saxons, which climaxed from 1459 to 1461, not the least of which was the attitude of the townships of Amlas and Fagaras, which, as previously noted, had never been particularly loyal to Wallachia ever since the rule of Vladislav II. It should be recalled that since 1453, both Amlas, and Fagaras had been detached from their Wallachian vassalage. Dracula demanded the restitution of the duchies, a demand that the Hungarian king considered an infraction of the treaty of submission signed in 1456.

It was undoubtedly for these reasons that Ladislas Posthumus in the last years of his rule (1457) began once again to champion various anti-Dracula candidates and members of the rival Danesti clan. Among the political foes were the old pretender Dan III, sometimes known as Danciul, his brother Basarab II, known as Laiota, the son of Dan II and Laiota's son Basarab the young, also nicknamed the Little Impaler (Tepelus). The latter two effectively ruled after Dracula's death. In addition, there were immediate members of his own family hostile to Dracula who were given support by the citizens of Sibiu. One was Vlad the Monk, his half brother; the other is a somewhat mysterious nephew, Nicolae Olahus, whose precise origin is obscure, although he is mentioned in documents as "ex Sanguinis Draculae."[57] It was therefore politically expedient for Dracula to eliminate these rivals or at least to circumscribe their field of action. A final reason for conflict with the German Saxons was Dracula's immersion into Hungarian domestic politics at the moment of great internal disorder and strife. Dracula decided to give his support to Michael Szilagy, who in turn championed the cause of Matthias Corvinus (Dracula was soon to marry into the Szilagy family) against Ladislas Posthumus, the ruling monarch. This participation in an internal feud, which had shaken both Hungary and Transylvania to its very foundations after the death of Hunyady at Belgrade, had additionally incurred the hostility of the German Saxons who had consistently given their support to Ladislas Posthumus and the Holy Roman Emperor Frederick III of Germany. With the final victory of Matthias Corvinus, who succeeded to the Hungarian throne as Matthias I on June 24, 1458, the new king explicitly wrote to the citizens of Sibiu to change their political attitudes toward Dracula, who was described as "our beloved and faithful friend."[58] The intervention of the Hungarian monarch undoubtedly improved relationships between Dracula and the German Transylvanian townships. There was, in fact, a temporary easing of tensions at this time.

During the winter of 1458-1459, Dracula's relations with the Transylvanian Saxons were abruptly broken. Dracula decided upon increasing the tariffs of Transylvanian goods to favor native manufacturers, in violation of the treaty he had signed. He also obligated the Germans to revert back to the previous custom of trading only in certain specified towns such as Cîmpulung, Tîrgoviste, and Tîrgsor. This action suddenly closed many towns to German trade where the Saxons had made a profitable business, including the traditional road from Rucar to Braila and especially to the Danube. Since the Brasovians continued to ignore these measures, Dracula proceeded to his first act of terrorism.

Dracula's first incursion into Transylvania was a lightning raid into the Sibiu district, in 1457, where he burned and pillaged castles, villages, and everything in his way. The Saint Gall manuscript describes the event in Alemanic succinctly: "Item zu hand darnach het er dorffer und Schlösser in Sibenbürgen by der Hermonstadt lassen verbrennen und geschlösser in Sibenburg daselbs und dorffer mit namen Kloster Holtznüwdorff, Holtznetya zu äschen gantz verbrennen. Item Berkendorf in Wuetzerland het er lassen verbrennen, man und frowen, kinder gross and klain."[59] Apparently, the men, women, and children who were not burned alive were taken to Wallachia and impaled. The region of Dracula's first Transylvanian atrocity, "Wuetzerland," or Wurzland, is the current Tara Bîrsei; "Hermonstadt," is the city of Sibiu; "Holtznüwdorff" is Hosmanul; "Berkendorf" is the village of Benesti. All of these are still villages in the immediate vicinity of Sibiu. A purpose of the raid may well have been that of capturing Vlad the Monk and thus warning the citizens of Sibiu who were spared not to give shelter and protection to other rival princely candidates.

The main period of Transylvanian incursions occurred two years later, between 1459 and 1460. In 1459 after secretly recalling his own Wallachian merchants from Transylvania, Dracula apprehended four hundred young Transylvanian trainees, "mere boys who had come to Wallachia to learn the language" (according to Michel Beheim), together with their thirty coach drivers; all were assembled in a room and burned alive.[60] Callous as this action may appear, Dracula looked upon the young Saxon apprentices and coach drivers less as legitimate trainees than as spies sent by the merchants of Brasov and Sibiu to learn about the native methods of production and what we would call marketing conditions.

Dracula's best known and most dramatized atrocity occurred early on the morning of April 2, 1459, in the town of Brasov. According to the Saint Gall text, Dracula looted the Church of Saint Bartholomew, which is still in existence, "stealing the vestments and chalices." He then burned the suburb of the city located near the chapel of Saint Jacob, and impaled countless victims on the hill surrounding the chapel (Kappelenberg, Tîmpa Hill). It was likely on this site that Dracula is described as wining and dining among the cadavers.[61] This episode is recalled by two famous prints, one published in 1500 at Strasbourg, the other published in 1499 at Nürnberg.[62] Both the episodes and the associated woodcuts did more to damage Dracula's reputation than any other single pamphlet or print. It is also likely that on the same occasion Dracula exemplified his perverted sense of humor, related by the Russian narratives. A boyar attending the Brasov festivity, apparently unable to endure the smell of coagulating blood any longer, had the misfortune to hold up his nose and express a gesture of revulsion. Dracula immediately ordered an unusually long stake prepared for the would-be victim and presented it to him with the cynical remark: "You live up there yonder, where the stench cannot reach you." He was immediately impaled.[63] After the Brasov raid, Dracula continued burning and terrorizing other villages in the vicinity of the city. He was not able, however, to capture the fortress of Zeyding (Codlea), still partially standing today, but for his failure to do so, he executed the captain responsible.

Dracula's vindictiveness and violence extended through the spring and summer of 1460. In the spring (April) he was finally able to catch his opponent Dan III (Danciul): he forced him to read his own funeral oration and then decapitated him—only seven of his followers were able to escape.[64] During the summer, in early July, Dracula captured Fagaras and impaled all its citizens—men, women, and children—states the Saint Gall manuscript.[65] One month later—the German narration specifies "on the day of Saint Bartholomew," August 24, 1460—Dracula raided the town of "Humilasch," evidently Amlas, and burned it, impaling all its citizens, with the priest leading the procession, a belated revenge for its continued defiance since 1456.[66] Although statistics are very difficult to establish, particularly for that period (and the German figures must be viewed with caution), there were more victims on the night of Saint Bartholomew in 1460, in the town of Amlas—twenty thousand may have perished—than were butchered by Catherine de Médicis in Paris over a century later. Somehow Dracula's Saint Bartholomew has escaped the eye of the historian while that of Catherine de Medicis has made her the object of great moral reprobation. However, Catherine's choice of the night of August 24, at a century's distance, could be more than a coincidence.

A few Transylvanian townships and villages affected by Dracula's terrorism, according to the German narrative have survived: Neudorff, the present village of Noul Sasesc, in the Brasov district; and Talmetz (Talmesh), near Sibiu; some like Thunow and Bregel cannot be positively identified and have probably since disappeared. From other Romanian sources we know that some villages like Sercaia and Mica, in the Fagaras district, had been so completely decimated by Dracula's vengeance that they had to be recolonized and repopulated a century later (the number of victims there could have reached thirty thousand altogether). The authenticity of these narratives is sufficiently attested by the precision of the geographic locations.

After 1460, Transylvanian raids somehow subsided as events compelled Dracula to turn his attention elsewhere. However, it is little wonder that the Saxon merchants exercised their initial revenge by being instrumental in Dracula's arrest in 1462, as "an enemy to humanity," and more permanently after his death by reviling his reputation for posterity.

The essential trait of Dracula's personality, reflected in his domestic policies both in Wallachia and in Transylvania, is his cruelty. From this point of view, Dracula emerges as a murky character from *1001 Nights*, an Oriental tyrant, a monster who may well vie with Ivan the Terrible, for the title of the most gruesome psychopath of history. The historian Bogdan believes that Ivan the Terrible modeled some of his own tortures on those of Dracula.[67]

In this view what impresses one first is the number of victims Dracula made within the short span of a six-year rule. It ranges from a minimum of 40,000 victims to a maximum of 100,000, an estimate made by the papal nuncio, the bishop of Erlau near the end of Dracula's career in 1475 (this undoubtedly includes his Turkish war victims as well). Apart from the Turks these victims included men of all nationalities (Moldavians, Wallachians, Transylvanians, Bulgarians, Germans, Hungarians, gypsies, and Jews), all classes (boyars as well as peasants), all religions (Catholic, Dissenter, Moslem, Orthodox), and men, women, and children. By our insensitive standards of twentieth-century brutalities these numbers may appear insignificant. However, the figure far exceeds the so-called massacres of the fifteenth, sixteenth, and even eighteenth centuries. The night of

Saint Bartholomew in Paris, which made even Ivan the Terrible indignant, accounted for only 5,000 to 10,000 victims, while during Robespierre's reign of terror (1793-1794), no more than 3,500 to 4,000 victims perished on the guillotine.[68] The number of Dracula victims, even if exaggerated, is all the more telling by comparison to the French massacres, when it is recalled that France's total population in 1715 was 18 million inhabitants, whereas the total population of Wallachia in Dracula's time did not exceed half a million.

It was, however, not only the matter of killing on a massive scale that shocked contemporaries, but the manner and refinements in imposing death. Dracula's favorite method of execution, which has immortalized him among artists of crime, was impalement. According to the various narratives—German, Russian, Hungarian, Turkish, Romanian—there were stakes permanently prepared in the courtyard of the palace of Tîrgoviste, in various strategic places, in public squares, and in the vicinity of the capital, with Dracula often present at the time of punishment. Usually, it is said, the stakes were carefully rounded at the end and bathed in oil so that the entrails of the victims should not be pierced by a wound too fatal when the victim's legs were stretched wide apart and two horses (one attached to each leg) were sent cantering in different directions, while attendants held the stake and body firmly in place. Not all of Dracula's impalement victims were, however, pierced from the buttocks up. Judging from several prints, the men, women, and children were also impaled through the heart, the navel, the stomach, and the chest. Nor was impalement the only form of punishment: Dracula decapitated, cut off noses, ears, and sexual organs and limbs. He blinded, strangled, hanged, burned, boiled, skinned, roasted, hacked ("like cabbage," specifies a German narrative), nailed, buried alive, and had his victims stabbed. He also exposed them to the elements, to wild animals, built secret trapdoors to drop the wretches on a cunningly located stake below. If he did not practice cannibalism, the German story teller mentions that he compelled others to eat human flesh. He also made use of the wheel, hot irons, and other forms of medieval torture. Turkish sources state that on one occasion he smeared salt and honey on the soles of his captives' feet and allowed animals to lick them for indefinite periods of suffering. The papal legate Nicolas Modrussa, perhaps with political intent, recapitulated some of the stories related to him by King Matthias, about the refinements of Dracula's cruelties. Let us quote his own words to Pope Pius II relating how, shortly before 1462, Dracula had killed forty thousand of his political foes:

> *He killed some of them by breaking them under the wheels of carts; others, stripped of their clothes, were skinned alive up to their entrails; others placed on stakes, or roasted on red hot coals placed under them; others punctured with stakes piercing their head, their navel, breast, and what is even unworthy of relating, their buttocks and the middle of their entrails, and, emerging from their mouths; in order that no form of cruelty be missing, he stuck stakes in both breasts of mothers and thrust their babies onto them; he killed others in other ferocious ways, torturing them with varied instruments such as the atrocious cruelties of the most frightful tyrants could devise.*[69]

Tursun Bey, a Turkish chronicler at the end of the fifteenth century, depicts the following macabre scene, which completes that of Modrussa:

> *In front of the wooden fortress where he had his residence, he set up at a distance of six leagues two rows of fences with impaled Hungarians, Moldavians and Wallachians. In addition, since the neighboring area was forested, innumerable people were hanging from each tree branch, and he ordered that if anyone should take one of the hanging victims down, they would hang in their place.*[70]

Literary descriptions such as these coined the caption "the forest of the impaled."

In addition to physical torture Dracula had a predilection for various forms of moral torture: he liked to obtain confessions prior to punishment, extracting admissions of guilt, to put a man in the wrong before he was executed. Dracula placed inordinate stress upon the use of words, and greatly prized dialectical talents: a clever answer to a twisted question could occasionally save a man's life. Those who failed to pass the ordeal, however, faced certain death.

In evaluating such physical and moral tortures, it is self-evident that they must be viewed in the light of the standards and morality of his time. Mass killings, the execution and torture of political opponents, together with their families, were hardly Dracula's inventions. Dracula's age is that of the War of the Roses, the massacres of Perugia between the Odis and the Baglionis, and the Roman struggles between the Orsinis and Colonnas, which have left an impressive horror tale of their own.

Nor was Dracula's mentality very different from that of Louis XI, "the Spider King," who had a predilection for hanging young boys on the branches of trees; of Lodovico Sforza, "the Moor," Pope Alexander the VI, Sigismondo Malatesta, or Cesare Borgia, whose crimes are only too familiar to the student of west European history. Given the specific circumstances prevailing in his principality, Dracula's motivations for crime were at least as cogent as those of other Renaissance despots. Mass killing of political opponents and the creation of a new loyal nobility was the only acceptable method of meeting the combined danger to authority and consolidating central power.

Even the favorite torture, impalement, though never in history practiced on so wide a scale, was not a Dracula innovation. It was known to Asiatic antiquity and practiced by the Turks, as well as by other Balkan rulers, including Dracula's cousin, Stephen of Moldavia. In 1473, Stephen had 2,300 of his Wallachian prisoners impaled through the navel.[71]

Contrary to Bogdan's view, Dracula's crimes cannot be dismissed on the grounds that he was an aimless killer. If a streak of insanity cannot altogether be excluded, there was a definite method woven into it. Terror, the order of the day, was used as a psychological device to frighten the impressionable Eastern mind. It was rarely used, as has been clearly demonstrated, for the sake of terror alone. A good many other Dracula massacres can be justified on moral grounds or had a utilitarian purpose or both; the episode best described as the "death march" of the citizens of Tîrgoviste from the capital to Dracula's castle was undoubtedly the obvious example combining both motives. It was aimed at punishing the guilty boyars, and at the same time, destined to serve the defenses of the Wallachian state.

No matter how carefully we account for Dracula's crimes, it is a matter of record that in the end he was abandoned by all his people. Many of his contemporaries, even his henchmen, may have felt that no one was really safe from impalement at the hands of the "monster." Indeed, no matter how hard we explain Dracula's crimes, one cannot completely adopt the adage "tout comprendre, c'est tout pardonner," and some of Dracula's atrocities may well have been motivated by a streak of irrationality. Dracula, in other words, was probably capable of butchery without valid reasons.

Although unwilling to indulge in a Freudian analysis of Dracula's personality, the nature of some of his crimes, particularly vis à vis women, suggests sexual abnormalities which have never been explained by historians. The ritual and manner of impalement, watching his victims eat flesh, the cutting of sexual organs, all point to a morbid sexual deviation. In this connection, one anecdote mentioned in the Russian story seems to confirm Dracula's anger toward women. On one occasion, relates the Slavic narrative, one of Dracula's mistresses pretended that he made her pregnant. Dracula was so angered by what he evidently expected to be a lie that he first had his mistress examined; then, realizing that he had been made an object of ridicule, had her womb cut up from her sexual organs to her breasts. When the unfortunate woman lay dying, writhing in excruciating pain, Dracula cynically remarked: "Let the world see where I have been."[72]

What verdict can reconcile Dracula's evident attraction for women with the savagery of his sexual crimes? The answer that suggests itself even to a nonspecialist is that Dracula may have been partially impotent and that he derived his sexual satisfactions in other ways: by watching the mutilation of women, the cutting of sexual organs, and scenes of cannibalism involving the eating of breasts. Furthermore, the very ritual of impalement would help focus the precise nature of Dracula's infirmity. The pleasure derived in watching the stake painfully penetrating his victims' buttocks may have provided a substitute satisfaction for his own inadequacy.

As we review Dracula's domestic and Transylvanian policies, several factors seem to stand out most vividly. Although Dracula seems to have suffered from "a bad press" already in his time, most of his so-called acts of atrocity were not, at least qualitatively, very different from that of other despots of the Renaissance period. Barring the few qualifications noted, Dracula's mentality and his political thinking can be labeled as representative of an age that witnessed the final disappearance of feudalism, the emergence of the centralized nation-state, and the rise of a middle class. In the case of Dracula's state, the arguments for "modernization" were all the more cogent, since he faced imminent danger from outside, threatening the very existence of his principality. Bearing this in mind, even terrorism by impalement, which we have in most instances explained on rational, moral, and utilitarian grounds, might also help account for the irrationality of a few of Dracula's murders that we have accepted as fact. A study of Dracula's foreign policy, to which we shall now turn, may indeed provide us with the final clue.

[1] The documentation traditionally labelled *internal* by Romanian historians includes only a handful of letters and edicts, most of which are published in P. P. Panaitescu and Damaschin Mioc, eds., *B. Tara Româneasca Documenta Româniae Historica* (Bucharest, 1966). These shed very little biographical light and are useful mostly in terms of Dracula's whereabouts. They refer to acts of donations to monasteries and individuals. The two oldest chronicles of the land, the Cantacuzino and the Baleanu chronicles, mention almost nothing about Dracula's reign in Wallachia. The two best critical editions of the chronicles are Constantin Grecescu and Dan Simonescu, eds., *Istoria Tarii Romînesti 1290-1690. Letopisetul Cantacuzinesc* (Bucharest, 1960), and C. Grecescu, *Istoriile domnilor Tarii Romînesti de Radu Popescu vornicul* (Bucharest, 1963). Wishing to research the archives of each individual monastery of Dracula's time, the authors of the present work were officially notified by the Romanian patriarchy that all the monastic archives (Cozia, Tismana, Cotmeana, Govora) had been transferred to the Manuscript Division of the National Archives in Bucharest and the Library of the Academy of the Romanian Socialist Republic.

[2] On Ambras Castle see Lilly V. Sauter, "Ein Schloss in Tirol," *Du Atlantis*. n.d. See also Aloys Primisser, *Die K. K. Ambraser Sammlung* (Vienna, 1819); Eduard Sacken, *Die K. K. Ambraser Sammlung* (Vienna, 1855); Alphons Lhotsky, "Die Geschichte der Sammlungen," *Festschrift des Kunsthistorischen Museums* (Vienna, 1941-1945); Kittenger Hubert, *Schloss Ambras bei Innsbruck* (Innsbruck, 1949). For specific reference to the archduke Ferdinand II see Josef Hirn, *Erzherzog Ferdinand II von Tirol* (Innsbruck, 1885); Laurin Luchner, *Denkmaleines Renaissancefürsten Versuch einer Rekonstruktion des Ambraser Museums von 1583* (Vienna, 1958). Some art critics believe the Dracula painting to be of the Nürnberg School. The artist is unknown. For a good reproduction of the painting see Nicolae Iorga, *Portretele Domniilor Romani dupa portrete si fresce contemporane* (Sibiu, 1930), p. 23. Iorga also has a book of reproductions on Romanian princesses: *Portretele Doamnilor Români* (Bucharest, 1937). For an analysis of Dracula's portrait see I. P. Hasdeu, *Studii critice asupra istoriei române. Filosofia portretului lui Tepesu. Schita iconografica* (Bucharest, 1964). Also see P. P. Panaitescu, "Vlad Tepes o problema psihologica," *Convorbiri literare* 76 (May-June 1943): 331-348.

[3] Peter the Lame, prince of Moldavia, was Mihnea the Bad's grandson. He ruled Moldavia in 1574-1577, 1578-1579, and 1582-1591. Constantin Gane, *Trecute vieti de Doamne si Domnite*, vol. 1 (Bucharest, 1932), pp. 121-122; Nicolae Iorga, *Istoria Românilor*, vol. 2 (Bucharest, 1937). On his tombstone at Bolzano one can still read the inscription: "I Petru voevod of the royal Corvinus family." Gane, *Trecute vieti de dodmne si domni* (Bucharest, 1932), p. 121.

[4] W. Peters sent the photo of the painting (oil on wood) to Professor Dinu Giurescu at Bucharest for identification. The latter confirmed the fact that this was a painting of Dracula. Peters has since completed a short study on the painting in manuscript, which has been used by the authors. George Jordan, a student of Professor Florescu at Boston College, took the first color photo of the painting during the summer of 1970.

[5] For reproductions of these engravings see Ion Bogdan, *Vlad Tepes si naratiunile germane si rusesti asupra lui* (Bucharest, 1896), portraits III, IV and V at the beginning of the book. One should note the gradual distortion of features. Far better reproductions are contained in Iorga, *Portretele domniilor Români*, p. 24. An unusual woodcut is included in a German pamphlet dated Leipzig, 1493. For reproduction of frontispiece see C. I. Karadja, "Incunabulele povestind despre cruzimile lui Tepes," *Inchinare lui N. Iorga* (Bucharest, 1931), pp. 196-206.

[6] G. Constantinescu, *Magul de la Snagov* (Bucharest, n.d.), p. 34.

[7] Bogdan, *Vlad Tepes*, p. 18.

[8] Nicolas Modrussa had been sent to the court of Matthias Corvinus by Pope Pius II to organize an anti-Ottoman crusade. G. Mercati, "Notizie varie sopra Niccolò Modrussiense," *Opere Minori*, vol. 4 (Vatican City, 1937), pp. 247-249.

[9] In a letter dated March 5, 1458, from Tismana, Dracula endowed the monastery of Tismana all the villages it owned during the reign of his father, Dracul, exempting them of princely obligations. (Written by Radu Gramaticul (the copyist.) State Archives Bucuresti, 11/2.) (Tismana IX/91.) (Copy at the Library of Ac. of Rom. Soc. Rep., XX-46.)

[10] "His [Dracula's] princely residence was a wooden fortress." From Mihail Guboglu and Mustafa Mehmet, *Cronici turcesti privind tările române*, vol. 1 (Bucharest, 1966), p. 199.

[11] For a good plan of Dracula's palace see N. Constantinescu and C. Moisescu, *Curtea domneasca din Tîrgoviste* (also translated into French), Bucharest, 1965, p. 7.

[12] Cîrstian is one of Dracola's envoys one frequently encounters. The original letter is in the Sibiu State Archives, formerly the Archives of the Saxon University. There is a copy at the Library of the Academy of the Romanian Socialist Republic. See Bogdan, *Doucmente, privitoare la relatiile tara romanesti cu Brasovul si cu tara unguresască in sec XV si SVI*, 1413-1508 (Bucharest, 1905), pp. 322-323, and Eudoxiu de Hurmuzacki, *Colectiune de documente privitoare la istoria Românilor 1199-1849*, vol. XV-7 (Bucharest 1876-1912) p. 146, doc. 146.

[13] The actual document first mentioning the fortress of Bucharest, written in ancient Slavonic, was signed by Dracula, "Io Vlad Voevod." The date is September 20, 1459. It was discovered half a century later, and the original manuscript is preserved in the manuscript room of the Library of the Academy of the Romanian Socialist Republic. The foundations of the old fortress have recently been excavated under the supervision of the archaeologist Panait Panait. See Florian Georgescu, ed., *Istoria Orasului Bucuresti* (Bucharest, 1965), pp. 79-81; Constantin C. Giurescu, *Istoria Bucurestilor, din cele mai vechi timpuri pîna în zilele noastre* (Bucharest, 1966), p. 51.

[14] Giurescu, *Istoria Bucurestilor*, p. 47.

[15] Ibid., p. 50.

[16] Library of the Academy of the Romanian Socialist Republic, Doc. CLXX-2. Among signatures witnessing this historic document were Jupân Dragomir Tacal, Jupân Voico Dobrita, Jupân Stan, Jupân Stefan Bratul of Milcov, Moldovean Spatar, Iova Vistier. . . Tocsaba Stolnic, Stoica Paharnic, Gherghina Comis. (The document is badly torn.) A copy executed by an Italian artist is housed in the Museum of the City of Bucharest. It had been executed on the orders of G. D. Florescu, a prewar director of the museum.

[17] Written from Bucharest. Dracula endowed the village of Godeni to the Boyar Bira and to his brother Godea, exempting them from taxes and services. Library of Ac. of Rom. Soc. Rep., no. 5236 f. 64-65.

[18] The most recently published hunt for Dracula's castle, which, like all others, ended in failure, is Gene Smith, "A Sentimental Journey to Dracula's Home Town," *Saturday Evening Post*, March 27, 1965, pp. 76-79. Recent research and excavations, however, seem to suggest that there was at one time a castle near the site where Stoker located it. Raymond T. McNally and Radu Florescu, *In Search of Dracula: A True History of Dracula and Vampire Legends* (Greenwich, 1972), p. 28.

[19] Constantin C. Giurescu, *Istoria Românilor*, vol. 2, pt. 2 (Bucharest, 1937), pp. 121, 123.

[20] Ibid., p. 152.

[21] Rev. Ion Stanciulescu, "Cetatea lui Tepes, cetatea Poenari (mss) p. 4.

[22] Ibid., p. 5.

[23] The identity of the boyar, Gherghina, governor of the castle, is controversial. We know that he enjoyed a very special status of autonomy, unlike other castle governors who were representatives of the prince. He also sat on the council of the boyars. *Istoria Romîniei*, vol. 2 (Bucharest, 1962), p. 330. Some historians think he was the uncle of Prince Radu the Great (1495-1505), the eldest son of Vlad the Monk. We also know that Vlad the Monk's first wife was Gherghina's sister. Giurescu, *Istoria Romînilor*, vol. 2, pt 1, p. 121. Popular folklore, however, considers him as an illegitimate son of Dracula. He was, in any case, a powerful figure. For his genealogy see George D. Florescu, *Divane domnesti din Muntenia in Secolul XV^{lea} din Tara Româneasca* (Bucharest, 1943), p. 320; St. Nicolaescu, *Documente Slavo-române cu privire la relatiile Tarii Românesti si Moldovei cu Ardealul în sec. XV si XVI^{lea}* (Bucharest, 1905), p. 9, footnote.

[24] There was a Hungarian governor as late as 1526. Giurescu, *Istoria Romînilor*, vol. 2, pt. 2, p. 533; vol. 2, pt. 1. pp. 150, 152.

[25] Henri Trenk (1820-1888) was a painter and designer of Swiss origin. He settled in Bucharest as a young man, and together with the Romanian archaeologist Alexander Odobescu he went on an expedition to the Arges region of Romania in 1860-1861. During that expedition he completed three paintings of Castle Dracula in a romantic style. They are all located in the Archives of the Fine Arts Museum in Bucharest. The first painting is dated 1860 (Fine Arts Museum, no. 4205). The second painting is dated 1861 (Fine Arts Museum, no. 4292). The final painting in the series, entitled "Ruins of the Castle," is not signed (Fine Arts Museum, no. 4204). See Stela Ionescu, "Expozitia documentara Henri Trenk (1820-1888),"*Muzeul de Arta at R. P. R. Sectia de arta grafica* (Bucharest, 1965). See also G. Oprescu, *Pictura Romîneasca în secolul al XIX^{lea}* (Bucharest, 1943). Butculescu's aquarelle was kindly lent to the authors by George D. Florescu, who owns it.

[26] The director of the project, the archaeologist Ion Cantacuzino, told the authors that the work of saving Castle Dracula would be completed by September 1972. He has recently given the authors a report of his finds. Although small in terms of its size, and as far as castles go, virtually a ruin, strange as it may seem, Dracula's fortress continues to fascinate all and sundry. When the Romanian encyclopedia *Cartea Româneasca* was published, the editors decide to reproduce a facsimile of the castle under the letter *T* (for Tepes). *Dictionarul Enciclopedic Cartea Româneasca* (Bucharest), p. 1,917.

[27] G. C. Conduratu, *Michael Beheim, Gedicht über den Woivoden Wlad II Dracul*, (Bucharest, 1908), pp. 40-41.

[28] Guboglu and Mehmed. *Cronici turcesti*, p. 199.

[29] N. Simache and T. Cristescu, *Cronicile românesti*, vol. 2, p. 4. Also see a variant of that chronicle: "He also gave great punishment to the citizens of Târgoviste, for an insult which was inflicted on one of Vlad's brothers. Thus on easter day when the citizens were all dining and the young ones dancing the hora, he surprised all of them without warning. All the adults were impaled and the stakes surrounded the city of Targoviste. The young ones, their wives and the maidens in their best dress, as they were clothed on Easter day, he took all of them to Poenari and they worked at the castle until the clothes fell off their backs and they were left naked. It is for this reason that they called him the impaler and he ruled fifteen years." Simache and Cristescu, *Variante ale Letopisetului Cantacuzinesc* (Buzau, 1942), p. 20. Anton Balota has made a study of the various versions of stories in neighboring villages concerning the building of Dracula's castle. They all indicate the existence of a historic epic tradition linked to the history of the construction of the castle in the second half of the fifteenth century. See Á. Balota, "Povestirile slave despre Vlad Tepes," ms. (Bucharest, 1967), app. Also see Petre Ispirescu, *Viata faptile lui Vlad Tepes* (Bucharest, 1942), pp. i-ii. (Extract from review *Fat-Frumos* printed at Cernauti.) For a different version concerning Dracula's motivation for this massacre see P. Ispirescu "Povesti despre Vlad Voda Tepes, Cetatea

Poenari," *Fat-Frumos* (Cernauti, 1935), pp. 1ff. The house ledger of Archbishop Neofit, containing a report of his travels in 1747, contains another version of the building of Poenari. (Manuscript of the Library of the Romanian Socialist Republic, n. 1 #2606, f. 26.) For other accounts see C. Radulescu-Codin, *Ingerul Românilor, povesti si legende din popor* (Bucharest, 1916), pp. 83–86. Another literary episode mentions the possibility that one of the foreman, Manole, had walled his wife within the castle wall, causing it to tumble constantly. Balota, "Povestirile."

[30] Impalement was an ancient Asiatic torture borrowed from the Tartars and Turks by Romanian princes during the fifteenth century. Decapitation (for boyars) and hanging (for commoners), burning at the stake, tearing a man apart, all had been standard methods of punishment since the birth of the principality. Tortures such as mutilation (cutting off hands and ears, etc.), hitting the soles of the feet (Turkish) with hot irons, making an incision in the nose, were also not "invented" by Dracula. The pale was even used by the religious-minded Prince Radu the Great who threatened malefactors with impalement at the scene of the crime. Martha Andronescu, *Repertoriile documentelor Tarii Românesti publicate pina asi, I, 1290-1508* (Bucharest, 1937), p. 778. Another somewhat similar form of torture, practiced in Bucharest up to the first decades of the nineteenth century, was nailing the criminal on the pillar by one ear and exposing the victim publicly.

[31] The destruction of a boyar and his family is recalled both by Chalkokondyles, *Expunerile*, Istorice by V. Grecu (Bucharest, 1958), p. 281, and by M. Beheim in Conduratu, *Michael Beheim*, p. 81, verses 91-100. A native document during the reign of Mircea Ciobanul, dated April 1, 1551, also recalls this episode. *Documente privind istoria Romaniei*, vol. 3 (Bucharest, 1951-60), p. 4. Also see story no. 7 in Saint Gall narrative, McNally and Florescu, *In Search of Dracula*, p. 192.

[32] G. Florescu, *Divane domnesti*, pp. 167-171.

[33] N. I. Serbanescu, *Istoria Manastirii Snagov* (Bucharest, 1944), p. 32, n. 7.

[34] Russian narrative, story no. 6, McNally and Florescu, *In Search of Dracula*, p. 198.

[35] G. D. Florescu placed an interesting manuscript on the origins of Cîrta at the authors' disposal.

[36] A great many of the Russian and German narratives as well as Romanian folklore stress Dracula's association with priests and monks, both Catholic and Orthodox.

[37] There is a great deal of controversy surrounding the reigns of Vlad IV, "the Monk." Although a monk, contrary to the practice of the Orthodox church he married twice, a boyar lady called Rada and later Maria, who gave him five children (the eldest, Radu the Great). It is interesting to note that both his wives became nuns and assumed religious names. It is possible that Rada became the nun Samonius, and Maria, the nun Eupraxia. The historian Bogdan, on the other hand, takes Vlad the Monk to be Dracula's son and considers him a degenerate. Bogdan, *Vlad Tepes*, pp. 50-51; G. Ghibanescu, "Vlad Voda calugarul," *Archiva* 7 (1896): 140; Al. Lapedatu, *Vlad Voda calugarul* (Bucharest, 1903); Paul Cernovodeanu, "Stiri privitoare la octitorie a lui Vlad Voda calugarul: schitul Babele 1492-1493," *Glasul bisericii* 19, no. 5-6 (1930): 483-497.

[38] Thus Radu the Great is known for his peaceful reign, 1495-1508, and his donations to the church. He basically gave Wallachia its ecclesiastical structure, creating two bishoprics (Severin and Buzau). We find his name associated with the foundation and endowment of a great number of churches and monasteries in Wallachia and at Mount Athos. He is often confused with his illegitimate son, Radu VI of Afumati, 1522-1553, 1524-1525. Stefan Andreescu, "Radu de la Afumati sau Radul cel Mare," *Magazinul istoric* 3, no. 2 (February 1969): 94-95; Alexandru Lapedatu, "Politica lui Radu cel Mare 1495-1508," in *Lui Ion Bianu: Amintire* (Bucharest, 1916), pp. 191-223.

[39] For Snagov see chap. V, nn. 31 and 32.

[40] The only indirect reference to a Dracula endowment to Snagov is an edict of Mircea Ciobanul, dated June 26, 1558, which endows certain properties to Snagov, stating, "and I have read the old books of Vlad Voevod Tepes." Library of the Academy of the Romanian Socialist Republic, ms., f. 21. It would be illogical to suppose that Dracula, having made donations to his other great monasteries in Romania (Comana, Cozia, Tismana) and possibly abroad at Athos, Rossikon, and Philoteiu, should have ignored Snagov. The villages of Cracimari and Babeni were likely endowed during his reign. Serbanescu, *Istoria manastirii Snagov*, p. 32.

[41] According to tradition, the church of the monastery of Comana was built by Dracula in 1461—he then made a donation. See *Documente privind istoria României veac XIII-XV*, p. 132. Subsequently destroyed, it was rebuilt by Prince Radu Serban in 1588 and again in 1699 by Prince Serban Cantacuzino. Prince Radu Serban was buried there in 1640. Comana also houses a famous chronicle written by Mathew of the Mirs. Among other famous men buried at Comana is Metropolitan Longhin Brancovici (seventeenth century), a presumed son of Michael the Brave. The palace of Radu Serban, in the vicinity, and its powerful walls are now in ruins. Until detailed archaeological research is made, one cannot definitely ascribe the construction of Comana to Dracula. Also see N. Stoicescu, "Bibliografia monumentelor feudale din Tara Româneasca," Craiova, 1966, pp. 93-96. The monastery is located very close to one of three villages named in honor of Vlad Tepes.

[42] Ascribing the construction of a recently excavated church at Cetateni to Dracula is mere speculation by Dinu Rosetti, the archaeologist who visited the site with the authors in the summer of 1969.

[43] The authors of the present work, together with Professor Giurescu, took a trip to Strejnicu in the hope of finding the original Dracula inscription at the spot where it had lain forty years before. The aged priest was still there, but the inscription had vanished. We were told that it had been moved to another church at nearby Ploesti. Needless to say, our venture at Ploesti was another source of frustration. It was only after a lengthy goose chase, leading to various museums and churches in Bucharest and elsewhere, that the authors were told that the Dracula inscription was located at Iorga's former school of Valeni de Munte. It seems that on the eve of World War II, shortly before his assassination, Nicolae Iorga had taken pains to remove the inscription to his mountain retreat for safekeeping. Constantin C. Giurescu, "O biserica a lui Vlad Tepes la Tirgsor," *Buletinul comisiunii monumentelor istorice* 17 (Bucharest, 1924): 74-75. Also see G. Zagorit, "O noua manastire zidita de Vlad Tepes," *Copii neamului* 1, no. 4 (April 1, 1922): 12. Some historians think that Dracula founded another church at Târgsor.

[44] Panaitescu and Mioc, eds., *Documenta Romaniae*, p. 198.

[45] Among the better known collections of historical ballads referring to Dracula are C. Radulescu-Codin, *Ingerul românului; Legende, traditii si amintiri istorice adunate din Oltenia si din Muscel* (Bucharest, 1910); *Din Muscel, cantece poporane adunate din Oltenia si din Muscel* (Bucharest, 1896); *Comorile poporului, literatura, obiceiuri si credinte* (Bucharest, 1930). Petre Ispirescu, "Viata si faptele lui Vlad Tepes Voda," extracted from Cernauti review *Fat-Frumos* (Cernauti, 1939, 1942); *Povesti despre Vlad Voda Tepes; opera postuma* (Cernauti, 1935, 1936). For a more recent compilation see V. Adascalitei, *De la Dragos la Cuza Voda, legende populare românesti* (Bucharest, 1966). For Transylvanian folklore see Ferencz Kóos, "Az ördög voda. Elbeszeles," in *Szekely naptar* (Târgu-Mures, 1869). Also see the interesting monograph of Rev. Ioan Rautescu, *Câmpulung-Muscel; monografie istorica* (Câmpulung-Muscel, 1943). A very recent doctoral dissertation on the subject still in manuscript is G. Ene, "Figura domnitorului muntean Vlad Tepes in legendele istorice din comuna Arefu-Arges."

[46] We have relied on a comparative study of all Dracula ballads and narratives placed at our disposal by the late Slavicist Anton Balota, a researcher at the

University of Bucharest. This manuscript is to be published by the *East European Quarterly* in 1974.

[47] Mihail Popescu, ed., *Legende istorice ale Românilor din cronicari.* (Bucharest, 1937), pp. 16-18.

[48] Russian narrative, story no. 4, McNally and Florescu, *In Search of Dracula,* p. 197.

[49] Russian narrative, story no. 5, ibid.

[50] Nicolae Vatamanu, *De la începuturile medicinei Românesti* (Bucharest, 1966), p. 79.

[51] Ispirescu, *Povesti despre Vlad Voda Tepes,* p. 21.

[52] Ibid., p. 14.

[53] The division *internal* and *external* conventionally adopted by Romanian historians treats Transylvania as a "foreign" land, which it was until 1918. Given the fact that relations between Transylvania and Wallachia were so close that Dracula had fiefs in that province (Fagaras and Almas), one is tempted to consider the Transylvanian documentation as "internal" documentation.

[54] On the commercial importance of Brasov see Nicolae Iorga, *Negotul si mestesugurile in trecutul românesc* (Bucharest, 1906), pp. 89-90. Also see Radu Manolescu, "Evolutia schimbului de marfuri al Tarii Romanesti a Moldovei cu Brasovul în secolele XIV-XVI," doctoral dissertation (Bucharest, 1961). Also see note chap. 1, n. 23.

[55] Bogdan, *Documente,* pp. 316-317.

[56] Conduratu, *Michael Beheim,* pp. 45, 46-47, 49.

[57] Nicolae Olahus was the son of a boyar, Manzila, from the Arges region, a relative of Dracula's. He is undoubtedly one of the most fascinating figures of the Transylvanian Renaissance. Serious study on all aspects of his career have only begun. Among many works, he left a fairly detailed description of Transylvania and Hungary in which he showed pride for his Romanian origins. Referring to Transylvania, he carefully distinguishes between its "nations": the Hungarians, the Saxons, the Székelys, and the Romanians. (*Hungarie sive de originibus gentis regni situ divisione habite atque opportunitatibus,* 1735.) Olahus was also the first Romanian poet writing Latin verse. On his family origins see S. Bezdecki, *Familia lui Nicolae Olahus* (Bucharest, n.d.), pp. 63-65 (extract from *Anuarul Inst. de istorice).* For his career see George Ivascu, *Istoria literaturii române* (Bucharest, 1969), pp. 61-62; S. Bezdecki, *Nicolaus Olahus primul umanist de origine romîna* (Anineasa-Gorj, 1939); Th. Vojteck Bucheo, *Nikulás Oláh a jeho doba* (Bratislava, 1940).

[58] Hurmuzacki, *Documente,* XV-I, pp. 48-49.

[59] Saint Gall ms., story nos. 3 and 4, McNally and Florescu, *In Search of Dracula,* p. 192.

[60] Conduratu, *Michael Beheim,* p. 32.

[61] Russian narrative, story no. 10, McNally and Florescu, *In Search of Dracula,* p. 199.

[62] Ibid., pp. 106, 116.

[63] Russian narrative, story no. 10, Ibid., p. 199.

[64] The decapitation of Dan and that of his followers (only seven escaped) is related in Conduratu, *Michael Beheim,* p. 32, verses 111-130 and in most of the German narratives. Also see a letter dated April 22, 1460 in Nicolae Iorga, "Lucruri noua despre Vlad Tepes si Stefan cel Mare," *Convorbiri literare,* 35 (1901): 149-162, and 38 (1904): 152-159, 381-383. For greater detail on Dan's rule see Iorga, "Un voivod necunoscut," *Studii si Documente* 11 (Bucharest, 1906), 217; C. Kogalniceanu, "Dan fiul si Dan nepotul lui Mircea cel Batrîn," *Convorbiri literare* 60 (1923), 371-376.

[65] St. Gall ms., story no. 25, McNally and Florescu, *In Search of Dracula*, p. 194.

[66] Conduratu, *Michael Beheim*, p. 41.

[67] Bogdan, *Vlad Tepes*, pp. 44-45. There are Russian prints in existence depicting Ivan the Terrible nailing the hats on visiting dignitaries' heads.

[68] L. Godechot, *Les Révolutions* (Paris, 1963), p. 169.

[69] G. Mercati "Notisie varie sopra Niccolò Modrussiense," Vol. 14, pp. 261. Some researchers think that the papal legate deliberately exaggerated Dracula's misdeeds to justify the action of the king in imprisoning Dracula. Even discounting the papal dispatch, however, the evidence attesting to Dracula's cruelties is overwhelming and is derived from too many unconnected sources.

[70] Guboglu and Mehmet, *Cronici turcesti*, p. 67.

[71] For Stephen's treatment of political prisoners see A. Boldur, *Stefan cel mare voivod al Moldovei 1457-1504*, vol. 1 (Madrid, 1970), p. 137.

[72] This is a variant of a story related by P. Ispirescu. McNally and Florescu, *In Search of Dracula*, p. 208.

4

Dracula's Foreign Policy and the Turkish Campaign of 1461-1462

Dracula's foreign policy, specifically his wars and his campaign against the Turks in 1461-1462, represents by far the most richly documented segment of his extraordinary career.[1] Most of the documentation can be labeled *external*, and much of it stems from the pens of Dracula's enemies. Among the most significant sources, are the writings of the Byzantine and Turkish chroniclers. Of the Byzantines the most exhaustive coverage, but not necessarily the most accurate, is the account of Chalkokondyles who takes the Turkish point of view; Michel Doukas and Kritoboulos of Imbros are undoubtedly more impartial. From the Turkish side the campaign of 1462 is covered by half a dozen contemporary historians. By far the most vivid and complete is the narrative of a Serbian janissary from Ostrovita who fought in the Turkish ranks and was an actual eyewitness throughout the early phases of the war. So was the Turkish chronicler Enveri, who can be called a participant.

The campaign of 1462 can also be studied from a Romanian viewpoint. One of the most fascinating testimonies on the beginnings of the hostilities, which includes Dracula's lightning attack upon the Danube, was dictated by Dracula himself in Latin. He wrote a lengthy letter, dated February 11, 1462, from the captured fortress of Giurgiu to King Matthias.[2] Two other letters were allegedly signed by Dracula at the end of the campaign in November, in the city of "Rothel." [3] The purpose of the first letter was to impress the Hungarian king with Dracula's acumen and to enlist his support in the anti-Turkish crusade. One measure of the value of this testimony is the accurate statistics it contains on the number of Turkish victims. Another native source, which has only recently been discovered, is an account by a veteran in Dracula's army which may have been inspired by Dracula himself and contains information on the famous night attack.[4]

In addition we have used the occasional references in the Slavic narrative and the German poem of Michel Beheim, particularly relevant in describing the circumstances that led to Dracula's capture. The Germans were informed accurately only on the events close to their Transylvanian border with which they were familiar, thus proving that his narration has to be taken with a great deal of seriousness. Romanian oral tradition will also be found helpful in dealing with Dracula's escape across the mountains from his Transylvanian castle. The writings or commentaries of Pope Pius II; the reports of his representative at Buda; the accounts of the court historian, Antonio Bonfinius; the dispatches of the representatives of the Venetian Republic in the Hungarian capital, Pietro Tommasi and Balbi; the five or six Serbian chronicles—all help to fill important gaps, here and there. Various interpretations have also been given by voyagers to eastern Europe, pilgrims to the Holy Land such as William of Wey, and some historians who wrote shortly after these events, Italians such as Felix Petancius and Anton Verancsics, and Germans like Sebastian Münster, who has invaluable material in his *Cosmographia Universalis*.

Whether friendly or hostile, most of this testimony emphasizes Dracula's heroic role, which made a deep impact on what was left of the crusading cause in western and central Europe. Several Italian writers in the following century were so impressed by Dracula's heroic epopee that they labeled the inhabitants of his Wallachian province "Draguli," in honor of their prince.

Dracula's foreign policy cannot be divorced from events at home. It has been already said that his persecution of the boyars and his decision to create a strong personal army were mainly motivated by his concern about the Turkish military menace on the Danube. One reason for the elimination of the older boyars was their pro-Turkish policy of appeasement, which Dracula viewed as subversive. It is clear from the foregoing that the supreme objective of Dracula's foreign policy was to free his principality from all vestiges of vassalage to Constantinople, which had been conceded at the end of his grandfather's, Prince Mircea's, reign. Only the incursions against the German-Saxon merchants of Transylvania during the years of 1458 to 1460, which must be looked upon as a temporary tergiversation, prevented Dracula from fulfilling this central objective.

In order to secure this aim, Dracula needed allies. In his view the pivotal alliances centered on his two neighbors: King Matthias, who ruled in Transylvania and Hungary to the west, and his cousin, Stephen of Moldavia, to the north. Since with respect to foreign policy at least, Dracula was a medievalist, in his efforts to obtain unity among a wider number of central and west European states, he attempted to rekindle enthusiasm for a renewed crusade against the infidel, involving at least all the remaining independent powers of central and eastern Europe. There are indications that Dracula imagined himself as another "Wallachian White Knight" capable of assuming the mantle of the great Hunyady himself, his former patron, with the wider objective of expelling the Turks from the whole Balkan peninsula.

In spite of his great bravery and tactical skill, and one or two moments of near success in the winter of 1461-1462, destiny was not to make such an ambitious role possible for Dracula.

Certainly political and diplomatic circumstances in both eastern and central Europe and in the west did not presage success in directing a crusade against the Ottomans. In eastern Europe the fall of Constantinople in 1453, a greater psychological than military setback, had meant the final collapse of a beleaguered Byzantium, the officialdom of which had few qualms in making peace with their Turkish protectors and masters, whom in many instances they preferred to the Italians. Even the duchy of Athens, ruled by a Florentine duke, finally surrendered to the Turks the year of Dracula's accession to the throne. Within the South Slavic lands, the last vestiges of Serbian resistance completely collapsed by 1460, and occasional opposition in Bosnia, badly subverted by the Bogomil heresy, ended three years later (1463). In the Balkans all that was left in the hands of the Christians by the time Dracula began his attack on the Turks, was Albania, still in the hands of Scanderbeg, the rebel who continued a desperate resistance until 1466. Another instance of successful resistance was that of Montenegro, a Serbian mountain principality that the Turks were never able to conquer. Both the latter military resistances, however, were strictly defensive, isolated, and in no way capable of joining Dracula from their respective mountain hideouts. The republic of Ragusa and a few harbors on the Dalmatian and Greek coasts, in addition to some islands in the Adriatic and Aegean seas, were still in the hands or under the protection of the Venetian Republic. Indeed one might say that in southeastern Europe the Venetian Republic alone represented a major naval power still capable of dealing a devastating blow to the Turks. However, in spite of the pleas of its emissary at Buda, Pietro Tommasi, who asked the Venetian senate repeatedly for military aid, the merchant republic participated in the crusade only in 1463, when Dracula was safely placed in a Hungarian jail.

The situation in central Europe was not much more propitious for a crusade. Hungary was still in the throes of internal disorders and strife, which had racked the kingdom since the death of Hunyady. This climaxed in the struggle for power between the forces of Matthias Corvinus, Hunyady's son, and those of the Hapsburg Holy Roman Emperor, Frederick III, for the Hungarian crown. There was, in addition, difficulties with Bohemia ever since the Hussite rebellion—the Taborites were finally defeated in 1434—but memories died slowly. King Matthias of Hungary, to whom Dracula had sworn fidelity, had been very liberal with promises only: "With the help of God, I will descend in Transylvania and unite with Dracula."[5] Words such as these, however, remained on paper and were not to be translated into fact until after Dracula's defeat, in spite of the sums of money that Matthias had already collected from the papacy for the purpose of a crusade. Undoubtedly Dracula's persecution of the Transylvanian German townships in 1459-1560 did not help enhance his chances of obtaining Transylvania and German aid, if only in weaponry, which he had often sought.

Neither was George of Podebrad, king of Bohemia (1458-1471), too interested in fighting the infidel, who did not really threaten his border. He needed all his efforts to restore the badly shattered authority of the crown of Saint Wenceslaus which had followed religious and civil disobedience.

The Jagellon King Casimir IV of Poland, "Cneaz of Lithuania" (1447-1492), was at least morally committed to military effort after the indignities suffered by the Polish army under King Ladislas III in the debacle at Varna in 1444. At first it seemed likely that the Polish king might at least attempt to improve the bad relations that existed between Wallachia and Moldavia and reunite the two against the common Turkish enemy. A letter to that effect was written on April 2, 1462, to Prince Stephen of Moldavia. But Poland was too distant and too involved in its own struggles against the German Teutonic Order to do much more than protest by diplomatic means. Ivan III, Grand Duke of Moscow, was even more geographically remote from the scene than Poland and was clearly preoccupied with internal feudal and religious strife. Abroad his initial objective was to escape from dependence on the Tartar yoke.

By far the most invaluable and loyal ally to Dracula should have been the principality of Moldavia. We have as yet too few documents to write a complete history of Moldavian-Wallachian relations during Dracula's central reign—these inevitably present certain intriguing and unresolvable problems.[6] Given the facts that the two families were related by marriage (Stephen was Dracula's cousin); that they had spent several years together at Suceava as students and been educated together; that they had fought side by side against Poland at the battle of Crasna in 1450; that they had fled to Transylvania in each other's company after Stephen's father's assassination in 1451; that Stephen had reconquered his Moldavian throne with Dracula's help in 1457, in accordance with an oath that the two cousins had taken to come to each other's aid; given all these facts, Stephen's hostility to Dracula in 1462 seems quite unaccountable. The prince of Moldavia not only turned down Dracula's demands for military aid but also betrayed the trust of his cousin by collaborating with the Turks at the worst possible moment in the conflict, by attacking the fortress of Chilia on the Danube delta, which was nominally under Wallachian control. For those who admire the Moldavian prince, this Turko-Moldavian collaboration represents one of the most difficult problems to explain away from the point of view of personal ethics as well as of state obligations. The only possible answer is the argument of *raison d'état* invoked by most Romanian historians, apologists of Stephen.[7] Stephen was thinking less of his treaty obligation to Dracula than of the survival of the Moldavian principality, should Chilia fall to the Turks. The Moldavian prince, moreover, had a valid pretext for attacking Chilia; though *de jure* it belonged to Dracula, its garrison was principally composed of Hungarians. Moldavia also had to play a cautious defensive policy on its northern frontier, since Poland, in spite of the words of Casimir IV, constituted a more immediate threat than the Turks. First token submission to Poland had occurred in 1455, and it is conceivable that Stephen preferred more amicable relations with Turkey in order to be able to deal more effectively with his ambitious northern neighbor.

Finally, the situation in western Europe was not calculated to strengthen Dracula's crusading zeal: the achievement of national unity and the centralization of power by individual despots were the dominating Renaissance themes, not crusading—essentially a medieval—survival.

Only in the Italies, badly torn by particularists' interests of its warring city-states, did crusading interests win the allegiance of a typically mundane Renaissance pope: Enea Silvio de Piccolomini (Aeneas Silvius), Pius II. Pius II, in essence, was the only major figure who had encouraged Dracula's action and had raised the necessary funds for the anti-Ottoman crusade in accordance with the traditional, worn-out clarion call of "Dieu le veut!" However, as a realist, the pope was not sanguine of success: one month after his coronation, at the Congress of Mantua, Pius II remarked that the odds were against such an enterprise, cynically observing: "Albani exhausti sunt, Hungari fessi, Valachi exterriti or extincti nisi opem ferimus aut fugere aut sese dedere et cum perfide Machometo Christum blasphemare iogentur."[8]

What were the causes for the outbreak of Turko-Wallachian hostilities? Dracula's relations with the Turks, in a sense, followed a pattern identical to the numerous tergiversations of his father, Dracul. After his release from Turkish captivity, Dracula had become the sultan's official candidate to the Wallachian throne in 1448. However, with his defeat, he proved ingrate to his Turkish protectors and fled to Moldavia and later to Transylvania, unwilling to risk reproof or renewed imprisonment.

In spite of his oath to the Hungarian king, in the initial years of his reign at least, Dracula's relationship with the Turks was correct, and insofar as we can ascertain, he fulfilled his obligation of vassalage. The first indication that here might be problems in preserving amicable relations came from Dracula's own pen. In a letter dated September 10, 1456, written to the city elders of Brasov, Dracula revealed his real thinking, only a matter of days after his inauguration as prince:

I'm giving you the news . . . that an Embassy from Turkey has now come to us. Bear in mind and firmly retain what I have previously transacted with you about brotherhood and

peace . . . the time and the hour has now come, concerning what
I have previously spoken of. The Turks wish to place on our
shoulders . . . unbearable difficulties and . . . to compel us not to
live peaceably [with you]. . . . They are seeking a way to loot
your country passing through ours. In addition, they force us . . .
to work against your Catholic faith. Our wish is to do no evil
against you, not to abandon you, as I have told you and sworn. I
trust I will remain your brother and faithful friend. This is
why I have retained the Turkish envoys here, *so that I have*
time to send you the news.

There follows a typically machiavellian precept:

You have to reflect . . . when a prince is powerful and brave,
then he can make peace as he wishes. If, however, he is
powerless, some more powerful than he will conquer him and
dictate as he pleases. This is why by this letter we ask you
with love . . . to send for our sake and yours without delay, 200,
or 100 or 50 chosen men, no later than the Sunday which
immediately follows. When the Turks will see a Hungarian
army, they will soften [their demands] and we can tell them
that more are to come.[9]

In spite of these entreaties, the expected help from
Transylvania never came, a fact that may well have angered
Dracula and encouraged his Transylvanian incursions in 1458-
1460.

Reference to the detention of the Turkish envoys leads us to
suspect that this episode may well coincide with the famous
scene described in the German, Russian, and Romanian
narratives of the nailing of the turbans on the heads of the
Turkish ambassadors. Some historians are inclined to assign
this incident to 1462 on the eve of the outbreak of hostilities.[10]
We tend to differ from this view on the following grounds: Since
the first German manuscript mentioning the incident is dated
1462, and since news from eastern Europe traveled slowly, it
seems hardly conceivable that such anecdotes could have
reached western Europe in so short a time. Moreover, in itself,
the provocation is not sufficiently serious to account for the
eruption of hostilities, since more likely than not, the Turkish
emissaries survived the ordeal. The Russian narrative
describes the incident in the following way:

At one time, some envoys, from the Turkish Sultan came to him; when they came and they bowed to him according to their custom, they did not take their turbans off. Dracula asked them: "Why do you do this towards a great ruler?" they answered, "This is our custom, my Lord, which is that of our country." Dracula then answered, "I too wish to strengthen your law so that you may be firm," and he ordered that their turbans be nailed to their heads with small iron nails. Then he allowed them to go, telling them: "Go and tell your master that he is accustomed to indure such shame from you but we are not accustomed. Let him not impose his customs to other rulers, who do not wish them, but let him keep them in his land."[11]

The point of this act of vengeance was not so much directed against the suzerain power as to teach the Turkish or any other representatives at his court a lesson in protocol and international good manners. Dracula's egomania and his sense of national pride would accept no slur on his "sacrosanct" person or the honor due to his state. The Russian narrative further explains:

Whenever there came to him an envoy; from the Emperor, or from the King, if he was not properly attired and was not able to give answers concerning [Dracula's] punishments, he was impaled, being told: "I am not guilty of your death, but your master, or you yourself; don't reproach me with anything, since your master, knowing you to be simple and uncultivated, has sent you to me; a wise ruler. Therefore, your master has killed you. But if you yourself have dared come to me on this mission, then you have killed yourself."[12]

Language such as this was one way of reaffirming even to the suzerain power the fact that Wallachia was a sovereign state.

Despite *de jure* submission, it should be emphasized that Wallachia continued to remain an autonomous state. In fact, since Dracula's main objective was to escape from Turkish vassalage, it is essential to spell out more precisely the articles of the so-called capitulation treaties that regulated the relations between Wallachia and the Ottoman Empire. These capitulations may have been officially reaffirmed by Dracula in 1460 in a treaty, although the original document has been lost and only a manufactured copy of that treaty exists.[13] Among the stipulations were the following obligations: (1) a yearly tribute of ten thousand gold ducats *(haratch)* sent to Constantinople each year, preferably brought by the prince in person, and (2) a yearly visit to Constantinople to kiss "the hem of the Sultan's coattail" as a token of submission. No prince could be formally invested before appearing at the sultan's court. Dracula likely presented himself in person in 1456, in 1457, and as late as 1458, thus arousing the suspicions of Christendom. The limitations on Turkish power imposed by the same capitulations also deserve to be stressed. The prince and the boyar council remained in control of the land and enjoyed all the attributes of sovereignty: they administered the laws, minted coins, conducted diplomacy, enjoyed the privilege of making war and peace and even that of granting asylum to Moslems as well as to Christians. Although officially linked to the patriarchy of Constantinople, the native Wallachian church continued to be autonomous, with native bishops as incumbents. Additionally, the Turks did not have the right to settle in the country or buy land north of the Danube, nor were their merchants allowed to transact business on Romanian soil. Another limitation on Turkish power, which was bitterly resented, was their inability to collect the child tribute in Wallachia. Turkish recruiting agents could only enroll youngsters from Balkan provinces integratedly linked to Constantinople for the janissary corps.

Taking the overall tense Turko-Wallachian situation resulting from Dracula's double dealings into account, the reasons for the final breakdown of relations and for the opening of hostilities must be sought in Turkish attempts to enforce these "infringements" of the capitulations, and extend the terms of these treaties to Turkish advantage. The tribute had been paid regularly by Dracula only during the first three years of his reign, although one finds it difficult to conceive of Dracula's kissing the hem of the sultan's coattails. From 1459 to 1461 onward, however, perhaps because he was preoccupied with the problems of the Transylvanian Saxons, Dracula had technically violated his capitulatory obligations and failed to appear at the Turkish court. This is why when negotiations resumed on the eve of the outbreak of hostilities, among other demands the Turks asked for the payment of the *haratch* tax unpaid in the last three years.

There was another surprising new Turkish demand which had never been stipulated before and represented a clear infraction of the capitulations. This entailed the request for payment of the child tribute, no fewer than five hundred young boys destined for the janissary corps, the infantry elite composed of recruits from other provinces of the Balkans, with the help of which the Turks had conquered the peninsula.[14] Indeed Turkish recruiting officers had occasionally shown themselves in the Wallachian plain, particularly in the province of Oltenia, which was particularly accessible from Bulgaria, and where the quality of manhood was best. Such incursions had been resisted by Dracula by force of arms, and the Turkish beys who were caught in hot pursuit across the Danube, were apt to find themselves on the extremity of a stake. In fact, such violations of territory practiced by both sides were considered as added provocations and embittered Turko-Wallachian relations. Raiding, pillaging, and looting were endemic from Giurgiu to the Black Sea coast, particularly as the line of the Danube did not always coincide with the common frontier. The Turks, in fact, had succeeded in securing control of various fortresses and townships on the Romanian side. Taking advantage of Mohammed's expeditions in Asiatic Turkey, Dracula had also proceeded to encroachments of his own on the Bulgarian side.

In retaliation for Dracula's spirit of noncooperation, the Turks had for some years, perhaps as early as 1458, given encouragement to Radu, Dracula's brother, who had faithfully resided at Constantinople since his liberation in 1447 and who already at the time considered himself as the prospective candidate to the Wallachian throne.

Before deciding on a final dethronement, Sultan Mohammed decided to give Dracula a final chance. (This episode is mentioned in Michel Beheim's poem as well as in the Turkish chronicles.) He invited Dracula to come to Nicopolis on the Danube (the town of Schylta in the German narrative) to meet the bey of Rumelia, Isaac Pasha, who represented the sultan. The latter was instructed to persuade Dracula to present himself at Constantinople in person and explain his misconduct during the last few years, which so adversely affected Turko-Wallachian relations. If the German narrative is true, Dracula, apparently in a submissive mood, was prepared to come with gifts to Constantinople, agreeing to discuss the frontier, but unwilling to pay the child tribute. It is unlikely, however, that he actually proceeded to Turkey, as Beheim infers.[15] He was much too astute for that, knowing how his father had been tricked before. The official pretext for his refusal to come to Constantinople, relayed to the sultan through the bey of Rumelia, was that if he went to the Turkish capital, his enemies in Transylvania would seize power in his absence.

From a Turkish point of view one must view the sultan's final trickery with a certain understanding. There was obviously no basis for genuine and sincere negotiations. Dracula's refusal to come to Constantinople simply confirmed earlier suspicions, of which the Turks were only too well aware, that Dracula was at the very same time negotiating with the Hungarians for an alliance and possibly for a marriage. The Turks decided first to attempt to ensnare Dracula in a well-planned ambush. The men entrusted with this mission could not have been better chosen; Chalkokondyles mentions a clever "Greek devil," Thomas Catavolinos (Greeks were already at that time beginning to be used in Turkish diplomacy); the other delegate was Hamza Pasha, the "chief court falconner," governor of Nicopolis, a man who was known for his subtle mind. Their ostensible mission was to discuss a mutually acceptable frontier on the Danube and once again to persuade Dracula to come to Constantinople. Since they suspected Dracula would refuse the latter, in essence their secret mission was to capture the Wallachian prince alive.

This episode is of itself sufficiently dramatic to bear extensive comment, and we are fortunate in possessing a very comprehensive testimony on the precise circumstances from Dracula himself, in a missive worth quoting in full, since it represents one of the most fascinating documents on the early phases of the Turko-Wallachian war. The original manuscript was accidentally found in the 1920s by the Romanian historian N. Iorga in the Munich archives.

Dracula's letter describing the event is dated February 11, 1462, and is addressed to King Matthias from the city of Giurgiu, by that time safely in his hands:

In other letters I have written to Your Highness the way in which the Turks, the cruel enemies of the Cross of Christ have sent their envoys to me, in order to break our mutual peace and alliance and to spoil our marriage, so that I may be allied only with them and that I travel to the Turkish sovereign, that is to say to his court, and, should I refuse to abandon the peace, and the treaties, and the marriage with Your Highness, the Turks will not keep the peace with me. They also sent a leading counselor of the Sultan, Hamza Bey of Nicopolis, to determine the Danubian frontier, with the intent that Hamza Bey should, if he could, take me in some manner by trickery or good faith, or in some other manner, to the Porte and if not, to try and take me in captivity. But by the grace of God, as I was journeying towards their frontier, I found out about their trickery and slyness and I was the one who captured Hamza Bey in the Turkish district and land, close to a fortress called Giurgiu. As the Turks opened the gates of the fortress, on the orders of our men, with the thought that only their men would enter, our soldiers mixing with theirs entered the fortress and conquered the city which I then set on fire.[16]

In that same letter Dracula describes the subsequent campaign that took place along the Danube up to the Black Sea during the winter of 1462, which in fact constituted a *de facto* opening of hostilities, without so much as a formal declaration of war. Thus in a sense Dracula can be looked upon as the aggressor.

The Danubian campaign represents the initial successful phase of the Turko-Wallachian war, and Dracula was actually on the offensive, attempting to duplicate Hunyady's successful amphibious warfare during the 1440s. Much of the campaign took place on Bulgarian soil, controlled by the Turks. From the mention of place names in Dracula's Giurgiu letter (many of them exist to this day), it is possible to reconstitute the progress of Dracula's forces along the Danube. We also have precise mention of the number of casualties inflicted:

I have killed men and women, old and young, who lived at Oblucitza and Novoselo where the Danube flows into the sea up to Rahova which is located near Chilia from the lower [Danube] up to such places as Samovit and Ghighen [both located in modern Bulgaria]. [We killed] 23,884 Turks and Bulgars without counting those whom we burned in homes or whose heads were not cut by our soldiers . . . thus Your Highness must know that I have broken the peace with him.

There follow some gloomy statistics of men killed: at Oblucitza and Novoselo, 1,350; at Dîrstor (Durostor, Silistria), Cîrtal, and Drido-potrom (no trace of latter town), 6,840; at Orsova, 343; at Vectrem, 840; at Turtucaia, 630; at Marotim, 210; at Giurgiu itself, 6,414; at Turnu, Batin and Novigrad, 384; at Sistov, with both marketplaces dependent upon that town, 410; at Nicopolis, Samovit, and Ghighen, 1,138; at Rahova, 1,460.

To further impress King Matthias with the accuracy of this account, Dracula sent through his envoy, Radu Farma, two bags of heads, noses, and ears to Buda.[17] Those who were captured by Dracula, including the Turkish leaders, Hamza Pasha and Thomas Catavolinos (the latter two were beheaded at Giurgiu), were taken to Tîrgoviste, and impaled in the hills in the vicinity.

The character of Dracula's campaign along the Danube had several objectives. First, it had a liberating aspect. With the invasion of Bulgaria proper, countless Bulgarian peasants joined the Christian ranks and greeted the Wallachian leader as a deliverer from the Turkish yoke. Later, when the Wallachians were compelled to retreat, many Bulgarian villagers sought and obtained asylum in Wallachia, fearing Turkish reprisals. It also had a crusading character, continuing the efforts previously made by the great Transylvanian warrior Hunyady, Dracula's mentor, whose objective had been the destruction of Turkish power in the Balkans. "Your majesty must know," wrote Dracula to King Matthias in the famous letter of February 11, "that I have broken the peace with them not for *our sake*, but for the sake of the honor of Your Highness . . . Your Highness' Holy Cross, and for guarding all of Christianity and strengthening the Catholic law."[18] Second, Dracula had a strategic aim—to destroy Turkish power along the Danube by burning fordable towns and potential food supplies and dispersing the population. The purpose of such strikes was to make a Turkish invasion of his country, which Dracula now judged inevitable, more difficult. Also, from a psychological point of view, and knowing the impressionable Turkish mentality, Dracula undoubtedly made use of terror to frighten the Turks.

The early portion of the campaign, which stirred the admiration of Europe, compelled the Turks to action. Dracula was sufficiently a realist to anticipate the full furor of the sultan's revenge. Destroying Danubian beachheads and port facilities was one way of gaining time to allow those succors he had asked for from the Christian camp to arrive. In the last-minute scramble for allies, Dracula had made his main pitch with the king of Hungary, Matthias:

Gather your whole army, your cavalry, and your infantry, bring them to our Wallachian land and accept to fight with us here. If Your Highness does not wish to come personally, then kindly send your army to the Transylvanian region of your realm . . . if Your Majesty does not wish to give your army, then only send as many as you wish, the Transylvanians and the Székelys. And if Your Highness is willing to lend help, then be good enough not to delay and let us truly know your mind. Please this time, do not delay our emissary [Radu Farma] who is bringing this letter to you. Send him back to me immediately and swiftly. Let us in no way leave unfinished what we have begun, let us push this affair to a conclusion. For if the Almighty will listen to the prayers and wishes of Christianity, if he will favorably listen to the prayers of his unworthy subjects, he will give us victory over the Infidel, the enemies of the Cross of Christ.

Despite his indulging in optimism, Dracula knew only too well that the odds were stacked against him. He prophetically warned the king of Hungary sixty-four years before the disastrous Hungarian defeat at Mohács (1625) that: "Should, God forbid, we come to harm, should our little land perish . . . it will not facilitate things for your highness and it will be to the detriment of all of Christendom."[19] Less eloquent entreaties had undoubtedly already been sent to the Venetian Republic, where Dracula, at least, gained the sympathy and support of its envoy at Buda, Pietro Tommasi. Other emissaries were sent to Pope Pius II, to Casimir IV of Poland, who showed sympathy, and to Stephen of Moldavia, his cousin. However, apart from papal finance, which never got to him—the money was pocketed by King Matthias—all that was obtained was sympathy and pious declarations of support. In the spring of 1462 Dracula found himself facing the Turks alone. When the Christian powers finally decided to join the crusade in 1463, the Wallachian prince was behind bars in a Hungarian jail.

The extraordinary exploits on the Danube, however, were greeted in western Europe by mixed awe, admiration, and praise. It seemed as if the days of the great Hunyady had come again. A new hope of liberation spread throughout the enslaved lands of Bulgaria, Serbia, and Greece. At Constantinople itself there was an atmosphere of consternation, gloom, and fear. Some of the Turkish leaders, haunted by the awesome reputation of the Impaler, "Kazîglu," had apparently contemplated flight across the Bosphorus into Asia Minor. The jubilation manifested in the eastern Christian camp is reflected in the comments of an English pilgrim, William of

Wey, returning from his travels to the Holy Land and stopping at the island of Rhodes, where he arrived on August 19, 1462: "Istud audientes milites de Rodys pre gaudio pulsabant campanas et cantabant Te Deum ad Dei laudem et honorem . . . propter quod dominus magister de Rodys convocavit milites frates suos et ordinavit ad instaurandum civitatem cum frumento et vino duobus annis."[20]

With the improvement of the weather in the spring of 1462—the Turks rarely fought winter campaigns—Mohammed the Conqueror finally set out with the bulk of his army, leaving Constantinople on April 26. The Greek chronicler Chalkokondyles speaks of a great army having been assembled: "the largest Turkish invasionary force since that which conquered Constantinople in 1453"; he estimated the total number of soldiers at 250,000 men.[21] The precise number of soldiers in both camps is still an unresolved problem. On the Turkish side one can hardly give credence to the exaggerated testimony of either Chalkokondyles or Doukas (100,000 men) or Tursun Bey (300,000 men). Even if we accept the statement that the army was as large as that led by Mohammed against Constantinople in 1453, the latter did not exceed 80,000 men. The Venetian envoy at Buda, Tommasi, was probably more accurate than the Turkish or Byzantine chroniclers when he estimated the total Turkish army at 60,000 men, a figure that seems reasonable.

On Dracula's side there are some contradictory views concerning numbers, totals which are cited with an evident parti pris: the smaller his army, the greater the disparity, the more heroic his exploits. Inevitably Wallachia experienced at the time the closest thing to a levée en masse, which entailed the mobilization of all able-bodied boys and men from the age of twelve upward, which may even have included gypsy slaves. The Slavic story gives us a total of 30,900 men; the papal ambassador Nicolas Modrussa, 24,000 men; Tommasi the Venetian envoy, 22,000 men.[22] In addition, Dracula had to divert a certain number of soldiers to fight his cousin, Stephen the Great. Including the latter contingent, we tend to accept the figure given by the Slavic narrative as close to the truth, which roughly gives a proportion of two to one vis-à-vis the Turks.

In its vast majority the Wallachian army was composed of peasants, whether free or serfs, and was officered by viteji, men promoted in battle and drawn from the ranks. It would be a mistake, however, to assume that the boyars did not collaborate with Dracula, for most of the new nobility at the time were his own appointees. Together with their retainers, these new boyars probably composed 25 percent of the total army. Only the older families of the land, who had been persecuted by Dracula, stayed aloof and sought refuge in their mountain hideouts, waiting for the outcome of the fray and pinned their hopes on the candidacy of Prince Radu, who accompanied the sultan. They were to join Radu's cause at the appropriate moment, with devastating consequences for Dracula.

There is one surprising fact about the Turko-Wallachian war of 1462: In spite of, or perhaps because of, the abundance of documentation, there are still many unresolved questions concerning the precise route followed by the Turks and the chronology of some of the main episodes; even the identification of place names sometimes remains in doubt. According to Chalkokondyles, the main Turkish army led by the sultan himself was transported by 25 triremes and 150 ships and sailed up the Danube through the Sulina channel to the port of Braila, which was burned by the Turks. Another supporting Turkish force left from Philipopolis in Bulgaria to effect a junction with the main Turkish contingent. It was logical to presume that the Turkish landing across the Danube would take place at a strategic location where disembarkation would be closest to the Wallachian capital and the centers of Dracula's power. Juncture of the two Turkish forces probably took place at Vidin, which was reached in the first days of June. Vidin was one of the few cities along the Bulgarian coast that had not been destroyed by Dracula during the winter campaign and had port facilities for the Turkish boats. An initial attempt at disembarkation across from Vidin at Calafat ended in disaster. The Wallachians, whose scouts and spies evidently followed the progress of the Turkish armada along the Danube, were prepared, and a volley of well-aimed arrows from the best archers compelled the Turks to scurry back to their ships. A more ambitious attempt was made a few miles down the river, although there is some controversy concerning the precise location of the Turkish disembarkation. The most logical place for a landing mentioned in some sources was the city of Nicopolis seventy miles east, which lies across the Romanian townlet of Turnu (badly damaged by Dracula) and opposite the confluence of the Olt River—the valley of the Olt had provided a traditional Turkish invasion route.

The Turkish chronicler Enveri, an eyewitness, states that the crossing was completed on the "sixth day of the feast of the Ramadan" (Friday, June 4 [1462]) at nighttime, the Turkish soldiers being transported in seventy boats and barges.[23] Another Turkish eyewitness, the Serbian janissary Constantin of Ostrovita, gives us a detailed and graphic account of the whole operation: The crossing of the Danube apparently took place at night and was made possible by a Turkish cannonade, the cannon fire being directed against Wallachian emplacements on the other side:

When night began to fall [states the janissary], "we climbed into the boats and floated down the Danube and crossed to the other side several leagues lower from the place where Dracula's army was standing. There we dug ourselves in trenches setting the cannon around us. We dug ourselves into the trenches so that the horsemen could not injure us. After that we crossed back to the other side and thus transported other janissaries across the Danube. And when the whole of the infantry crossed over, then we prepared and set out gradually against the army of Dracula, together with the artillery and other impedimenta we had taken with us. Having stopped, we set up the cannon, but until we could succeed in doing this, 300 janissaries were killed. The Sultan was very saddened by this affair, seeing a great battle from the other side of the Danube and being unable personally to come there. He was fearful lest all the janissaries be killed, since the Emperor had personally not crossed. After that, seeing that our side was weakening greatly, having transported 120 guns, we defended ourselves with them and fired often, so that we repelled the army of the prince from that place and we strengthened ourselves. Then the Emperor having gained reassurance, transported even other soldiers called "azapi" akin to our "drabanti." And Dracula seeing he could not prevent the crossing, withdrew from us. And then, after the Emperor had crossed the Danube following us with a whole army, he gave us 30,000 zloties to be divided among us.[24]

The order of disembarkation apparently was janissaries first, followed by the azapis, then the Asiatic soldiers from Anatolia, the sultan, and the bulk of the cavalry from

Rumelia. In the Turkish ranks was Prince Radu with four thousand Wallachian horsemen, who figured prominently in the vanguard of the Turkish offensive.

From this point onward because of the hopeless disparity of numbers, it is clear that Dracula was not able to fight the Turks in open battle. He was compelled to adopt the classical tactic of the outnumbered—strategic retreat—and resorted to what for lack of a better term can be labeled the "scorched earth policy." As the Wallachians abandoned their own native soil to the Turks, they reduced the country to ashes, burning crops, poisoning wells, herding the cattle northward, and consuming all that they could not carry with them. All the villages were empty of people, the houses destroyed, with the peasants usually accompanying the armies in the retreat. The boyars and their families, hearing of the impending attack, withdrew from their estates to the mountains with their belongings. A few kept themselves hidden in the island monastery of Snagov near Bucharest where they also stored their treasures. When the Turks reached the central plain, they saw remains of villages reduced to ashes, contributing to an oppressive heat. It was so hot it is said that shish kebab could be roasted on the steel netting of the Turkish soldiers' uniforms. To further delay the progress of the Turks, Dracula combined "scorched earth" with guerrilla tactics, where the element of surprise played the most vital part. His veteran cavalrymen knew the terrain well and generally maneuvered at the dead of night under cover of the vast Vlasie forest. Despite such delaying tactics, the Turks maintained their advance. The precise route through which they passed was first from Turnu to Slatina, a mere village in those days—along the Olt River and then eastward to Pitesti and Tîrgoviste. Slatina was likely reached within a matter of three days' march (June 7). "Within a week," states Doukas, "they reached Dracula's capital of Tîrgoviste but found neither men, cattle, food nor drink."[25]

At this point we may note certain disagreement concerning the precise route followed by the Turkish sultan. According to Professor Eric Tappe, who bases his interpretation on the account of an anonymous historian, the sultan continued to proceed northward along the Olt in the direction of "the mountains of Brasov"; a report from Balbi, the Venetian envoy at Constantinople, also refers to the Turks "apresso la montagna." Thus, concludes Tappe, "it may be that the Sultan penetrated from the Danube opposite Nicopolis, to at least the foothills of the Transylvanian Alps. In that case he may have passed near Tîrgoviste."[26] If this interpretation is correct, the Turks were more interested in destroying Dracula's military power, perhaps in capturing him alive and seeking out the boyars, their women, children, and chattels hidden in the mountains, than in securing the capital city. Hitherto, Romanian historians had taken it for granted that the main Turkish objective was the capture of Tîrgoviste.

Although some of the documents seem to substantiate Tappe's theory, his hypothesis raises serious problems and presents new riddles. Simplicity's sake would tend to make us rally to the traditional view put forward by N. Iorga, Barbu Cîmpina, and others.[27] Clearly the Turks could not have considered themselves "masters of the country," nor could Radu have effectively posed as prince of the land, unless Tîrgoviste had actually been captured.

It is thus likely that by the middle of June, Sultan Mohammed was in a position to attack Dracula's capital. The gates of the city had been left open, but the defenders were still manning the cannons and directing its fire against the Turkish army. Mohammed II apparently chose not to secure the Wallachian capital. The reason given by the chroniclers for this extraordinary decision was the frightful scene that greeted the sultan in a narrow gorge one mile long, just outside the city. There, the sultan's eyes caught sight of the remains of over twenty thousand mangled, rotting men, women, and children, which included many corpses of impaled boyars and what was left of the prisoners of Giurgiu caught during the preceding winter. During the course of several months the elements and the blackbirds had done their work. It was a scene horrible enough to discourage even the most hard-hearted. Overawed by this spectacle, Mohammed II ordered the Turkish camp to be surrounded with a deep trench that very night, but soon reflecting on what he had seen, the sultan lost heart. The oft-quoted statement that, in fact, indicated admission of defeat is reproduced by Chalkokondyles: "Even the emperor, overcome by amazement, admitted that he could not win the land, from a man who does such great things, and above all knows how to exploit his rule and that of his subjects in this way."[28] He also related that the man who performs such deeds should be worthier of greater things. The sultan then gave orders for the retreat of the main Turkish force and started eastward for Braila. Among other woes the plague had just begun to make its appearance within Turkish ranks.

Shortly before and perhaps accounting for the sultan's decision, Dracula delivered his notorious night attack, aimed at killing the sultan in his entrenched camp, which constitutes by far the best documented single battle of the whole campaign. The night attack, states Enveri, occurred on Friday, June 17, three hours after the setting of the sun, and lasted to 4:00 A.M. It likely took place in a mountainous region in the immediate vicinity of Tîrgoviste. The testimony is sufficiently interesting to quote from three different sources, two of them pro-Turkish (Chalkokondyles and the Serbian janissary) and one of them pro-Romanian, an anonymous soldier in Dracula's army. The account attributed to Dracula's veteran, and possibly dictated by Dracula himself, was enclosed in a dispatch of Nicolas Modrussa, the papal legate to Pope Pius II; it is dated 1464 and is evidently of the utmost importance:

The Sultan besieged him and found him hidden in a certain mountain where the Wallachians (Dracula), supported by the natural strength of the place, had enclosed himself along with 24,000 men who had followed him willingly. When he realized that he would either perish of hunger or would fall into the hands of the very cruel enemy, and reckoning that both eventualities were unworthy of brave men, he dared commit an act worthy of being remembered. Calling his men and explaining the situation to them, he easily persuaded them to enter the enemy camp. He divided the men so that either they should die bravely in battle with glory and honor, or else if destiny were favorable to them, they should avenge themselves against the enemy in an exceptional manner. Thus, making use of some Turkish prisoners who were caught at twilight when they were wandering imprudently, he penetrated at nightfall with a portion of his troops into the Turkish camp, all the way up the fortifications, and during the whole night he sped like lightning in all directions and caused great slaughter, so much so, that had the other commander to whom he had entrusted the remaining forces been equally brave, or had the Turks obeyed the repeated orders of the Sultan not to abandon the garrisons a little less, the Wallachians undoubtedly would have gained the greatest and most brilliant victory. But since the other commander [a boyar named Gales] did not dare attack the camp from the other side as had been agreed upon . . . Dracula provoked an incredible massacre without losing many men in such a major encounter, though there were many wounded; he abandoned the enemy camp before daybreak and returned to the same mountain whence he had come, without anyone daring to follow him, since he had caused so much terror and trouble among all. I learnt by questioning those who had participated in this battle that the Sultan lost all confidence regarding the situation. During that night he secretly abandoned the camp and fled in a shameful way. And he would have continued in this way had he not been reprimanded by friends and brought back, almost against his will.[29]

Testimonies on the Turkish side give a slightly different interpretation of the same event. According to Chalkokondyles, Dracula entered the Turkish camp with his seven to ten thousand followers and drove the panic-stricken Asian troops backward. With the help of torches and candles the Romanians tried to reach the sultan's tent. However, they erred, and instead headed for the tent of the two vizirs, Mohammed and Isaac. This enabled the Ottoman cavalry to mount their horses, and the guards around the imperial tent alerted the sultan. All that Dracula accomplished was to create a massacre in the heart of the Turkish camp. The Wallachians withdrew at daybreak. The sultan then ordered his best troops to pursue Dracula, with the result that two thousand were taken alive.[30] The interpretation of the Serbian janissary who was actually an eyewitness is more interesting and more relevant than that of Chalkokondyles:

Although the Romanian prince had a small army, we always advanced with great caution and fear and spent the night in ditches, but even in this manner we were not safe, for during one night the Romanians struck at us; they massacred horses, camels, and several thousand Turks. And when the Turks had retreated in the face of the enemy, we (the janissaries) repelled them and killed them. The Sultan had thus incurred great losses.[31]

Although the details are sometimes confusing and imprecise, the episode of the night attack certainly deserves all the fame it has received both in Dracula's time and in the legend that has been built around it. It undoubtedly constituted an act of extraordinary temerity. It represented Dracula's last-ditch attempt to save his capital. He knew that only the assassination of the sultan might sufficiently paralyze the Turkish army to effect a speedy withdrawal. The night attack also helped demonstrate how accurately Dracula's spies had described the topography of the Turkish camp, for the whole operation could not have been performed without foreknowledge of the location of the various tents. Popular tradition states that Dracula himself had entered the camp in Turkish disguise earlier to survey the location of the various Turkish tents and the fortifications, although Chalkokondyles does not seem to believe that particular story. The losses incurred by the Turks were undoubtedly heavy. According to Balbi, the Venetian diplomat, Dracula lost five thousand men and the Turks fifteen thousand, although these figures appear rather high and may have included minor skirmishes that followed the actual night attack.

Bitterly disappointed at the failure of the attack, which may in part have been due to the defection of a Romanian commander, Gales. Dracula manifested unusual cruelty toward his own men, if the Slavic story is correct. He ordered those who had been wounded to be examined. Whoever was wounded in front was recompensed and given a title; those who were found to be wounded in the back, however, were immediately impaled, with the scornful remark "You are not a man but a woman."[32] No matter what the details, this episode deserves to be ranked as one of the most fascinating in the whole campaign and certainly forms part of the popular Dracula epic which has since been romanticized by a number of Romanian novelists.

Whether the Turks' initial thrust was in the direction of Tîrgoviste or directly northward to the mountains of Transylvania, the initial phase of the Turko-Wallachian campaign undoubtedly proceeded northward from the Danube. The second phase, on the other hand, which began in the middle of June, was directed eastward toward the Danube delta and the Black Sea. It is even conceivable that at the very moment when Dracula made his night attack the sultan was already on his way eastward to effect a juncture with Stephen of Moldavia. In any case, whether it is the night attack or possibly the "spectacle of woe" beheld by the sultan near Tîrgoviste, both or either of these episodes could represent the dividing point between the separate phases of the Turko-Romanian war.

After that date Dracula proceeded with the main body of the army toward northeastern Wallachia by way of Buzau. The reason for his concern for the security of that portion of his principality was inevitably Stephen of Moldavia's intervention. As already stated, Stephen, hearing that Dracula was harassing the Turkish army, joined the Turks, and together they went and fought to capture the fortress of Chilia, which belonged to Dracula.

Professor Giurescu justified Stephen's attack on Chilia for reasons of strategic necessity—to secure Moldavia's southern frontier.[33] It seems that on this occasion, at least, ingratitude and the abandonment of a mutual pledge had not paid off. The Moldavian chronicle informs us that on June 22 Stephen was wounded in the ankle by a projectile hurled from the fortress while besieging the Danubian port. This may have been a factor in Stephen's decision to abandon the siege. His campaign had barely lasted eight days, probably from June 18 to June 25. There is an uncanny sequel to this story: According to the account of Stephen's physician, one of the earliest detailed, medical diagnoses in Romanian history, Stephen's wound was either so profound or so badly doctored that his death on July 2, 1504 was an indirect consequence of it.[34]

Stephen renewed the attack on Chilia only in 1465, and this time captured the fortress from Dracula's brother, Prince Radu. Chilia finally fell into Turkish hands in 1484. There is no question, however, that it represented a major Turkish military objective, recognized by Sultan Mohammed II himself when he stated: "We shall never conquer the Christians as long as the Vlachs possess Chilia and Cetatea-Alba, and the Hungarians possess Belgrade."[35]

Dracula, at least, never got to Chilia to join the Wallachian and Hungarian garrisons. On his way eastward, several skirmishes took place with the Turks, Radu's forces, and the Moldavians. They were undoubtedly military defeats. In one major encounter, two thousand Wallachians were killed and their heads brought on lances to the sultan. This seems to have been the turning point in Dracula's fortunes. If this last battle occurred in an attempt by Dracula to relieve Chilia, it may have actually been fought on Moldavian soil. But it is likely that the siege of Chilia had already been abandoned, and that the Moldavian and Turkish forces encountered

Dracula in the northeastern part of Wallachia. The historian Petancius identifies the location as Vasilium, which may well be the modern Romanian village of Vizirul, on the road from Braila to Calarasi between the rivers Buzau and Ialomita.[36] The defeat likely took place by June 25 and June 29.

By the time of the Moslem festivities of the Bairam, which follow the feast of Ramadan, which occurred on the twenty-ninth of June in 1462, Mohammed II was in Braila, on his way down the Danube. On July 11 the sultan was back in Adrianople with the bulk of the Turkish army. The principal phase of the whole campaign had lasted barely one month. In its briefest outline, Professor Tappe summarizes it as follows:

The Sultan crossed the Danube at Nicopolis in the first half of June. He advanced northwards into the foothills of the Carpathians, turned eastwards, and was attacked by Dracula near Viziru; then finally he recrossed the Danube near Braila reaching Adrianople before the middle of July. Before the autumn one of Mohammed's objectives had been achieved, namely the deposition of Dracula; this was due more to internal pressure in Wallachia than to Turkish arms.[37]

After the withdrawal of Mohammed and the main Turkish contingent, the character of the war changed radically. Indeed this last epopee leading to Dracula's flight across the Carpathians should more properly be described as a civil rather than a foreign war, even though Turkish soldiers were still involved. While in Braila, Sultan Mohammed formally appointed Radu as commander in chief with the mission of destroying Dracula and taking over the princely office. The Turkish contingent, under the command of the pasha of Silistria, was to support Radu's actions, but the new candidate was to rely essentially upon native support. The Turks, stated the Venetian representative Balbi, had deliberately fostered this conflict in order to confuse the Wallachians and avoid the impression of a national war against a common foe.[38] What they had failed to do by force of arms they succeeded in accomplishing by diplomacy. Thus, in the final analysis, it was less a matter of tactics than of politics. The last battles pitted Dracula not so much against the Turks, but against the powerful Romanian boyars who ultimately and decisively rallied to the cause of Radu. "The Romanian boyars realizing that the Turks were stronger, abandoned Dracula and associated themselves with his brother who was with the Turkish Sultan."[39] So ends the account of the Serbian janissary. Even in this phase, however, which might well be labeled "the war between the two brothers," at least two victories were gained by Dracula, one on July 26 and the other on September 28. By early November, though still residing at his headquarters at Braila, Radu was recognized as prince of the land by the boyar council and by King Matthias of Hungary.

Dracula's escape from eastern Wallachia to the Transylvanian Alps and his capture by King Matthias entail the problem of insufficient historical documentation. With much circumspection, the historian once again has to fall back on anecdotal sources and native folklore. Since some of the events leading to Dracula's escape across the Transylvanian border took place in the vicinity of Dracula's castle, we may well refer to "the castle epic," now scientifically studied by the Institute of Folklore in Bucharest.[40] Contemporary historical sources, however, come to our rescue only after Dracula crossed the Transylvanian border (the commentaries of Pius II, Antonio Bonfinius, Michel Beheim, Pietro Tommasi, Balbi, etc.). From Dracula himself we possess only the "Rothel letters" for that period, allegedly written on November 7, but suspicions have been cast on their authenticity.[41] In default of conventional sources it is the historian's privilege to rely upon his intuition and ordinary common sense.

Abandoned by the majority of boyars who defected to Radu, Dracula's army simply melted away. It was but natural in these circumstances for the escapee to attempt to reach the Transylvanian border and seek help from the Hungarian king, his so-called ally whose assistance he had so far sought in vain. It was equally logical that Dracula and his few partisans should avoid the plain and the major cities, by the middle of September safely under Turkish or Radu's control. Under the circumstances, what hypothesis could be more reasonable than to presume that Dracula should direct himself toward his famous castle hideout on the southern slopes of the Transylvanian mountains, which forms the Hungarian-Wallachian frontier, a logical point of departure for Brasov where the Hungarian king had established his headquarters. After all, the castle had originally been built by Wallachian slave labor specifically for some such emergency. The precise road traveled by Dracula from eastern Wallachia can be reconstructed. It is likely that he traveled within the protective shadow of the sub-Carpathian mountains, crossing the rivers Teleajen, Prahova, and Dîmbovita, quite high up near their source. In that manner Dracula likely passed through the villages of Cheia, Sinaia, and Cetateni. In his flight he certainly made use of the small mountain fortresses that Wallachia's early princes had built, high up on peaks that commanded a panoramic view and offered virtually impregnable hideouts. Tradition states that Dracula sought refuge in the castle rock at Cetateni overlooking the Dîmbovita. Finally, he crossed the Arges River, a few miles to the west, and reached his impressive mountain eerie.

There is one valid argument for the authenticity of the stories collected from the villages surrounding Castle Dracula: All the narratives end precisely at the moment when Dracula crossed the border into Transylvania, thus once again demonstrating that no matter how imaginative the peasants could be, they only relate events that they personally witnessed.[42]

We are tempted to paraphrase one of the more classical folkloric narratives of Dracula's last moments of resistance on Romanian soil. Knowing of Dracula's hideout, Prince Radu ordered the Turkish forces to pursue his brother along the valley of the Arges River. Reaching the village of Poenari, they encamped upon the very bluff of the castle that had so recently been dismantled by Dracula's boyars. The hill of Poenari commanded an admirable view of Dracula's castle on the opposite bank of the Arges. The castle itself had been so completely dismantled that it could be put to little strategic use. From this vantage point, the Turks set up their cherry wood cannons. At Poenari to this day there is a field known as "Tunuri," or "the field of cannon." The bulk of the Turkish janissaries descended to the river, forded it at much the same place where the Tartars had crossed it a century before, and encamped. The Turkish bombardment of the castle began without too much success, owing to the small caliber of the Turkish guns and the thickness of the castle walls. The orders for the final assault were to have been given the following day.

During that night, one of Dracula's relatives enslaved by the Turks years before, mindful of his family allegiance, decided to forewarn the Wallachian prince of the great dangers he was incurring by remaining in the fortress. Undetected during the pitch-dark, moonless night, the Romanian, who was a member of the janissary corps, climbed to the top of Poenari hill, a short distance from Dracula's castle, and then, armed with a bow and arrow, took careful aim at one of the dimly lit openings in the main castle tower, which he knew contained Dracula's quarters. At the end of the arrow he had pinned a message advising Dracula to escape while there was still time. The Romanian-born Moslem witnessed the accuracy of his aim: the candle was suddenly extinguished by the arrow. Within a minute it was relit by Dracula's Transylvanian wife; she could be seen reading the message by the flickering light. What followed could evidently only be recalled by Dracula's intimate advisers within the castle, who were witnessing the scene. Peasant imagination, however, reconstructed the story in the following manner: Dracula's wife apprised her husband of the ominous content of the message. She told him that she would "rather have her body rot and be eaten by the fish of the Arges than be led into captivity by the Turks." From the upper battlements she then hurled herself from the dungeon, her body falling down the precipice below into the river, which became her tomb. A fact that tends to corroborate this story is that to this day the river at that point is known as "Rîul Doamnei," or the "Princess's River." This tragic folkloric footnote is practically the only mention anywhere of Dracula's first wife, permanently enshrined only in local memories.[43]

Surrounded by an overwhelming Turkish force, Dracula decided to attempt to escape across the mountains and seek the assistance of King Matthias. The flight to Brasov labelled by the local peasants "Dracula's escape" has all the elements of a melodrama. Dracula supposedly escaped through a secret passage leading to the banks of the river, and the horses were allegedly shod backward to elude pursuit. Both the ascent and the descent of the Fagaras mountains was no easy task, since there are no passes at that point. It was a matter of climbing three or four thousand feet to the summit, still a challenge to the most experienced Alpinists. The upper slopes of the mountains are rocky and treacherous and often covered with snow or ice throughout the summer. Dracula could not have attempted such an ascent without the help of local experts. The precise escape route was mapped out by peasant leaders from neighboring villages. Popular folklore still recalls the names of sources of rivers, clearings, forested areas, even rocks, which have a role in the story of Dracula's escape. The task, however, of reconstructing the journey is difficult, because many of the place names have changed. It is more than likely that Dracula rewarded the men who had helped him escape—even if the actual "rabbit skin" scrolls on which these Dracula donations were inscribed are never found.[44] There is an ancient tradition in the village of Arefu that these rabbit skins are kept somewhere, carefully hidden by the descendants of the families thus endowed.

As he reached Brasov, where the Hungarian king had established his military headquarters since November 3, instead of the expected aid, Dracula was treated coolly and within a matter of weeks, was arrested, brought in chains, and taken to the Hungarian capital where he remained technically a prisoner for twelve years. This extraordinary action, the change of heart of King Matthias, with whom Dracula had discussed a marriage contract, only a few months earlier, presents the historian with a problem even more difficult to resolve than Stephen's defection or Dracula's abandonment by the boyars. The action of the Hungarian king is the less accountable in light of the historian Bonfinius' statement that Matthias had finally decided, with papal financial support, to come to Dracula's aid. For a time, indeed, pretenses were kept up, and the two leaders appeared to be discussing common strategy at Brasov. The German chronicler Beheim tells us that "fünf wochen oder mere sy also pei einander waren."[45] Then suddenly, after five weeks or more, negotiations broke down and Dracula was arrested by King Matthias at the castle of Königstein (Piatra Craiului in Romanian), no longer in existence, six miles across the Transylvanian-Wallachian border. Dracula was apprehended by the Bohemian soldier of fortune, Jan Giskra, in King Matthias's service and brought back in chains to Brasov.[46] According to Pietro Tommasi, the Venetian representative at Buda, Dracula's arrest took place on November 26. By December 6 the Hungarian king, his new prisoner, and the Hungarian army had left Brasov for Buda, and Prince Radu, long since recognized as the legitimate ruler of Wallachia, had moved to Tîrgoviste.

What had caused this drastic reversal of alliances? One explanation is that King Matthias had in the meantime been informed of the "Rothel letters" (November 7, 1462), the originals of which we have lost but a copy of which is contained in Latin in the commentaries of Pope Pius II. In two separate statements, one addressed to Stephen and one addressed to the Turks, Dracula begged for forgiveness from his enemies, promised to join in an alliance with the Turks, and willingly offered his help to seize the person of the Hungarian king. According to most Romanian historians, these letters are forgeries fabricated, possibly, on the orders of the Hungarian king to justify his nonintervention in the crusade and his arrest of Dracula. Moreover, Matthias needed justification for not having spent the subsidy that Pius II had placed at his disposal. If we believe in the "Hungarian plot" theory, it is also conceivable that King Matthias deliberately fostered and encouraged the dissemination of German anti-Dracula horror literature to destroy Dracula's reputation in the eyes of Christianity. Another theory holds that unknown to the Hungarian king, these letters were manufactured by the German Saxons to destroy Dracula's reputation, a belated revenge for the persecution and terror he inflicted upon them during the 1459-1460) period. Although the king of Hungary was more innocent on this view, Matthias secured the opportunity to justify the arrest of a so-called ally and to recognize the rule of Radu.

Most of the Romanian historians have considered the "Rothel letters" as forgeries for yet other reasons. The style of writing, the rhetoric of meek submission, was hardly compatible with Dracula's irascible character, and no one has, as yet, identified "Rothel" precisely. Furthermore, to say the least, it would have been foolhardy and unconscionable for Dracula to write a letter of submission to the sultan and to Stephen at a time when he was technically on Hungarian soil.

It is just conceivable, however, knowing of Dracula's previous change of heart, that the letters were genuine enough. F. Babinger, the biographer of Mohammed II, emits this theory, although without proof.[47] Other historians have variously identified Rothel as Turnu Rosu (Rotherturn), Ruchel, and even Rucar, the frontier town.[48] In any case the decision to proceed to Dracula's arrest had probably already been taken before the so-called Rothel letters were sent.

Who had won the war? The Turks or Dracula? There is a controversy among historians concerning the outcome of Mohammed II's campaign and its sequel. In view of Mohammed II's decision to withdraw, can Dracula be considered the real victor in this particular campaign, as many historians contend? Many contemporaries, travelers in the Balkans, in the eastern Mediterranean, and even in the west, had prematurely returned with tidings of a "great Dracula victory" against the Turks.

Since news traveled slowly in the fifteenth century, all these commentators were in fact referring to the early portion of Dracula's winter Danubian campaign. Most of Romania's nationalist historians of the nineteenth century and even B. Cîmpina, who has done most research on the campaign,[49] credited Dracula with a brilliant victory over the Turks. The Wallachian prince, however, according to Cîmpina, was cheated out of this victory by a "boyar plot." Such a view is hardly acceptable. Although Dracula had inflicted far more severe punishment on the aggressor than he had suffered himself, he was finally compelled to abandon his capital and his throne. Ultimately he was pursued by his brother's forces and hounded out of the country. Radu the Handsome took over and governed the state in the name of the Turks. Rarely in history does one speak of victory when the alleged victor is expelled from his own country, as was the case in this instance. This, in essence, is the view of such notable historians as A. D. Xenopol, N. Iorga, and C. C. Giurescu. Dracula would hardly have been abandoned by the boyars had he defeated the Turks. Even if battles were won, these were pyrrhic victories which so exhausted Dracula's forces that he was unable to exploit his advantages.

In the last resort, Dracula lost the war because he was not able to command the allegiance and support of his own people—not only the boyars—who had rejected him. He had lost the allegiance of the boyars because of their desire to collaborate with the Turks; his continued "terror tactics," however, ultimately made his rule unacceptable to all and sundry, even to the peasants. Herein may well lie the final explanation for Dracula's isolation and universal abandonment. Prince Radu and the boyars simply decided to terminate the heroic phase of Romania's struggle against the Turks, which had bled the country dry, and revolted against Dracula's medievalist crusading conception, no longer shared elsewhere in Europe. Instead, the boyars and Radu decided to capitalize on Dracula's heroic resistance by diplomacy and negotiation. The country needed peace and tranquillity to recover from its losses in men and natural resources. It was perhaps in the long run more important to spare the Romanian population from complete exhaustion. Nevertheless, Dracula's heroic and dramatic exploits did impose upon the Turks a lesson that they were not likely to forget easily and may provide the final explanation why the country continued to preserve its autonomy, rather than be converted into a Turkish province. Following Dracula's demise the tribute was in fact reduced from ten thousand to eight thousand ducats, Prince Radu thus exploiting the courage of his brother to the advantage of his country. In the long-term historic view, Dracula's campaign was indeed a dramatic contribution to Romania's struggle for survival and independence and in that sense can be labeled successful.

---

[1] Primary sources of Dracula's campaign of 1461-62 are extensive. *Expunerile istorice* (Historical Expositions), ed. Vasile Grecu (Bucharest, 1958), by the Byzantine chronicler Leonikos Chalkokondyles, is the basic and most extensive work. Michel Doukas, *Istoria Turco-Bizantina* (Turkish Byzantine History), ed. Vasile Grecu (Bucharest 1958), has more limited material on Dracula, but contains data not found elsewhere. Kritoboulos of Imbros, *Din domnia lui Mahommed al II^{lea}* (The Rule of Mohammed II), ed. Vasile Grecu (Bucharest, 1963), and Georgios Sphrantzes, *Memorii* (Memoirs), ed. Vasile Grecu (Bucharest, 1966), contain briefer references (one sentence in the case of Sphrantzes). The Turkish chronicles of Tursun Bey (who personally participated in the campaign of 1462) and those of Enveri (perhaps the most important source of Turkish information) are invaluable. Tursun Bey's chronicle *Tarih-i Ebu-il Feth-i Sultan Mehmed-han* was written between 1497 and 1500 and has been in part translated into Romanian by Mihail Guboglu and Mustafa Mehmet, *Cronici turcesti*, pp. 67-68. In the same volume also see the anonymous chronicle *Tevarih-i al-i Osman*, pp. 93-94, 198-199, and Kodja Husein's (1570-1650) work *Beda-i ul veka'i*, pp. 454-455. The Serbian chronicles (six variations) all refer to Dracula's military exploits: *Stari srpski rodoslovi letopisi*, ed. Stojanovich (Karlowitz, 1927). One should not forget references in the Slavic story and in Romanian folklore. The narration of the janissary Constantin Mihailovici of Ostrovitza, compiled between 1496 and 1501 in Poland, is invaluable, since the janissary was a personal witness. See Maria Holban, *Calatori straini despre tarile române*, vol. 1 (Bucharest, 1968), p. 126. Lately a testimony possibly based on Dracula's personal account and evidently written by a Romanian veteran has been discovered and is of the greatest importance: "Cronica lui Tepes," contained in *Cronicile Slavo-Române, din Secolul XV-XVI*, ed. P. P. Panaitescu (Bucharest, 1959), pp. 197-219. For this document also see Serban Papacostea, "Cu privire la geneza si raspîndirea provestirilor scrise despre faptele lui Vlad Tepes," *Romanoslavica* 13 (Bucharest, 1966): 163. An Albanian slave in Turkish service has an interpretation of his own dated 1463-1464, "Relatia scavului Albanez," *Columna lui Traian* (Bucharest, 1883), pp. 40-41. The English pilgrim William of Wey had heard of Dracula's exploits on his way to the Holy Land. See Eric Tappe, *Documents Concerning Rumanian History* (The Hague, 1964), pp. 17-18. Of particular interest are the reports of the papal envoy to Budapest, Nicolas Modrussa, *Opere Minori*, vol. 4 (Vatican City, 1937), pp. 217-218 (see G. Mercati, ed., "Notizie varie sopra Niccolo Modrusiense"), and those of the Venetian diplomats Pietro Tommasi and Balbi. See the latter's report dated July 28, 1462, published in *Monumenta Hungariae Historica, Acta Externa*, vol. 4 (Budapest, 1907), p. 168. Most of the diplomatic correspondence is included in Nicolae Iorga, *Acte si fragmente*, vol. 3. With J. Dlugosz, *Historica Polonica*, vol. 2 (Leipzig, 1712); Antonio Bonfinius (1434-1503), *Rerum Ungaricarum decades . . .* (1st ed., Basel, 1543); and Sebastian Münster, *Cosmografia*

universalis, bk. 4 (1550), p. 920, we are finally removed from eyewitness accounts or from the period itself. In spite of the research in foreign archives done so far by Iorga and others, there are undoubtedly many foreign sources, including the Papal Archives that are susceptible of yielding valuable new information on Dracula's campaign.

2 The letter was found by the historian Iorga in the Munich archives. We have used its Romanian translation from Nicolae Iorga, *Scrisori de boieri scrisori de domni,* 3d ed. (Bucharest, 1932). The letter is also included in Bogdan, *Vlad Tepes,* pp. 78-82.

3 These letters were published in the commentaries of Pope Pius II, published by N. Iorga, *Acte si documente cu privire la istoria Românilor* (Bucharest, 1900), pp. xxxi, lxxii-lxxiv. The language and composition of the letters incline most historians to believe they were forgeries. (Iorga, *Istoria Românilor,* vol. 4 (Bucharest, 1937), pp. 141-142, Conduratu, *Michael Beheim,* p. 154, and Cîmpina, "Complotul," p. 623.

4 For the Latin text and Romanian translation see Papacostea, "Cu privire l a geneza si raspîndirea povestirilor," pp. 164-165.

5 *Columna lui Traian* (Bucharest, 1883), pp. 34-35. Venice and Transylvania had also promised their help to Dracula.

6 The literature on Stephen the Great's reign is vast. For documents see Ion Bogdan, *Documentele lui Stefan cel Mare* (Bucharest, 1913); Grigore Ureche, *Letopisetul Tarii Moldovei,* ed. P. P. Panaitescu (Bucharest, 1958). Among the better works are Nicolae Iorga, *Istoria lui Stefan cel Mare povestita neamului românesc* (Bucharest, 1904); Alexandru V. Boldur, *Stefan cel Mare voievod a l Moldovei 1457-1504, studiu de istorie sociala si politica* (Madrid, 1970), and *Studii cu privire la Stefan cel Mare* (Bucharest, 1956). For the beginning of the reign of particular interest to Dracula's career see N. Grigoras, "Inceputurile domniei lui Stefan cel Mare 1457-1459," *Studii si cercetari stiintifice* 8, fasc. 1 (1957): 35-62, and "Cândaa intrat Stefan cel Mare in Moldova," *Anuarul Liceului National* (Iasi, 1942-1945); Emil Diaconescu, *Vechi drumuri Moldovenesti, contributiuni în legatura cu luptele lui Stefan cel Mare pentru ocuparea domniei* (Iasi, n.d.); Ion Bogdan, "Contributii la istoria Moldovei între anii 1448-1458," *An. Ac. Rom. Mem. Sect. Ist.,* 2d ser. 29 (Bucharest, 1907); Ion Ursu, *Stefan cel Mare si Turcii* (Bucharest, 1914) . For Romanian culture during the time of Stephen the Great, by far the best compendium is M. Berza, ed., *Cultura Moldoveneasca în timpul lui Stefan cel Mare* (Bucharest, 1964). See in particular the study by C. Nicolescu, "Arta m epoca lui Stefan cel Mare," p. 259. This volume also contains an excellent bibliography by Serban Papacostea, p. 641.

7 The emnity between Moldavia and Wallachia continued under Prince Radu. From 1465 Radu was almost continuously at war with Stephen of Moldavia (who took Chilia from him in 1465). It was largely in order to defend himself against the Moldavians that Radu built the fortresses of Craciunas and Teleajen. In the autumn of 1473 Stephen invaded Moldavia, defeated Radu, and established Basarab Laiota on the throne. Stephen took Radu's wife, Maria Despina, with him to Suceava and Radu's daughter Maria Voichita, the Moldavian princess whom he married in 1480 (his fourth wife). Radu briefly returned to Wallachia and was killed in battle by the boyars of Basarab Laiota.

8 *Orationes politicae et ecclesiasticae,* vol. 2 (Lucca, 1757), p. 69.

9 Iorga, *Scrisori de boeri,* p. 161-162.

10 Cazacu, "Vlad Tepes," p. 98.

11 This is a translation of the oldest Kirillo-Belozersk Russian manuscript. See Russian narrative, story no. 1, McNally and Florescu, *In Search of Dracula,* p. 196.

12 Russian narrative, story no. 12, Ibid., p. 199.

13 For the so-called capitulation treaty of 1460, see Cazacu, "Vlad Tepes," p. 83-86.

14 The child tribute was very arbitrarily imposed. In Turkish provinces it was levied every five years. See B. D. Papoulia, *Ursprung und Wesen der Knebenlese im Osmanischen Reich* (Munich, 1963).

15 Tursun Bey affirms the contrary, stating that Dracula yearly came to Constaninople. Guboglu and Mehmet, *Cronici turcesti*, p. 67.

16 Iorga, *Scrisori de boeri*, p. 165. For the capture of Hamza Pasha also see T. Nicolau, "Cum a capturat Vlad Tepes pe Hamza Pasha," *Revista Militara* 81 (1934): 63-88, and *Doua erori istorice* (Bucharest, 1934).

17 Iorga, *Scrisori de boeri*, p. 166.

18 Ibid., p. 165.

19 Ibid., p. 166.

20 Tappe, *Documents Concerning Rumanian History*, p. 19. A good study on Wey is that of Fr. Pall, "Notes du Pélerin William Wey à propos de opérations militaires des Turcs en 1462," *Revue historique du Sud-Est Européen* 22 (1945): 246-266.

21 Grecu, *Expunerile*, p. 284-285.

22 Bogdan, *Vlad Tepes*, p. 24. For figures on both sides, see Cazacu, "Vlad Tepes," p. 102. Cîmpina, on the other hand, accepts Chalkokondyles' figure of 250,000. Cîmpina, "Complotul," p. 604.

23 In the text Orudj, in the month of the Ramadan, corresponds to June 4. Guboglu and Mehmet, *Cronici turcesti*, p. 42, n. 49.

24 The most recent translation of the text relating to Dracula's campaign of the janissary of Ostrovitza is that of Maria Holban, *Calatori straini*, vol. 1. For this particular passage, see p. 127.

25 Grecu, *Istoria Turco-Bizantina*, p. 432.

26 "Dracula and the Campaign of Mohamet II" (manuscript originally presented at the International Congress of Byzantine Studies at Istanbul in 1955), p. 4. (To be published in *East European Quarterly* in 1974).

27 For Iorga's interpretation of the campaign, see *Histoire des Romains*, vol. 4, pp. 163-165. Also see "Victoria ostii lui Vlad Tepes asupra lui Mehmed II-lea," *Studii* 15 (1962): 533-556; "Complotul boierilor si rascoala din Tara Româneasca din Iulie-noiembrie 1462," *Studii so referate privind istoria României* 1 (1954): 599-624.

28 Chalkokondyles provides another anecdote which adds to Dracula's stature. Having caught one of Dracula's men, the sultan asked him about his master's whereabouts, which the soldier admitted knowing. However, although threatened with death, the latter refused to reveal his master's hideaway. Mohammed II marveled at such temerity and stated that with a large army Dracula would have accomplished great things. Grecu, *Expunerile*, p. 289.

29 Papacostea, "Cu privire la geneza si raspândirea povestirilor," p. 165, n. 1.

30 Grecu, *Expunerile*, p. 290.

31 Holban, *Calatori straini*, pp. 127-128. Enveri also mentions the night attack as a witness Guboglu and Mehmet, *Cronici turcesti*, p. 42.

32 Russian narrative, story no. 2, McNally and Florescu, *In Search of Dracula*, p.196.

33 Giurescu's reasoning is contained in "The Historical Dracula," ms., p. 13. (To be published in *East European Quarterly* in 1974.)

34 "Stephen was wounded at the leg when he attacked Chilia. He succeeded in capturing Chilia but the leg was affected throughout his lifetime . . . in his old age he suffered terribly as a consequence of that wound." Finally, he sought the help of foreign doctors and appealed to Venetian Matheus Murianus. When the latter came to Moldavia to treat Stephen, he himself fell ill (1502), and Stephen sought another doctor, Alexandre of Verona The latter actually set out for Moldavia, having been paid three hundred gold pieces in advance, but he became lost on the way and was never heard of. At the time of his death in July 1504, however, Stephen did have an Italian doctor (Liornardo do Massari) and a German doctor from Nürnberg, Johann Klingensporn. Neither of them was able to make a precise diagnosis of his recalcitrant wound, which simply refused to heal. One can make quite a case of the story in terms of "draculesque." Iorga, *Istoria Romănilor în chipuri,* pp. 314-316.

35 Cited in E. Tappe's "Dracula and the Campaign of Mahomet II," ms., p. 8. (To be published in the *East European Quarterly* in 1974.)

36 Felix Petancius, "Felicis Petancii cancelarii segniae dissertatio de itineribus aggrediendi turcan ad Vladislaum Hungariae et Bohemiae origine," in I. G. Schwandtrer, *Scriptores rerum hungaricarum* (Vienna, 1746), p. 371.

37. Tappe, "Dracula and the Campaign of Mahomet II," p. 8.

38 Cîmpina, "Complotul," p. 622.

39 Holban, *Calatori straini,* p. 128.

40 For "castle epic" see folkloric references in P. Ispirescu, *Povesti despre Vlad Tepes,* and *Viata si faptele lui Vlad Tepes Voda,* and C. Radulescu-Codin, *Ingerul Romănului.* Also see thesis in manuscript of Miss G. Ene (Bucharest, 1970).

41 See note 3 above.

42 Romanian peasant stories refer only to events in the vicinity of the castle. The German narrative (Beheim) gives us an account of Dracula's capture at the Castle Königstein and the events at Brasov across the Transylvanian border, while the Russian narrative deals with the events during Dracula's imprisonment at Buda.

43 This particular story was related by the priest of Arefu. Ion Stanciulescu, "Cetatea lui Tepes," ms, pp. 6ff. In Ispirescu and Radulescu-Codin there are other variants of the same story. Also see Adascalitei, *De la Dragos la Cuza Voda,* for a story entitled, "Dracula's Escape," p. 58, and "When Dracula Escaped beyond the Mountains," p. 51. The local priests and village teachers in the various villages around the castle have proven to be of invaluable help to the present authors.

44 Professor Pandele Olteanu, author of a monograph on the origins of the language in Dracula Slavic tales, *Limba povestirilor slave despre Vlad Tepes* (Bucharest, 1961), who has done extensive research in the castle area, informed Professor Florescu in the summer of 1967 that the parchments with Dracula donations on rabbit skins still exist and that they are carefully hidden by peasants from the Arefu region in their homes. (One such expedition with Professor Olteanu was planned but never came to fruition.)

45 Conduratu, *Michael Beheim,* p. 55.

46 Ibid.

47 *Mahomet II le conquérant et son temps 1432-1481 la grande peur du monde au tournant de l'histoire* (Paris, 1954), p. 248.

48 Conduratu thinks that Dracula resided for some time at Rucar on the Wallachian-Transylvanian border. Conduratu, *Michael Beheim,* p. 99.

49 Cîmpina, "Victoria ostii lui Tepes," p. 555.

5

Imprisonment, Third Reign, and Assassination (1462-1476)

The final stage in Dracula's career must be divided into two phases: (1) his lengthy period of Hungarian captivity, according to the Russian narrative extending over twelve years (1462-1474), and (2) his liberation—the diplomacy and campaign that preceded his third reign, lasting barely two years, from 1474 to 1476.

The period of Hungarian imprisonment or house arrest is the least documented segment of Dracula's whole career. Beyond the Russian narrative (which is the most extensive source), a brief reference to Beheim's song, Modrussa's description of Dracula's physical appearance, occasional references by Bonfinius, and a few dispatches from Venetian diplomats, we have next to nothing in terms of written documentation.[1] (The Ambras portrait was painted at the time.) By way of contrast, the 1474-1476 period, particularly the years 1475 and 1476, presents the historian with rich documentation, mostly internal and diplomatic. Among others, we have Dracula's personal correspondence and that of his chancellery officials, written for the most part in Latin to the Hungarian king and to various Transylvanian officials, and their answers. These letters, all precisely dated, the originals of which are located in the archives of Brasov and Sibiu, emanate from such Transylvanian towns as Arghis, Turda, Medias, Brasov, Stremt, Merghindel, and Balcaciu. At the end of the year 1476, when he was reestablished on the throne, Dracula wrote from Tîrgoviste, Bucharest, and Gherghita, a Wallachian fortress. In addition, we have a fairly rich external diplomatic correspondence for these years from the usual vantage points such as Venice, Buda, and Constantinople.[2] Only the circumstances leading to Dracula's assassination and burial are obscure and can be pieced together by reference to local tradition in the vicinity of the island monastery of Snagov.

We can only speculate on the precise route Dracula traveled to Buda after his capture at Castle Königstein. Since we know that the royal Hungarian party reached the Transylvanian town of Medias on December 11, 1462, the obvious journey should have been Brasov, Medias, Turda, Cluj, Oradea, Debreczen, and Buda.

Both obscurity and controversy center upon the actual site of Dracula's imprisonment. The Russian story seems to be precise enough on that point: "And he was imprisoned at Vísegràd on the Danube above Buda for 12 years."[3] Michel Beheim refers to the place of imprisonment as "Iersiu" (Wissurd) in his poem.[4] Both the palace and the fortress prison at Vísegràd did, of course, exist in Dracula's time, and the ruins of the summer palace of King Matthias still survive. The palace is located fifteen to twenty miles up the Danube, on the famous scenic bend, high up on a hill with a commanding view of the river. Solomon's tower, where political prisoners were held, lies at the foot of the hill, on the edge of the banks of the Danube, and has been completely restored. Within this large complex, which is today the scene of careful archaeological investigation and partial reconstruction, was centered the flowering culture of the Hungarian Renaissance. Like the Medicis of Florence, King Matthias evidently liked to think of himself as a true patron of learning and art, and used Vísegràd to impress foreign visitors with the material splendors of his age, reflected in the countless artistic treasures even recently discovered in the main palace.

Careful investigation by the authors in the local library and archives, however, did not reveal the name of Dracula on the roster of eminent political detainees at Solomon's tower.[5] This in itself does not necessarily invalidate the veracity of the Russian narrative. It could simply mean that Dracula was not in a strict sense a political prisoner but may have been under "house arrest." The late Romanian Slavicist P. P. Panaitescu, on the other hand, believed that the actual place of confinement was not Vísegràd. Within the context of the Russian narrative he believes that "Vísegràd" refers to the fortress of Vàcz, which is located near Buda and also lies on the banks of the Danube. According to his interpretation, Vísegràd means "small fortress on a height" or "on the confines" of a city, precisely the case in point with Vàcz.[6]

One way of reconciling both these theories is by viewing Dracula less as a political prisoner in the strict sense—he may indeed have actually been imprisoned at Vàcz or elsewhere at Buda—and more as a personal detainee of the Hungarian king placed under "house arrest"—by no means a unique situation. As such, if Dracula stayed at the Hungarian court, he must have accompanied the Hungarian king on his frequent trips to Vísegràd. Dracula had established quite a reputation for himself and must have been an object of interest and a conversation piece among the diplomats and courtiers in the entourage of the Hungarian king. It is, in fact, more than likely that the first anecdotal histories (Russian, German, and Latin), to which reference has often been made, were written at the time of Dracula's imprisonment.

The only reference to Dracula's life-style in prison is a short anecdote told in the Russian narrative: "It is said of him however that even when he was in jail, he did not cure himself of the evil habit of catching mice and buying birds at the market, he punished them by impaling them. He cut off the heads of some, others he had feathered and then allowed them to go. He learned to sew, and subsisted on that during his period of imprisonment."[7] Most Romanian critics consider this particular story apocryphal—just another way of blackening Dracula's reputation. The accuracy of the remaining segment of the Russian narrative dealing with Dracula's imprisonment makes us doubt that the author would have inserted just "one fabricated" anecdote. In any case the intention of the author of the Russian story, unlike the German narrator, was never that of defaming Dracula.

The problem of Dracula's remarriage while technically in jail or under house arrest also poses formidable problems, not the least of which is the precise identity of this second wife, whose name has never been revealed. We do know from Dracula's own mention in 1462 that a marriage contract with the Hungarian royal family was in the offing. The Russian story tells us that the lady in question was "a sister of the king."[8] One Romanian author, C. Gane, identifies her as Helen Corvinus, a cousin of King Matthias. An argument that that author uses in support of his contention is that Dracula's descendants from that moment onward added to their nomenclature the additional title "from the royal family of

Corvinus" and adopted their coat of arms.[9] Most Romanian historians, however, and George Florescu, one of the country's leading genealogists, state that Dracula's second wife was a member of the Szilagy family whom Dracula had supported in the struggle for power that followed the death of Hunyady.[10] The Szilagys in any case were related to the royal Corvinus family.

In the Russian story the question of remarriage is linked to Dracula's conversion to Catholicism, which in turn was his passport to freedom. The relevant citation deserves to be quoted in full and requires a careful interpretation:

> *With the death of the Wallachian prince [presumably Radu, whom Matthias had previously recognized] the king sent an emissary to Dracula in jail with the question: "Should he wish to become prince in Wallachia as he had been before, then he must convert to Catholicism. Should he refuse, he will die in jail." Dracula, however, was more attached to the passing pleasures of this world than to life eternal. This is why he abandoned orthodoxy and gave up the truth; he abandoned the light and received darkness, since he could not endure the temporary difficulties of prison. Thus he prepared for the eternal martyrdom; he abandoned our Orthodox faith and received the Catholic religion.*[11]

It was only after his renunciation of Orthodoxy that the king gave him the hand of his "sister" in marriage and decided to consider him the official candidate to the Wallachian throne.

The only way of making sense of this whole complicated question of imprisonment, conversion, liberation, and remarriage is by stating that Matthias gave Dracula a kind of Hobson's choice: he must convert to Catholicism, obviously an essential precondition to marriage with the king's relative, and only then he might once again be considered an acceptable candidate; in case of refusal he would die in jail. The Orthodox apologists, and authors of the narrative, express righteous indignation about Dracula's decision to abandon "the truth faith"; but could he really afford to do otherwise? Dracula's religious convictions were not particularly profound; nor did his faith arise from any inward principle. Hence conversion to Catholicism posed no particular "conscience" problem. According to the German narrative, Dracula may have considered Catholicism or even conversion to Islam before.

Surely, taking his ambition into account, the deal offered by King Matthias was tempting enough. The throne of Wallachia in Dracula's eyes was certainly worth a Catholic mass.

What is more difficult to gauge is the precise date of Dracula's remarriage and conversion. The Russian narrative affirms that the episode occurred "after the death of the Wallachian prince previously recognized by Matthias," undoubtedly Radu the Handsome, which was in January 1475.[12] In that eventuality the date of remarriage and conversion would coincide with the full length of Dracula's official imprisonment, more than twelve years. Common sense, however, makes it difficult to envisage Dracula wooing a princess of the royal family, spending his honeymoon, and having two children behind prison bars. The Russian story comes to our aid in affixing a more plausible date for the happy event. The narrative adds that "Dracula had two sons of this [Hungarian] marriage and that he only lived for a short time afterwards, *approximately ten years.*"[13] Since Dracula died in December 1476, by deducting ten years one can trace Dracula's remarriage and liberation back to 1466; this allows for a period of only four years—1462-1466—of technical imprisonment at Vàcz or Vísegràd. Such an interpretation, we think, seems reasonable enough.

When Dracula was released from jail, presumably in 1466, after his remarriage, he was "given a house in Pest, opposite Buda," where he lived with his Hungarian wife and where likely the two sons referred to in the Russian narrative were born. We know next to nothing of his life in Pest beyond an anecdote that obviously aroused the attention of the Russian chronicler and caused a good deal of mirth at the Hungarian court. The narrative describes the incident in this manner (we are freely paraphrasing): A thief had apparently broken into Dracula's house, and a captain of the Hungarian guards pursuing him had simply followed onto the threshold of Dracula's house without a formal search warrant. Dracula avenged himself, not against the thief but against the unfortunate Hungarian official, stabbing him to death on the spot. When the municipal authorities went to complain about this strange behavior to the Hungarian king, Dracula justified himself in his inimitable and characteristic manner: "I did no evil; the captain is responsible for his own death. Anyone will perish thus who trespasses into the house of a great ruler. If this captain had come to me and had introduced himself, I too would have found the thief and either surrendered him or spared him from death."[14] The probable authenticity of this episode is sufficiently guaranteed by what we know of Dracula's character.

From the point of view of the Hungarian king, Matthias, Dracula's liberation and marriage into his family reestablished the *status quo ante*. No matter what his past sins, Dracula could reassume the role of "leader" of a Catholic crusading army. He was actually given the rank of captain by the Hungarian king. The king could now justify the use of papal funds and prepare his protégé for an opportunity to reassert his authority in Wallachia and lead the crusade against the Turks.

The use of Dracula as an instrument of the Catholic church and of Hungarian power was not viewed benevolently by the Orthodox world, as the author of the Russian story readily admits: Wallachia was no longer safe for Orthodoxy. And it was all the more essential for the Orthodox powers to strengthen their political ties to the sister principality of Moldavia. As early as July 5, 1463, a marriage contract was sealed at Suceava offering a Ukrainian princess, Evdochia, the daughter of Prince Olelocovicz of Kiev, to Dracula's Moldavian kinsman Stephen who, like Dracula, had been married before.[15] By this marriage, Stephen had a daughter, Helena, born in 1483, who was in turn given in marriage to young Ivan, the son of the Grand Duke, Ivan III, who succeeded his father in 1498. The Moldavian princess presented her husband with a son, the pathetic Demeter, who for a brief time carried the hopes of a permanent Moldavian-Russian-Orthodox connection. This parenthesis is relevant not only because of the Orthodox connections, but because the famous Russian narrative may have reflected Helena's political and religious viewpoint.[16] We are, however, anticipating on events. The danger posed to the Orthodox world by Dracula's conversion to Catholicism simply produced delayed reactions reflected in the Russian narrative.

From the moment of Dracula's remarriage and conversion, his active candidacy to the Wallachian throne was a *fait accompli*. Radu, always considered as the instrument of the Turks, was defeated by Stephen the Great in the spring of 1473. His successor, Basarab the Old (the son of Dan II), known as Laiota, a member of the Danesti clan, became prince for the first time on November 24, 1473, and with one interruption ruled until the beginning of November 1475. He was, however, totally unreliable from a Hungarian point of view. It was evidently in Hungarian interests to officialize Dracula's investiture as leader of the western crusade. He was by far the ablest and the most distinguished strategist available in the Christian camp. As such, the newly created "captain" moved from Hungary to Transylvania to receive the command of the frontier district of that province, a situation not very different from that which he enjoyed in 1456 during the days of Hunyady. Unlike the previous situation, however, the provinces of Amlas and Fagaras previously held by Wallachian princes were left under the control of the German Saxon cities, which status they had enjoyed since 1469.

The first record of a military action in which Dracula participated against the Turks is in 1474 when he was placed in charge of a Hungarian contingent, collaborating with the forces of Vuc Brancovic, the Serbian despot. The papal nuncio, the bishop of Erlau, reported the brutal cruelties committed against the Turks, stating that Dracula was spearing the Turks with his own hand and impaling the separate pieces on stakes.[17] Dracula once again used terror to frighten his enemies. Some historians also believe that Dracula and his Hungarian contingent participated at the great battle of Vaslui (January 10, 1475), on the side of Stephen the Great, fighting the Turks and Basarab Laiota, possibly 100,000 strong.[18] This important battle had been described by the contemporary Polish chronicler Dlugosz as a notable Christian victory. Stephen also received warm praises from Pope Sixtus IV. This was the first occasion since the battle of Crasna (June 1450) that the two cousins found each other fighting on the same side, and undoubtedly helped allay the bad feelings that had been caused by Stephen's defection and attack on Chilia in 1462. From this moment to the end of Dracula's career the two cousins remained loyal to each other. Forgetting previous differences and promising each other mutual aid and support, a formal compact was signed in the summer of 1475 by Matthias, Dracula, and Stephen. This was to be the cornerstone of the renewed anti-Ottoman crusade sponsored by the pope.

The winter of 1475-1476 was spent by Dracula and his family in Sibiu. In a letter dated August 4, 1475, written from Arghis in the Hida district of Transylvania and signed "Wladislaus Dragwlya," Dracula sent one of his boyars, Cîrstian, later to become governor of Tîrgoviste, to ask permission from the citizens of Sibiu to allow construction of a house for him and his family.[19] Replying to this request on September 21, the king of Hungary sent two hundred florins to the mayor of the town to help Dracula defray the expenses.[20] The money was received on October 13, and Dracula's letter of acceptance seemed to indicate that he had not as yet settled in Sibiu but was residing in the neighboring village of Balcaciu (October 13).[21] On January 21, 1476, the Hungarian diet formally gave its support to Dracula's candidacy to the Wallachian throne, as did the governor of Transylvania, Johann Pongrantz. By February 1476, Dracula's hold on Transylvania was so firmly entrenched that Basarab Laiota retaliated by writing to the citizens of Sibiu that he no longer considered himself as "their friend," since Dracula was living among them.

It was not until the summer of 1476—twenty years after his previous restoration—that serious plans were finally made to regain his throne, which was still officially occupied by Basarab Laiota. Supreme command of the expedition was given by King Matthias to Stephen Báthory (1414-1493), a member of the Ecsèd branch of that fascinating and powerful Hungarian aristocratic family which had for some time been linked with the Balkan crusading efforts; a namesake, another Stephen, had fought with Dracula's father and perished at the battle of Varna. The main reason for Báthory's command was the fact that the bulk of Dracula's army was composed of Hungarians and Transylvanians. Although his services during the campaign were not great—Báthory could not read a war map—Stephen was richly rewarded by the Hungarian king, being given the governorship of Transylvania from 1479 until his death, a position held by many of his successors. Stephen Báthory was the great-uncle of the notorious "blood countess" Elizabeth Báthory (1570-1614), held by Gabriel Ronay to be the only authentically documented case of a living vampiress.[22]

Although Stephen Báthory was technically commander in chief, actual military leadership was collective. Stephen and Vuc Brancovic each commanded his own contingent. In fact, Dracula, who knew the terrain best, was militarily in charge. On July 25, 1476, Dracula and Báthory held a council of war in the town of Turda (Transylvania) to discuss the details of the projected campaign. Stephen the Great was to launch his attack with 15,000 men from Moldavia, toward eastern

Wallachia. Dracula, Báthory and Vuc Brancovic, the Serbian despot, would attack from southern Transylvania with an army of roughly 25,000 men composed of Hungarians, Transylvanians, Wallachians, and some Serbs. By July 31 the main contingent had reached the town of Medias in central Transylvania, and the army traveled along the usual route of Balcaciu, Merghindel (both these placed are mentioned), Fagaras, Codlea, and finally Brasov, which was reached in October. Dracula had previously made several attempts to assuage the ruffled feelings of the Brasovians using the good offices of János Vitéz, the famous diplomat and humanist at the court of King Matthias, as his own personal representative (October 7). By October 7 the Brasovians, in whose district Dracula had committed so many of his crimes, were wooed into subservience by extensive commercial concessions and a renewal of trade relations.[23] Oxen, horses, and grain were to be sent from Wallachia in return for manufactured goods. None of the usual limitations were placed as regards the places where the Brasovians could trade, as has previously been done. In return, however, Dracula spent a good deal of effort sending two of his envoys, Ion Polivar and Mihai Log, to extract a promise from the citizens of that town not to protect Dracula's numerous political enemies who had sought refuge there. Indeed, Dracula's diplomatic activity on the eve of his third return to the throne is quite impressive. Another envoy of whom we know too little, called Ladislas, who reported to Dracula from Buda, kept him regularly informed on events in Moldavia and of Stephen's participation in the campaign.[24] Both Ladislas and Janos Vitez were also instructed to keep the Hungarian king, Matthias, informed of the progress of the forthcoming anti-Turkish campaign.

The actual offensive from Transylvania into Wallachia proper began in early November 1476. The allies directed their first offensive against the city of Tîrgoviste, the capital of the province, undoubtedly traveling along the most direct route, the Dîmbovita River via Bran and Rucar. The Wallachian capital was besieged and captured on November 8, after a skirmish in the vicinity of the fortress. Dracula himself reported the capture of the city in a letter to the Brasovians on that date.[25] (Its capture was also reported by Jacob Unrest.) On November 11, still continuing to travel along the valley of the Dîmbovita, Dracula's army was on the way to Bucharest, evidently the major objective of the campaign. We possess an interesting letter dated November 11 1476, dictated by Stephen Báthory to the town officials of Sibiu declaring that the greater part of Wallachia was in Dracula's hands, that "All the boyars except two are with us," and euphorically assuring the citizens that "even the latter will soon join us."[26] Bucharest was captured on November 16, and on November 26 Dracula was reestablished as prince of the land for the third time in his life in what can then be described as the new capital of the country. In a letter addressed to Pope Sixtus IV, Matthias confirmed the fact that Dracula was once again in control of the country and that he had agreed to renew his pledge of loyalty to the Hungarian king. By December 4, this happy news had reached Buda and Rome.[27]

According to peasant tradition, within one month, or at most two, Dracula's bloody, mangled, headless body was discovered by some monks from the monastery of Snagov in nearby marshes and secretly interred in a crypt facing the altar of the main church. Every moment since his accession during his brief third reign was dominated by the certainty of death: the odds against Dracula's survival were simply too great.

That no chronicle speaks of a bloodbath during these few months may indicate that the dissident boyars chose to make themselves scarce during that time. The partisans of the Turks and of Basarab Laiota had withdrawn to the mountains and had vowed to kill Dracula. As a Catholic he represented antichrist in the eyes of the Orthodox religious leaders. Most of the boyars had been too deeply implicated on Laiota's side to hope for permanent reconciliation and mercy. To the sultan, Dracula was obviously unacceptable. Even the Transylvanian Saxons, in spite of temporary appeasement, were unreliable and continue to give comfort to Dracula's political enemies. The moment that Báthory's Hungarian force and Stephen's main contingent would leave the country, Dracula was clearly exposed to great dangers, for he had had little time to consolidate his strength and rebuild a force loyal to himself. The fact that he was aware of these dangers is proven by his unwillingness to bring his wife and son with him to Wallachia, where undoubtedly they, too, would have been assassinated. Stephen of Moldavia, who had no great faith in the loyalty of the Wallachians, had left a small contingent of two hundred bodyguards to protect their newfound master. The loyalty of the Moldavians was Stephen's way of expiating his previous infidelities.

The final battle took place near Bucharest. Dracula's opponents were the boyars, the Turks, and the partisans of Laiota, all personal enemies of the Wallachian prince. How they were able to surprise Dracula's small contingent, comprising no more than four thousand men at most, including his Moldavian contingent; who actually killed the Wallachian leader; how the Moldavians fought and died— these elements of the battle have not been clearly preserved for posterity. There are several disputed versions. One of the most extensive and the most colorful is contained in the Slavic narrative, although it must be taken with a certain caution because the author of the story was clearly not a participant or a witness but had information from hearsay. The Slavic account of Dracula's assassination runs as follows: "Dracula's army began to kill (the Turks) and to pursue them without mercy. Then out of joy Dracula ascended a mountain in order to see how his men were killing the Turks. Detaching himself from the army, one of those around him, taking him for a Turk, hit him with a lance. Dracula, seeing that he was being attacked by his own men, immediately killed five of his assassins on the spot with his own sword. However, many arrows pierced him and he died in this manner."[28] Like a lion at bay, Dracula must have defended himself formidably. All but ten of the two hundred Moldavians perished at the side of their new master.[29]

We beg to differ from the interpretation of the author of the Slavic story; Dracula's death undoubtedly took place in the course of battle, but likely the assassin was either Laiota or one of his paid hands. According to Bonfinius and to the Turkish chronicler, Dracula was then beheaded and his head sent to Constantinople, where it remained exposed in Turkish fashion for all to see that the dreaded "impaler" was really dead.[30] It took about a month for this calamitous news to reach western Europe; only in February 1477 did the envoy of the duke of Milan at Buda, Leonardo Botta, write to his master, the famous Lodovico Sforza, "Il Moro," that the Turks had reconquered Wallachia and that Dracula had been killed.[31]

Strange is the fate of the Dracula epic. The legend was born in Transylvania; it spread westward to the German lands and eastward to Russia. The heroic moments took place on the Danube; the dramatic ones at the castle and in Hungary. Death came in a little clearing of the Vlasie forest on a marsh near

Bucharest. According to tradition, Dracula's final resting place was an island, the isolated monastery of Snagov, which perhaps more than any other structure, religious or otherwise, connected with Dracula's name bears the imprint of his tortured personality. What makes the blood-stained history of Snagov unique is the fact that, unlike castles, essentially edifices built for war, it was a monastery—admittedly at one time a fortified monastery, but nevertheless a place of worship. According to the old Romanian chronicles, the monastery of Snagov was built by Dracula; the chronicles are very precise on this point, and most of the older historians have accepted this as fact.[32] Just as we discussed the development of a "castle epic," there also exists a "Snagov saga," equally vivid and still alive among the peasants of the villages surrounding the lake.[33] In the imagination of these people, the awesome figure of the Impaler still dominates the little church and preoccupies their superstitious minds. Dracula has succeeded in stamping his whole personality profoundly upon the bricks and stones of the only surviving chapel, which he allegedly built and in which, according to tradition, he lies buried.

As archaeological excavation on the island and popular folklore have confirmed, the monastery of Snagov originally occupied an area immeasurably larger than that presently occupied by the church one can see today. The original monastic complex must have extended to the full length of the island. It was evidently fortified; the original walls extending to the edge of the lake were for added protection, for it was known that in a time of peril both princes and boyars stored their treasures at Snagov. In addition to three original chapels, which include the Chapel of the Annunciation (Buna Vestire), by far the largest (built by Vladislav II in 1453), the monastery contained cloisters for the monks, farmhouses and outhouses for the boyars and their mounts, a princely residence, probably a prison, and a mint (coins had been found on the island). Snagov, in fact, like many medieval fortresses, was a little town all its own, naturally limited by the size of the island. Of this vast structure nothing is left standing today.

The original monastery of Snagov is a much older ecclesiastical foundation, and can be traced back to the fourteenth century.[34] What is of interest to us is the extent of Dracula's contribution to the monastery. Here, as in the case of Castle Dracula, it is perfectly plausible to say that Dracula was in some way responsible for its completion. Snagov is

certainly not the first ecclesiastical edifice in Romania founded
by one prince and completed by another, and, as very often
happens in the erection of larger buildings, the name that
history associates with it is less that of the original founder
than that of the person who completes it.[35]

Many of the popular folkloric traditions in the Snagov area
are clearly fictitious: one popular ballad relates that Dracula
had a vision from God telling him to establish a place of
prayer near the scene of his father's assassination at Balteni.
Other stories are more specific and may contain an element of
truth. One ballad relates that Dracula's contribution was the
completion of another church on the island monastery just to
compete with his enemy Vladislav II, who was responsible for
the construction of the Chapel of the Annunciation. It is far
more certain that Dracula converted Snagov from a poorly
defended monastery into an island fortress. With his morbid
concern for a "refuge," he could find no better natural
fortification than the island surrounded by the dense Vlasie
forest, which commanded some sort of a view and was protected
on all sides. Even in winter, when the lake is frozen, a cannon
shot from the island could break up the ice and thus drown any
incoming enemy. It was by simple accident that the fortress
monastery fell into the hands of Radu's partisans during the
Turkish campaign of 1462. The monastery at the time had been
taken over by anti-Dracula boyars, who had hidden their
treasures in the vault of the church. According to the peasant
stories, the monks, fearful of their lives, threw these treasures
into the lake to avoid tempting the Turks. There are many
peasant stories concerning these treasures at the bottom of
Snagov lake. It is likely that Radu and his partisans also used
the monastery to store their wealth where it was
comparatively secure.

Other peasant narratives make mention of other Dracula
crimes on the island. Apparently Dracula's intention had been
to transform the island monastery into a prison and establish a
torture chamber for political foes. In a tiny cell the prince
would invite his intended victims to kneel and pray to a small
icon of the Blessed Virgin. While the prisoners were praying, a
secret trapdoor controlled by Dracula would open, sending them
deep into a ditch below, where a number of pales stood erect
waiting to pierce the body of the would-be candidate.[36] The
discovery of several decapitated skeletons, with their skulls
placed on the right side near the abdomen, lends further

credence to the theory that the monastery was used as a place of punishment in Dracula's time.[37] Yet another story relates how a great storm blew upon the lake the day of Dracula's internment, a storm that tore the Chapel of the Annunciation from its foundation and blew it into the lake. To this day, the peasants in the villages neighboring the lake say that whenever the waters of Snagov get unduly agitated, one can hear the muffled noises from the bell of the chapel's steeple tolling at the bottom of the lake.[38] Only the heavy, beautifully carved oak door of the chapel—one of the most beautiful legacies of fifteenth-century Romanian sculpture—which tore itself loose from its hinges, was seen floating down to the village of Turbati, where the Romanian archaeologist and novelist Alexandru Odobescu found it, when he was visiting a convent.[39] The nuns had apparently used it for their own chapel. When he read the inscription on the door, he was amazed to find it was dated 1453 during the reign of Prince Vladislav II, Dracula's predecessor. The carved door is now located at the Bucharest Art Museum.

Many of the immediate members of Dracula's family were in some way connected with Snagov. We have already mentioned Radu's role in 1462. Perhaps simply for reason of filial piety, Dracula's son, Mihnea, repaired the monastery after the extensive damage done to it by the Turks during the campaign of 1462 and endowed it with additional land. Vlad the Monk, Dracula's half brother and political enemy, may at one time have become abbot of the monastery, though he is not officially so listed. (His religious name was apparently Pahonie.) Vlad the Monk's second wife, Maria, took the veil and lived at Snagov as a widow, assuming the religious name of Eupraxia. She lived at Snagov for several years, together with her sons. One of these, Vlad V, or Vladut, spent all his early years at the monastery before becoming prince in 1530. The son of the latter, yet another Vlad, known to history as Vlad VII, "the Drowned," who briefly ruled between 1530 and 1532, may well have met death in the lake. Others say he drowned in the Dîmbovita River.

A great deal of violence has occurred at Snagov since Dracula's time, wrought both by man and by the elements of nature.[40] Storms of great intensity have occurred on the lake, doing inestimable damage to the buildings on the island. During the winter, the place is constantly heavily snowed under (Snagov in Slavic means snow). The peasants say that when the lake is frozen and the cold, merciless *crivat* wind from the Romanian steppes blows hard, it scoops the snow from the lake and hits with such violence that it can bury the whole island several feet deep. The present abbot told the authors that in preparation for winter, food has to be stored, since the island is completely isolated from the mainland. Like other places in the vicinity of Romania's capital, Snagov has felt the tremors of earthquakes, including the one in 1940. The monastery, however, has suffered far more from the violence of men. Only a small portion of this brutal history is enshrined in the inscription on the walls and the cold stone tombs of the existing church.

Like Alexander I of Russia, Dracula carried the mystery of his life to his grave. In his death, as on so many occasions during his turbulent lifetime, Dracula left problems unsolved. Among many riddles, one of the most perplexing is the precise location of Dracula's tomb within the monastery of Snagov, if indeed it lies there, as popular tradition will have it. During the year 1931-1932 the archaeologist Dinu Rosetti and George Florescu were officially assigned by the Commission on Historic Monuments to dig around the monastery and elsewhere on the island, and to make certain investigations at the site of the princely stone just beneath the altar where Dracula's decapitated body was supposed to have been laid to rest. Many interesting finds were made, which were publicized in a monograph edited by the History Museum of Bucharest, directed by George Florescu, entitled *Diggings at Snagov*.[41] Among these were archaeological remains that indicated that the island monastery was a very ancient historical settlement. The quantity and variety of coins that were dug up also confirm the use of Snagov as a treasury and mint since earliest times.[42] One of the main interests of the Florescu-Rosetti discoveries, however, centered upon the place where, in the eyes of the people, Dracula lay buried, in front of the altar of the church. Popular legend has various reasons for choosing the altar site as the location of Dracula's grave quite apart from its preeminent position. It is claimed that the monks purposely had Dracula's remains placed at the foot of the altar—contrary to usage, the tombstone rests in a north-south direction—so that the priest and the monks could read the Gospel and say prayers for the permanent repose of his troubled soul standing above the tomb. The trampling of the cleric's feet undoubtedly helped erase all inscriptions. Among the many graves in the monastery, this particular tombstone, though not of princely proportions, was more ambitious than most. When the stone was removed, however, to the utter amazement of the researchers, there was not even a casket. Dracula's presumed tombstone covered a huge empty grave containing the bones of various animals, some ceramics, and other archaeological finds dating back to the Iron Age.

Further exploration in various parts of the church revealed an unopened tombstone, on the right side of the entrance near the door, a most unusual place for burial in an Orthodox church. What struck the researcher team immediately was the precise coincidence in the size of the tombstone with that facing the altar, and the solidity of the crypt built of heavy brick and mortar. Within this tomb was a casket still partially covered by a purple shroud embroidered in gold. Much of the casket, as well as the remains of the cloth cover enclosing it, had rotted away. Within the coffin lay the pulverized bones of a human skeleton (far too pulverized to reveal the presence or absence of a skull) still clothed in tattered fragments of a thick yellowish brown silk vestment, the sleeves clearly discernible, with large round silver buttons linked to filament cord. Judging by the position of the sleeves, the hands of the skeleton were resting on the right of the pelvis. Not far away were the remains of a crown worked in cloisonné, embroidered with terra-cotta circles alternating with golden claws, holding a turquoise jewel. Adding to the mystery, there was also a woman's ring, which at one time contained a jewel, hidden behind the fold of the sleeve. Rosetti told the authors that he had found identical rings in Nürnberg and other parts of the Germanys dating back to the fifteenth century. He firmly believes that Dracula may have been involved in a joust or tournament somewhere in western Europe, and should this be his grave, the ring represented a token of courtly love from an unknown lady admirer.[43]

Were these the last earthly remains of Dracula? Those responsible for the find, notably Rosetti, believe they were; so does Rev. G. Dumitriu, an Orthodox clergyman from a neighboring village who has done a good deal of research on the problem of the tomb and who is convinced that Dracula's Hungarian wife is also interred at Snagov.[44] In this way scholarship tends to confirm the deeply anchored belief of the people.

There is no need of learned scholarship, however, to find suitable explanations for the desecration of Dracula's original tomb. These seem to suggest themselves. One might go so far as to state that, given both the terror that Dracula's name inspired and the vandalism that was permitted on the island during the latter part of the nineteenth century, when it was virtually abandoned, it would have been little short of a miracle for Dracula's tomb to have survived intact. Dracula's remains may have been removed from the more exalted position near the altar and reinterred for reasons of priestly fears. He was too wicked a prince to be so close to God on the altar footsteps. To cover up an act of desecration those responsible took the precaution of having all writing removed, and may have substituted a plain slab of stone. As an additional symbolic gesture of contempt, the bones of various animals and other ancient remains present on the island may have been thrown into the empty grave, while at the back of the church near the portico, unknown to all, they laid the earthly remains of the tyrant, where any church visitor could trample him under his feet. It is also symptomatic that there exists no mural or portrait of the prince in this, his church. If such a portrait existed at one time as is the custom when a prince is buried, it was either washed away or painted over. Those who desecrated Dracula's remains and mementoes were thus responsible for immortalizing both a hoax and a sacrilege.

No one knows for certain when the opening of the grave originally took place, and it would be unprofitable to go into the great variety of theories that have been advanced on the question of who was actually responsible for it. Some have suggested that it occurred when Snagov was under the control of the Greek monks during the eighteenth century. The Greeks were not as interested as their Romanian colleagues in praying for Dracula's soul near the altar. Others think that the desecration took place on the orders of Metropolitan Filaret, who became metropolitan in 1792, on the pretext of making some repairs on the church. A similar action could have been taken by Ilaron, bishop of Arges, at the beginning of the nineteenth century. In fact, any bishop, archbishop, or abbot, Romanian or Greek, might have given the necessary orders. It could also have been the result of vandalism by the peasants themselves from villages in the vicinity of the lake, simply looting during a time in the nineteenth century when the monastery was abandoned.[45]

The enigma of Snagov remains unresolved and awaits the historian brave enough to pick up the slender clues that archaeological investigation has so far produced.

---

[1] Michel Beheim refers to Dracula's imprisonment; Conduratu, *Michael Beheim*, p. 55. So does the author of the Russian story (story nos. 15, 16, 17), McNally and Florescu, *In Search of Dracula*, p. 200. Modrussa's literary portrait is also from that period. Papacostea, "Cu privire la geneza si raspindirea povestirilor," p. 163, n. 3. For other facts concerning Dracula's imprisonment see N. Iorga, "Lucruri noua despre Vlad Tepes," *Convorbiri literare* 35 (1901): 149-162.

[2] For excerpts of that Transylvanian correspondence and of the Italian correspondence, see Bogdan, *Vlad Tepes*, pp. 31-36.

[3] Russian narrative, story no. 14, McNally and Florescu, *In Search of Dracula*, p. 200.

[4] Conduratu, *Michael Beheim*, p. 55.

[5] Professors Florescu and McNally undertook a trip to Vísegràd in the summer of 1969. Two recent guides to Vísegràd are Cseke Laszlo, *Vísegràd* (Budapest, n.d.) and *Vísegràdi Lakotorony* (Budapest, 1966).

[6] Panaitescu, "Viata lui Vlad Tepes," *Cronici Slavo-Române*, p. 8.

[7] Russian narrative, story no. 16, McNally and Florescu, *In Search of Dracula*, p. 200.

[8] Dracula actually mentions that "we were going to celebrate the marriage" in the famous letter of February 11, 1462; Iorga, *Scrisori de boeri*, p. 164.

[9] Gane *"Trecute Vieti,"* p. 117.

[10] G. Florescu's genealogy in manuscript. (To be published by *East European Quarterly* in 1974.)

[11] Russian narrative, story no. 15, McNally and Florescu, *In Search of Dracula*, p. 200. The Russian story insists that Dracula sold his soul to the devil in order to escape from forced labor in jail, which was hardly plausible. The German St. Gall manuscript tells us that Dracula "renounced his faith." Another printed German pamphlet (fifteenth century, Leonardus Hefft, Latin manuscript from Munich, no. 26, 632, fol. 495) says that Dracula converted himself from the Moslem to the Catholic faith. Bogdan, *Vlad Tepes*, p. 30. Antonio Bonfinius, Matthias Corvinus's official court historian, generally well informed, tells us that Dracula, once baptized, was immediately restored to the Wallachian throne. G. Sincai, *Hronica Românilor si a altor nearmuri*, vol. 2 (Bucharest, 1886), p. 66.

[12] Russian narrative, story no. 15, McNally and Florescu, *In Search of Dracula*, p. 200.

[13] Ibid.

[14] Russian narrative, story no. 17, Ibid.

[15] Stephen the Great was married four times. His first marriage was to Marusca, who died before becoming a princess. He had two sons by her, Ilie and Alexander. By his Kievan wife, Evdochia, who died in 1467, he had three children: Bogdan, Peter, and Helena. By his third wife (1472), Maria of Mangop (of the Comnenus family), he had no children. Finally, he married Maria Voichita (1480), the daughter of Radu the Handsome, whom he captured. By her he had two children, Maria and Bogdan, who became prince. Gane, *Trecute Vieti*, p. 41.

16 A. Boldur: "Un Roman Transilvanean—autor presupus al povestirii ruse despre Dracula," *Apullum* 8 (Alba Julia, 1971): 75.

17 Iorga, "Lucruri noua," pp. 155-156.

18 Likely, however, Dracula did not get there in time. There is an interesting report from Moldavia. Shortly after that time there was a diplomat called Ladislas who kept Dracula informed of Moldavian events.

19 There has been a great deal of discussion concerning the genealogy of Cîrstian, evidently one of Dracula's chief boyar officials. Somehow he managed to continue in office after Dracula's demise, and we find him holding the title of Vornic from 1483 to 1504 under various princes. He died in 1522. Some authorities believe he was related to Dracula.

20 The letter of Matthias Corvinus to "Thomas magister civium civitatis Cibiniensis" is in the Sibiu State Archives. A copy is at the Library of the Academy of the Romanian Socialist Republic. See Hurmuzacki, *Documente*, 147, p. 86, 15-1.

21 This letter is also signed Draghwlya. The original is in the Sibiu State Archives, and a copy is at the Library of the Academy of the Romanian Socialist Republic. It is published in Bogdan, *Documente*, doc. no. 266, p. 328, and Hurmuzacki, *Documente* 148, p. 86, 15-1.

22 Gabriel Ronay, *The Truth about Dracula*, (New York, 1972), p. 93. The Báthory family traces its ascendants to the thirteenth century. It may have been of Romanian origin though Magyarized like the Hunyadys. There were two branches, those from Sombyo and those from Ecsèd. Among the most illustrious members was Stephen Báthory of Sombyo, prince of Transylvania and Hungary (1571-1576), who became king of Poland. Relations between the descendants of Stephen Báthory and the descendants of Dracula were not always good. The most dramatic episode was Michael the Brave's defeat of Cardinal Andrei Báthory, who was governor of Transylvania, on October 28, 1599, at the battle of Selimberg. Fleeing the field of battle, the cardinal was caught by a Székely who by a strange coincidence was called Blasiu Ordög (Hungarian for devil) who killed Báthory and personally brought the head of the defunct (later the body) to the Wallachian prince. Michael had him buried at the church of Saint Michael at Alba Iulia. The papacy punished the whole Székely people for the crime by ordering them to keep fasting for a century. The last of the well-known Báthorys, Gabriel (elected prince of Transylvania on March 3, 1608), indulged in Dracula's pastime of massacring Brasovians. He was also apparently a ladies man, for he was assassinated by two Hungarian noblemen who wished to avenge the insult inflicted by him upon their wives (1612).

23 This document in which Dracula conceded the very commercial concessions for which he had previously burned the citizens is in the archives at Brasov, doc. 773. A copy is at the Library of the Academy of the Romanian Socialist Republic. Also see Bogdan, *Documente*, pp. 95-97.

24 See the report of Ladislas, Dracula's envoy to Matthias Corvinus, dated Buda, August 7, 1476. He is described as a "famulus" of Dracula and could have been either a Hungarian or a Romanian. Some historians state that he could have belonged to the noble Hungarian family of Ladislas Drakulya of Semtest. Could this family itself have been related to Dracula? See Holban, *Calatori straini*, pp. 139-143 and chapter 9. The other Dracula diplomat, Bishop János Vitéz, was sent on several secret missions to Brasov in October 1475. Documents referring to him are in Brasov State Archives, doc. 189.

25 There is a woodcut in existence depicting Dracula's attack on Tîrgoviste. On November 11 Basarab was still within the fortress of Bucharest. Two weeks later he had fled across the Danube to the Turks. See a letter of King Matthias

to the papacy. N. Iorga, *Stefan cel Mare: documente descoperite in archivele Venetiei* (Bucharest, 1874), p. 80.

26 Bogdan, *Vlad Tepes*, p. 22.

27 In a letter to the papacy, Matthias describes Dracula in this way: "Dragula capitaneus meus, vir imprimis Turcis infestissimus et admodum bellicosum, de mea voluntate et disposicione per incolas regni illius transalpani in vayvodam solita solemnitate est assumptus." Bogdan, *Vlad Tepes*, p. 35; Teleki, *Hunyadiak Kora*, vol. II, pp. 575-576.

28 Russian narrative, story no. 18, McNally and Florescu, *In Search of Dracula*, p. 200.

29 Antonio Bonfinius, the historian of King Matthias, states that Dracula's head was cut off and sent to Mohammed II. *Rerum Hungaricarum decades* (Leipzig, 1936-1941), vol. 4, p. 6.

30 Bogdan, *Vlad Tepes*, p. 36. n. 2.

31 "He [Dracula] built the castle of Poenari and the holy monastery of Snagov." Simache and Cristescu, *Letopisetul Cantacuzinesc 1290-1688*, p. 69. Also see Simache and Cristescu, *Variante ale Letopistetului Contacuzinesc*, p. 20. For academic works see V. Bratulescu, *Manastirea Snagovul* (Bucharest, 1933); V. Draghiceanu, "Manastirea Snagov" (communicare), *Bul. Com. Mon. Ist.* 24, fasc. 67 (1931): 91; "Inscriptiile de la Snagov," *Bul. Com. Mon. Ist.* 26, fasc. 67 (1933): 42; Rev. G. Dumitriu, "Pe urmele unor sapaturi," *Amvonul* 21, nos. 4-6 (Bucharest, 1942): 9-14; N. Iorga, *Sate si manastiri din România* (Bucharest, 1905), p. 166; "In marginea Snagovului," *Floarea darurilor* 2, no. 25 (Bucharest, 1907); "Câteva indicatii asupra manastirii Sangovul" (Valenii de Munte, 1926); G. Mandrea, *Manastirea Snagov* (Bucharest, 1900); E. Mihaileanu, "Snagovul," *Boabe de Grâu* 2, nos. 6-7 (1921): 318-329, also published separately (Bucharest, 1933); St. Nicolaescu, "Vechimea manastirii Snagov," *Bucurestii*, no. 1 (1935), pp. 108-112, also published separately (Bucharest, 1936); "Manastirea Snagov si usa de stejar cu sculptori de sfinti a bisericii Buna Vestire ctitoria lui Vladislav voevod 1453." *Bucurestii*, nos. 1-2 (1936), pp. 118-128; Col. Popescu-Lumina, "Cine a facut manastirea Snagov," *Universul* 55, no. 269 (October 3, 1938): 4; D. V. Rosetti, *Sapaturile arheologice dela Snagov* (Bucharest, 1935); N. I. Serbanescu, *Istoria manastirii Snagov*; Stefan Andreescu, "Snagovul si Tainele lui," *Magazinul istoric*, year 3, no. 10, 31 (October 1969); 42. The archives of Snagov have now been transferred to the State Archives and the Academy Library.

32 Very little work has as yet been done on the "Snagov saga," and most of those works are romantic rather than strictly scientific. Among such romantic works we would list the following: *Câteva ore la Snagov (Opere complecte)*, vol. 3 (Bucharest, 1909), pp. 10-71; Armand G. Constantinescu, *Magul de la Snagov* (Bucharest, n.d.). More recently, G. V. Rogoz sets the whole atmosphere to her novel *Vlad fiul Dracului* (Bucharest, 1970) with a description of Snagov. See prologue, pp. 1-10.

33 The prewar Romanian encyclopedia states: "Dracula founded Snagov in 1457 where his tomb is shown." *Enciclopedia României*, vol. 2, p. 248. Most historians have accepted this fact: "The monastery of Snagov was built by Vlad Tepes during his first reign around 1457." D. Stanescu, *Viata religiosa la Români* (Bucharest, 1906), p. 43. "The great, the cruel Tepes built the monastery of Snagov." Iorga, *Istoria Românilor în chipuri si icoane*, p. 103. Dr. Frunzescu has 1470 as the date for the foundation of Snagov. (Dr. Frunzescu, *Dictionarul topografic si statistic al României* (Bucharest, 1872), p. 449. C. St. Bilciurescu has 1457. See *Manastirile si bisericile din România* (Bucharest, 1890), p. 158. Rev. G. Musceleanu simply states that Snagov was erected during Dracula's first (in fact, the second) reign. *Monumentele strabunilor din România* (Bucharest, 1873), p. 41. I. Popescu-Bajenaru thinks Mircea the Old was the

founder. I. Popescu-Bajenaru, *Schitul Balteni* (Bucharest, 1912), pp. 18-19. Yet others attribute its foundation to Mircea's brother, to Staico, to Vladislav, and to Radu I. See St. Andreescu, "Snagovul si tainele lui," *Magazinul Istoric* 3, (October 1969): 62. Col. Popescu-Lumina, "Cine a facut manastirea Snagov," p. 4, attributes the foundation to Dracul in 1446. Alexandru Odobescu found an icon with an inscription (today in Moscow) according to which the monastery was founded by a boyar or Prince Vintila or Vlad on June 7, 1431. A. Odobescu, *Câteva ore la Snagov*, p. 363. The author, however, cannot identify this Vlad. See Florescu, *Divanele domnesti*, vol. 1, pp. 67-69, n. 1. Iorga seems to agree with this view that a boyar Vintila was the founder. N. Iorga, *Istoria literaturii religioase a Românilor pana la 1688* (Bucharest, n.d.), p. 10. I. Lupas, *Istoria biseridi ortodoxe române* (Bucharest, 1930), p. 33.

[34] Sometimes the opposite is true. Such was the case with Dealul, which was begun by Prince Radu the Great in 1500-1501, but terminated by Neagoe Basarab. It is, nevertheless, in the popular mind associated with Radu, its original founder.

[35] Serbanescu, *Istoria manstirii Snagov*, p. 33.

[36] Dinu Rosetti, "Trei enigme," *Tribuna României*, no. 6 (February 1, 1973).

[37] "This is why sometimes when the wind blows and the waters are deeply agitated one can hear sounds of a bell emerging from the bottom of the lake." Odobescu, *Câteva ore*, p. 32.

[38] Ibid, p. 31.

[39] Another possible victim of Snagov may have been Vlad "the drowned," the son of Vlad V 'Vladut,' who according to some historians may have drowned in the lake. Others say he drowned in the Dîmbovita river in 1532. He is also buried at the Monastery of the Hill.

[40] The most notorious Snagov crime was assuredly the assassination of Constantin Cantacuzino. See the Baleanu Chronicle, *Istoriile domnilor Tarii Românesti*, p. 131. Also, N. Balcescu, "Postelnicul Constantin Cantacuzino," *Magazinul Istoric* 1, pp. 380-411. An accidental tragedy was the burning of the bridge linking Snagov to the mainland during the nineteenth century. "The bridge burned completely during a whole day and a whole night." Odobescu, *Câteva ore*, p. 19. It was never rebuilt. During the Ypsilanti uprising, the Turks had established themselves in the neighboring monastery of Pantelimon, and caused great hardships to the nuns at Pasare Monastery. The latter were then evacuated to Snagov until the signing of the peace. A. Mironescu, *Istoria manastirii Cernica* (Cernica, 1930), p. 179. Yet a third incident was the mass drowning of convicts on their way to the monastery in the 1860s (the monastery had temporarily been converted into a jail) when a hastily built pontoon bridge collapsed under their weight. Ion Tic, "Snagovul asa cum este," *Illustratiunea Româna* 10, no. 30 (1938): 2-3. Today a wooden cross in front of the church shows the place where these victims drowned.

[41] The monograph was published in 1933. The D. Rosetti, *Sapaturile archeologice dela Snagov*, vol. 1 (Bucharest, 1935).

[42] The secret mint probably dates back to the beginning or middle of the seventeenth century in the reign of Mihnea II (1658-1659). According to Rosetti, coins of all countries were imitated, including those bearing the effigy of Gustavus Adolphus of Sweden (1611-1633). Coins of an earlier fourteenth-century period were also found. Ibid., p. 28.

[43] Rosetti, "Trei enigme," p. 6. Also see Rosetti, "Unde este mormintul lui Vlad Tepes," a communication to the History Museum of the city of Bucharest (Oct. 12, 1966) and P. Anghil "Un episod Shakespirean din istoria nationala: Tepes" *Gazeta Literatà* 14 (January 12, 1967); 1, 7.

[44] Rev. G. Dumitriu, the priest at the village of Snagov, with whom the authors often conversed, has made the study of historical traditions in the

area, particularly pertaining to Dracula's tomb, his lifelong hobby. He revealed the result of his studies in "Pe urmele unei sapaturi." In addition Rev. Dumitriu has collected quite a number of the popular tales from villages in the Snagov area. These certainly deserve to be published to arouse the attention of scholars.

45 In 1873 the priest Agatanghel notified the ministry of cults and the metropolitan "that during its abandonment, the monastery was thoroughly looted by neighboring villages." He demonstrated that the doors, the windows, the floors, door cases, and window cases were taken out of the walls and stolen. Only empty walls remained. *Arhiva Stat. Mln.* Instruct., doc. 704/1867, fol. 74r., and *Arhiva Stat. Min. Instruct.,* doc. 704/1870, fol. 154r.

6

Dracula's Heirs

The history of the immediate future of Dracula's family and the ultimate fate of Dracula's descendants has inevitably aroused the interest of scholars and the public at large, and to this day the topic has never been researched. A great deal of misconception has centered on both these themes, because of the fame of Dracula's name and the many claimants who have posed as "Dracula heirs."[1] It is thus timely to expose some myths.

With reference to Dracula's family, the author of the Russian narrative is the only source that gives us news of the whereabouts of Dracula's Hungarian wife and his three sons. After Dracula's assassination at Bucharest, the family stayed for some time at Sibiu, then left Transylvania for Buda, where two of Dracula's sons were seen by the author of the Slavic story as late as February 1486 in the city of Buda. They were residing at the Hungarian Court and were presumably brought up by King Matthias. Yet another son is mentioned, who had taken up residence with the local bishop in the Transylvana city of Oradea. (Oradea at the time could be described as the center of the Transylvanian Renaissance, and Nicolae Olahus, the famous humanist bishop-to-be, resided there.) "He died in our time," states the author of the Russian narrative presumably around 1486 when the manuscript was first completed.[2] "I saw the third son," he added, "the eldest, whose name was Mihail, in Buda. He fled from the Turkish Sultan to the King of Hungary. Dracula had him by a woman before he was married."[3] It was but natural for Dracula's family to leave Sibiu, never particularly safe, and seek refuge with the Hungarian king, Dracula's relative. Eufrosin, the transcriber of the Russian story, however, makes a slight confusion concerning Dracula's sons. The eldest, undoubtedly the son of the unknown Transylvanian woman referred to, was Vlad, who became a claimant to the Wallachian throne and died about 1485.[4] Mihnea the Bad, or, as the Russian chronicler refers to him, "Mihail," was Dracula's second son of the Hungarian wife (not that of a Transylvanian woman). He was probably born shortly after his marriage (circa 1466). The Russian narrator is correct in noticing the presence of a third son at Oradea, although he does not give his name, which has been lost to history.

Mihnea the Bad, Dracula's eldest surviving son, ruled Wallachia briefly from April 1508 to October 1509.[5] The sobriquet "the Bad," coined for him by the Romanian people, is sufficiently accounted for by the monk Gavril Protul, chronicler of the period, who was struck by the enormity of Mihnea's crimes.

As soon as Mihnea began to rule [April 1508], he immediately abandoned his sheep's clothes and he plugged his ears like the asp. . . . He caught all the greater boyars and worked them hard and cruelly confiscated their fortunes and slept with their wives and daughters in their presence. He cut off the noses and lips of some, others he hanged, yet others he drowned.[6]

All this had a familiar ring: "Tel père, tel fils." If Mihnea's crimes did not assume the proportion of those of his father, it was simply due to lack of time and opportunity. Expectedly, Mihnea was stabbed to death on March 12, 1510, in a public square facing the ancient Roman Catholic Cathedral of Sibiu, where he was worshiping. He was killed by the Serb Demeter Iaxici, a partisan of a rival candidate to the throne, Neagoe Basarab, who became prince of Wallachia two years later, on January 23, 1512. Gavril Protul's venomous condemnation of Mihnea may also, in part, have been colored by the fact that he was in the pay of the latter prince. Mihnea the Bad is buried in that same cathedral (today the Saxon Evangelical Church of Sibiu), where his tomb can still be seen. He must have been about 56 years old at the time of his death, if the date of his birth, 1466, is correct. History knows of two women whom Mihnea married: the first was Smaranda, who died before 1485, and the second Voica, who was left a widow by her husband's assassination and bravely brought up her two sons, Milos and Mircea, as well as Mihnea's only daughter, Ruxandra. The whole family continued to reside in Sibiu. Milos, the eldest, was born about 1480, but was never considered the heir to the throne by the father.

Mircea became coregent with his father from 1508 to 1509. He was elected prince of Wallachia on October 29, 1509, styled himself Mircea II, and ruled very briefly until January 1510. He must have been a strong and brutal man, for it is said that he caught some of his father's assassins and killed them single-handed.[7] After he was expelled by his boyar enemies, he once again sought refuge in Transylvania, and on two separate occasions, in 1512 and in 1521, he tried unsuccessfully to recapture the throne from his political foe, Neagoe Basarab. After living in Transylvania for some time, like many of the Draculas, Mircea took residence at Constantinople, continuing to intrigue with the Turks in an attempt to regain his throne, but never succeeded in doing so. He married a Serbian sometime before 1519, when he was still residing in Transylvania. Only her name—Maria Despina—is recorded by history.

Of Dracula's grandchildren, by far the most successful was Mircea's sister Ruxandra, first married to a Wallachian boyar called Dragomir in 1511, who survived this marriage barely by one year, dying in mysterious circumstances.[8] A second marriage was immediately arranged by the ambitious mother with no less a person than Bogdan III of Moldavia, known to history as "the Blind," though he was in actual fact one-eyed. Bogdan was the son of Stephen the Great, and the marriage was celebrated with a great deal of pomp on August 15, 1513, at Jassy. It was yet another occasion in history where these two powerful families of Moldavia and Wallachia, the Musat and the Basarabs, were connected by blood.[9] Prince Bogdan survived the marriage to Dracula's granddaughter by only four years; he died prematurely in the full vigor of manhood in 1517, without leaving any children, and his widow, Ruxandra, disappeared from history. Both Prince Bogdan and Ruxandra are buried in the famous monastery of Putna, the mausoleum of Stephen the Great.[10]

Prince Mircea II had a multitude of children by his Serbian wife, no fewer than twelve, six boys and six girls bearing familiar Basarab names. Of the girls, little is known, except that one of them married a boyar who held the office of chamberlain at the Bucharest court in 1591. Of the boys, the oldest, Milos II, "the One-Armed," styled himself "son of a prince," and was a perpetual candidate to the throne, spending most of his life in exile, first at Kaffa (in Asia Minor) and later at Constaninople, where he married about 1550 and died in 1577.

For Romanian history only two of Mircea's sons are important: one is Alexandru II (Alexandru Mircea), the fifth child; the other is Peter the Lame, the tenth. Both were brought up in the Turkish capital to ripe middle age and hardly knew their country of origin before ascending to the throne. During their long stay in the Turkish capital, both sons married into powerful Greco-Italian families, members of an increasingly wealthy and influential community that was soon to be identified with the lighthouse section of Constantinople—the Fanar. Peter the Lame married Maria, daughter of the powerful Amirali family, about 1565. Alexandru married Catherine Salvaressi, a fascinating woman who came from the Pera district of Constantinople. Catherine Salvaressi has left a correspondence with her sister Maria, who sojourned in Venice for long periods of time, of invaluable help to the historian.[11] The letters reflect a sense of the instability inherent in the princely title during the sixteenth century. On one occasion she wrote to her sister: "Today we are, tomorrow we are not, in accordance with the wishes of God. We are in the hands of the Turks and we do not know where we shall be up to the end."[12] Both the Amirali and the Salvaressi families had a good deal of influence with the sultan, possibly owing to patronage of the powerful Cantacuzino family. Both princes, who were well past middle age, eventually became candidates to the Wallachian and Moldavian thrones.

Alexandru, who was to style himself Alexandru II, and Catherine were greeted in Bucharest as the first lord and lady of the land, in June 1568. At the time, they had only one son, whose name was also Mihnea. Following Dracula and like his grandfather Mihnea the Bad, Alexandru II can be considered as one of Wallachia's cruel and wicked princes. He began his rule with the usual boyar massacres and killed almost on the scale of his great-grandfather. Three of his most famous victims are interred in the monastery of Snagov.[13] It was possibly because of his massacres and because of boyar complaints that an edict for the deposition of Alexandru II was signed by the sultan on April 30, 1574. However, with the powerful support of his wife's family and because of an extravagant expenditure of *bakshish*, Alexandru II made a comeback in May 1574, and he ruled until September 1577 for a second time. In that year, after yet another boyar massacre, Alexandru was poisoned by boyars. Like Dracula, both he and his wife, Catherine, had turned to the building of churches to pay for their sins. Catherine founded the monastery of Slatioara and Alexandru built the monastery of Saint Troita, later known as the Church of Prince Radu, in Bucharest, where he lies buried. With Alexandru II's assassination, his widow fled into exile and lived to a ripe old age, dying in 1590. The only authentic mural painting of Alexandru II and his wife is at the monastery of Slatioara.

The second ruling son of Mircea II was Peter the Lame, who liked to style himself (in memory of his great-grandfather Dracula's marriage into the Hungarian royal family) "of the royal Corvinus family."[14] He was born about 1530, the tenth of Mircea's children. Like his brother, Alexandru II, Peter spent all of his youth at Constantinople in the company of powerful Greek and Italian patrons and friends of his wife. Since his brother occupied the Wallachian throne, only that of Moldavia was left open. Thus at the respectable age of forty-five, Peter first became prince of Moldavia on June 14, 1574, replacing a tyrant, John, by name, also known as "the Cruel." Following Alexandru's pattern, Peter's fortunes went up and down. He actually ruled and was dispossessed on three different occasions.[15] Unlike most of the Draculas, Peter was known essentially as a weak prince, a tool in the hands of the boyars, who preferred a comfortable exile in the west to the continued struggle for power. He is known in history chiefly for his amorous pursuits. The marriage with Maria Amirali was not a success, for when he was deposed in 1579, she did not follow him into exile, even though she returned to him three years later when he regained the throne (1582). A little later while still on the throne, Peter fell in love with a beautiful gypsy woman, who was probably an attendant at the court in his wife's retinue, and became his mistress. Court practice made it impossible for Peter to marry Irina—princes were supposed to have only one legitimate wife—but he went to the extent of having her baptized and having her assume a Christian name. He also coined her surname: Irina Botezata, which simply means, Irina the Baptized.

When Peter fled into exile at the court of the Holy Roman Emperor Rudolph II, he left his legitimate wife behind and took with him the gypsy slave Irina. (Their relationship may well have been legitimized, since Peter was no longer prince of the land.) He was given a residence at the castle of Zimmerlehen in the Austrian Tyrol, where for a few years the former prince maintained the semblance of a court, even with a court dwarf in attendance. Irina died only a year after their arrival at Zimmerlehen, on November 3, 1592, still young and beautiful, and was buried at the Franciscan cemetery of Bolzano. It was rumored that she died of heartbreak, because this romantic prince had fallen in love once again—he was past sixty at the time—with a beautiful Circassian woman of humble rank named Maria, who lived with him at Zimmerlehen up until his death.[16] Peter himself died on July 1, 1594, and was buried in a chapel near the Franciscan church of Bolzano next to the woman he had loved. Their tombs can still be seen today in this pretty Tyrolean village.

Peter the Lame had but one son, Stephen (or Stefanita), who was born of his gypsy wife and had accompanied him in exile. After the death of the father, there was an attempt by some Moldavian boyars to bring back Stephen and the considerable assets that his father had taken with him in Austria to Moldavia. Emperor Rudolph II, however, resisted that move, and the Society of Jesus sequestered the legacy and took over Stephen to keep him safe from the Orthodoxy. Stephen was placed in a Jesuit school at Innsbruck and later at the Mariani congregation. He died of consumption in 1603 and was buried beside his father and his gypsy mother. The inheritance of the young prince, which included the famous portrait of his ancestor Dracula, now located at Ambras Castle near Innsbruck, was confiscated by the Society of Jesus. It was likely given to Ferdinand II, archduke of Tyrol.[17] A portrait of Peter the Lame and one of his son were also placed in the Ambras gallery, although both have been lost. We are fortunate, however, in possessing a reproduction of the portrait of Peter's son, Stephen, which is one of the most beautifully finished portraits of any Romanian prince.[18]

With the death of Stephen, the male Dracula line could survive only by way of Alexandru II and Catherine's only son, Mihnea, born in July 1559.[19] In 1577, after his father's assassination and with the help of his mother, who became regent, Mihnea made a brave attempt to pose his candidature, and precariously maintained himself on the throne up to 1583. He was barely eighteen years of age at the time. Expelled by a boyar coup, Mihnea was to spend the next two years in company with his mother in various places of exile, which included the island of Rhodes, Tripoli, Tunisia, and Venice. There is a letter in existence dated September 18, 1584, in the Venice archives, sent by Mihnea to the Grand Vizir, Sinan Pasha, in which he implores the sultan to give him back the throne.[20] His mother's family, the Salvaressis, were still sufficiently influential and had enough money to obtain the throne on behalf of their grandson. Mihnea thus became prince for the second time on April 6, 1585. He had been married early in life by his mother to a boyar lady (1582) called Neaga or Neacsa of Cislau, a pious woman of whom we know very little, except that she built several monasteries in the Buzau district which have since disappeared. History has preserved the name of a second wife, another boyar lady by the name of Voica or Visa, who was certainly illegitimate. Mihnea was probably separated from his first wife, Neacsa, at the time of his second reign.

In May of 1591, one year after the death of his powerful and fascinating mother, Catherine, the Turks deposed Mihnea for the second time. His efforts in placating his Turkish masters by raising new taxes upon the country had not paid off. Mihnea came back to the Turkish capital, and possibly in order to save his neck, adopted the law of Islam together with his eldest son and assumed the name of "Mehmed Bey," the name of Dracula's worst enemy, Sultan Mohammed II. Since by Turkish law he was allowed a harem, he had innumerable wives and children bearing Moslem names, which history has preserved. He died in Constantinople and was buried in an unmarked grave in 1601. It is because of his conversion to Islam that Mihnea had been labeled "the Islamized."

Apart from the children born in the harem at Constantinople, Mihnea the Islamized had five other children, four sons and one daughter. Of the sons, only one survived with male heirs continuing the direct Dracula line—Radu Mihnea, the son of Visa, one of Mihnea's Christian wives.

Radu Mihnea, the fourth son, born about 1585-1586, returned to Wallachia after completing his studies at Constantinople. He was one of the most fascinating figures in the history of Dracula's direct descendants. He came to power following a historic moment in the history of all three principalities, Wallachia, Moldavia, and Transylvania. One of the descendants of Vlad the Monk, Prince Michael the Brave, had just accomplished the traditional dream of all Romanians—namely, the unity of all three principalities under one realm, rather a premature stroke of genius, which ended with his assassination. Given the endemic political instability, Radu Mihnea achieved an almost unique record, ruling no fewer than on six different occasions: four times in Wallachia and twice in Moldavia. His first Wallachian rule, from 1601 to 1602, occurred a few months after the assassination of Michael the Brave.[21] In contrast to cruel predecessors, such as Alexandru II, or to weak personalities, such as Peter the Lame, Radu Mihnea was a splendid, mundane, Renaissance-style prince and a patron of the arts. He was probably one of the best educated of Romanian princes, versed in languages, and brought up by the monks of Iveron, the Romanian monastery at Mount Athos. He also liked luxury, and the fiscality of his extravagant court bore heavily upon the country. He began the nefarious practice of introducing Greek sycophants at the palace and found sinecures for them. Finally, he enhanced the cause of Romanian nationalism, since his rule in Moldavia coincided with the reign of his eldest son, Alexandru; thus *de facto*, for the second time in history, the two principalities were under one sovereign. Radu Mihnea died in 1626 at Hîrlau in Moldavia. His body was carried to Bucharest where he was buried at the Church of Prince Radu, completed by him but begun by Alexandru II. The church was later placed under the protection of Mount Athos.

Radu Mihnea's only legitimate wife was Arghira Bartolomeo Minetti, an Italo-Greek of whom we know very little. By that wife he had five children, three boys and two girls, who must be considered as Dracula's last surviving direct descendants. The eldest was a boy, another Alexandru, known as "Coconul" (cocoon), because of the tender age on which he first acceded to the throne.

Alexandru Coconul ruled on two occasions: initially in Wallachia from 1623 to 1627, then in Moldavia from 1629 to 1630. The interchanging of thrones was a practice increasingly more frequently adopted by the Turks. Another characteristic abuse, foreshadowing the eighteenth-century Greek period of rule, was the distribution of lavish sums of money at Constantinople to purchase the throne.

Two years before his death, Radu Mihnea had arranged what appeared a most brilliant marriage for his son, Alexandru. The bride-to-be was Ruxandra Scarlat Beglitzi, the daughter of a powerful Greco-Italian prince-maker at Constantinople, who had consistently supported Dracula's heirs. This was one of the high moments in the history of Dracula's heirs, for both father and son ruled: Alexandru at Bucharest, Radu Mihnea at Jassy. With a great deal of fanfare both courts were making preparations in Bucharest eagerly expecting the Greco-Italian heiress. Ruxandra not only was wealthy and had powerful connections but was described as one of the most beautiful available young heiresses of Constantinople. While the bridal cortege was traveling through Bulgaria on their way to Bucharest, a terrible calamity occurred which later destroyed the marriage: Ruxandra caught the dreaded smallpox, which permanently disfigured her beautiful face with unsightly scars.[22] During the wedding ceremony it is said that she covered her face with a veil to deceive the entourage of both princes. Alexandru Coconul, however, soon made the terrible discovery; nevertheless, for his father's sake, he kept his wife at court for some time, this being dictated by political motives and the need for Beglitzi's money. Eventually, however, Alexandru III repudiated his wife and sent her back to Constantinople. He never married again nor had any children. After losing his throne for the second time on April 29, 1630, he fled to Constantinople.

The year of Alexandru Coconul's death, 1632, witnessed several. important events. It was the year when Wallenstein finally defeated and killed the Protestant hero, Gustavus Adolphus the Swedish king, on the blood-stained battlefield of Lützen, thus terminating the Thirty Years' War of religion in Germany; in that same year the long ailing Richelieu finally breathed his last, allowing his nominal master, Louis XIII, to govern France without his strong hand; in England the Stuart king Charles I finally decided to flee London, thus ushering in the English Civil War. In eastern Europe the king of Poland, Ladislas IV, had just given up his mad bid to rule distant Moscow; the Ottoman Empire had temporarily forsaken Europe and was busy fighting the Persians. In distant America Lord Baltimore had just received the privilege of founding the colony of Maryland. Within this framework of events, unknown to all, on June 26 of that year at Constantinople died Alexandru Coconul, the last direct male descendant of Dracula, sixth generation of that line, the last ancestor of a man who had inspired terror and awe throughout Europe some 170 years before. He was heirless, penniless, unpraised and unsung, completely obscure, and a subject of the Turkish masters whom Dracula had fought. His very grave is unknown, and there are no paintings of him. Thus, miserably, died the last of the Draculas. One feels a natural compassion for his tragic plight.

---

[1] Among the less serious studies is Leo Heiman, "Meet the Real Count Dracula," *Fate*, March 1968, pp. 53-60. It is the story of "Count" Alexander Cepesi who operates a blood bank in Istanbul and poses as a Dracula descendant. Various members of the Cantacuzino and Basarab Brîncovan families have better credentials as "descendants" through the female line.

[2] McNally and Florescu, *In Search of Dracula*, p. 21.

[3] Ibid.

[4] George D. Florescu, "Dracula's Descendants," ms. (To be published by the *East European Quarterly* in 1974).

[5] Mihnea the Bad had a reputation of evil almost rivaling that of his father. A letter quoted by Bogdan dated January 7, 1509 stresses his cruelty toward the boyars. It states that "the whole country trembled in fear." He was also responsible for massacres in Brasov and Fagaras. We possess a few anecdotes about Mihnea reminiscent of those of his father. "It is said that he had a poor man (who had come to ask him to reduce the tax) hung in the following manner: As Mihnea asked the unfortunate man whether he had a wife, the latter answered in the affirmative. Then the Prince said: 'You will pay the tax' and the poor man answered: 'If I have to pay the tax because of my wife, I prefer to separate myself from her. Upon hearing this, Mihnea answered Dracula-style: 'Although you may wish to separate yourself from your wife, I, for one, will not allow you to leave,' and he ordered that he be placed on a pitchfork." Bogdan, *Vlad Tepes*, p. 73. Mihnea was finally defeated by the Craiovesti boyars who were as exasperated with his cruelties as they were indignant at his Catholicism and persecution of the Orthodox church. For further biographical details on Mihnea the Bad see Al. Lapedatu, "Moartea lui Mihnea cel Rau," *Convorbiri liteare* 50 (1916): 314-325; "Minhea cel Rau si Ungurii 1508-1510," *Anuarul istoric* 1 (Cluj, 1921-1922): 46-76, also published separately (Bucharest, 1922).

[6] G. Ivascu, *Istoria literaturii române* (Bucharest, 1969), p. 77.

[7] For further details on Mircea II see Giurescu, *Istoria Românilor*, vol. 2, pt. 1, p. 144, and Gane, *Trecute vieti*, p. 55.

[8] Ibid.

[9] See chap. II, n. 6.

[10] For Putna Monastery see M. Berza, "500 ani de la constructia Manastirii Putna," *An. Ac. Rom.* 100, no. 16 (1966): and 1967 511-578, and N. Constantinescu, *The Putna Monastery* (Bucharest, 1956).

[11] Gane, *Trecute vieti*, p. 102.

[12] Giurescu, *Istoria Românilor*, p. 328.

[13] The three sons of the boyar Dragomir were decapitated and interred on the orders of Prince Alexandru II at Snagov. The mother of these young men then took the veil and returned to the monastery to pray for their souls. Serbanescu, *Istoria manastirii Snagov*, p. 49.

[14] Very little work has been done on Peter the Lame. For his domestic policy see *Istoria României*, vol. 2 (Bucharest, 1962), pp. 921-923. A more specialized work on peasant rebellions under his rule is N. Grigoras, "Despre rascoalele taranilor moldoveni în vremea domniilor lui Petru Schiopu 1574-1579 si 1582-1591," *Studii si cercetari de Stiinte Istorice* 11 (Iasi, 1960): 227-239.

[15] June 14, 1474, to November 23, 1577; January 15, 1578, to November 21, 1579; September 2, 1582, to August 19, 1591.

[16] Iorga, *Istoria Românilor in chipuri si icoane*, p. 44.

[17] Gane, *Trecute vieti*, p. 122.

[18] Iorga, *Portretele domnilor române*, p. 66. The painting of Prince Stephen was located at Ambras but has since disappeared.

[19] Giurescu, *Istoria Românilor*, pp. 256-257, 324-328.

[20] Gane, *Trecute vieti*, p. 108.

[21] He ruled again in Wallachia from 1611 to 1612, 1612 to 1616, and 1620 to 1623, and in Moldavia from 1616 to 1619, and 1623 to 1626.

[22] Gane, *Trecute vieti*, p. 223.

7

Dracula in Literature—
From Hero to Vampire

The Dracula image followed two distinct, opposite paths—one within Romania and the other beyond the frontiers of that country. The literary representation of Dracula in the West from the fifteenth-century German pamphlets on Dracula progressively amplified the horror theme, until Dracula became a vampire in Stoker's late-nineteenth-century English novel. But in Romania, subject to varying qualifications, such as the image of Dracula as buffoon, the heroic trait prevailed. There is a wide gulf between these two literary traditions exemplified by the use of the two different names, i.e., "Vlad Tepes," the Impaler, in Romania, and "Dracula" abroad. This fact in itself makes it difficult to recognize that one is speaking about the same man.

The initial Dracula apologist may well have been Romania's first internationally known humanist, Nicolae Olahus (1493-1568), the foremost representative of the Transylvanian Renaissance.[1] Olahus had good reasons for coming to Dracula's defense: since he was related to him. This Dracula kinship was further strengthened when Olahus married the sister of the Hungarian king Matthias, another relative of whom had become Dracula's own wife. When Olahus was compelled to flee with the widow of the Hungarian king Ladislas following the Hungarian defeat at Mohács in 1526, Olahus took up residence at Innsbruck, only a few years before Dracula's great-grandson Peter the Lame arrived there. Apart from his political and ecclesiastical preoccupation (he became primate of free Hungary in 1553), Olahus was a scholar who conducted a vast correspondence with all the important representatives of the Renaissance, including the "prince of humanists" Erasmus. Among various political writings, which included reference to his native Transylvania, Olahus has left us an interesting biography entitled *Atilla*, written in Brussels between 1536 and 1537. This was a timid attempt to gloss over the crimes of the "whip of God," and portray the Hun as a man of justice and

learning. Most literary critics thought that under this literary
disguise the author was eulogizing King Matthias. Matthias,
however, had never been particularly noted for cruelties. Might
it not be pertinent to suggest that Olahus may have in fact
undertaken the first apology for Dracula, his kinsman? The book
was first published in Vienna in 1718, indicating the manuscript
had not met with approval in its own day.[2]

This later date is relevant; only a few years earlier the first
Transylvanian intellectuals availing themselves of the
educational opportunities afforded to them by the establishment
of the Uniate church, traveled to Vienna for study.[3] One of the
most fascinating representatives of the Latinist school was
undoubtedly Ion Budai-Deleanu (1760-1820), theologian, lawyer,
geographer, grammarian, historian, and political scientist
acquainted with the works of the *philosophes*.[4] From our point of
view, he was the author of a remarkable epic creation perhaps
unique in the history of Romanian literature. By a strange
coincidence Budai-Deleanu's epic, *Tiganiada*, was based upon the
life and times of Dracula, a song poem with the Wallachian
prince leading an army of gypsy slaves against the Turks. (The
work was not published until 1875).[5] One over-admiring critic,
M. Dragomirescu, may indeed have gone overboard when he
referred to *Tiganiada* as "the most significant heroic comic epic in
universal literature."[6] Nonetheless it is remarkable when one
reflects that the Romanian literary language was barely in the
process of formation. Budai-Deleanu, like Homer, sought a hero
to be immortalized above all other heroes of Romanian history.[7]
In his eyes Dracula was "the Brave," not the "Impaler," leading
his disorganized gypsy army in battle array, with the help of the
angels and the forces of good against the Turks, the evil boyars,
and the forces of Satan. In comparison with Stroker's *Dracula* the
whole plot is turned topsy-turvy. The encounters are at times
burlesque but narrated in a powerful verbal orchestration
perhaps unsurpassed until Mihail Eminescu's time. The work
contains satire, humor, sarcasm, and a good deal of ideological
content critical of absolute monarchy. The poem is Voltairean in
its distrust of men, Josephinist in its rationalism, and
revolutionary in its attack on boyars and kings, for whom Budai-
Deleanu has little respect.[8]

Uncannily Budai-Deleanu introduces the female vampire
Strigoaica in his plot, as well as other spirits of evil, with which

he was all too familiar in his native Transylvania, but they are not linked to Dracula; vampires are, in fact, his enemies:

> *At nightfall the vampires fly*
> *When the beautiful ladies take their walk*
> *Breaking the bones of people.*[9]

Budai-Deleanu also speaks of "unclean spirits who never sleep but fly all over at night," another obvious reference to vampires. In an eerie sort of way the vampires fly in the direction of the Retezat region of southern Transylvania "towards a mountain which lies between Wallachia and Transylvania."[10] Dracula's castle lies not far away. To a scientific historian such quotations are truly startling and unaccountable!

When the current of Transylvanian cultural nationalism crossed the mountains into the principality of Wallachia, it was natural that the heroic figure of Dracula should be exploited by Romanian nationalists to give the movement for independence precedence and paternity. Most of the Romantic historians of the 1848 generation—Gh. Lazar, N. Balcescu, I. Eliade Radulescu, Aaron Florian, A. Treboniu Laurian—were at least in part responsible either for romanticizing Dracula's career or for explaining away his crimes.[11]

Beyond romanticizing history, the men of the generation of 1848 were interested in dramatizing Dracula's career by other literary means. Since it was dangerous to teach Romanian history in the schools, plays with nationalizing themes were an effective way of reaching a wider audience. The public was bound to recognize the obvious message in Dracula's spectacular anti-Turkish campaign in 1462. Besides, under the camouflage of literary endeavor, one could occasionally overcome political censorship. The first Dracula play was not so fortunate. Its author was Ion Catina, and his Dracula in two acts completed in 1847 was not allowed to be performed because of the tense political situation existing in Wallachia on the eve of the revolution of 1848.[12]

The claim of having actually produced and performed the first Dracula play, *Vladu Tzepeshu drama istorica in cinci acte,* thus belongs to an obscure dramatist, G. Mavrodollu. He was able to show it to Bucharest audiences in 1856 when a more liberal administration no longer considered such a play subversive.[13]

Dracula did much better with the poets than with the dramatists. One of the most prominent figures of the generation of 1848, Dimitrie Bolintineanu (1819-1872) sounded the clarion call praising Dracula's military valor.[14] In highly stylized but beautifully versified rhymes and with a sense for the musical sounds of the Romanian language, Bolintineanu recalled the highlights of Dracula's career in his "Battles of the Romanians."[15] The well-known episode referring to the nailing of the turbans on the heads of the Turkish envoys is innocently dismissed in the following manner:

The assembly of soldiers
Shout with people
Long live the Impaler
The terrified Boyars jump through the window
While Dracula drives spikes into the Turkish envoy's heads.[16]

The boyars, as in the poem of Budai-Deleanu, are the allies of the Turks, whereas Dracula becomes popular in the broadest sense, not only as a national but as a social crusader. In 1863 Bolintineanu wrote a historical novel based on Dracula's life in the same nationalizing vein.

One may wonder why the subject of Dracula was not taken up by Romania's most prolific nineteenth-century poet, Vasile Alecsandri, while he was writing folkloric ballads and praising the heroes of old. Part of the answer may lie in Alecsandri's Moldavian origins—he was more interested in eulogizing Dracula's cousin Stephen the Great. However, one gets the impression that, as in the case of Mihail Kogalniceanu, the enormity of Dracula's impalements had hurt the sensibilities of the Moldavian poet. In his *Legende* Alecsandri associates Dracula with other bloody Turkish tyrants "intrinsically evil and unworthy of note."[17]

In addition to hero worship, the period of national awakening was also characterized by reverential nostalgia about the ruins of the past. This mood was created by the poet Vasile Cârlova (1809-1831), who in his brief and tragic career composed an ode, "Ruins of Tîrgoviste," Dracula's capital city. Forgetting impalements, he recalled the past greatness of Wallachia's ancient capital and gloomily mused upon the fact that his fatherland was still under foreign rule in 1828. Much the same nostalgia characterizes some of the verse of Grigore

Alexandrescu, also a native of Tîrgoviste, who wrote, "The Shadows of Mircea at Cozia," Cozia being the monastery where Dracula's grandfather lies buried and frequently visited by the grandson.[18]

It was both awe and sentimentality that impelled the critic and archaeologist Alexandru Odobescu to describe his solitary encounter with the spirit of Dracula at Snagov—the alleged burial place—in the Romantic style of a Walter Scott. Linking the presence of Dracula's presumed earthly remains to the weight of the crimes and other unwholesome incidents that that monastery has endured across the centuries, Odobescu's reflections at the lake site leave the reader perplexed by the impenetrable secret of the Dracula story.[19] Snagov, perhaps more than any other single memento of Dracula's stormy past, has continued to be a source of dramatic inspiration for novelists and poets, much of it inspired by superstitious reverence linked to the fact that Dracula is associated in the popular mind with that particular monastery.

After Romanian nationalism was made safe by the achievement of union and independence, "heroics" were no longer needed as an aid to patriotic education. Novelists and dramatists could afford the luxury of drama for drama's sake. One remarkable novel deserves to be mentioned in this connection, even though it centers on Dracula's son; this was Odobescu's *Mihnea the Bad*, completed in 1860. The plot focuses upon the murderous struggle between the Draculestis and Danestis, a Montagu-Capulet kind of affair—although it involved rival branches of the same dynasty. The end is truly Shakespearean: Mihnea the Bad is evidently "damned," and the last words of an agonizing Dracula—called Dracea in the plot— are drowned out by the "rattling of handcuffs and chains of the slaves strewn all around the cellar." Although in essence a "dramatic reconstruction," Odobescu's *Mihnea the Bad* drew its inspiration from genuine historical sources—the work of Gavril Protul, an abbot from Mount Athos, who was genuinely indignant at the crimes of Dracula's son.[20]

A much greater degree of dramatic and comic license was soon to be taken with Romania's revered historical figures, including Dracula. Mihail Sorbul, born in 1885, a future director of the National Theater in Bucharest, was in this respect a product of an iconoclastic *fin de siècle* generation.[21] His artificially stylized tragic-comedies had no purpose other than to amuse the public. With this in mind Sorbul sought incidents in Dracula's life that would lend themselves to comedy. He chose the extermination of the needy and the sick, when Dracula at the height of festivities set fire to the building in which they were. The play was entitled *The Feast of Beggars* (Praznicul Calicülor). It is interesting to note that precisely at the time when Dracula "the vampire" had established himself as a literary success in England, Dracula "the hero" had degenerated into a buffoon in the country of his birth.

Only in Dracula's birthplace in Transylvania, still unredeemed, were national heroes still needed, particularly after the compromise of 1897, when the Romanian population suffered under the hard hand of Magyar bureaucrats. Under the innocuous title of *Love and Revenge,* a Dracula novel saw the uncertain light of day at Brasov in 1877. It was written by Ion Lapedatu (1884-1878), a native of Sibiu (where Dracula owned a house), who after studying at Bucharest and Paris, returned to Brasov where he taught for some years at a secondary school.[22] He found a review with the harmless title *The Bee of the Carpathians*—a perfect vehicle for disseminating his historical novels, which could thus escape the eye of the Hungarian censor. This was history repeating itself. The Transylvanians experienced the same pressures under which the Moldavo—Wallachians had labored at the beginning of the century. With this one difference, there now existed a free Romania which, no matter what the official policy of the government, was essentially interested in their desires for self-determination.

Among Romanian poets there was one conspicuous isolated voice crying in the wilderness protesting the amorality of the government and the indifference of men of letters. This was the voice of Mihail Eminescu (1850-1889), undoubtedly Romania's greatest poet.[23] In a famous invocation, *The Third Letter,* Eminescu in a final verse turned back to Dracula, but for reasons different from those of his predecessors. The poet had a good understanding of Romanian history, having studied Hammer and Cantemir. He was at the time composing the verse for one of his great dramas, *Alexandru Lapusneanu,* another villain whose crimes bear many similarities to those of Dracula. However, Eminescu's appeal to Dracula was no mere trumpeting in the style of Bolintineanu. Rather it reveals the mentality of Hamlet, deeply disturbed with his times, which from his vantage point were hopelessly "out of joint." Eminescu was indignant at the · mores of Bucharest society, at the perfidy of politicians, at the faithlessness of diplomats whom he considered responsible for the loss of Bessarabia, and at the literary iconoclasts who took the names of the heroes in vain. In despair he appealed to the giants of old to rise from the dust under which they had been laid to rest in order to regenerate Romanian society and political life. They alone understood the true meaning of patriotism and showed genuine love of the fatherland. In a final invocation that was to be immortalized and is often quoted, Dracula is called back to life and asked to use his drastic methods against the Philistines. The poem—sometimes labeled his greatest patriotic poem—is permeated by a note of deep despair and a sense of abandonment. Eminescu was to survive the poem by only seven years, dying in the flower of his manhood at age thirty-nine, with Dracula's mission of exterminating the antipatriots still unachieved.[24]

During the period following World War I only one man skirted the poetic depths of Eminescu's *Third Letter*. This was Ion N. Theodorescu, better known by his pseudonym Tudor Arghezi.[25] In a poem entitled "The Impaler Prince" (Tepes Voda) Dracula is initially placed on a high philosophical pedestal, but is soon brought down to earth by his cruelty. Arghezi cannot quite condone shoving sticks into the rectum and throats of men even for the sake of reforming mankind. In a satiric spirit, however, he pokes fun at boyars and hierarchy:

> *With due concern for class distinction*
> *For the magnates be they Wallachian or Turks*
> *Dracula reserved special stakes*
> *So that there be no question of violating rank*
> *The Vizirs were impaled at proper height*
> *On the nimble tops of poplar trees*
> *And for the saints be they abbots or bishops*
> *The Impaler reserved holy and sweet smelling wood*
> *While the courtiers and friends in the hall raised their wine glasses*
> *   honoring his deeds*
> *Dracula pondered on the kind of stakes that would befit them*
> *   most.*[26]

Apart from Arghezi's poem, the interwar period produced no work on the Dracula theme. Of several third-rate playwrights only two deserve to be rescued from oblivion and figure on the fringes of literature. One is Ludovic Daus, who wrote a play entitled the *Impaler* performed at Bucharest in 1930.[27] The performance was not a success, perhaps because Daus belonged to the historical Romantic Samanatorist school, which was no longer in vogue.

The public at the time desired to be amused; this probably accounts for the degeneration of Dracula into a figure of fun. Pastorel Teodoreanu, a journalist of talent who wrote novelettes, had precisely such a purpose in mind.[28] Everything sacred and historic went by the board in Teodoreanu's plays. Dracula's name and the chronicles of old were lampooned and transformed into comic personages. Dracula's great-grandson became Trasca Draculescu and dies in despair, because his wife, an adolescent of seventeen, had died in his arms on their wedding night when he was ninety years old! [29] The cycle had turned completely. From its lofty heights the Dracula epic had descended into Rabelaisian buffoonery. In the mood of impending national disaster that preceded the outbreak of World War II, the literary critic George Calinescu summoned sufficient courage to write a poem called "Life" and reassigned Dracula the increasingly difficult task of saving the Romanian race. Calinescu, however, was less reverential to Dracula than was Eminescu. Instead of addressing him "my Lord," he calls him a madman. Written in 1940, the appeal even to this madman came too late as Greater Romania faced dismemberment.[30]

During the last decade of the Socialist period, coinciding with the rebirth of interest on patriotic themes, Dracula like other Romanian legendary heroes has made a most remarkable comeback. A number of plays, poems, and novels commemorating Dracula's deeds of valor have enjoyed success. Only a few examples will help illustrate this point.

In 1967 there appeared a historical novel called *The Ancestors*, by Radu Theodoru.[31] One of the reasons for the success of this and similar novels, largely centering on Dracula's career, is concern for historical truth, no matter how dramatized. Theodoru calls upon an imaginary chronicler, the Chevalier d'Ossau, a Basque from Béarn, whose papers he had allegedly found in Spain and who had fought for both Dracula and Dracul. The reconstruction is sufficiently close to reality to appear authentic. Dracula was, of course, the hero, but his heroism was bounded by the realities of historical fact. A second historical novel, by Georgina Viorica Rögöz, *Vlad the Son of the Devil*, is a powerful plot written in the best tradition of Sadoveanu's historical novels.[32]

In a totally different modernistic vein a poem entitled "Dracula and His Wife" appeared in 1968 signed by Elizabeth Isanos, a respected surname in contemporary Romanian literature.[33] The subject of Dracula has also been kept alive in plays that have been performed by student groups and repertory companies. One such play was getting good reviews at Galati and Piatra-Neamt during our visit there in 1969. It has since enjoyed success in Bucharest. Dracula the hero has also caught the imagination of the young. In 1964 there appeared a pamphlet written by G. Popescu, *Vlad the Impaler;*[34] it was no longer in print by 1967. In 1969 there appeared a regular column in a review for the young, *Cutezátorii,* on "the Times of Dracula." At a much higher level the noted literary critic and director of the Library of the Academy of the Romanian Socialist Republic, Serban Cioculescu, occasionally enlightens his readers on Dracula topics in *Contemporanul.*[35]

From this very sketchy review of the treatment of Dracula in Romanian literature it seems obvious that the Impaler has been exploited by authors with various *arrière pensées* corresponding to the needs of each period, varying from uncritical adulation to satire. It is worth noticing, however, that at no time does Dracula ever correspond to Stoker's Dracula, which has immortalized the subject in the West. Even when vampires are mentioned, as in the case of Budai-Deleanu, they are Dracula's opponents, not his friends. Romanian literature has not generally avoided the vampire theme, but Dracula, the vampire from Stoker's novel, is virtually unknown.

As late as 1946 a Romanian scholar, Felician Brînzeu, in an article on Dracula in Turkish literature attempted to account for the sources used by a Turkish novelist who had written a Dracula vampire novel.[36] After a lengthy examination of plot, Brînzeu innocently concluded that the Turkish novelist had obtained his material from a Hollywood Hungarian scenario writer. Mr. Brînzeu, in other words, was acquainted with the Bela Lugosi-style Dracula horror movies, but simply ignorant of the fact that all these movies were based upon Bram Stoker's novel! It is indeed strange to reflect that Stoker's book, which enjoyed such an extraordinary success and had been translated into dozens of languages, including Japanese, was by a strange omission never translated into Romanian. Only now, a

Romanian translation of Bram Stoker's novel is under way.[37] The chances of its setting a new Gothic trend in Romanian literature, however, are remote, since old literary modes inspired from abroad are not generally encouraged. It remains to be seen whether the current interest in Dracula in the West, and the public's increasing taste for genuine historical personages, will set a trend in reverse and inspire novelists, dramatists, or even scenario writers with a real appreciation for the life of the real Dracula, the man.

But no matter how heroic the image of Dracula was generally portrayed within the confines of Romanian literature, he would have permanently remained a comparatively unknown figure to most Europeans and Americans had his life not been successfully fictionalized beyond the Romanian cultural milieu. It is generally assumed that it was Stoker's novel that gave Dracula his evil reputation in fiction, but this is not so. Stoker's novel is not the isolated creation of one man's imagination; it is rather the culmination of a complex series of specific elements in western European literature.

The historical development of those literary traditions are important here. Because of the number of Italian Renaissance humanists at the court of the Hungarian king Matthias Corvinus, it is understandable how Dracula's fame was initially passed on to the West. A Croatian of Italian origin, Antonio Verancicz (1504-1573), demonstrates how far the reputation of Dracula had spread by the sixteenth century. Verancicz even labelled all the inhabitants of Wallachia as "Draguli," and the name caught on among subsequent Italian writers.[38] But this image did not inspire major works in Italian literature.

In France interest in Dracula, under his name Vlad, had developed from Dracula's own day when Walerand de Wavrin had fought in Dracul's army and had known Dracula as a young man. In general, Dracula was known in French literature, if at all, as "Vlad l'Empaleur," as a fighter against the Turks, a ruler who was cruel, but only to his enemies. This combination of cruelty and heroism was firmly established by Prince Dimitrie Cantemir (1673-1723), the great figure from the Romanian cultural Renaissance, who wrote *Histoire de l'empire Ottoman*, in which Dracula's remarkable campaign of 1462 was included. Directly inspired by Cantemir's work, the great French poet Victor Hugo, upon returning from the island of Guernsey in 1875, composed a poem entitled "Sultan Mourad" and included it in his famous *Légende des siècles*.

In Victor Hugo's poem Dracula again emerged as the valiant fighter against the Turks. Hugo wrote:

Vlad boyard de Tarxis appelé Belzebuth
Refuse de payer au Sultan le tribut
Prend l'ambassade turque et le fait périr toute
Sur trente pals plantés au bord de la route
Mourad accourt brulant moissons, granges, greniers,
Bat le boyard, lui fait vingt mille prisonniers,
Puis, autour de l'immense et noir champ de bataille
Batit un large mur tout en pierre de taille,
Et fait dans les creneaux pleins d'affreux cris plaintifs,
Maçonner et murer les vingt mille captifs,
Laissant des trous par ou l'on voit leurs yeux dans l'ombre,
Et part, après avoir écrit sur leur mure sombre:
«Mourad tailleur de pierre, à Vlad planteur de pieux.»[39]

In Russian literature, also, the historical Dracula was presented as a basically heroic figure. In fact, the old Slavic tales in Russia provide a clue to a fairly long-range *postmortem* development of the Dracula image, since copies were made all the way up to the eighteenth century. In Russia the Slavic manuscripts about Dracula, principally the Kirillo-Belozersk (1490-1491) and the Rumiantsev versions (1499-1502), were recopied until the story temporarily dropped out of sight during the sixteenth century.[40] (The newly found evidence by L'urie refutes the common assumption that the Dracula story was utilized in the sixteenth century in Russia as a covert attack on Ivan the Terrible.) The fate of the Dracula story during the sixteenth century in Russia was similar to that of the "Story about the Indian Kingdom" and the Serbian "Aleksandria," both of which had been included by Eufrosin in his collection of stories, along with the Dracula tale, back in 1490-1491. Those stories all fell prey to the powerful Russian ecclesiastical censorship against "useless stories" and *belles lettres* during the sixteenth century. However, during the seventeenth and eighteenth centuries, the Dracula tale cropped up once again in Russia, as did the "Story about the Indian Kingdom" and the "Aleksandria," because by that time, "worldly" or belletristic works were again permitted circulation in Russia.[41]

But these later copyists tried to "correct" the apparent ambiguity of the old Dracula image. Dracula became somewhat less of a "devil" (the very reference to the devil is dropped from many of these later manuscripts) and more of a fighter against the Turks, much as he was in Romanian literature.[42] However, significantly, this expurgated "heroic" Dracula did not catch on with any major Russian fiction writers during the seventeenth and eighteenth centuries. Furthermore, the "heroic" Dracula story did not inspire any major Russian literary works in the nineteenth or twentieth centuries.

The old German and Hungarian portrayals of Dracula stand in marked contrast to most of the European literature in their appraisal of Dracula. Specifically, the anti-Dracula image in old German literature was embellished and kept alive by Hungarian fiction. In fact, parts of the fifteenth- and sixteenth-century Dracula stories in the old German manuscripts and pamphlets, as well as sections in the accounts of Münster and Beheim, belong really to the field of horror fiction rather than any strict history. But the circulation of those old German pamphlets by means of the coincidental invention of the printing press, which made them "best sellers" by the standards of the times, was largely confined to the immediate period before and after Dracula's death.

Following the Dracula portrayals in the German pamphlets it was in Hungarian literature, in particular, that Dracula was consistently portrayed as a villain rather than a hero. As early as the sixteenth century, Hungarian historical ballads, inspired by fifteenth-century historical events, appeared about Dracula. One such song was printed by Gaspar of Heltai in Cluj in 1574. It had as its express purpose praise of János Hunyady and defamation of Dracul and Dracula, who were treated as Hunyady's enemies after the fatal battle of Varna.[42] A similar poem was written about 1560 by Matthias Nagybanki, a priest from upper Hungary and printed also in 1574.[44]

Dracula was also portrayed as a villain in a play by Adam Horvath about Hunyady, published in 1787 at Györ. In the play Dracula, seeking revenge for the murder of his father and brother, betrays Hunyady to the Serbian despot Brancovic. The play was first performed at Buda on July 15, 1790, and published in rewritten form as a drama in three acts at Pest in 1792.[45]

An obscure Hungarian writer, Miklós Jesiku, wrote a novel, published in 1863, that takes place at the time of Dracul, Dracula's father, and in which Dracul and Dracula are confused in the narrative.[46] The Calvinist priest Ferencz Kóos also published a work in 1890 in which Dracula played a negative role.[47] It is thus clear that Hungarian literature embodied a basically evil Dracula. And it is the emphasis on the evil Dracula that fired the poetic imagination of the English horror story writer Bram Stoker through his contact with the Hungarian scholar Professor Arminius Vambery.

Beyond general European and specifically Hungarian literary influence upon Stoker, one must also cite the image of Transylvania in English literature, since Transylvania plays such an important, if mysterious, role in the Stoker novel. In writing his story, Stoker was influenced by the generally vague English picture of Transylvania as a far-off never-never land, a land of the mysterious and the occult.

The real Dracula's reputation had initially come to England via a pilgrim to the Holy Land, William of Wey, whose narration has already been referred to earlier in this book. The first commercial treaty linking Romania to England had been signed during the reign of Queen Elizabeth by Dracula's own great-grandson Peter the Lame on August 27, 1588, when Peter was prince of Moldavia. This event probably focused some slight attention on the Romanian principalities. Shakespeare mentioned Transylvania in his play *Pericles*,[48] and Ben Jonson referred to a Moldavian prince in his play *The Silent Woman*.[49] Beaumont and Fletcher refer to the palace of a Moldavian king.[50] But the English public generally took this name, Moldavia, to be the designation of a mythical place. The first good English map of Romania was done by Peter Heylyn and printed only in 1628 in *The Microcosm*.[51] Transylvania continued to remain basically an unreal, strange place in the minds of most Englishmen up into the contemporary era, a perfect setting for a vampire. (Even in the recent musical *My Fair Lady*, based on Bernard Shaw's *Pygmalion*, the prince of Transylvania is considered to come from an imaginary land.)

In Stoker's day general interest in Transylvania and Transylvanian folklore had been stimulated by Romania's Queen Elizabeth of Wied, who wrote under the pseudonym Carmen Sylva in collaboration with Vasile Alecsandri from 1880 onward.[52] The Romanian queen also dabbled in the occult, as did Stoker, and this preoccupation may also have fit into Stoker's image of the area. Further interest in the area was generated when the granddaughter of Queen Victoria married Ferdinand, the heir to the Romanian throne in 1893, two years before Stoker began working on the first draft of his book.

The first installments of Sir James Frazer's extremely influential book, *The Golden Bough*, began appearing in the 1890s. This may have had an influence upon Stoker's presentation of the mythical aspects of the vampire image. Frazer himself had noted that nowhere in the world was there such a wealth of materials about vampirism as among the Romanians of Transylvania.[53] Some of the Romanian folklore about vampirism may also have come to Stoker from Emily Gérard's book, *The Land beyond the Forest*, in 1888. She wrote: ". . . every person killed by a Nosferatu [vampire] becomes likewise a vampire after death, and will continue to suck the blood of innocent persons 'til the spirit has been exorcized by opening the grave of the suspected person, and either driving a stake through the corpse or firing a pistol shot into the coffin."[54] For general information Stoker might also have drawn on E. Mawe, *Roumanian Fairy Tales and Legends* (London, 1881); E. C. G. Murray, *The National Songs and Legends of Romania* (London, 1852); and Emily Gérard's essay, "Transylvanian Superstitions" (London, 1885), a short reprint from *The Nineteenth Century* (vol. 13, pp. 130-150), a journal to which Stoker himself contributed.

The major elements of Bram Stoker's ritual acts to kill vampires are already found in the Romanian folklore of Transylvania. According to Frazer: "Among the Romanians in Transylvania . . . in very obstinate cases of vampirism, it is recommended to cut off the head and replace it in the coffin with the mouth filled with garlic; or to extract the heart and burn it, strewing the ashes over the grave."[55] Garlic has traditionally been considered by men across the centuries as having medicinal or magic powers. But one author has claimed that it is not generally used as a method of warding off vampires, except in Romania.[56] Stoker's method of killing the vampire by decapitation and a stake driven through the heart is in accord with most Romanian and east European folk beliefs.

In Stoker's novel Dracula sometimes changes into the form of a mist or phosphorescent specks; the Romanian vampire of folklore, or *strigoi*, sometimes comes as points of light shimmering in the air.[57] Stoker's vampire can also turn into a wolf or bat. Some Transylvanian folklore links the bat with acts of vampirism.[58]

A relationship between Dracula and the Transylvanian region of Bistrita just as Stoker described it is not wholly groundless. There was an old Szeckler family in this region, who were named "Ordög," which is a Hungarian equivalent of the word "Dracul," i.e., the devil. In his novel Stoker states that the people of the Bistrita region spoke the word "Ordög" before Jonathan Harker is picked up in the carriage heading for the Borgo Pass.[59] The full name of the Ordög family was Ordög Moses (Moysei). The family was one of the oldest in the region.[60]

Stoker was not a meticulous scholar, so that the real sources for his poetic imagination will probably remain obscure. But his novel indicates that he was familiar with some of the works in English about Transylvania and the prevalence of vampirism in that part of the world.

In his novel Bram Stoker often acknowledges his debt to the Hungarian scholar Arminius Vambery as his main source for the specific connection of Dracula to vampirism. For example, Stoker wrote:

> The Draculas were, says Arminius, a great and noble race, though now and again were scions who were held by their coevals to have had dealings with the Evil One. They learned his secrets in the Scholomance, amongst the mountains over Lake Hermanstadt, where the devil claim the tenth scholar as his due. In the records are such words as "stregoica," witch, "ordog" and "pokol," Satan and Hell; and in one manuscript this very Dracula is spoken of as "wampyr," which we all understand too well. There have been from the loins of this very one great men and good women, and their graves made sacred the earth where alone this foulness can dwell.[61]

Vambery himself was certainly familiar with Engel's *History of Moldavia and Wallachia*, in which there was specific inclusion of the Dracula pamphlet in the National Museum in Budapest which portrayed Dracula as a berserker, a bloodthirsty monster. Vambery was not only familiar with the consistent image of Dracula as an arch villain and clever ruler in Hungarian folklore and history, but also knew that Hungarian vampire stories often associated the word "Dracul" with acts of vampirism. In fact, in 1886 the publication of an article identifying the word "Dracul" with vampire stories may have lent impetus to Vambery's influence on Stoker.[62] Vambery was undoubtedly also conversant with aspects of Romanian folklore in which the vampire beliefs were highlighted, as embodied in an important work in German published at Hermannstadt in 1866.[63]

In his novel Stoker states about Dracula that "he dared even to attend the Scholomance, and there was no branch of knowledge of his time which he did not essay."[64] Stoker himself may have acquired some ideas about Scholomance, "the devil's school," and "the tenth scholar" through Gérard's book *The Land beyond the Forest*. In that work she wrote:

I may as well here mention the scholomance, *or school, supposed to exist in the heart of the mountains, and where the secrets of nature, the language of animals, and all magic spells are taught by the devil in person. Only ten scholars are admitted at a time, and when the course of learning has expired, and nine of them are released to return to their homes, the tenth scholar is detained by the devil as payment, and mounted upon an ismeju, or dragon, becomes henceforth the devil's aide-de-camp.*[65]

Dracula, the one who inherited the dragon emblem from his father, became the tenth scholar at scholomance, the devil's assistant mounted on a dragon.

All the evidence indicates that Stoker drew not only upon his own imagination but upon some history, ethnography, and folklore in the writing of his novel, yet there are two other important ingredients in the novel: (1) the tradition of the Gothic horror tale, especially as it relates to vampirism, and (2) Stoker's personal experiences. Such historical research is as relevant to the theme of this book as the study of the gradual unfolding of the historical Dracula image in literature, because Bram Stoker was equally attracted to the vampire theme, and he linked the highly developed literary tradition on vampires to Dracula in order to create one of the most powerful Gothic horror tales in the entire history of literature.

The popularity of the "Gothic novel" has already been developed in English literature long before Stoker wrote in that tradition. There were two basic trends—namely, the "rationalistic" and the "realistic" approaches, the presentation of terror as distinct from horror. The late eighteenth-century Gothic novels of writers such as Ann Radcliffe (1764-1823) represented the rationalistic approach. The horror was only apparent; it was all explained away at the end of the story by scientific detective work. The mysteries dissolved, and they were all discovered to have had quite natural explanations. The story had all been only an illusion of the supernatural, not the real thing. There was terror in such tales, but not true horror. The other tradition, that of the realistic Gothic horror, was fostered by the Romantic movement in the nineteenth century.[66] Stoker's Dracula was the culmination of this tradition. The Romantics revived the spirit of the late medieval and early Renaissance tales from the historical Dracula's own day. Horrors are presented by the Romantics as facts of daily life. The horrible, the unthinkable, did really happen. The sheer shock of this approach made it appealing to the new vast public of readers in the nineteenth century.

It is the development of the vampire theme in English Romantic literature that is especially relevant to any in-depth understanding of Stoker's novel. In English literature John Stagg had written a ballad called "The Vampyre" in 1810. In that ballad the heroine Gertrude is struck by the "deadly pale" of her Lord Herman and "the fading crimson from his cheek." Herman tells her how his friend Sigismund, recently buried, visits him every night. Herman himself then dies and Gertrude sees the vampire Sigismund appear that night. In the morning Sigismund's tomb is opened and his body found "still warm as life and undecay'd" and "With blood his visage was distain'd, Ensanguin'd were his frightful eyes." A stake is driven through Sigismund's heart and the ballad ends.[67]

Curiously, both the real vampire image and the real Frankenstein monster were developed in English prose about the same time and at the same place. It occurred during an important summer sojourn in 1816 at Geneva, when Percy Bysshe Shelley, his second wife, Mary, her sister Jane, and Lord Byron and his personal physician-in-attendance, John Polidori (1795-1821), went on a holiday. In Geneva the group first moved into the Hôtel d'Angleterre and then rented adjacent villas along the perimeter of Geneva. At the Villa Diodati, the teen-ager Mary wrote that a "wet ungenial summer" with rain "confined us for days to the house." In order to amuse themselves this gifted group decided to read German tales of terror. One night in June, Byron suggested, "We will each write a ghost story."[68]

At night, by candlelight, in Byron's Villa Diodati, they told each other various ghost stories. Before the end of the summer the eighteen-year-old Mary, inspired by a philosophical discussion about galvanism, the possibility of instilling life in dead matter, and a nightmare, had begun to write her novel *Frankenstein*. Mary Shelley wrote her story to show in a sympathetic way the failure of a would-be scientific savior of mankind. Her Dr. Frankenstein was meant to evoke pity. The public turned it all upside down. The Frankenstein story came to inspire an endless run of stories and films in the twentieth century about the "mad scientist" who wrongly tries to go beyond nature's laws unlike God-fearing ordinary mortals. The unholy Frankenstein monster destroys his own creator.

At this very time Byron had sketched out a plan for a tale about a vampire, but he never finished it. In the fragment left of the story Byron has his vampire living in the present, not in the past. Most of the former Gothic horror tales, such as Ann Radcliffe's *Mysteries of Udolpho*, had situated the monsters in a faraway past. Byron's monster was a contemporary, just as Stoker's Dracula would be eighty years later. It was the twenty-year-old Polidori, an Englishman of Italian descent who had studied medicine at the University of Edinburgh, who took over Byron's idea and wrote a story based upon it. Polidori called his story simply, "The Vampyre."[69]

In April 1819 Polidori's tale "The Vampyre" was printed in the *New Monthly Magazine* under Byron's name because of a misunderstanding on the part of the editor of the review. Goethe declared it to be the best thing that Byron had ever written; Goethe had himself delved into the vampire legend in his own *Braut Von Korinth*, which had been published in 1797.[70]

In Polidori's "Vampyre" a young libertine, Lord Ruthven, a character based loosely on Byron, is killed in Greece and becomes a vampire. He seduces the sister of his friend, Aubrey, and suffocates her during the night following their wedding. Two years after the publication of his vampire story, Polidori, who had been unsuccessful at literature and medicine, swallowed poison and died. Only the vampire myth itself remained popular, along with the resultant image of the satanic Byronic lover, and other writers tried their hands at creating an attractive fictional vampire figure.

During the 1820s there was a popular vampire craze quite similar to the Dracula craze in the twentieth century. Polidori's "Vampyre" was the basic inspiration for all the takeoffs in French and German literature, drama, and opera. Inspired by Polidori's story, Charles Nodier and Cyprien Bérard produced a two-volume work entitled *Vampyr* in 1820. On June 13, 1820, the play *The Vampire*, written by Nodier, T. F. A. Carmouche, and Achille de Jouffray, opened with music by Piccini at the Theater of Porte-Saint-Martin in Paris. It ran sold-out performances, was a commercial success, and spawned more plays, such as a vaudeville *Vampire* and *The Three Vampires* at the Paris Varieties Theater.[71] In England J. R. Planché brought Nodier's melodrama

The Vampire to the English stage in 1820 as *The Vampire or the Bride of the Isles,* set in Scotland; the play was republished in Baltimore in 1830. Planché also wrote another play entitled *Giovanni the Vampire, or How Shall We Get Rid of Him?*[72] Even a Polchinella vampire emerged in the Parisian puppet theaters. Alexandre Dumas Père in collaboration with Maquet composed a dramatic paraphrase of the Polidori-Ruthven vampire.[73]

One of the most famous adaptations of this theme which appeared in the German music theater was Marschner's opera *The Vampire* with libretto by Wilhelm August Wohlbruck. The libretto was based on the 1822 German translation of Nodier's *Vampire.* The opera was first performed in Leipzig in 1828. J. R. Planché produced an English version of Marschner's opera. The action in this opera was significantly situated in Hungary—a land that was destined to become the legendary homeland of the vampires in the works of Le Fanu and Stoker. Another German opera, *Vampyr,* music by P. von Lindpaintner and libretto by Cäsar Max Heigl, was performed in Stuttgart on September 1, 1829. Both operas claimed that the story line was "after Byron," but actually they went back to the Polidori-Nodier melodrama.[74]

One of the high points in the development of the vampire theme came with Thomas Preskett Prest's popular penny-novel, published in 1847 in installments, entitled *Varney the Vampire or the Feast of Blood,* which was reprinted in 1853 and recently republished in 1970.[75] The vampire myth is the central theme in this story, which is set in 1730 in England, during the last years of the reign of Queen Anne. Like Stoker, Prest studied the vampire legends and historical data in detail before he wrote his horror story. Varney was supposed to be based on the life of a real person who cremated himself, as described in the novel in 1713. Prest's story tells about the Bannesworth family which is persecuted by Sir Francis Varney. Varney sucks the blood of young Flora Bannesworth, captures her lover, and wreaks general havoc upon the family. Curiously, the author depicts Varney as a basically good person driven to evil by circumstances. He tries often to save himself, and in the end of the story, in despair, Varney commits suicide by jumping into the crater of Mount Vesuvius. Bram Stoker borrowed many of his themes for Dracula from *Varney the Vampire,* such as the methodical search for the vampire, the black cape worn by the vampire, the vampire's attractiveness to his almost somnambulistic victims, the stake, and the religious overtones.

Near the end of the tale, Varney is confronted by a rival, a Hungarian vampire who is much like Stoker's Dracula, created some fifty years later.[76]

A watershed in the development of the vampire theme in English literature occurs when Dublin's famous author, Joseph Sheridan Le Fanu (1814-1873), wrote one of the greatest vampire stories of all time, *Carmilla*. Le Fanu's *Carmilla* was published in 1872 in a collection of tales of terror entitled *In a Glass Darkly*. Bram Stoker read it, was fascinated, and began thinking about writing his own horror tales as inspired by Le Fanu. A short summary of Le Fanu's story reveals the link with the Stoker Dracula theme. In the Carmilla vampire story the heroine Laura welcomes a strange girl named Carmilla into her father's castle, and they become close friends. Laura feels that she has somehow already met the dark beauty Carmilla in her childhood nightmares. Real suspense and curiosity is sustained in the novel, because until the end the reader does not know whether Carmilla is the vampire or not. Finally, "formal proceedings took place in the chapel of Karnstein. The grave of the Countess Mircalla was opened." The dead Countess Mircalla turned out to be Carmilla herself! The author emphasizes that her "features, though a hundred and fifty years had passed since her funeral, were tinted with the warmth of life. Her eyes were open; no cadaverous smell exhaled from the coffin."[77] Furthermore, her "limbs were perfectly flexible, the flesh elastic; and the leaden coffin floated with blood. . . ." The killing of the vampire in Le Fanu's novel was in the eastern European tradition, as used by Stoker later: "The body, therefore, in accordance with the ancient practice was raised, and a sharp stake driven through the heart of the vampire . . . the head was struck off . . . body and head were next placed on a pile of wood, and reduced to ashes. . . ."[78]

Le Fanu also hazarded the problem of the origins and spread of vampirism: "Assume, at starting, a territory perfectly free from that pest. How does it begin and how does it multiply itself? I will tell you. A person, more or less wicked, puts an end to himself. A suicide, under certain circumstances, becomes a vampire. That spectre visits living people in their slumbers; they die, and invariably, in the grave, develop into vampires."[79]

There is an entire chapter in the original Stoker Dracula manuscript that was inspired by Le Fanu's story, but it was not published until after Stoker's death. In the chapter entitled "Dracula's Guest," Jonathan Harker leaves his Munich hotel, the

Vierjahreszeiten (this hotel still functions there; the present authors stayed there in 1970), and goes for a coach ride into the countryside. The coachman refuses to take him to a village which has been deserted because of vampirism. In a snowstorm Harker stumbles into a graveyard, where he finds a beautiful woman with red cheeks and red lips asleep upon her bier. The inscription reads: "Countess Dölingen of Gratz in Styria. Sought and found Death 1801." Le Fanu's vampire Carmilla was a countess whose activities took place in Styria, who had committed suicide, and who had been laid out in just such a tomb. Stoker paid his intellectual and inspirational debt to Le Fanu in this way.

It was solidly in this "realistic" vampire horror-story tradition of Polidori, Prest, and Le Fanu that Bram Stoker wrote his horror story. There is no attempt to explain away the vampire by any rationalistic phenomenon. Stoker's *Dracula* was also historically the last of the great Gothic romances.[80] It brought to a high point most of the ingredients of the horror story. Yet even after one has traced the image of the vampire and the realistic horror tale as it developed, especially in English literature, from Polidori to Prest, from Prest to Le Fanu, and from Le Fanu to Stoker, there is still an important ingredient that went into the Dracula novel, namely, the personal experiences of Stoker himself.

Stoker claimed that the actual idea for the book *Dracula* came to him in a nightmare. After talking with the Hungarian scholar Arminius Vambery and after dining on too much dressed crab, Stoker attests that he fell asleep and had a dream about a vampire who rises from his grave at night to go about his ghastly business.[81] What is the significance of Stoker's dream?

As Jung has pointed out: "No dream symbol can be separated from the individual who dreams, and there is no definite or straightforward interpretation of any dreams."[82] Therefore, the historian must probe into the personal life of Stoker to find an answer for his vampiric interest and the circumstances that stimulated that interest and forced it to come out first in a dream and then in a novel.

Bram Stoker, born in Dublin in 1847, christened Abraham Stoker after his father, who worked in the chief secretary's office at Dublin Castle, was affectionately called Bram throughout his whole life.[83] Young Bram was very sick and feeble. He was entirely confined to his bed for the first eight years of his life. He did not even feel the experience of standing upright during those years, since he was never able to do it. Like his Dracula, while other "normal" people were up and about in the daylight hours, Bram spent his days and nights flat on his back in bed. He felt the helplessness of being bedridden. He was as bound to his bed as his Dracula was later bound to his coffin and his native soil. It was Bram's mother, Charlotte, who took care of her invalid son and exerted a strong influence upon his early childhood fantasy life. She recounted Irish folk tales and some real horror stories to her invalid son. Charlotte, an Irishwoman from Sligo, had witnessed a cholera epidemic there in 1832. Later in life Bram still recalled his mother's horror stories about cholera. The fearsome, unstoppable spread of cholera was similar to the vampire pestilence in Stoker's *Dracula*. Obscure diseases and medical diagnoses were part of Bram's personal childhood experiences, and later they formed an essential part of the atmosphere of his Dracula story, which is dominated by a strange disease and many medical uncertainties.

Bram, who was finally able to, entered Trinity College, Dublin, in 1866, where he exhibited more interest in theater than in his studies or any career in the Irish civil service. He regularly attended the performances at the one large regular theater in Dublin, the Theater Royal. One evening in August 1867, the nineteen-year-old Bram saw a performance of *The Rivals*, in which the noted actor Henry Irving starred. Bram was enthralled by Henry Irving's performance. His description of Irving strongly resembles his later description of Dracula with "long web-like hands" and "penetrating eyes." The towering figure of Irving was to dominate the rest of Stoker's life like a Dracula. When Irving returned to Dublin, Stoker was again in the audience in 1871. At this time Stoker became specifically interested in vampirism, principally because of the popularity of Le Fanu's *Carmilla*. Stoker's adulation of Henry Irving and his interest in vampirism coincided. On December 3, 1876, Stoker heard Irving render Thomas Hood's poem, "The Dream of Eugene Aram," at a small gathering in Dublin. Stoker was so stunned by the event that he broke into hysterics and cried in a fit of uncontrollable emotion.[84]

Bram abandoned a job in the Irish civil service in 1878 and went to London to work full-time for Henry Irving, his Dracula. Much of Bram's time was taken up with making tour arrangements for Irving and his company. But he also began writing his own tales. In 1881 Stoker published his first long piece of fiction, *Under the Sunset,* a book of stories for children, which had undertones of horror. In it was the terrible kingdom of the King of Death. The description of the castle of the King of Death strongly resembles that of Castle Dracula. Stoker also published other short horror tales in the late 1880s, and some of them foreshadow the Dracula tale.

While in London, Stoker met the prominent Orientalist Sir Richard Burton. Burton had translated the *Arabian Nights,* in which there is a vampire tale, into English, and in 1870 some eleven tales about vampires from Hindu sources in Sanskrit. Specifically, Mrs. Isabel Burton had called attention to the fact that there were in all twenty-five old Hindu tales about "a huge Bat, Vampire or Evil spirit."[85] Stoker in his reminiscences mentioned how impressed he was by Sir Richard Burton's accounts and by his physical appearance—especially Burton's canine teeth.[86]

Hall Caine, the writer and critic, spent long hours in conversation with his friend Bram Stoker. Caine later recalled: "I remember that most of our subjects dealt with the supernatural, and that the wandering Jew, the Flying Dutchman, and the Demon Lover were themes around which our imagination constantly revolved."[87] In fact, Stoker's dedication of the Dracula book "To my dear friend Hommy-Beg" is to Caine. Caine was baptized Thomas Henry Hall, and Hommy-Beg ("little Tommy") was the nickname by which his grandmother addressed Hall Caine.[88]

Another factor that helps explain Stoker's Dracula image was the terror of Jack the Ripper in London from August to November 1888 which was similar to the Dracula terror. As the *East London Advertiser* stated: "It is so impossible to account, on any ordinary hypothesis, for these revolting acts of blood that the mind turns as it were instinctively to some theory of occult force, and the myths of the Dark Ages arise before the imagination. Ghouls, vampires, blood-suckers . . . take form and seize control of the excited fancy." [89] The fear of seeing the body cut up was summarized by Thomas Bowyer, who stated after he saw what Jack the Ripper had done to Mary Kelly: "The sight I saw was even more ghastly than I had prepared myself for, all those lumps of flesh lying on the table—it was more the work of a devil than a man."[90] Living in London, Stoker's imagination must have been fired up by the inexplicable sadistic blood murders of Jack the Ripper. The Ripper stalked London in much the same way that Stoker's Dracula walked the London streets in search of his blood victims. Like the Ripper, Dracula's blood murders inspired feelings of terror, and the police were unable to apprehend Jack the Ripper, just as they could not trap Dracula in the novel. In the Stoker novel only the learned Dr. Van Helsing is able to stop the vampire scare.

The Oscar Wilde scandal in London society may also have excited Stoker's imagination in his presentation of an aspect of Dracula's character. The Oscar Wilde case erupted at the very moment when Stoker was writing his novel, but the connection with Stoker himself was old. When Bram Stoker was young, he had been a friend of Oscar Wilde's father, Sir William Wilde, a famed Dublin eye and ear specialist. The young Stoker had frequented the Wilde home in Marrion Square in Dublin, and Stoker had studied at Trinity with Oscar Wilde.[91]

In Stoker's novel Dracula is presented as a person with exotic interests. He is the outsider *par excellence*. He moves in Victorian society, but is not part of that society. His sexual interests are highly peculiar, just as the sexual interests of the scandalous Oscar Wilde were considered to be unsavory. The Oscar Wilde scandal stirred up almost as much interest as the Charles Manson case today. Oscar Wilde, born Oscar Fingal O'Flahertie Wills Wilde (1854-1900), became the epitome of the *fin de siècle* esthete. He wore his hair long, dressed in velveteen pants, and sported sunflowers. Wilde's novel *The Portrait of Dorian Grey*, in which the hero remains outwardly young while his portrait takes on his many sins, may have inspired Stoker's presentation of the vampire as one who remains outwardly young. Wilde spent two famous years in prison in Old Bailey and Reading Gaol from 1895 to 1897,[92] precisely the very time period when Stoker began and completed his Dracula story.

Stoker was himself also actively involved in the occult. His latest biographer, Harry Ludlam, fails to mention that, like Joris Karl Huysmans and Montague Summers, Stoker belonged to an occult lodge called Golden Dawn in the Outer. Stoker's fascination with the occult, rituals, and symbols is evident in his Dracula story.[93]

The reality theme in Stoker's novel seemed to respond to the collective wish of his day. Stoker lived at a turning point in European intellectual history, "the second flood tide of Romanticism," at the end of the nineteenth century. The previous heyday of scientism was over, and the collapse of positivism opened new horizons of uncertainties about man and nature.

Bergsonian philosophy and psychoanalysis were being born
when Stoker's novel was published. Stoker can be seen as a
reflection of both the past Romanticism of creaky doors, murky
castles, and old medieval settings and the new Romanticism of
"collective unconsciousness," the repository of common
memories that all men share, Jungian archetypes, primordial
symbols common to all mankind like the vampire. As such,
Stoker's own novel proved to be later immediately realizable in
the visual media of theater and especially the modern film.

The fame of Stoker's Dracula even spread to Turkey. In
Istanbul in 1928 there appeared a Turkish adaptation of Stoker's
novel entitled *Kasîgli Voyvoda*, by Ali Riga Seifi. Dracula is called
the Impaler, but he is a kind of ghostly vampire who haunts the
familiar Bistrita castle. The author evidently based a good deal of
his story on Stoker's novel, though the plot has been arrayed in a
Turkish context; for example, Dracula comes, not to London, but
to Istanbul. Also, the historical context is more ample than in the
Stoker story; Mohammed II appears, as well as Dracula's night
attack. Dracula the vampire is killed by a stake. Another Turkish
novel about Dracula entitled *Akinda Ahina* was written by
Turhan Tan.[94]

The popularity of Dracula the vampire king evidently goes
beyond strict historical data, ethnography, Stoker's personal
experiences, the Gothic novel, or the vampire theme in literature.
Its appeal seems to rest on a symbolism, common to all mankind,
and that is the subject of the next and final chapter of this book.

---

[1] Nicolae Olahus was the son of a boyar, Manzila, from the Arges region, a
relative of Dracula. He is undoubtedly one of the most fascinating figures of the
Transylvanian Renaissance. Serious study on all aspects of his career has only
begun. Among many works he left a fairly detailed description of Transylvania
and Hungary in which he showed pride for his Romanian origins. Referring to
Transylvania, he carefully distinguishes between its "nations," the Hungarians,
the Saxons, the Székelys, and the Romanians (*Hungarie sive de originibus gentis
regni situ divisione habite atque opportunitatibus*, published in 1735). Olahus was
also the first Romanian poet writing Latin verse. On his family origins see S.
Bezdecki, *Familia lui Nicolae Olahus* (Bucharest, n.d.), pp. 63–85. For his career see
George Ivascu, *Istoria literaturii române* (Bucharest, 1969), pp. 61-62; S. Bezdecki,
Nicolaus Olahus primul umanist de origine romîna; (Anineasa-Gorj, 1939); Th.
Vojteck Bucheo, *Nikulás Oláh a jeho doba* (Bratislava, 1940).

[2] Piru, *Literature Româna veche*, pp. 45–46.

[3] Radu Florescu, "The Uniate Church, Catalyst of Romanian National
Consciousness," *Slavonic and East European Review* 45 (July 1967).

[4] Serious scholarly research on Ion Budai-Deleanu has just begun in recent years.
There exists an impressive recent monograph by Lucia Protopopescu, *Noi
contributii la biografa lui Ion Budai-Deleanu documente inedite* (Bucharest, 1967).

Budai-Deleanu was also the author of a forgotten historical work on Transylvania, still in manuscript, in which he defends Dracula. *De originibus populorum Transylvaniae comentatiucula cum observationibus historias criticis*, Library of the Academy of the Romanian Socialist Republic, no. 2719-2720. For his historical contribution see A. Cioranescu, "Opera istorica a lui Budai-Deleanu," *Cercetari literare, vol.* 2, published by N. Cartojan (Bucharest, 1936), p. 109. For useful bibliography on Budai-Deleanu see Ivascu, *Istoria literaturii române*, pp. 66-89.

5 A good study on *Tiganiada* is Savin Bratu, "Locul Tiganiadei în istoria idiologiei noastre literare," *Limba si Literatura* 13 (1967): 35-54.

6 Citation of Mihail Dragomirescu in his course on Romanian literature quoted by Ivascu, *Istoria literaturii române, p.* 329. Ivascu agrees that *Tiganiada* is one of the great heroic-comic epics in European literature.

7 In the prologue, Budai-Deleanu guarantees the historicity of his plot on Dracula. He claims to have consulted Byzantine writers and also that Wallachian chroniclers "know the fact that Dracula armed the gypsies against the Turks," a fact that can hardly be substantiated, but which seems plausible enough. Even the actual plot of the *Tiganiada is* said to stem from a source that Budai-Deleanu found at the monastery of Cioarei in Transylvania, evidently fictitious. The legend of the castle in the vicinity of his village, the customs of the gypsies, the fantastic tales about the vampires of the Retezat mountains—all these are popular elements of "the national baggage of his [Transylvanian] childhood." Budai-Deleanu, *Tiganiada poema eroi-comica* (Bucharest, 1944), p. 9. He dedicates the poem to a nonexistent "Mitru Petrea, a well-known minstrel." Budai-Deleanu, *Tiganiada* (Bucharest, 1967), p. 11. One original manuscript of the *Tiganiada* (ms. 2429) is to be found at the Library of the Academy of the Romanian Socialist Republic. The first complete critical edition was published in 1944 (Gh. Cardas), then republished in 1953, 1959, and 1967, the latest edition which we have used.

8 Budai-Deleanu was evidently acquainted with most of the works of the philosophers. He had undoubtedly read Jean Jacques Rousseau's *Social Contract;* he was acquainted with Montesquieu's *Spirit of the Laws* and most of Voltaire's satirical work. He had, of course, personally experienced the meaning of Josephinism (1765-1790). Budai-Deleanu's ideal constitution is described in jest by one of his characters as "demo-aristocratic-monarchical."

9 Budai-Deleanu, *Tiganiada*, song number 5, verses 74-77, p. 143.

10 Ibid, song number 6, verses and explanatory note, p. 151.

11 A sample of such works are: August Treboniu Laurian, *Istoria Românilor din timpurile cele mai vechi pâna în zilele noastre* (1st ed., Iasi, 1853); Ion Eliade-Radulescu, *Prescurtare de historia Românilor sau Dacia si România* (Bucharest, 1861); Aaron Florian, *Idee repede de istoria printipatului Tarii Româneste* (Bucharest, 1835).

12 C. D. Aricescu had heard of a play entitled *Tepes Voda* in two acts, by Ion Catina (1828-1851). Ivascu, *Istoria literaturii române, vol.* a, p. 584. Catina also wrote another play (never produced)called *Dan,* possibly referring to one of Dracula's political foes whom he buried alive in 1460.

13 Cazacu, "Vlad Tepes," p. 131.

14 Bolintineanu was of Macedonian origin. He studied at the famed Saint Sava school in Bucharest where many of the future revolutionaries were being indoctrinated in the new nationalist current brought from Transylvania by Gh. Lazar. He later joined the secret revolutionary society Brotherhood (Fratie)and with the help of I. Ghica and N. Balcescu organized the revolution of 1848 in Bucharest. It is at that time that Bolintineanu's career as a poet began in earnest. He was the editor of the revolutionary newspaper *The Sovereign People* (Poporul Suveran). After the failure of the revolution he went into exile, first to Transylvania, and later to Paris, where he continued his activities as a poet and journalist. He later traveled in Asia Minor, Egypt, Palestine, and his native

Macedonia. He left us an account of these peregrinations. He was able to return to Wallachia only in 1857 after the victory of the allies in the Crimean War. He held various political offices under Prince Alexander, including that of foreign secretary and minister of ecclesiastical affairs. Like other Dracula enthusiasts, he became insane at the end of his life and died in poverty. For an adequate biographical sketch of Bolintineanu see the introductory study by D. Pacurariu in D. Bolintineanu, *Opere alese* (Bucharest, 1981). Also see the preface and chronological table in I. Roman and Aurel Martin, *Legende istorice si alte poezii* (Bucharest, 1985). Another work, now outdated but of some value, is Aughel Demetriescu, "Dimitrie Balintineanu," *Anale literare 1*, no. 2 (1866).

[15] Bolintineanu wrote several other historically inspired poems: "Sorin sau taierea boierlior la Tîrgoviste," an antiboyar theme undoubtedly in part inspired by Dracula's massacres; "Mircea cel Mare si solii," reminiscent in some way of Dracula's reception of the Turkish ambassadors, but referring to Dracula's grandfather; "Cea de pe urma noapte a lui Mihai cel Mare" (1867); "Muma lui Stefan cel Mare"; "Daniil Sihastru"; "Legende noi" (1862); "Legende sau basme originale în versuri" (Bucharest, 1858). He also wrote historical plays and popular historical novels: *Sase drame istorice; Stefan Voda; Viata lui Vlad Tepes Voda si Mircea cel Batrân*. For a critique of these and other works see Ivascu, *Istoria literaturii române*, pp. 462-464.

[16] D. Bolintineanu, *Legende istorice* (Bucharest, 1966), p. 25.

[17] G. Calinescu, *Vasile Alecsandri* (Bucharest, 1965), p. 76. Alecsandri showed no greater fondness for Tepelus (the Little Impaler), Basarab IV, and other Turkish "tyrants." He preferred to praise Stephen the Great and Michael the Brave.

[18] G. Cosbue's (1866-1918)poem, "Pasa Hassan," centers on Michael the Brave, but the historical characters are intermixed (Mihnea is mentioned)and all, in part, inspired by the traditional heroes of Romania. G. Cosbue, *Versuri alese* (Bucharest, n.d.), pp. 259-260. Other historically inspired poems: "Pe pamântul turcului," "Cântece de Vitejie," etc.

[19] Alexandru Odobescu (1834-1895). Interestingly enough, Odobescu, after studying at Saint Sava and Paris and holding minor political functions, turned his interests to archaeology and history. Odobescu established for himself a reputation as an archaeologist and ended his career as professor of archaeology at the University of Bucharest in 1874. These same interests prompted his famous speculations concerning Dracula's tomb at Snagov, not as yet excavated in his time. Like Bolintineanu, he died insane, taking poison in a fit of depression in 1895. Although hardly a professional historian, Odobescu's intuitive insight and imagination succeeded in giving life to some very dry documents and archaeological finds by original interpretations often approaching the historical truth.

[20] See Calinescu, *Istoria literaturii române, p.* 132.

[21] Mihail Sorbul's name was Smolsky. He was born in 1885 at Botosani, Moldavia and enjoyed a great success as a playwright at the National Theater in Bucharest. (Sorbul also for a time directed the National Theater in Cluj and the Bucharest Opera House.) He won the National Theater prize in 1937. Some of his plays simply took over the great historical themes of Sadoveanu's novels, such as *Neamul soimestilor.*

[22] Ion Lapedatu should not be confused with the distinguished historian Alexandru Lapedatu whose works on Mihnea the Bad and Vlad the Monk we have cited. See chap. VI.

[23] The work on Mihail Eminescu (1850-1889) is vast. He is one of the few Romanian poets whose works have been translated into English. The best biography is undoubtedly S. G. Galinescu, *Opera lui Mihail Eminescu* (Bucharest, 1969).

24 M. Eminescu, *Poezii* (Bucharest, 1969), p. 542. While composing his *Third Letter*, Eminescu did considerable research on Turkish history, getting much of the information from Hammer, *Geschichte des Osmanisches Reiches* (Pest, 1834), pp. 65-67. With *The Third Letter* the patriotism of Eminescu's poetry is finally fulfilled. D. Murarasu, *Istoria literaturii române*, vol. 2 (Madrid, 1955), p. 18.

25 Tudor Arghezi was born in 1880 at Bucharest of humble parents. At the time when Stoker wrote his novel *Dracula*, Arghezi was a chemist in a sugar factory in Bucharest. He later became a monk at the monastery of Cernica just outside the capital and served at the patriarchy in humble capacities. In 1905 he left Romania and sojourned in various west European countries. He eventually resumed his literary career within Romania, won the national poetry prize, and became one of the great literary figures of the interwar period. The construction of his verse, his unconventional vocabulary, the boldness of his expression, rank him as a founder of a school.

26 *Versuri* (Bucharest, 1940), pp. 105-106.

27 Eugent Lovinescu, *Istoria literaturii române contemporane, 1900–1937* (Bucharest, 1937), p. 213.

28 Al. O. Teodoreanu (Pastorel) was born in 1894 in the Dorohoi district (Moldavia). He can essentially be described as a militant journalist.

29 Lovinescu, *Istoria literaturii române contemporane*, p. 261.

30 George Calinescu, *Opere* (Bucharest, 1965), pp. 191-192.

31 B. Theodoru's novel *Stramosii* was already out of print in the summer of 1969.

32 *Vlad fiul Dracului* (Bucharest, 1970).

33 Magda Isanos (1916-1944) was a poetess of some note who died prematurely and wrote on themes dedicated to world peace and the solidarity among nations: "The Song of the Mountains" (Cintarea muntilor), "The Country of Light" (Tara Luminii). *Literatur româna contemporana* (Bucharest, 1964), p. 235. The authors do not know the relationship between Magda and Elizabeth Isanos. The poem "Dracula and His Wife" was published in *Cronica* 17 (Iasi, 1968).

34 Gr. Popescu, *Vlad Tepes*, (Bucharest, 1964), is essentially a work of popularization for children without real literary merit.

35 E. G. Serban Cioculescu, "Istorie si literatura," *România literara* (July 1971).

36 Brînzeu's conclusion on the problem of the sources used by Ali Seifi in his novel *Kazîgli Voyvoda* (Istanbul, 1928) is the following: "Only one admissible hypothesis is left in terms of a common source [for the Turkish novel]. Hungarian writers are often used as authors of scenarios for American films." F. Brinzeu, "Vlad l'Empaleur dans la litterature turque," *Revista o istorica românia* 16 (1946): 70.

37 Cioculescu, *România literara*, p. 5.

38 Cazacu, "Vlad Tepes," p. 129.

39 Victor Hugo, *La legende des siecles*, vol. 2 (Paris, n.d.), p. 31. See I. C. Bistritianui, "Pe marginea poemului Sultan Mourad de Victor Hugo," *Anuarul Liceului Coriolan Brediceanu din Lugoj*, 1941.

40 L'urie, *Povest' o Drakule*, p. 73.

41 Ibid., p. 77.

42 Ibid., p. 81.

42 The Cluj typographer Gaspar of Heltai indulged in hero worship of Hunyady, extended it to his son Matthias Corvinus and the consequent defamation of Dracula. Heltai also published the chronicle of Ivan Turoczi and a Hungarian edition of Bonfiinius chronicle in 1575. See Andrei Veress, *Cântece istorice Vechi unguresti despre Români*, pp. 5, 7, 14-16.

[44] Matthias Nagybanki's poetry, probably based largely on the Bonfinius chronicle, was written in 1560 at Nagyszombat (Trnava), and published at Debreczen in 1574 under the title *Historia az vitez Huniadi Janos vajdanak.* . . . Cited in Veress, *Cântece istorice,* p. 7.

[45] Ibid., vol. 2, pp. 46, 84.

[46] Ibid., vol. 3, p. 173.

[47] Ibid., p. 253.

[48] "The poor Transylvanian is dead, that lay with little baggage." Act 4, sc. 2. See R. V. Bossy, "Românii si Anglia pe vremea lui Shakespeare," in *Buletinul Bibliotecii Române* (Freiburg, 1968), pp. 1-14, esp. p. 9.

[49] Jonson has one character named La Foole refer to "the prince of Transylvania " See M. Bezâ, *Papers on the Romanian People and Literature* (London, 1920), p. 20.

[50] In their play *The Knight of the Burning Pestle,* written in 1611, Fletcher and Beaumont confuse Cracovia with Moldavia in act 4, scenes 1 and 2, and later in the play they mention the hall in the palace of a "King of Moldavia" (act 5, sc. 2). See Bossy, "Românii si Anglia," pp. 20-21.

[51] This map was probably based on that done by the Protestant reformer Honterus in 1531. See Nicolae Iorga, A *History of Anglo-Romanian Relations* (Bucharest, 1931), p. 22.

[52] See Carmen Sylva, *Pilgrim Sorrow* (London, 1884); *Heart Regained* (Boston, 1888); *Shadow of Love's Dial* (London, 1895); *The Band of Dimbovitza* (London, 1892); *Legend from River and Mountains,* with *Alma Strettel* (New York, 1896). See G. Bengencu, *Carmen Sylva* (Paris, 1904), p. 121.

[53] Sir James G. Frazer, *The Golden Bough* (London, 1890).

[54] Emily Gérard, *The Land beyond the Forest* (London, 1888), p. 193.

[55] Sir James G. Frazer, *The Fear of the Dead in Primitive Religions, vol.* 2 (London, 1934), pp. 85-86.

[56] Tony Faivre, *Les Vampires* (Paris, 1962), p. 92. But see also M. Olinescu, *Mitologia Româneasca* (Bucharest, 1944), pp. 26, 40, 495; Agnes Murgoci, "The Vampire in Rumania," *Folklore* 37 (1926): 325.

[57] See Stoker, *Dracula,* pp. 155-156, 238; Murgoci, "The Vampire in Rumania," pp. 321, 345.

[58] Heinrich von Wlisocki, *Volksglaube und Volksbrauch der Siebenbürger Sachsen* (Berlin, 1893), p. 163.

[59] Stoker, *Dracula,* p. 6.

[60] Information about "ördög" came from Zsigmond Bagoly, from Bistrita-Nasaud, and also from a local archivist of Hungarian origin, Peter Bodnov. On the ethnography of the Bistrita-Nasaud region there is an unpublished mimeographed paper by Pompei Boca entitled "Monografia etnografica a Judetului Bistrita-Nasaud" at the Museum of the City of Bistrita.

[61] Stoker, *Dracula,* p. 265.

[62] "Dracula poveste ruseasca despre strigoi," *Contemporanul România literara* 10, no. 2547 (1886), and a variant had been published in *Tara Noua,* nos. 21-22 (1885), under the title "Logodnica strigoiului" (Bride of the Vampire).

[63] W. Schmidt, *Das Jahr und seine Tage in Meinung und Brauch der Roma'nen* (Hermannstadt, 1866).

[64] Stoker, *Dracula,* p. 334.

[65] Gérard, *The Land beyond the Forest,* p. 198.

[66] See Mario Praz, *The Romantic Agony* (1st ed., 1933), trans. Angus Davidson (New York, 1956), and Sir Devendra P. Varma, *The Gothic Flame* (1957).

[67] We are indebted to Sir Devendra P. Varma for this information. See Varma, ed., *Varney the Vampire* (New York, 1970), pp. xxii-xxiv.

68 Mary Shelley, *Frankenstein* (New York, 1957), p. 6.

69 William Polidori, *The Vampire, a Tale* (London, 1819). Recent edition with an introduction by Professor Adams (Pasadena, Calif.: Edition Castle Press).

70 For Goethe's work see Dieter Stürm and Klaus Volker, *Von den Vampiren oder Menschensaugern* (Munich, 1968), pp. 15-20.

71 Ibid., pp. 551-553.

72 Margaret L. Carter, "From Polidori to Prest," in Varma, *Varney the Vampire*, p. xxxiv.

73 Stürm and Volker, *Von den Vampiren*, p. 552.

74 Ibid., p. 553; Carter, "From Polidori to Prest," p. xxxiv.

75 Thomas Preskett Prest, *Varney the Vampire or the Feast of Blood*, ed. Sir Devendra P. Varma (New York 1970).

76 Sir Devendra P. Varma "The Vampire in Legend, Lore and Literature," in Varma, *Varney the Vampire*.

77 Joseph Sheridan Le Fanu, *Carmilla*, from *In a Glass Darkly*, with introduction by V. S. Pritchett (London, 1947), cited from Ornella Volta and Vabrie Rivo, *The Vampyre, an Anthology* (London, 1963), p. 84.

78 Ibid.

79 Ibid., p. 86.

80 Harry Ludlam, *A Biography of Dracula*, London, 1969, p. 179.

81 Ibid., p. 99.

82 Carl G. Jung, *Man and His Symbols* (Garden City, N.Y., 1964), p. 53.

83 Most of the subsequent biographical data comes from Ludlam, *A Biography* of Dracula.

84 Ibid., p. 44.

85 Sir Richard Burton, *Vakrim and the Vampire Tales of Hindu Devilry*, ed. Isabel Burton (New York, 1969), p. xi.

86 Bram Stoker, *Personal Reminiscences of Henry Irving*, vol. 1 (1906).

87 Ludlam, *A Biography of Dracula*, p. 97.

88 Ibid.

89 Tom A. Cullen, *When London Walked in Terror* (Boston, 1965), p. 83.

90 Ibid., p. 192.

91 Ludlam, *A Biography of Dracula*, p. 32.

92 Frank N. Magill, ed., *Cyclopedia of World Authors* (New York, 1958), p. 1,158.

93 Stürm and Volker, *Von den Vampiren*, p. 574.

94 Brînzeu, "Vlad l'Empaleur dans la littérature turque," 16, pp. 68-71.

8

Son of the Devil, Vampire, or Tactician of Terror?

The fact that the name "Dracula" is inextricably linked with vampire symbolism requires further historical explanation. An attempt must be made to understand not just how but why Dracula became a household word for "vampire" or "monster" in the Western world.

Vampire symbolism became attached to Dracula essentially because his real life lent itself to being mythologized in that way. Dracula's thirst for blood was well known, as was his fixation on impalement. His seemingly tortured "demonic" acts stirred the imagination of most past authors, and descriptions in many of the sources fed into the image of Dracula as a kind of bloodthirsty monster. The very word "wütrich" in the German sources signified bloodthirsty berserker or monster. The author Bram Stoker merely elaborated upon poetic references in the old Dracula tales and connected them with the general Transylvanian folklore about vampirism.

The general belief in vampires is one on the most universal themes in the history of mankind. Stories about vampires resemble each other from one end of the world to the other. Vampire tales exist in wholly disparate civilizations where any "borrowing" remains physically and geographically impossible. Therefore, the historical evidence seems to suggest that the vampire may belong to a common store of images which psychologists term "symbols."

Many people assume that when one uses the word "symbol," one of necessity refers to an "unreal" event, but, in fact, most symbols have some historical or particular meaning, as well as a universal significance. Although the symbol transcends the historical event or person referred to, it continues to relate historically to that event or person. The problem is that the historical meaning has become unclear through the passage of time, and a great effort must be made to uncover the actual levels of meanings behind the given symbolic expression. A "symbol," as Jung defines it, "possesses specific connotations in addition to its conventional and obvious meaning. It implies something vague, unknown, hidden from us."[1] This is the case when one deals with the vampire symbol in reference to Dracula.

Furthermore, Jung insists on the importance of dreams as the principle source for symbols. He writes: "I have gone into detail about the origins of our dream life because it is the soil from which most symbols originally grow."[2] And he goes on to explain his view because: "In dreams symbols occur spontaneously, for dreams happen and are not invented; they are, therefore, the main source of all our knowledge about symbolism.[3] Stoker got the idea for his Dracula vampire story in a dream, and in this way intuitively hit upon a kind of universally recurrent symbol among mankind.

In Stoker's novel, when the English real estate agent, Jonathan Harker, sets out in a coach for Castle Dracula, he remarks, "I could hear a lot of words often repeated, queer words, for there were many nationalities in the crowd; so I quietly got my polyglot dictionary from my bag and looked them up. I must say they were not cheering to me, for amongst them were "Ordog"—Satan; "pokol" —hell; "Stregoica"— witch; "Vrolok" and "Vrkoslak"—both of which mean the same thing, one being Slovak and the other Serbian for something that is either were-wolf or vampire."[4] Those lexical references are fairly accurate. "Ordög" does signify devil in Hungarian and "pokol" means hell. "Strigoaica" can signify "witch" or "old hag" in Romanian. Stoker was also correct in stating that the Serbian and Slovak words may, at the same time, signify both vampire and werewolf.

The vampire is known historically under many names as: *Vrukolakes, Brykolakas, barbalakos, borbolakas, bourbolakas, bordoakas, bourboulakas, bourdoulakos* in modern Greek, or the ancient *katakhanos, baital* in Sanskrit, *upiry* in Russian, *upiory* in Polish, *blutsäuger* in German, etc[5] There does indeed appear to be some common association of the vampire and the werewolf symbols, as Stoker surmised, since they often merge together or are confused. This is probably because the term refers to two of the strongest human taboo subjects, namely blood-drinking and flesh-eating. The vampire drinks human blood; the werewolf eats human flesh.

One can find stories about the vampire in ancient Tibetan manuscripts, and ancient frescoes in Nepalese monasteries portray the bat as a kind of god.[6] Those two images apparently fused quite early in human history for the following reasons: Both the mythical vampire and the bat belong to the night. Primitive man lived in caves. In the evening at dusk bats flew out of the caves. In the morning dawn, before the sun rose, bats flew home to rest. During the day they seemed dead. Man must have developed a fear and an awe for night-flying creatures which belonged to the twilight zone. Vampire legends themselves can be seen historically among ancient Hindus and ancient Egyptians.[7] In these ancient legends the dead sought renewed life specifically by drawing out blood from the sleeping living beings. In China Tsze-Chan reported in the "Tsachwen" the existence of vampires in 600 B.C.[8] This idea was also prevalent in ancient Babylon and Assyria.[9] It existed in the Old World and the New. Among the ancient Peruvians there was a class of devil-worshipers, known as *canchus* or *rumapmicuc*. They sucked the blood from sleeping youths in order to gain renewed life. The victims died, depleted of their blood.[10] The Aztecs assured the continuity of the sun by sacrificing the hearts of prisoners to it incessantly; their blood was destined to renew the fading energies of the sun.

In Homer's *Odyssey*, Odysseus presents a blood-offering to the shades in Hades in order to bring their souls and consciousness back to them. In Greek mythology there are the "Lamia," who are kin to the vampire. These are ghastly women who lure handsome youths in order to drink their blood and eat their flesh. Lamia was once a beloved of Zeus; she went insane because of the jealous wife of Zeus, Hera, and Lamia killed her own children and became ugly. During her sleepless nights she wanders and steals children from their mothers.

Early in the Christian era, the sage Bhavabhuti composed masterpieces of Indian supernatural fiction. Sir Richard Burton, whom Bram Stoker met personally in London, translated these tales into English and, in his preface to the 1870 edition, wrote: "The Baital-Pachisi or twenty-five [tales of a] Baital—a vampire or evil spirit which animates dead bodies—is an old and thoroughly Hindu repertory." [11] Burton's wife, in her preface to the 1893 edition of her husband's work, specified that the story was "the history of a huge Bat, Vampire or Evil spirit."[12] In the tale of the hero Vikram he finds the vampire hanging from a tree like a kind of a bat.[13]

The vampire is similar to the Hindu god Shiva, since it is a destroyer and a creator at one and the same time. It represents the theme of renewal, the *éternel retour*, from life comes death and from death comes life in an unending circle. The vampire takes the life's blood from the living person. But if he does not kill and instead mixes his blood with that of the living person, that person, in turn, becomes an "undead." And so the cycle of life and unending death continues on.

Although vampire stories can historically and geographically be found over most of the known world, the most highly developed and prevalent vampire mythology belongs to eastern Europe and the Balkans. The very term "vampire," which has come to be used in many languages, is apparently of Serbian or Turkish origin, thus indicating its prevalence in those parts of Europe.

According to Sir James Frazer: "In eastern Europe, from Prussia on the north to Macedonia and Greece on the south, the belief in vampires has been and still is rampant. Vampires are malicious ghosts who issue from their graves to suck the blood of the living, and stringent measures are deemed necessary to hinder or arrest this horrible proceeding."[14] During the seventeenth century Valvassor traced some of the practices associated with vampirism to the Balkan region in his work, *Ehre des Herzogtums Krains*, published in 1687.[15]

The first vampire of renown in the eighteenth century was a Hungarian named Peter Poglojowitz, a peasant from a small village in Hungary. After his death in 1725, he was disinterred, and there was fresh blood flowing from his mouth and his body was uncorrupted. The peasants burned the body.[16] In 1751 a Dominican friar, Augustin Calmet, wrote his *Treatise on the Apparition of Spirits and on the Vampires and Ghosts of Hungary and Moravia*, which contained a number of authenticated vampire stories.[17] According to the Hungarian folklore specialist Lund Degh, "Horror of the living dead is a very common belief with the Hungarian peasantry."[18] The Hungarian vampire Poglojowitz and the Serbian vampire Arnold Paole from Medvegia in 1732 stimulated the interest of eighteenth-century medicine, particularly the matter of impaling the corpse and burning the body as medical cures for this phenomenon.[19]

Vampire legends are also highly developed in southeastern Europe, particularly among the Greeks. For example, the Greek island of Santorini, the most southerly of the Cyclades, was notorious for its "vampires." Father Francois Richard, a Jesuit priest, stationed on the island, connected the belief in vampires to the fact that "Greek priests and bishops, when they launch the ban of excommunication against a person, always add this anathema and after thy death thy body shall remain incorrupt and entire."[20] According to Orthodox Christian belief, the body of anyone bound by a curse will not be received by the earth; the body will not decay. This includes criminals, bastards, magicians, and Christians who convert to Islam or Roman Catholicism. The bodies of those who die under ban of excommunication are thus doomed to remain "incorrupt and entire" after death. They cannot enter heaven. The earth will not receive such bodies until they are set free by official absolution. Such "undead" ramble at night and spend only daytime in their tombs until excommunication is lifted.

According to Montague Summers: "In Roumania the vampire tradition extends back into the centuries, and there is perhaps no supernatural belief which is so strongly prevalent both in city and market-town as in the villages and remoter country districts. . . . It is hardly too much to say that in Roumania we find gathered together around the vampire almost all the beliefs and superstitions that prevail throughout the whole of Eastern Europe."[21]

Most Romanians believe that life after death will be much like life on this earth. There is not much belief in any purely spiritual world. So it seems natural to them that after death such an "undead" would walk the earth not as a ghost or spirit, but as a living creature. It is interesting to note that in all the regions of Romania, most of the genuine authenticated vampire "cases" were reported from Transylvania, particularly northern Transylvania, the scene of Stoker's Gothic plot, which stories Vambery, the Hungarian orientalist, undoubtedly described in detail in the course of his conversations with Bram Stoker. Quite often, in fact, reference to Hungarian "border town vampire cases" specifically referred to the border towns of Transylvania which, up to 1918, were an integral portion of the kingdom. Indeed, particularly during the first half of the nineteenth century, there had been an extraordinary number of reported vampire stories stemming from a certain region of central and northern Transylvania; coincidentally enough these were intimately associated with Dracula's name: in the Black Cris district, the Fagaras, Bihor, Hunedoara, Oradea, Deva, Mures, Metes, the Hateg, Turda, even the Borgo Pass region. One famous female vampire case, by a strange coincidence, originated in the village of Dragonesti, located very close to Dracula's birthplace in Sighisoara. Another so-called authenticated story came from a tiny village of Apateu (Black Cris) where soldiers had to be stationed outside the house of a widow to guard her against the return of her dead husband, who was supposedly a vampire. Ironically enough, this particular case, as many other similar stories, was written in Hungarian and published at Oradea—another center of Dracula interest.[22]

One possible explanation—purely a theory—accounting in part for the prevalence of vampire beliefs in Transylvania, assumes that the Tibetan Mongols, who had the belief in both the mythical vampire and the bat god, as we have already shown, came into contact with the East Asians who migrated into Transylvania. When these people came from East Asia to Hungary, they brought with them these beliefs to eastern Europe, in general, and to Transylvania, in particular.[23] Further evidence supporting this theory can be offered on the basis that vampire beliefs are particularly strongly anchored among the Székelys of Transylvania, who claim to be living successors of the Huns. It is interesting to note in this connection that Stoker refers to Dracula as of Székely descent. Legend has it that Attila himself was killed by the bite of a bat.

Further proof of the profound roots of vampirism in Romanian folklore is attested by the number of terms referring to various species of vampire in the Romanian language.[24] Few languages in fact can equal the inventive terminology adopted by the peasants in their oral traditions (some of these being of foreign origin—borrowed from their neighbors). *Strigoi* (feminine *strigoaica)* is a spirit that can take the form of various animals (such as wolves, dogs, blackbirds, and chickens). It sleeps during the day; at nighttime, however, it meets other kindred evil spirits and holders of evil intent. The female *(strigoaica)* species are incredibly cruel, far more wicked than the male consorts. They suck the blood of children, spoil marriages, can cause impoverishment and even complete destruction; they spoil harvests, prevent cows from giving milk, cause disease or even death. Whenever a series of evil, untoward, and unaccountable tragedies succeed each other at frequent intervals, the peasants of the community or district thus affected immediately suspect the presence of a female or male *strigoi*. Since the *strigoi* are often demon birds flying at night, this helps account for fear of night-flying bats in Romanian culture.[25]

The *moroi* or his female mate—the *moroaica*—is a different species of the undead breed. He usually represents the spirit of an unbaptized child who wishes to taunt and torture his mother.[26] The *vîrcolac* takes the form of a werewolf, and in popular superstition he is also linked to a child whose parents neglected to baptize him. His presence, like Stoker's vampire, is chiefly connected with the appearance of the full moon. In fact, he supposedly has some control over the moon and can cause total or partial eclipse.[27] The *pricolici* clearly corresponds to the classical vampire, the "living dead," who rises from his grave at night, in the form of a man or of a wolf or dog; hence, the fearful spine-tingling howling of dogs and wolves at night may be a sign of his presence.[28]

The term *iele* (always feminine) refers to a collection of nasty female vampires who always travel about their sordid business in numbers, perhaps for safety, generally in threes or sevens. They particularly attack men during their sleep and have various kinds of awesome powers, paralyzing him or driving him to insanity. Since, in their idle moments, they generally "play" on grass, the peasants keep an eye for burned yellow patches in the morning, indicating the places where the *iele* were feasting during the night before.[29]

The *sburator* in a sense comes closest to Stoker's vampire portrayed by Bela Lugosi in films, though he need not cause fatal vampirization. He takes the form of a handsome man, enters the house through the window at night, and kisses women during their sleep—often without the latter realizing the intrusion—except for the fact that they are tired, terribly tormented, pain-ridden, and agitated on the following day (reaction similar to those of a man vampirized by the *iele*).

The *zmeu* has really more of a mythological or fairy tale connotation. Like the *sburator*, he flies at night and has some sort of a hairy tail. He is not as wicked as the other vampires, but has extraordinary powers even though he is feeble-minded. With his brethren, he lives in castles usually located in the mountains—once again an obvious link to Dracula. His chief interest is that of kidnapping the daughters of powerful men, who then have to be saved by the gentle Prince Charming (Fat-Frumos).[30]

Other such terms are: *nagoda* (weird spirits which appear particularly in the Wallachian tales), *joimarite* (female evil spirits); *lighioane* (unclean spirits), not to mention the more conventional ghosts *duh, stafie, naluca, vedenie, fantoma, muma-padurii, dracoaica*—an evil woman. The conventional word "vampire," borrowed from the Serbs, is hardly ever used in Romanian folklore.

It is also to be noted that in popular literature all kinds of vampire metamorphoses are possible. The *pricolici* can transform himself into a *vîrcolac* (werewolf), and the werewolf himself, in turn, can become a *strigoi*, in a progressive degeneration in terms of wickedness. There are, after all, degrees of iniquity even among the vampires of Romania.

With so many evil spirits roaming the fields and villages of Transylvania, it stands to reason that the people have traditionally sought all sorts of instruments of defense, and in the course of the centuries they developed a formidable array of weapons to combat and neutralize the forces of darkness. Thus, just as popular folklore is included in its vampire terminology, the people are not entirely helpless in terms of defensive weapons.[31]

The serpent-dragon associated with Dracula has occupied a most respectable place in ancient Romanian mythology. There was evidently an ancient dragon-shaped god, portrayed in various forms, who was worshiped, perhaps even in pre-Dacian times. The most remarkable portrayal of this semihuman, semidragon, winged serpent is the "Fantastic Serpent," which the present authors saw at the history museum of Constanta, though little is known about it. The symbol of the Dacians, the ancestors of the Romanians, was also a dragon and the dragon supposedly had great powers in the history of the Romanian people, not necessarily all evil.[32] Dracula's father was a member of the Order of the Dragon, and according to some authorities, as has been previously demonstrated, the very name "Dracula" may be derived from "dragon." According to peasant ballads in the original princely chapel at Curtea-de-Arges, now disappeared, the bas-relief of the dragon originally rested, sculptured upon the orders of Vlad Dracul.[33]

Possibly, because the dragon often takes the form of a large winged snake, he has continued to live as an element of good luck with the people of Romania and Transylvania—though he has survived in a diminutive sort of way in the common and humble garden snake which has tremendous powers of defense against evil in popular folklore. The common garden snake (*sarpele de casa*) lives in the cracks of walls of peasant cottages, in the animals and the household garbage upon which it feeds—or else in the garden itself. No matter how frightening he may appear to the young, he must never be killed, since he is the guardian angel of the house and has magical powers for good. Should he perchance be killed, runs a popular proverb, good fortune will inevitably be driven away.

Beyond the garden snake, the people have other weapons wherewith to combat evil. The traditional preservative instrument is, of course, the Christian cross, often to be found to this day in isolated places, as in the middle of a field or on mountain tops in Transylvania. In such instances, the cross protects the wayfarer from evil. It is also worn by men and women around their necks and hangs in a prominent place in individual households. The modern cinema viewer knows the overwhelming powers of the cross against the vampire—a belief widely held in Romania and certainly not "invented" by Bram Stoker. Ikons painted on glass or on wood are frequently seen in peasant households with spiritual attributes of defense against evil.[34]

Another classic weapon immortalized by Bram Stoker is garlic (*usturoi*), long known by the eastern Europeans for its medicinal value in combating a great diversity of ailments. Beyond its medical curative merits, garlic, in popular practice, is used as a spiritual "talisman"; allegedly the vampire cannot stand its smell. The peasants make garlic crosses on the panes of windows, usually on the feast day of Saint Andrew, to preserve the house against evil spirits. Cattle are protected from harm and milklessness (which vampires can cause) by smearing garlic on their horns. Garlic is also placed on window frames, on doorknobs, or on locks to preserve the house against vampires who cannot endure this smell.[35]

If all else fails, there is always the possibility of *descîntece*, or incantations—really spiritual incantations, forms of popular exorcism chasing away evil spirits. These rites are performed by elderly experts in each village, usually women, occasionally gypsies. They are most effective against anyone who has been vampirized or even given the evil eye, and can be used to defend people, animals, and plants. In the case of humans who suffer from dizzy spells, high temperature, nosebleeds, headaches, fainting, and other forms of sickness, these incantations or the actual exorcising ritual performed by the Orthodox church can cure the symptoms of possession or vampirization.[36]

Other popular talismans include charm bracelets handed to women and young girls on the Ides of March (Mîrtisoare). These contain crosses, hearts, anchors, often the number 13 (which in Romania brings good luck); the small black patch made with ink or cinders on the foreheads of children, rather like the Catholic ceremony on Ash Wednesday; spit; red ribbons; and countless other symbols that defend man against evil spirits, which often vary from region to region. When it comes to finally killing the vampire, there is no alternative to the method used by Bram Stoker in the novel— the stake is inevitably used, evoking Dracula's favorite method of torture.

When unparalleled and persistent tragedies occur in a specific village, or if there is a period of unprecedented drought, or if cattle go berserk or are devoid of milk; when chickens cease laying eggs; if the plague or other epidemics spread and harvests fail; when there are natural tremors, massive inundations, or simply if people die without good reason in mysterious fashion, then inevitably the people suspect the presence of a vampire haunting the vicinity. Incantations, talismans, crosses, and garlic are no longer sufficient defense.

Prior to using the ultimate weapon, the peasants might drive stakes into the burial place of those who have recently died. In the case of a prolonged drought, for instance, there is a special ritual. Holes will be made around a suspected vampire tomb which is then filled with water. Wooden stakes are then driven into the soil around the tomb. Stakes, which are occasionally nicely carved, made of fir trees, often adorn many village cemeteries and are usually used in a symbolic way as a "preventative," as are the clay puppets made by peasant children in which pins are carefully stuck in the manner of Dracula.

If all these measures fail, one has to resort to the ultimate instrument of vampire destruction, which is used sparingly and reluctantly because, quite apart from the repulsiveness of the act itself, it entails desecration of the hallowed ground of the dead. Certain sturdy peasants are then picked to dig up the graves of those who have recently died—usually in the past few weeks when the calamities have begun to occur. Likely, among the corpses thus uncovered, they will find one still tepid, permanently ruddy and flesh-colored, completely pliable, and slightly turned rather than facing the sky, as an Orthodox Christian is supposed to be buried. These are the obvious signs of the vampire. Then the ritual has to be performed: a stake, whether red-hot and made of iron or simple wood, has to be driven through the victim's heart to keep the body in the grave. In other instances, the body is simply burned—another device Dracula frequently used in Transylvania. The fact that in the eyes of the people Dracula's body has never been found helps perpetrate the myth that he still is an "undead" who has not been successfully dealt with. The evil that existed within his family also contributes to the myth. The discovery of his brother, Mircea, turned head downward in his tomb, rather than upward, once again helped perpetrate the vampire lore in Dracula's family, although, in this case, there are evidently other explanations (he was probably buried alive by the boyars).

The connection between the historical Dracula and the vampire has by now hopefully become clear. The problem next to be uncovered is his possible connection to the bat.[37] The bat is a symbol closely identified with the subject of Stoker's novel. The bat is the only mammal who fulfills an old dream of man— it can really fly all by itself and seems to defy gravity. In order to fly, man has had to fashion artificial wings and then flying machines. Allegedly man is fearful of the consequences and inherently earthbound—a fear still prevalent among those few who obstinately refuse to travel by air. In Greek mythology, Icarus and his father fashioned wings to fly, but Icarus flew too close to the sun; the heat melted the wax that held the wings to his body, and he fell into the sea. Man wants to "fly like god" but, at the same time, is afraid of "defying his own nature" in that way. If God had wanted man to fly, goes the argument, the Creator would have given him wings like a bird or a bat.

The bat is a close relative of man, which may explain the attraction-repulsion feeling most men have toward these animals. Most experts hold that the bat is a very particular kind of mammal called chiroptera. It is definitely not a flying rat, as is popularly assumed. Bats' "wings" are really elongated webbed hands; the head is erect like a man's head. Another trait, which draws an obvious analogy to man, is the fact that the bat is one of the most versatile creatures in the world. The vampire blood-sucking bat, termed by scientists *Desmotontidae* (or *Desmodus rotundus*), does not exist anywhere in Europe. It was found by Cortez in the early sixteenth century in South America among the Mayan Indians who worshiped it as a god. Cortez and his men were apparently the very first Europeans to see a real vampire bat. Not long after the followers of Cortez returned to Europe, rumors about "blood-sucking bats" followed through European literature. Because of the association with blood (whether sucked or lapped) and generally because of the fear they both inspired in men, the mythical vampire from the Old World was then mentally linked in popular imagination and mythical literature with the blood-sucking bat of South America.

This symbolic identity seems all the more plausible when it is recalled that, rather like the vampire, the vampire-bat is a champion of agility. It can stalk with its body reared like a spider and creep over its prey in search of a place to make its painless gash with its surgical incisor teeth. Then, as the blood spurts out, the vampire-bat licks it with its tongue. It has a skull-like face. Most authorities hold that the vampire bat subsists on blood alone. To complete the analogy to the vampire, the vampire bat can fly and walk, dodge swiftly, turn somersaults, and do all this with speed and efficiency.

However, to be quite technical, contrary to the beliefs of most naturalists (Androvindi, Shaw, Currier, Buffon, Gervais, Hensel, Goeldi, Darwin), the vampire bat is *no blood-sucker;* it laps up blood with its tongue and consequently, in the strict sense, represents a false kind of vampire. Within this group of "false vampires" there is another species, *Megaderma lyra,* which is known to capture and devour birds, other bats, and even mice. Real vampire bats do not generally attack men. They usually confine their tastes to cattle. The only real danger to man is that the vampire bat—like all bats, in fact—is known to be a carrier of rabies, an additional reason why they are feared by the Romanian peasants. In general, however, bats are clean animals which spend a good deal of their time preening themselves like cats.

In the symbol of the vampire bat is also hidden an aspect of sexual pathology experienced by some people at the sight of blood. The male vampire is, of course, no ghost and is often portrayed like the incubus. He can and does have sexual relations with women, as the female vampire tends to kiss, sleep with, or otherwise assault young men. But there is a certain perversity in the sensual joy that some persons feel at the sight of flowing blood.[38] Blood, "the source of life," flows out and the sexual deviate laps it up. In medical language, such persons are known as "living vampires." Cases such as these are classed under "fetishism," which is a fixation on some "abnormal" experience. What, for other people, is just "dessert" becomes the real meal to the fetishist; the minor becomes the major for him. The fetishist is so enamored of "doing his thing" that he is oblivious to everything and everyone else. He does not transfer his love of his particular perverse sexual experience to the personality of his "beloved" or partner but remains wholly fixated on a particular element of the human anatomy-in this case the flowing blood. Such persons are said to be afflicted with haematophilia; Gilles de Rais, renowned as Bluebeard, and Elizabeth Báthory were possibly afflicted with such an illness.

Beyond the case of the person who enjoys seeing blood flowing during coitus, there is a further aberration of erotic blood lust known as haemotodipsia. Such persons desire blood, not only during the act of coitus, but at other times. In fact, their whole sexual satisfaction comes from blood. In such cases, the sex of the victim is not important; they literally get their whole sexual satisfaction through their teeth and mouth. What coitus is to the lover, the bite and the sucking of blood is to the haemotodipsiac. The tooth is an old phallic symbol, and in such cases the tooth assumes the function of the penis. Dracula enjoyed watching blood flow; he apparently liked to eat among his bleeding victims. It is conceivable that, coupled with his sexual insufficiency, Dracula could also have been classified as a haemotodipsiac.

This blood fixation is also often tied up with necrophilia. For example, "the vampire of Düsseldorf," Peter Kürten (1883-1931), who had begun by bleeding animals and ended by bleeding people, before he was tried and hanged, often went to the graves of his victims.[39] At the grave he disinterred the bodies and derived some sexual joy from disturbing these dead bodies. The dead subject was passive and he could do whatever he wanted to do with the corpse. He could literally dominate his dead sexual partner. Just as in Romanian folklore, the vampire and the werewolf are very closely allied and often confused, since the same term may signify either or both of them, so, in pathology, such necrosadism is mixed up with a desire of cannibalism. The subject desires not only to drink the blood from the human body, but to eat the flesh. He wants to become "one" with his "other" by drinking the blood and eating the flesh of his "beloved."

Leaving pathology aside, for the "normal" person, the final symbol of the Dracula vampire story may be the return to the womb: Lewin's oral triad—the desire to eat, to be eaten, and to sleep. It is part of the human sucking instinct which evidently develops while the human being is still a fetus; it is forcibly and suddenly interrupted at birth. Stoker's Dracula, the vampire, has the desire to drink the blood of another, to have his blood drunk by the other, and to sleep in his native soil. In this way, Dracula the vampire may represent the ambivalent link between the desire for life and death in the human psyche.[40] The vampire, Dracula, is driven fatalistically to drink blood in order to continue his existence. But he is not happy. In fact, he admires the repose of the truly dead. "Oh how wonderful it must be to be really dead," Dracula exclaimed. He cannot help himself. In order to survive, he must drink the blood of the living. On the one hand, he wants to live really, and on the other hand, he wants to die really. But both options are not meant to be his. He is not really alive and not really dead; he should decompose, but he does not do so. He is doomed to live on as an "undead." There is something pathetic, if not tragic, about Dracula the vampire.

By reading the Dracula novel or seeing horror movies on this theme, one can allow the fantasy and taboo of blood-drinking to work itself out. The blood-drinking urge can be satisfied in this way. The vampire will remain within fantasy life and need not really rise from the grave of the unconscious to go about its ghastly business among the living. The Dracula *within* remains under control, because one allows the Dracula *without* to continue to walk symbolically among the living through horror stories and films.

In addition to the vampire symbol and its relationship to bats and to blood fetishism, the Dracula image has, from the outset, been connected with Satan. Repeatedly, in the course of this book, the current authors have highlighted the fact that Dracul, in Romanian, means the devil, and Dracula, son of the devil. In the Bible, it is specifically the serpent devil that tempts Eve in the Garden of Paradise. He tempts her to eat of the forbidden fruit to gain the knowledge of good and evil. This serpent *speaks* like a human and reminds one of the old god

Proteus, who could transform himself into beast or man. In this case, it would seem that primitive religions survive in distorted form; some of the old gods of the pre-Judeo-Christian religion degenerate into tempters and slimy demons. The very fact that these early primitive gods were usually associated with the dragon suggests that, in popular legend, the devil may degenerate into a flying dragon or a vampire. In the imagination of the Romanian people, devil and vampire are inextricably bound together.[41] If this line of reasoning is correct, these gods of night could also, in the case of the mythical Dracula himself, be a reflection of some ancient pre-Christian blood-drinking religion in eastern Europe, traces of which have since been lost.

Although in Dacian mythology, the dragon can be a symbol of defense against evil, he can also represent evil itself. The dragon is a symbolic figure, a serpent with wings; Apollo, Cadmus, Perseus, and Siegfried all had to conquer "the dragon." The ancient ansated Egyptian cross, the hem Ankh, stands for life, whereas its antithesis, the Ouroboros, the serpent or dragon, denotes primeval anarchic dynamism. The Ouroboros among the Gnostics was represented as a dragon biting its own tail. The dragon with wings biting its own tail was the insignia of Dracula's Order of the Dragon. The dragon has generally stood for "things animal" and hence "the adversary" *par excellence.* This monster is the primordial enemy in the perpetual test of combat, as in Saint George and the dragon. In Christian mythology the dragon is also specifically the evil symbol of Satan, which can also correspond with Dracula's evil image. In Romania the dragon is occasionally typified as a huge monster with two fantastic open jaws, one trailing the earth, the other high up on the horizon, gulping everything in his way.

Romanian folklore is extremely rich in its references to the devil as well as its reference to the vampire. There is an endless number of words associated with Satan: *Dracesc, Draceste, Dracie, Dracime, Dracoaica,* etc. In addition, even in general parlance, the word "devil" is used to indicate nervousness or tension. The peasants' "Sunt plinde draci" implies "I am tense." The peasants say that the devil, like the vampire, is able to turn into various animals; since he has wings, he can also fly. During the day he lives in hell; at night he rules until the cock crows at dawn.

The popular image of the real historical Dracula also demonstrates the inadequacy of the usual moral, political, and psychological categories. Unable to face up to the actual implications of the historical Dracula's tactics of terror, almost all previous authors have generally transformed him into a common satanic theme. Interpretation of his life has thus been clouded with mythology from the fifteenth century to the present day. But one should try to come to terms with the real Dracula's use of terror as a legitimate form of rule and place his rule in a wide historical context.

One of the reasons why most writers have taken refuge in references to the devil when dealing with Dracula is that there is a bias against his kind of use of fear and violence. Supposedly, most human political systems are characterized by a reliance upon reason. The consistent use of violence and terror has been relegated to some faraway places, or else terror has been analyzed as part of a recent temporary aberration attributed to totalitarianism as found in Hitler or Stalin. In short, when dealing with the tactics of terror, man has proved generally incapable of separating out "what is" from "what should be."

In referring to the use of myths, Professor E. V. Walter has pointed out how "one corner of the mind remains ungratified by explanation that would submit human choices as the cause of complex phenomena. For ages, mythology occupied that corner." He concluded, "Although the mythic component can never be purged from the process of rational explanation, still its influence may be controlled."[42] Such demythologizing is definitely the case where one deals with the Dracula image. Terror has been socially supported in simple societies as a way of dealing with political resistance.[43] As shown by the evidence previously presented in this book, Dracula's tactics appeared to have received fairly wide popular and social support in his own country.

At this point some clarification of the use of the word "terror" seems in order in this context. The word "terreur" apparently appeared first in a modern language in the fourteenth century in a French translation of Livy's *Ab Urbe Condita Libri,* by Bechorius, a French Benedictine.[44] Terror is the feeling of fear which humans share with animals. It is thus to be distinguished from rational fear, which is a human feeling. The tactics of terror specifically refer to the seemingly indiscriminate yet systematic use of violence in order to achieve control as practiced by Dracula, as well as other leaders in history.

In the ancient world terror was an essential part of the power system known as tyranny.[45] In this context the reader should recall that Dracula was called "a great tyrant" in many of the old German pamphlets. In Dracula's day the German sources also compared his tyranny to that of Nero and Domitian and thus, unknowingly, hit upon similarities in those distinct regimes of terror. The reigns of Marcus, "a bloody cruel tyranny," and that of Sulla, as described by Plutarch, also fit into this historical development of the tactics of terror.[46]

Examples of some northern Italian Renaissance rulers from the Age of Despots also offer relevant similarities to Dracula's methods. In referring to Ezzelino da Romano, Frederick II's vicar in northern Italy, the historian Symonds wrote:

> *Is there in fact such a thing as Haematomania, Blood-madness, but if we answer this question in the affirmative, we shall have to place how many Visconti, Sforzeachi, Malatesti, Borgias, Farnesi and princes of the House of Anjou and Aragon in the list of these maniacs.... Ezzelino's cruelty was no mere Berserker fury or Lycanthropia coming over him in gusts and leaving him exhausted. It was steady and continuous. In his madness, if such we may call this inhumanity, there was method; he used it to the end of the consolidation of his tyranny.*[47]

Those very words relating to Ezzelino da Romano may well apply to Dracula, since he, too, followed these tactics consistently and not in any isolated acts of blind rage.

The reign of terror as practiced by Ivan IV of Russia (Ivan the Terrible) against his boyars reflects a similar attitude toward the many uses of terror.[48] Finally, the period of the Terror during the French Revolution from the summer of 1793 to that of 1794 popularized the term in a modern context.

Perhaps the most relevant example for our study of Dracula as a tactician of terror concerns the ruler Shaka (1816-1828) who ruled at the zenith of Zulu power. The Englishman Flynn reported:

> *Following a military encounter Shaka decided to punish those who had been cowards. On the first day of our visit we*

had seen no less than ten men carried off to death. On a mere sign of Shaka—viz., the pointing of a finger, the victim would be seized by his nearest neighbors; his neck would be twisted, and his head and body beaten with sticks, the nobs of some of these being as large as a man's fist. On each succeeding day, too, numbers of others were killed; their bodies would then be carried to an adjoining hill there impaled. We visited this spot on the fourth day. It was truly a Golgotha, swarming with hundreds of vultures.[49]

This tale of the procedure of impalement is reminiscent of the episode when Dracula ordered those men killed who had been wounded in battle in the back (and not in front). As in the case of Shaka, Dracula impaled his own men and left them in full view as food for vultures. Lest one assume that Shaka's methods were erroneously recorded by Flynn, another account helps confirm the veracity of the incident. On December 5, 1825, an event similar to that described by Flynn occured and was recorded by the eyewitness Isaacs. About three hundred Zulu veterans came to salute Shaka and he ordered some to be executed as cowards. "The victims were then dragged away and beaten as they proceeded to the bush, about a mile from the kraal, where a stick was inhumanly forced up the fundament of each and they were left as food for the wild beasts of the forest, and those carnivorous birds that hover near the habitations of the natives."[50] Once again the methods used by Shaka were remarkably similar to those employed by the historical Dracula. The victims were impaled "up the fundament of each" and left to die from exposure. Like Dracula, Shaka received strict obedience from his subjects, was successful in battle, maintained discipline at home, and was feared and respected by his enemies. The point behind such references here is to demonstrate that there was indeed a method in Dracula's "madness." He does not merely stand out as some isolated historical example of a perverted demon of extreme sexual pathology or as a universal dragon symbol. His method of execution was designed to inspire terror and instill into his subjects a "respect" for his law and order.

With a final look at the legitimate use of terror, our book has come to a full circle. Dracula is, of course, first and foremost a precise historical personage in flesh and blood, living in the middle of the fifteenth century in a remote geographic area of eastern Europe called Wallachia. He spent most of his years in neighboring Transylvania, where he was born. During his lifetime, he commanded admiration because of his heroic exploits; he inspired fear and respect because of his terrorism, and anecdotal interest because of his "pathological" cruelty and "perverse" sexuality.

In spite of these traits, Dracula would undoubtedly have remained a permanently obscure and irretrievably forgotten provincial governor on the confines of civilization buried under the dust of the heavy documentation recalling his existence, no matter how deified by popular folklore or native literature, were it not for one saving feature. By one of those historical incidents that happen only rarely in the course of human existence, a Dracula myth was created by Transylvanian refugees who traveled to the West, which happened to respond to a certain taste for the fantastic among the fifteenth-century reading public. By even stranger coincidence, this mood also coincided with the invention of the printing press. Those twin circumstances made Dracula a best seller in the West four hundred years before Bram Stoker wrote his famous book. In history, everything seems to be a matter of coincidence, timing, and dates. Without the invention of the printing press, there would have been no Dracula myth, any more than Christopher Columbus could have sailed to America shortly thereafter without the invention of a compass. Had western Europe been in its medieval frame of mind, there would have been little interest in demons or adventure. Without the "modernism" of the Renaissance, both Dracula and Columbus would undoubtedly have turned their formidable energy to medieval crusading. In the circumstances, neither of them would have found a patron, whether a Hungarian king or a Spanish queen.

Created in the fifteenth century, the cruel mythological monster of the German tales was by 1897 to transform itself into a permanent symbolic figure, i.e., Stoker's vampire, which still endures today. This extraordinarily powerful figure seems to respond to a very basic spiritual need trespassing upon the mysteries of life and death. It was in disguise, rather than in his historic form, that Dracula has assumed the status of a universal archetype, which transcends the limitations of time and defies geographic localization and human mortality. Therein lies Dracula's real fame and the permanency of his appeal. It is the case of the myth completely overshadowing the historical figure.

Yet the particular flavor of these unusual stories lies precisely in the historicity of the plot. The mere manufacture of an imaginary Shelley-type Frankenstein may represent a fascinating intellectual gymnastic in terms of its horror, yet it can have little credibility. The real fascination of Dracula lies in the fact that he existed, that he was real, and that Transylvania can actually be found on the map. But the present authors can hardly claim to have solved the final mysteries of Dracula's life and death.

This book stands clearly in the tradition of seeing both the historical and the symbolic aspects of Dracula. Dracula belongs to history as well as to myth. Like his name, which was associated with the dragon, the vampire, and the devil, so was his life related to the terroristic practice of impalement.

In conclusion, behind the mythical Dracula image lies hidden not only symbolic significance but the tactics of terror as means of social integration and political control. In a very real sense, Dracula merits an important place in any history. His real life will probably continue to fascinate and puzzle historians now and in the future. It is our hope that our study will contribute to a further revival of research into the complexities of the real Dracula.

---

[1] Carl G. Jung, *Man and His Symbols* (New York, 1964), p. 20.

[2] Ibid., p. 39.

[3] Ibid., p. 55.

[4] Stoker, *Dracula*, p. ff.

[5] Max Vasmer, *Russisches etymologiches Wörterbuch* (Heidelberg, 1953), vol. 1, p. 168, and vol. 2, pp. 186-187.

[6] Sir Devendra P. Varma, ed., *Varney the Vampire or the Feast of Blood* (New York, 1970), introduction pp. xiv-xv.

[7] Ibid., p. xiii.

[8] Tony Faivre, *Les Vampires* (Paris, 1962), p. 25.

[9] Sayre, *Ancient Empires of the East*, p. 146.

[10] Arraja, *Enterpacion de la idolatria de Piru*, pp. 21ff., cited in Spencer's *Des. Soc.*, vol. 2, p. 48.

[11] Burton, *Vikram and the Vampire* (New York, 1969), p. xvii.

[12] Ibid., p. xi.

[13] Ibid., p. 35.

[14] Sir James George Frazer, *Fear of the Dead in Primitive Religions*, vol. 2, (London, 1934), p. 83.

[15] Valvassor, 1687 anno *Ehre des Herzogtums Krains*, III, IV, cop. 10, p. 335; III, I, XI, pp. 317-319; II I, VI, cop. 4, p. 295.

[16] *Wiener Diarium* (Anhang) July 21, 1725 (1728; new ed., 1734), p. 25. Also Michel Raufft, *De masticatione mortuorum in timulis,* cited in Weitenkampf "Gedanken über wichtige Wahrheiten aus der Vernunft und Religion," pt. 1 (1735), p. 108, and also cited in Ornella Volta and Valeria Riva, *The Vampire* (London, 1963), p. 19.

[17] Dom Augustin Calmet (1672-1757), *Dissertation sur les apparitions des esprits et sur les vampires et revenants de Hongorie et de Moravie* (1st ed., 1749; 2d ed., 1751; republished often thereafter).

[18] Lund Degh, *Folktales in Hungary,* trans. Judith Halasz (University of Chicago Press, 1965), p. 349. On this subject she wrote: "A well-known figure in the spirit world of Hungarian myths is the *liderc* or *ludverc,* a nightmarish creature which appears in either sex. The *liderc is* not unlike the vampire, a well-known creature in popular tradition all over the Balkans, though their characteristic features are not identical" (p. 349). See the old study by Heinich von Wlisocki, *Volksglaube und religiosen Brauch der Magyaren,* 1893. See also Tekla Domotor, "Ethnographische Forschung in Ungarn 1950-62," *Hessische Blätter für Volkskunde* 59 (1963): 665-674; Ivan Bulassa, *Kasscassi Mondak* (Budapest, 1963); Gyula Ortutay, *Hungarian Folk Tales* (Budapest, 1962).

[19] Calmet, *Dissertation,* cited in Volta and Riva, *The Vampire,* pp. 15-17, 20-21.

[20] P. François Richard, *Relations de ce qui s'est passe de plus remarquable d Saint-Erini . . .* (Paris, 1657).

[21] See Montague Summers, *Vampire in Europe,* cited in Faivre, *Les Vampires,* p. 128.

[22] See Sándor Márki, *A fektete körös ís vídeke* (Oradea, 1877), pp. 119-122.

[23] Varma, *Varney the Vampire,* p. xviii.

[24] See Alfred Poissonier, "Contes populaires de la Roumanie, le strigoi," *Courier de Bucharest* 1, nos. 8, 9, and 11 (1856). Also Marcel Olanescu, *Mitologie Româneasca* (Bucharest, n.d.), pp. 494-501. Winterhalter, "Wahn und Aberglaube bei den Walachen," *Sat. Sieb. Woch.* 4 (1844): 181-182.

[25] Arthur Erdélyi, *Erdélyrol* (Cluj, 1849), 60-63; I. Nadejde, "Despre strîgoi si strîgoi ce sau strige," *Contemporanul* 3 (1883): 194-199, 264-268— , 317-320, 345-352, 494-500, 545-548, 611-614; Dr. Negrescu, "Strigoii din judetul Vilcea," *Casa rur* 2 (1891): 191-192; Ioanu M. Petranu, "Schite istorice despre 'Strigoi,'" *Transylvania* 15 (1884) 90-92, 102-105; E. M. Vacano, "Nationelle Aberglauben Der Vampyr," *Epoche* 5, no. 464, (1872); George Vuia, "Diferitele datine pentru asiedarea mortiloru cu privire la arderea cadavereloru," *Transylvania* 7 (1874): 258-263, 265-268; D. Bolinteanu, *Calatorii la Românii din Macedonia si Muntele Atos sau Santa Agora* (Bucharest, 1863), pp. 91-92.

[26] S. Fl. Marian, "Mitologia daco-romana," *Alb. Carp.* 3 (1878) 86-89. Iohann Karl Schuller, *Das Todaustragen und der Muorlef* (Sibiu, 1861).

[27] Dr. S. Schullerus, "Zur Sagenkunde," *Korresp.* 14, no. 3 (1891) 1-29; Frederich Wilhelm Schuster, "Deutsche Mythe aus siebenbürgischen Quellen," *Archiv* n.s. 9 (1870) 230-231, 401-497, and 10 (1872): 65-155; G. Dem. Teodorescu, "Miturile lunare: vîrcolacii studiu de etnologie si de mitologie comparata," *Convorbire literara* 23 (1889) 3-25, 110-140.

[28] G. I. Pites, "Siste, pricolici necuratu," *Revista Noua* 3 (1890) 391-393; "Walachischer Aberglaube," *Sieb. Bote* 61 (1846) 16; Henrik Wlislocki, *Märchen und Sagen der Transilvanischen Zigeuner* (Berlin, 1886), pp. 76-78.

[29] At. M. Marienescu, "Ielele," *Familia* 9 (1873) 97-101, 109-111; Lozai Saineanu, *Ielele, Dânsele, vîntoasele . . .* (Bucharest, 1886).

[30] V. A. Urechia, *Patria româna Notitie etimografice . . .* (Bucharest, 1868); C. C. Stamati, *Musa româneasca,* vol. 2 (Iasi, n.d.), pp. 523-524.

[31] I. G. Sbiera, *Povesti poporale romînesti* (Cernauti, 1886), esp. pp. 314-318.

32 G. Nandris, "The Historical Dracula," *Comparative Literature Studies*, pp. 376-377.

33 Pavel Chihaia, "Deux armoires sculptées appartenent aux voevodes Vlad Dracul et Neagoe Basarab," *Revue roumaine d'histoire de l'art* 1, no. 1 (1964): 151-166.

34 G. Dem. Teodorescu, *Incercari critice asupra unoru creditente datine si moravuri ale poporului Romậnu* (Bucharest, 1874), pp. 114-115.

35 *Dictionarul Enciclopedic Illustrat Cartea Romậneasca*, p. 1392.

36 G. Dem. Theodorescu, "Consideratiuni . . . asupra descântecului de 'apucat' sau 'inclestat,' " *Columna lui Trajan* 6 (1875) 133-135; Grigore G. Tocilescu, "Descântece Superstitiuni si poesii poporane din plaiul Prahovei," *Revista istorica archeologica si filologica* (Bucharest, 1884), pp. 385-386; Ioan Reteganul Popu, "Ceva literatura religiosa a poporului nostru," *Timis* 1 (1885): 63-65. One of the best books is Dr. Moses Gaster, *Literature populara romậna si un apendice* (Bucharest, 1883), pp. 406-429.

37 The latest book on bats is Alvin Novick, *The World of Bats* (New York, 1969).

38 Leslie Fiedler, *Liebe, Sexualität und Tod* (Berlin, 1964); Krafft-Ebing, *Psychopathia Sexualia* (Stuttgart, 1894), cited in Stürm, *Von den Vampiren*, pp. 528-529.

39 Cited ibid., p. 530.

40 Thanks to Dr. Joseph Bierman, "Dracula, Prolonged Childhood Illness and the Oral Triad," ms.

41 See F. Voronca, "Cum se trateaza dracul în Bucovina si alte coredinte despre dracul la români." *Romậnul* 35 (1890) 80-81; Marcel Olanescu, *Mitologie Romậneasca*, pp. 26-44.

42 Eugene Victor Walter, *Terror and Resistance, A Study of Political Violence* (New York, 1969). See also E. V. Walter, "Violence and the Process of Terror," *American Sociological Review* 29 (1964) 248-257.

43 Walter, *Terror and Resistance*, pp. 279-280.

44 See Jerczy Waciorski, *Le terrorism politique* (Paris, 1939), cited in David Spitz, *Political Theory and Social Change* (New York, 1967), in the essay by E. V. Walter, "Theories of Terrorism and the Classical Tradition," p. 148.

45 See Samuel Dill, *Roman Society from Nero to Marcus Aurelius* (London, 1925), esp. the chapter "The Aristocracy under the Terror," pp. 1-57.

46 See Plutarch, *Selected Lives from the Lives of the Noble Grecians and Romans*, ed. Paul Turner (Southern Illinois Press, 1963), pp. 146-185 186-221.

47 John Addington Symonds, *Renaissance in Italy*, vol. 1 (New York, 1935), pp. 55-56.

48 For one of the most recent comments on Ivan's actions see George Vernadsky, *The Tsardom of Moscow 1547-1682*, pt. 1 (New Haven, 1969), p. 169.

49 Cited in Walter, *Terror and Resistance*, p. 184.

50 Cited ibid., p. 135.

Bibliography

Primary Sources

Dracula Letters, edicts (both internal and diplomatic) we have drawn upon. Most of these are published in collection of documents mentioned below.

September 6, 1456, Tîrgoviste. Dracula swears oath of fealty to King Ladislav the Young of Hungary. (Latin) State Archives Brasov. (Bogdan, *Documente*, doc. no. 257, pp. 316-317; Hurmuzacki, *Documente*, 79, p. 45, 15-1.)

September 10, 1456, Tîrgoviste. Dracula to citizens of Brasov asking them to send two hundred men so that he can negotiate with the Turks for a position of strength. (Latin) State Archives Brasov. (Iorga, *Scrisori documente* (Bucharest, 1912), pp. 9-10; Bogdan, *Documente*, doc. no. 258, pp. 317-318; Hurmuzacki, *Documente*, 80, p. 45, 16-1.)

February 14, 1457, Tîrgoviste. Dracula complains to citizens of Brasov that they gave asylum to Vlad the Monk. (Latin) State Archives Brasov. (Bogdan, *Documente*, doc. no. 259, pp. 318-19; Hurmuzacki, *Documente*, 82, p. 47, 15-1.)

March 13, 1457, Tîrgoviste. Dracula asks Saxons of Sibiu *not* to give shelter to a Romanian monk who styles himself son of a prince (Vlad the Monk, his half brother). (Latin) State Archives Sibiu. (*Archiv für Sieb. Landesk.*, n.s. 21, 351.)

April 16, 1457, Tîrgoviste. Dracula endows the village of Troianesti to Cozia Monastery. (Slav) State Archives Bucuresti, 11/1 Cozia. (Copy at the Library of Ac. of Rom. Soc. Rep., 20-45.)

June 12, 1457, n.p. Dracula endows privileges to the monasteries of Rusicon at Mount Athos. (Slav) Library of Ac. of Rom. Soc. Rep., uncat.

1458 (?), n.p. Dracula promises to keep the engagements he undertook toward his patron Szilágy and promises to keep peace with the citizens of Brasov. (Latin) State Archives Brasov, doc. no. 193.

March 5, 1458, Tîsmana. Dracula endows the monastery of Tîsmana all the villages it owned during the reign of his father, Dracul, exempting them of princely obligations. (Slav) (Written by Radu gramatical, the copyist.) State Archives Bucuresti, 11/2.

(Tismana 9/91.) (Copy at the Library of Ac. of Rom. Soc. Rep., 20-46.)

May 25, 1458, n.p. Dracula's letter to Gaspari asking for artisans from Brasov. (Latin) State Archives Brasov. (Copy at the Library of Ac. of Rom. Soc. Rep., 17-53). (Bogdan, *Documente*, doc. no. 255, pp. 319-320; Hurmuzacki, *Documente*, 87 p. 49, 15-1)

June 13, 1458, on the banks of the Dimbovita. Dracula to citizens of Brasov recommends his emissary to them. (Latin) State Archives Brasov. (Copy at the Library of Ac. of Rom. Soc. Rep., 44-1.) (Bogdan, *Documente*, doc. no. 261, p. 320; Hurmuzacki, *Documente*, 87, pp. 49-50, 15-1.)

September 20, 1459, Bucharest. Dracula endows to Andrei and other boyars privileges, exempting them from various services. (First mention of "citadel of Bucharest.") (Slav) Library of Ac. of Rom. Soc. Rep., uncat. (Alex Bunceanu Collection, ms. 170/2.) (Copy at History Museum of City of Bucharest.)

December 1459, n.p. Dracula's comments to Michael Szilágy in connection with peace negotiation. (Latin) Library of Ac. of Rom. Soc. Rep., Slav F VII 9 XIII.

1459-1460, Tîrgoviste. Dracula endows the monastery of Buna Vestire of Cotmeana a number of villages and exempts them of taxes (Slav) State Archives Bucuresti, Cotmeana N as, F 32.

June 4, 1460, Cetatea Dimbovitei (Bucharest). Dracula asks the Saxons of Brasov to allow Wallachian refugees to return. (Latin) State Archives Brasov. (Bogdan, *Documente*, doc. no. 263, pp. 320-321; Hurmuzacki, *Documente*, 96, p. 56, 15-1.)

July 26, 1460, n.p. Dracula asks the citizens of Brasov to keep the peace, since he has problems only with those of Fugaras. (Latin) State Archives Brasov. (Bogdan, *Documente*, doc. no. 263, p. 321; Hurmuzacki, *Documente*, 97, 56-57.)

August 10, 1460, n.p. Dracula to citizens of Brasov about commercial affairs. (Latin) State Archives Brasov, Fronius Collection, no 303. (Bogdan, *Documente*, doc. no. 264 p. 322; Hurmuzacki, *Documente*, 98, p. 57, 15-1.)

September 1, 1460, n.p. Dracula endows to Filoteu Monastery a year's sum of four thousand aspri. (Slav) Library of Ac. of Rom. Soc. Rep., 595/10.

February 10, 1461, Bucharest. Dracula endows the village of Godeni to the boyar Bira and to his brother Godea, exempting them from taxes and services. (Slav) Library of Ac. of Rom. Soc. Rep., no. 5,236, fols. 64-65. (Original document, Professor Sapcaliu of Cîmpulung.)

September 27, 1461, n.p. Mention of one of Dracula's acts concerning the village of Calugareni, signed by Grigore Iogofat. (Slav) History Institute of Ac. of Rom. Soc. Rep.

Before 1462, n.p. Dracula orders the customs officials of Rucar to let the citizens of Brasov know that the rumors concerning a Turkish invasion are false. (Latin) State Archives Brasov, doc. no. 175. (Photostat at Library of Ac. of Rom. Soc. Rep.)

February 11, 1462, Giurgiu. Dracula's letter to Matthias concerning his Turkish campaign and massacre of twenty thousand Turks. (Latin) (Written by Radul Farma, probably Radu gramatical, the copyist.) Municipal Archives Munich, ms. 19,648, fol. 69.

November 7 or 8, 1462 Rottel (Turnu Rosu?) Dracula's so-called letter of submission to the Turks. (Latin) Only copy available in the commentaries of Enea Silvio de Piccolomini (Pius II), probably dated 1464. Most historians consider the letter a forgery.

August 4, 1475, Arghis (Transylvania). Dracula to Saxons of Sibiu asks for one of his boyars, Cîrstian Percalab (governor) to obtain permission to build a house. (Latin) State Archives Sibiu. (Copy at the Library of Ac. of Rom. Soc. Rep.) (Bogdan, *Documente,* doc. no. 265, pp. 322-323; Hurmuzacki, *Documente,* 146, pp. 84-85, 15-1.) *Note:* Dracula signs himself "Wladislaus Dragwlya Waywoda parcium Transalpinarum:"

October 7 (1475?), Mirghendel Traghii. Dracula sends one of his emissaries Vitez János in a secret mission to Brasov. (Latin) State Archives Brasov, doc. no. 189.

October 13, 1475, Balcaciu. Dracula has received and acknowledges to the citizens of Brasov and Sibiu receipt of two hundred florins given him by Matthias Corvinus. "Nos Ladislaus Draghwyla."(Latin) State Archives Sibiu. (Copy at Library of Ac.of Rom. Soc. Rep.) (Bogdan, *Documente,* doc. no. 266, p. 328; Hurmuzacki, *Documente,* 148, p. 86, 15-1.)

1476 (?), n.p. Dracula instructs his emissary Vitez János not to allow anyone to cross into Wallachia without his permission. (Latin) State Archives Brasov, doc. no. 180.

October 7, 1476, Brasov. Dracula gives merchants of Brasov commercial privileges as in the time of Mircea the Old and Dracul. (Latin) State Archives Brasov, doc. no 773.

November 8, 1476, Tîrgoviste. Dracula informs the ruling citizens of Brasov that he has beaten his enemy Basarab Laiota, who has fled to the Turks. (Latin) State Archives Brasov, doc. no. 145.

N.d., n.p. Dracula denounces his enemy Aldea. (Latin) State Archives Brasov, doc. no. 164.

N.d., n.p. Dracula sends two of his boyars, Ion Polivar and Mihai Log, to Brasov to extradite two enemy boyars. (Latin) State Archives Brasov, doc, no. 166. (Copy at the Library of Ac. of Rom. Soc. Rep., Slav F 7-86.)

N.d., n.p. Dracula demands justice for his men whose rights are infringed upon by Hungarian customs officials. (Latin) State Archives Brasov, doc. no. 173.

N.d., n.p. Dracula demands the extradition of a thief who has stolen merchandise from one of his subjects. (Latin) State Archives Brasov, doc. nos. 176 and 177.

N.d., n.p. Dracula sends oxen and cattle herds to Brasov. State Archives Brasov. (Copy at the Library of Ac. of Rom. Soc. Rep., Slav F VII 37 XIII.)

Other Archival Material

German fifteenth-century chronicle by Leonardus Hefft. Copy of Andrew of Ratisbon about Dracula's conversion to Catholicism. (Latin) Municipal Archives Munich, no. 26,632, fol. 495.

Neofit bishop. The House Ledger of Archbishop Neofit. Ms. Library of Ac. of Rom. Soc. Rep., no. 2606/26.

German Manuscripts

Lambach manuscript, Lambach Monastery, Codex 327, manuscripts of the fifteenth century. Published by Wilhelm Wattenbach. "Uber den Walächischen Woiwoden Wlad IV, 1456-1462," *Archiv des Vereins für Siebenbürgische Landeskunde*, n.s. 27, no. 1 (Hermannstadt, 1896): 331-343. Also published by G. C. Conduratu in *Michael Beheims Gedicht über den Woiwoden Wlad II*. Mit historischen und kritischen Erläuterungen Inaugeraldissertation. Leipzig-Bucharest, 1903, pp. 115ff.

St. Gall manuscript, St. Gall Monastery, present-day Stiff Library, no. 806, manuscripts of the sixteenth century. Discovered around 1882 and published by G. Baritiu in "Manuscript despre cruzimile lui Vlad Dracula," *Analele Academiei Române*, 2, pt. 5 (1882-1883), sec. 2, pp. 11-14. Also published by Bogdan, pp. 90-105, and Conduratu, pp. 101-105.

Beheim's poem. Title: "Von ainem wutrich der hiess tracle waida von der walachei." Discovered by G. Conduratu and published in his *Michael Beheims Gedicht über den Woiwoden Wlad II*, pp. 29ff. Also published by J. Bleyer. "Ein Gedicht Michael Beheims über Wlad IV, Woiwoden de Walachei (1456-62)," *Archiv des Vereins für Siebenbürgische Landeskunde*, n.s. 32, no. 2

(Hermannstadt, 1903): 10ff. See also Michel Beheim, *Die Gedichte des Michel Beheim*. Band I. Gedichte Nr. 1-147 herausgegeben von Hans Giele und Ingeborg Spriewald (Berlin, 1968).

German Pamphlets

"An deme quaden thyrane Dracole Wyda." No date, publisher, or place of publication. Location: Magyar Nemzeti Museum, Budapest. M. H. 705. Copy at the Biblioteca Centrala Bucuresti, 49763413. Portrait on the title page which corresponds as a slightly modified version to the one on the 1488 Nürnberg edition. First published by J. Ch. Engel, who found it in the library of Count Széchényi at Budapest, in *Fortsetzung der Algemeinen Welthistorie durch eine Gesellschaft von Gelehrten im Teutschland und England ausgefertigt* 49, bd. 4, abth. 1 (Halle, 1804), no. 72, pp. 75ff. The tale ends with Dracula's imprisonment in Buda and release in 1476. Old Low German: Engel thought that the text was in Transylvanian Saxon dialect (p. 80). K. M. Kertbeny, who knew six German editions of the Dracula pamphlets, also thought that the language of this one was Old Saxon from Transylvania, when he added a modern German translation to his edition of the pamphlet. (See K. M. Kertbeny, *Ungarn Betreffende Deutsche Erstlingsdrücke 1454-1600* [Budapest, 1880], pp. 328-332.) Bogdan rejected Engel and Kertbeny's thesis and correctly demonstrated that the pamphlet was not in Transylvanian Saxon dialect, but in Low German. Date: Engel dated it soon after 1477 (pp. 75-80). C. I. Karadja dated it around 1480, before 1484 ("Incunabele povestind despre cruzimile lui Vlad Tepes," *Inchinare lui N. Iorga* [Cluj, 1931], pp. 196-205). C. Borchling and B. Claussen dated it around 1483. (*Niederdeutsche Bibliographie* 1 (Neumünster, 1931). Nos. 66 and 367 refer to "Dracula.") The unpublished incunabula catalog at the Berliner Staatsbibliothek had the date "1480," but corrected it to "1485." (Under the title "Historia Dracole Waida, Blatt 8617ff.) H. Raab dated it "around 1483." ("Zu einigen Niederdeutschen Quellen des Altrussischen Schrifttums," *Zeitschrift für Slawistik* 3, nos. 2-4 (1958): 334.) Aside from the scholar Striedter, all the previous experts held that this text found by Engel was the oldest text. Striedter states that it cannot be dated before 1488. (J. Striedter, "Die Erzählung vom Walächischen Vojwoden Drakula in der Russischen und Deutschen Uberlieferung," *Zeitschrift für Slavische Philologie* (1961), p. 403.) Bogdan, when he republished this pamphlet in his 1896 work *Vlad Tepes*, placed its publication at Lübeck and attributed the publisher as probably Bartholomaeus Gothan. H. Raab attributed it directly to Gothan, as if that were a proven fact, which it is not, and claimed that it could have been published either at Magdeburg or at Lübeck "Zu einigen Niederdeutschen Quellen . . .," p. 334). But Striedter challenged whether Gothan ever really published it (Striedter, p. 403). The latest research on this aspect by Striedter rejects the old thesis that this pamphlet in Budapest was the original "Stammvater" for all the others (Striedter, pp. 401-404).

Nürnberg: Marcus Ayrer, 1488. Location: Landesbibliothek, Weimar. Portrait on the title page is very similar to the Budapest copy. High German: According to Striedter, this edition is the "Stammvater" for all the others (Striedter, pp. 401-404).

"Dracolewaida." No date, publisher, or place of publication. Location: Bayrische Staatsbibliothek, Munich; Landesbibliothek, Stuttgart; Biblioteca Academiei Române, Bucharest (Sturdza edition); photo from the Stuttgart copy at the Biblioteca Centrala Bucuresti, 497635. Portrait on the cover can be seen as a slightly modified version of the 1488 Marcus Ayrer-Nürnberg text, possibly published by P. Wagner around 1488. High German.

"Historie von Dracole Wayda." Leipzig (no publisher cited), 1493. Location: Manuscript Division, State Public Library, Saltykov-Shchedrin, Leningrad. Gravure portrait shows Dracula in soldier's uniform; it differs from all the others. N. V. Varbanets traces the publisher to Martin Landsberg ("Nemetskaia broshiura 'Ob odnom velikom izverge' Leiptsigskoe izdanie 1493," *Povest' o Drakule, p.* 185).

No date, publisher, or place of publication. Title: we did not have the opportunity of seeing it. Location: Only known pamphlet at Wolfenbüttel. Copies at the Biblioteca Centrala Bucuresti, 497638, where it is cited as Lübeck, Steffen Arnder, 1494-1498. Low German: Striedter claims that the low German pamphlet in Budapest was probably the basis for this one (Striedter, p. 404). Karadja does not cite this pamphlet.

"Ein Wunderliche und Erschröchenliche Hystorie von einem Grossen Wuttrich Genant Dracole Wayde. . . ." Bamberg: Hans Sporer, 1491. Woodcut portrait: a simplified version of the woodcut portrait on the pamphlet located in Budapest. Plattdeutsch. Location: British Museum (reproduced in photocopy by Ilona Hubay), 795, 1491, Dracola Wyda (Vlad IV), 6406. See Robert Proctos, *An Index to the Early Printed Books in the British Museum* (London, 1960). Copy at the Biblioteca Centrala Bucuresti, 497636. The British Museum copy, acquired in 1846, belonged to the Frenchman Henri Ternaux, who probably wrote on one of three blank pages: "Ce petit volume imprime à

Bamberg en 1491 contient l'histoire des cruautés de Vlad V
Dracu, prince de Valachie, surnommé Cépélussu ou
l'empaleur. Kogalnitschan l'historien de la Valachie ignorait
l'existence de cette édition quoiqu'il en cite d'après Engel
traduction en bas-allemand."

[Dracole Waida] "Hier facht sich au gar ain grassenlichen
erschrocken ystoren. . . ." Augsburg: Christoph Schnaitter,
March 14, 1494. Cross of Christ on the cover. Location: Two
copies at the Bayrische Staatsbibliothek, Munich;
Kantonsbibliothek, Solothurn; Staatsbibliothek, Zwickau; copy
at the Library of the Romanian Academy, II, 198676; also copies
of the four texts at the Biblioteca Centrala Bucuresti, 497637.

Nürnberg: Ambrosius Huber, 1499. Title: no opportunity of seeing it.
The text is identical with that of the pamphlet located in
Budapest. Cited by Karadja in 1931.

"Hie facht sich au gar ein graussemliche und erschrökenliche
hystorien. . . ." Strasbourg: Matthias Hupfuff, 1500. On the cover
is a woodcut depicting Dracula dining amid his impaled
victims. Location: Staatsbibliothek, Berlin; Stadtbibliothek,
Colmar; Library of the Episcopal Seminary, Mainz; Royal
Library, Copenhagen; copy at the Biblioteca Centrala
Bucuresti, 497639. Published by Karadja in the original
language in 1931.

"Von dem Dracole wayda dem grossen Thyrannen." Nürnberg:
[Johannes Stuchs], n.d. Tentatively dated c. 1515. Location:
Preussischer Kulturbesitz, Marburg.

No date, publisher, or place of publication. Title: no opportunity of
seeing it. Small portrait on the cover. Tentatively dated c. 1520,
M. Ramminger, Augsburg. Location: Copy at the Library of the
Romanian Academy of Sciences, from the Sturdza Library; copy
at the Biblioteca Centrala Bucuresti, 497642.

Nürnberg: Jobst Gutknecht, 1521. Title: no opportunity of seeing it.
Cited by I. Bogdan, *Vlad Tepes*, p. 87.

"Von dem Dracole Wayda dem grossen Tyrannen." Augsburg:
Mathias Francken, n.d. Tentatively dated c. 1530. Location:
Staatsbibliothek, Berlin.

No date (Ms 1485 mentioned by Library curator), publisher, or place
of publication. Watercolor portrait—the only one of its kind
found so far (reproduced on book cover). Location: The Philip
H. and A. S. W. Rosenbach Foundation at Philadelphia. See
Frederick R. Goff, *Incunabula in American Libraries* (New York,
1964), D-366, p. 221. This is a copy that has been ignored by all
previous scholars. It has been conjecturally cited back to c.
1488, Peter Wagner, Nürnberg.

Slavic Manuscripts in Russian Archives

Kirillo-Belozersk Manuscript

1. Oldest version. Original: Manuscript Division, State Public Library, Saltykov-Shchedrin, Leningrad, Kirillo-Belozersk collection, no. 11/1088. Copies: Kirillovskii Historical-Artistic Museum, no. 2967; Lenin Library, Museum collection, no. 8779. (See L'urie, *Povest'*, pp. 117-122; also Sedel'nikov, pp. 621-659.)

2. Tikhonravovskii version. Manuscript Division, Lenin Library, Moscow, Tikhonravovskii collection (collection 299), no. 379. (See L'urie, *Povest'*, pp. 123-125.)

3. Zabelinskii version. Original: State Historical Museum, Moscow, Zabelinskii collection, no. 451. Copies: State Public Library, Saltykov-Shchedrin, Leningrad, Titov collection, no. 2796; State Public Library, Collection of the Lovers of Ancient Literature, no. 195; Archive of the Geographical Society of the USSR, R. 114, op. 1, no. 17 (notebook no. 6); State Public Library, Pogodin collection, 1606; Lenin Library, Moscow, Undol'sk'ii collection (310), no. 632.

4. Western Russian version. State Historical Museum, Moscow, Barsov collection, no. 604.

Riumiantsev Manuscript

1. Oldest version. Lenin Library, Moscow, Riumiantsev collection (256), no. 358.

2. Library version. Main text: State Public Library, Saltykov-Shchedrin, Leningrad, Q. 17, 169. Copy: State Historical Museum, Moscow, Museum collection, no. 3860.

3. Published version. Lenin Library, Moscow. Collection of the Society of History and Russian Antiquities (205), no. 286.

4. Barsovskii version. State Historical Museum, Moscow, Barsov collection, no. 1521.

5. Uvarovskii version. Original: State Historical Museum, Moscow, Uvarov collection, no. 848. Copies: State Historical Museum, Uvarov collection, no. 152; Lenin Library, Moscow, Beliaev collection (29), no. 1529; State Historical Museum, Barsov collection, no. 2134.

6. Kholovskii version. State Library (Lenin Library), Moscow, Tikhonravovskii collection (299), no. 283.

Combined Manuscript

Central State Archives of Ancient Acts (Moscow). Collection from the Archives of the Ministry of Foreign Relations (181), no. 613/1121.

Secondary Sources

Adascalitiei, V. *De la Dragos la Cuza Voda legende populare românesti.* Bucharest, 1966.

Andreescu, Stefan. "Snagovul si tainele lui." *Magazin Istoric* 3 (October 1969); 62.

Anghel, Paul. "Un episod Shakesperean din istoria nationala; Tepes." *Gazeta Literara* 14 (January 12, 1967); 1, 7.

Apostolescu, N. *Cetatile lui Negru Voda si a lui Tepes.* Bucharest, 1910.

Babinger, Franz. *Mohammed le conquérant et son temps 1432-1481, la grande peur du monde au tournant de l'histoire.* Paris, 1954.

Baritiu, Gheorghe. "Manuscript despre cruzimile lui Vlad Dracula." *Analele Academiei Româna,* 2d ser. 5 (1882-1883), 2, pp. 11-14 (Includes text of Saint Gall manuscript.)

Beheim, Michel. *Die Gedichte des Michel Beheim.* Band I Einleitung Gedichte Nr. 1-147 herausgegeben von Hans Gille und Ingeborg Spriewald. Berlin, 1968. (Deutsche Texte des Mittelalters herausgegeben von der Deutschen Akademie der Wissenschaften zu Berlin, Band 60.) See also Gille, Hans.

Bentley, Juliette. "Vlad Voivode Dracula." *Supernaturel* 2 (Bournemouth, 1969).

Betzdechi, S. *Familia lui Nicolae Olahus.* Cluj, n.d.

Bianu, Ion. "Despre istoricul Ion Christian Engel." *An. Ac. Rom.* 38: 64.

Bleyer, Jacob. "Beheim's Gedichte über Drakul und der Historische Wert Quelle." *Szazadek* 38 (1904): 874-882.

——————. "Ein Gedicht Michael Beheim's über Wlad IV, Woiwoden von der Walachei (1456-1462)." *Archiv des Vereins für Siebenbürgische Landeskunde* n.e. 32, bk. 1 (Hermannstadt, 1903): 5-39.

Bogdan, Ion. *Vlad Tepes si naratiunile germane si rusesti asupra lui.* Bucharest, 1896.

Bogrea, V. "Inca o pomenire germana despre Tepes." *An. Inst. de Ist. Nat.* 2 (1923).

Bolintineanu, Dimitrie. *Viata lui Vlad Tepes Voda si Mircea cel Batrin.* Bucharest, 1863.

Bonfinius, Antonio. *Rerum Ungaricarum decades....* 4 vols. Leipzig, 1936-1941.

Bratulescu, Victor. *Manastirea Snagovul.* Bucharest, 1933.

Brînzeu, F. "Vlad l'empaleur dans la littérature turque." *Revista Istorica româna* 16 (1946): 68-71.

Budai-Deleanu, Ioan. *Tiganiada.* Edited by G. Cardas. Bucharest, 1967.

Catina, Ion. *Tepes Voda* (drama in two acts). 1847.

Cazacu, Matei. "O domnie necunoscuta a lui Vlad Tepes din anul 1848." *Viata Studenteasca,* December 11, 1968, p. 6.

—————. "La Valachie et la bataille de Kossovo." *Revue des Etudes Sud-Est Européennes* 9 (1971): 131-152.

—————. "Un viteaz frate a lui Vlad Tepes." *Viata Studenteasca,* October 23, 1968, p. 6.

—————. "Vlad Tepes erou de epopee," *Magazin Istoric* 4 (June 1970): 25-31.

—————. "Vlad Tepes: monografie istorica." Master's thesis, Bucharest, 1961.

Chalkokondyles, Leonikos. *Expunerile istorice.* Edited and translated by Vasile Grecu. Bucharest, 1958.

Cîmpina, Barbu. "Complotul boierilor si rascoala din Tara Româneasca din Iulie-noiembrie 1462." *Studii si referate privind istoria României I* (1954): 599-624.

—————. "Victoria ostii lui Vlad Tepes asupra lui Mehmed al II-lea." *Studii* 15 (1962): 533-556.

Cîmpina, Barbu, and Stefanescu, S. "Lupta condusa de Vlad Tepes pentru consolidarea rezistentei tarii Românesti împotriva primejdiei Otomane 1456-62." *Istoria României* 2 (1962): 465-477.

Columna lui Traian. Bucharest, 1888. (Includes diplomatic dispatches referring to Dracula's campaign of 1462 and narration of an Albanian slave.)

Conduratu, Grigore C. *Michael Beheim's Gedicht über den Woiwoden Wlad II Drakul. Mit historischen und kritischen Erläuterungen.* Inauguraldissertation, Leipzig-Bucharest, 1903.

Constantinescu, Armand G. *Magul dela Snagov.* Bucharest, n.d.

Constantinescu, N. A., and Moisescu, Cristian. *Curtea domneasca din Tîrgoviste.* Bucharest, 1965.

Critoboulos of Imbros. *Din domnia lui Mahommed al H-lea.* Edited by Vasile Grecu. Bucharest, 1963. (Also see English translation, which is much inferior: Kritoboulos of Imbros. *History of Mehmed the Conqueror.* Translated by C. T. Riggs. Princeton, 1954.)

Csabai, Stephen. "The Real Dracula." *Hungarian Quarterly,* Autumn 1941, pp. 327-332.

Degaudenzi, S. L. "Mythe et réalité: le véritable Dracula." *Midi-minuit*, no. 22 (Paris, 1971) .

Dlugosz, I. *Historia polonica libri XIII ab antiquissimus temporibus*, vols. 1-2. Leipzig, 1711-1712.

Documente privind istoria Romaniei: B: Tara Romaneasca veac. XIII-XV, N.p., n.d.

Doukas, Michael. *Istoria Turco-Bizantina*. Edited by Vasile Grecu. Bucharest, 1958. (Probably the best critical edition of this text.)

Draghiceanu, Virgilius. "Manastirea Snagov." *Bul. Com. Mon. Ist.* 24 (1931): 91.

Dumitriu, G. "Pe urmele unei sapaturi." *Amvonul* 21 (1942): 9-14.

Ebendorfer, Th., *Chronica Regum Romanorum*. Mittheilungen des Institut's für österreichiesche Geschichtsförschung; III Erganzungsband. Innsbruck, 1890-1894. (That edition contained only selections from the chronicles. A new edition of this chronicle was published in 1968.)

Elekes, L. *Hunyady*. Budapest, 1952.

——————. *Matyas es Kora*. Budapest, 1956.

Eliade, Mircea. *The Myth of the Eternal Return*. New York, 1954.

——————. *De Zalmoxis à Genghis-Khan. Etudes comparatives sur les religions et le folklore de la Dacie et de l'Europe orientale*. Paris, 1970.

Ene, Georgeta. "Figura domnitorului muntean Vlad Tepes în legende istorice din comuna Arefu-Arges." Thesis, Bucharest: Institute of Folklore, 1970.

Engel, Johann Christian von. *Geschichte der Moldau und Walachey. Nebst der Historischen und Statistischen Literatur beider Länder*, vol. 1. Halle, 1804. (Actually vol. 4 of the *Geschichte des Ungarischen Reiches und Seine Nebenländer, Lübeck*, pp. 75-80).

Fine, John V. A., Jr. "Fedor Kuritsyn's 'Laodikjskoe Poslanie' and the Heresy of the Judaisers." *Speculum* 41 (July 1966): 500-504.

Florescu, George. *Divanele domnesti din Muntenia în secolul al XV-lea, dregatori si boeri 1496-1501* Bucharest, 1929.

Florian, Aaron. "Vlad Tepes." *Muzeul National: Gazeta Literara si Industriala* 2 (1837-1838): 21.

Gane, C. *Trecute vieti de domni si doamne*, vol. 1. Bucharest, 1943.

Gérard, Emily de Laszowska. *The Land beyond the Forest*. London, 1888.

——————. "Transylvanian Superstitions." London, 1885. A reprint from *The Nineteenth Century*, vol. 13, pp. 130-150.

Ghibanescu, G. "Vlad Tepes, studiu critic." *Arhiva* 8 (1897): 373-417, 497-520.

——————. "Vlad Voda Calugarul," *Arhiva* 7 (1896): 140.

Gille, Hans. *Die Historischen und Politischen Gedichte Michel Beheim's.* Berlin, 1910.

Giurescu, C. C. *Transylvanià în istoria poporului român.* Bucharest, 1967. (Also in English translation.)

Giurescu, C. C., and Giurescu, Dinu. *Istoria Patriei.* Bucharest, 1971.

Grecescu, Constantin. *Istoriile domnilor Tarii Românesti de Radu Popescu Vornicul.* Bucharest, 1963. (One of the most recent editions of the Baleanu Chronicle.)

Grecescu, Constantin, and Simonescu, D., eds. *Istoria tarii Românesti 1290-1690. Letopisetul Cantacuzinesc.* Bucharest, 1960. (One of the most recent editions of the Cantacuzino Chronicle.)

Guboglu, Mihael, and Mehmet, M. Mustafa A. *Cronici turcesti privind tarile române,* vols. 1 and 3. Bucharest, 1966.

Gündisch, Gustav. "Cu privire la relatiile lui Vlad Tepes cu Transilvania în anii 1456-1458." *Studii* 16 (1963): 681-696.

——————. "Vlad Tepes und die Sachsischen Selbstverwaltungsgebiete Siebenbürgen's." *Revue Romaine d'Histoire* 8 (1969): 981-982.

Hasdeu, Bogden Petriceicu. "Filosofia portretului lui in Tepes. Schita iconografica." *Studii critice asupra istoriei Romanei.* Bucharest, 1864.

Heiman, Leo. "Meet the Real Count Dracula." *Fate,* March 1968, pp. 53-60.

Holban, Maria. *Calatori straini despre tarile române,* vol. 1. Bucharest, 1968. (Contains among other valuable sources the Chronicle of Walerand de Wavrin: the Epistola of Michael Bocignoli of Raguza [published before 1512]. The Chronicle of Serban Janissary of Ostrovitza and treaties of Felix Petancius, *De aggrediendo Turco,* the narration of Ladislas, Dracula's servant, also contains work of Antonio Verancsics [1504-1573], *De Situ Transylvaniae Moldaviae et Transalpinae,* referring to the inhabitants of Wallachia as "draguli.")

Hubay, Ilona. *Egykoru eysaglap Drakula vaydaral.* Budapest, 1948.

Hurmuzacki, Eudoxiu de, ed. *Colectiune de documente privitoare la istoria Românilor 1199-1849,* vol. 15. Edited by Nicolae Iorga. Bucharest, 1911. (This volume contains a large number of documents on Dracula's reign drawn from the Transylvanian archives.)

Husar, Alexandru. *Dincolo de ruine: cetati medievale.* Bucharest, 1959. (On Castle Dracula, pp. 36–47.)

Ionescu, N. "Despre uciderea lui Mihai Voda Viteazul si despre cruzimile lui Vlad Dracula doua documente istorice." *An. Ac. Rom.,* 1883.

Iorga, Nicolae. *Acte si fragmente cu privire la istoria românilor,* vol. 3. 1895–1897. (Among other documents, mostly drawn from foreign archives, the reports of Jacob Unrest, Pietro Tommasi, and Marino Sanudo are of particular interest for Dracula's third reign.)

——————. "Les aventures serrazines des francais de Bourgogne au XVieme siècle." *Mélanges d'histoire générale.* Published by C. Marinescu. Cluj, 1927. (Contains interesting letter dated February 2, 1443, by a Franciscan monk.)

——————. "Cronica lui Wavrin si românii." *Bul. Com. Ist. 6* (1927): 57–148.

——————. "O cronica munteana în greceste pentru secolul all XV-lea." *An. Ac. Rom. Nem. Sect.* Ist., 3d ser. 19 (1937): 147–151. (Analyzes Chronicle of Jacob Unrest.)

——————. "Lucruri noua despre Vlad Tepes si Stefan cel Mare." *Convorbiri Literare* 35 (1901): 149–162. (Contains letter of Dan [buried alive by Dracula] dated March 2, 1460, and one referring to Dan dated April 22, 1460, papal dispatches on Dracula's Serbian campaign of 1476, and testimony of Bishop Erlau. Also letter of April 22, 1460 [from Pruda] concerning the decapitation of Dan by Dracula.)

——————. *Scrisori de Boieri. Scrisori de domni.* Valenii de Munte, 1932.

——————. *Domnii români dupa portrete si fresce originale.* Sibiu, 1930.

——————. *Histoire des Roumains et de la romanité orientale. Les Chevaliers,* vol. 4. Bucharest, 1937.

——————. "Inca ceva despre Vlad Tepes si Stefan cel Mare," *Convorbiri Literare* 38 (1904): 381–383. (Contains facts referring to Wallachian history drawn from Melk monastery in Austria.)

——————. *Cîteva indicatii asupra manastirii Snagovul.* Valenii de Munte, 1926.

——————. "Contributii la legaturile literare românesti cu Rusii si Ungurii; I-Ceva nou despre povestea ruseasca a ispravilor lui Vlad Tepes." *An. Ac. Rom. Mem. Sect. Ist.* 21 (1939).

404   A Biography of Vlad the Impaler

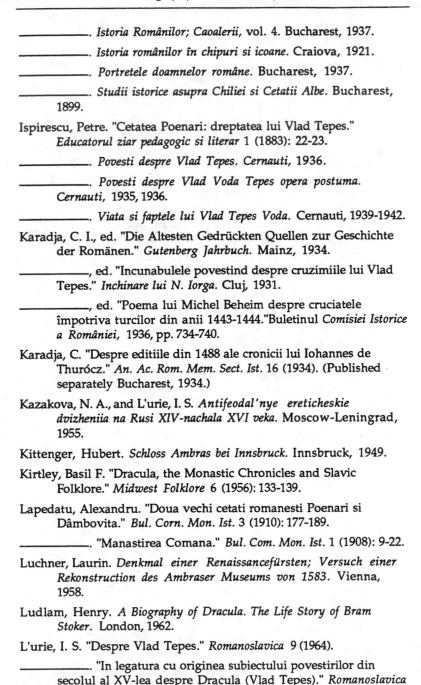

_____. *Istoria Românilor; Caoalerii*, vol. 4. Bucharest, 1937.

_____. *Istoria românilor în chipuri si icoane.* Craiova, 1921.

_____. *Portretele doamnelor române.* Bucharest, 1937.

_____. *Studii istorice asupra Chiliei si Cetatii Albe.* Bucharest, 1899.

Ispirescu, Petre. "Cetatea Poenari: dreptatea lui Vlad Tepes." *Educatorul ziar pedagogic si literar* 1 (1883): 22-23.

_____. *Povesti despre Vlad Tepes. Cernauti,* 1936.

_____. *Povesti despre Vlad Voda Tepes opera postuma. Cernauti,* 1935, 1936.

_____. *Viata si faptele lui Vlad Tepes Voda.* Cernauti, 1939-1942.

Karadja, C. I., ed. "Die Altesten Gedrückten Quellen zur Geschichte der Romänen." *Gutenberg Jahrbuch.* Mainz, 1934.

_____, ed. "Incunabulele povestind despre cruzimiile lui Vlad Tepes." *Inchinare lui N. Iorga.* Cluj, 1931.

_____, ed. "Poema lui Michel Beheim despre cruciatele împotriva turcilor din anii 1443-1444."Buletinul *Comisiei Istorice a României,* 1936, pp. 734-740.

Karadja, C. "Despre editiile din 1488 ale cronicii lui Iohannes de Thurócz." *An. Ac. Rom. Mem. Sect. Ist.* 16 (1934). (Published separately Bucharest, 1934.)

Kazakova, N. A., and L'urie, I. S. *Antifeodal'nye ereticheskie dvizheniia na Rusi XIV-nachala XVI veka.* Moscow-Leningrad, 1955.

Kittenger, Hubert. *Schloss Ambras bei Innsbruck.* Innsbruck, 1949.

Kirtley, Basil F. "Dracula, the Monastic Chronicles and Slavic Folklore." *Midwest Folklore* 6 (1956): 133-139.

Lapedatu, Alexandru. "Doua vechi cetati romanesti Poenari si Dâmbovita." *Bul. Corn. Mon. Ist.* 3 (1910): 177-189.

_____. "Manastirea Comana." *Bul. Com. Mon. Ist.* 1 (1908): 9-22.

Luchner, Laurin. *Denkmal einer Renaissancefürsten; Versuch einer Rekonstruction des Ambraser Museums von 1583.* Vienna, 1958.

Ludlam, Henry. *A Biography of Dracula. The Life Story of Bram Stoker.* London, 1962.

L'urie, I. S. "Despre Vlad Tepes." *Romanoslavica* 9 (1964).

_____. "In legatura cu originea subiectului povestirilor din secolul al XV-lea despre Dracula (Vlad Tepes)." *Romanoslavica* 10 (1964): 5-19.

————— "Literaturnaia i kul'turno-prosvetilel'naia deiatel'nost' Efrosina v kontse XVV." *Trudy Otdela drevnerusskoi literatury instituta russkoi literatury. A.N.S.S.S.R.,* 17 (1961): 130-168.

—————. *Povest'o Drakule.* Moscow-Leningrad, 1964. (Contains the Kirillo-Belozersk manuscript in the oldest version, pp. 117-122; Tikhonravovskii version, pp. 123-125; Zabelinskii version, pp. 125-135; western Russian version, pp. 135-139. Also the Riumiantsev manuscript in the oldest version, pp. 140-145; library version, pp. 145-150; disseminated version, pp. 150-159; Barsovskii version, pp. 159-162; Uvarovskii version, pp. 162-172; Khokhlovskii version, pp. 172-178; and finally, the revised edition, pp. 179-181.)

—————. "Povest'o mut'ianskom voevode Drakule." *Russkie Povesti* XV-XVI vv. Moscow-Leningrad, 1959.

McNally, R. T., and Florescu, Radu. *In Search of Dracula, a True History of Dracula and Vampire Legends.* Greenwich, 1972.

Mandrea, G. *Manastirea Snagov.* Bucharest, 1900.

Manolescu, G. T. "Moneta lui Vlad I Dracul," *Revista din Iasi* 1 (April 1908): 210-212.

Mavrodollu, G. *Vlada Tsepeshu, drama istorica în cinci acte.* Bucharest, 1858.

Mercati, G., ed. "Notizie varii sopra Niccolo Modrussiense." *Opere Minore,* vol. 4. Vatican City, 1937.

Midi-minuit fantastique, nos. 4-5. Paris, 1963. (A special edition devoted to Dracula.)

Minea, Ilie. "Pierderea Amlasului si Fagarasului; contributiuni la domnia lui Vladislav II si Vlad Tepes." *Convorbiri Literare* 48 (1914) 169-181, 271-286, 412-421, 519-528, 785-806.

—————. *Principatele române si politica orientala a împaratului Sigismund.* Bucharest, 1919.

—————. *Vlad Dracul si vremea sa.* Iasi, 1929.

Münster, Sebastian. *Cosmographiae Universales,* Libri 6. Basel, 1572. (Also 1550 edition. English edition, 1558).

Murasan, Camil. *Iancu de Hunedoara so vremea si.* 2d. ed. Bucharest, 1968.

Murgoci, A. "The Vampire in Rumania." *Folklore* 37 (1926).

Nandris, Grigore. "The Dracula Theme in the European Literature of the West and of the East." *Literary History and Literary Criticism.* Edited by Leon Edel. New York, 1965.

——————. "The Historical Dracula: The Theme of His Legend in the Western and Eastern Literature of Europe." *Comparative Literature Studies* 3 (1966) 367-396.

——————. "A Philological Analysis of Dracula and Rumanian Place Names and Masculine Personal Names in a/ea." *Slavonic and East European Review* 37 (June 1959): 371-377.

——————. "Rumanian Folklore." *The Aryan Path* (Bombay), April 1954, pp. 164-169.

Nicolaescu, Stefan. "Manastirea Snagov si usa de Stear cu sculpturi de sfinti a bisericii Buna Vestire ctiria lui Vladislav voevod 1453." Bucharest, 1946, pp. 118-128.

——————. "Vechimea manastirii Snagov." Bucharest, no. 1 (1935).

Nicolau, T. "Cum a capturat Vlad Tepes pe Hamza Pacha." *Revista Militara* 81 (1934) 63-88.

Odobescu, Alexandru. "Cîteva Ore la Snagov." *Opere complecte,* vol. 3. Bucharest, 1908.

Olteanu, Pandele. "Lexicul povestirilor slave despre Vlad Tepes." *Revista universitatii,* seria stiinte sociale filologie, nos. 2-3 (1955).

——————. *Limba povestirilor slave despre Vlad Tepes.* Bucharest, 1961. (Contains nineteen Slavic stories and Romanian translations.)

Pall, F. "Le condizione e gli echi internazionali della lotta antiottomana del 1442-1443 condotta, da Giovanni de Hunedoara," *Revue des Etudes Sud-Est Européenne* 3 (1965) 456-457.

——————. "Notes du pélerin William Wey à propos des operations militaires des Turcs en 1462." *Revue Historique du Sud-Est Européene* 22 (1945): 246-266.

——————. "Stiri noi despre expeditiile turcesti din Transilvania în 1438." *Anuarul Institutului de Istorie din Cluj* 1-2 (1958-1959), pp. 9-28.

Panaitescu, P. P. *Istoria României,* vol. 2. Bucharest, 1962.

——————. "Povestirile slave despre Vlad Tepes." *Comunicare la Inst. de Ist. Acad. Rep. Pop. Rom.,* 1952.

——————. *Viata lui Vlad Tepes. Cronici slavo-romîne din sec. XV-XVI publicate de Ion Bogdan.* Editie revazuta si complectata. Bucharest, 1959.

——————. "Vlad Tepes. O problema psihologica." *Convorbiri Literare* 76 (May-June 1943): 331-348.

——————. *Vlad Tepes si naratiunele germane si rusesti asupra lui.* Bucharest, 1896. (Contains Slavic texts, the Saint Gall German story, and some crucial Dracula letters.)

————, ed. *Cronicile slavo-române din sec. XV-XVI, publicate de Ion Bogdan.* Editie revazuta si complectata de P. P. Panaitescu. Bucharest, 1959.

————, ed. *Documente privitoare la relatiile Tarii Românesti cu Brasovul si cu tara ungureasca în sec. XV d SVI. 1413-1508,* vol. 1. Bucharest, 1905. (Contains numerous letters of Dracula, of his political opponents, and of Transylvanian officials from Brasov and Sibiu.)

Panaitescu, P. P., and Mioc, Damaschin, eds. *Documenta Romaniae historica. Tara Romineasca 1247-1500,* vol. 1. Bucharest, 1966. (Document nos. 115-121.)

Papacostea, Serban. "Cu privire da geneza si raspîndirea povestirilor scrise despre faptele lui Vlad Tepes." *Romanoslavica* 13 (1966). (Contains analysis of commentaries of Pope Pius II and so-called Dracula narration on 1462 campaign.)

Piccolomini, Aenea Silvio (Pius II). *Commentarii Rerum Memorabilium.* Frankfurt, 1614.

Popescu, Grigore. *Vlad Tepes.* Bucharest, 1964.

Popescu-Bajenaru, Ion. *Un schit istoric in codrul Vlasiei. Schitul Balteni si vecinatatile.* Bucharest, 1912.

Puchov, Jan (archbishop of Prague). *Siveta wsseho kronika skrz pracy zygmunda mladsiho z Puchowa.* Prague, 1554. (Inspired by S. Münster's *Cosmographiae.*)

————. *To jest wypisanii o polozenii krajin neb zemy y obysiejych narodnow wseho swieta . . . Prelozena od Jana (a Zikunda) z Puchowa.* Prague, 1554.

Radulescu-Codin, C. *Din Muscel cântece poporane.* Bucharest, 1896.

————. *Din trecutul nostru legende, traditii si amintiri istorice.* Bucharest, 1923.

————. *Ingerul Românului. Povesti si legende din popor.* Bucharest, 1916.

————. "Legende asupra lui Tepes." *Copii Neamului,* 1922.

————. "Legende traditii si amintiri istorice adunate din Oltenia si din Muscel." *Ac. Rom. Din viata poporului român, culegeri si studii* 10 (May 22, 1910).

Rogoz, Victoria. *Vlad fiul Dracului.* Bucharest, 1970.

Ronay, Gabriel. *The Truth about Dracula.* New York, 1972.

Rosetti, Dinu. *Sapaturile arheologice de la Snagov,* vol. 1. Bucharest, 1935.

Rudorff, Raymond. *The Dracula Archives.* New York, 1971.

Schulerus, Adolf. "Michael Beheim's Gedicht über Wlad IV Drakul als Historische Quelle." *Korrespondenzblatt des Vereins für Siebenbürgische Landeskunde* 27, no. 5 (1904): 49-59; and 28, nos. 2-3 (1905): 38-39.

Schwob, Monika Vt. *Kulturelle Beziehungen zwischen Nürnberg und die Deutschen im Sudösten im 14 bis 16 Jahrhundert.* Munich, 1969.

Sedel'nikov, A. "Literaturnaia istoriia povesti o Drakule." *Izvestia po russkomu iazyku i slovestnosti* 2 (1929): 621-659.

Seifi, ali Riza. *Kazikli voyvoda.* Istanbul, 1928.

Serbanescu, N. I. *Istoria manastirii Snagov.* Bucharest, 1944.

Seton-Watson, R. W. *A History of the Roumanians.* Cambridge, 1934.

Simache, N., and Cristescu, Tr., eds. *Cronicile românesti. Letopisetul Cantacuzinesc 1290-1688*, vol. 2. Buzau, 1942.

Simache, N., and Cristescu, Tr. *Variante ale Letopisetului Cantacuzinesc,* vol. 3. Buzau, 1942.

Smith, Gene. "A Sentimental Journey to Dracula's Home Town." *Saturday Evening Post,* 238 (March 27, 1965): 76-79.

Smochina, N. P. "Povestea despre Dracula." *Moldova noua,* 5 (1939). (Translated from the Russian.)

——————. *Povestirea slava despre Vlad Tepes.* Iasi, 1939.

Stahl, Henry H. "Cetatea lui Tepes," *Neamul Românesc,* September 1921.

Stefulescu, Alexander. *Manastirea Tismana.* Bucharest, 1909.

Stoker, Bram. *Dracula.* New York, n.d.

Striedter, J. "Die Erzählung vom Walächischen Voivoden Drakula in der Russischen und Deutschen Uberlieferung." *Zeitschrift fur Slavische Philologie* 39 (1961): 401-404.

Tappe, Eric. *Documents Concerning Romanian History 1427-1601 Collected from British Archives.* The Hague, 1964.

Teleki, I. *A hunyadiak kora Magyar orszagon 10.* Pest, 1853. (Contains letters written by Hunyady referring to Dracula.)

Theodoru, Radu. *Stramosii.* Bucharest, 1967.

——————. *The Tismana Monastery.* Bucharest, 1966.

Thalloczy, L., and Aldasy, A., eds. *Monumenta Hungariae Historica. Acta Externa,* vols. 1, 3, and 33. Budapest, 1907. (Also see vol. 5 in this collection, edited by Ivan Nagy and A. B. Niary, *Magyar diplomacziai emeleket Matyas Kiraly Korabol 1458-1490,* vol. 2, Budapest, 1876. For Dracula's activities after liberation from jail, p. 273.)

Thuroczy, I. G. *Der Hungern Chronica inhallend wie sie anfengklich ins land kommen . . . von irem ersten König Athila.* Nürnberg, 1534. (Also see *Chronica Hungarorum ab origine gentis.* Latin translation by I. G. Schwandter. Vienna, from 1746.)

Turhan-Tan, M. *Aknidan Aknia.* Istanbul, 1936.

Vambery, Arminius. *His Life and Adventure with/by Himself.* London, 1884.

——————. *Story* of *My Struggles: The Memoirs* of *Arminius Vambery.* 2 vols. London, 1904.

Varma, Devendra P. *The Gothic Flame.* 1957.

Veress, Andrei. "Cintece istorice vechi unguresti despre români." *An. Ac. Rom. Mem. Sect. Lit.,* s. 3, 3 (1934): 1-40.

——————, ed. *Bibliografia româna-ungara.* 3 vols. Bucharest, 1931-1935.

Vernadsky, George. "The Heresy of the Judaizers and the Policies of Ivan III of Moscow." *Speculum* 8 (1933): 436-454.

Viskovatyi, K. "O sekule Drakuloviche (Draguloviche) iugoslavianskikh narodnykh pesen." *Slavia* 14 (1935-1936): 160-163.

"Vremea lui Tepes," *Cutezatorii.* Bucharest, 1969.

Walerand (Chevalier), Seigneur de Wavrin *Anciennes chroniques d'Engleterre.* Edited by Hardy. Master of Rolls Series. London, 1891. (Portions affecting Romanian history.) Also see N. Iorga, *Buletinul Comisiei istorice a României,* vol. 6, pp. 16-148. Bucharest, 1926.

Wattenbach, Wilhelm. "Uber den Walächischen Woiwoden Wlad IV, 1456-1462." *Archiv des Vereins für Siebenbürgische Landeskunde* n.s. 27 (1896): 331-343. (Includes text of Lambach manuscript.)

Wolf, Leonard. *A Dream of Dracula: In Search of the Living Dead.* Boston and Toronto, 1972.

Xenopol, A. D. *Istoria românilor din Dacia Traiana.* 2d ed., vol. 4. Bucharest, 1914.

——————. "Lupta între Draculesti so Danesti." *An. Ac. Rom. Mem. Sect. Lit.,* 2d ser. 30 (1907) .

Zagorit, G. "O noua manastire zidita de Vlad Tepes." *Copiii Neamului* 1 (April 1, 1922): 12.

——————. "Vlad Tepes: citeva fapte necunoscute." *Gazeta Cartilor* 2 (April 15, 1922): 1-3.